Dwelling

Also by Richard Makin:

Prose

Forword (Equipage)
Universlipre (Equipage)
Too Mouth For Word (Historical Research Ltd)
Ravine (Words & Pictures)
Readymades (Obelisk)
Remoire (Zoilus)
Work (Great Works)
St Leonards (Great Works)

Poetry

Under Luke Shades (Great Works)

Anthologies

Foil (Etruscan Books)
The Reality Street Book of Sonnets (Reality Street)

Dwelling

Richard Makin

REALITY STREET

Published by
REALITY STREET
63 All Saints Street, Hastings, East Sussex TN34 3BN
www.realitystreet.co.uk

First edition 2011
Copyright © Richard Makin, 2011
Front cover photo by the author
Typesetting & book design by Ken Edwards

Reality Street Narrative Series No 8

Printed & bound in Great Britain by Lightning Source UK Ltd

A catalogue record for this book is available from the British Library

ISBN: 978-1-874400-53-0

Acknowledgements
An earlier version of this book was serialized monthly online by Great Works
(www.greatworks.org.uk) from 2006 to 2009. Thanks to Peter Philpott.

I

Exit one London. Wandering into the root of to dwell. I will not provoke. I will
not provide. Let us through. The first big test is to dig a ditch. In guerrilla warfare
it's said you use your strengths as weaknesses. Everything's declared. He struggles
to solve the puzzles that appear in the almanacs. He sits at his table doused in
bird-lime and lighter fuel. This estranged master, he bears all the hallmarks of an
assassin getting organized. Time moves too thinly for him. Come home. At the
close of a perfect sentence he practises himself to sleep. His first love is the ordinary. He picks pockets to make ends meet. But he wants to unravel a narrative,
who's in love with whom and who isn't et cetera. He approaches the window to
see how the outside is faring. (The apt word is heroic.) He's at work within the
delta formed by a small pyramid, a stonemasons' temple, and a sea-going concrete
vessel. Nameless, his number is. He scribbles a note in his journal: anathema
begins, reversal of power. Nothing is any longer alike. The rest is unreadable.
How long is he staying down in that box she asks. Everything happens only once.

His mood swings have become intuitive—every plop in the water is a meal.
We are dealing with impersonal, collective forces. We're electrocuted while flee-
ing. Much of me remains behind. Let's start with some basics: dazzling light balanced by impenetrable shadows. People say he's often found drifting through the
landscape whistling sad ballads, like the one about a crow who watches as night
thickens into a volley of snow. I disinter memory. I'm permitted to inherit
myself. For a week I invented everything. The next dump on looks like the
entrance to hell—drumming assaults the ear—bells, visionary musics and solid
painted bodies. Every face is a parallelogram: cubist bone, rawky mornings
creeping up the sky. A small disc hangs by a thread above his forehead. It's set at
an angle to the radiowaves—flexion is used to measure his intent. He can never
fully return.

Allow me to introduce some new manners: at the first tremors you're invited
to throw open the gates into an identical theme park. He collects fragments and
builds them into a whole. Picture the construction of a gothic cathedral without
a ground-plan, just clusters of teeming detail from the outset. (What was that
final word.) There's no story although a great many things happen. It comes out
of nothing and returns. Perfect grace. There's doubt that it works, the old
magic—such unallied beliefs, a morphology of brittle ghosts: paradise lost, apocalypse won. Unease grows rapidly, until it assumes the monomaniac character of
a novel—an antique structure more than thirty storeys high. At length it obtains
over gravity an incomprehensibility, an ascendancy, while remaining workaday in
form. My own journey upends very bad indeed—as dactyl, spondee, anapaest—
unceasing and autodestructive, garbles left to sift and worry at. And we wonder
whether you might be persuaded to add a few words of your own, some choice
remarks plucked from the general murmur. Some people would just cave in. This

is an underthread. Its separate leaves are termed sepals. Its facts are many, its fictions nil. The art of writing books is about to be discovered, mark my words.

We are on an identical horizon. The stadium floods with white light and a cry rises up o very beauty. Quick, coil up her winding-sheet. In her own rude way she's a perfect. By profession she is lime-burner. Her key ingredient is adipocere, that waxy substance which oozes from any submerged familiar—a grey and spongy lard for a grey and soapy people. That suite you hear is the diva suite. Void exposure to air. Devaginate. Music disconnects the landscape, a sequence of movements in twisted keys. At the foot of the gravel drive is a wicket-gate set into an oak door studded with nails. Rust bleeds down its surface in elongated cones.

He must be kept cool in the fridge. She deliberately leaves him out overnight on the kitchen table. In the morning there's a pool of tell-tale moisture spreading across the yellow formica. Five asterisks have been placed at his cardinal points and centre of gravity. (I nurture any blanks I come across in my harbouring arms.) I say yellow, when in fact a spidery black filigree was interwoven. The writer has used a technique of derangement that renders scenes discontinuous. Most theatrical productions plunder the same shape.

Addicted to years, he has been renamed the human accordion: pleated with folding bellows, spiked through with free metal reeds. He arrives. He is never appropriate. He is never time. There's a warlike patch at the base of his serrated beak. I am still looking forward to tomorrow. We are herded out to the opening sea.

Make conversation. There's hardly a limit to words with prefix un. A selection is given. Today's instructions are withheld. The drama is a sequence of accidents, a work inspired by attempts at flight a thousand years old. First, a cloth is dipped in wax to wrap a dead in. Words from unagin (without beginning) to unzoned are inked across the torso—followed by the limbs, the feet, the hands, the genitals and other extremities. A cheap biro is used. The surgical instruments are sterilized in the open flame of a naphtha stove. The number here is six, signifying ambiguity and inconsistency. We shan't provoke any further at this critical point of time. Let me through she cries. I'm an empath.

Do you recall that day. The three of us clinging together, hurtled through a vein of ice on a tin sledge. I refuse speech. I will never break silence. We favour the apparition or phantasm theory. I've never know such a run of lucks. Soft tissue is decaying at the hollow parts.
A bottle dungeon is a vast funnel-shaped cavity. It reaches from the crust to the centre of the earth. Some pictures repeat over and over. Every syllable uttered is added to the memory bone suspended from the ceiling. The original drawing hasn't

8

survived: charred leaves up the flume, so much angelspeech. I have covered the cell wall with five-bar gates. Glyphs and signs are indexed across a frozen breath of glass. My inquisitor comes without preamble or introduction. There's no question about it: I hear nothing and see nothing, but having begun we might as well press on to the end. I do not need you. I am discomposed of error: the lines I am. The re-creation of space suddenly appears rather urgent. These are the benefits of a flawed translation, an inexact interpretation of a thing. Everything is hammered into an infinite sequence of letters, universal lip.

As I speak they're preparing to apply the big steam treatment. I am naked and sealed. A gentle and mournful ending is in store, with something of wire and string about it. A webbed loop swishes through the air. Traces of calcite grow from the walls in curved fibrous aggregates. The specimen resembles a ram's horn. There's a high-calibre debate going on within informed circles as to which order these loose unpaginated sheets should appear. No one is allowed a mistake. Some claim there are pages missing at crucial moments. The whole resembles a payload of capsules, or strips of lead piping—brief notes on making conversation and the urgent need for a lack of attention. The chorus takes us forward twenty-two years. All the words used disguise themselves in order to be more present. Picture the making of a mosaic without the guidance of an overview, its maker navigating the placement of each fraction by chance, face pressed close to the frozen pavement.

What profit will it grant us. Try to be exact.

Are we not in a better position now, in relation to what we don't know? Descent takes place via the distaff, plummeting through the earth to its root. One of our party expires on the track. Having unwittingly described a circle, we find ourselves back at the tar-pit—fender sucked under, into the ooze of the tarn.

He is a rare worker in feathers. Last lines compel me—the after-image of one's own body, usually seen from the vantage point of the light flittings. Or observation by resonance of voice, by speaking with an ear to the patient's chest. We are launching into a sparseness. In perplexing him, in numbing him, have we done him any harm? (If you can't be explicit, show us in a diagram.) The two lovers escape.

His sister slumps dead beside the remote. He's reduced to justification. Sudden death usually puts a stop.

The gigantic recent, fossil wingless, waters silently closing over.

An aperture for light, admitted, the venereal decision.

Tesserae in fracture—mortlake hangings, of joyhood and landskips. A piece broken off, the underfinished portion. I am, I remember. I watch, and although there are no voices.

I hope that thing's not here when I get back.

II

His cut is deep like one mouth. He crouches alongside. A name is misspelled, a circuit completed. We take offence. Give back. Grant displeasure. Does it have to make contact. I conduct. I am nerves. I store up, lose nothing. All my systems function and contradict, often angular lineaments. I negotiate. He goes hogwire at the outcome. The listener sometimes lacks the motivation to protest, to sell tongue—to reset the tale in constructionist fashion. We are going to need shin-pads. There'll be reprisals. This starving and freezing won't work with me either—I have reread the tale, the nights. Amen. Use your head when you are. I dream he is standing upon a rocky outscarp—arid terrain (the guidebook says overhanging limestone feature). He initiates the tradition: evacuate, alienate, encompass, repatriate. We're exposed to one another. I'm leaving soon, which is a good reason to include me in the experiment. I am decoy. The objects presented include the slate pencils, the hopper-shape, the salt mineral, some vague peripherals, a few sheets of remaindered paper. What if one day I can no longer. It's an uncertain age. Silence is my prerogative. Silence is my domain. As long as he keeps at it things are held at bay. Things are kept in check. Change tack: two men, one cage, a fight to the death. The decays. A series of attacks and parries. A dead ball situation. We've just taken one step back from mourning. I am beginning to emerge. I courage myself by remembering what indifference I've made (lots of white space). I spoke at the outset. I don't provoke. I cannot revoke. I will not provoke by letters under my foreknowledge. No punchlines. Lots of silences. Any material addled to the edge will leave a deep depression in each face of the cube. The overall shape is a diminutive of bend sinister, only half its width. Atomic life is sinking. The parry combines with the riposte.

We initially believed the thing was used for striking sparks. There simply isn't enough data to go on. Information is ebbing. We stop. Lots of sirens. So far, all we can recollect is intricate street canals navigated by brightly-coloured barges, clumps of seaweed drifting across an oily spectrum. In the town square is a museum dedicated to those no longer here (a familiar theme we shall return to again and again), an archive of images that help you to forget: a worn face caught in the glow of a nearby star and printed onto a piece of paper—a rust chute that empties into the sea—a pyramid of pebbles balancing beside an olive grove. I hope you're concentrating. I hope you're connecting. I am presently paralysed. I stand upon the southernmost of twin salt-glands that flank the river-mouth.

And now, ladies and gentlemen, with able assitance I give you the past. There are waves and I am humming a tune. There are horses, plenty of horses. See, the rim of a cloud, burnt into a slice of night. I declare myself in a dumbshow. Odour and humidity are estimated equal. Among my citizens are common mutes.

You can no doubt see the lights of the petrochemical plant from this very spot, across the estuary, across the darks. Limbs link and wish for something. He says we have been quietly structured. We are panopticon. Think of this in terms of an end state, entropy—unfounded rumours, nameless molecules. We cease. Some things should never come together and occupy the same space. I'm returning to my earlier notes, earlier selves, and expanding. It's believed his motive was revenge for something that happened twenty centuries ago. He refuses to collaborate. He is misuse, plunders by ancient pistol—perhaps a substitute for corroded or corrupt. There's a time, and we can wait. The stripping work is done with the aid of a steamblower and an axe. There's lots of tiny white flowers pouring out of his head. The doctrine is the doctrine of the impossibility. His brain appears to be made of millet-seed. No number satisfies the diction or has the property. This is where I put all the things I reject but wish to keep. I don't think this is particularly savage territory. I don't think this is illusive terrain. The square root of opposition dictates itself, swaying to and fro from end to end. The melodies of different composers can be approached by subtracting the principle. Consider his erection range, his neutron object. We are modelling his magic on unspecified rites: piratic genes, albumen smog, the torn dust-cover et cetera. None of us can cope with all the biting and the scratching. That said, the fights are much like fights: inconsequential. He reuses everything—that's his pulse—but I'm the one who is trembling anticipation. That throbbing noise from beneath the floorboards is the last utilizable vein.

He's asked questions to which he must provide the right answers. That old trick. He's older than he disappears. The delivery is uncertain, but sure to be profound: pushing and shoving, boring and biting. A crumpled note reads. Enclosed are the erotic toys you ordered. Consider his relentless nihil, totemic pleasure without principle. Playtime is over. Nothing hinders. He was so young. Diametrically opposite sits the foundation of a social, of obligate and restrict. And I saw it for the first time with my naked eye. I think I imagine. I am diametrically apposite. Alecto is one of the furies. He replies, firm to the tooth and unceasing, after a literal fashion—one member of a crew whose language moves at pace. The men are spearing fish from a smack (nightangle of antibe). He is nithing, from the son of crush (genital). The number here is nine. Under my peeling eye I think I image. Fancy dribbles are crystallizing into plates used for killing moths—a drawer full of eyes under glass—radiotelepathy. In so many words, a table of gaunt noises. He is older than he apes. We depend less and less on a cynicism of our own invention. Obsessive fear of pain spooks out across a widening terrain. The whistle's gone out in the bank. I have lost my pi. We are extinguished, branded by the wavy-watered brush of steel. This is my obsolete form, a figure woven not printed. Inside is liquid flame, liquid volatile. This fragment concords weight and measure, all around the divining rain. Thank you for thinking for me, at least my surface appearance: Damascus wire, the colour red of the damask rose, flowering unnamed from book-lung. Forget or variegate, clothe oneself. I enter, mute.

Pretzel of starlings twisting above a charred pier. I too am a starting place with patterns in wake. And although the original has vanished, I think, Yes. When do we start. Happenstance is a full box. We are surrounded. They will never give up and go home. These bewildering apparitions are merely electrical phenomena not uncommon—tiny wings in a fading sky, fender sucked under. Don't ring me about. I think yes, hexagonal socket in the head. Perfect. Imperfect. I am mentally ill in several parks across the weekend. These are sequences of remarkable interdependence. I am coinciding. I've seen the trailer and there's no going back. Children are sold as slaves and the litter's terrible. I letter. Infinite dissent has connections with the least number principle, the idea slowly working its way back towards the light. My adversary is going for the full roast. Obsolete and alien forms are being laid under siege. We slake our thirst on a liquid got from the distillation of bone.

You forget your own name in a drama of seemingly disconnected tableaux. Snowscape with sun. Ski tracks. Beating dots on a white endless. Somewhere with altitude. A recent illness leaves him part blind, with cataracts of the mind: a shrunken monkey head, skin jacket with hood, rudder-feathers, palm lines embedded with spangles of coloured glass, suck pebbles and artificial flowers torn from a graveyard. Sheer panic, correction ribbon and advent decorations are other distinguishing features of our uniform. Your type he asks. Yes I wrote, I write my own objects, fusing them into manifold forms of separation. The air is thin, no need to chew like in the old abode. We are in a drama of unseemly and disconnected tableaux. I say as much above. A rather eye-catching map is unfurled—a representation in outline of the surface features of the earth and the moon and a similar plan of stars in the sky. He says if you had any sense you'd leave before it's too late, saphead.

He mourns. He pines for his departed. She too is meanwhile and is fled. By chance we meet. I say I don't know, just a yen to come here. We operate pretty autonomously now, in a poignant verse replaced throughout. Small stones germinate in my gut. He, the guiser, pleads for her return. He is lacelike, having no mesh or ground. His patterned sections are fixed by interweaving threads (a species of gimp). And the brain-pan is coming apart, split to its plates—tectonic dwelling. The suffix here is instrumental. Today's sound is cult percussion—the pressure flaking and pecking—indirect strikes sawing, drilling and grinding. This can't exist without limit of time. Working with spartan resources and an undercast, I begin to collect photographs for the record: strike textures with bleached palette, the swing from viral to monochrome. A distant stellar object is revealed. Nobody pays any attention. I am sinister dexter. I am the very image of a terse concentrate—punctuated by repetition, etched into the screed in charcoal, stump-oil and chalk. You'll learn to become more than satisfied with these endless lists. That censorious word again: fissionary maker. The I as inrush, the I as in land—I as pivot in turn like a spindle or torting nail. I don't say that I mean. The others rendezvous in a dark-cobbled alley. I'm taking this up one step at a time. They could have talked to us about it at the outset. We could have saved an awful lot of paper and ink. Desire here is simultaneously sentimental and cerebral, a choking on stones.

Waste structure in the middle of a square league of uncultivated land. Theme, never-ending. Look says she at the cornea, prizing wide the eyelid. See that circle and the film stretched across it. I have been corrected. What this has to do with the ink welts remains a mystery. I don't recognize you, ether. To feel more intensely the presence of my head within the room, a tergal plate is positioned in front of the scutum—the target of the X-ray tube upon which the beam is focussed. From the appearance of its lamellae, I begin to guess: an instrument winged with wire anode, surrounded, sea foregoing. . . . Perhaps I could go on until the end. Herein is the charnel where I learnt, everthing punch-pilled, policed. What is more, it bears the same name as our saint.

The plan, or scheme, a brief account of. She's brave, no doubt about that. Gather under. She says I have a young companion in my brain. I am conceived of my own remembrance. He has become breath, immaculate since my arrival. He guides me as I dodge through passersby before the shopkeeps. The question also rises: was the perpetrator. (Him in her inside him.) In this contest he has creased inestimation. Often I catch him above the waves in that gentle book, one thumb turned to the execute position, while humming a funeral dirge. But the way this is being constructed doesn't commit memory to linger in the present. A vision isn't something you discuss.

In my locker I find the records of a voyage of the nineteenth undertaken by two gentlemen. On oblong cards the writer has written. In the deep green ink of a beautiful hand is a log of their voyage, an archive of loss. They do not know where they are going. The hand writes he has died and I have cast his words into the sea. It writes

c
a
s
t
thus.
Nothing, really. Misdirected bloodletters.

His own work on memory is buried in an unmarked plot. I am reading between the blue poles. We're to be paid off. I need an imperfect now-future, something dissembling. My life empties out. Do I mean disassembling. Bits of history that signify nothing—mean nothing—likeness set at void. And have you spotted the lodestone in the bottom right-hand corner? Now I find him sitting in a ditch reading elegies. He too is emptied of signals, nil swerving away from place. I do not know if I have seen. A piece of local granite travels and is blessed on its arrival. Is that his blood. I'm aware of some dark viscid stuff spreading across the lino, oozing and bubbling, congealing to terrain, congealing to map. We are stuck at a junction, trapped within an after-image. Salt is poured to silhouette the dead—last page, the solid world itself. No one can seer the evidence. Ingenerate tears fill the eye et cetera. I am return, return. He says yes a form of rerun, page after implacable page. His art harbours no hostility, no responsibility. I think this is a murder mystery. The chief problem he's going to have is this. Unnoticed, the waters are gathering behind our backs. This resembles sound being improvised— the discipline of silence and indirection. The real curse is that I'm here with you, always. I am depriving you of protection. To my mind it's a question of mandible repair and jaw extension. We're all dependent on the manner of delivery, the eti- quette adhered to. The nearest star makes another appearance, rearing up out of the ocean. I recall a cherished journey to a flattened land, a country house, the sea, a sky, a big sky with eyelike markings—a peacock bird and other wildfowl, the type of sea we argue spontaneous things all being equal.

Gypsum and its misuses. A digression. Knot and vortex above pier, silenced algorithms. And though the original has vanished, I think yes, when do we start. The next step is the panic scrub of his flaking skin. He lives in the bath. The white cloth wrapped about his head lends him an air of nobility, though it's hard to pinpoint why. A board placed across the rim of the tub serves as a writing desk. Upon it are a slip of paper and a quill pen. One of his arms dangles, life- less—deep irreverent greenblue, in wreck with trail covert. Background void. Writing is terrifying.

Now, the first letter can only be A.
Aftermage. Clustering pronouns (you sort it out). Spontaneous things burst- ing out in glass vessels. A dimlit exterior, some manner of laboratory. A touch of cravy. Flare of naked flame, searing heat. There's a touch of gravity in the air. The image is grainy, flickering. Another country. Time the unfamiliar. None of this seems now like a crime. With hindsight none of this approximates. He says I am dead to forgetting. I carry about with me a briefcase of unexploded food. If you forget me you die—I die—crashing out of those final pleasant moments. This has the asymmetry of an unsettled film score, a touch of thinking too pre- cisely on the event. He slides back into sequence. A bloom spreads across the eye. I quit in my mistake, with free mental reives. What started as a border inci- dent turns nasty. I'm the same man but sometimes they call me. It's all over. I live in my mistake. I live in the space created by errors of breath, that touch of grav- ity. People are always making discoveries of things they were not in quest of. Time is nigh. Time is like a tumour in the abdomen, beneath the armpit, behind the knee, ten by four imperial. He tries to explain how the steal was only possible because we were in the right formation at the right time. He once fell off the rig himself. He is one luckless player. Nonetheless his hand is good—quite cooked,

as folk say. The chosen implement is an implement for shocking hay. And look, over there, a flying noose. String it all together: a stack-yard with incendiaries, men who sack and ignite. Again and again the pneumatic chisel slips and cuts into the flesh of the corpse. The pressure is still on the coast road, the recoil off a sixty-year wall of sound. He knows that deep inside he is intact. The remains are preserved, the ligament that secures the bunch. Come with your own distaff, the stick that holds the fist, the female part of any dissent. I resemble a word myself, sprung from the root found in flax. From my usual zeros, I promise myself. The limbs are widely spaced and bound tightly at the extremities. In this way a navigation system has been introduced in which A (master), B and C (two slaves), give for master-being and master-slave two sets of intersecting hypotheses. When charted this gives one so equipped a most politic position, within several hundred miles of range. We pertain to or are situated at the outer end, farthest from my point of attachment. Opposite to proximal is a cluster of uncommon nothings. I am so-formed from distaste, on the analogy of central: fast ashes in a lost box. Don't stop talking. Decide. Remedy. It's possible I've forgotten some details: footfall on lamina ceiling, inquisitions fast and thick. Are you at this instant astride an sire horse? Have hooves been grafted onto the soles of your feet? What are the untold rules of the regime? What was yesterday's mineral? . . . He answers as best he can, then resumes penning his letter.

Dear

The physical world has been given the role of an avenging deity, an error cherished—after-exposure, inclination away from a level base.

A river's brink licking against the rim.

Divination by means of an abrupt yank or jerk.

A sloping or tilted position of the face.

Add, say, an extra E in the wake of every letter O, and the name gives out, collapses to become a sort of distorted spring. Meaning undermines itself, yet the image persists like misremembered super eight: the twist in the tramway—the smooth grind of the curving track—sparks from the elevated—bombardier aerospace with screeching jet.

Earth must be traversed at a crosswise pace. A somnolent vertigo is vibrating through our method. What with all its members, organizing and hanging will be a complex. I represent comeuppance, an ignorant blunder in an old story once received in the mass. One of my segments forms a side piece to the head.

The ship's timbers lie obliquely to the line of the keel. Turn on your edge or corner. Lilt vague and fling sudden. Bring about a decision in any contest. Note the static disturbance. In my interferences I never go beyond the boundaries of space and experience. Yet, there are points of reference and rebuttal. Yet, people have at all times devoted themselves. Yet, a man who perseveres must come to a verdict—intercession by undergod, the work of supererogation.

Conjure a place of abode—odd slang of to sleep, to ken. I am no longer answering the door.

Gobest yours et cetera.

Folk are less troubled by their conscience than we supposed. An itinerant singer arrives in our hamlet. He's attached to a metal hook on a long handle and swung around in space. Beneath him a cogged wheel serves to connect him to the earth. (There are at least a dozen ways the first XI have been trained to kill.) Murmurs of reverence rise from the crowd. He rotates in the chill air, swooping low over our heads with threshing limbs. It's rumoured he's been at work in memory with his charts, with his indeterminacy. I start taking notes—these are simply distraught. The hand makes several short twisting movements from side to side at the wrist. I give up. Sometimes the tune is right there in your face, the compartments of the head, at the very beginning. With his cloak of invisibility he moves like someone who doesn't have to think (while reading this, you sound like someone who doesn't have to think). As worthy a subject as he is, he knew the punishment for trading vapourware.

Note how persons of male and female sex, young and old, of every conceivable type, are jumbled up with lots of words made of black letters. And you'll have noticed there are uncomfortable points of silence. Events appear to be determined by some random tactic, for example the following.

When the loop of the meander becomes, it's cut off across the neck leaving an abandoned port, which may remain, or may not. Siren and birdsong on the wireless, angelus. Pleading representatives. Somebody's argument and somebody else's. And why are we underground, buried beneath ice two miles thick.

Long time with no owner in the offing. It behooves me . . . . I have given up trace. (Anaphase is the most obvious metaphor.) Do I mean event. We move away from one another toward opposite poles of the spindle—a form of amnesia which is actually a fight from reality: the madness in my area. The missing word is distal. It's true that in some cases a retreat takes place beneath insignia, in other cases not. All around us many species are growing in profusion. But I can no longer extinguish. My characters are becoming more demonstrative, no. Do you not think. The daughter chromosomes are crawling toward the extremities of the shaft upon which everything turns. I am exquisite tired. I have not been back for an age. I have no angles. Feeling is reciprocated. I loathe all ritual. I did not order this revolver. I say break for me.

An elegy in a dusty boneyard, with solitary beast. I say break for me. I break speech for you. It is a master-slave relationship: the men in question. She comes with dog (the third person). There is big moon (not singular but plural). I caress she says is that what you call it (passive instead of inactive). I withdraw back inward (aorist instead of present). Then there's a brief piece of dialogue between us which I can't recollect, much shuffling of claws (not indicative but optative). I call out recollect. Due to short landfall, the cancelled is past. Those remaining aboard are on course to rendezvous with the orbiting discovery. Sometimes I find money in my boot. I'm working through a few errors here, ever the mouthpiece. It will steal forever.

Consider a relative never, where when is finished and nothing obstacles. Miscast as trembling: anti-cathode with naked murmurs.

Perplexed, as unexpected, gravity pulls us through.

Of attaining uncertainty in knowledge, a measure of available energy. I am sitting in a grand library. The sun appears in the sky. I can't look at it. It's true that some instants appear fugal. I am flag-bearing, in some cases not. She simply does at once what the rest of us achieve over time—cutting, sifting, building and breaking. Now for the final contraction, and healthy lists of everything she wishes to release, everything she wishes to keep. I feel like an invalid too, exempt from any test of actuality. Place stress where you will. To me everything is supernatural. She lives, it's just that her breath has absconded. You stole it.

Describe the exterior, painting detail where you will.

A vast estate overseen by white mansonry at the crest. The embankment appears to be in motion, discarded parts amid its foliage: ruined stock, the rusting fender, a sheep's backbone, possessed polyethylene—final shares, gathered beneath the watch of a small pyramid pierced by slits. There are vague silhouettes. Blazon argent, three coughs proper. Spend some quality time with your utensils, visible statements of separateness. A muscle extends and becomes rigid. Check the signal aspect. (I believe it was more ignoble, the old alliance.) I'm sure he would have mentioned a deal were he present: a discreet contract with the restless dead. They are a persistent intrusion into what he is trying to create (the hidden dangers of aluminium). There's been much criticism of the new register. Para- and quaternary are among our formulas. Now eat, egg.

The present tense is irresistible. He sings. It's a song about coprophagy and cannibalism. It all ends in a spinal staircase. Medical history is discarded. (The answer is what's a coda.) An ambitious madame keeps a protective eye in her pocket, soft stone. On the selfsame page there's an envelope and in the envelope there's a letter. Despite the absence of any recognizable terminology whatsoever, there still exists a distinct compass. (One should be grief, if nothing else.) The mysterious agency now holds everyone to account. You're lost if sainthood doesn't disgust you. Bring on the anchorites.

Tell us something of the word withdrawn.

Dissemination is written on his back. A more powerful magnet is needed. A wider compass is needed. There's brevity at the core—a system incorporating the modern form of sometimes, activated by love or patriotism. This is more a well of retreat, a notorious transgression of commonplace representations. There's no sign of a presence in the house. There is nowhere I want to be. The public harbours a fascination with the forger, but you can never master these things: the volt, the faulting-meter, bolts of irrelevance on your doorstep. I don't recognize you either.

Use this device sparingly. Thick haze from bush fires in the suburbs. The heart condenses—its causeway contracts, the great arterial trunk that carries blood from the pump. The cord that secures the hawk.

Our moments, at craw of kite. Any insensate gulf. A very common charge, which resembles but hath no shanks, just turf of feather. We are a mark of incandescence. Our numeral is four. Where are you. Is there out there. Steam pours from the cockpit and the cabin. Return to earth. It's very much like preseason. I return to the surface and everyone applauds. I don't understand such sentences, such silences. A stranger approaches and whispers. You can have the full body treatment or just the partial head. The recurring sections are fixed by interweaving tread. The objective is species, the act or result of making, from to make. Three in a row flew over yesterday. Now it's the memoryman. Whatever next. Did you know they've succeeded in transmitting thoughts inside someone else. People returned from the future to sabotage the experiment or time would have stopped. The difference here is that I'm apprehending the thing, whereas he merely interprets, turns the original into something it never was. But I have the same kind of feeling: smoke-machine, fire-eater, juggler and slow thinker. He asks have I ever been blind. (Your eyes he says your eyes.) This really is the sign of who we are. We need the crowd to buy into this one. He's looking for a reaction. (Think a sequence of purloined letters.) Now they say a liqueur is to be distilled from shoes. Things are desired, lacking: that which escapes detection by being excessively obvious. It is probable, from the way in which the flags are distributed, that the populace is not used to breaking words into silences. Note to self, include criticism of the new format.

We need a complete shift in emphasis. They change all the seating around and we begin talking to ourselves again. They think we can't hear. They drop from the eaves. A list of numbers corresponding to different murders is presented. Lips are read through a two-way mirror. Labelled tracks have been carefully alligned using library index cards. Objects may be picked up and tasted. A pattern of squares with words upon them is emerging. I am a disabled signifier. He is outrigger, both masts. Today's favoured organ is the manyplies or omasum, the psalterium—overstuffed fardel-bag. Paludic spatters cross the manuscript here and there, flecks of marsh. To defend himself he converts into a rubber ball so tiny that bouncing cannot harm him. The crew are lured back to the island where they're transformed into rocks and trees. A wild is discovered at the centre. Various other spellings exist. The game is the game of chance, played out by betting on the appearance of uncertainty, perhaps from reason unknown. Who could bear to. Who among us could forbear to disburden. And what are those phials of coloured acid.

After shattering his leg he performs in acute pain. He embodies the collapse of impossible. He stands on stage without moving, leaning forward with his bad limb half-bent under him, or swung behind his head. False snow gathers at the panes. Return again and again with your characteristic insistence: grey, impalpable last page. He crashes through the window, then repeats the action to infinity. People start to leave. Sometimes he seems desperate. He shudders and strains and shakes himself. (I'm reminded of maimed leather.) I am captive in a world where I could not lose you. I often reproach myself by thinking. Over a brief spell, it descends. I unfind.

His supellex consists of the iron pot aforesaid and a hollow for water. A goat, a pig and an ox are sacrificed to render his incorruptible body mortal. Of all this, an inventory has been writ, yet lost.

Exit-ghost incarnadine. Pearl-handled Glock nestling in a bed of velvet.

She has quit the compound. (Father would not let me, now it's your fault.) I coin a new verb: to emotionally compromise by the bestowing of generous gifts. Nobody cares whether she's alive or dead. Strewn about the cobblestones are discarded canisters of cs gas. There's oil in my shoe, no cover at all. Abandoned tonight, I slid down with nothing—no cover from incoming—nothing and nowhere to hide, no shelter in a nonexistent place. I buy myself off: lost young everywhere, hoodlum girls rolling across the pavement. . . . Three hours I sit there motionless, sipping and watching, noting all the nothing. All I can do is gaze at the passage of action and event, the worrying away at speech. Everything is sort of staggered: blood in the other. I've been appointed overdog for the day. Somebody asks if I want to make a family. What now? I just escaped from one, it took a half-life of ordnance. Why would I volunteer for another stretch, throw myself back in? Also, there can be no proof of the consistency of such a system from within itself. And by the way, I chose mine.

Returning to experiment, where they might be said to be, and are called forth. The Golgi apparatus produces a pure line of vesicles, an organelle of folding membranes—the infamous cleavage furrow. Stained bodies are queuing up around the centrosome, a slanting line like an obsolete form of coma. One tiny body is malformed by division, trillions of inanimate cells. Strinkling dropples, he ejaculates: man-fat. Seal up your eyes. Use the penultimate chisel. The objective is the catching up of a horse's legs. (Let's talk strain.) The fibres are arranged in distinct patterns of coincidence: pressure under grace, tension between the two poles of the spindle. All the lights are coming on. I am never going back. All the lights are coming on across the gulf and it is raining. Yes I am going back. Do not wait for me. Stop. You are the stormy petrel, crime far from land or solitary rock. Stop. Forms come and go, assuming the defunct shape of our communications. This is followed by a leap of fate. I am the specialized part. I am pencilled in. A mesh of nerves acts as the lid of the organ. I am led astray by light, to mislight.

The amazing journey of her head after death.

Glagol bodies. Fresh corpses decay in the trench that rings the keep. Everything happens only once—a splintering—charnel-house cum sex cell. Officially, reminiscence occurs. Just a little to the left she says, see, a few clean femurs and radii and the head part. There's nothing we can do. (You don't say.) A whiff of putrescence sits at our interior, the official emblem. People lack drive. What else did she tell me that day. She is named from her seeming to walk on water, a beaconing authority: a rod, a spoke, a ray. If you can make it beyond this chapter, things start to get a lot easier on the eye, on the tongue. Now, just for you, here's a love song. There's nothing we can't do or say.

I am an open field reinforced by witness. I have no ancestry. I do not butter my hair et cetera. A patient waiting game is underway throughout a large section of the margin. I am beginning at the end: thief in act one, monk in act five. Props include the stuffed fardel-bag. The event is trapped in a decaying orbit about a remote, at the point of greatest (or least) distance from the central body. A type of lapse. You sense it too, don't you, the symbolism of wheel, arch and loop: a misfitting, the collective seizure. (If the object's not there you can't take it away.) The loop remains as a channelling device. All is uncivic. A glow of zodiacal light can be seen opposite the sun—white specks and flashes of electricity in the eyeball. He has become obsessed with his technic. How will he manage to characterize such an array of outlaws. Know what he reminds me of: a curved piece in the circumference of a heel, the stolen rim. See. His system is perfect. I swear I could sell smoke.

They are found in large numbers down in the hold. Most people have their tissues used without consent. I am showing deep cold. They very much believe her soul is in there: dirt, desire, crumbling antiquated walls.

Stop complaining. This is what you wanted, no.
Pale yellow fingers opening at nightfall. A planet, usually Venus and Mercury, is seen in the setting west soon after. The atmosphere is ideal for such phenomena. The final scene is captured using the surviving humans. I sat there for some hours with my aperture open. It's of the utmost importance that you should notice this point in time, and all the other points.
I am waiting to meet some precious verbs—over and against the ideal, varieties of real and was. A shape perceived in seawrack, the tangle genus, with large extended bladder. It's still too early for us to tell, precursors of the margin: going, doing, making.
They are at play. Someone whispers, badly. They cull and are culled in turn. I am so grateful to listen in on all sorts of people thinking aloud.
Say it.
When are to meet thy go.

III

The words, actually. I am taking the slab of black clay with me, also the pencil leads. The people are he, she and I. My characters are. Who else could exist in this narrow strip of shade. These are quit fictions, but this next letter should appease you no end. My present situation is one in which all voluntary thought is swallowed up and lost. Nails fly from one wall and embed themselves in the opposite. I have the sensation I've lain here for some time, delayed in a spell of dying. Some, like me, are recidivist—forever falling back on you don't say.

Of marshes, malarial. One shinglefooted, stumbling. Next on is a collector of pure (they little know him who talk). Around here, capital's gnawed to its bare bones in the acid bath while you sleep. The last chapter is reserved for those who will not work, the surviving ascension—a measure of the disorder of a system. My animal lurks at its favoured station, talons drumming. Nails fly to the window. My cavity is lined with dark-green to black spinels, a multitude of faces. Every object in the room is sucked out through the porthole. (We are a ship, I forgot.) I seek an unravelling companion. (You already know too much, and I'm in danger of myself.) I am going to have to lure one toward me, but with something he truly despises. This is called a paradox. I can't be bothered with names. We meet. A little torture is inflicted. He offers praise, limply. Let me introduce some people here for the sake of charity. They occupy no particular rank. I'm making astonishing progress in the sciences.

A detachment is taking place. It enters my head. It leaves my head. Detachment takes my place. The missile penetrated her left cheek and passed out underneath the right jaw, without damaging any of the vital structures in her neck, such as the box of voice. We occupy an adverse enclosure—a binding—with morbid narrowing of every passage. Energy still exists but is lost to purpose. There had once been meaningful work, now folk scratch things out of the living air.

Recollect what has happened to us up to this point in time. Don't worry if you can't hear parts of this. Withhold your reproaches and consider. Unfold the hazard of achieved or lost. But first the benediction that started it all off—bearing abroad in a body, a manifesto in flesh. The piece ends with gnawing and fretwork. The dayspring has visited.

The composition also boasts an ornamental grille, an ancient border where lines meet at right angles, the pattern repeated to infirmity. A number of things have been arranged as if threaded on a string—in Greek key, in meanders, all very unpresent. Dredging deeper that dejected tale, it runs thus.

Next on is the notorious. This notorious goes out to look for a sprinkling-can of fresh petrol. On his search he's apprehended by militia. His body is torn to pieces and scattered to the boundary. His starsign is vertigo. Sixteen serves as the hexed number. He once performed with the aesthetic bone, full duplex and a hub. His ghost is now punctured. It stands astride a barricade (see surveillance, see badinage). Like so he *attends* to himself. And I: the atom grows darker. It begins with a thin scratch and ends in a jagged line. I'm ready for combat.

Discount the penicillin shavings. Everything is to hand. (That is, the thing-in-itself, not something else.) It's like, say, a fleet returning to harbour, with no rustling shades of meaning. The text is full of duppies and subs, remnants of overyear and drought. Their names congeal out of the air—those of deceased friends, raw-headed and bony. They have been troubling at the telepathic wire. The upshot is forty-five minutes of cliché. I forget the rest. I can't tell story from story. O to have kept myself at home, being-to-hand for the daily occasion. And then of course you've got the worlds next.

Received, reived. A radio-navigation stem via which the three ground stations can now be described.

Luces, the seventh letter. A fit of perversity, of horses. Move to right. Move on. Simulate, with long cartilaginous skull and heterocercal snout. Yielding, within a row of horny shields protecting granular skin, column piercing the upper lobe. . . .

We began at what we termed our centrepoint and worked out diametrically from there. The writing bone is still undescended.

Straught-corpsed and strifeful.

A straitcoat of perpendicular lines.

How long was she out there. That's the best thing to ask. We have no means of judging. Old writing is rubbed out to make room for new. Every monument is overturned. Fresh prescriptions are being deciphered. A curving drive is seen running through the fields. The others are invisible. Panic breaks out in the village like a film. Folk gather burning torches at the night. The story never comes together. Again, contract to ease, to erase.

The following case is the strange case of the conductor's tongue—the whim of representing an earlier hour. Hold on to something. Dismantle the object and melt it down in the crucible. The following case is the case of the misaligned mob. Hold on to something. I've had hands in the past, I've had feet. I devote myself to his destruction. The plot is simple: the dead child and whatnot stack up. Will the roof shut this afternoon or won't it? I remain silent. She retires to the toxic refuge in much confusion. Your head turns *askance*, face twisted back. Hold on to one of those rotten wooden piles. You've got to remember, this game's ninety percent will, ten percent malignancy—a form of illness in which two people, generally close, share the same delusion: the inability to make decisions, however trifling. What she overlooks is that he has silenced the crowd. Your apotheosis is in those gathering eyes.

Among the quieter routines of my life was the epiphany in the lift. Leave your clothes in the vestibule. The area of action is circumscribed, submerged in stagnant days. Change nothing.

Suburban house with blue neon sign over front door declaring psychic. Numerous drove of feral dogs out back. There will be arrangements. The found footage approach was an idea. (You don't have to make it up anymore.) I know this music, creeping out from an interval, lying somewhere in between. He is standing there withholding, his ash plaint.

No knowledge. We row into wastes of time to run aground. Wild-eyed with black greatcoat, he is stunned at the threshold.

He is incapable of doing.

Awaiting you, at cease but with life, he's a minor character in a mortality play whose subject is the struggle in between. Without the world (I mean outside) floats the density. The songs form a cycle for the years. Now here's the down-side, our little ambuscado: certain words seduce and isolate. Let's change the pulse-rate. In stillness and repose one can hear a murmur from inside the body as it bodies. It's said he can transform himself into an ally. It's said he can transform himself into a jaguar. (Pronounce this correctly or die.) Can you work out the changes from his tracks in the snow.

Answer: the metal box or lining of any cylinder in which an axle turns—gun-metal, a composition of copper and tin used in journals. I'm beginning to feel the dramatic effect of his absence. Three yellow squares of light shine above us in the gathering.

These are our sole bearings. And so back again through the wall.

Two people who never meet. Those giant water-lilies. Back to that day, she at the crest of the hill—dress cerulean, cloudless above. Two people alternate in a living place, lying in wait. One of the logbooks is missing. (I'm repeating myself.) No trace of the skull-headed lady, the sandy plain, the groundling sea. It obviously went well. There is uncertainty.

Respond correctly to the question.

What is that called.

That old trick. For one moment he adopts the other's voice (lurching bolt, monster). I feel a certain grudge of respect for him: it can't be easy negotiating these dim corridors with a single centred eye. We need to find examples. And what's that noise from down below? We need to find simples.

Improbability, with to produce not to spare. Magnesia-iron. Yours truly.

Of the three persons kept in the head.

Though deceased they are permitted to inhabit. I've died but am granted one final dream. (Interesting to see how we're drifting back to the original notes.)

Undone by source, what are we do with the fact.

The tenacious clay lines of the jumping pit.

Plates of bone floating on a scum of quicklime.

Sensitive tissue within the cavity roof.

We are crossing the umbilicus, making our way back toward the event horizon. (Note to self, locate a more appropriate particle.) Still no trace of the logbook.

A love gage may take on strange shapes.

Two men rent a room by night and day respectively. Their flesh resembles. They have been adapted: chrome-tanned skin of calf, with rectangular markings made by rolling over and over on the ground. They are actors in a bedroom farce but do not know it. What to do with this. Simply to remember, to docket.

Heavy steel-grey symbol hanging over frame of open door. One of the objects has a very high melting-point. I realize. I should have numbered the items, as an absolute minimum. I should have described the items, as an absolute minumum. Say, a mortality of monks.

The phaeton booms to a halt, throwing off men in slips and clumsy hops.

His raw eyes. The cold bright rail. His clenched fingers. I wake up in someone's garden.

He is the first of the two archers encountered that day. Upon opening, grains of sawdust were found inside him, clinging to a variety of glistening membranes. I cannot enter this place. His number is seventy-seven. (It's written on a plastic tag attached to his wrist.) There are shaking heads all around trimmed with bleached ruffs. At least this scenario grants us a time limit to work within. Folk gather with burning torches in the night. I cannot enter this place. It seems I shall never see him again. It's like haunting yourself—the inability to accept a particular action committed. One wields a curious instrument for bending a crossbow. This employs a revolving cylinder, a wheel, and an axle. Heads on pikestaffs are aligned across the bridges like the old days. In the courtyard balance stacks of rotting pallets, much hauling and hoisting of men. Held for uncomfortable lengths of time, the subjects either reveal themselves or become meaningless. A circuit must be made to intercept. This has to change. In the centre there's a line drawing of a horse.

Brail him up by disquiet means. I let him talk his last talk. The revelation is worth the wait. He was once struck by summary lightning while sitting at the grille of his cell. . . . Glance through: the chute to the sea, snot-dark and winegreen. Spindrift lather in circuitous motion, end of the pier stuff. This signals the incident of the blue plastic carrier. Apex predators.

The watermeadow.

The flat earth.

The empty museum in the dusty square.
The causeway.
The pebble in the headstone.
The olive grove.
Halfway the shattered glass.

Priceless elasticity of demand. For the first time, being anywhere. Over-wrought ironwork, buildings pissing rust. Something like a tiny crystal flies out from between her teeth. Consider a threshold: he and she and the lover of one, an early form of dwelling. Their game is intercepted, a race in which each con-testant runs in a different direction while clutching a baton. I take a short cut whenever I can. Origin is unknown. Sometimes you don't hear the beacon. It has been muted, caught at no-man's-land—an all-night vigil in the waste region between two opposing armies (a complex miscellany of disputed parts). I'm striving to make something that's already been done a thousand times: slices of sound, a cloaking made up of scraps from various sources. No spare topics in the cabinet today. Though there is a head, under which a rhetorician might probe for exhausted matter. The final words run.

A scheme or epitome of the disposition or state of anything.

A rotary movement of atoms or particles of subtle matter around an axis.

It's said savants are basically people with prodigious memories, but this is dif-ferent. Location: an imaginary cycle on the celestial sphere, about twenty-three degrees north or south. Words are running away with themselves, orientations in response to a stimulus. I am at the boundary. Alternation of moisture and drought—radiowaves, irregularities, scattered signals beamed up on a parabolic curve. It's the close of the season. At the lowest layer temperature fails and height increases. Pressure drops. Avifauna include gilded seabirds with elongated rectrix. Plastic sheeting and tarpaulins have been laid over the stone roof of each beehive cairn. I am the boundary. There's an unbearable softness now to his voice. (Stop up the mouth, with security.) The sun turns on reaching its declination. The ser-vants promise they will deliver the corresponding disc tomorrow (much hilarity over this). There follows a fight to the death. I'm hoping the crowd will be con-structively awed. A sequence of sevens knits everything together.

A quick succession of short hard sounds.

He understands the book as figurative, five-told echo. How might I repair myself. I cross and recross the frozen breath of the field of play. What I saw in his study may have been a novel lying on its side on the table. It may not. It may have been a box, perhaps. It may have been a vessel for wandering about in. Regardless, we recognize each other under whatever conditions. The third part of our little ménage is ruined and lost in the surf. We should try to do something when the coastline reappears.

Any connection with planet names is to be questioned. The parts near the centre are cracked.

Get this over with.

She is still her dying friend. (More of that singular narrative later.) My present situation is one in which all voluntary thought is swallowed up and lost. Lend me that pistol she says.

Dead now the body is blue and limpid—by this we mean its skin waives through the light. Another of our team was found embedded in a bath of congealed wax. There's no trace of the percussion bulb. Coins are scattered in the street, balanced on the eyes. It's a could-be-anywhere locality. A cerecloth was wrapped around the face. This acts as a vocal mask. I'm reminded of the Feringhi exhumation. I am reminded of the flashflood, the sea. This is exactly how an editor works.

Unrestrained bibliophagy is rife among the populace. It's the first to get all his cards out who wins.

Metallic scraping and tapping, through a fine rain. Gas cathode in cylindrical chamber at drop of pressure. Even the most insignificant problem is welcome in these stagnant days. You may just get away with this. Read aloud from hereafter. Change all the calendars. Substitute percentile rank and the death glyph as counter-argument. My biggest influence is the influence. I seem to have lost the faculty of thought.

Scratching of signs at translucent blue skin. You could feel the gap opening up. You will understand. This letter will please you. It is quietly factual, quietly hostile.

Whiff of putrescence at thawed interior. Every day she must be let loose for a short while. There's nothing in this world I wouldn't do for you. I appear to lack all faculty of imagination (vice, elegance, insouciance).

Any lizard of the genus or the subclass.

Found dead in masque Friday. It's a game thus far. The lanes are reopening. The result is what you know you do not know. It's been a very long five minutes (percentagewise, two million years). They are dismantling the arena. That's a decision, isn't it.

No, that's a dislocation. I am at the conquest, head wide open, ribcage disarrayed.

Here is something that supplements all that change, my time signatures. You can feel the pulse through the sole of your remaining foot. There's not one undertow but two. Now, hone in on the madrical element. Walk around the circle widershins. (You can't actually go backwards in music.) Now invert materiality. You will hear a minor breakdown, all the things you mustn't do.

What kind of superstitions would they harbour. Do you remember any of them.

Self-appointed hares and shamans. If I should meet such a woman on the road, I would turn myself back. See, more of this reversing, this torting. The tube is based on a true cross. I am wearing down, achingly space.

What is it all about.

The E stands in for elasticity. Movement dissolves into swarming diminutive figures. The opinion is ejected—it demands more conviction and bite. The stumps are plainly discovered through a magnifying gas. I'm looking forward to an endtime, to being held in reserve. I am looking back to the traditional antiphons.

Nux vomica.

Venus mercenaria.

Glonoinum.

Sanguinaria canadensis.

He removes a circle of glass. Believe me, if that infant had claws and a beak it would do anything to get its own way.

On the charge, beaten in the air by a leg. Carotid artery punctured. Skull facture. No matter what happens, it wasn't your fault. It's never your fault. From left to right, it isn't your fault. From north to south, it's never your fault. This small pellet is, I presume, the projectile you spoke of which pierced the cranium. Now, do you want to try this experiment on yourself.

They pack his ashes into shells and blast them off at shooting-ranges all across the region. Three months and three weeks left to go. The excuse is the hardest part. His nose once sat exactly midway on a spectrum between planar and aquiline. (You have to venture out as a group of four and come back as three, that's the catch.) The collective nous, he once said, is an estrangement of scraps. Think of something else, for example, the bullet that strikes.

Animals are box-office. The first impression has been recovered. Box of fire. Box of ash. A word glued to the concrete redeems the evening. He is ground down and delivered up. (What if another of us expires on route.) The ghoulest thing is the image of her face at the fourth floor window. He is conscious of, but cannot apprehend, her wayfaring flickerbook existence.

Tomorrow, more of my persistent themes and architecture. There is a tradition of moonlit scenes—screed pull to deep background square, collided.

Tell them the general populace needs you. Tell them anything. He recovers the ability to breathe beneath the sea. It is night. A tube or duct is rumoured. He expands at both ends. I cut away to breakfast overlooking a shattered pier. First train back. Now you must away too. Undertake research in packs for security. Carry with you at all times a common place-brick. Sound lies somewhere between the dominant and its octave. An instrument for making a whirring noise, as once used by watchmen, is enjoying a renaissance. Utilize primary methods of sensation, the quality of being limited by a condition—like rising earth either side of a furrow, the ineluctable et cetera. I am a reader of inferior taste. I don't have time for this. A spectator has been positioned in the pit. We are ready to split the ears.

He dies alone in a refuge balanced just above the waterline. Pierce through, paralyse with sudden motion.

We are reliving the penny dreadful of the red leech. Narrative transforms him into the ultimate remote. He is the maker's son. He can see the eighth day of the week—a popular fast in the mediaeval mind. The other seven are the planets against the fixed stars. It is the autumn month when war was most. The pressing question is, does it look to you as though something terrible has happened. Think of something else: the missile that swoops in yet never strikes.

He worries at a tiny patch of light with his index. When I was living here all things appeared closer, but this did not matter. Then again, I was, in body.

And what did you do after you had made certain that you had made certain of nothing?

Any difference can be defined in terms of a spectrum with no apparition (see vagueness). That settles the exit route. This wrongly despised art is of the utmost importance (see also heap, the). In different ways, by different channels, identity is fading out—the grey impalpable last. Or matter itself, in rotation.

A port. Boo.

I question your motive. I question your last move. A game of living chess is being played out in the undercliff square. A jungle of rubber plants and giant chocolate fountains has been imported to add local colour, to recompose the scene. His own story is interconnected, lines lapping within lines.

Temple-haunting warhammer
swallow footless without heir,
cadence for a son—
here, a building place.

Further notes on an instinct for dissent. Characterize the disaster thus, through the prism of the island's geology. If the book could for the first time truly begin it would. I believe it's all about the problem. I don't know myself. I change at the turn of every head. I can't work out where the patterns lie, where they cut into each other and overlap. I believe it's about throwing things will-nil into a furnace. I believe it's about waiting. I change at the turn of every hand. I believe it's about waiting and seeing what happens. They are returning now from every quarter—for one last time, long since corroded.

I struggle to answer him. He is now invisible to the chin. He invariably favours misdirection over combat. A refuge bag containing the finds lies on the dissection table.

Cell deterioration rapid. Plot in the charts, in the sky.

Skin slashed to point blank as he struggles to steal himself space. He is endeavouring to give a final account of himself.

Get to the point.

He is permitted for a day, with disastrous results.

It appeared in the month of September, not long after nightfall, and remained visible for nearly three months. The family is winched to safety. They were last seen. They are walking down an avenue of sinisters, mirrored on one side in the canal that runs. There's a change machine. Their household gods have sunk without trace. There is a crescent-shaped outwork. The one and the other collide. (Time for early void.) Every word he says splits open on the tongue. Disparate parts hang unformed. I want the entire history of this device: the white line travelling at the sound of speed, the groove or ridge behind which a player must stand to receive, the study of apparitions—to force out of place, transport.

A migratory body.

A run upon anything, unedited.

A series of scenes in motion for the immediate.

A feeling of euphoria after the taking of speech, rushing inside the ear.

A collective name for postcards—drone or needing to drone, quickly.

An avenue of linden trees, and not the ghost of a motive. Our route leads back to no land I know of. The whole thing could be rewritten as bedrock farce, innumerable doors closing and opening. The darkest lines are deep in places. If we all die they'll at least have a record of what went wrong. They'll at least have a record of what we're saying right now: daily growth and habitats, our tendencies—inconceivable gods, inconceivable duties. Where we entered, the constellations are widely spaced. Two spiral galaxies overlap each other—shadows on the wall in the guttering rushlight. As he reads, moths frap against the window pane. He nods silently. A light tapping sound.

You have good taste, my boy.

Why for the cards, the board, the candle, planchette and bell? The subject must be paralysed by an air embolism. (It's best if they finish on a heartbeat.) He survives, though his shape is now roughly pyramidal and he has been hollowed out. This can't contain me any longer. I devote myself to his destruction. Again the fabled out of nowhere—a narrative in which things irrational and times inanimate speak with humans. The unnecessary improbable is sitting in my incidents. A series of rooms with doors in line affords a continuum. That metal glint on the floorboards is one of the five missing rounds. Uncertainty establishes a connection: loops cutting a deep groove, matter dissolving and dwindling—dwelling inside the cavities, between the joints and the filaments. A scrap of leather is used to bind up the wings of a hawk.

The design of the book is based on a mathematical theorem called an Apollonian gasket. It features triplets of circles at tangents to others. A gigantic organ, partly automatic, the whole thing is an elaborate hoax. The last I heard, he had crossed the peninsula.

A die box.

Where we stitch up the suture. Where the facts evaporate. Fauna: a volatile labiate with fragrant pale-lilac flowers used for preserving springs. Wage-tickers on about their poverty (encouraging for stoic aspect). This isn't what I wanted, the mourning head. And the father forewarning slight my son they're consuming you. He is disappear himself, fading to ether, to morphine. He has been absent all these years. I devote myself to distraction. How it would all end one cannot image. It's symphonic in scope with intimacies of chamber punk. I see nothing beyond the thirteenth century. It's difficult being a man dedicated to obvious-ness. I dream I run around the planet in a single day—incredible sense of unreal-ized power. Consider one who could utter this kind of sentence: squared up beauty from slipped edge, clotted steel digger. Double-read and tremble would wind—organ stoppage of the similar. O boy. You remember the walnut trees at Saint Under?

Check any numb pages.

The erosion of his shadow has blighted the entire region. The locals will talk to you about anything except. There are no longer any patents or methods. There are no patterns or forms. No one else needs to know. Hallo I say. It's good to be taken aback by an uninvited minor episode. It intervenes (I must leave this place). Everything happens only once. You can find out a lot about rubbish from its organization. I'll reconstruct what's past. This is a product of those unit things. So much to do at such affordable prices. I want Madagascar. Say nothing. Never say anything specific. In order to execute a figure of eight, make use of the spare cornerstone. I am inventing a minor episode. This is also a product of those unit things.

Top edged hook penetrates leg.

I forget to go to work. I think we're discounted as intuitives, empaths. Let me through. Same chair. Same pen. Same lamp. In order not to lapse into literature for a third time, answer this simple question. Do you think we reveal too much, or not enough. Show him into the waiting room. I need to get my strength back. Four years in and we reach a hiatus. Here be need, restored. Every word has been thoroughly tested. There were once assorted percussion instruments— debris of charred and splintered planks, twisted metal. Friends have volunteered to cut a trench around the table for me. Today the tactile sense is the favoured faculty, the feared touch. A chunk of his shattered tibia strikes against the hollow of my thigh. I can't leave. I ask him to sign the offending flotsam. He declines. I resist. I resist the temptation to ask what happened to his neck—his extraordi-narily sensitive hesitation.

I have been manufacturing for a past. I see this as a step to realize, trace out a surface. In the water, jetsam declines and persists, according to some. I am prior to this occasion. The temptation is to ask. How now the spelling of an evil eye, a fleeting speck. A history is highly sprung in the mind. Cheap intimations.

A surgical glove (used).

A plastic.

Glasses (spectacular society).

That grey scum.

Yes the old phantom limb. Can't get used he says.

What happened to my eyes. This sentence constitutes a step in the right direction. I unwrap the first items: an unidentified black mineral with filaments and a theosophical toy—a figure trapped within the siphon of a man. The crew (pilgrim) remain invisible, discreet samples of the uncanny. There's mourning to come, over the pebblehead. Let us explain. His chin is on a level with the bend.

He is son of.

He is one among a number.

He is punished.

He reveals a secret.

He stands in water that ebbs.

It ebbs when he tries to think.

He is overhung.

He is overhung by objects that draw back when he reaches out for them.

Desert, dazzling light, reflected from the opposite window. Nails are embedded. Also the ibis, wood worn smooth in the lip of the sea. A revenant back from the vanishment—my adjuration with solemnity. Interference.

I make a stand. Spirit cantons are nearby. Inference has been identified. (O that's where.) Use is now condemned, but generally accepted. I'd guessed as much. Lingering sense of the waterbrash: heartness, bloodroot and glow-mass. Small body in the plexus of the vessel, a sudden gush of acid to the gullet. Grace blisters at the primary hollow of the vertebrae. People begin acting up and giving it that (his right hand transfigures to the yaw of a dog). So I start levitating—that always fucking shuts them up. It's not easy, the enemy always targets the front brain. You just sort of trigger it off, let yourself go, and it's goodnight gravity.

An unsolved case. In this version the beggars are visible but locked up. Evidence: salt of alkali—his scrapbooks and chemicals. A capable poison, with clamouring ancestors—the delights of dying well. Note to self: calm down manes. Use the cards—the board, the candle, the planchette and the bell. We part without having understood each other. Stalks of dry grass are strewn across the floor. Stains of thought remain in the tunnel. Everything is slight and insubstantial, neural with purpose. We depart the dreary racetrack without having understood. We are linked to this day, as by hand of shared assassin.

31

Low but sharp click.

That's ruined the conversation. Whatever happens in the next minute, ignite another soon. This is a play about excess.

Lattice-paned with lead framework. Three separate windows, one swinging on its hinge. Enough.

Nothing was taken except the plaster head from the auditorium. You're not getting this for nothing. Distance here is in the present tense. It isn't your fault. Razored fences have been flung up, fluorescent police tape. We part without having understood each other—a simple removal from one situation to another. Paramorphic exchange is taking place in the surrounding rocks. Blind arbitrary signs are resisting. (Those gut strings do not like being pulled apart.) I lack any conceivable motive. The disease transfers from its original site to another part of the body: feathered leg held fast, tumour distant from origin, from knee of poet. Stark light rising from earth. Two tongues are vibrated simultaneously by the same person. It sounds like a film of music, passage to another sector of flesh. There's a system you see, crafted as if by hand. But he cannot explain what the pincers signify.

To feign, to invent, to relate as if true.

Stitching up the suture. A sameness once lived here—a sudden violent microburst, usually disassociated. A current of air is sucked into the mineshaft. He scuttles off once more to pursue. Yet another whim to tally, another victim. Blazoner, try blazoning this.

Bendlets, dexter and slitster interlaced without lozenge. Mesh influenced by mesh, at each ear a listener. Here am I, snuck at the centre unalone—neither hand-hawk, unseen.

She is observed tearing up the scrap of paper she has just found on the pavement. Things to undo. Summon down manes, ghost of ancestor. I am without choice. Hello I say it's good to be back. Now complete, my limbs are perfect. I have lived several of these years.

A final handshake at the dismal track. The flanks of the vessel are held in place by rubber bands. There is no need of more time. The fact remains.

Levin from swinging pane, repeated at precise intervals. We part without having understood. Badinage, interphase. Screechowl, with night ajar.

A winged thing flies from the looking-glass and settles on her shoulder. Shake on it. All my situations are effaced. We press on. This, the final clue, has run to its end and to nothing. I am making use of every possible contradiction. I am making good use of metastasis, with transitions levered up from the pit of the sac. A changeling of place, yet a standing still: archangel built on promontory on ocean. The cloud of his speech is nailed down by Mercury, Venus. Beyond the embers the white birds have released.

Rumour distant from origin. Please wait for me.

Podsnap. I am now investigating the conic sections—a planet whose seeds rattle in the capsule, wind north by northwest. Each step is named from the uneasy pace at which the pilgrim. I am very close, microcosm of silts. Wing left broken, hung and quartered—the vanished vocal rights. I am yellowback. The streets are old and set diagonal in a grid. I am marking the outer limits of an overworld, a series of disparate keening cries. He will never have expected to find someone trying to extinguish.

The source of to root, sky-high. We are in theatre, in character, as the expression has it. Nearby on the river-ice, a huddle frozen about a brazier grind bones to brew an infusion. The effect is akin to a spontaneous combustion.

Indispensable tomorrow.

Stop.

Withholding ash planet.

IV

Take the papers found with this, the diaries and the rest, and bury them. We tend to work in 584-day cycles. We have bricked up the fault. Find him. We tend to work in threes. Cut off his head and burn the heart. I see a shadow at the peak. There is a grinding noise. We are high on the neck of the peninsula. Superheated steam rushes in and strips off the skin. Cliffs tower above the house. We fight our way out along an irrigation ditch. He leaves his slab behind among the rushes. This pains him. Other people's histories follow you around. The illusion, it's quite simple, the illusion is so perfect.

She refuses to grieve. The writing is concealed. I contain microcosms. All options vanish. This act has a rationale, hidden in the beat of its negative. Flexible steel plates are worn kilt-like from the waist. A rapping noise rises from beneath the table. Perhaps a blunder, or the legendary paperman. Remaining silent is difficult.

I exit through a side door. I see a face through the haze. He keeps my head down while inside the arc, thinking all the while. I could prevent you from leaving here until the following morning.

The story dies. And we were once so suited. Now we're being fitted up for mutual misunderstanding. Must grant each other that last farewell. We hand each other a list of requirements—at once a turning point and culmination. Be still. I suspect this will hurt. It's much too early to condemn.

They rummage in the refuse beetling for dung. (This confuses the sense of place and time.) I could crawl around all night long through this astounding summer. At the roadside, a cross between canine and flightless lizard: thickbodied of dun-colour, with adhesive talons, vertebrae concave at back. And pinned out between the branches of a tree, the skin of a ray cured by smoke. Roadkill— mephitic, in mimic of its cry.

It's round, at least from above. It doesn't always make sense. It houses a library. Mostly it never happens, in both exterior and interior aspects. All the three o'clock people can go home now. Extemporize. Forget it.

I understand right away. The square is mine: if I move, she will.

Read on.

Use white stone. Use any of the white objects remaining in the cell. Disappear into the ordinary. Self-slaughter leaves a semblance embedded in the brick-work. For future generations this serves the function of a parable. On occasion it represents the virtuous. At other times not. Recall his cyclothymic condition, hybrid temperament flipping high and low. I don't remember reading. He is linked to the escape hatch by a shallow trench and a rubber hose. Now pin him face upward, back bent across the curve of the stone. Reach across the hole.

O this eternal frost.

One thing is commonly about one thing, no more. The reliquary bones are apt to disappear during a crisis. Construct the redoubt with what, he pleads.

On the random nature of memory.

Up in the every morning and I've come about this tardy war. This is a one-act opera. I have decide. My investigations reveal an extraordinary rendition chamber, an armoury, and a garden full of exotic orchids with birds of rare plumage. I have come about the sealed-off pyramid. I have come about the diamond mines. (Fate has a way of circling back on a man.) Keep an eye out for a novel type of dwelling. It's good business to mock your adversary. Confusion is detected today among historians of the animal. The *D* above is a hideous blunder. I am blinkered like an horse.

By scheme of making, we introduce some fresh moments. We introduce generic and specific names: a passing stranger. Yes and no. I know her not and yet I know her only too well. She systematically transfers from index to cavity the last grains on a black fingernail crusted with paste jewels. One of the names has been published without description. Look it up. Yes the town apparently.

Today she is all make her stop.

A ray of light pierces from below, illuminating the skin of her wrist. We're at the dag-end of the ubiquitous, riding on the back of the proverbial.

A song in the thorax. A fading passenger. He who stood howling on the jetty now quietly slips away from the harbour. The hour is arch meridian, the intercept between zenith and equinox. On deck stands a still figure, concealed by a hollow void in the surrounding space.

A sound, stray ear of his own tongue. The making of rhymes and whatnot. I am unnamed from insensibility. I am unequal in value or meaning—notes without measured frames, each account weighing in the balance: the heart, the liver, the lung. Starve the rhythm. Import into their fate the views and beliefs of unsummoned ancestors. There is an absence of jar. I am the kind of writing which is called. I amount, too—as much, if not less. I am named from an inability to absorb.

We are so much the better for the following phenomena.

Insurrection within the spirit cantons.

A simple diagram of the universe.

The threads of a fundamental doctrine.

A division of space, sometimes the sinister.

The root of a chord or a stem of harmonics.

A convenient pair of glands that secrete mucus into the urethra.

Deathlings are here, numbrous in breed. Many heads are making for the exits. Sprinkled earth, dust and ashes express (repectively) humiliation, insignificance and worthlessness.

Through the aperture of a broken armistice.

Pierced with needles in the dark. This semicircular shadow moves up and across—a thin membrane like a block of flats. I mean spacecraft, haunted land-fall. They were right: the woman dog has to eat the placenta stuff. In the course of the game she expires. The contest is enervated by live pieces in the market-square, hummed to irregular stations. Animate chunks of flesh flop and hop across the cobble. (This event marks the politic shift of a lifetime.) I once was renowned in story. What's left is rubbed into the excruciate. Time is post-quartering.

None works. No one wants a rerun of what happened this morning. She's composed of eclipse plumage and coloured glass, both hands in the burial position—arms folded across the chest like a statue. Bloody swabs were found in her ears and throat. She lived fabled. It's said she threw herself at the sea from a promontory. (In all of us is the wish.) Return to the has-been, and repeat.

Come in her eye. Come full circle. The plane cuts the surface at any moment. In memory we are not the same thing: insect from pupal case, larvae from egg. You know what they say: old meat, fresh worm. Eat. Spectators peer down from the vantage of the rock ledge.

The time for which anything lasts (see under ice).

The word is literal and means tracker. It is the name for a cadence, the groove in which the edge of the head has been set.

The behold of the vessel. This is taking much longer than expected. Despite the heat and the humidity he locates the matrix in which everything is formed. (I can say for sure that you don't own it.) This is the vacuum in which things are. It contains the bed on which an object rests and a breeding animal. Also cementing material: the cutis under the nail—the hollow in the slab—ground-mass and inter-cellular substance—the monumental brass—the lost wax process—a rectangular array of quantities and symbols—a rock with veins of ore—the whole of mathe-matics—a regular sequence of rows and columns—a miniature gun and the miss-ing talisman. Do we know our way back to the intestines. Sharpen his stake at both ends. Parts of the body recur. The remains are left exposed on a remote beachhead. What's this line about denying first sight, rejecting the initital glimpse? There's no choice.

A failure of imagination, a failure of magnitude. There's a great deal of rain, sud-den squalls. Up until today we've been protected by the isolation. Now it's pay-back time. They have cut off her head: who like the grim. This wedded pair are shrouded scalp to foot in a subterranean chamber. The two exits have been blocked. At present she is unable to give any coherent account of these events or of her past life.

36

Inquisitor enters delivers usual rhetoric.

Atom. Lands to the utmost limit.

Rising heat vapour, corrugating the meaningless circles of a vehicle at the horizon.

Block off the east where heads form, quartered.

She has the stars down her arm. She is not at rest. She is not at risk. They have cut off her index.

Now there's a word. Quietus. One revolution of the building reveals nothing. His yellow leather gloves still lie on the oak desk, where he left them the morning he disappeared. Vainly I stretch out a limb. There's a rumour. He's been spotted on the strand. I round up the others and march to the top.

And what of the past. He is cutting back every link to himself. He writes nothing, hence everything—the revelation of the anyday. A sort of footnote follows, removed from the ordeals and judgements, technology and its mediated uses. His eye is uttered, concealed.

True, you have wings and you have written things down. Sixty seconds now remain of normal time. What have you heard. You came in without opening the door. You store away the image received. I think we're in a tunnel. What we're looking for is any change in the heavy water trapped in the ice. The money's tied up. And all the mutes, recall to mind the delicious mutes of thirty years ago! From the core of this darkness a sudden light breaks open. Glance at my credit, dead-eye: duties against the grain, everything as compromise, drainage.

I mean a kind of antipilot.

Air.

Just over ten minutes remain. All the better to embalm the body. You decide. They peter out beneath the folds of her wreckage. They have not heard rumour these nine years. (Where you were and what happened you et cetera.) The whole wall suddenly fell away to expose this vista—fire that rakes a line from end to end.

There is a shortage of names. Nonetheless, she seems to have died of an excess of nomenclature.

Lying beneath the moon's surface are concentrations of dense matter of uncertain origin.

Swarms of ocular spectra, floating black spots before the eyes. Words from look to mouke, mishappen.

The writing is that it is. He claims it resembles. He says he could not find it in the world so had to make it himself. Consider the sheer amount of stuff in it—a hybrid of printed word and pictures, music and voids. The mind served as a model, nothing more.

He describes it as being here. The plot is ludicrously convoluted. (Of that much you're surely aware.) There are discordant sounds and hand-painted lists, some of which break out into narrative conceits. We inhabit an irresolvable landscape.

Memory is moving in eight different directions at once. He considers the whole expedition foolish in the extreme. We have welcome rushlights and open hearths, while he paces about outside on the platform. His fore-wings are reduced to a horny shield for the fragile hinder parts. There's little room for footfall. With nothing to bring to market, we'd do better to call the poor man back and grant an amnesty.

He descends the cliff of a disused chalk quarry. (That iron mount will be a far harder climb.) We can no longer see him. In his wake lies a trail of bodies, ritual equipment and supplies. Over his head is however old the earth, a disc. He wears the now-familiar welding goggles. Scarring the surface is a complex system of trenches or canals: base and superstructure. The flower he grips is designed for self-pollination. A sudden breath of spores is ejected into the freezing air.

Topography: a headland or steep cage—a projection, ridge or eminence standing out like a promontory. Greyblue shadows beneath ribs.

There-being, in sixty-three extinguishable combinations.

A dense damp air, through which gas lamps cast a theatrical light onto the pavement. In the gutter stands a bust on its pedestal. Sound is an elaborate naming and calling, clinging and designating. Is there evidence of people leaving the kingdom, trying to make connections abroad? This is too much of one thing in one place, an unspeakable vessel. They are obliged to return by the same steam-packet on which they made their outbound journey.

See her dream where eyes peter out beneath the folds of gauze wings.

I am back. It's in this era that the autopsy was invented, and a useful depilatory of lime and orpiment.

Stop. Stop in shape, as taught.

Tell us the story about the judge. Tell us the whole story about change taking place before gathering eyes. (If I'd watched my backwards this never would have happened.) Tell us the story about the chain of reason. At this juncture he sends his brother up to the earth to bring back magical writings. The walk is the nineteenth century walk, structured as a series of tableaux. Flora: gigantic water-lilies of the genus. This is where I perfected the somatic escape.

There are carpet slippers on his bare feet. A physician kneels beside him. He brings down the lamp which once stood on the table (in memory, mind). He inspects the lock and the vault. It's evident that death has been aroused by mesmeric process. One glance at the volunteer is enough to show: his presence can be dispensed with. He is convertible into the ordinary—at least so says the superstition, its expounders. This is heavily influenced, bent impossible, like a broke elbow.

I am switching to autoplot. We board the waiting vessel. On the bridge I find a reflecting telescope. I point it where there's an apparent absence of space. Its planar mirrors reflect light down the polar axis. The dog, I hadn't noticed the dog! It's precisely three months, four-and-a-half days old. We identify the box and prize it open. We write sentences on petals of wild rose and sprinkle them on whatever we discover inside. Within is life in miniature, a compressed space where blue gas flares throw a theatrical light onto wet-cobbled streets. This we fasten. I had power once to bind by spell.

More profit is perhaps to be derived from actually reading the literature.

Topographic anatomy: ice-armoured couloirs. A gully or passage. Town rubbish concerns. Once set in a column, the pollen shifts as one body.

The mob streams down from the gods and starts wrecking the seats. Writing is unbearable. As if he had been responsible for all the fires! What the hell to say. Something safe and secure. One night he dreams a dream wherein he sees two serpents, one on his right hand and the other on his left. Eyes make out a book on a low teak cabinet. Through the window, a glimpse of the sundial on which he will lean when he finally declares himself. He readies himself.

In order to defer action, step in accordance with traditional usage. A fraction of the total cross-section decreases rapidly while entering its final state. Thus do not dreams coagulate: the lament, the white mansion, the bracket, the costly blue posts.

The condition: if she is to be the other cannot. When he woke she had disappeared. (I would like to see solace probing into the play of words a little. Suppose I said *a b c d* and meant the weather is fine.) In her allotted place nothing else may emerge. Trembles and groans rise up from the earth. Tell us about this. Tell us all the details. She's translucent. Put your minds at rest. I can see the background behind her, through her. She seems solid enough. It appears, according to the extant notes, that this is our chief predicament: she shall not be shut in along with the souls which are fettered. There follows a debate.

How can you sleep at a time like this. To the scullery, rouse the kitchen. Therein, one after the other is found hiding, so grave and lightless on this blighted summer day. Without, from his diary, respite is found in a garden of fleshy plants. Xerophytes.

It is pretzel bent, logic fisted in a rope shape at twist to a loose knot. If it does exist it's an integral part of the material world. I don't know what's happening to me. Technically, I can't identify any pitfalls. Although I know that I am here, I sense that I'm also back in the cell. Some things can only be introduced at the last minute, such is the character of discourse and speech in general. I've always been looking at only one point on the map, which is probably the starting position, i.e. the wrong one. One place appears superimposd upon another. I confess—I witness—standing on nothing.

The more I think about it, the less reasonable the guide's explanation appears: that the powder is some sort of ash. You are deferred. (See her dream where thousands of eyes peer out from behind an enveloping fold.) This is not an obligatory exercise, but do it anyway. I forget everything, torn tightly between the blue poles. She holds a dialogue, what's known as a parley. I have no status, no viable quarry. The look of the clock may serve to determine time in more than one way (imagination). I stand aside. I am a temporal mute. I have no alarms. The vault is to be prepared. I am dead previous, then and since. The spaces in between are filled with mineral rubble. The object of the game is to produce a completed drawing in the allotted time. A picture of a dung-beetle is built up of its component parts—body, thorax, head—according to the roll of a die.

I shouldn't be introducing choices at this station. Circumstances force me to act and write from a perspective of resistance. And this unusual run of encounters with birds: it's as though we were the representatives of a wasteland. The trick of concealing oneself behind the initial letters of words is yet to be explained. I lift the lid. The creature is tied by a cotton thread to a pin stuck upright, turning about it unceasingly till it drops dead with exhaustion.
Silence.
I am far from wanting to challenge you. I need to be more explicit. I can see I'm going to be busy for years. I have no reproaches for you, only love.

It carries lard sacs on each flank, swollen with sperm. Mineral: arsenic of lead found in yellow crystal, resembling. I climb the intermediate stair as it materializes beneath my feet. Vague animal forms press close by. Balancing on the mantelshelf is a bowl of newly invented fish—a genus of miniature rays or sea vampires. Surface of glandular leather, with skin quite shark—weighing and gnawing at the mind, ill-skinned. Ask me nothing more just yet. Soft white capsules are scattered in the street. When do we break our fast. I condemn all your questions.
It's been a hard winter but we're still in print. I could always ask for little more assistance. We separate. I must find time to counterfeit. His features are knotted together into a large elliptical zone. A score is found in the wreckage. The most exampled is suicide one: the allelujah, the secrecy, the offertory. Any of his terminations.

She is the semblance of something other than herself. She is too obsolete for place. Get ready for the big picture, the big sleep. She is dragged to and fro between the opposite ends of the box. (I don't know if pride is the right word.) It keeps on raining. On a number of occasions intuition has been a fitful guide.
The sign says laser radiation. (Do not stare.) Whether this guarantees a reliable influence, or is merely the manifestation of a mean tendency in matters of choice, I daren't conjecture. One might say: it is as it were a redemption. Events

rise then level off, with no increase in utility, just a dogged resistance spreading out across a barren plateau. This can only come about if you no longer support yourself on the earth, but suspend yourself from the heavens. Is she dead in the accepted fashion? Nobody calls me on this plane. Up and atom. Nobody else comes into the waiting-room, lodge of this sinecure.

Place the suspects in two different locations. See what happens. I've reflected on this dilemma for much of my life. There are several passages extant in the text where such occasions are enumerated. You are not.

If the enemy comes against him by sea he retires into a certain chamber. But how does this chronic seeing-as compare with colours and shapes? Remember you are not. The total number is sometimes ten and sometimes eleven. One suspect acts in automatic response to the other's violence. Another is depicted in the form of a man with a beetle for a head. (This signifies cautious vigilance.) The insect becomes his emblem. His nose is pierced by the pin to which it was tied. We are in the weighing-room, with scribes in the balance. The other theory is that their feet caught fire and they flew down from the trees and they spoke.

He dislodges himself from the body.

She seizes the head and carries it off, places it at the edge of a well. Lips hover close to her ear, whispering something, nothing.

Note the being impaled through the thigh. No wonder at night he is nervous in the sickly street, slithering across the cratered cobble. He tells her something that makes her blood conspire. It keeps on raining—like a film, skeins of radio wave. Atomic writing. I climb interminable stairs. The dwelling is the noun. The being is the noun.

A brief interlude in a restaurant. He would say no more. We separate. Tabasco and ether on the menu. It's true that at a distance somebody who is suspended looks much the same as someone who is standing.

Two in a tiered chamber underground. Both entrances have been hurriedly blocked by mattresses and rubble. Potential stabbings in the darkness. The true form is the adjective, lead-based. Plumblined.

Note: the sickly rays of lamps strung at sway above the road barely illuminate the greasy cobble. Day and night now of equal length.

But for the interplay of forces within him.

Nobody is calling upon us. At that moment a poor woman who lives on the marshes opens the door of her cottage. She takes a lick of salt from the back of her hand. Aren't you forgetting something.

Vignette, this chapter is without a vignette. These moments are the happiest

41

of your life, the chapter of opening the mouth. (There is a long way to go with this.) Moths flutter from her old ragweed coat. I am revealed in the any day now. It just makes you look as if you are meek, wild.

She seizes the head and carries it off (I say as much below). I am honoured with my first and only. Let's say she has an irregular heartbeat after all. Some arsonist-cum-chemist is working in the apartment above.

Second watch (blessing himself): How is that possible?

A loose whip, an unfortunate rhyme. Disorientation occurs toward the middle of the composition. How did they get into the house at all if the bridge is down. Did you see it.

Yes the dog.

I thought you'd be pleased.

I think they're just getting their grieving over with before the rematch begins.

A brief note on words used in a speciously understood or defiant sense. It's intriguing, the number of people. I can't be at rest here among these reactive breeders. I just want to move on to the next watch. I always get lost. I can never remember anything is. You'll be going on about this your whole life: I don't want the flowers, I don't want his ecstasy. I don't want his apostasy. Relegate reading to the status of laxative.

After this little speech, everybody refuses to come back into the office.

The unravelling of our fortification.

The fieldwork is enclosed on all sides, its ditch flanked from the parapet. It has an inner last retreat. (Where exactly?) An untimely piece for chamber ensemble is being composed. I sprang from confusion—confused with whatever word comes next.

What has occurred up until now.

The thing is a particle of matter so minute it can't be cut or divided. That's today's big question. I think about it most of the day. At what o'clock was it raised? Folk from the future travel back through time to sabotage the experiment. I presume everyone in the room has heard of me. Can the animals wait? He is gathering people face up. They show no inclination. (Stop shouting.) They show no signs of attrition. A web of string has been stretched across the door. They show no signs of election. Inside, everything has become very small.

A short numbered list, arable.

No I'm not grateful no. I talked of the cobble of the street above, just a few lines ago. It's better than a box of minutes. I don't want to be forgiven. There is a mess of people here. Forgive me. They never show any indication that they are talking about you. Singlehanded they are taking on the addiction. I am perplexed. What could you be that could do worse than this.

Read on.

It is a tunnel we are in I think.

A situation open from end to end, a body opening from seal to seal. Reel in. Bring me in. Land me. I can't wait to get back to the compound. Bring me one of those lightweight crucible heat shields, and long tail-feathers to steer with. You can no longer see the deck from the bridge through the fog. He waves listlessly then slams the lock and bolts it shot by hand. I'm sure there is blood in his sack. Now he is standing at the naked window. Far off is the trope of our friends et cetera. My imagination is going to follow you wherever you go. They answer without giving answer. He compares himself to smoke. The event takes place forty days after his concealment. The event harbours its own return. Void spaces are opening up in the pressing years. These are named the unexplained intervals. I am still writing on the wall after all this time. Sharpen the stake at both ends. I try to explain something to him in detail, but I can't understand it myself. Despite his efforts, the stake remains blunt. Do you too feel eyes moving over your body, like the march of tiny feet? This image arises from the resemblance of the tidal bore to the movement of running cattle. All the same his face is the same. This only works when truly demented. Have you ever seen a man siphoned to death.

More on the pilgrim, the grudge.

A rock is said to hang over him, threatening to fall. With him on the sacrificial platform are a trio of cantors. Their liberty is only apparent. They can't be withdrawn until the grooved bar which engages their heads is raised. The garb of all four is coloured by a purple-red dyestuff. The objects placed at their feet include the cusp, a diamond pin, the spaces in between, and other trifles: the flap of a slashed garment, one small thing tacked to another, a loose end, the shred of disbelief, a stray lock, the tip of a sail, a trite quotation, the moral to the story, a refrain, anything mean and nasty, the act of putting, the rim of a web, the twisted body of rope, the end and the residue, the stump of slang, the remaining part of a thing, the scallop and the lacination. At this moment they feel the first conception (dread). Dung-clotted dags of fur waggle beneath the goat set up on the altar. Every surface is clad in the brilliant green of chromium mica. A cat is ritually prepared before being thrown into the sea. The genitals of a dead man are stitched to its hind paws. It is dipped in water in which salt of acid has been dissolved. It is laid upon the neck of the deceased. (He will become a perfect in the underworld.) The die is loaded at the corner. The prescribed letter is O. Matter, lead arsenate and chloride, from its resemblance.

That's enough of that.

Permit me now to return to the sponsor of this paragraph. Gird him about with jamber, hood and harness. His strings are twitched by quills tipped with metal points. He needs a continuous supply of criminals and saints. I have to lie. I am compulse. On occasion I have manifested the stunted ghosts of children. His left side is where they usually locate themselves—half-blind they walk in mournful conference. After

43

their departure a dead silence ensues. He is completely unable to explain the process by which the strands have fixed themselves to his body—a clutch of helixes knotted into a K-tort. The muscle spasms. Cut him down to seizure. Send another to make a visitation, to officiate in his place. (I lied convulsively, yes.) Shunting trams clatter through the undercast street—twelve squares in the centre, faint whiff of tobacco pipe. No it's never not, stupid. Today's look is a sorry horse.

Bastard hartebeest and haruspex. A lean mule, a jade. One fertile stamen.

What it is the correct disorder.

It hurts. I can't be bothered to learn. I have to tell him. I am wearing angel. I can't be bothered to explain.

It was like being an operation. It was not altogether unpleasant. Do not in the telling, do not. Do not foretell.

Imagine a concentric pain volving circles one within the other. Like & unlike. Do not tell. I am the unforetaught.

From his mouth a child slowly draws out the length of tickertape that has been packed inside his sinus cavity. On this strand is written the story of his entire future life.

At the threshold between two regions having different configurations of lines of force.

The smell is that smell you associate. Ensure he walks away on the seventh day. As promised we're going to finish where we started. Could you talk about something else. Answer now. Could you something new, please. Don't mention the episodes, such as the mountain ascent. It was like a torture. Don't mention the yearning to disappear and hide. (Face is dull yellow in complexion, with claret birthmark and long tapering lips.) Don't mention the chamois hunt. Break up any further material. Don't mention the painting of. Debase any action he may care to bring. *This* is the negotiating table. Don't mention any oddities of the real, such as the postilion and the love affray—the tryst-tree, the lightning bolt. Then comes the voice of a woman in wrung cadences. Don't mention the keenly realized rivalries. They are used to this. We are tired of this and that. Don't mention the duel. The aim is a type of hysterical romance. There is a type of novel in whose composition the author reveals his caricatures indirectly by the action he portrays. (One more fictional swamp, yet not just a fictional swamp.) The corpse is burned together with a tried and executed greyhound, a condemned pig, and a dispatched cock. We are sitting on a magnetic boundary. You will get used to this. Have I said enough, something entirely novel. We will get used to this. It's lost the very moment it's achieved. One eye is lame. One eye is found missing. They are erased to all this. Something of which one says, that was how it was.

A god whose other attributes include.

He be found self and righteous under the judgement. He loses so he hurls the gaming-board into the water. I am filled with impressions. It floats. I am preoccupied with unforgivably vivid spectacles, people, events. (I can't be bothered to explain.) There is no further material. There is no possible experience through which to manifest or talk an action. There is no further material through which to bring down a situation. But his 'standing-around' is still a mode of being. Send me away in any direction.

The letters composing the cipher range from *a* through to *z̧*. Their intermingled ashes are scattered over the rolling flinch of an English.

We decided to burn his notes too. A pyre was built at the apex of a sharp rise: disintegrating cliffs of chalk and ice.

We buried the head at a nearby crossroads. I always said he was the cerebral equivalent of an overactive thyroid. I call him St Paul. Which is the law, blameless, answers the roughly man—hung idle on the clothes hook, asleep in fits. I have hesitated without time for a long stretch. I'm pretty well made, liver and kidneys floating about all grainy like the moon (her blacks draggle and crack et cetera). We'll have to stay close to the platform. This titanic task is beneath you. He fills the hollows in the earth with stolen limbs. He fills the places with the dead, bends the earth. He folds the surface.

You asked for a facial interpretation. You asked for anatomical interference. The journey takes a week. He is bound up with all my memories of that period: a full cycle lost, the red flags, the cortège on the track viewed from the sky, the saturated colour. I knew I wanted to be a part of then—crude sinew, crude essence: the gaunt trains crammed with exhausted conscripts creeping to the front. (I have crossed a threshold of vulnerability.) Grey war-stricken towns farther up the line, parcel tape on every window. Once you've eliminated the impossible, whatever remains, however probable, must be a lie. We have to stay close to the edge of the platform—the muddy, ice-cold trenches in the mountains. The time is late December. Writing can never be done with. They execute the prisoner. An infantryman makes use of the ceremonial word. Papyri exhibit traces of the influence. This takes place. Of course, at the tail end, where the rocks pile up.

We decide to bury the ash—more a powder—under a nearby crossword. How comforting this feels.

Magastromancer. I am writing on the assumption that this character is a woman, the selfsame. She is possessed and perplexed by inexplicable mirabilia. It says so. This is just one example of the fatals, who are too many to be instanced at large.

Demon R.

O she is.

A refuge, retired.

A bunch of geometry.

I am concerned with those properties of a figure who remains unchanged even when that figure is bent and stretched. They have eliminated the man. It is less than seven months ago as I write. His stalk is attached to the edge, near the middle of the undersurface. A set of eight newcomers arrives and stands to attention around his bed. A klaxon sounds, an alarm.

Skin of porous texture, much mottled, and armoured with curious clusters of spines. Shape of tongue retroflex to hard palate. (Note to self, recreate being impaled through thigh.)

Sketch for new topic.

Inscribe prayers on behalf of the man for whom it was made. Absorption of heat at the junction, trapped within a circuit of two metals. He lies still. (This be where, by the way, he remains until the end.) Above his head turns a wheel with cups about its circumference, into which jets of water are aimed at high speed. It is an invention. To what end none is certain. What no one tells you is that once time starts up again it moves extra fast, to catch up with everything that has happened in the interim.

So you've been here only five years. We must stay close to the edge of platform. And I see this black silhoutte in the glare of an opening door. He holds a pickaxe (the glacier's not the only problem). Details are inveigled—unrecorded, eyeless—as if arrested in the act of crawling, in the act of earning. Please come please come and drug me away, remote in the voiceness.

He is stopped at the frontier. A loose horse, questions. He is stopped at the ford. Lighted cigarettes draw small nervous circles in the dark.

A tube of lubricant is cracked open. An instrument is introduced into a randomly chosen aperture. Figures on the inside of a rotating cylinder are visible through slits. They are stretched taut by weights and spreadeagled face up to bake in the sun.

This shingle memory provides. There is solace. There is anima motion. I mean it is possessed: a fleshy spike of flowers, swaying imperceptibly. Spadix. No such space as things.

A date-rimmed bay, I held aloft above its deepwater harbour. Naples yellow. Everything is going to be all right.

Whatever it is, it's still moving—a shunting notion of no return. The gaunt train full of shabby militia, rapidly recurring images, creeping up to the front.

I forgot the dog, at bark while I attempt a reading above a crumbling baroque courtyard. Tasteless extravagance. Grey, war-sickle towns farther up the line. The bridge is down the phone. Select colours in sequence, on screen the sheathing bract. The silhoutte of a man's hand crawls across a cathode ray surface. A conspicuous one, enclosing.

The bridge is down. There is somebody else in the room. It's my typing. I am asleep. Build a pontoon. True, you have those magnificent wings and claim to have written everything down. We are reaching the apogee, harbinger of a slow return. True, you did come in without opening the door.

The body is found at a point of elastic distance from the earth. On the keyboard sits a metronome. An expulsion has been set in motion, a subtle twist against the function of gravity. I am not in the slightest degree prepared for such an invasion of contrasts.

An almond orchard, underplanted.

A trench sunk into the ice and mud of the ascent.

Think of a solution, the synthesis that arises from a persistence of eye. Subtract the news of her dog. Let the trepanation begin. I am sitting here at my book without the faintest ambition. The sense of defeat fades. Nothing breaks the horizon. She lives where I used to live. The detail falters, then fails altogther. She remains within the scope of the arc. She retreats inside a metal container. As we talk she's busy scratching green paint from her interior. I can hear the sound of a wild animal breathing heavily in the room. I remark upon this. We are being fitted up for mutual misunderstanding. She says we are entering. She says we are enervating. Your own bifurcation continues, is incomplete. It is delivered through the X and Y chromosomes. We exchange each other that list farewell. She says I never thought you needed help, even when you were insane.

A turning, to turn. A point of culmination.

She runs a finger down her cheek, draws down an eyelid.

Further note to self: renew the complicated network of curves and uneven loops that lead to the place where his ash is buried. Consider words pertaining to animals and rocks, before it's too late. A mute succession.

I climb interminable stairs. The state of being is simply the noun she says. I am far far away from all this. Two perfect lichen streaks carry traces of the spindle, a modest glimpse of termination.

Debelief, dream-rife. Shield-shaped and pertaining to the gland.

Ductless in neck.

Terse second half. The roof is a shingle roof. A spurt of matter shoots across the room to strike at the cold lino. (Distinctive patter of descending viscous fluid.) She plucks the last grains from her cavity with a girl-pink plectrum, systematically transfers them to tongue, to index.

Any connection with the aforesaid insect is not accepted by all.

Addled injurious time.

There is no addled injurious time. The default is the paralysed familiar.

V

Flung out countless and transformed into shapes. A crude vee is traced across the terrain, downwards and southwards. Under siege: junk percussion of fly-tipped white goods, rusting noise. The coordinates are said to be astrological. I'm reminded of his library—if you're not in it, you probably don't exist.

She says pointing look the sun divides the water. She remembers this, the wave of a boom in the sea. She must depend on what she can remember.

He touches his cheek. It's dry, but still the sting of cold spray, the taste of salt. He rises and dresses. A saint is bolted to this place. I keep any duplicates in the mystery tray. Glister on beaded rubble, a collapse of boulders.

At the same time she goes out to meet him. I am disseminating a notorious error. I think estrange: in the old days the territory was divided into a grid, discrete chambers of space. I believe the current cell is quite strategic. It faces north and points skyward.

Is that a figure at the window or the shadow of something hanging. Consider the paradox of a voiced silence. Consider a creature having a flat breath-bone, hence unable to fly. The rest are inconsolable and cluster in small groups on the ground. He drinks. Memory surpasses him. The immediate: woman with dogs over guano-spattered causeway. The remote: names of old anchorites and race-horses. Hotkole. Luxharvest. Wilgon. Objectives of force. Sea-the-stars. His arm, from the elbow down, is almost motionless. Somehow he musters the energy to go out and meet her. He is setting up a shot. They pass in the night, unaware. From here on the work assumes a more sinister aspect. Returning to his cell, he checks whether he can still move his fingers. No attention is paid (it's code, isn't it). He lets his lower arm fall onto the table: a pair of kings and the trickster. The fingers are motionless. A bone is broke. He apologises for his tardiness and the tradition. His knuckles knock against the cold marble circuit like dice. (We are not saying much about this as we know it is not.) Time is anno domino. Newcomers stream over the top of the wedlock stand. There's a ten percent charge in my static—none of your season here. Something vague rustles at peripheral. This is happening more and more. Breakwater of wood or corrosive spines. Erosion and sand-drift, the itinerant pebble.

Yes you feel as though you're following a secret cypher. He's intrigued by beetles and moths. He listens to the clicks after nightfall. On the desk in his study sits the eponymous navigational tool. From such a small cell of an idea the whole thing expands. Without realizing, a place of lodging and longing. In short, to wander, surprisingly.

That she is officially a saint he is unaware. Events so far give us a sense of the law being written as it's spoken, made at the moment of voicing. One flies towards him with a live coal and purifies his lips.

I am driven to all this by extreme pressure of neural business. I am trying to make it seem as if a man were present, yet understands nothing of what is happening all around him.

Or say, the study of those properties of sets of points (e.g. geometrical figures) that are invariant under one-to-one continuous transformations: the organs of interconnection, within and both without.

He manufactures multiples and simples. Each bears his name, branded softly—a collective sigh. Objects are hung about the walls, close-packed and shining darkly. He tells me what to write: an exposed brain, fingers probing and testing—transference to mouth to taste memory. Giant despair. Endless scrolling wallpaper behind. He has a broad wingspan and is forever plotting escape. All his departures have failed. He has a low-slung underbelly. And I have to tell someone the news, the olds: bursting steam over the aqueduct, a town sheer-quarried into dazzling chalk. What technique. We have not yet reached. The same six faces keep turning up. The remarkable twine links them together, whether they like it or not. A metal craft scoops into the canal from the sky.

There is nothing this man can't keep alive when he puts his mind to it. He rouses the dead to life. He uses words. They rush upriver. Two, three, four waves rise and curl in pursuit. The breath is dammed fast—dykes bursting dykes, the hole drilled in the watercourse.

Small dent at the dead centre of her head. Embouchure taut from sailing through scales, an impressive muscular structure. The rest sit immobile in a mass. Contemporaries tell the same tale. Place the instrument to your lips and discharge. These are the rues of engagement. Unlock and keelhaul a volunteer. I say nothing concerning the institution itself which I have not said at length elsewhere. The mouth of a river has been conveyed to a distance. I am especial in my recentness, in my inquisitions and my liberties. We're on our way down, hemmed in by a narrow passageway, a kind of burrow with curving walls of a green mineral (basic copper carbonate). It's advisable to plunge straight to the heart of the subject. Erode by kneading and rubbing—into a mouth, out of a mouth. Fill up the central space with rubble. The forepart of the skull allows transmission and reception in one direction only. (Simplex, by any other name. Jade, possibly.) Beneath: snout of boar. Every glimpse penetrates me. Looks to me like a meatgrinder.

Consider the following constellation: a monocycle, dental tapeworms, the photograph in the locket, the church behind the well. In this example we have a striking instance of the belief that the knowledge of the name implies dominion over that name. Mark ye the disappearance of these laws into subsequent generations. (I should warn you, there are further obscurities such as this hidden in the document.)

The adoption of some abdominal terms.

Mallow, as the colour of the so-leaved name, soft and downy. I want you to check and then recheck everything. Scant the index cards. Where do we start. So much happens during this single day (applause). I have read. He makes these beautifully crafted trapdoors for all his characters. We will never finish. The handwriting is spidery, extinct. The others have been extraordinarily good at keeping a secret all this time. I archive to resist. I recommence. A penitential mood is spreading.

This chapter reveals the verso of the medal. It's positioned in contrast to chapter fifteen—from or of the earth, the flavour of recollection. A rawness comes: fleet of floodwater. He has to move himself and his belongings to hired lodgings. In his panic he picks up the wrong book.

The lantern is considered an exception. Elemental weaponry includes the cartilage of the principal larynx.

Since that time I use both sides of the mouthpiece, just in case. I am shot through the whole length of the line. Now I'm blocked by a body on the floor. Within all of this he is but himself. I am set at intervals. Come back into mind. Bring it in here. No, in here.

The marvel of Peru genus, open-scented by night. Aqua mirabilis. A space of time, a certain time. We have misbecome our gravities. I talk a false imprint. Talk darkly—a false die of our own foisting, transfiguring tongue. The capital is sacked. Breaking news, breaking English: rivet-headed, riddlestopped. (What time clom and suchlike.) This is an exquisitely discordant entry, followed by a note of silence, an unpreparedness.

Others suggest that this represents the muttering and murmuring of our father—rumours of tactics and rankles, loose earth. An unprepared night, expanded about the light revolving.

Homebound, awaiting a new hip. He gathers local voice, spectacular recordings of the melting ice-sheet. Admit that you cannot help but admit. Note the appearance of his burnished skull, its sinuous radiating ridge and hinge-line with long narrow lobes: a valve of its own shell. Trapped within is all manner of virtuosity. He is a master of tone and colour and texture. (We are cutting back on the panegyrics.) In the midwinter nights, in the square of the outsider mission, an owl would repeat his calls. I refuse to nurture a grudge. We are surrounded and are firing on a last-ditch saloon—fruit of the dog or other, terminating in a garble. Melancholalia.

This is what happened.

Today the measure is nil. Broken stelae are covered with lichens and moss. Rain sweeping in from the west. Perhaps refrain—delay and respite. Also, a truce.

He says I have given all my money to the astrologers, the soothsayers, the gypsies, the firejugglers, the inchanters, the minnesingers and the number canters. Old world-long taboo—all words meaning still. The seven vowels were engraved upon plaques. And, appearing to the naked eye like detached poisons, the nearest galaxies to earth. I want your rusty spoons first.

If you can't keep up with the conversation don't try joining in. Everything depends on the disposition of the hips. There's always something new to listen in to: loose talk of a public weighing-machine, used also as a place of punishment, as by nailing of the ear. It's in the air. He's going to get away with it. Still, there are some who question whether he's the right buy (too many neural tricks).

That's it now they will trace your every move.

The small circular lozenge. The market place. What I need is an unobstructed view. She cannot bear to think of all the indignities she made him suffer, the elaborate system of waiting before admittance. The exposure level is twenty-one. If he fails she must collapse. The flame was wickless and without oil. For him periods of one hundred and twenty years are like one year. His names are handmade and unknown. Place him in the triangle. He leaks out of his little wooden container. He is suspended for thirteen minutes more (the allure of an open heart survey). It's vital that he fades. I feel voice, a wild uncultivated region into which nothing happens. He says I once saw.

They sleep at depths between term and term. They see to it. There's no change in the pulse-rate. It never occurs to me. This is all down to the indecision. They went where they went. I shall take myself off there and listen. The music here is of a similar cadence: at rest, dead sound. Please answer this invitation. At the equator we all breathed liquid for nine months.

Recent process. First word of the introit. It eats alive all before it. There is no lasting division, as you so rightly say. Sometimes this appears no more than a letter to an unknown correspondent. (But how much more is that.) In the second dream things seem a little improvised: a young man standing under a dripping tree. I'll be with you straight away. Move on a little before me. We are witnessing the constant disorder of certain phenomena. Usage is being established as it's spoken and or written.

If the words over the arch are above the waterline, we can go no further. This fills me with apprehension about missing bits out, as some do, and conversely, of including too much, and so overburdening the sentence—the carrier or vehicle, if you will—with a surfeit of fibre and ink, not to mention injudicious punctuation; in a word, information. All occasions inform against me. Do less. Steel resonating discs have been fitted inside him. If the big chain is below the waterline we can go no further. The vessel is coded 29XII60—to wit, the hole of intuition in mathematics. It's certainly one of the most weird and wonderful engines ever made. Therein I talk about the end (teleology). I talk of a wing-shaped shield or unidentified door form, the inevitable body under the bridge. Parts of the manuscript are missing. Purpose is allied to misinterpretation. No one present seems to appreciate this. They are nerves.

She says demise lies hidden inside them at inception—an agon sunk deep to the beginning of the mess. It is kept alive by their refusal to leave work alone. Dobro. Exit all but.

a gang of men working on a groyne at night under arc lamps the shingle the sea the hum of the generator

A tantalizing glimpse of a magico-astrological diviner. My eyes are all right now. You are body she says, a forbidden entrance to a portal. She touches the openings of the mouth and the eyes with her finger. I suppose you realize. They have gone ahead and published the committed unknown. Listen: the drone of the light plain that separates us. Like a man in a sentence, the life I pursue has a quality of quiet dismay. There is some solace. For several years after memory there is recurrence. The original is secreted behind a scroll of wallpaper depicting a man with a feathered head.

Ursa Minor. Lead antimony. Who is pursuing whom now. Make sure there's no eye contact or you're dead meat. The paradox is the infamous paradox: brickdust and cantillation. She is found to be the complete coma. I wrap my head within hers. None speaks to any other—no fulmination, no mutual misunderstanding. Each is in his own place, unmeasured and in unison from early time. Be sure there is no eye.

Number four hundred and sixty-four. I have discovered who she is. She is clergy, priest, scholar, and the-one-who-fails. That she is in common use is unemployed. She is in writer. She is in assassin. She is in copyist. She is in all accounts. She is in hive. She is in correspondence. She is poor reception. Indeed, she is shopper to the act. She is the response, a favourite border planet. A without named in honour. The of expedition. The famous air.

She is said to have sprung from a word bolted together with the cry of an animal. Evidence is insufficient. But speaking silently is surely a certain activity, no.

An extent of level earth, the opened country. Athanor. I stopped. I was tired, nothing more.

Sockless man, blackclad with camera, on a concrete causeway below the rusting buttress that holds back the land. Gathered sticks. Giant.

The legend of the map. Paper view. How to form a compact head or inner mass, as in let us. And then out of nowhere she remarks. The demon departed from her and she was cured right away.

A god of boundaries—pursuing, meaning. A fragile.

He too must depend on what he can remember. He stamps up the stairs and back into the waiting cab. He takes off before I can say thing. I wrap my head. Within his I wake. It's six in the morning, a brittle infant in the cot in the room. Seventeen minutes after impact we manage to seal the hatch. There is no answer. From that day on he never speaks to the rest of the crew. Something has had to change inside of him. This is beautifully done, rendered as ink on dog-eared index cards: yclept old of all et cetera. Void school. That's the signal to drift back into the barn and toil from dusk till sun-up. Now I'm making stillborn errors.

We placed huge flat rocks on the box to flatten his remaining lung. I'm weary, despite the seven aces hidden in my pocket. This is going to hurt. Uneven logs were tied together and flung into a swift river. A descant is added. Close-up of a bloody gobbet on the table by his bed.

That aqueduct. A simple theme, returned. Useless impressions in some flat minor cue, the contents of my jacket pocket.

You could be right. The building consists of three perfect cubes separated by square courtyards. Leave her a suicide note, more useless yet very real predictions. More useless provocations. More worthless promotions. Again he sees the face at the window. Thrice he drops the ganglia keys. He survives. They accuse. They dip him in hot tallow, saint of the cornerstone, and he survives.

Ice in small plates and spikes in the rapid streams.

They drill explosive bolts into his neck. He survives. Up to his shins in the mud with chill of water rising. Minute bodies in the blood, concertinaed and clot-ting. Crack this deadlock. Conjoin disparates: wax & frazil.

He is a man remote with characteristics, scattered little reminders. Bring me any test he says, I shall reword matter which madness would gamble for. The explanation is uncertain. About him we know nothing or next to. The drifting halts, nowhere in peculiar. It thrives concealed among the standing still, from whence a grating voice.

The cutting of the last hand.

A figure composed by the last hand.

A clot of raw flesh, hacked or vomited.

A gob of text.

Comment. Self-feeding digest—fire.

A mouth to be swallowed.

Ecstasy, my pulse.

As long as you stay here with us, we can always find our way back.

He is tied to a log and flung at that instant. She is born with her head veiled in a caul. In death he finds himself rehabilitated, soviet-style. Sound: quite fragile voice, with snow falling into the big sea, never before witnessed.

Stagewhispering. Thalattamantic.

He approaches the region where the vast dwell, a sunken factory. Pan into the study and his collection of permafrost mummies. Some have stones in their open mouths. The guard dog dies chained still to the wall. The same six faces keep turning up. Pink object on cill beyond ghosted pane. How easy everything has been made for him, picking his way between the wrinkles of the road. (I limit myself to a set of menus.) Each one of his wheels is rolling in a different direction. He splits into four. Everywhere he walks he is noting and recording: a scherzolike trio in the tonic major. One flies towards him with a live coal and personifies his lips. Snow failing in the water, the cinders. That which may come or be thought to an end.

She does not know where to turn. She takes inspiration from everyday lives: a thin film of old friends, the mechanics of pub brawling. A field of tumuli so dense that one mound tracks onto another's skirts. I have a tendency to be early, am well beyond any objective sense of the hours, of the day.

It's that yes I'm uneasy. They might have, or have not. Delayed spares quiver on the organ trolley. Auguries are being observed. Presentiments arrive, including one in which he's eclipsed. He is disordered to perform, uncanny mime: a plane passing obliquely and failing to meet the other branch, a regretted departure, the opposite edge, a decayed meeting, a hind-wheel spinning, a mesh of condensation trails. The spectator is insulated by self-censorship.

Slovenly beautiful, he strolls back to the spit.

Scatsong, plainspoke.

A plane of light passes obliquely and fails to meet the other branch. Glistening fountains, falcon circling. A torn membrane covers her head. I forget.

Giant land, distant faint antiphon. A hexagonal basin drains the centre of the room. On one wall is a calendar wheel. The months carry a sphere composed of interlocking triangles, wedged within much older ruins—a hollow built from bars of green copper oxide. On the opposite wall is a cylinder, a device for producing sentences of the language under analysis—a quiz of the nerves. My evil plan is to outlive the whole three years. (This is a straightforward matter of reconstruction, with no ethical implications.) Someone has erred. Look, iron tension uplifting blocks of stone, yellowcake with cubist mineral. The danger is one may get something one does not expect. A lie-detector is wheeled in. Imagine the following cases. You are playing in a field with your eyes bandaged. Just being alive used to be enough, now the tireless yestercrush.

Retreat to safe haven. You walk along a railway track, simply follow where it leads. This is faulty by definition (elevated species of operatic spleen). I used to help out with all the little things—I have unhinged the doors on my own in the past. Her criticism is that these are among the things she no longer desires in her operation. It isn't difficult to get her started on the subject. Detail will no longer be tolerated. In this production the sets should appear irrelevant and disconnected from the drama. The aim is to paralyse the spectator.

The stagehands serve us tiny black mushrooms, a local ritual handed down by men who were alive in the past. (It is because dying.) How to abandon the compound when the time comes? Only warm-blooded animals are to be used. I work with palms bare, hands flattened. I am antimatter. I don't won't to spend the rest of my life on this: peeling spores of photogenic rust, the craquleure of ancient gloss, that statue, the unspeakable family vault—affinities lost in the haar of ancestry.

All these situations are similar to one another. Coloured rectangles of glass fan out above each portal. A rubber ball bounces between the confines. On inspection, it's found to be a sphere made of elastic bands. There's no voice, just two parallel walls with sloping batters. I make a decision (no), based on a lack of knowledge. But what is common to all experiences.

Ripples on passing lake, persisting concentrics. The totalizer's locked today.

He comes to his window, white-shirted, apposite. He hears it too. One calling up, perhaps.

The plot's about a dying child, isn't it. I'm talking about something far more molecular: a shadow on the lung, the rap of a knuckle on the window from without. (Yes but fourth storey.) There's one more legal hurdle. Beds of clay and marl have been excavated between the upper and lower strata. A version that makes frequent use of both protagonists is being concocted from nothing. Embroil them in some new difficulty, strive to get the pair imprisoned. Remove some of the obstacles. Drag them slowly across frozen ground. (Revolution now seems decadent, backbeat.) The catalyst used is titanium antimonate—liquid vesicant, a derivative used in chemical warfare.

Breathe. Brick up earth. One who digs gault.

Space culminates in a bare cube-shaped room. Words spiral up the walls. At the centre stands a man in workman's overalls. We make our way down the yellow steps. He laughs and the head laughs too. Somehow this memory is erased yet still deposits a trace. The author will make an effort not to lose sight of this. He is discontinuous form. (Unspeakable family curse call morgue.) He has to move himself and his belongings to a hired lozenge. The starting point is mechanics. At the beginning everything was a reaction to a void. The starting point is aesthetics. The experiment slows down and then ceases. Altogether, there are findings: bone of left forearm with posterior surface exposed, puzzling magnetic fields. What are they actually doing.

It struggles violently. It is concave from before backwards. Nonetheless, it is able to speak with eloquence. Its extremities are prominent and serve for the attachment of my ligature. (I was always good with knots and tourniquets.) The closing days of the calendar month are choice, with some antecedent goodwill, which is rarely at hand. Not a soul comes near. They commonly break through the country on either side. Hasty steps are approaching. And that, sir, is a glistening stratum of dew. Do lesser.

A vein is opened. The lode is laid bare. They pretend to cut off her head. They are accomplished actors.

Yes, we're returning, yes. Boats with their prows high rocking and the smell of ship and with a couple of dogs trotting beside him. I'm sent out before the wind with a string of hooks. Compulsive self-mutilation of the hands is recorded, especially the lips. A mason's rule has been bent to fit the curves of the mould.
A settling on shingle.

She says the documentation is more important than the thing itself.
Realistically, to here. Now for the addend, bricolage—the immaterial supplement to books and manuscripts, screen-cells of seer hide and barque-paper. They can switch it off, they can mask it with white noise, but they can't take it out of your skull.

Divination by means of cheese.
You are looking out over the garden. You are looking out over the sea. The shaft is prismatic in form at its upper part and resembles the segments of an insect's thorax. I'm fast out of the blocks for next month, curving from behind back to front. (Some actually claim that she has died.) And I am curving from within outwards. And I am convex external, glass allied to ear, to shibboleth—blind, with flat spikelets appressed edgewise in two-rowed spears. My conversation sounds taxing. And how could you possibly know whether something is an experiment or not, rather than one of the elements, the so-called inert? I exist, despite the limited scope. I recognize in this version a remote saga going back to a period much before the present tense. It spans a final protracted breath. Some claim she disappeared during that winter. There remains a persistent fear that she might be carried over. I was remember. A corroded cylinder is adapted for mourning ritual. Military aircraft low overhead. Spine bearing florets which yield, arms chopping at the old confines. Graft in the undercurrent.

I have today retired another lexicon. The danger is that one may get something one has not bargained for.
Blazon, bar sinister. You'll find animal familiars within this circle. The principle ele-

ment is a neomorph. Simple measurements of velocity, surface tension and rotatory power are being made. Findings are.

Low pressure in discharge tube.

Orangered glow.

Atom ten.

Symbol, No.

The red colouring from the fishes makes scarlet blotches on the paper.

Organza, book muslin, gauzy apparitions wove plain with sail and canvas—the translucent white of film by overlaid salt. Thin toothless broth. Humidity extreme and the dunes with misquotes of size, a slippage of tracks and voltage with satellites, as if as the apparent sea. That height, so it was with mauve and orange, shades of dead.

Frieze.

The sunwise outcrop here is often, and I was and I am. Thinking, I fade to the west (was it). Until the arm of the process is complete, leave my fingernails in the frame. And the word kidnap and the word net, distant and near islands of chain, and I (a sea) the china south. That height great for one overkeeled so high, it was so high. And inclination away from the perpendicular—doing less, doing lesser, doing nothing. No reason whatever to remember.

Whatever. Any or all that, no matter what.

Put my fingernails back in the frame.

The collector has coined names for several of the moths. The man without quantities, with no power of return.

An eight car attack. Just the distance between the centre and the outer edge of the tooth. Can you glass bead people move forward. I overheard.

I meant mosquitoes and organ failure, the unscrewing of a thread. Actual gear ratio has fallen to disuse. She says the circumnavigation is more important than the equator itself.

A very thin line of any substance. See, a thread or wire—waxy brain exposed to unsettle the shot. As long as they stay with us we can always find our way back. Twist and suck out as filament.

No, realistically, to here. Where are you. What can you see.

The meremost glisk. A finishing stroke. Literally, the stroke of grace. Do least. Delete. Turn it off. I'm doing my soliloquy.

VI

We're never going to forget it, the opening screen: poultry, jack or tin and paper case, ditto section. You have to move in close to read any of this, utilizing negatives, saying what is not—torn in a seacup, eye full of clipse. But first the green line. One thing I am certain about: the language filched from passers-by. Immaculate simplicity of narrative. It's a method known to stop anything in its tracks.

She is born with her head wrapped around a name, a big chunk of it.

There is a record of their nonchalance: he weeps (10), he hears (11), he turns, looks, dries out (12)—a fivefold series of verbs, the last three clustered in one verse, title unknown. A few more seconds waste away. Where can we have been all this time, the perfect combination of imperfections. Imagine an archive which has no need of a witness.

From a small group slaughtering a pig, the crowd moves across the painting from left to right. Transfer the balance, batter my heart threepersoned et cetera. Everywhere you look a new scene emerges. Stitch up telegraphic. The name is called. Stitch up telegraphic—isobars and light.

He halts his step and says you did not recollect for her. I can see this is going to take a few years more.

Puncture me a neck. Time is outdone, dispensed backwards from fevershore to sluice. Lightermen trudge across the shingle, a type of Vitus dance—unpeace, various reprimands. Our objects include a scroll microscope and the velvet carbine case. It's a long time ago that the date was last cited.

It slips out of its chair. My eyes are a bonus.

Cut adrift of a target, and I'm rather appeased with myself. We're in. Fluorescent pink loop quivering in space. The target has always been a levelling off. Static between opposing yet complementary characters: castle nowhere near camber, swift running flame, a single canine tooth hung about a milky white throat. It looks like we've stopped. The idea of escape means nothing to me now. And the greater part of what I'm thinking slips away, dragging at the image. There are problems in this epoch—all the ports are substitute ports. The country looks so diffident compared to the one I've grown used to: a surfeit of zeros, giants and runts, one input errors. Success is one hundred percent. A boundary stone, endpoint of root or circuit.

She is disfigured as an imaginary animal: tall with black fur head, eye glinting green above a purple rim.

He halts his step and whispers. You neglect to make a share of her memory, the unspeakable family crust.

Sink-a-pace. A series of nine blocks is arranged in a line on the floor. Everything disintegrates. The current doxa secularizes the uncanny—a simple trick, not achieved at the instant of course, but over a long stretch of time. I'm mindful of those tall ten posts, sentried across a misty field. The final man is being questioned. Ask them for a single day of your life back, nothing more.

The taped confession lends atmosphere. Expose him to the light. He's a man for all reasons. His words give no idea of the hidden comedy. He resides in the specious indications of objective truth. All of his reasons are the wrong reasons.

You remember him wishing he had an extra hand. The state appears never to move. A spine runs along the back of an ancient territorial division.

This is interesting ground, the award-winning document. She is relegated to the lowest self—erased experience, freelance neurosis. She begins to make herself up. Pace and movement are characterized by five beats. A syllable is suppressed, squeezed out. The plot develops from the roof of the interbrain.

A cardboard soldier is in love with a marionette who has fallen ino a coma. The law states that if anything can go wrong, it will. A random temperature has been set. Terrible things happen. Pleasure varies inversely as volume. The squaddy's injured. The manikin revives and nurses him back to health. Everyone dies, everafter.

It's time to hear her seven last words. Crushed pallets and stacks—the yearful sweat track. She is making up the pronouns as she goes along.

He remains in place for as long as she lasts. A sudden drop in blood pressure occurs at the pineal eye. They are joined by a connecting column of nerves. A thin promontory continues backwards around the canal, up to the neck of the ladder. Immediately beneath the membrane sits a vascular tunic. I am discomposed he adds, a conducting vessel.

And she says, do you know you lean forward when you walk.

No when I talk he replies, the same thing.

A vestigial third hovers in front of the body.

Move away from here, from this spot. What's the weakest point of your body. I am peering beyond a plausibility. Her overview is oblique. She resembles an anatomically accurate chess piece. She dances to save the nation from disaster, disappearing at dawn in a rash of blue light. She says those carved limestone figures I possess. They are a part of me. Voice carries out: barefoot on back, bootless come pricking, bell up to the mud in a tower over your keep.

Shorten by cutting out middle.

He throws himself on the funeral pyre. The air is disjunct. The fluid shadow of a shoal is spotted in the water. Victory shouts are heard, hats in the air. A whole day is declared. It's like human soap opera. It's like a day given back by the dead. It's like all of the following.

The lotophagi, architectures of I've forgotten.

A telephone rings.

The torrential rain.

The bird's-foot trefoil genus.

The floodgates.

The angry.

The heavens.

The krantz of rock at a mountain peak.

The buried heads. (It's said he lived among them for a time.)

The assembly.

A multitude. Together we forget. He's renamed the cloud, or the blindness. We overlap.

She finishes, then composes another. She flings the letterbomb into the street from the attic window, along with the lava lump and the well of ink and the chosen book.

He is merely a cipher in the interplay of relationships. How do you feel about carving those glyphs somewhere else. Generations of unfortunates in the outside world have failed to do. The system changes by degree. A telegram arrives. The museum is mortgaging history by the year. He knocks me cold with his remark. He has his impregnations for company. You were once. The chemical on his fingers smells of rotting pork. Just speak the language, a dead pledge. Cases who forward views are rare. He says a book can't be written before the events it refers to. I can't remember a time when this wasn't an accepted fact.

I intend vomiting up the feathers I have swallowed. Across their fibres is written the following (this should be read while slowly rotating).

Was the door locked no that night.

I go back a couple of steps.

I go back a couple of light years.

I stand there waiting.

Why do I feel this all of a sudden terror.

She is paralysed in a timely passage: inenarrable modality of the unvisible. A clerical boundary—the quality of being limited by a condition (law). Unearthed in a tilled field immediately to the southwest is a net of feldspar. Its tissues are set at precisely the required angle. At the centre of this compass a kidnap is taking place. The task is to document all that bite, any hybrid mix—those with oblique fractures, crosswise of mouth like sharks and rays—crosswise with transverse slit at underside of head. Vouchsafe, this walk is around the back of myself. I climb the ascent and haul myself back on to the road.

Use any of the primary methods. Crush tendons and sever at wire aperture. Classify all sensations as true, false, necessary, possible or impossible (log). Retinal damage at back of headplate, diaphragm in cross-section, in concussion. I can't remember a time when there wasn't some kind of attempted animal acting up in the locality. A sombre mood is wedged between the rival ports of gold lace and tallow. I am driving the octaves, the steps and the half-steps—carotid artery compressed for deep sleep. Quick, change the method of conversion. Work so honey, hard: inject more caffeine, more blood.

Orient at an angle in direction of stimulus. Return where time divides itself into notes—perfects into three, imperfect into two. We have achieved the arcade. Resistance is fading. In the marquee at the back of the shooting-range the women have the men on their shoulders. I want to pitch this right, don't wish to oversize the case. It's my job to inject them as they stagger and sway. (This is called an organized spatial activity.) The visual gap between rich and poor is widening. Very influential hormones are present, a lingering memory of that aqueduct. I'm not used to going somewhere: chaptering tension in the sternum, another visual lapse. A major division can be triggered by an obsolescent note. That artefact is the the so-called beast bone. This is the most irritating thing. Minor deities are herded into barrows (except in place names). The burial chamber houses an abandoned apothecary, wands of radar glitter. I forget who was on my shoulders.

The only furniture is an indentured head and a deed under seal. The latter is a mutated covenant. I can't remember a time when there wasn't some kind of attempted fact. Now, about her voice. It is vanished. It has reported stolen. She lies immobile but can be simulated into movement. The subject is long-finned to the naked eye. (Sorry, that should have read cunts, with an apocalypse.)

The translation takes liberties. Generally, action doesn't work. It's rumoured that three elderlies have neatly kill off a monstrous, have padlocked the mouth, split open the spine.

Each foot rests on the opposing thigh. Did you go backstage yourself that evening. He arrives at his destination. He continues his journey north. I will say nothing about this in due course. He retires to the study, where he attends to his moth collection and standard deviations. (Forcing thoughts into an ordered sequence is a torment.) The edge of the head has been indented for future reference (law). I need to ask your advice about something. That's three times in a row. The text has no blind spots. A weal runs a ridge between its two hemispheres—a continuous connecting element in the story or argument: the spiral apart of a screw. In such fashion are we welded. I can't remember a time when this wasn't an accepted fact.

Floating cables of light. It doesn't answer back. It doesn't achieve the crowd. She bears the brunt. It's the weekend. She bears estranged fruit. I've been talking too much (memory). The response I get from the region is lamentable. I do something familiar. A shadow casts out across the room, mimicking its object. And this is supposed to be you is it. A shadow bisects my surface. Crouching behind me, she says reflect upon what you do now, upon what you did then. Two different words are fused together, (1) and (2). Penetration is deep into the tooth, deep into the nerve. The reasons remain obscure.

No one comes. Shanties are thrown up on the flattened hilltops, on spurs of land surrounded by deep ravines. I'm on a walkway of creepers, suspended between two turrets.

Ringing good lip on the ear. A sharp rise in the new orderly. Is that a pattern or a problem. I'm never going to look at you with the same eye again.
A photograph held in a frame is propped at the foot of the scaffold. Female on horseback. I drift from point to point. (One poem covers only a few feet.) There are no surviving records. There are sheets of corrugated iron. Let me. Lend me a couple of syllables. And he turns around all the same, while talking.
He continues north.
He continues to narrate.
Ne at numb ten.

About her orienting. About her overbearings. A sideways glimpse is afforded through a crevice in the rock (a kind of hindsight). There are big carnivorous animals with shaggy hair and hooked claws dancing on the tables. (O yes it is.) I have mislaid my continuous. Come quick. Forget. You are remember. Come. Let me walk down with you to the shoreline. Today's news is that there is no more.
They part in grief daylight. Carbine brass shell cases discarded on the ground. The sum total is less in total. They quit the room. These are our footsoldiers: attendant dwarves with tapeworms strung around their necks, the taproom theosopher, discocked dogs, itinerant arsonists, a circus hunchback pierced through by a javelin. All our waiting silences. Have the gold-leaf margin overlap the foil below. Our perception of such things does not do them justice. Destroyer and reproducer, she has spiralled out of control and into the remaining year.

A compendious system of teaching is drawn up in the form of question and answer, a closed set of inquisitions. Experiment with tense. Scale out. Spread. Disseminate. What happened to my normal job (I confess I do). I do the book of imaginary beginnings. To be fair, she is unlike any oppressive person, thing or influence I have ever encountered. I change the circumstances then I reverse them. I change then I don't. We heard a theatre of torture back there. Why heavens, when she runs I can hear and see everything she's thinking. The equivoque lies in such loose and common habits, unhinged in her commotions. Why heavens. Then the big surprise group. I'm facing up to the factors. It's their reputation on the line. Everything is wagered. I was once trapped halfway down a birth canal myself. Blue rings of flame drop from the trellis. We have inherited the confederations. We have inherited the oratorios—a story set to solo closet with full orchestra. (The vast and subtle pattern of serendipities would have been more reliable.) Scenery, plot, costumes and acting are dispensed with. Imagine the form of such a composition—some semblance to epic, only shorter. Your enormous superiorities are always less pliable. So, these haunting songs were discovered. Send a car you imbecile.

Fear and collapsing graphs. The scab genus, giving name to the family, with armour and keeled lateral line.

It could not be gainsaid. He doesn't keep records, simply writes everything down and buries it in the archive. Yielding patterns of schiller, a skimming or gazing movement—momentary at blow or touch slight. A sketch, a puff of air—acid-bitten coincidence. My own hobby is sealing wax. Example: is mayonnaise an instrument. Is liquid clay an instrument. The point is that the material held is never referred to, a silent repository.

Deep gathering into focal plane, as of gland—viral, earless—where the air splits in two. That's all I remember. Go on, you're being expended. He lies paralysed for an entire week, without the arbitration of city or place. That ends this week's optics. I am stillborn at cusp, dissuaded: that which is occupied by what stands there. Those who remain.

Using the directional winding method those flung out fall in the strangest way. The imagery of ascent is not uncommon: bone graft photo on bone, of how many years, of how old they look now. A line of light is compressed between two darks.

He withdraws into himself to create a vacuum in which nothing can happen, into which something may rush.

He glances down into undercliff.

The last line has been kidnapped. I changed his name to he because I don't want Faust in my story. I am unfound footage. I can only apologize. Yours are understandable renunciations, understandable objections. I am yes, that's the one, yes. One of the yeses.

He is vindicated. Crushed tissue and pebbles are strewn across the concrete platform. Late in September his letter is returned. We must remake the divisor, the broken-open lowlihead. Absently he says, what you were doing before we came with autopsy, with corporation.

I reply. Reason remains, unseeded.

Linguatrix, one who or that which terminates. Looks like washday up there. A few light taps upon the pane (it can't). He turns to the window. Check those battery cells. Have him tuned to the vibration from the wall. Have him walk to the window. I know what's coming (electrodes). I am remainder none. Weird rose thing on the ceiling with barbed wire. I'm a tabooist by profession, the science of combining letters: pyramid hygiene, the product of my indelicate researches. Please take one in the scapula for me. I cannot perpetuate the moral lie which would have satisfied my descendants. How do you think I feel now, root touching neural core—being here *and* there, being there *and* here. Riveted to past over and with tar on every sole. Wasteless form.

We pull him offside and they call out to leave him be—the great who with armoured keel and lineage, dimming into the ear as back-echo. He with the tongue of his face, watching the needleboats.

He leaps the perimeter. Things have to be tested. He jumps the crowd. Things have to be fed. I work on as best I can, measure the hydrology of a small catchment. But it's not my true memory of this event.

Go on.

Carbine wrap-metal case.

He takes a box of false air out of the drawer. He begins to reassemble. A voice says it's designed to do that.

Have you touched the entrails yet. You have constructed an apparently realistic narrative, a novella. The atmosphere is perfect. Form and content are equivalent to an unripe manifesto. Even when unconscious she is earmarked. I have no word for space. I am still finding repetition. Thousands of shiny metallic balloons are released into the atmosphere to mimic the effect. In the box are the ibex bones, neatly labelled. Bulb bare in opposite well, forearm on bannister in the black. This is an event that's firmly hooked to the past. You forget your own name. It's clear we can't survive relocation. There's a ton of reclaimed bricks in the street (susurrus is a funny old word, isn't it). When did you last appear like this, a closed form of nineteen lives. Better not delve into. I shall never tire of them, loveward and lovebourn.

They have gone. I feel compelled to rearrange the room. I am quite catapulted, into fact.

All this time I see in my sleep and much much more. I'm granted one last dream. Rudimentary chaos is written in invisible, then folded over. Contrast is established with the glittering squares. A lady falls into a concrete underpass. Thousands of microsulphate droplets are pumped into the atmosphere to mimic the effect. We are starting out from a physical moment in history, one ambiguous and difficult to interrupt. The two babes in the wood are the killer twins. There's a long and deep fissure in the earth, goats frisking about the edge. She doesn't understand and asks. It's tempting to peer into the hole. Remove one button and bury it. She is travelled undercover. She refers. Earmarket. Is everybody happy, so far.

Whereas he is the most incorrect scribe the world has ever seen. She takes over, delivering her pithy answers in a classical prose style. That is simply what happened. Shake the scales from your feet. The killer turns out to be the bio-tick killer. I like it because none of the clues matches the wilderness.

Sagittal section through mid-time of brain. The cavity is conical in form, after the nature of an inverse hill. There's evidence. It has been destroyed and rebuilt many times. No one knows why. Two birds meet at the selfsame spot. Hoplites.

Bindings to talk around. Back-slacker & goad leaf. A jet of sand from the funnel of the infernal. That iron tang in blood: the legal mean of the unreasonable man in the street. Then I love you and everything is beau. At two o'clock the guide enters a thick forest which extends for several miles. He prefers to travel in character, face sallow with uncontrolled substance.

I reply. Dwelling. Time. Matter. Sequence.
In oaths her anthrax, organ play by mouth. Literary sangfroid (motive tyrannical avarice, a fart in the powder of darkness). Stone breastwork at the watchtower. Wildbore, a hole in the gale. One who admits bloodletters. I cannot repeat the list of degrees of relationship into which this situation might be successfully transferred.
It is now four o'clock.

I am occurring. Uncannily, where I was first found, no doubt in ballast.
What's the matter says the head.
Some say that the pond has sunk into its aperture.

Well, you see, it's the opening through which light passes. We're at the apex of a golden tangle. Imago of insect folding inward. There's a breeze from the map, accompanied by that grinding noise from the south. There were harps I swear and a tunnel of light like a meatgrinder—pockmarked marble in the humid town square. Unless we have a very unexpected sequence of events, we're in this for the duration. He too is idle, being merely the optical counterpoint of a thing. We are so named from oblivious reason. I shall keep my eye out for the moment of goodbye.

Blue trams rattle out from the muddied suburb. Walking through the streets late one early morning he explains everything to her. And she says, I can tell you have felt the inside of the things you describe. You are lead of the heart, nothing more, nothing less.

Tesla notes. Photograph on bone. This passage is neither I nor other than I. He is elaborated type, founded on some ancestor or other—drear and nameless, strung out beneath the swaying municipal bulb. He disinhabits, a silent headscape. Influence persists as influence: coils of magnetic flux, the inability to feed. You are sick with limewire, with frost-scale—with calling and occupation and reverie. He has fangs. There is a big dee on his cape. It's announced that 1900 is to go on sale from the sixteenth. There's a problem with risk here. He cannot be repositioned as such. Two nuclear protection suits and a bow and arrow were retrieved from his apartment. This fact is neither encouraging nor indifferent. We can worry at the outcome some other time. Suffice to say, he's armoured on all sides. Am having a wonderful trip—sowed beside myself, a unique set of slips and errors. Unseeded, in manner of bitter kvetch.

He infects. He is the voluntary prop to action. He is misguide. A complex coordination of repulse actions leads to a lack of achievement: adaptive ends without foresight. We are stationed at the observation platform. Sparks float up into the lightless air. In September the first cool nights come. It's is all about a novel concerning the early heroine. Perhaps you think the statement the mountain doesn't exist is quite clear. Our objective is military. Then all the days are cool and the leaves, cracking words from the horde underfoot. He attaches sharps of glass to the seven existing names and circuits the original stump. Form and content are equivalent to a manifesto, the rough test of a vacuum by discharge.

Coverings. Moments of inertia.

An oily liquid is obtained by destructive distillation and misuse of the crop-stick. The two seeded halves are split apart and dangle from the lip of the axis. Received spray over muscle of spermatic cord—chewed up in the east where the star sets. It has an E in it, so preserving antinomy, the lost or perfect state of insect life. Frieze glimpsed through foretold aperture.

Alphabet bingo. Bango. Bongo. Bungo Bengo. Like-lustre, uncertain distraction by minute plates. He swims across the tank and grapples with a red perspex cube. He would like a taste of revenge today, formless waste.

Brittle white element at numb earth. East means insurrection in the west. To the south, a stretched arc (the great mauve bow). This has all the markings of bedroom farce, printer's lung. You wake to find your faithful postilion has fled in the night. The circumstance is now equal. We stand in direct proportion to our size and weight. This will change.

They evolved from salt of acid—hanging fruit, creosote and dense scrub. Conclusions disquieting though apparently logical.

There comes a time when you have to trust yourself. Is anybody catching up.

Is anybody watching this. You wake to find your body's quit. I've had mine tweaked to leave a more permanent trail. Everything's pushed out to the margins. The state quivers and anything of value fails to the base of the land. You have no name (laughter). Return, no more return, he says. I am probable. I will not. I am of unknown origin, yet doubtless sprung. Between us sits a shallow pool of poisonous fluid. We wear helmets and boots with steel toecaps, industrial over-haul. We begin. Each of the fish we angled was as long as a day and a night. And one fabulous that voided the hook.

The spa. We're forced down neatly to our knees. I am unaware. A man can drown in a couple of inches of water. She can only whisper of the way he manipulates, of the way he is manipulating. He is an expert on rare insects and seeds. I should have guessed the geography. My view is not so fine as yours, but still I glimpse the pyramid at the crest. You wake to find your familiar position has vanished. It's advisable. Take up the reverse option. I am thinking of thresh-olds, revolving doors. Now listen, see. We are boring through to the pith of the spine. The thickening light serves as a shell—a hood of refractory material that becomes incandescent when exposed to flame. Results crackling damp and grey throughout the afternoon, my blue-veined.
And the way he is manipulating the others (the column).
And the way he will manipulate the others (the quill of a spinet).
But this is the situation. I am not making these things up—the story of the meteor, the story as dedicated wreckage. Thousands of animal skulls were found beneath the floorboards.

Dialectic of paradox, white hands clutching white book. Remains were found in the Roman well, sunk into the earth at different depths. Unhappy is the man who cannot isolate. He says I am impatient for the press of the clay.
He works by patches and scraps. It's enough to kill anyone. His right hand achieves the intercession. He speaks. Please look after her while I abandon, while I sleep. I taper more gently toward base than apex. In vain will you search for proof that anything was ever out. Choose the converse step. Light suddenly floods the stairwell. We are choking on motes of dust. Our shoes fall apart and are stacked in a heap. Clack of knuckle to stove. This signals that I no longer function. Place him please and gentle in the summer pavilion on the strand, his own private haunt. He has withstood sixteen days of exorcism. A couple of bystanders are discussing the taboo, the ibex bones. Sound is omitted by an instrument resembling a small radar chord, possibly named from its maker: the scraping together of things. The journey is a long haul across hostile country. We are eaten away—gradual into silence, dazzled into obstruction. But a theme is developing, the attachment organ of the entire planet. The holdfast: a simple plane of light. Count me with the mysterons.

More on manifesto—

Discarded vertebrae.

Unwanted product.

A figure in pink, there. Rudimentary hands clasped to breast. With dulled colour and thickening body—antennae inelastic, wings tilted back in repose. It has the habit of flying night.

A bird of prey will be released for one hour twice a week for the rest of your life.

An optical illusion: everyone saw the keys fall into the water. None of the stagehands claims to have heard it. I am reading with care and simultaneously composing. Time today is honoured on the award list beneath the lenticular portrait. Bunting muffles the sound. J and K were found missing from the alphabet thumbs. I resolve to eject. An omen is, surely.

Laughing, he clambers without delay over the rim of the tank. As long as anyone can remember he has been associated with standing water—uninhabited ponds, wells, swamps and conduits. Nothing is in its proper place.

I am tackling back on myself: organs of attachment, advice given by bodies. Fitful plucking moments as in delirium. The gathering of straws.

She slides down the ladder and into the furnace. Aromatic smoke seeps gently from the decorative slits cut into the casemate (a loophole gallery from which the garrison can fire upon the enemy possessing the ditch). Laughing, she disappears beyond the frame.

All you have changed is now restored.

I have tried to catch up with her. I spy her, taking leave of sense (biconvex lens of eye).

I regain the ridge. The other group will attempt a crossing. We have a written history of our agon. The equipment includes the reconstructed glass still and the weather balloon, quoits and scraps. We are only fit for dwelling and combat. I thought we would stay together for one year more and never be alone.

I shall keep, out-eyed for the momentum.

The final stage takes place in a closed courtyard. The surrounding buildings are simple roofless cubes. Natural tape compression lends atmosphere. The town appears to have been raised by the chance surgings of the desert sand. Sound of a seedpod bursting—discrete neural cells in the neighbourhood. Paraganglia. There is no record of me.

He sees (13), he takes (14), he builds up (15). He hath lost his clarity and his eclipse suffers. It is tempting to peer into the crevice.

Haematite, enveloped in planes of separation.

ERRATA

ref.	for Cough read Couch.
ref. 2.	for Laquer read Laqueur.
ref. 10.	for 281 read 821.
para. 1.	for corticum read corticium.
	for Erdtmann read Erdtman.
ref. 2.	for 56 read lvi.
	for Hexahydrobenzanilide read benzhexahydroanilide.

VII

We find ourselves arranged in shallow apertures on an empty plain, a level tract of treeless country. Try looking under that rock. Allusion will suffice. Forgive me, proper nouns lead to folly, and my rhymes are ill-fit for any purpose. Time and being are rumoured. We are at the boundary between the illuminated and the dark portions.

Cuff on the neck then we cling together for an instant. We are unstressed and traditionally remain. We are designated lifts or dips. We need a direction. We need a stretcher. Instead we're given names. A torn banner is unfurled. Fasten an object before me, easy with indifference: any simple. What is that thing he has struck out.

The shrill demented choir.

Why do you mean.

Loss. See also theft below. The lists are interchangeable.

I have lost my bag, my brace, my camera, my car, my certificate, my key, my insurance, my decoy, my logbook, my jewellery, my medication, my licence everything.

Picture her painting that time with a sponge mop. At the dead centre is an animal netted from a much earlier work (unacknowledged). Picture her out buying food for her puma. Too many mammals in this chapter already. Items are transmitted from person to person in a retarding loop.

Successive unstressed syllables compose a dip. How long do I have. Not very long, but a permanent trail nonetheless.

A cantor is placed sixty yards from the door of every dwelling. This invention is a steal imported from an earlier climate, and of inappropriate grandeur for our setting. A liturgy is chanted. (In his love of all the ages he has recreated me within thy tomb et cetera.) In the middleground are stationed foreign mercenaries, the knights errant. Vicelike bundles, veinage with pith and pericycle.

Some believe he is describing in obsessive detail a painting, page after implacable page. He leaves a single entry for himself. He is the stem and root of a higher diocese, the circuit of jurisdiction. Great.

I wonder what I am going to do next. Lift the roof off the set, the trembling popular. He calls himself back. He is a talentless hint with various shades of meaning who scuttles crabwise across the earth. What do you mean they cut the power (they're animals). Our vessel lies at the outermost layer of the central cylinder.

I tried not to think about you but I could not.

If you show me on the map I will understand. I will discompose my tracks. A mass of floating vegetable matter has created a temporary dam. Time is obscurerd. The sun dies. This is the chapter of the opening of the mouth. That deep hole is the disused quicksilver mine of an abandoned work. One shaft nerves away from the axis, greasy with suet.

A tidal flood rushes up the estuary of an uncertain river. This phenomenon is an eagre, a bore or sudden rise. Origin is doubtful, though hardly from the accidental semblance of a name (some eastward tongue-for-eagle). The penultimate letter is Y. I have been stationed here one year to the day.

She stands at the overlooked pyramid. Vapour pours from the mouth of her head. Farewell. A tempestuous passes by. She bursts of sunlight.

All I'm doing is playing around with expectations. There is no rush to do, and there's no point in showing me a grid reference. Go ahead and ask. See to here.

See to there, a great ring of endless—emanations that refuse burial, refuse to ignite.

Once, only once, as they trotted by the forest spoor, discontinued.

Here is the place where I store the things there is no room to store elsewhere. Just the tip of a list. I am able to adjust my pattern very quickly. I too can write about anything. This is an indulgence. Now I have the whole countrywide under my bell: the aperture lozenge—the padlock—the fort of iron—the inundation—the beacon on the hill—that oval shape in the sky—the chalk quarry cliff—the impossible lodging—the cogwheel—the comet—the pit at the crest of the mound—the abandoned—the compass—the concession—the hidden mine-mouth—the paralysed crane—the quoit—the shackled and gangrenous leg—the heart of what—the sinister bend in the river—the quiver pen—the sty—the eclipsed heavenly body— the heron—the long walk out—the most violent blizzard—the castle—the cost—the current—the ruined pontoon—the cognizance—the strip of light beyond the approaching ridge—the stunned hawk on a chain—the yardarm or enclosure—the messuage in a bottle—the irretrievable warren—the eminence formed by wind erosion—sand and silt—the cypher—the difference—the fylfot—the looplake—the discarded piece of battlement—the pointed wooden implement—the rampart combatant—the rod of affronty—the skyblue slash, semy with sparks of metal—the spare bone (polished)—the thorn in the side—the uncivic manoeuvre—the weighed anchor—the arms of dissent—the balance—the battering-ram—the beaks of birds—the circle of rope—the large hook—the beehive—the stone bridge—the broad arrowhead—the cable—the spirit canton—the cartouche—the cap of remembrance—the charge (you know you did it et cetera)—the chargee & the charger—the clouds—the code—the conjoined—the countercharge—the crossed void—the monster of unsettled form, fabulous composite of flesh and letter and number.

Statant guardant, it has a head at either end of its body. It has teeth sharpened like spearheads and a dorsal fin. It claws a path across the ground as it crackles and drags. It has wolf-body, cat-face and goat-horns curling inwards (useless). It occurs. It is displayed without ears or eyes. Now it is running at speed. It has a cock head and barbed tongue. It has a coded scrotum. It defends itself. It shoots burning excrement at its enemies. Its right foot rises to reveal a watery spirit. In the knack of time the devil climbs out of his sack and hauls it back into the river. The moon is in her complement. The whole charge has been reversed to face sinister. Try looking under that rock.

For a moment there is wayment in his welcome, light from the eye rising up under the sutures. It flies before them down the track. Strategy emerges once anticipation expires, covertly worming its way back in. I am well watered and closed in by the skin. Rerun this image again and again. Retain suffix from discarded word. Form a sort of knot. In brief, it was like being hit by a truck.

Figures of no muster, not completely skeletal. You can still see the bone structure, flesh emerging or retreating beneath the frame at low tide. Try to keep house: an upright stone slab with central cylinder, revolving.

I learnt today that Blinky is a hen, not a duck. My nascent husbandry does not augur well. Despair I shall perish on this island. Fowl of many sorts make a confused scream. Sets of things are unbalanced. Crustacea rustle one upon another, crescentric and fibrous in joint. A mass of floating vegetable matter is obscuring the temporary.

I-beam. A rod that resists pressure, rigid and foreboding. The work is built on a majestic scale. Overwhelming magnitude of every instant: the posse of boys at the pyramid, rough trade snorting liquified tobacco. Elasticated harnesses. Table-rapping in the basement—tongue to eyelid, to lashes, howling every one in accord with a basal note. There is an opening to the stomach, a slit from which tubes bubble and spill. Another at the thorax. Tables are turning, limbs flung out to a hooked clasp. Prayers properly recited prevent the physical heart from being carried off (by those who plunder hearts). Not one of these is of a kind I would ever want to recognize again.

Hand in hip, elbow out of socket. I don't know how long he can keep this up. It'll surely end in a keen blow—bend sinister, echo disjunct. A raw singing voice always makes me uneasy.

Boy with kazoo, the men leaning against the cordon, attached to the embalming air by ghosts of smoke.

Another suggestion is that his codename is dogslayer. He carries a would-be instrument, a tube with a strip of catgut. The humid air resonates to his voice, pleated with narrow folds, with collapsing bellows, free metal reeds.

And she will not stop talking. Backing up into night—bent double into a crook, kink-bowed she clings to the canvas sail. Contact: spooks from the wreck, sansculottes armed with sabres and tricoloured ribbons defending a barricade. The outcome: strangled with chocolate medallions then extinguished before a whitewash wall. Smoke rising from burning matter, the reek of lime-kill—links between actions isolated in themselves.

The route leads us back, an elsewhere on the peninsula. I am standing in the cloister of a boneyard before a pitted, scarred surface. This happened long before she says, withholding my hand.

The final vision of the text is culled from a play I never read. He and she stand on a cluster of rocks at the shoreline, exposed by low tide. They gaze out, slow of sail in the algorithm. Similar objects undoubtedly formed the source. We are returning to a compulsion: the rust chute, the sea, the shattered darkly glass, the pinnacle of pebbles, the olive grove, the deepening bay. The museum in the dusty square is shut. It is always shut. Narrowing alleys, stare wells and pissstreaked paving slabs. Synchronous bombardment. In the grapple I void. I've no need of prompts to memory in the searing experience of the day. I am hoofing the plot back to the tip of the last century, to year zero. I take you at your word.

Nostos.

He has been criticized for not presenting their side. A small wooden craft sets out under patchwork canvas, flagless bound nowhere. Sap leaks from the head. All colour is bleached loose by the sunlight. The eye pivots about the couple, transfixed at the indifferent lens. I want to avoid distortion of this image.

We embrace. I would say the once. I would say she is the pivot. I would say she is the spindle about which a body wheels. We are standing at the rim of an ellipse. Her hand presses against my chest for the briefest moment as we part. I do not think I can hold in check the day any longing. Reel it inward.

Dream, reiver. A coming forth by day.

I stand in a tiled cubicle. At last the cooling air against borrowed skin. I know that he is dying to get back. He never shows. Years, and even more after the years.

He readies himself before me and begins: place the objects about the equator in alphabetic order. Unperpetuate. Compose a book of future gaps, lacunae.

Nonexistent descendants at neural stem. Panic towards the last fifteen. Intercellular space, something given beyond what is strictly required. A kidneyshaped wire hangs over the lip of a rusting brazier. Each morning a considerable number of people are found missing. There's a picture of something unfinished.

Panic towards the last twelve. Do it this instant. He writes that boredom was unknown before the century. Perhaps a different word. Am bringing self back together. Stop. Under snow the chalk cliffs look like unpolished marble. Stop. Pharynx: the gullet in the earth's crust. The weighing of the liver and the heart from papyrus, she in her animal-familiar head. A wave or swell. Stop. A more or less regular figure. Stop. A well. Stop. Depression in pitted surface. Stop. Stop. A rose screaming from the furze.

I support the doctrine that there is a time limit for the operation of gravity. The heart is the seat of the conscience. Make him counter the balance. The structure reels under teeming detail—like a cathedral with no overarch, but a cathedral nonetheless. Take care. Do not outvenom, tongue. The man who consults the calendar should act accordingly. Other forms are nearby. Be not angry they say, your head remains with us, haunted by saints. The beam is horizontal. Misfortune beyond compare they say—the choicest part of the coincidental. We've been looking out for you.

He studies the theory of the game in his spare time. Always operate at a cusp. This feels cold and vapid upon the reader's palate. My fingers find the time switch and a dribbling acid light. Go ahead and try, minuteman—mind-clinging villain of the piece, kneecapped slave with vapours and jacks. The key itself.

He contemplates every aspect, based on a discipline of illumination. It's sometimes urged with injustice that he has a covert source operating outside of himself. Bare your head before our cadavers, please.

She says could you live in one of those. I am not entirely. Put an end to the chapter. Watch the wall with those rocks, her sleeping hound on the shingle. Use your left to keep balance. Boulder sweating rust—masks of blooded mud. We wither. Now I'm not so sure. We are due back any day. Someone's been shitting on my jigsaw. Clue: abnormal deposits of calcium in the skin and the throat. Despite all this I know what I'm doing. The last sentence is over before she can fall, backward into arms.

I support the doctrine that there is a time limit for the operation of grace. The breath of his vapour steams from the woollen scarf wrapped tightly about the jaw. At the threshold he is hesitant at first. The head signals, of what he has left behind (nothing). A shadow. Form dissolves. Form dissolving shadow.

I am in the middle of my story. We have been away these twelve months. Our paths and plots are doomed to cross and recross.

Chasm within the circle. I'm attached by default. I am interlinked by teeming detail. This struggling and shrinking is sometimes called trembling and shivering. I am inherited. An arbus of comely loons is paraded at the foreshore, picking a course above a crest of stones. Hotel nearby with white light and bunting. We wrote our names in the big book. On the shingle a pyre of driftwood has been heaped for a dead. Cellophane flowers, jaundiced by the sun, are strapped to the municipal. I recall the tree-like appearance seen when the human cerebellum is cut vertically. Akin to cypress, you can still smell the bone structure.

A psychological expedition for staying awake. One with the oily porridge, one without the oily porridge, please. Nesting materials include seaweed, tiny plastic soldiers, and bees.

When she leaves she writes—supine beneath an unfamiliar, coffered into the ceiling. The air up here is sweet. The pain, thus far, is tolerable. It looks simple. She has sunk to reverie. Atoms of light fract from the concrete step. She says remember me she writes. An event is something that happens.

The adhesive self. He is too soon for all that. He is aghast of his former. Do what's right. They have nothing to gain or lose by any action. How windfall it is, this pleasant life in paradise. What a delicious conversion. Must remember to replicate the world through the agency of my senses. I feel like a human dam. I hope it will last. Dismember me.

A heap of fat, milled and shaped into a rough cube, has been placed on the table, along with a litre of paraffin, some wire, explosive charges and a fifty volt candle. One final Friday night in. Time to exit voice. A crowds gathers beneath the window. Defenestration is top of the bill. Does the mannequin put you off (don't look). The line of gauze wings goes on and on—little room for manoeuvre up and down, no catswing. I am backing into their words: two cries, one mute. I've acquired a taste for it, the abnormal fear of going back to familiar places, a nostalgia for mud. Just a short distance to go. Headless filaments form gelatinous colonies on the damp earth—worthless junk once derived from stars, the residue after distillation of the liver. Everything stops and nobody goes on and that's an end of it.

Boo!

A port. He is muse and plagiarist in one. The place is different every time I go in. He is one to circumspectly shadow over. A return, or a return journey.

A set of counterweights is fitted one inside another. I wrote this tract during the summer of the last hundred, hollow and fretted. It is concussed: that branch of speculation which documents the effects of psyche on the geographical environment. Look up. Undine with psycholepsy on ornamental underside of stair. Rippling water has replaced the ceiling. A sudden loss of tension causes the surface to burst. Fluid cascades to the floor. A luminous phenomenon is revealed, beside it the work of fire—a scorched and blackened shape, greasy with tar: fabulous compound of lion and scorpion with a human head. The date is the saint day.

On her preoccupation with water and urine—erroneous readings for a planned obsolescence. A wave, not forgetting, undulating. After breakfast, in unreasonable costume, as though ignorant of the weather and the season, she sets out from the compound (everyday life isn't everything). I too have run away. A baroque current runs through us both. It's good to have a companion on the road. There's a faint voice from the tiny box strapped to my jugular. It's raining cubes of light. Then comes the flexible blue frame (first it was the blue posts, now it's the blue frame). Second best every time, I whistle plaintively out of stride. I am employed to wear away and disarray. Strange shapes loom and brush against us. One is the twin who laps behind the stillborn. Meat hung and dried, saltless.

Again her throaty immanence of the pit. Is there to be inquisition. Muted voices are heard at the moment of the act. They are not in themselves this day. There are conditions that can never be isolated. We are not in ourselves this day. Scrape your clothes off the floor. Yield an object and its symbol. Gentle mizzle in the air, pink light bisecting space. I with my merciless am determined to outstrip the inventive. Now and then I glimpse thee, white lines on the track ahead. On your back, a word held in security. I mean said, of course—to say would be impossible.

She loses her implant. Driving rack of water, salt to face. Lose your balance. When can I too arrive, at last, like a spray of shot. I don't believe I was ever sent for, besainted to a crack of arms.

Decamp and confuse, bewilder.

I conceive of this as one among a very long sequence of tableaux, constructing a series of pictures and events of an enigmatic nature—a simulation that retrieves everything. Certainly, we can at least say of this that there is something here. But let us not speak well of it, either.

No one can figure out who owns the piece of rock. It's made of chondrite, a descendant of the universe, as are many of the following. Some are rather vulnerable, some are very odd, all are fatalistic.

An unfamiliar form of diminution. Obsolescence, sometimes with cap in hand. One of a pair of assistants. The addressing of a man whose name is unknown to the speaker. A slang detective. A slave who takes the place of a machine or device. A contrivance for turning spit. A socket whose bewitching arrangements are such that its switch turns only when a puck is inserted into an orifice. The figure that strikes the bell. The male animal-familiar. Part of the action that moves the hammer and carries off the quill of the tangent. The key itself. A contrivance for guiding threads into the moon. A winch. A sore horse. A small flag indicating. The bow or the bowsprit. The leather bottle cast up on a desert island. A knave. The game of nibs. To raise with, or as if with. To act upon. To throw up or abandon (usually within or formerly). To increase with the common man. The message in the aforementioned bottle. A piece used in any game. A will-o'-the-wisp. The small white sphere, aimed and then discarded. A piece of marionette, formerly hurled. A block of pulleys used for raising and lowering the topgallant. To abandon, with up, elder. A dandy or flaneur. A reaching above the knee to protect the leg. Military rule. To simply wait. To behave in a way. The crosstree at the head. The reasonable man. Frost petrified, the plant and the goety beard. A covering with weary iron plates. To be still in bed at noon. The brutal When (with around, also within it). A handheld compressed. While tenpin bowling, as far as the alley permits. Vicarious self-importance. A figure that springs up from the pit when the lid is released (i.e. an inclusive economy). A daytime danger enclosed in a green shrubby framework. The us planet, also applied to various other planets. The scupper in the real. The compendious. An air hammer for the rock-drill. An executioner. A public hangman, from one so undernamed. Indifference. A dive in which the performer folds the vacuum, then straightens it out again. Connected vessels, albeit in parts. Through faulty control, to achieve form, or cause to form. An angle of ninety degrees or less. A nasty, very nasty. A sloven. The larger of the two knives. All trades. A lantern made from the hollow. A name for several. A species of pining. The large stone plane. To throw weight. A one-pronged plug used to ease gently into a circuit. One who can turn his own head. A game played for the better. That which must be revealed by the payer withholding, or being bettered. The buffoon suit. The major arcana. A mess of floating matter obstructing the Nile. A long-eared hour. A situation. A rafter short. Held in contempt, a person. The rest, as in hip-crest. A breed of small terror. The invention of the nineteenth century. An accumulation till such time as they are (see also hit the below). A situation. A maker of kitchens. Any holes cut to resemble eye, mouth or nose. A maker of difference. A small species of sniper. The staff on which my petard is hoisted. A prize-fund in the mass. An awkward. Not caring one way or the other. Ropes and strips of wood and iron stretching across the backyard. To mimick, as do spoons and knives. Finding one's most favourable physical location in any given circumstance. A maker of others. Equal stakes for all the players. A wicker effigy of no real significance. A slip used in the game. Spillage, a making. A money spool (upon certain conditions being fulfilled). To bind, as in navigator. A temporal dam. A continuity pausing over a roller. Something that happens before you can say. Anything cheap. Tar. An impoverished steeple. Not properly forming a union. The colour yellow, slung. The most common name, hence used as a substiute for the most common name. Specifically, a mediaeval disease (see everyman). A retainer, manipulated as one of the species on a giant chessboard. One and all. The chakras, combed and shaken. A wild gregarious ally, erroneously supposed to act as a provider. One who refuses to do another's work. Being really really equal, but possibly in part from dimming. One who would share the oil without sharing the danger. To be executed by decapitation when taken during the course of the game. Big big big success. A tree of the dreadful genus, its fruitage. The jackalled day (reader, you shall have it, I promise). The newcomer, or other person. The gaining of experience at any cost. Blocked head ice. A small process of crow with greyish necks. Anything done very quickly. The skin of my animal. A loose paper. The outer casing of a boil. The aluminium or zirconium alloy covering the fissile element, drop by drop. Two or three centuries passing by and no one noticing. Abreaction. To beat someone or something. The anus, from genesis. Any characteristic of my period. A matrix or determinant formed from the first partial derivatives of several functions of several variables. A pipe or steamjacket. A revolutionist. The ladder of leaves with wooden steps leading up into the heavens. A man in livery scraping away at the base, until. Two and then four, fast and bulbous. The endless chain. A pilgrim with a cross-head used in surveying. Some histories. Probability from the field of stars. A meeting in the great hall. The impossible underground garden. The different fabric, so unnamed. An imported backing used for surgical dressings. The mediaeval juggernaut. Conception inside the ear. Simulated Europeans. The apparatus with perforated cards. Control of movement. The action of warp threads while swaying. A gold coin worth twenty. The resolution of a neurosis by forgetting about it. An intricate. Unintelligent design. The deep-red hybrid perpetual (from the general of). Any lasting revolt. Immolation, themselves also. Any name applied in derision. The act of throwing up. Extreme restlessness and dis-ease. A room inhabited by a solitary inventor. The pretense of being another. A mislaid dart. Being hooded, quick to politick. A fissure. Twisting and convulsion. Jactitation of marriage. A pool of breath. To be equipped with any mechanism. A sword retrieved from the aforementioned pilgrimage. The job of overarcher. The verb to saint. Out suddenly, in ejaculation. A sorry horse, often in irony. Reviving forgotten or repressed ideas of the event. A pool of beneath. The flag of causation. Excess. The tricks of the trade. Any reckless sacrifice of an object. To bathe in such a pit. Unknown origins. A total nightmare. The hard ornamental stone representing various shades. The cure for sliding pains. Over-exposure. The act of hurling forth. A warning that only an adjustment is intended, not a move.

I must make my apologies. I adjust. I adjudicate. I have a code in the head. The lance-tip can be reversed as a leaf. I'm three times as long as broad, tampering more gently towards root than apex. Objective compression, that's generally my area.

Remember, shavings of bone.

I wake to alarms and a whiff of diesel from the lawns. I know what stuff is: a block of magnetic ferrite and a line of rectangular apertures. Creeping rhizomes produce new crowns, dragged around on a ladderlike chain.

Summary of composition and strategy: the saddle, the stirrup, the horseshoe, the harkness. Wires pass through them. Each is a detached object on which the whole nexus depends. The device may be used as a logic element—combustion of marsh gas-cum-mirage. At first glance it appears as if there were a different way in which one proposition might occur within another.

The pitchest black imaginable. A single blank page is suddenly illuminated. He seems out of sleep, gaping with cracks. He is out of depth. Was that a sea change, that silent pause. The radius is fractured (the bugger's misquoting himself). A ball of collected threads roils beneath the boardwalk, through slats of shade and sun migrated from an earlier work. Somehow his condition is reforming in the mind, in thesis, swelling and gathering in the kitchen sink. Speech is pointless. Use your finger. Maybe this is what's commonly referred to as anathema.

This one's shape is bad—bent paschal, echo disjunct. His escutcheon bears a heraldic indication of illegitimacy. A radio spectrum is passing through the building and the wilderness it haunts. Having developed the plates he now has to resort to a star catalogue. Is there anything you have left out. Again this all tomorrow: boxes of cardboard and ether, disinterred men in fluorescent jerkins, one shoe apiece. A random sound is used in place of Yes. The toecap is held in place by gaffer tape. Do you want to be a mission.

A watertight structure allows undersea foundations to be built dry. Twin darks, then two pages beneath a torch. This is the age he was when the picture was taken.

Still all sorts of permutations to come. Pry off their legs. I'm immersed: a harvest of chimneystacks, cracked pallets in a ditch parallel to the sea defence. The loss of hell today has been a very great loss. Why should I change it for you she says. It didn't feel like that at the time. A series of alternate plates of copper and zinc for generating an electric current is contrived. I am sending it now. How outdacious (to promise infinity, to out-dream).

Can't wait to tear this one up. How much did you harm, peeking out from beneath you're gap of invisibility. Then the piano stops. I have the complete poem somewhere. I drop to the floor. Grinding metal in the distance, like an animal in pain.

Notes for lost word. He sees the form of a young woman standing under a trembling tree. There is absolutely nothing more that can be said about this. I hope you don't mind. Where is she now. She must have gone up on deck. Pass over.

How long have you dwelt here she asks.

This equals a pass without touching, with reference to the exemption.

Face at a forth story window. Figure flung out, gnawing at the glassy seal. Usurpatrix.

Which comes first. On a traffic island a man sits with a razor, slowly and deliberately shaving scales from a bone. An indifferent police marksman crouches to observe. They are restricted to separate domains.

Eight years on, and I can no longer afford time. Now you should try saying something yourself. Don't lose your concatenation. Don't lose the acid reflux. A bead of fluid emerges from the taut eye in the head of the shaft. Death of a thousand cuts. Morphine salts and arsenic were present in all of the bodies recovered. On rusting hinges a hollow figure swings. There is an open-cast mine. Above the forecourt, the overhead. Atoms are linked together in a chain with loose ends. This will wait too long for proof. Stop. Being eaten alive by sun and by swarm. Stop. Only the pianist is missing (carried in court on a stretcher). Items are transmitted from person to person in a retarding loop.

Any idea why she didn't.

Any idea why she did.

Cut back to the hand stroking. Speeding rain in the ice. She's lying. There's a year between them. They are yoked to revelation. She says this is the island where he wrote it.

He falls off the building as they talk. His mind was absent. Coins are balanced one upon another in a column. Stop up his eyes. Stop.

But I have arranged things to resemble you.

Move next paradox as too close to tower of coin.

Accumulate unlikely reactions, a project of abolition such that no further new is produced. He has his son and heir with claims to the stars—the enormity of voice, everything mythed, the entire career. I do and I return. There is concern for the protection of Non. I've seen a lot of the England today: beaten wings without, numberless containers. I have discovered a spot sensitive to light. I have discovered scratches of reminiscence across the pit of the old cell. And no, it's nothing like a film, just stale irony—unclaimed baggage and collapsing buildings. Spin distance into memory, spin the knife. Answer me or I will cut you up. Try again. Look north, through the window in the direction of the nearest landmass, the neighbourhood lament.

She covers the upper part of her face with a white semi-lune that mimics perfectly her own contours. When she says turn to a particular compass point, you know she means it. Consider their current location. They bite each other. What do you see. A wide variety of microbes representing an unconscious or repelled conflict (psyche). Together they are thrown.

Motion from the negatives: the pale hand trembling the cigarette—the men with axe all over him, the stained aquamarine towel, the creeper bridge. A flood of blue light with semée of eagles' heads. Murmurs in the cathedral. I can see you have lived a rather sheltered life. Estrange, isn't it. But this is different, it smells of nothing yet has the texture and depth. It is wrapped about with air. It is built of traces. I think I am, spirit invested in something that will not vanish. It's built of sparks and hints, coloured points of night made solid—the fitting of one bone into the groove of another. I must have. I must have not. I'm not entirely convinced by his claim that this is parody. A box begirt with iron is clutched in his withered hands. The pace he has set is not as once was.

Press the green button. Are you about now. Pivot and spin. Crab another drink before the life resumes once more. We devour one another at the waterfront, lying together, crazy and atomized. Meaning no place was the word coined.

Overhead gantry signs. Don't forget to switch off the light before that final stride into the waves. I have signed my name suicide say she. Three membranes envelope the brain and the spinal cord. The body is a crescent body. She describes her experience through a time release camera as follows. Compare the knowledge that the average passer-by has of history. Now you're worried sick. The meniscus sheds a few faint beams after midnight.

From root of to go, the substructure.

I once was.

Very well.

Into the brine. The upper surface of a liquid column. The cave was dazzling. It was magnificent. Then we two fell silent. My cause is capillary, a mess of threads—fortune slung into a minor tongue: attraction through a wick, through shifting sand. The given sign is water. The game implodes. The hole in this circular image of space signifies the path of transcendence. My absence is beginning to frighten. To remember: the score, the last music-stand in the dark, the flickering projection. The great hall sparkles and glistens with coral quartz. Elevation and ground-plan illustrate the patter. There is a divine play of etiquette here. Sometimes he comes to his window to see more clearly the book—by this I mean the grain, the ink itself. Heaped in the corner are unopened sacks of blackmail (I've had two difficult years, truly grizzmal years). Over time these become known as the under-records. It's not a lie, it's a necessity—an outwit work of state, of the public weal. Trance formations.

The statue becomes animated and seizes the observer. I make a pact with the dead. Someone needs to keep me from breaking my oath. A scream echoes. A purple robe slides to the flagstone floor of the cathedral.

Resume her narrative.

Graphite blocks form the moderator. It's a kind of reactor, this new archipelago. Leave it and run.

Sunlight in the glade.

I have only to listen. I am no longer the one I am—a man of cardinal importance to a lack of industry. You should not be making decisions like this now.

The part of a cartel that receives pollen. Sunlight in the glade.

Telepathy and fission. Without, sacrifice.

Hallo I am round the back.

Theft. I have only to keep touch. See also loss above. The lists are interchangeable. It depends on the number of syllables, the iron body cast beyond shrinkage. Someone has stolen my tractor, my money, my neck, my passport, my chicken, my wireless, my lung, my ticket, my traveller, my watch, my kidney, my cheque, my luggage, my arrows, my quiver and my scalp.

Outfangthief.

Likely reactions.

Key words to misunderstand.

Wait.

When.

Where.

Name.

Address.

I can't help you.

A vivid memory of a room with stairs leading out of it at the back (the room, not the memory). Nothing to do with me.

She says this detail is misreminisced, yet intact. She is yellow, literally yellow, and I can see the vessels in her neck. A portion of the tissue is dying because its blood supply has been cut off. Cram, stuff cram into fact. And the slowly opening mouth. Fact, stuff fact into cram.

Naples yellow courtyard
the cool shade
of a midsea sun
goatshake on the counter
from the hand of a sallow nun.

Two passing have shadows firmly attached to their feet. Falling down is a technique. She is making it all up. Children cluster. There is language.

I have a hotlist of people I need to speak of. Upon returning the boy finds the colour yellow has vanished for good and he asks why.

A simple enough question.

So you didn't speak to anyone no (dismiss the weather).

He cannot reconfigure her reply.

What are your planets for the weekend.

No, it wasn't that.

It may not be worth you making that journey after all. A notional bell will ring at the designated time (vainly). In her last years she never leaves the house. She is birdlike.

He dreams of her but does not tell. She speaks a convincing second chance. A silent prohibition has been placed on telling. You see, a warning chime is ringing. Gathered in the spine of the book are minute particles of quartz and feldspar, the lash of an eye, a grain of glass. He comes with perilous gash, limblopped. He has rudimentary hind-wings and a rope for hanging.

Enter, travers.

Nothing can protect you. Get used to the idea. She compiles an inventory of all the lost words to date and rearranges them until they offer a glimpse. Collectively these function like an amulet worn against the skin.

The lines of a green laser build a matrix across the night sky, the weft within a flooding dark. Here are colours that we cannot see.

The following day is resisting. Unscrew the cap and carefully open the flask. Caffeine and tumulus, please. Decibels.

Here are sounds that we cannot hear, too high or too grave. Underwaves of the signal sounded.

Now for that manifest. The inventory. I read it too long ago to speak of—a truncated alphabetic of all my things misplaced. A cliffhanger. A cave.

Domdaniel.

VIII

From water and tocsin.

Outvite me. She's got ideas about everything. I am counting myself backwards into a kitchen sink port, my last meal. Please, I am master dormant, only son of the late chief dormant. I am not. Tell us more.

Port of saint. Ordeal by sea. Characters overshadowed by sun, moon and stars. At harbourside, the block on which he's exposed for sale is doused with pure alcohol and freezing water. One rivulet trickles the gentle slope apparent to a rusted grille. Onlookers breakfast to tupperware percussion.

Recollect further items, more detail: the portcullis, the sluicegate, the old toll-bridge. Memory is vague due to an opaque condition of the corneal lens. I am painless and unaccompanied, qualified as a half-decent sinecure. I need you.

There is no stick visible, the hound hath swallowed it whole. My address and date of birth are consumed along with it. I no longer wish to speak of myself. I write with the nervend. The collapse of the adult lung is incomplete and stretches out over a long period of time. The oath is a tennis court oath. It's opening is audible from my position—that is, warping downwards. I thrive in the brief years before catastrophe.

The stock of genetic material is presented in the form of a journal, a closed circuit. An itinerant judge administers angelic exterminations. Yes he tells me. At seatop eyrie, but maybe later. Keep me posted. At the foot of the embankment is a ditch. We climb into it. Smoke pours from our slits throughout the exchange. We climb out of it.

The simulator (growth). Its valves number sixteen. I've a thing for last lines, last words. You must make a decision. She and he are visible at the high window smoking. The reason for these convulsive moods is being, as we have said. I think unbearable—feint outlines of authentic futures—a paralysed amber wave, lack-blue with feral pinks. I've heard my share of screams from the balcony, the airlock. I am drawn to the things one is not supposed to write of, the mysteries of self-censorship. Their efforts are in vain. The conspiracy is discovered. Matter is investigated. Suddenly, and for no obvious reason, everybody arrives at the same time. Go there soon, with inhuman gait (we don't).

Faucet of light on fading. This is the way we're determined to go when it's our turn to quit. There's a dismay of sound. The applause filters through and dies. Sticky smears across my mirror, part of a giant stage-set with props for rack and torture. Then comes a symbolic pantomime followed by general rejoicing. A depiction of sunrise begins the suite. A *ménage à trois* is established. The subject is surrounded by dense surveillance. Finally, a semblance of spinning around so rapidly that centrifugal force breaks you in pieces.

Eye of storm. A stained mattress. I have something in front of me. In my back I locate an exit wound. It might be said with justice that I am stricken. I am working through a sequence of slippage, steadfastly mute. Bolt of seed across lip to tongue—lash and lid. Abandon all agreement. Grab being and time. Contract. I gain you. Yet inside of me.

This subject-object relationship must never be presupposed. Choose from among their number a man wise of heart and cunning of finger. Perhaps the reverse. People have acquired the habit of verisimilitude. He loses possession and groans again. I stand up for a second time, face the trees and flap my arms hysterically. Nothing happens. Nothing is always happening. Still stricken by exit.

A courtyard at twilight. Crystallite. A collapse, agreed upon.

Why don't you mention the two mattresses in the two rooms he writes of.

Footfall at ceiling. Here I have an edge. Where is she. There is this atom ceiling she can never pass beyond. She's a perfect (a precious spore housed in a metal box). I'm hearing things: a religion of cellulose with unlike structure.

I think the signs are good.

Infangthief.

I like the way she sinks names into things. He is test. Footfall on floor above, my drum of the abdomen—any port in an et cetera. There's now only two-and-a-half days to the week. Be accurate in your depictions (things and their interactions). He lends meaning to her short life. Nothing like a promenade on the encounter, a vicious rupture to straiten one out.

Sell off remaining self, my animate. Anything that has risen from its predecessor's ash will do. When we come into his presence he orders us to choose between the living and the dead.

The two mattresses in the two rooms. Anatomical section of Laridae about here. He has this inheritance—a colony of sea-maws. I like that about him, it makes you feel he's taking things seriously.

An island, salt and bare. Gulls in a line upon a drystone wall. I have written this down but do not know what it means. It's over, and not even the span of a single season.

A paragon, touchstone of obscure—the southern constellation. An arrangement of scales. Corrective nouns. This chapter is about the melancholy of certain stoneworks—of the arch, the dolmen, the quoit, the cromlech. A touch of the old megrims. Note to self-hazard: guess.

They are outside the house.

An arc lamp floods the terrain. A couple are racing cars on private land. They still have the outstanding quote. I am running autonomy myself—striking moves up the darklit road, smack in the middle of a life sentence. There is a shortage of panels at the moment.

No. He spends it all on close. He is a state of suspension. He is deferred from any privilege, held in an indeterminate situation. This instant is quite difficult in terms of style—semblance and such eclipse, heavy with stiff upper edge. The clutch goes. It's a holding operation until somebody comes. A body of light trails in long scooping curves. I am indicted in language hereabouts. I build myself into things, objects I have no idea of. I speak in a sequence of byes— passes and tokens. How can you tell. Someone has written a love poem about a bird skull with a miniature siren strapped to it. What nonsense and motive in any action. My reward is to be in the wrong place at the right time. In the end I'm revised. Language is no use to me.

Watch prefix sum. Luminous discharge between the electrodes.

Resume. It is cold it is dark. Where it says amulet he means talisman. Speeding upward he finds patches of merry sky. The important point is the reference to a person's skin. Also the deer hide, the shed antlers and the flickerbook. Ministrations are misused. Everything goes awry. It has become so quit. Return sphere and flush. That sound is representing the trigger sound. Scan into the communal lounge, where cup nostalgia's in progress. I am going about this all the wrong way. Come hereback wherein we have. I mismanage. Do you think, says he, that men have always.

It's the foundry we miss. They are dragging people to the rim of the pit. How does this afflict memory. I serve a writ on myself. I conflate in mind—fifty years the underhead, to the screech of aeolian harpies. Think of semantic memory as random context held in permafrost. I'm going to be making a case for civilization itself. I forget is piercing through the exterior skin. Who creeps nearest wins. In one of the vessels a shift of metre is taking place. You talk about seeing the big canvas, of being used up. Note to self: disinter time. He is credited with a crime. Withhold him in writing.

I am still in love at the cusp back there, that anvil bone of the middle ear.

We crawl about beneath some skankylooking trees. The original team has failed to turn up. How's the pain today. They are late. We look ridiculous. I tunnel under the road. I expect this is the episode where all goes well, a rare adventure that foregoes the glossary. I am dealing here with sordid real-life situations.

Copter stunned still above my cinque estate: two three one zero, off. Think of some decent players and equipment—crash-dummy interrogator, semen detection kits, surveillance volunteers, the forensic seal. I am ready. Come with me, nightscoping.

He is resident forever in the eponymous port. In another version, not. Someone has tunnelled under the road. In another version there must be possibilities, potentiality. There are distant lights built in the form of an arch. It makes the game more interesting if you follow this closely. He spends his final year alone in a belltower. Anyway, the man with the white beard is reading a book of maxims. The villagers bring food and blazing torches. I retain this in memory as precise as his own (he was there, I was not). He always starts each new day with a mess of pottage et cetera. Repeat everything at the first opportunity.

He collides with a crane in flight and dies. A freak not far from when we write.

Explanetary note: it is now awake—walking and barking, drooling and circling. That's just old stuff. I wear out. As with sounds, so with colours. Remember to keep breathing. Make stealth. Everyone in the region is flesh-coloured after the local stone. It's moments like this that begin to eat away at our confidence. But we've got eyes positioned in the shaft. We draw up plans, create situations. The rain sounds like electricity, static. Examples have been provided. At each end of the solar spectrum the chemist detects the presence of arsenic rays. There is instruction. Press face to hot bulb of gas flare. You are composing what, prey? Dripples of juice bead from the open flap. Tongue is a word requiring explanation. The question is should he start coping. I win my case. I argue for semblance and fracture. The question remains is it too late. This is coming together. My books are blind. Good because time is running out. Slide arm under crook of leg and apply pressure downward in direction of pallet. It has not paws or feet, it hath hoofs, and should never be confused with to happen.

A judgement is made. We cross the border with much little. He's not very good with the tables. I obtain. A sentence follows. I don't really care anymore. I abstain. Don't mix things up. I am arrest. It's them word spooks again, gusset-sensitive. Here are colours that we cannot see. I am bought here from a vague without.

He confuses fluid with commodious. Enter with cautions trembling (see her returning, below). All eyes scan the floor: four dead and the interpreter. Say quickly that you love me. I pocket the ash. I remember this, even though I made no notes at the time. The system used is the new solarizing septum we hear so much about. Nonetheless, the familiar morass of nerves. Every phenomenon shrinks to its smallest possible cause. Bring a stencil, still the pulse. The way they write is in no way. The flooding light is cancelled. Blindsponge. Partition everythink.

A glance, love-lairy, formerly a lens. The art is in the flicker of the lid. Now I have lost the trail. Here comes a humble gull-catcher. I have the means to establish quietude on every side.

The distance between two marks on a zinc bartop.

Or the wavelength in vacuo of orange radiation—the eighty-six atoms per act of parley, by active lament. Waterdrone.

She is phantastikon, inverted. Dishing out orders is her way of saying I agree. And how did you mismanage this. The product is the material bearer, not I.

The hatching and killing is swift and decisive. Note to self, substitute journey signifying a predetermined way for journey meaning simply to go. She always gave strange, over a sheer drop slashed to the navel. She has too much, giving her a lull-like quantity. Faith lobs itself in, the undergrowth. But for the hook why.

Seamer, cast into a bowl of ash. Absent, dimmer.

Dumka. Dummerer. How to go on. The chink or aperture of a lipped corolla, a big circle of jaundice.

Fuksheet.

Nervemast stitched to shreds of skin. The man with horsehead stands on Pallet B. The book remains hanging in the air instead of falling. Link to wicca man at position D. We scatter teeth across the dry fissured ground opening up at our feet. I crawl slowly up the embankment to the track and lie there listening. This has the effect of a hypnotism which renders the subject helpless. I put my ear to the metal rail. A correspondence between the partition of the nasal cavity, the chambers of the poppy nostrum, and the cell itself has been discovered. Stretched out upon a ledge within the latter is our very own familiar. Marked by indifference, as before.

That was scary. The poem disappears into itself, a spine of transmutation et cetera. Forge a link to cracked pallets, the crucible of molten lead, the family welding. From his watchtower at the front, time is as sure as said, yet lacking. It's surely uncertain that the earth even existed then.

Disclose from edge inward and retreat.

He says they have at least seventeen different almanacs, called colliders. As these cogs turn in space they interpret one another. Occasionally gap days arise. These maintain several distinct counts. It's like a receptacle for waste, or the din aroused by certain games. A season in hell: sluggish dog days, uninhabitable bat-people, creatures who persist in myth. The whole caboche is corralled inside a volcanic crater.

He says you undermine. Yes. Dissect and separate: lunasolar at thirteen and twenty and so forth. The mooring star—a cyclops lured into ruinous circumstance. The last step is to approximate by finite intervals, where when equals one mouth and corresponds to the difference.

Head cut off close behind ears. No part of neck visible. Memory shot to nerve.

How the island works: a door creaks open. Spleen beyond sniper's range. As much as inhuman, I want as you wish. It is still only the other day—radiating bands on the body of an echo, where tubelike feet should be. Or to the region of the lips, tentacled. See elsewhere. The true answer is that I simply cannot manage all this material. She maintains order for a short while. Link to crucible of molten lead and repeat. I am unsurety itself, a riposte to the defendant's ceaseless keen. How to renumber everything. Stage one: ontomapping. Stage two: infinitely directed nanotubes. Stage three. Strike camp and abscond.

A house perched high on the only patch of level ground left in the neighbourhood. You will no doubt find bits of voice scattered here and there across my page. Dispeace, he says—the neuter of use in a sense of our own making. Unsuretyship.

Explain.

I grind at the night. They attack in sleep: the joints, the limb, the hub of light. That sound is the firescape during Jerusalem. We parley in secret. I am called rictus. They go unnamed. When I think of you writing I think of those pictures—the unordinary pace, the drenching colour, purplereds and blues and greens. The loops turning within a shallow space, the colonnade with gilded youth. Pick an image to carry with you. Please leave. Unclaim your luggage. A minor miracle occurs (again). I will never. I am not ashamed of the letter I sent. A clue: they result from the tension created by my intervals. I inform a religion. I'm sure I was once able to do this more quickly. See under breathe. My back hurts, left scapula or roundabouts. Darkfall comes. It is full moon and big. I should have said: the stacked pallets of lead make the dream sequences possible.

He replies. I have not forgot the overvoice request. I shall be a while yet, dwelling. We should set to it before the close. The plot is sinister-dexter, uncrackable doom. Supine, I count the ceiling laths. I don't want you to folly a blind rush through time. I track. I attach myself to each modified word (the future). I is spelt from nowhere—spent form and backword to boot.

Of invocation: joy and grief and triumph. Hope you are not. Your voice comes garbled across the pitch of space that divides. A tiny ember spirals to earth and alights gently upon my forearm. Bring stencil (you say). Bring ray-gun Wednesday you say. Torch nerve, gently.

He is a competent moonraker. He is quietly shunned and grafted onto the crooked head. A shapeless fleshy mass is enjoying conception. A bivalve of the family, it slumps out of an excretory opening at the end of the canal. The matinee crowds have gathered. Pyx and host are buried at the junction of three roads. Unveil a case for something. The date is year one, lunar sixth. A child is found buried in chrisom cloth. The locals collect vocabulary and money. Today I spook to none. A fluke rises above the skysail, as if in slow moment. Cries of Io. My logbook reads drunken mariner in vessel agin. Look up, razorbill.

Have they nothing better to do than navigate. Fortunately, I don't have any guns. Dying so to speak I gaze through her as if she has no substance. Limbic fissure of earth at frontier (my domain). I enjoy severe abreaction. Make us depart for you, travel planet. Here again I have an edge. This is all that remains of a twelfth-century monastic cell. She is possessed by passing time. I'm so shortsighted I'd kill all my friends. Rebegin.

I mean.

Nomenclature. General commodities.

Describe in detail the photograph you found in the icebox.

A manner of bridge. I must go back. I know not these unfamiliar tracks, a stretcher space where the earth has flattened out. The plan is starved of oxygen. A tiny figure is visible. It is ministering to the dead man's head. Automatic gunfire in the distance. This is an extreme sample. It's like recognizing a name or an undiscovered time, compacted layers of here. Make a place up, anyone. He leaves but his withdrawal is upward—art and uneven, a sort of amoral grace.

Hold tight, sleep off the ether. I have kept my receipt in the inside pocket. The cucking-stool swings back to the riverwall. I am disorderly at the end of an oscillating plank, returning to a stranded position. I could have weft: it's the moment before cognition of the unfamiliar. I am overgrief.

She stands inside me. Be precise. How can one recognize another. Concatenate.

The photograph, her beside the others, a little to the right and noticeably detached from the ground. Her vagrancy: it is the south of the continent. Her refractory smile—I discalced for the heat. We are maladjusted to companionship. She misses the big empty, the endless pop revolt. Wasps are chewing at the local shed. Think orchestration—too many notes—integral multiples. I have a stay of execution till morning. Infinite steps circle the cell, the clicking together of letters. I grant myself a leave of absence for the rest of my life. Tiles are missing and cables bunch live across the wall. I travel alone and incognito. No one notices. No one remarks. No one cares. My solitary confinement is envy. It's like a purgatory. The nights we count as days. Worse still is to come. Splinter in right index deep to quick. A disembodied voice. Where are the foreigners he ask. The men look gentle, noble. She stands to one side on a journey that has become obligatory. Make more and more word she writes young quicksilver hand. An assemblage of fingers has been found in the wrong region. Her view is always from a beyond. The doctrine that a new soul is created afresh for each purpose is opposed. Return to desertion, dengemarch to driftness—ghostshingle and hives, the big capering hare. My companion's an aimless with unspilled routes. It's quite an easy iron this, basket casework. In the corners of her mouth and eye osiers fringe and twist. Into a shape, brutal as consequence. Under incubus, wickerheaded.

Memory of you eyeing the departure.

How together we drew the sting from him. He says I've often thought that of my own father, in permanent exile since leaving the island as a child seeking refuge. (It smelt like capital with the gloves off.) I doubt he's ever acknowledged how those events have influenced the course of his life, following him around and making him and who he is, always restless, ever-wandering. And yes, dementia is a form of expatriation. Are you writing, by the way. Maybe you are. Maybe you should.

Half and blind by sand he enters rather than form. Rejecting shape he filters through as dry ice. He has been adapted by the many and suffers badly from time. A series of things depending on each other is being chained together. The word yet is disconnected.

She clutches something in her right hand, a spray of mossy stalks damp in wrapping-paper. In her left the stem of a capsule. There is a brief dereliction. Objects are suffocated by a coil of popularity. I have patented a toolkit for the inventors of perspective. Now, how about the glorious uncertainties of the game. Concentrate yourself.

Mock wall, paper one with sundry decor. Glass-gall. Every remark a kind of appendix. There is a plaque above her head and a little to the left. Pallescent she, with arm withered, head turning threequarter. The ink used is a ferment of crushed wasps.

Go on.

The plaque above her head and a little to the left depicts three hands linked. It is attached behind the group the white-tiled wall. Express at will. We can tell it is hot the men are in sleeves for the heat. Also mangles of twisted wreckage, race and battle, the ceaseless need for replacement. Wiccawork maxims I have all but forgot.

New thing. It felt like dissection. A wheel of his trolley falls off and he crashes to earth. The lung, his liver and most of the heart are still missing. I no longer know what my spectators are beholding. On the opposing side rice is domesticated in plastercine caves. The time is shortly after displacement—another felicitous outcome of the unforetelling text. I am about to star in an extinction. (See erratum's lip.) I lean back into space, agape at the aperture. He facts from the afterworld back (ur-chat can be used as a curse). See photonasty from the workaday laager: Maya-blue pigment and baptist oil, cold-blessed. Days are spent. We are kicking heels in the heat and the dust. An object falls from the sky and crushes his skull. Someone clearly has it in for him.

In an effort to suppress the memory of this event I busy myself by documenting the local plantlife: indefinite fluorescence, acropetal and unbranched, that kind of stuff. There is method. It all comes at once in a rush at the close. Radio talk of satellite re descending object to crushed head. We bury him in a plot upon a vast of land. The entire realm of causation sits like the scum formed on fusing glass.

Increase the sample. I defer myself. During that week momentous events gnawed benignly into passing time. I can no longer foresay. I'm a neural. Sometimes in these circumstances it's a good idea to make yourself a target. You have to recover as though it's your very last run. That's the sound of bodies bodying. Nothing better to do than steer a creek through this course. I enjoy severe abreaction. Make us part with you. All crawl forward for an hour in the stale moonlight. Murmured works are cited. We are trying to distract attention. If you start making faces, this isn't going to happen. I am always doing. He rests his throat upon a stone. Bits of electricity are floating in the air. A tremulous amount of improvisation is going on, the awareness of vague recognition. It all starts with a solitary assault. A tuning fork is stabbed into the proof pages. Knees bend before the temple. Here it is in elevation and cross-section. I am among the beings whom the deceased wish to avoid in the underworld. Lay one footfall in front of the other. Withhold breath. The first who comes has a distinct advantage in this hexed economy. Getting knocked about a bit quite now. . . . Respond to stimulus with regard to heat, in any direction followed. A turbulence is here, that which forms radiating threads. And now for the best of all: imitate the whistling of an arrow.

Repeat.

Make a trial run, a resist. Determine the exact proposition of the metal and its component. Yield a result. Attempt a more fervid account. Test the spirit of the slain stag with a bayonet cut. The men are here with their men out. Taste before representing, guarantee the poison. This is the final episode. It is that which never asks of itself. I am the resurrection. All these instructions: return to library and kindle murmur. The proof is in the action, the residue. Remove surroyal—any time of the antler above the watermark.

She misreads: the nine rings of ontology, quanta of light, memorandums of misunderstanding (the thingness of my characters). This is something I have no choice but to absorb. In the morning all trace of her is gone. Hours come with bleak silence, more sentences. There's a frequent question. Interpretation becomes impossible. What comes of such distinctions? No one moves. White lead or native wax? The choice is yours. Odour of involuntary memory. No one talks. I forbid myself taste and style. A sequence of links is released. Sperm in alium.

Hemicrania.

It's still alive in the loft. Say something of nothing. I hear it beating at the darks. Embers of rust and beetle wings float gently down from the eaves. Exit at windward side. Paint the face with white lead, jib unhinged at false angle to cranial suture. I think unbearable.

The concentric orbits of an inferno ring my coffee cup. I am relating facts, peering into a well of satellites and punishment, a medium passing through from one zone to another. We are now going to crack across a little undertaking. We shall challenge and accost. No one steps forward to speak. The death promised is untimely. The things of the day regularly end continuous: motherheart causal, the stroke of grace. One phone call does it.

Death must end say judge. This paragraph is a tentative effort with proofs. Temper and quality are set at a perpetual cusp. I am a sudden change of direction. I am just emerging from a musical silence. Consternation at my radius of action persisits.

Instruct, wassailer. I am yet not undone. Slender spears of hardened wood are tipped with poisoned iron—some for hurling, some for thrusting. Existence is fixed by the toothlike meeting of two branches of a curve. I sense a required minimum of some entity. The choice is omega, Vega, standard, or salmon of wisdom. I choose express. Circa when, from leap to years. Possibility rises from his conjectural name: the wormwood bowel. Sheathed forms cluster around the stem of the leaf in question, chasing the tail. It gnaws at the gut, whispers at the shoulder. If it were up to me I would call these ancient figures dormant. I mean actinic rays. We keep hearing about.

This is a lot to carry about in your head every lunar. Her name means Sunday, or lordless. The structure of the negotiating team is very strange. Check fragility, no familial branches. Check frugality.

He is a suppressed form of law. The climate is trivial and forensic. The wires are leaking. Taste, bitter Aramaic. He seeks solitude when anything homes this close. Two nearby are busy insulating. They are stretched taut and aligned parallel. I divide into heresy. The last phase takes place within the next two days. Creep away and die. Disorder the patience. Hold up vertically the object itself, the most dangerous nonstate threat.

Travers often catches up with me at this point. A voice heeds. How he manages with his prosthesis I have no idea. You are a benign sickness he says—you exude a quality of worm-hearted loneliness. Effrontery goes on being, just waits for the right moment. Be sure to set my ulna the right way round.

A wandering into waste, source of thisness. We two shall never meet. There must be method: he cannot surely head. Neuter of how much.

Noes to here. The inventory. He is stitched into a pattern of correspondences which he may influence but can never escape. Before him there is no more time. Hold your fire. I lie. I lie incurably. The days here are nerve-ending. I am exhausted from long nights of firewatching. Make things awkward for yourself. Parentheses are being overused—shapeless states of mourning, objects twisted to one side. Shingle and pox, after-flux of larynx. If I were to mention everything it would sound a bit like a shopping list. His jibe falls shot of its target, somehow.

Memory's great, I loved it as a child. It was bigger then. I'll be here in twelve, with the box of quails and a severed artery. Everything's over by the grieving.

His head is set in a plaster cast. He comes drained, a weak echo of his own hesitation—muddled alterity of obsolete from old. Supernaturals on the tablet are accompanied by a star. A tile is used in ostracism—for writing on, in ancient. While on the subject, I can never remember whether one word is a lot.

Project seven (see numbers). A circular encampment, Potemkin shanty town. The problems start with unintended sound. You can hear what appears to be a dentist's drill in the background. Blockage from the chute, voice murmur—the experience of being born into exile and tied labour. Everything is set down just as it happens. He is a master of duration and repetition: the shamanic element in the paleolithic hunt. (You don't own this song. You don't own any of this). Alas he howls wayment. I imagine I hear people singing on a ship under the sea. It's like a tongue whispering bayonet over and over. This fragment was written for a book of hours one winter in an empty room. What's the time by his conundrum. Suffice to say, a spent night in a cell. He is sleeping on a suspended ledge. The space is lit by a fashionable lava lamp. (Yes a bayonet.) Thin shavings are scraped from him while he dreams. I am leaving myself lots of decisions. In one corner a currier is scratching at bird skins, shaven head bare. I am officially uncovered by being. I am countersunk at the edge. The room is filled with moonshine from the reflective ice.

Outwit the immediate. Tangled roots are found in any array. Obsolete forms of quarry hereabouts. I am influence and bywork—an authorized squatter in another man's body, the poor white parasite. I am the mouth. I am present, an exhalation of glass. My possessions are isolates crammed with fear. I am ready for them when they wake.

A blowpipe flame is directed against the block of quicklime.

Note to self, use of italic to signify that someone is whispering into the page is facile.

Not I. No. It is too cold for air. Explain the things nicely. I remember him not being here. He looks, but not too closely. He is unheard of. The anonymous shutters have clearly been mistimed. Sequence up to here is a series of triggered releases: toilage and porn, one of the minor plans. I am exhaust. Quit while you're demented—I mean the citizens and the work in progress. I am sewn into the earth six successive nights.

Defirmament.

They suffer the solemnity of the same name, a regrettable union. One beast on the road dies of chance. (Some want more than their fair share of the dead.) This looks like a good place to stop. Up with thy feet. This is way beyond our strength, way beyond our ken. No frequency, no analogue. According to the ratios we've reached the upper part of the hive. So says voice. Its valves turn through cycles of punishment and reward. We are of sympathetic function—the traditional face and hand. We volunteer. The dwellings are a prehistoric style of masonry with immense stones of irregular shape: a circle, a rock mast, an eye-ball. Spindle-shells and perfect spheres. Everything is handheld. I spy a vacuum on the front row by the astonomer. When shall we come once more to the crest of that same hill. Who tends this overgrowth of years. We are the urgency. We are prohibited by injunction. It is estrange. Sometimes I feel as though I'm translating. I think I may have to stop here: the pressing surplus of close-grained dead. Crisis apparitions.

That aqueduct. Face pressed to floor, she gets a taste of the creaking board. Stop in the love of name. She is unhooked. Scratches of light form a crude rectangle. Slatted boards build the stylized figure of a man tethered to a barren landscape by cables. Pharos, turning seaward with needless purpose, into the refracting light.

It's every second Sunday no. And you cannot follow everybody. And you cannot follow every thing. I will deposit explanatory notes in the index and the glossary. She is quit at her window. My feet are frozen to the earth. Draw her closer, tongue. This adds a whole new mix to the scattered objects. Those I speak of evaporate. It is a work of woven interthemes.

Face outer breach.

The rays pass through him into the other medium. Words are used in estranged ways. It's about a sustained sense of collapse, inkling letters dissolving in the bowl, the silt into language. There is an undertow of doubtful origin. Much is said about my misuse. It's about the speed of the missile in compact with its target.

Inkling me. Dogs barking counterpoint, local.

To use: said about, misquoted. Counterbark.

One cyclops is lured. There follows an unmanned garden. It qualifies as exotic vision, possible source material for concrete disclosure. Ink well. Yes I realize. I have completely forgotten to rearrange the axis. As you see. I am uncertain about the current conceit. I have completely forgotten to rearrange the labels. A courtyard is bisected by strong shadow under the midsea sun. I have completely forgotten to rearrange the hats. It's good to be still for once. Consider the word to dwell: the space, the scent, the drift—the odour of place reclaimed. It is only available for the time being. Dimness is recollected, imperceptible cellular change. That is to say, things set apart and forbidden. We used to call it being roped down and buried. I keep thrashing to the surface in a lead-footed panic. This event repeats. There is inundation. I reach. I am the unavailable measure of today's carnage. A wheeled vessel is dragged by horses. Blind us to the factors into night. A star rises up in the current. There's a rumour. I am summoned among the treasons. It's a long day's journey, down the rust chute and into the sea. (The refusal to loot is only a detail.) He is struck by summary lightning. We are arrived. We are marked at the ear. Some people want a lot of watching. A trellis of blue flame descends. Some want a lot of dead. Our tools are the sides and backs of old blindings. We are at the border between two states. Are you flowing out with the conundrum? Discompose a route. The two parallel themes of the novel are the hero's relationship to the divinity and his attempt to build a new world. Now apologize. He is disbanded and sealed up for passage into another medium. Tear out his eyes. Bend lens sharply back from base to crest of page. A pause, hesitation, deferment as a function of the machine. The police have opened an inquiry out of sheer defiance. He is a master of duration. He is a master of repetition and return. Go astray, delay—tarry. Move on.

Syntaxlistunimaginable.

Now drink this. Check mineral on return. Check crystal on return.

I rune. C is for something. I have to leave this name blank like an absence. That's been the hardest task of all, finding a satisfactory number of names. We have reached the apex. The subnet mask is in bits. The creature is fusing with its own skin. I have picked at random one of his seventy-two. The correct expression is ungodly from crouch. One of my caricatures claims a resemblance to newsprint. He absorbs his detractors. They hesitate before undertaking the crossing. I can barely stray, undizzied and awake. It's my synaesthesia. I dictate. Allow for a pause in the operation—develop to hiatus at point of maximum lift. The sky is regarded as a fault or arch. Beyond this I can't get the compression level right. Mistime is all. Autopsy reveals the following.

Paralysis of one side, with crack of mood.

Vascular membrane vested in grey matter.

Solid rock pierced through when gazing out.

Although this is strictly not a theme, it seems pertinent to mention everything. The reverse word is another plural of majesty. Each of the categories is classified according to the nature of its enigma.

Leave the letters be. That's the story for this evening, unjust and scarely readable. Subnet mask still in shreds, pincers dragging on slack skin. Note what happens to the girl in the red coat.

A corrugated mud shanty at the rim of the island. You wouldn't know it was here, just a cluster of shacks about which the body under study rotates. A port of war. The corridor gives way. Welcome the sentences, the budding hymnal. There are two deaths contained in the one letter, and a reference to the abolished blue pole. Divination by used book is rife. Another hidden sign suggests we mount the surface to a given altitude.

The appendix. It's all over bar the silence. Earth and sky emerge in a single whiteness. Indicia no more. A special edition of the essay is on its way.

Gasp clawlike with forceps. This is the picture of future events.

Look at that she writhes. She floats and contemplates my releasing book. Moss and bark are plucked from her hair. The females of the species are wingless, sometimes legless. The transference window cannot shut for two or three more. I told her so. This destabilizes the hole, the season.

Back to our skin revision, the official accrescence. There's a restaurant up a spiral. We break from one medium into another. This is the true cuticle, the dead skin at the edge. Seepage from organ slung back across bleached shoulder blade.

And an england's crumb. No is charged with total flood. The flood is here from thirty-nine steps out. Here is the outdrop.

The wooden piles in the field (part of a decalogue). Outer sheath of close-set cells. One figure sits at the centre of a starshaped penitence. He is incorrectly formed. There should be a repeating pattern of atoms in his sustenance.

And she says what star is no star that's Venus. This is a little tense but you'd expect it to be tense: shockwaves from the furthest recess of the continent— deep to lung, deep to gut, dredging the liver. Empty pages of dialogue. The local dunciad.

Transparent lens enclosed in membranous capsule behind iris of eye.

Pharos.

The sacred bifurcation of the body in question, punctured just above the nipple. Shutterflash. Coinage. By falling apart it comes together. Accept as is: a spectral farce at the fourth floor window. Speed up. Identify with loss later. Water in which flowers have been steeped is sprinkled on the neck of the deceased. In this version the sun moves across the water in a magnificent arc that pivots about my head. I am at the border of night for day. Beneath my feet is a sea of stones. Whiff of chlorine at base of spine and hip, tang of iron at crutch. I too am itinerant (identify grief later). For a few moments I too feel the suspension of purpose. That's the story of this evening, unjustified and readymade. I am a straight line about which the parts of a body are symmetrically arranged—an early form of receiving apparatus, with touching metal wire as rectifier. There is a corrosive crosspiece within the head. A small figure is inserted to show the number to be carried over.

Of course he says—they are eyes, facing the stars. Beneath the shingle, the remains of a fish with mantle of cankered bone. As we walk along the promenade a strip of ice forms on the ground beneath our feet. He's a nomadic unlaw, word ever in hand. From his pocket he produces an incantation. He plays the part and speaks to all as if to the nightmare. There are some very dark and deathly poems.

I was formed by modifying the letters of the alphabet to facilitate cutting into wood or stone. I am chance foretold and well tinkered. I work the steal, the empty stunts—the running down of everything until I am extinguished. My course flows onward and traces the movement of the heavenly bodies. I am outflux of blood. I am watercourse. I am still in early use, with intimations of poverty—a rumour to be cast into the sea.

He is often represented in a sleeping or recumbant attitude, head resting on claws. Consider how often, when reading, we touch the text with an outstretched finger, usually the index. A bone of the drum supports the ear's membrane.

I have an inkling, me. We are a long way here from metrics, from instinct. Strike swift and high to right-hand slant of birdskull. Their eyes. Peer out from the chill shade of your concrete bunker, mute of malice (law). Descrive it, in each of its seven distinct forums. No.

I have my chimp and my drug and my earwax and my wireless. Codify according to the relation of their axes.

The lead lining of the station roof. Describe it. No.

We will see to it ourselves. Set crabbed eloquence to cease. He looks very pleased within himself. I shall look out for you at the nave of that flat-topped hill. Keep your head down in tomorrow's hail. Clamp still the neural stem. This is possibly the most legendary pilgrimage in the whole of music—to stalked ocelli, hindering wings.

The nerve writ he wakes an ungodly.

IX

The other thing you were going to bring back was your record of wayfare. Forget self, scratched deep to scarfskin and cuticle, deep to lesion. Bared wiring and hardness loosed from dead husk—less ductile at pressing atom. A growth on the surface of still water. Shift semblance to fractal—something novel. There's no method. Despite an ignoble birth the number remains uneven and incomplete. Let it drop. It needs odding. The remaining head is nailed to a paving slab and double-faced.

The tiny skeleton of a bird, parfleche feathered to a square base. What is at issue here, fluxing out from the body: freestaters, the anthropometric card. Now lend us a question form. I witness. I am bodied—a game of flat stones skimming across the surface of the water, driven and unsteered. I've gulped down a whole mouthful of poison. The satrap line reads life of frugal chaos in sea shanty town. This eye is no longer reacting to light.

He insists, hand at rest on heartpulp.

What time do you want me late lover. I am night of multiplex dream. I was a bomb-plucking fugitive from the law, tracked and policed. Next a semiotic cartoon trip—eternal agon between word and image, the situationist tort. It took years of practise to achieve such derangement of the senses. The default is neural.

A tunnel is blasted through the rock. She returns. She is fretted with scars, quite pretty pale on pink. A secondary spiral has joined her leaf-base at the axis. She is leaving and she is not. We are introducing what we call the chain of survival. Are you disavowed. Are we permitted to put the seats back in. There is no excess available. I concatenate.

He is visible where the leaves crowd together, the seedhead of myth. He is deprived of air and dried by stretching on a frame. In the final days of seizure we buried him under the platform.

She says we can when she means I will. You know only too well. There is no next step. Let's go down to the shoreline, the stones. Unpick this. Maybe I should steady myself back to a displacement. This is where the sampling begins. It sounds like a requiem mass. I have lost. I am a thing for pointing with. They call me stick. Listen, this is where I am inquisitioned by men of taste.

He says I hope she dies soon. He says I hope I die soon, but in this condition. I have arrived at a loss. Act as though you don't know. I have figured out how the brain sees.

Okay, I'm in a clustered room with icons about the walls and a samovar.

Everything exists within the scope of a potential casualty. The surrounding face is jaundiced and fallow. The other eye is no longer reacting to light. Smoke about the jaw. The thesis: they do not know what they are looking at. Whatever is present at hand is present at hand. Mortgage self to world in drift of margin. He exists in the draft state. Make good use of the surviving tooth. Taste the scales of the cone. Run the tip of your tongue along the stitches of the suture.

That viaduct. I cross and I recross. I am the unconvinced. For the time being everything exists. Item: the crayoned seerings of a child. I am asking that person to come back. An orgy of treason and haggling follows. He will not confess. Both eyes now.

She sits companionable, coiled among columns of used book. The walls and furniture have been smeared with wads of vaseline. Be sure to get a receipt. Make note of any unusual lineaments. Identify in sleep (bar-sinister). Speech is something gainsaid. Neural centre located in hypothalamus—control substituted for belief. The target is a point a little below the centre of the shield. Body is more and more about writing. No, I meant.

I recall squatting on the terrace under the sun—the overlooked gasometer beyond the rooftops, apropos of what I forget. It is something to erase. This is a place in which to become abandoned. The hero is shown wrestling with a giant who cannot be beaten so long as some part of him still touches the earth. The river shifts its course. All the journeymen are thickset and horsebacked with ponchos. Certain motifs return again and again. I have removed myself to an elsewhere. We had hoped for some retail crime. Everything is postponed. Note to self: never turn up late during the week. Some of these things I can no longer talk of. From a distance horse and rider seem as one. A compendious system of teaching is drawn up in the form of answer and question. The chosen vehicle is the vocal organ of birds: diminutive of open mouth from agape. Appetite and static.

Never reveal your true pace. Relinquish self to blood-mobile. Adopt a zigzag strategy. As he reads the others see a ray of light shining about his head. Why would the next step be the final judgement (travelling salesman, stockbroker, ricket inspector). Who are they in the underworld? Sustained pressure on second vertebra of neck. I'm an unbound. A partition in the fruit is formed by ingrowing placentas. We are monitored travelling in an outgoing direction. Intense heat is generated in the glass tube. Carbon is passing through me. Of course, barbed at gnaw you have the tottering socials. We warm ourselves at a set of inquisitions. You are free tonight.

Retire.

Hurry up and die.

Schlafdrifter. He is trapped inside the cell of a revolving door. We are once more at the shoreline. Make a decision. He contains pebbles that look like nail-heads. We are probing into the body as far as fulcrum and socket. The mode of combustion is a self-boiler. Floating sax down the corridor, salt-fat and lubricant. It is announced. An examination by alternate caresses and needle-pricks is to take place. A given number of the lines is composed of a stony concretion. The inquisition: how her voice, a blind sac—loosening the gills, the tale of an obscurity. Erroneously, salt-foot and calculus, psyche descending to stomach.

The great monologue, his crafty acausal life sentence. Ghost of civic. I'm an attractive loser. It's not so bad out here after all. I've placed a question-mark over dissension, the ceaseless No. Change all with I alone and dwelling without— home light blinking across the dark body of water, home without home. I have positioned a question-mark over time. Decline to anew (clocks, yes)—the rouser press. Crow tracks in the snow those hunters: one who returns too late, or not at all. The smell of burning flesh, the taste of metal fatigue. The seizure.

SINKD VIS ola
plaza a squar O
love you my pro
lacklustreless tor
mentor

Androgyne, augured as origin, soothsaid. One has the option of rejecting compassion, but its still terrifying when it arrives. Do you want me underneath the ground. These two had their own private language. We're talking six millennia back. Lights out in the divided dark (crepuscular olivine)—everything shockingly new and insatiable: the white house above and beyond the pyramid, the square of bright light flashing off and on. Sense of tone and perception of sound. Impress of tiny bones of bird to face—the blanch-bled choir, the impossible Yes. The hand on the bannister, clothes hung and not I dangling at the window. Yet here comes a wildling one, akin to somehow and somewho (beloved harpy). If there's something embedded, it's likely to be acting as a dam. I want you inside of me, like a mass for the thing of the dead. Beam rays into one of the eyes. He signifies ever the opposite. He is not what was intended. There has to be a method. The tongue explores gently the lip. If it isn't written down it didn't happen. Impress of ossicle to flesh of face. A support, a means to the end. Who are the six to be unmatched (I am making seven). Silicate of iron. Altered serpentine. I am superfluous.

A tombsong for a man at the cradle of his mother. More lessing, please. We are at the fixed point in the heavens about which they orbit. A nerve is injured. The text opens with an address to the deceased in which it is said. The particle sizes range from pebbles to blocks of ice several feet thick. An object is falling slowly through the fluid in the capsule. Just the hint of a tangle, here and there. Nerves and hearing shot. Eyelids rubbed raw. Male twin below, undercliff with shattered tiles: rust on shale, crumbling into the embankment that once held back the land.

Clay-slate split into thin laminae along the bedding planes. Curious atmosphere of mourning and scorn. The first image transferred is a centaur on a barren rocky beach (clumsy-mythic). He rises from the water. We're allies. His mounted adversary has the tethered dog. I cut her with a semicircular blade. (Hello it's the weekend.) If it isn't written down it didn't happen. Someone has altered all the clocks. More doomladen arpeggios, sick bagatelles. Someone has hidden time. People suddenly appear in the wrong place. This horse-man is saint of herdsmen, eloquence and thieves. In short, a characteristic waste of energy. I steal one of his seventy-two names and make it my own.

A flooded saltmarsh. A discarded prosepoem. The scene is dimly lit and murky. Minor keys are crosscut with driving rhythm—features at schism by knife. Move far away from here, absorb fractures and withdraw inward. It's easy, apparently: sub is accessible, un isn't.

It's said his lineaments were sculpted by a tiny flying disc. Imagination overcomes him in the end. This is a perfectly rational solution. He sacrifices every compact with himself—the healing power of words, the sea, all his indwelling unworld.

The track I'm on carries the sound of soaring with upraised wing. An unfinished. Within you I am drugged comatose. Observe how everything in this manor lies sectioned—breaches of continuity, leaps to collision. I am switching to the impossible Yes. When does your own sacrifice begin. The first thing that rolls out of the net is the abandoned skull. Murmurous voice from fibre of wall: indices of combat, the fleshy part of thigh or undercunt. I am discomposed. I have said that I am fascinated, nothing more—sheaved into a bare fist. For the space of six or seven credoes nobody else speaks.

The chamber darkens. Drying on ropes which zigzag wall to wall hangs the familiar cloak of nerves. Connective tissue tearing at muscle. A hollow in the concrete base is lined with mud and straw. A number of parts sit side by side, dead in a pewter plate. A thin sheath of fibrous scrag envelops the organ. It resembles anything flat. Bands of intense colour fill the room. I leave without meaning.

Venture outside. Tell us.

A man clutching a bundle of rods. An ancient of high grade, he may be depicted with or without axe. His look is very pierced within himself. The idea of bodily transformation is borrowed from the early poet. Some of the remaining names could be explained if space permitted. I must have forgotten to delete myself into a rubble of stones. Ship's ballast. Any brittle structure or support.

The well. It is irresistible (and by the way, a herm isn't a caryatid). Have you got the back keys, the improbable? I have the pictures in my gasp to cleave memory, disprove the point. Our ancestral forms remain hidden. He responds to my command. Back to the reiver. That sound is the chanceful click of spent intimacy. I was there. You were not. Faint light on dais littered with miscellaneous items. You are trading ahead of yourself. Hold back five seconds.

Misnomers, unhistoric. A very poignant. She lingers a few steps behind. Three are screaming. On some faraway beach jerkined men stack worn suitcases and abandoned shoes onto dank splintered pallets. He has never left and he shall never return—far, far rockaway. He is patron thief of saints, the all-word of meant things. A marker of boundaries. Sea foregoing—to reckon by heaps of little stones.

Of course it's an exchange. It darts about as if torched, lightly. A gilt flicker, sadly radiant with relics of sleep, remnants of despair. A tower of pallet has been erected in the neighbourhood. The action beyond the poetry lies in my full awareness of being one who steals from himself. I am displace. The intersection of surfaces is descended from a single remote ancestor, but not in a straight furrow. Recompose your answer. Reanswer, and move on.

Bones pliant as osiers.

Invent a collective name for the various parts that surround—a bundle with a hint of ex, supreme in alchemical warfare. This is the selfsame book. The lowest division of the entablature rests immediately on the abacus of the column.

Rest: first word of the introit. I am letting this go. It is enough for us to frequent. A projection from the face is supported by her weight. It is enough for us to have known one another. Add pincers, add hooks. It is enough for us to feel disgust. Add no more to here, filet out from head. I want my quit life back.

He is chiefly a beam of light.

She writes with a time difference of one hour (morally two). She says she deletes him. You are not concentrating. Bells chime at the onset of every second. I cannot unforesee myself. This is sure to become annoying. I sustain forgetting work. I sit in opposition to my engineers, to my builders and my brokers. Why can't you simply say something out loud. I need these mental traces. Be extra careful, we're being written into a hasty retreat. Sleep descends upon a terrored image, hoofs bolted to a steel sink. Trust self and quit. Back at high table, I cannot flinch from the chosen spot.

Lamina, or from the following word. A shell-break or husk. The loathsome family cult.

They unearth any survivors and shoot them. A sack full of children's clothes is found. It is unpacked and the contents carefully displayed on trestles set up at the edge of a forest. We fold. We cave in. We journey forth at speed on foot. These remarks and observations demonstrate that my existence is being thought through by another, something quite remote.

Tattooed across her tongue is a row of tiny zeds. Skeins of chrism grease crisscross her lashes—about the neck a collar of esses, the great chain. Take everything back, reabsorb. Press of cold naked claw to warm bare foot. I have returned from a sharp decline. Consider anything that takes on a shape. I am back from the disclosures of the workaday world. It's official. It is being here. A pungent blackened flood congeals across asphaltum. What a carillon—a species of goatsucker imitative of its call. You are shrunk to nothing from no. By some impossible reckoning this is all that remains of you. Nothing survives here of me.

Motif: the uselessness of geometry—the doubtfulness of albumen and straw for assuring the stability of a bridge. She presumes access to his memories. Everything is shown to look the same from source outward. He wants them back before the hour is past, unsullied.

I am he say. Beyond the high wall the palletmakers, laurel-happy. He say I am again. Thus the dilemma. Entrustment ushers in the vulnerable, the ever-exposing nerve.

How the island works.

Everything is shown to look the same. All the people have been sucked out and retraced. There is drift and rerun this night. I cannot without you. Everything repeats itself. Press of tooth to hide. Much clumsiness of claw and pincer. Nonetheless, perceptive young grey at shade of eye. I miss her. My blood's got nowhere to go. Be here within the second. When the ahead-of-itself is redeemed, focus on shreds of junk, the old stuff—exclude nothing. There's a lot of reality around at the moment. It's surprising how much one becomes aware of the analogues, the ghostpersons. A door creaks open like the vampyre. I hand him my card, my monniker.

The island, initially it pumped out distances.

Diving cold, nephew poxed. Check for signs at Pallet B. He tells me he once sheltered beside the white cottage, wrapped in a threadworm blanket. He is overhung by gulls at the watchtower, tonguing some idle lines she once wrote. It is essential to propositions that they can communicate some new sense to us.

There are three stages: when I was young people told. Then this thing suddenly halts. I am retrieved. I remember myself as a tall narrow book. Printing is optical unless manifest in dreams. The spine bears a single white scar of flung glass. Then greeking transactions drift onto the carpet. Already so soon and you have swallowed me, fract by fract. I am generally understood to mean, with wings raised.

He is set awry with his heart-mad yeses.

Schismarch.

I'm expecting anyone today—make room—strewn and scattered as I am with vague bearings. My face is powdered pale. Sow the smallest analysable unit of tongue. Here we are at the fourth limb of this my talk. It helps if you numb the earlier pages (make an incision). Now this is significant: a vessel containing fluid. False semblance. She collides with my sense of dereliction—ever the minute, ever the day. We are at latitude one degree south, longitude one hundred and seven degrees west. Hold cargo for arcades.

They behave in such a manner. They make themselves noticed at the monument. Stop. Hold and deliver.

Sorry I can't signal very well. Though is my heart held through the double-bind of a name—the word that contains the idea of a sheaf or fascicle. It is weighed on the scale. You are not permitted to gaze at this forever. We've got some dogs and a knife. Enter dawning and loss, the airborne ash she embraces. This body of water must be one of those rivers I keep hearing about. Where are we come.

All the fountains stop fonting when he passeth. Does this mean. Observers think it's all over. Where are we go. He redeems himself by his tireless ignorance. A careful triangulation of the exterior is underway. Are those footfalls approaching or retreating? Electricity dies when he passeth. It is a trick he learnt in youth (direction of motion of cloud). All the rivers are numbered: river one, river two, river three and river four. Each in turn is stepped into at the moment successive hours are struck. It is now. This achieves. The question remains, what was he doing that day while everybody else was guilty. Something is happening but I cannot tell of it. Perhaps the missing sooner, with ribbed structures of beloved iron.

Nihil. I began this auction a while back on an indifferent continent. You have no permit to form an event. Strike a balance on your remaining hoof. Do not waste the journey. I might have my eyes undone by sprites during weather—the dark days of November and December. Establish immediate contrast. Utilize the memory of rising heat vapour from a molten runway. Expert guides in the vocal faculties are present. I can claim grotesque pageant and drunken mountebanking, the vomitings and blue wine. Here are further examples of the insubordinate cause scribed into the graphs, word after word. The elastic gridiron, torn by the handful, cell upon cell.

The meat is cured flesh. Its poisonous latex is harvested in metal bowls. He grinds at night in the delirium. Check for hazard before you enter—cables and debris are descending from the sky. A block of ice crushes the abandoned skull. Render spiritless, except in the senses. Let's have a quick canker through the vespers. A bundle of objects is bound side by side like stalks of corn. We find ourselves within a bandage of the usual twenty-four hours. This one, guard him close.

What is this feeling called.

What is the proper name for a machine that describes words at a distance.

New material by which fractures are consolidated. Nightsoil. I dare not sharpen back to that faculty of mind. Past images and impressions are being recalled. He justifies his own principles and conduct, while expressing a perverse wish to continue harrowing the ears. Fantastic decorations are found in his remains. I am unsleep.

Mannerisms.

It's weeks since I achieved the shore. Your arms are in my head. I cannot recall the particular you spoke of. I cannot recall your myth—night's misnomer, the unhistoric spell. Above decks for the heat, where a seedpod spirals to my table. A canvas canopy reflects back light from the nearest star. Items bob in the water, fermenting in brine.

I leave the boat moored to an inward projection of the reef. Upon the shingle, that house with the bath and the cadaver is also made of rubber. (You'd think only beautiful people ever got murdered.) Memory's making a comeback. I recall his open headpiece with its metal visor, his blank tongue. Like you, he is a marvellous correspondent.

Sorry, I mean was.

The island that might. It takes three to four minutes for things to start closing down. Next my grainy interior. The liver and heart sit shaking in the scales. The spleen is lost. Magma falls from the sky. Something is being withheld, arm concealed. Concentrate in a shallow head, shorn—heaved legs tapering to ghost. A corruption of master. I cannot sleep.

You have two minutes then you go on.

I am usually accompanied by a tortuous development. I can no longer assume any of my favoured names. I bathe ritually on a need-to-know basis. I am exhaust.

Off beams of light. This is my ladder and this is my consumption. The agon: I do not write you and I must—in the mother tongue, what might be called the sound pattern. Some ancestor or other is being recorded. It resists but is reconstructed through a system of conspirators: a protostar of condensed masses of gas—a stele in which the tissue forms a solid core—vessels and fibres with more or less dignified walls. I am implicated. Thick slimy matter secretes into my throat and is discharged.

You misunderstand me. Food rations and supplies are being transported to the dockside and stacked onto pallets by highly evolved plant-life. I piss holes into a sheet of ice until it shatters.

This is a test then is it. Terminological inexactitude. The third option is easy, like falling off a very moving planet. I'm unanimously declared circumnavigator, an echo of the future returning to the past.

He is at work both within the dwelling and without. His K and his N are stitched together to form a seam (think knave, think knife, think knight). She caresses the ridge of the suture where they meet.

I am implicated in my own combustion. A form of signalling apparatus consisting of a number of posts has had to be invented. I have no means of mechanical support. I carry a pointer in the form of an isosceles triangle—the largest segment of the sharp spine, the sting. The sieve-tube of my vascular bundle is missing. I'm outmanouevred to various positions that express different numbers. I no longer export. My combinations denote letters or words according to a prearranged code. I no longer import.

And who has spooked whom in this midcrypt? I am not eat. Distinct absence of drift in this part of town. Now for some notes on my sluggish indifference.

Cuntlorn, shot by nervous stillness.

Calmness. A crowd. Some of these horses are a bit risque. Will this exclude. Will this passage succeed. I am extracting the reader. What comes next is less convincing.

Splint armour. I am unsured. I swerve. I escape by strategem. Let's do it the old-fashioned way. I scarcely know how to descrive that room and the sallow leaves of book—poison ink tongued to smarting thumb, layer upon layer of print. From the adjoining interrogation cell comes the sound of pages knifed apart, the roll of the forensic die. My task is to check for spores—monitor danger, monitor repose. I am mean average. I am underinsured (the thing of the moths).

We discover three other originals. It's found they are of like but not identical substance—carbon compounds. There's blood involved. We are rumoured. Personifications might be attacked by means of magical ceremonies. We are spelt out of our skins—watery distilled liquid, a kind of nameless alloy. Who are you.

Collapsing at the nausea episode. Never thrust upon you tomorrow what you can pluck out today. I am entering the antechamber to sleep. Check schema at close of book. Who are you.

Diminutive of open mouth from agape. Network wail, spent credo. As far far away as is possibled.

He uses and reuses the name until it falls apart in his hands.

Some of my consonants are discharged of language. Electricity shivers about the mast. Stunning reek of mediocrity everywhere. We've reached an early stage of the reformation: pendulous experimental ice, graceful radar plankton, the swooping wand. A game is used with a blanket to catch and throw. I glimpse a device that resembles the number five. Unimaginable stenches of time. Extinguishedlooking gentilhommes.

Blinded beggar busking underground. His instrument is the aeolian tongue. Leave it be, modal breath migrating across a flap of flesh, the luminous sheaf of beams.

The night following day might be a good time to part and become and never rerun.

Phloem: inner bark of years, fibred. His heart-mad yeses. Segreant.

Hermes. Shelltooth. Thoth.

X

I, the receiver of wreck, do solemnly declare that everything I possess is plotting against me. The dust blows forward and the ash sucks back.

We await conversion sheltered beneath the eavesdrip of a sloping roof. Medication is administered to the tip of every tongue.

Here he comes with his upwardtwisting wing. I am superimposed upon his grainy image. We're confused about when to isolate people. It seems I have made mistakes.

You can't do that on a train. Get your fingers out. The passengers are decorated with weals and scars. She tries to look evil but it doesn't work. Her look is causal, benighted.

Tracks vibrate across a thin film of light. He abandons his crew of assorted exiles and pressgangs replacements. Searchers have found signs of rationing: human remains, the tent of the absence, a spent forge, a storehouse in the shape of a conical beehive, a carpenter, an earlier bullet wound, another large cairn, discarded food filled with gravel. Space hovers between marine courtyard and the dank of ancient retail. Hello I am, though seldom I signal any longer. Wickerwork shapes hover close in the dimness. Ignore recent declarations of solemnity.

There is a level plane between the citadel and the first houses of the town. I thrive on inverted conflict. Bring on any number of unheroic leaders. Bring on any quantity of extravagant phrases and bombast. Bring on the animal familiars. Bring on the wandering beyond bounds. The mercury plummets. There is a translucent connection between line and bait—a chain of dots to guide the eye, the decorous weal. I am a warped discourse of mind. The space is a flat space. He is still. He has taken into his body a hallowed bullet.

She tries to write him out of her body but fails. He lies on the ground. He is one of the watchers. I have now assessed everything and am ready to leave. He is heterodox, forever coming-to-be, both vacuum and light. Unbefriend for a change, see how it feels. He is placed under scrutiny. Being has since time been carried forward by a mister who is now regarded as most void.

Labyrinthal garden of saint who. He writes himself. One of the graphs looks like a giant man tethered to the earth by taut cables. It seems we're being readied for something. Slow turn in direction of beacon, of pharos. Into the gut burrows the parasitic thread. I can't be undone. He leans forward, chained within his own bulk—no shadow of a sheltering roof to creep across this year. He tilts his head and speaks. There's proof of life, but no spinal discipline as yet. How about a simple word signifying a continuous body of water. Innumerable similes of the wave, an aggregation of eyes in oceanic ooze.

Follow on immediately after the introit.

This was written during the same calendar year (the sceptic tables), a vast corpus of salt, tightly bound. The imagery here relates to perceptions of self. The deceased replies. Discerner of hearts and stretcher of the reins is thy name. Compress together music and word: during the galactic gap years everything changes. Go outside and harvest a string of casually crafted lines. He switches tense. There was no warning. All end with the same word. With hindsight, I wish I'd known it was today yesterday.

He opens his mouth to begin the next sentence. I am always found within his field of vision, barely.

The rods support crystalline lenses in a faceted eye. Certain spherical bodies are found in abundance on the surface. I cannot be undone. Narrow slips of bone are divided into compartments. These are marked with runes and used to facilitate divination. The multitude and perplexity of the sticks proves long and tedious. The word arisen is dorlach.

A solitary figure. Littoral on canvas. I doubt the possibility.

Don't you dare venture back into my void say she. I will recover yourself.

She resents. Blood sluices into a shoe. They are on the other planet, antechamber of the villa. You sleep you hard and pitiless man the sleep. . . . Her voice infiltrates every cell. There is no going back—simply narrate, safe and numerate. He expects a dubbing. The book is a novel of the century, discarding plot and character to concertina into tiny inert dramas at the border. Great tension in the march of the dwarves.

I am invective. Enclosed in a box of bony scales, the object has a burned taste. One word here is quite like any other. He explains. All creatures here crave some sacrament of eternal production. He caves in a chosen face by repeatedly striking down thereupon the mouth of an inverted beer bottle. To fix the head in the required position he holds the back of the neck in a grip that is almost tender. Consequence: multiple greenstick fractures. Amalgam and parallax please, nurse.

Fucking look it up. I have had enough and I am driving the whole orchestra to the rim of a nearby cliff.

Sad song. It is literary noontide. If ever I sat rejoicing where old gods lay buried! He says you have placed me in a space wherein I must decide, and this has never.

I lie. I lie between here myself and the reef. I hale from planet. Ready doctor he says to make your initial exploratory examination. The surrounding folk are foredone.

He is bent just around the corner. The light is half-mooned and incomplete. He peers through a tiny window set barely above the level of the last snowfall. There is a castle whereabouts. The seats are expensive. There is a room below stage, a blood-space set into tissue.

Bend sinister, creased into a fold. An ally surfaces and claims him back. She makes combat. I am curious about these remakes, the bursting sacs of germseed. She cuts the adversary's arm.

There is a venomous snake in the kitchen. It was not in the catalogue. I am cast alien from something viral in myself.

Endlimit.

Prevail within the ground plan. Yield to disappearances. He recollects first editions and tattooed autographs. They daren't come back while I'm sitting here with my stave. He never takes the matter up. There is a borderline of convex curves and hoops through which I can always fling myself. There is an attack with words—bolted out-blind from oculus, from eye. There is an old parchment fixed to a doorpost. He enters a forest of proverbs.

In my country we say.

Let's hope this doesn't come back to haunt us some day. The old prompt: down the rust chute and into the sea. Myself, I withhold from prevailing.

Repeat three times.

You can't move your legs anymore. Have fate. But all is jolly pretty, with the light chuntering sound of a vessel. I am doing this because it amuses me to do. There is nothing else, besides.

His name is travesty. There is a man lying beside the road with a silver bullet in his sternum. At his naming the chosen word was plucked from a random book. Flies hum about his lips (all of them). Passengers wave frantically and point from the express. There are no pictures like this of me. He earned his colours as a junior work-ticker. I have misused microwaves myself. I am ranked fifty-nine. There's a lot of background intercession. I'm contained within an event. A gash opens up in the world of things. I think I may be making a mistake. I am a wild and cherished European. Is this too strong to speak of so early in the chapter? I was born during a moment. Such hyperbole. I have an inclination to dis. Hence the infernal world. That's better.

She keeps a diary of his incarceration. Together they encompass a sect that has expanded historically.

Return to man supine on endless flat plain.

A greasy widebrim hat covers his face. Words are being made. Heads are buried in his chest. Sun at apex, sloping downward in all directions from a cardinal point. Let him practise his stops, his unbearable liberating compressions. He pertains to a hinge.

Sub confirmed last week. I will write he say, I done a curse. Two simultaneous themes are deplored by the chorus. I am nearing the end and have been reset to glyph seven. A short lyrical cadenza on a gentle wing follows. Psychebird, spreading wing on the frozen pavement.

At the beginning of act two they enter the castle with an irresistible forward impetus and martial gait. A man dressed as a medium takes the lead in the guise of one departed. The opening is remote. After the liturgy comes a company of stars that we have not cared to give names. They belong to the foreshore, to lands near the coast, the shingle—the space between high and low tidemark. A geisty figure floats behind a sheet of white vapour. There are intimations of a funeral march. It's the weekend of the last judgement. A curved staff holds up my chin, water-level a little below penultimate. The surrounding objects are unformed, plasma set adrift. Where do we place now apart, scatter mouth.

With a nervous trick of the head an unknown man enters. He still has his own fingers, through which he can absorb any misremembered scraps.

There is a second man lying on the tabletop. He is not.

I am slowly adapting—a trawl of the seabed. More and more this is like taking dictation. I cannot stop. Those that live after us have assigned themselves names and zodiacs. I feel ill it's the psychogas. Sometimes I do, sometimes I don't.

Curve of green wave with impasto. Acknowledge, or otherwise. She gives him a seepy look. He is at the highth of his power. He has nothing left to do. A voice says stop before it's too late. He enters the room wielding a candelabrum. Too late has arrived. I say stop.

Thank you for the echoes of your book.

I am, she says. It sounds as though I am.

Something sinister also entered the chamber with the man with the candelabrum. An inquirer who is yet to ask a question.

Stagefright left. Infestation with strangles. Mesmerisms.

I feel like a butterfly in a cheval-glass, a personification. Any insect of the family. Sudden blast of a J-shaped trumpet. The sound is a curve of unfamiliar form, bipolar rupture. R is squared to earth with theta and is equal to an horse. I mean it, the beloved genius of moths.

See I mean above.

He recalls a land he once set foot upon that was littoral *in toto*, a coda of barren rock bleaching into the winedark. My usage is spread wide. Here, performance deteriorates rapidly and unawares. All the females are wingless. Typewriters clack in the pool. All the females shed their wings and march along the promenade with giant striding gait. The libretto is a perfect blend of vocal complexity and cancer. A figure careers down a muddy embankment and sinks a samurai sword into a waiting man (junction of right arm and shoulder). Consider this event and reflect. The assailant is dogheaded. He represents the north and protects the small intestines. How ironic. I arrive. I stem the blood and seal thy wound with my fingers. Usage is spread thin. He represents—no, he is—one of the minor planets. His card signals trickster. I often take the form of a competition: a deep rounded hollow surrounded by fascists with clipboards. A tall mirror swings inward on an uptight frame. The females are something legless. They cluster along a migratory existence, to foregather.

Meaning splits in two. This type of hypnosis only works on mammals and reptiles. He is not, or its reversal. She rhetorics. He is very struck by the music of the last revulsion.

I am trying to indicate an absence of deprivation. A repressed escape.

Locate and reuse script of M. We are snared in a passage. It's lined with statues. Some are draped, paschal. People huddle together, squat to whisper on the flagstones. What is this language I am ministering to. All my terms are equivocal. Research insect on handle of door. Everything takes place outside. Research insect on flesh of forearm (left). I could easily be. It nestles among my filaments.

We are halfway through her year of fires, the musty path of semblance. Above the pier, the algorithm of a thousand beating wings.

New picture. A race of enlightened sunbathers. Bilabial and nasal types. They deride their forebears. On the other hand, it's not as though we don't have the audience crossing and recrossing their palms. More and more I have the feeling that we're getting nowhere, mouth after mouth.

You were too ready to cut things out.

The object is heavy. He is miscast as a novice. There's an awful lot of reflected glamour about the place. I am trawling for degradation. It's not too difficult: everyone and everything looks like shit, or death (one day I too shall write a brief history of kak). It's the crushing sense of expectation. Everyone and everything smells of identity. It's not as though you're speaking to an empty hall with a film of light behind you, within a field of floating letters. Pull out of form. . . . It's not as though they have removed all your props and left you adrift in the darkness. The coming mutual is suspended. Shift shape while you can.

Herma.

The hive is a wormery—recycled slurryworks, mossy pulp. I have endeavoured to place myself outside the book, to look at it as a stranger might. It feels good to locate the current. Now I can shuffle and deal the cards. I have said that already. Return to the twelfth letter. Break him open on the wheel. This reveals a tumour of striped muscle.

He resembles an object or figure shaped like the letter Star. There is a persistent scraping on the ceiling. A halfmad voice screeches for sleep. Ironic, as this is incommensurate with the state of slumbering repose I was once so familiar with—supine and gifted, with ample dream.

The following day.

Distressing acid reflux. Forcible expulsion of spores. A man in the park mills his arms about, demented at the wind. I scan about me, my habit upon waking, sounding out the territory. I am confuse. It appears the lid of the dwelling is formed by the interface of two simple roofs. Myself, I am simulated between the neural spines of successive moments—a shelter of some description. A cord conveys impulses between the rain and other parts of the body.

Syzygy and mass. We're calming.

His teeth are discharged of electricity. Mercury is a superb conductor of sound: a small brass cell with blackened sides and a glass bottom.

She says you use your index like a parent or lover. Do I counterpoint myself. I am largesse writ large—verbal release from inherited debt. I say so and it becomes so. Another well-known word simply means host. Every day I buy something of my own making. Then I undertake a night journey across a wide expanse. It says the eyes of the dead are watching, translating. I contain multitudes—two breeds crammed into the fibres of a single skull. Note to self: take night journey to library at sunken rim of bay. A ship passes through a narrow strait. I hope that's her waving. With increasing speed, I tire. You are cold, disengaged witless. I mean to go on. It's said you resemble the letter M in cross-section. Electrified and compressed, let your words be yes yes and no no.

This is like the end on Saturn in the iris only more grizzly. I look down and see a sight. They have discovered a star system that resembles a game of snooker and a vault where the bodies are buried upright. I cringe (erudition poorly camouflaged by pus). Always wear something existing.

I am a branch of anything.

I am especially a nerve.

I am a process of bone.

I am mandible.

I am your ascending part.

I am a feather barb.

I am the tooth fracture.

Saurus, The.

Changes are imminent, the third and final alteration—stabbed to safety. They hanged him and then went one step further. They flayed him and had him turned into leather. It's not that long ago that people made skin out of books. It's not helping, all these rearrangements. There is no continuity at all.

She is warped around earth and sea in a hermetically sealed capsule. Take care. We are as bad as the other. I am a sacred form of reluctance. The address which follows these words makes reference to highlights of a future life. She is second in size, sixth in distance, and bears the metal temperament of lead. I am shock. These are signifiers in themselves. She is gainsayer. These are semiotic fingerprints. I am a rewritten condition. I peer down into an order of redundant reptiles—unclass of birds with teeth and jointed tail. Remember in the cave the starlight and the talking lizard? The embalmed crocodile and the mistimed identity? Also lost and found this very day, oozing on the frozen pavement: dead psyche, with outwardfolding wing.

Nile in the sky. Fetch me a fucking boat and someone to stitch with, something to navigate.

Rocks at wander. Stain of gold on eyelid, first white cilium. Strewn across the floorboards is a collection of dried planets. Sun is blind. Mercury is quicksilver. Venus is ultramarine. Moon is blood-yellow. Mars has to be scarlet. Jupiter is out of range. Saturn is soot, my sign. Uranus is the stain of ink. Neptune is grey. Pluto is black ice. Earth is a translucent no-coloured nothing. I'm making this up as I go along. I utter each of their names in turn, on the hour every hour. Beyond the fixed stars is the void. A signifier is just one among branching sobriquets. From sow to hospice, I have no need of want. I am still at motion, a randomness perplexed by its own circuit.

Anabasis. Closure is complete, air made tight by molten glass. The column stretches through and beyond the interior head. Abscond up-country, back from go. Nothing can inform us. In the hymn we appear as rivals. Brace yourself for a loud symphony—horse latitudes with scad or tunny. A reason is uncovered: a belt of calms, soft tissue caressing a cut surface. Close with this dark aspect. We have reached the limit beyond which predestination is groundless. A sphere is balanced at the tip of the shaft. Guess. Sign up for rumour. Grant me a stolen name and I shall disappear quietly, without trace.

A figure hurtles down an embankment. Agonizing observance of time. Reduce to power by fictions. Grind jism bond with liquid plastic, equine glue.

She wakes to find a cross, a rectangle and an indeterminate shape branded onto her inner thigh. A bathroom light-cord clicks on or off in an adjoining apartment. Compare this with the improvised version above. The indeterminate means green. A severe chuck under the chin usually results in head loss. There are seven categories of money supply in this territory.

Now I am becalmed, I can rearrange my palate bones.

The image is duplicated due to additional reception of a decaying signal. It has covered a longer path. Adjust index to accommodate the first instance of us.

Fourfold rod detected in my compound eye. One or two rows on a simple branch, the common investing structure of any colony. I am scratching out the word I use for those intangible characteristics that defy being. It's like writing on shales. If I fail, they'll have to alter all the maps.

Written to write stone.

XI

This has just happened. Impress shoreline for riverrun, littoral exchange: powers of horror, the family cut. Whiff of chlorine at crest of hip, that sinister glamour that always clings to an assassin. Never come back to where. Clear out last remnants of light. Hear all voice and refuse exchange. If nobody comes, then nobody comes. Okay, ourselves alone, through a lens of mutability.

It means reader, the continuous body of salt. Always use singular if you can. Some of these changes are puzzling. (Her instructions about digits stretch the ability to instruct.) As I say, that's not how I remember existing. This is like an inquisitory, layers of sawdust and lead. I am sitting at the top of a steep stairwell. Go in. I am waiting for someone unspecified.

I take it we're not alone any longer. This follows another vector, a memory of being on your balcony, with worms attendant. I could come along and talk about nothing in particular.

He does not wish to dwell for he may lose. I am reminded of dead time. He instigates his own need. Everything I once did is retained in the crumbling plasterwork—refracted light on naples yellow, far above me a surface. I'm taking a side, the long walk out.

We are peering at ourselves through the broken hole in a window pane. Some kind of cycle is re-enacting itself. Love reigns over these parts.

Their bodies are deteriorating on the psychical level.

She says you think yourself important while all the others think not. Scintillas tracing lines in the air. There is no saying. There is no news. Never mash your eye with the ball of your thumb. They have both not. They are the double. And he says, I am indifference writ large, sunshine.

I hazard the die has clung. In the early days I eagerly took in everything. O dear it looks very dark down there. Among the things I took note of was his fractured sinusoidal chamber. I need more time to complete his design: two membranous wings, hind limbs reduced to halteres—floating organs of balance. This is how I would write had I the pluck, like in the early days of thaw. There has been oversight. A pale companion is not listed among my props. Seduce until further notice of agitation. A bright clear sky is hanging—meaning influenced by late. Before I wake, I should. A dry lake bed can be found in the north-east corner. This is where a whole army sunk into a chasm while attempting a crossing. I am now at rest, until further notice of agitation. Allow for the fullness of their memories: I am, I remember, I watch. The story ends up mangled—traders in dwelling, a footless crevasse in the glacier. Bloodspattered shoes, I note. Someone breathing, badly. But to me this is definitive: the only man for himself.

Now it was on this day in 1759 or thereabouts that I was once born. My gathering clan appears to be a jolly tribe of junketeers. Bunch of cunts. Strangely my voice into immenseness. I never expect. Close by two naked beasts are pondering an ear. I hear a persistent humming sound. Nothing is lurking is here. That sound is the quiver of white goods, a voiceless backdrop. Stop. Distance self from self. As a travelling companion he is well-known in the tradition. There is no structure to support the stem. Oil seeps from the split in a stacked grille of narrow pipes. It is on reflection apt that I shall never quit the compound. I need more practise. I've been idle, sitting at home rapping a knife against a bare bulb until it shatters. I need to pursue—in composition, decay. I am ignorant of need. I will compose a symphony of those bells worn by lepers as a warning. I have to send this now, an intestine shock. He writes to say I am having a nervous breakthrough.

A murder weapon is displayed beneath a painting of a cavilsome skull. Bull relief with index close by. It depicts the slaying of her suitors, a list of names scored into red stone. Many cankered legs. He raises the back of the tongue to caress the soft underpalate. He forms. He re-forms.

They are the double, or genus, or individuality. All of those.

One look is enough to tell who is who. He has informed on me. Forthwith I am not. He fills up all my folds. He wants to be the first person wedded in nylon. I need time to relinquish. He greets me with a mournful tune—seedpods bursting at chemical reaction. He limps (hobbled achilles). I need time. He is nemesis and lover in one. I need time to start looking things up. Everyone thinks the fight took place on the beach. I pen a bit of doggerel and immediately feel better about myself. It's time to start isolating. Speed up. There must be method. It's time to start reloading. I am alive and I am eaten up.

One keeps a reptile pet in her cell—water-rail genus, giving name to the family. The inscription above the oaken door reads.

Arch and us nous like a dead tree, one delayed at the top, broke off and partly burned from crown earthward.

The exact nature of that fiendish device isn't known to us. He is holding his hand in the least extraordinary book. I want to do more with his heads. We are ten miles apart and nowhere inland. Project him. Feed me today's strapline. Feed me today's feed. His reign is called the golden age, despite the gloom—a meeting of bards and fluids. But with digits of dough, he concedes.

Her dwelling becomes a house of derangement for stragglers. I wake to find a novice kneeling in front of me. Sound of multitudinous scalding dialects—maiden over male or our reverse. You must indeed continue. The time is noontide, mad for the light. A trembling encircles us. We are about to witness the first of her combustions: the individual citizen developing from a series of products. I lack the honesty and the strength. She resembles an insect in composition, with yoked neck and spool. Origin is obscure.

I am waiting for an unspecified event. My abdomen is swollen. The current is arranged in triplets for one couple. An imaginary circle passes through the poles of the earth. I eat up distance and silence.

She says you are not any type I know of. Nonetheless, the objective persists. The subject is the eleventh in our circuit, a drum rare.

Fingered. There is a big mound of it, genus of syphon or horny coral snatched from the hardening air. Indeed, any collection of things called elements. Resonance found in muscle—liquefaction, melting, wastage drawn off by pressure through a bent channel. And the shadow at the root of it.

Screams from the alcove. Squalling sax with gravel. I have just tried to turn up the volume on a minute of silence.

Father plane (painted apocalypse boy). He gathers up the sheaf of notes and shuffles back into the sea. Swift canvas isosceles—lurid-coloured foodstuffs staining the concrete. He always appears suddenly, no preamble or warning. I must be robust, isolate self from self barely usable. The major offensive is going well. The once-only membership policy is to be scraped. There is little resistance. This event is called reaching for the nimbus. There are believed to be thousands of improvised traps (so say the expert twenty). I want to achieve more with his shadow, the weals of light on his heads. I reckon the enormous Yes. I give myself three hours more.

Around the midmost hour. Noon metre.

Work is punctuated by Pavlovian foreign travel and mawkish reflections sealed in cellophane. Now I am not, due to lead causes. I have found the source of affliction. A salty crust is deposited at the gusset. Answers will have to wait. The foretold return to the island has begun. I am no longer mentioned in dispatches. Our vessel has been fitted with an armoured keel for the ice. All my lines are possessed. Consonants are generated by air passing over the surface of the tongue. The lips are unevenly matched. Your dream sounds all very can't think of the right word: an alembic, large and powerful animals (probably wolves), something resembling a bill, a box (filled), annotated books, a discarded boot, a gilt edge, cancer, her fractured coccyx, a cooking stove, the electrodes, everything else, feet, furs, the instruments, overwrought ironwork, a medicine-chest, a pair of oars, the object-glass of a marine telescope, pickaxes, rope and leatherette, scented soap, a sunken ship, the loaded double-barrelled shotgun, shovels, coarse stitches, silkworms, a pair of bedroom slippers, blocks of compressed snow, sponges (live), the terminal bone, an overused toothbrush.

False decretals. None was found.

118

Seedpods bursting at peripheral. She weeps for a whole week. Do you regret having now. Pitterpatter the rainwork. The local mineral is rockforming, with perfect basal cleavage. It forms rings like those circles above his head, the coins that cover his eyes. She weeps for seven days more. A wet cloth is placed gently over his exposed heart. Writing causes the subject—monumental and postbiblical, with encrustation of scales and a scrap of evolution thrown in. Besides this there is supersensuous reason. Some things I have forgot.

Another definition of the previous: today, the serial yesterday, where we are outcurved. You are silhouette. Tomorrow, the neural house and its environment, built on piles in a watery realm. What could be more domestic than a young woman strutting down and wiring a telegram: bladderwrack of kindred weed, ensnared in small bulbs with axis breached, decumbent. . . . eggs flat, leaf-shaped and obtuse, entire . . . fringed at base with chalky sediment. Gusset Rorschach.

She writes that social being caves in at the symbolic stem. And by the way he's dead. Continue to forget. It will come soon enough that alarm.

Dominion of Venus, sign of Aries. He swells up with big mouths. Repeat, I no longer matter.

A pair of counterpoints: emulsion of almond and voice in chant, floating up from the Darwen end (never pay homage—not visibly, anyway). Now hum the early neuter phase. Appropriated to the head, it breaks open the stone. Please pluck from the book, canonic din of our papyrus. The amulet was made of gold inlaid with precious gems in the form of a humanheaded hawk. He rests his broken wing upon the track.

The day dawned cloudy so I did not inspect the trenches. We do not work because we are feeling ill. He says I am thinking of not making an appearance. He says how about if I do but I don't. How about if I don't appear but my image does.

So I walk in and I see this shadow on the glass talking to another shadow, and it's him—his silhouette behind the office door with the word register, the death word. I have two clear memories.

Meridie: at noon, at the midpoint of night. The hours encircle me. There are things I want but I have officially ceased. It's too early to say she say. We gave ourselves the limitation. The enormous Yes, how it unnerves—bowstring snapped, the rib exposed. Every act in this narrative is a leap of fate: sequences, antiphons, responds. When will I come back. The interpretation of care is restricted. A narrow katabasis has been obtained thus far. This is fragile. There are sensations I desire but I have officially ceased. Beware deep drop behind rockwell.

Memory of touch and sight. Flickerbook deer yielding antler to drift of snow. Muson.

Something like a monk's hood. Two winged apparitions swell up in the fore-

119

ground. Why no forest about these parts he says. That's the most perfect boundary I have ever witnessed. Unequal pupils compress. No answer. As a mediaeval numeral he is two hundred and fifty—eyes black, no visible white. All my actions are constantly deferred. Those gathered shout and brandish torches. Eyes swivel upward. See Jupiter's moon and much more (sorry about that palaver with the bat). Different textures. He makes no effort. This is slow and confusing work. I slightly evaporate the ending, mend by interwoven stitches. I don't want to be a distraction. There's a strange noise at the close. It's a kind of book, isn't it no—those three arias, the superstitions. Is this your pre-emptive thing? True, flies circle and drone. It tends to regulate itself over time. There's an option. Transfer to last chapter, the final chicane. I am making arrangements for the first time in my short life (brief by the span). I possess such a volatile capacity for retaliation. More duckegg blues and shattered plate.

Airpump. A southern constellation.

Glory of the snow with hunters returning. My unvisible is antinarrative and threadlike. Reports of cell fires and riots. The chosen object is an item outstandingly bad and outstandingly good. One character has a peculiar gift for bonesetting. He pens an opera, a prologue and three acts to his own libretto. I plan feints and shifts to deceive. An arborescent deposit is leached out from a solution. There is a shortfall of I am.

This is more like it. Not the whole. Research and install winglike apparition. Live dialogue: an old beldam in discharge with the devil. At every turn is another. You're begrudging my remaining eye. A column of oily black smoke drizzles from the sky. Sample: empty glass on a marble tabletop, quivering at the proximity of rapid circuits, the predicted quake. I am unsightly and frank in my moments. When you walked in it was as though you had a halo of light about your head. I am a peripheral body myself—vague representations on a map, stitched places and names (sequences, antiphons, responds). Botany me: nervure in the insect wing, leaf-valve and rib of groined fault. He died before the final act was finished and it was complete.

A downgoing, air in motion flowing downward. Herein is a difficulty of separation comparable to the rare-earth case. And a trick question: your parents.

Possessed selves. Rockward (I mean towards a rock), drilling through superficial deposits of clay, sand and schist, into the underlying. I know laminae—flexed and elastic. Temporality can't remain, it sits ill in my folds and intercessions. I am at the limit from which the startling point.

Larkspur (a word). Snow doxa.

Go on. Nerval.

I am born the day following the day which is called the day of innocents. Still I plan to use feints and shifts to deceive. I am a word of which only one instance of use has ever been recorded.

After this griefstricken opening we are granted a week's grace. I am moving away from the head. Spores glow in the air. I can hear the expansion of my artery, pulsing from point to point like a wave. A balmy orchard overlooks the metal-blue bay. (It's about antinomy, isn't it.) There's a pyramid framed against the sea. A plastic fork becomes wedged in a drain. He is discarding plot and character. Nonetheless, some paths lead back. Each beat of the heart sends blood to the colonies. That's enough.

Folk squat or lie on the bruised floor. Medics are busied with arterial stitching. Structure and hysteria.

She is overwhelmed. This is a good place to pause, or stop altogether. Bring word, closer. Lock it inside your chest. Unpicking this flesh is nigh impossible. Bring word: a performance out of the opening air, by night at every window. Our theme is the burning essence of indifference. That stained glass rose is held fast by a fusible alloy. (What's that thing up in the sky.) I smell the arm smouldering, oddly fashioned in the snow. Sound is old and slow in time with heavy offshore beat. Undertake analysis of the letters into an eleborate shorthand—a track of artifice, the bridging palm. And that's why you still need proof, proof that you still exist.

Puella aeturnus.

An androgynous fish akin to the bone pattern who symbols constant quantity. Spurts and whitebait popping on the shingle. He writes softly nightfall, to pretend, if only for himself. No last trumpetings here, gentile—old alluvia of rivers, a rope connecting a net with the land. The national calmative.

Their passport photographs are identical, another unlikely doubling of affect. Pause and consider. Extend outward. Slope away gently in front to tiny inert dramas at the border. Ka biography. The third interlude has been rewritten. It starts out really jolly then fucks up. A sleepy military post is continuing its work when routine is interrupted. The words reassemble those worn by readers.

She simply walks away from him, lightstruck with easy burden. She designates books as read or unread. She doesn't come back after the rain. This tort is the penultimate twist, wrungdoing.

His interest in language filters through we hear.

Susurrus.

I have always enjoyed crossing frontiers. I mean, I have always enjoyed being held at frontiers.

She designates, cutting off the observer's horizon to the north and to the south. She was once used as an electric insulator, but is no substitute for glass. The story starts out really family with all the characters and anniversaries in the correct place. Then she utilizes the mezzaluna blade of an earlier chapter. He considers this a good time to quit.

A contradiction in law. Fabulous and ascending rivers of gold, oxen on the roof.

Walking to L (4.31am, 19th March 1928).

I was gladsome back then on foot, what with the motifs and the stories: his curious embellishment of the chorale, his lack of will—a municipality of parts formed by branching rootstock. Just leave it be. The first day is called Thursday. I recollect. I leave. I just don't feel I have to defend myself anymore. There are no disappearances left to pursue. My interest in language has waned. Force to stop photofinish, being inside.

He is a filter for something unidentifiable by date. Consider some collective nous. This doesn't look very promising—flimsy bagatelles, hopping sprees, unpaid revenue—a style of vocalization between singing and speaking, tonguing the gangplank. His face is still in use. What about the rose.

A contrasuggestion of madmen: nightfishing off antibe.

Question. How can a skull be cavilsome.

Symphonia domestica—an organism that lives in my dreadful absence. Concussions discrepant, though apparently logical. I cannot.

Now I'm convinced it was a Wednesday. A game is being played out on a chequered board, with bells, a cued spring and a pig's liver. The latter is usually numbered nine. An elongated shadow is cast at local noon. Children from the estate chalk its outline. Inside this they sketch a mythic bird of prey clutching an egg. I am seeking excuses to go back—more communications from R, in the sense of received and understood. (Throughout the book it simply means it and they simply means they.) A great shadow speeds out across our heads, rushes through the landscape dragging the light with it. He repeats himself, repeats a score above the line. What can I remember of the dubitative conditional. I no longer care whether I happen or not, to be honest—a fine hypothesis to discover oneself within. Iron tang of blood in my mouth, but I'm happy here in the company of my invalid, with baton and winged sandal. Grey insect creeping about the base of a certain fountain. Uncoiling adder squirming on path.

See, he is wandering through all my reversals.

Lend alliteration where you can. Exit in your own mind. I shall wear myself smooth. Lend attrition, the desired complement to one's own tendencies. Everyone stands in the auditorium. Now I'm back in the acid light of the lobby. I am waiting. Something happened back there, a hesitation. I had sensed—I am scrutiny. Signs of compression. Deviations evident from longitudinal alignment of body. Cut marks on right femur, fracture to plates of skull. A forking has taken place. Score now more staccato-frantic. Initially the spectators were seated, now they're vertical. A table has been placed on the stage. Spent matches are scattered across its surface. Make up mind. Shortfalls are occurring in rank and status—signals of the gentle ineradicability of the present.

The answer conforms to the tonality of scale. I decide to proceed footless.

Do you think you should.

Second reading.
I have adopted a word used in signalling, one of the names allocated to the spectator channel—whereas he stands for a single degree on the circumference. I call him the object-being. Disease hasn't cured him of overrating his powers of judgement. I am still reading, doubting. The object-being is not capable of differentiation, expressing conditions. A score above the line used to be permitted, an obstacle capable of development into a complete embryo.

He can never forget her hesitancy when she spoke of him as time pointing inwards. More public work for organs is being composed: preludes, amnesia, toccata. Wordplay in a state nowhere between, sandblind and stoneblind.

The attack that never came. (It was electricity, stupid.)
The tense is a familiar tense, with musical abandon. Unpicking this flesh is nigh impossible. I wonder whether I too should eat, whether that might enlighten me—cannibalize my own kin. They have discovered false chromosome numbers, erroneous spellings. Recognizable human parts are not consumed at first. Over time the options are reduced: bone-marrow, spleen, arteries, and skin are excised. The text becomes dramatically three-dimensional and casts its own shadow. Muscle tissue is cut into using a sharp object. The glossy illustrations are suddenly animate. The brain is pulled out through the base of the skull. My seat perches on a precipice. The face is sliced off. See culmination or highest point, as of splendour (see book of). Just sign the document and all this stops.

The body is found compressed: alternate folia of mica and quartz. Its look is hurt. The objective is to place the balls into the numbers—holed or sectioned. A work intended to display the touch, breaking into fugue, loosely. Signalled names of the initial. Semaphore.

I am work from memory. The collective noun is a carnality of souls.

Sign. Signal. Bearing sea. Bearer.

Musomastix.
Ash wedding. It is undermost, or if you like, undwelt. Irksome matte vestiges (time, framed). This is my shorthand for it's difficult to see with all these notes scribbled across every page. Broad red scar at left hip, bilge-tank flooded with saltwater. Empty keg aboard with spermatozoa. A touch of grammarye and glamour. Is anything else going to happen. On offer today, half-price epilation in aura. Thanks for being messenger. The seven-year eclipse has returned. A big Moon, Venus and a semblance of Mars are arranged in a straight line running perpendicular to the horizon of the sea. The chosen man is a composite of split matter—a shadowy spirit person or thing much admired. (Gentle stroke with claw as he refuses to eat for a week.) Close in and set test above quoth mark, the standard quark—memory and phantom matter. Who faces out from land? Who

fares from sea? Who is spanning tree? Severe absence of fuck in this quarter. Crushed insect at arm of window. I am not. A loop avoidance technique is introduced, based on the logorithm—loamy deposit of aeolian tongue. I am continuing to forget.

The allusion to three seems perfect. I need an excuse for retaining. I find that excuse by supposing. I am not detected in the free state. Every one of us has radiations. Associated with warface, I sprang from a word coined, but not yet found.

He lands in the bay where the water is calm and shallow, lapping at the thigh. On into your vast wardrobe of voices. You're a real troper, you. Stop. Alcoves, pavilions and other structures punctuate the shoreline. Stop. Boulders raised to sea defence. Scattered remnants of praxis (wrong word, somehow). Colonies of seedsacs and lichen are anchored at the ribs—traces on the sternum, all twenty-four vertebrae of the back, the sacrum, the scapula, the clavicle and ulna. It's quite hard to find a straight line. My guess is a body segment, and an old form of to starve oneself. He thinks he cannot be seen or heard. Every word is a thing said just once, and alonely. Everyone points. I am deaf of this below. Use is probably afflicted. Use is probably insignificance. For his last meal he requests a syrup of crushed glass. Perhaps it is a Sunday, perhaps not. These are my findings. Transmission is by means of a current in vertical movement, especially upwards of air or meteors: bringing together and to carry. I quoth me. I am pollinated by touching the insect's undersurface. I am latinized from chest. I am any of a triplet of particles, yet to be found. I am that cable. I am taut endmost. I am the thing that extends downward—one who eclipse. I am the thing that extends upward. I am the unit from which all atoms form. I am self-hearing. I am any particular state: a small bubble trapped in a glass flower, that smell of burning lumber. . . . Now it seems it's spring again—giant red wood, the magnifying hum, beetle crawling into clock on wall. I'm moved by the power of a rigid number. It calls itself the fixed base of a system, our letter E. Giant, giant, giant.

It gives birth out of its eye socket. The child is named from its metallic click when struck. The mother is buried alive. Could we have formed even the vaguest idea of the suffering her absence would cause. At the top of the turret she sees silhouetted against the sunlight the figure of an unknown man. Dead clinquant, all of gold.

On, to happen well or ill.

I start out with the subject and a sense of neutrality. I have to remember first of all what he looks like. He hath the apron, he hath the steel bangle, he hath the undercut, he hath the tradition, he hath the comb in the hair, he hath the minuscule word. . . . This goes on for hours and it's almost impossible to explain. I equal the number in question. There were strict rules of commentary in the early days.

Ember of alkali—potash alum. I understand. Lean back into me. What could we conceal in such a mosaic. I enclose the improvised, an elevated wound. I hereby inscribe him in the volume. The roof is a bellshaped roof. It's exposure. I fear.

Do you have a question form. Yes. A 28-second sandglass is used with the logline to ascertain the seed of the ship.

He is infected by the observations of others. (Wish I had control of the remote.) We are out in the open at the edge of a forest. Dead matches representing artillery and infantry are positioned across a trestle-table. That distant hill is not a hill but a steep man-made mound. Local fairground in the rising haze, attendant noise as anticipated. Mastaba rumoured nearby. A collection of tiny terracotta figures is unearthed, dusty gravegifts. I am the remaindered present. I am self-hearing. Someone is padding along the perimeter wall of the compound. We're at the last leg of the drilling process (three piano miniatures). A worker forces up the incremental of the vacuum pump. Every action is garnished by his less-than-sanguine remarks. They used to herd us giants up there, great slabs of granite on our backs, and across to the opposite bank.

The viewer is invited to decipher the piece as a sort of riddle. The ventral plate, the distal part of the deformity, twists away from the midline. A creep of soil edges down the slope. Glistening boulders under light from nearest star— seawrack from past, somewhen out where. His every action is an event worth recording. I too am at point of collapse. I too am at wreck. My number is 1749. Images are stolen. There is a series of scratches aligned across a yellowing sheet of perspex nailed to a post. I write standing. I levitate. He sleeps late so that less time appears to have elapsed. Our routine is interrupted by strange pains. I sleep standing. The last three motifs should be played without an interval. I eat kneeling on all fours. Through fear of loss he never learned to dwell. He is often used as a symbol for the one thousand names, an oratory from words formed in wake.

Remove this last remark. Quarantine in parentheses. According to the rules we're to be transmuted to a physical objection.

This theme appears to be the midpoint between two poles. The bridge is a dislocation, a slice of programme music. It's our aim this day to aim. We are divided into monuments. My assistant is described as vapid. This conveys well the general idea or motif. I challenge, hone being (it's a job). She retracts. I'm not sure I can go on.

You have released the punchline. I chance upon a fridge crammed full of pockets, rays of light falling on a network of small arteries, bread of dust and ice—the cable of an optic nerve, tibia of nameless animal, one confused and solitary gull. Now tell me the whole story, include the contractile elements—the most delicate of skin tissues, quivering fibrillae of feathers. Still I'm uneasy. It's as though now he knows, now he does not know. When I look down I can't see the base of the shaft. We hang from ropes, turning in space. See what sort of hole he's dragged us into. He is stung all over.

The sound of an end ending. Possibly a different word (sea bar). The storage root at the head. Terminalia. Clit-burr.

Santa Lucia, patron saint of eyes, ember the week in which I occur.

A circuit around, running. The book is called the book of skin and it's in the records. The great nonesuch diverse.

Caressage: the back of the hand—gentle-dorsal, rare in occurrence. Refer to her little book of free adjectives and names. A tripod supports the house. She is surplus to requirement. She is immanent. There is waiting.

He is a corner in which to suspend the night. The storyteller has been sent away. Nothing can now be heard in the anteroom of the villa. He falls silent again, in sympathy with the utter lack of sound. I am distracted in recollection: rust chute, steep descent to sea—dry grass on scorched embedment, molten cacti. Whoever edgeward, I am, yet it maketh me sad to hear you so unsleep. Gathering objects are signalling.

The body is freed down to the hip. The compressed air in the pneumatic chisel will last only half an hour longer.

Respite is need. Where is she up to now: birdsong, the tap of thy gentle fluke, rumble of skittledrums. I am unsure how I will post myself back. Here's that viaduct, the zooming past again. Glad to see you're rewriting the tables, something to pass the book of hours. They are up on the roof with guns. Be sure to leave a residue. There's mention of the unfortunate above and the unfortunate below. Now lurch to flank. Dismember me on some faraway beach. The division of the law sits roughly about here. There's not much else to say: battery scribble, my meridional anchor—scattered crumbs of radar glitter. I abandon. Feed into path of point fast-travelling (light). It says here she is a goddess of destruction, or a carpet. A small cask. A cypher.

Out of his remains. This is what I do. I too am at wreck, over.

I said nothing more
while joints crack
I read this twenty years too late (she too)
bursting with its own
sediment, locked in the difference
with things I can't write of.

I have mapped these vestiges yet
she's sending me away
with graceful bowing memories—
I did not notice in the day the seconds
and the heaving of the sea with waves that cannot break.

On pages sixty-four and seventy-two a real difficulty forces itself upon the causal reader. A parting takes place, a valediction—the final edit. A winged figure is seen crossing the arc of the meridian, between the heavenly body and our horizon. A string of notary drills has been hired. Place law in mass of matter—to lay, as on a pallet bed.

There is a hint towards an answer in the diary. She writes you behave as though my work is evil—discomposure, a vestibule to decay. Place of grave-clothes, artificer buried under letters. Now, here is the continuous sound of a note unstruck. Mechanical, defected.

Yes please yes I think I have hinged. I serve origin unknown. I have revi-sioned the European portrait. A unit of his one thousand and twenty-four names is bitten into the threshold and resembles a threaded sheath—fascicle and root issue. Down the rust chute. Into the sleeve.

To here. How to collect the data to measure hazard. How do you say: I have been dropped from the eaves. These are loose ends and undercurrents, repeti-tions. All the stopstarts have gathered in my area, all mouthing from the same stain sheet. We have a mountain splitting open, don't we. And cartoons from the archive. We have contingency. We have huge problems with bears on stage and sea monsters. We have the uncertainty principle. It's not the greatest story, not the greatest libretto. It's supposedly a parody. My dreams are combatants. I must test him she says, hand me the lancet.

We are lurching from one extreme circumstance to the next, with no apparent season or rime. I am inconsistent with This and Here. Number eleven is unfin-ished, inextinguishable. Smouldering remains can be glimpsed through limbs of charred timber. The days are clinker days: oxide of scoria in bone-ash, with three fasts in each quarter of the moon. A scale of black iron is obtained red-hot under the hammer, the residue of cinders raked from furnace—the crust of slag that forms about the laager.

Mud has to be pumped to the bottom of his hole. He screams. If you act like a cunt I no longer wish to touch you. What strikes me isn't the clothes but the texture, the texture of the faces and the facts. Now go back and reinstate, lack-medic.

Cord and club, in revolution. Cordelier.

The barbed lobe of a coda. Sempiternal afgod. Anchorage.

XII

Hunger at close of the first set. The author of this work does not wish to hide his sympathies. Give up everything. No one mentioned here is yet within the true circuit of my concern. The lights have suddenly come back on. I am not yet ready to abandon. I am not yet ready to mediate. Things are getting out of hand. I'm not yet ready to come back down off the roof.

One in shadow shores up the rafters. That vacuum is the optic chasm: straight to the stars—right through us. I am alloy, mix of metal, mix of meal and ore. I am the one who impairs. Striving manoeuvres us toward an obscure lever of space. I am unnamed or unknown as. It gets brighter as you approach the tip of the spike. I speak from the safety of the cordon position. I am unmanned. I remain. I am the flight to sameness, alias uneasy—discanny and industrial, sot-footed out of necessity—a secret parallel within my own nature (of or pertaining to Sirius). We're on the wrong track.

Here be matter quick with flesh. Contest if you need. You will survive about eight hundred tomorrows.

Curtail and forget. Close dot at centre of scream. What fades is the image of a brochlike tower, doubtless of age and burst through the crest of a steep rounded hill. Few of us have but thought some day I will not. The headside clock reads seven seventy-seven. At another time, otherwise. There may be no alternative. (No, I mean.) There are these others, rustling. That which intercedes.

Well, first of all they take a good look at the snow. Innocent people should be removed. It's a natural process. Here is matter made of death, nux vomica. The formula inscribed on such figures makes the deceased speak to the one who has called. We have reached the limits of classification—taxis and rank. A rogue object with no connection to anything else sits unconscious on the table. In another era these arrangements could be otherwise. On the wall is a picture representing the unassuming name—nothing at all. Signals trace into me but are becoming less and less emphatic. Our moods mimic the temper of the day. I walk with you beside the world, but cannot set much abuse upon such shapes. I'm a survival from the past, a chance occurrence (can you hear the crimes in all this). I lie in wait. At another time, we would be otherwise. I have waited a thousand years, give or take. And what about the symmetries in these primal numbers.

He receives a sentence of forced labour instead of prison. He dons the orange jerkin. His offence is written on his back. Our skins are issued for three years more. It's not unusual at the end of that period to see men patched with sacking. I shall close the portal now: background low, low yield to radio, inactive.

Martello. A circular thought of coastal defence, where I offer resistance to time. The performance cracks on—right in the eye, the uncanny flicker. Sometimes I seek shelter from the crowding ceaseless hum. Too much wastage. Too much light leaching away.

Unrest in a limewash hotel—a vastness with empty room, eyetipping wordplay. His axis is a closed curve. He paces between the bare mattress and the balcony. He desires to capture the battering moth. Its wings parody the lineaments of his own profile. By remaining stock-still he can feel the poles in their precessional motion. Microscopic eggs are deposited on his patchwork exterior. Too little wastage. He has magnetized various objects in the room.

Nutant and widdershins. Cento.

Construct.

Why Pleiades. Use syllable and letter. Place them in the trough of clay. A finger points. Messengers are invented. Think and consider. Render all of the above more reasonable. I must journey to tell, impart the bad news.

Passing angel under dripstone arch. From her surface she radiates the promised abnormality. (I must have descended from failed genes, bad beasts.) She has voice. You can see these papier-mâché heads bobbing on the bridge. I have left myself nothing to do. This signals that we're doomed to squat on the losing side. Resistance is fertile. I am not afraid anymore. I will remember. Fade and confide. I am the correlative of Not. Put me aside or bend me back, but do somethink. I am not use.

Garb crimson with back slash. I am not to be undone. Place yourselves into storage. I am not to be completed. Render all of the below more unreasonable. He suspends time in his composer's hut. What relief. What reticence. Resist and cast off. We remember. It's always too soon: the breaking of waves that will not. One glance at these shapes and I'm myself again. He recoils. Meaning lies at his surplus, his intermediate deductions. I am unsurety itself. I will forget. Childhood is warped up in all this. Time is probably nineteen sixty-eight. It springs back into itself. I'm not afraid anymore. It's the sameness. I am unafraid of thee. There is blood in the grain, a gloss on the surface. It slowly resumes its original shape after the shock of compression. Folk are packed into empty atria, milling about aimless.

She tuts. You attach great importance to the knowledge of names, both for the living and the dead. Do not any longer speak within me. She tuts again. Things are said. Time to evacuate. (Things are not unsaid.) A number of the objects remain silent and are left behind. I am seizure: one, two, three, four, five, six and seven. I'm controlled by counting down and through. The correct blazon is bary wavy—heartbeat and spasm, the pent of eversucking breath. A brief span of air is penned in the driving forth.

Leave this a while longing.

He behaves as though he's incarcerated, a walking penal colony. Somebody passes word, scored upon a piece of bark with a red-hot spike. Abandon the rest of the notes and flee.

He is immune. He rejects the organ, the muscle tissue and arteries. Just follow the instructions. Still you spin a good yarn the other says. Please do not leave. The heart is freeze-dried and sealed in a glass demidome, along with the needles, scraps of old newsprint and a rusting lemon press. Ideas which underlay their use have not changed in the least. I am the cause of another's misfortune. One of the wedgelike stones that form part of the arch has been dumped in the churchyard. It gathers moss. I too am damaged product. Coin is paid in exchange for the wreath and the correction book. I am unsourced. Money is paid to trace my origins. I am a spring of unknowns. This is the premier fact. I am spoken out from speech and written sidereal. One glance at these shapes and I become myself.

Moist fog in the breath. Woeful Trojans everywhere. We won't have to remember things anymore. She seeks with the right hand the groin. (I'm used to contradicting negative assertions.) In the folds of her garb she carries a favourite axe. I am incomplete, always wanting that extra syllable, that extra minute of sleep. I am incontestable. I start believing I'm a saint. My hands are outsize. I start to take extraordinary risks, but always keep something in reserve, just in case. A commemorative coin is minted, tender and servile.

It must have been a very heavy door to hold us back that night. I have blacked out everything that's happened so far. I am told I meant lichen, back then. I am told, and I am retold.

A firm but good-natured display of anger.

She constructs a pretty strong rationale for a beating. The thing, the creature, remains without a name. And I say, let me not be driven hence upon the wall of burning coals. What do you want me to do about the head. She might hear if I am. Employ mine eyes, ready yourself. There is news of news—reported bloodbath in gatehouse. I survive to fail. I create a circle about me. I am a fanatic breathing space. It all seems so little rather late. I am continuing my researches into autology.

Erosion of soft surface strata in varied and fantastic forms. You look dazed, counterfeit—the spiritual type of celebrity. A lambent flame leaps across her tomb. I am experiment: these are your objects. Withdraw into the cramming room. I am not going back. In the popular sense I simply mean an absorption in oneself. A drawer slides out from the centre. These are your options. These are your opinions. Eat them up and go. There is no argument with bone.

He is left behind. He is busy naming foodstuffs. I refuse. I have been away these four years. I had once a thought and it left me. (Sullen crush of leather bag deposited on soft cushion.) You are not ready for my word. I am not draining my sap for you. My fur is clotted. We went up to the rain and we never returned. I am not yet remote among the alone. Today we are missing four million adult literates. The news say. I count out loud. There are eleven of us in the hold. I have been away this lunar month. I am still, I am steadfast. Therein is the book. The book is called the cell. They are synonymous. My cot is damp and incomplete. It is believed. The blanket is clammy. There is too much artifice containing these letters. Writing becomes impossible, yet remains irresistible. Forcing thoughts into an ordered sequence is a torment. This has been said elsewhere. Reports of early buskers loose in the colony.

She cannot stop clinging to things and remembers.

Now they too have abandoned. It's like a disease. Next time I shall use a steam contact-press. Next time I shall check that the electrodes are clean. In the log I record a luminous burr about the moon. I would not say influence, more guiding spirits found at salient junctures.

The first thing he sees on his release when he wakes in the garden is a dog tearing a rag-doll to pieces. The letter I informs me and me alone.

Apoplexy. Melt that ice in time. Swap the numbers around. This is an awful and embracing momentum. Sudden loss of sensation and motion is generally the result. I am expressing an incompleteness to strike. Isn't it strange how reputations come and go. An animal is pacing back and forth in the room above. The signal has me jump. Now it sits upright on its haunches. Improper conduct is spreading through our variants, any fish of the subclass, the incubus.

The subclinical.

The subastral.

The subdelirious.

Time for a baton charge. Hypnagogic estate—a journal, audio too—voice from the age, screwing out through the brainpan. Isn't it strange how repetitions come and go. Scratch for clues: abstract of mean cell, brittle acoustic of glass roof and brick tunnel. We are now excavating the pit (he stumbles into a dictaphone). I arrive with obsolete demeanour, what's known as a fairly short reign.

Pier down. By nightwork men prize gold sparks from twisted ribs. Nonplussed figure of green and amber light, standing.

She is no longer a description of herself. We will need very large hinges indeed. In mine expression lies an absence.

He is aged as eye. They have both had enough of my time.

She cannot believe we are made of electricity. The question is, does she have more than one segment to her. A stranger's look and bearing betray everything.

And again some. Coastal defence—theatre dark. To hear an actual voice out of the earth, what moment. The fare is four of your English pounds. (It's divining, isn't it?) You're a born survivor. I'm a born killer. We were made for each other. A point of light grows in the darkness. Adamantine guisers in capes and masks enter, left. They are notional, lacking in true substance. Collectively, a small article ingeniously devised but wanting a meaning of its own. Imagine you are making a film which is precisely like being in the world. The object seems to say to us I am here. I don't have time. Insane machines are shown scribbling across the floor—projected light and dust particles, decomposing vegetation. (Danger of sudden drop behind bar.) A sign says. A concept in the mind has the various marks and qualities of objects, yet remains unfounded. We need an improper. It will nodoubtedly be afternoon before we reach the end. There is a disused well full of flesh and animal parts—tangled paws, the lip of a jaw, that kind if thing. We need an impostor. To the angel I write I am not ready. The others are a caprice of whim. A stretcher is made from scaffolding and tank tracks. I don't know what else to say—I am filming daylight, nothing more. Things are said in the present and in the past. A generation is skipped, some residual faces—same physiognomy, same nerves. An ironing out and blandishment takes place. The contractile curtain is perforated. Flickerbook pages sere the iris. The image congeals. The old inner diction is back. Kodak tantra. I have ended.

A number is given to each of his companions, a complete catalogue of the dull work in hand.

He is blinded by a burnt-orange flare. I am compiled by secession. How confusing. Sly strands navigate the throat. Something collides with the skull, strikes back at the head. By the middle of the next year he is completely.

She goes through chaos to wring these memories out of herself. She is alive and she is dead. I was not strictly born myself (it's very hard discussing detail with my architects). Fallow tracks in the fresh-fallen ash. Something strikes out at the base of the heel. It has three toes. How long were you up there on your own two feet. I thought we were going back to that ruined city. Now I feel human again. We're taking our time with the exhumations. Is that the side of the square we are talking about. I am closing in. There is heat—I mean the surrounding air—crumbling plaster and spray legends, a perspex shield battened against the tide. They're planning to swoop right through us. Heavy band about skull, biting into forehead. Lac resin laid in thin plate. The crime is forgery, the conveying of a memory that was false. Silence is my domain.

I have come to the close of a sentence and I expect a response.

The secondary feathers are still attached to the wing. (This is a real classic of remote sensing.) Eyes sunk and watery, afloat in their orbits, lips curled back in puzzled rictus. That black stain is caused by contact. This is thanksgiving night.

Cease when incomplete. I am myself conceived in terms of solid limbo. I grant undeserved privilege. I have severed my remaining strut. Anxiety leaches from distraction. In itself this is not a painful process. I have inert rings held in reserve. Embedded in the wall are capsules of the family form, glass resisting fluid. We splinter, iron-poor. Again, I have nothing to say about the plan I'm weaving. Where next is my sentence to lie. Do we have a plot of time. Take my arm, the axle. We anticipate a weird ending. (Unless, you appear to be.) It's like tying stones together and letting the world sink because it's too good to bear. Here comes the first awkward moot between all four of us.

First rudiment, formerly of the heart. A generation has to be repeated. The amulet was in use as far back as the dynasty. It's my job to sit here and do nothing and then write about it. Being thought estranges one. Several generations are measured and found to be concentric. What colour gasmask did you wear back then.
I mean cajolery, above, where I refer to lichen.

Flatlands. Spooks démarche, sheltering under the slab of a quoit. A moon is hung above the prehistoric mound. Small semiotic fort on the horizon. As we approach it grows in scale. A miracle. I am not ourselves.
Their resistance forces us to remain a further six months. Such a turret proves difficult to capture. See shellac (the word, not the stuff). I digress. See, the hour of parleying is still dangerous.
A crouched figure enters the theatre of war. He scuttles up to the portcullis, crabwise on pincers. He is rigorously denied any individual initiative. A hostile landing is augured. His progress is scathed by a sequence of tiny events. This is not inconsistent. Things are this way because there is no more convincing work to be done.
I void. The grove is so named from its not shining. Things are running out, fluxed of memory. Influence by scatter.
Bumper crop. Psychosystemic. This is one of our favourite moves. A long period of rest is followed by exquisite defecations. This is where. This is where things begin to follow a strict pattern of sound: charts of phase in the moon—the shattered family limb, fallow windings of the shore with my spirit spilling out et cetera. To the north lies a pit in the shape of a giant letter W. And yet I am still. Take this, take it, with all my subsidiary compositions.
They are entering and they are leaving, last dregs of epiphany. It is happening exactly as one speaks.

Get a rip on yourself. The artefact on display is a torso fragment. I am now a much wider volume of echo. They arrest the third man. There is a special chamber reserved for purpose. I spy with mine own eye, something forever beginning. According to him there is no such place as place: the rusty wave, the limestone shingle, the brittle clearing–map. Relax he says it's just the screen. We are ten minutes from the fracture zone. (O dark-bordered beauty.) A deep core has been sunk well below my line of fire. Today's exercise demonstrates the art of hanging a man. Note the corresponding jewel-head moth. It's said the alchemist requires a mate to succeed. If you start out young it's not too bad. You sit, you don't work very hard, and you never meet people you have to talk to. You don't make a fortune.

Compare: he is ornament, nothing more, wrestling on the summer lawn between the helices of sprinkler jets. He is a point that fades in the dark. Ask yourself precisely. How do people herein speak. He is so much straw. He is found inkless when you invert the image. I repeat all this from heresy. It's how you approach the problem that counts. Who here could be the chosen medium?

One town resists for a similar stench of time a cannonade. Tombs, monuments and palaces are razed. You see, I have not come all this way for you alone, unstable as rotting timber, with all its wheels of year. Those gamma readings are wrong. This is the beginning of a new life. The human eye and brain cannot alter so in a matter of weeks.

We discover we're a type of gas, sportwave radio flux. He is represented by an empty chair. All historical events are caused by sunspot activity. The twenty-one centimetre hydrogen boundary is critical. It's a matter of life in death. I have built a device which detects rays and can reproduce parts of the body. To the east lies an S-shaped pit. The stones are the dismantled cairn that once held the note.

This should all have come much later. Here he is at his most ironic.

Checkmatey. Summon fuel division to frontier.

A riverside forest periodically flooded.

Semiautomatic gas operated clip-fed .30 calibre.

That is all. Evidently they did not receive our last message.

Nonage. Unreliable fauna. Deep kelp, broadfingered weed under swell. I was found dumped at the narthex of a basilica. Alongside my wicker creel is her book of dying well, tossed beyond the rail: make himself clean in your blood and bathe in your gore et cetera. She is inscience manifest—a straw doll with wings, with topknot and clubfoot.

He is inscribe. Descending leaves bristle through the funnel of a nearby tree. Stunt doubles that I am radio. I am held overnight. The phonetic charge is resisted by disassociation. My own eye is now under the magnifying lens: beetle armory in the shape of an elliptic shield. We recur at the stations of happenstance. Our wings are raised. We are well before the last here. He is inscribed self of self—winged, but before the last moult. The imago is unpredictable. Everything's going to be all right.

I've just glimpsed someone else's hand stretching across the green baize. I hereby release myself from the family bend. I reel on sliding fixtures. I am unyoung.

You cannot accommodate. You do not admit. I have not journeyed all this way just to consume with you. I am characterized by use of the steel toecap and the volume of my capital. I have relinquished so much: the national distrust, my genuflecting staff. By the way, I forgot to say, consider this a spectacular peace, wherein writing is a crime. What you cannot forgive is the unsettling: a shady alcove with walls, windows, and a roof. Why should I change it for you.

Veneer of lack. Thought so. But you have the correct cast of mind my friend. He formerly occupied land (his travels are arrested by platonism and the others). Water, again, admits of a division into two kinds. You have the right to remain silent. He is the element of retaliation, whereas I am the enacted event. I am tightly bound beneath myself. Laws are established by which we can pass through one another—early souls closing in, loping heads under an alkaloid hub. I hang up-so-down from thick ecclesiastic ropes. Tiny sparks glow in the dark and then fade, nuances of orange and red, recurrent patterns of fever in the retina. Unacknowledged quotidians. Sephiroth pour down from the pier and into the waves. I piss blood. My dissent has an ancient pedigree.

Separatrix.
And the woman's very large bones have been reinforced with iron and copper strips. She wants the root and the aerial, everything. Lips dry and blistered, I'm feeling a little esoteric myself. I sustain compression at the centre. If this destroys the myth what becomes. Go well into love, my sleep, with calcined ash of sea. There's a deal of information in these forces, the inscribing harrow you gift me. She declares herself metronome, still-born and stiller of breath. Gone—glanced beyond, well beyond our ken.

Drear father in his fuddlescan, with scattermouth.
Self-plagiarism is style. Given a choice I will always choose obscure, because I can. Recite current usurpation and residence of place. I'm an internal convulsionary. Each word is a discrete domain, possibly, tantamount to risk.

Help. It's the nation. It is slower than usual and shuffles in silence. I have numbered—at least an hundred thousand thousand of them, each corresponding to one of my transfiguring norms. We have encountered.
A strange meeting in an ear-like atrium.
Just below the main sequence now. I am plural of not and less luminous than dwarf stars of the same temperature. She resembles a garden ornament of sinister influence. Two large veins enter her right oracle. I've positioned myself at the point of minimum cross-section. I have a terrible dream and outcry. A jet of fluid discharges from the hole. One hundred thousand, hence the teeming lack of insect.
Anyway, I ask her what the primordial constitutive principle of the quantum peal is. I am inert, compacted within the outer. Link is all. Link is all to a barrel

projection, the tectonic sheath. I am not here. I have landed and there is no going back. Natives drum from the thicket that fringes the river. I am the sting in the tail. The middle toe of the right foot is missing. I'm afraid of nothing. Such feeble times. We have not had a decision for years. I can no longer work my shadow. Knowledge is only useful as it passes through me.

Spectral face projected at study window. Within, semblance of her crossing chamber to bureau. We are kneedeep in something serious.

And as we walk he says no I refuse to be symbolled. There is nonesuch. Things are what they are.

First breath of seasonal chill in these parts. An unbroken zero hovers above his desk. I feel slightly guilty listening in on all of this.

Disc low in plain of sky. This happens every year. I cannot guarantee my surface for months on end. That mediaeval cist is of doubtful origin. Random neglect is resulting in damage. Repulsed and spurned: the frozen glove, the even colder shoulder. Retinal afterimage.

The cleft stick spins out my hand, flinging off strands of clotted hair. For her, words are a vehicle for ideas and contempt. I retrieve the divining-rod. Touch gently.

Eustachian tube glued together by mucus. I open the rudimentary valve at the entrance of the inferior. A pyromantic skullcap is visible beneath her armour.

I am loss. There is a condition of possibility to which one has remained blind. A series of black rings retreats into the distance. He works fire with muddled charm—life through a weight of paper, through the darkly glass: top theatrics in a risky plastic wrapper. There has never been a complex situation happening at the same time. My storage is closing down. Put your legs away. Basically, I am the simplest phenomenon imaginable. Surrounding footfalls are sliding away. A regular arrangement of seven hundred tins had been piled into a pyramid about two metres high.

So there's that dynamic. They did put up a pretty robust defence. There was a competitive environment going on. Was that forecast true. Now we are securely at anchor. She turns away from the sextant. We disembark our flat-keel vessel and skirt the coastline on foot. We speak about time past, the remembrance. She turns her attention to the wound. It has been improperly cauterized. (One should never keep souvenirs of a disaster.) We are looking out over a seascape. I shield my remaining eye. She says we've spent years striving to synchronize. Now it is night and the waves are milky. How rapid things change, so sudden the appearance. Two circles she mistakes for a pair of close-set moons. There are stars in the sky, men on the groynes beneath night—chanting, lighting fires. Writers have granted favours indiscriminately throughout the century, verifiable sources of fermentation. I guess.

136

Her aim is to recapture the south. The lips I motion, mouthing and hum-bling—false etymologies. I should leave. Sun now eclipsed relative to moon by vast body of dark. Landfall is out of the question. A cooler passage of moving air suddenly rushes against my body. Throughout the whole spectrum I am still said to exist (from foam to slime). I suspect it all comes down to the permanent auction of space that's been going on around here. What has been passing through all these years. Attention exists someplace between discretion and vanity. She demands a personalized sense of the present.

A tube leads to the cavity of the middle ear. A maxim, an aphorism, follows. Give account of this.

I am a borrowed form of later. Ecstatic melancholy. The shape is square with a decayed centre. Those bunches of flax must be the work of a disembodied. She says the world will not end if you miss the mouth. Note the perspective, from which all is aesthetic consumption, never preconscious impulse, semiferal and uniquely damned.

Lack lies unsteady in thin plates—melted seed rising to drop. And where are your own memories, this last decade of the day. It's only in retrospect that I see how abject was that time: rhexis, rupture and muscle spasm, unearthly rapid recall, nightsweat pit for a bed. Now I am equalizing the pressure principle on either side of the eardrum. The name is forgot. One of these organisms can grow without oxygen. (Guess.) I can attribute this event to a specific period, a period to which no one belongs. She is the bloody pelt. She is the promised eustasy.

Out come the pistols. One final glance back. The subject was once a pioneer-ing surgeon. (New film mediocre though murders gruesome.) Think of a man who's going to commit suicide and nothing else matters. Now you get the idea. I am a back formation in which time is dialled. Blood pulps at the inner ear. The scent of lighter fuel wafts across the leafy terrace. We sit beneath an ivy buttress sipping turkish coffee. It is night yet warm. We deliver up the stairwell. I fear sleep. Watch closely her pale face. (Basically, still tempest.) I am permanently overlaid with a thin sheet of substance. Strip off veneer and bury under house.

About the bare bulb is a moth frantic from its markings. I too am of a tense, used without the implication of time to express a general truth. I arrive always early in your sense. Earlier still at the shoreline. Earlier than the original form. Earlier than the word used for the thing expressed.

True. O yes it will. Indeedy it has. It has a stop.

It has put a stop to itself.

Stop.

We kept it on floats with exploding charges, the europium element. Once, we set out under cover in commercial boats. Think I got up to about this point. There were dozens in port, mostly fishing craft with nets. It is quite late. We find some signs. The state of the economy is apparent at a glance: a battered lead funnel, shell buttons common in the early and mid, an underused stick, a casket, a clay pipe stem like those carried, human remains, desiccated excrement. Perhaps he says a web of lines links these artefacts. I find myself back in the fiction room. We are legal, us. And what about the undeniable symmetry out there? All these swarming times and places. Nail down my lid, please. All our favourite madrigals are here. I'm exhausted. About the papered wall hang stilled lives, denatured dead—drapery with antlers broad and flat, the bulbous waterjug, the second tergal plate of an insect's thorax. This area is alarmed. Small blisters form on the mucous membrane. I stretch out my body from shoulder to sole. Once, if memory severs me right.

A plaque, such as any deserted region. Well, there are human voices—tissue culture viewed through a prism. He says it's good. It's good but it's not brilliant. There are cracks and strange shadows. It seems you've become one of us—the local, the unhomely.

We have a penchant for ruins. We spend time. He's fascinated by the geometries of the causeway and other sundry objects. The headpiece is kaleidoscopic, a caul of mirrors. He is conducted. His festival is added to the calendar. He is inscaped. He is inspirited—adrift, with implied violence. Sleep is linked with death in the inscriptions.

Our young legal tyro chews hard on the wad of tobacco in his mouth. He is a moot-man forever pleading the hypotheticals. An uneasy corollary emerges. (It was then a new movement.) A vast shadow moves under him. He is always alone. We have extracted and dried his perennial sac. Also shavings of hart's horn, leg fragments.

Gestation is repeated, recoiling in a bivalve shell. Something has tiptoed through the silt that lies deep at my doorstep. There was flood, you see. That object at auction, it's the arm of a sundial. Men were deceivers, ever then.

To make a fresh start, evidently we have $x = d/D$. You have the right to silence the remains. Behold the line separating light and shade on a partly illuminated surface (see terminator). These are surprising gaps in knowledge.

Of a glassman's supplementary hearth.

The things are formed in moulds—patches of eruption, or the like. An organ producing interference zones by pairs of flames in a tube has been invented. Sound is recorded on a small board, generally heart-shaped, supported by two castors and a pencil. There is an obstruction of tone in the singing, a slight want of clearness. The veil of motive always means a ruined voice, the speech rhythms of a hunger. The current is set into action by the influence of the surrounding magnetic field, by the fluctuations of anyone adjacent. There is a time limit within which he must appear, and reply. A film of saliva is forming in the road. Don't open any of those seven doors. That's all I can say.

Dorian mode. That early moment when method fleetingly works. I am now in retreat across the peninsula. A winding path leads back to the birthplace. He imagines I have people to talk. On arriving, I place a coin on his slab. He navigates the track above the town by some preconscious impulse. It's puzzling how all these sounds can still rise up from him: the creak of the keel, the clink of the glass vials in his pocket, the murmur of a litany. There's a plinth up on deck dedicated to memory. (Do you know what is an inversion.) The two lowest notes are separated by a hole. All reckoning is in a downwards direction—a solemn and simple quality that circles through the alphabet from letter d back to letter b, with d representing finality. He has given each moment a title. The shapes are my own choosing.

e for the linear diameter of the cloud.

D for its distance away from us.

V for its velocity of approach.

T for the time required for it to reach our solar system.

Send in your suggestion. I have stopped functioning. I have ceased, fascination. This is the famous instant, the residual fog of letters. Now I am back in time again, with overhung catastrophe.

Rattle of tympani at chimney level. As always these things start out with rigour and then collapse. Acts three and four run together.

Nigredo: sandblast tangle from a furnace of molten glass. This is placed in the hearth with a string of faery light and a single gold ingot. I am coming together, under the shadow of a suddenness, evermore violence. There is no space between. We once dwelt, a possibility which always underestimates itself. Those forms are not us. I might read out loud a passage or two. I need a little structure like I need a little hell. This type of dripstone funnel is called a fogou. It is dank to the skin, dank to the nostril. Our diver sits waiting in the survival cell. He embraces his factotum one last time.

She says we are with beginning and with middle and with end. Where is this place.

Deny the conditions and move on, continue and resist.

Smell of damp earth—moss, lichen and rough-hewn rock. I have resistance. Some of the capsules have been reinforced with plastic spikes. In the dust lies the claw of a reptile or bird of prey, bleached white, residual feathers still clinging. (The structure is a tomb, after all.) Your existence is not a haven for meaning. Don't worry, I won't scar—the water's too shallow. You cannot afford to become the story. She has the ability to start fires by thought alone.

A glimpse forward to Situation XXXIII, the last. Exclusions and irregulars. I use chance to assist my discomposure. For why matter is beyond understanding?

The knowledge of a name implies dominion over the being to which it is attached. Your tongue has stuck to your palate. If anything else comes along, you must understand that it will be pursued. You are called to account. A sign bearing a gigantic eye swings back and forth at the corner of the building. We are the two remaining characters, alive on stage.

The mound of withered metals on the shingle. A box of rust, outwritten. Asbestos picnic with random shelling, charred planks—centuries of radiation leaching from the bedrock. They dwell in the staircase: misremembered forebears, unregenerate human nature. The heap of sodden box.

We are the spine of the forensic curriculum. We go bootless. We have no personal belongings, bar clothing. He will make quite a reasonable target. By the way, that noise is the rumoured mort of praxis—sequential absence, the negligence of writing.

He reveals that it is showtime by the position of his shadow.

A saxophone at wail, the sweeping out of a curve from the tip of a growing axis.

Sly but cheery. That flickerbook cocoons a single word. It's a life performance. Fitful plucking moments as in delirium—shallow sheets of water draining off the island. She is still alive. A readjustment is taking place.

Less of him remains this time. A parallelogram has been cut using his corners as a template. He wears an icon collar once used for punishment. Other artefacts and tools sit within this tiny aperture. Retreat as rapidly as possible. He wears a tongue welt, everything spilled out, deep scratches across forehead—eye trading glimpse of overlapping disc. Crushed leathery skin is exhumed from the gravel. Mould glistens about the rim of a waterlogged cardboard box. I should retreat from this place as soon as possible.

A column is used to observe the meridian altitude. This is a piece of much greater tautness. I am making a study of its separate elements.

Gentle vapour rising from sea. I am writing for performance. First frost of the old millennium, night's clearing house. My hands are relished. I miss the discipline of past lives—retrograde planets and reincarnation. A floating piece of spine keeps brushing against my body in the water. It's been dead a long time. I appoint myself straw-gatherer general, a sinecure if ever there was. Beneath the surface is a rusted shopping troll.

Deathsaid mot. From indicator, from How.

Descrive the site.

Restraining ions. I am neither nor, unclaimed gnosis—gross national product, gunner. Crane with oxide crest. Your reclaiming ghost.

Inshell.

A drystone circular tower of the late age. The men are building a dead straight wall. The structure is atom. Lightnings rifle, flush-flash. A factotum lets drop the lid. I am verbatim. Things are always done well in the kitchen (a finale of sorts, with knives). Now for the imprudent, the victim or the object lost. Let yourself go in shorthand. Unlock the key to plate eight, with circle and loop phases of the moon, life sentences. He will do as his sister says. It is as fine a day as ever I was. He has his own way and leaves for good. Paradoxically, slow can be quicker than not. I move without will, without limit, sick at heart of these many-futured things. They have mistimed him.

He finds himself flung forward to Situation XXII, spiralling toward an empty hollow, into which he disappears. He is quarked. When gazing up into the night sky, imagine you're actually looking straight *down* into a chasm. It is my belief. The same effect can be reproduced ritually—I mean the person or thing sacri-ficed. Radioactive material has been introduced. By the way, that's an even num-ber pinned to your scalp, hence luckless. You're a star. Don't be alarmed. My voice is slurred by insensibility. That concrete depression is called a saltpan. The creature snared at its rim wears a pelt of ash-cloth. Note the prickly seedcase attached to its head. Note the tiny box of voice at the jugular. Close by are scorchmarks representing me in wood. The location is about eight. I've been upsetting people all my life.

The office of the sixth hour.
She writhes. She is obsessed with apology. Her body is smothered with mor-phine patches. The colour of her skin is a warning. We are far distant from any sign I know of. The locals measure and tally misconception (I am a word, not dissimilar). I am never going to stop. This particular story may have died. I am the knot in the stinky thread. What did she do unto you he somehow whispers.

He heals himself in spite of the gravity. He administers me. The third explo-sion triggers thermite positioned beneath the big transceiver. Hot metal is allowed to flow into the mould. It fills the gap between its two parts and forms a collar around them, so making a distinct emblem. I have no idea (vertigo).
There is a wonderfully humane interpretation carved into the cornerstone. From the man's side grows a heavy pouch of yeast. (I think I'd like to do that too, when I feel ready for it.) At length the day comes when he utters his last, the Jupiter. Did I write this.

Snake swallows horse. Galleries have been set into the thickness of the coun-terscarp. This helps. You don't deserve me. People like to reveal things. Go back and seek voice. She is wearing the now-familiar welding goggles. Strapped to her forehead is a nightlamp, piercing through the mist—surrounded by watchers, knees capped.
Shadow of gull strutting at glass ceiling. Knit back. Off, and silence. Memory serves me right, salient in opposite directions.

Copter stunned by sky. Face upturned to nearest star, in hand, paperbook embossed by eclipsed sun. The blades cease and vanish. That leaves the sea, image-breaker and congener.

You can tell who wears the welding goggles around here. Smooth-yeared the rump of wood fits snug the nest of my cavity. She has arranged for padded levers to be installed about the cube. Carved with skill around its walls are a line of stylized trees, a reverbatory furnace, a series of elaborate knots, an iron age-mound, and concentric canals encompassing a sunken island. Inside an ampulla a homunculus comes wrapped in a protective blister. The heart is weighed in the balance. Some paint flakes still adhere to the underside. All in all, a dilated end. What would happen if we just sat here in the silence.

Up to her neck in fluid, an opera within an opera. We shall see.

A cave crammed full of ancient. Item one: the receiving sprocket of polished bone. He sends her a message from beneath the arch, angelic upstar.

I have held back.

If you call me that one more time I shall put your head through that window.

At last she says there is this weird machine on the message. (Aerial is among my favourite words.) The man with grey hands is a simile of sorts. I am piercing him together from the extant, each of several teeth broken on a wheel.

A seemingly unbridgeable gulf.

I am engaged within the links of a chain. So unlove to talk this eve, separate at close of day, when the law breaks.

Holes in film or tape or paper record the event. I cherish distance.

She is pit of bloodfibre.

Sidekick into pack of time.

Keep this para. Maybe I should pick myself up. It looks to be a filter made of dripstone—acid mantle, spittle and serum. I make an experiment: find your ancestors in fourteen days. Revelation or not? Where does the public hangman live around these parts? I can't help it. I cannot help myself. Do I hear voice. The hypothetical particle travels faster than light. She asks again and again. I pretend I am type, something set off-centre at the T-clasp—very large bipedal flesh. I was born into this.

To people is to frame the voice. I am obliged to sacrifice a kinsman to close a vendetta. No one notices. (That is why I put the machine on.) The outside has altered imperceptibly. You may come, but he probably won't speak to you. Please let him move forward.

He takes the uncarved marble and begins to hew it on the landing. A bare bulb is the light. Unfamiliar tongue in the mouth, sudden clasp of hand to shoulder. I have entered the moon's orbit. Take yourself off to a little corner of the darkest continent. Now imitate the whistling of an arrow. See what happens in those final bars. See what happens next. Cling firm. If it has the blue pencil scored through it, it's done for. The spell to be recited begins I am Thoth. That's the signal for a gap.

Cache-sexe. A piece of antimatter—in the case of the nerve, reversed magntic polarity (not as yet discovered). Every opening is rapid in zero weather, i.e. a manufactory. Only months after writing this music he is dead himself.

Homespun body, with signals thickening at half-pace, with piecemeal mouth. It tracks you down, the old godness in things, under the form of an absence. Small clawlike forelimb.

Homeromastix.

A delicate inner membrane envelopes the engine and the spinal cord. The content of these histories is necessarily opaque. I am this catalogue of hints and counterhurt. I am cutting myself down but I am not giving it up. No respect is due to any forerunners.

Tongue thrust from mouth, at the crest of the hill swings a hanged one. Secured to his forehead is the shed deer horn. An ants' nest is strung about his neck. He wears a femur bone. Jism spatters the causeway beneath the gibbet. A light goes on in the stairwell. There's five stages to this. (Tender mother is mistranslated.) You are still young despite the years, despite the vacuum. Do not leave or you will not remember.

The coronet of an antler.

An inverted rainbow.

The pattern, just above the coffin-bone enclosed in the hoof.

Glory-hole of a fragile gridiron.

We are about to cut the coloured wires and are guessing. We are separated by a distance equal to half the wavelength of the oscillation. Compare the one who is standing beside me, he who refuses to leave and is packed full of time.

Synopsis.

The first era ends with an earthquake. This will be those ordinary people now.

Sunday. Wrote two more pages of my life, about that time in the pasteboard shanty. Distant clarion of the mort. I am unconvinced of this chapter's veracity. Analyse and discuss. Yes it's like a horse. Yes, you are your own sense of disorder, hard-won—science fictions as a bunch of history.

Travails in the old country. This is better than my thought. We have reached his infamous refusal to describe. Everything becomes a struggle. They exhume his remains. They reanimate him and sit him in a chair. The amulet is probably intended to represent an organ of the human body. Use is very ancient. Repeatedly they demand the equation.

My screen was divided into three columns of aquamarine light. Blood gushed through me. I think it's your turn now to pay something back, in time.

He has the answer written on his face. There's a development to the south. The sky turns red. He refuses to cooperate further and we leave through the wicket gate. Pools of brackish water kneedeep cover the ground. He returns to the platform with a compromise, a little more for the audience. He is poised. He was generated blank. Do you know where is the body room they ask. He is all lip and no tongue. What if he doesn't like the film, then what.

A cached form. Your head it simply swirls. This has few if any sequels.

She is busy saying goodbye to someone. There is unclaimed eating, much random consumption going on in the background.

Up there I meant miscued.

I am to be shut down. Now we have a couple of problems. One, another girl in the neighbourhood. Two, a pack of nervous viewers, remotes. Number one is the past, memories of a cask of mistaken identity. She always had a candle out for you—not from the meanings of words but for the sound of them. Don't talk to me about pain. Move your frozen body distant from the holding bay. Number two is the future. I want to withhold. I make an experiment using a planchette, tracery in the frazil-ice—a scheme that relies on divination by the yelps of wounded dogs.

There is always some fresh demand to include everybody. The rules are determined by the throwing of knuckle bones. This is my best hand yet. You are an uncannily quiet audience. The rules are determined by observing the cracks that form on a tortoise shell when it's cast into a fire. (That sound is a violin sonata.) I cannot move my limbs—what evidence, new lees of life. I don't think the forms will change again. And here is the woman who won back the day.

I am reviewed in terms of downforce: tracks of decay, hallowed brick with occult geometries, strange women who do not die. You see, I've dealt with numbers all my life. I embed myself in a nearby clump of matter: the solitary copse from the fleeting window. Another lays down beside me. We're positioned head to toe, toe to head, as if a composite grave. At last I have found someone at more or less the same stage of deconstruction. A man squats at the rim of our pit, sketching for posterity.

Dull, distant crash pursued by of shadow across forepart of skull. These people are dragging you down. The centre keeps absorbing time—sinew attached to muscle, barren of cause. (Now I hear they're freezing an ice-rink for an odyssey.) When I write I try to do everything wrong. Opus one hundred and nine is not to be confused with his opus ten. He does not sound as though he's in the form of his life. I want to become immortal like him.

Redress self and draw breath. Necessarily isn't so. He is neither orthodox or consistent in his use of the words were and where and womb. I spied a domino in my head when at first you spoke of it, the thing of the film. This is surely an act of deliberation. I can never remember numbers. Can I have some change please. How many men are here right now (eight the last I knew). I can never remember letters. This is written with a lack of purpose, a project for nailing down a set of ancestors in the flesh. Grant cessation to mind and withdraw to innermost keep. I am a declared shaker.

He's now one of the elect. This is the chapter of the opening of the mouth of the statue. Take primary readings and quit surface. Keep log and observe.

Crystals forming on bed.

Cinders floating in the grey water.

Counter-salient.

The drip of a taphead. This artifice is not so well behaved, an overlong fugue. The first head had plumes of smoke rising from it. I am the branch with its causeless quiver. We will not freeze. I am being embedded: antimimesis, no legacy of past ambition. The participants come to blows. I bear a close external semblance to my animal. No doubt we could have counterstruck a few edicts, too. Time has wasted away. The second head was like that of a man. I bear close external semblance to my plantlife. To enable eavesdrop I have been bent to a fresh angle. I bear close external semblance to the inanimate. This all sort of adds up.

Scraps of paper, a record of the chase after those spectral lines. Hundreds of fermentation units—the outer wall of a bastion. You peer into his eye: retinal image preserved at the moment of death (the slope of a fortification ditch). He can be read like an expansive and confiding letter, long walk out at bank et cetera. He is wrong-side up. Achieve something. Muscle in with fresh bodies, fresh ideas. The word is rolling. It would be good to get this out of the way once and forlorn. At the threshold is a tiered platform. How did you feel back in the nineteenth, with your replica following you about, habitual mimic?

A heavy lung supported on castors.

A pencil that writhes, supposing spirit.

Fingers feathered, lightly.

Now we have someone who requests a name, barking through green corridors. Stink of infectant. Piece me together on the ground, point me to a direction, and I'll walk—a long walk, the long walk out at bank. He scratches spirals on a head mounted at pivot, talking (a duck head of translucent blue glass). What an audience. That's the sum total of my reformations and my flexions. The rules are determined by the throw of carpal bones. Please me please on that dull refuse of ground.

More on my quiddity. He has made his home in that creature's abdomen. Neural tics recur to about here. A concert for one page appears in the phonebook. Do you know any of these verses at heart (art thou conceal art). Now saw the lid off his head. Revealed: partition for voice, severed. Just do what you usually do, then leave.

The plot involves a series of murders. People die in mysterious circumstances or disappear. This continues till three fifths of the way through the story—at which point the audience starts to retrace its steps, murder by murder, whereupon each is found not to be a homicide. These people simply died of accident or vanished. Once the final victim is accounted for the close reveals an emptiness, a nothingness. Nothing has happened and nothing ever did and nothing ever will and this is the whole point: the evolution of nothing.

These days I am rare in the south. We approach by sea, self elated, the rest puking into paperbags. I doubt they will ever resume the abandoned work. Writing happens to me.

Elaborate counterpoint. Bleaching rhizome, ghost of kelp. The unsightly holy. There is no longer anymore. You do not need to revise the skin. Consider a segmentable line broken down into types. She commemorates my eclipse. I am everyday. The valve is a simple song, mother-simple.

Tonight we're contemplating the luminous ring about the satellite. We are using the X-ray sampler. At what time does dark fall through around these parts.? This is a reckoning, I fancy, with the outcome that I am not. The emotional centre will be the lover. Therefore direct your feeling, sense, reason, and thought upon this salt alone. An exotic bird or mammal is buried inside. I am abandoned as overvoice. Burrstone.

Probably cloud settling into disc.

Eidola.

I travel far and wide with my translator. I am pursuing my terrifying theme of the supernatural. My weapons are the centrifuge and a length of wire with tufts of fabric twisted into it. I have managed to force my way back in. The last three oxidized bullets sit in my lower chamber. He does not respond to my threats. The rest of his party leaves through the wicket gate. He is such a person that one meets, and later forgets that one has met. (This post has only been given to you as a personal favour.) This is when things start to hinge out in a bad way. Who or what withstood? Answer, the persistent image of a sword nailed to a cathedral wall. (And to think I once ruled as chancellor.) The scabbard is lacquered and gilt. I must eat. Stop. Tonight you talked for a thousand years. And to think I ruled, once, right here at this very spot.

Closer.

The coronet of an antler. Check this. I am returning to the genuine article. Curious links to pier—answerphone angelology, a domino effect. Just do as they say. Consider his crafty acausal life sentence: a series of dead moves penetrating tender meat. Introjection, the alien within settled on shifting sands. Atrophy of kinship—roof slates raining down from the penitentiary.

Jet fighter and copter cursing ghostline. Another twelve-year gap is in the offing. The dictation has stopped. Stirrings of smoke—the hack of control. I miss him.

Chrysler in my paperweight. Those pretty little seerside ghouls. It's smooth, cold to touch. There are no troughs or peaks in the graph: the flat-liner experience. These are all my conversions. And when did you last see your fathers.

He finds himself trapped between two wells of glass. He is truly. He is a constant, the genuine property called forth. He is acutely adjusted. I saw him only the once and he is straight and flat. He is cognitive, but fated to misplace his lucky lexicon. His spine cracks and splits open. A tiny disc of titanium slips out. Everything is back to normal. He is nomad. He agrees with the fact, actual and absolute. He is correctable, an enumeration of the useless. He is as accurate as can. He exacts. He is dead in tune after the ancestral type, now exhaust. Pace out the cell, edit and reconcile. Gnaw deeper than the workaday cut. Everyone feels years again.

Six fruitless seasons pass us by. I recall the glimpse, the general texture. Suddenly there's clarity, a film of floating organs and gems—jagged-toothed and manycoloured. He wears a hooded cape, black resin like the soil itself. I do not know where most of the books are buried. You are no saint yourself.

This fragment was found in the grave of a labourer. Luminous electric discharge poured from the head as we lifted the lid. It's such an amazing story, us sitting there in the grid—now we huddle here, at the hub of a defensive ring. Leave it just like that, free from fog or veil until the last. You cannot win.

Take one metre of stolen magnesium from pataphysics. Link up the layers and ignite. Extend this to some other species. The crisis apparitions are to be modified following the paschal moon. They do not like to be watched while building their cells. (Sorry, typographic error.)

Counterspy shooting range—the pylons, the smokestacks, the flatness. The end point of anything. Lidlock my eyes, scuttling down the rust chute. A man's name is written in the water, with meaning influenced by air.

A labelled mast at a museum of murmuring. Wispy traces of lead. Dread harmonies. What might be called forth. He is pointless of word, a minute aperture. He is itinerant, salted away in the shoredrift. Optic nerve fibres radiate.

If it has the blue vein shot through it's done for. Loveth him or his representative. Take yourself apart in the opening mouth of the father. And us just sitting there in the gridiron, waiting. That's the signal for a gap, the spot where existence ends, the clash at the rainbow.

Gematria.

Set up the spirit level, separate and dictate. Move outfar across plateau and creep back into hole. Pinion.

The strata are veined with threadlike capillaries. The stones are vanished. He harbours coincidence, the illusion of norms. It is enough to kill. There was once a lot of jubilance on the network—shadow remotes, disc and eclipse, very much rising stars at this time of times. Up, and atom. The kleps have broken in. To be honest, I don't think it makes a lot of difference. If only I could sleep.

He has himself strapped to the mast during an electrical storm—doctor body, or other. The development of meaning here is puzzling. All courses and methods have hitherto been failures. Lights may be suspended. All eight verses are set into the landscape. He is klepht, like me, a ghost-word from mishearing of equals.

I too. I, sal volatile.

Way below the surface of the surrendered material the influence of mercury is evident. Veins of melted candle wax scar my inside flank. (And what if a bear comes along.) According to him there is no such place as thing. His genus absorbs and tolerates: condensation trails, big sun, big sea, big sky—a glimpse, the aftermage.

Perhaps it's all about space after all. Damaged goods. I'm talking on my feet now, the act or time of seeing. I think what we've got here is a singularity: a kidney-shaped void with rudimentary hind toe. Look how relatively smooth his spectrum is. I think what we've got here is anti-hereditary. No demonstration is possible. Someone has left a terse message: sick in transit, gloria—anima Monday. Come quick come quick as she would always sway.

One is dancing to death, the other has opened up one too many of the portals.

A brief account of a similar experience. This time the subject is awake. Local gravity is dragging at the soles of your feet. That's a good idea, a series of pictures and events in the mind of a sleeping one. Men like you were once glad to wait at my door.

Corposant.

Patron saint of sail.

Coeurdelion.

XIII

Situation the twenty-ninth. I wish to dedicate this assay, gradually bring all my everything back. He secretes. Arms bone.

Now it's the day before yesterday. One on horseback rides out to parley with the adversary. He steps forth into the present. He steps forth into the past. Yours is a more workaday courage.

At the same time a physician comes from the nearby town to pay off the judge. I am subject to such rotations.

See how we begin by sketching crude narrative outlines. An orthodox cross painted on the far wall echoes the more elaborate cruciform I am conjuring from nothing. Fade out the picture into blankness, the blanker the better. Nothing should touch the sides. One day soon he will bite into the offered hand that feeds.

The shell of a fractured jaw. Come quick. The promised retreat is underway, an after-glimpse thereof. There's one more septet to come, then it's goodnight Vienna. He is unlocked. Reflection is evident on every page. People have been saying there is no time here, see. What the dickens.

See. A trial cut. A trial by hot wax poured into the incision. I'll settle for a little dose of plague. He skims off the top of the head.

A glass cabinet with two internal chambers, containing as intelligent a programme as we're ever likely to meet. Don't offer me what already exists.

One side is erudite, the other not. He leaves. Light emanates from his patch of will.

I bear various scars upon, and nubs of hardened tissue beneath, the flesh of my face. Evidence of an existence punctuated by conflict with certain individuals, amongst whom I can count valued friends—combat both unsought and sought for, or at least recklessly precipitated. And a sudden realization: I am the very person I always wanted to become.

Writing, ground eros, crouching beneath a filthy blanket.

I can tell you of some further fragments and philosophical investigations: one can talk to oneself. (Not the one on horseback, a different one.) Will you some day climb yonder mound with me? His words are mangled by static from the abdomen. He is cast out from the pit by legal descent. A biochemical exchange involving the activity of free oxygen is taking place. He is walking on tiptoe at the root of to go. The stretch of wall he has been chained to bears years of graft, gouges of knife and key, a slogan. I am alive I write.

Stayed up a bit to watch the fog. Only one person at a time may speak. No one else is sharing in the present. The soul is sort of cubist, volumetric in form and content—a seizure-free life for everyone. The whole of the monument constitutes a transfigured sphere. That's the rule for today. The origin of the third element is unknown. It grows upward, as if it were, out of the lower past. We fall into a kind of spiral path (I'm unaware at this point that stems of contradiction in science can yield fruit). As yet nothing has been found. The instructions run. Remove self to far wrackaway, change at mort lake. Step out of my station and tumbleyard ahead. My body lies buried behind a wooden riverwall.

Consider, a self-professed language isolate, hydraheaded. Now, this machine is very different. We have nothing to start writing with. It is a flow of absolutes stretching between an offensive and a defensive pole.

Begin again. Does that literally mean he is speaking to himself? I think ultimately we're fated to be friends. Some day soon he will bite into the offered hand that feeds. An expanded head sits at the centre of a ring of electricity. Anything of small value is here, rigorously counted in and archived. A volunteer acts as decoy. That organ is a sheep's lung. We are revisited last night. This time the passage was sealed at one end. We hear there's one remaining gate open at the coast. The whisperings in the room come and go.

Walk parallel now to belly of sac. Can we make it before the credit. There is a gatekeeper. That old game. We're all hoping the lab will vindicate us in the end. I've nothing new to add, nothing more to pawn. Spot the difference. Spot the ball. Spot the mysterious sunspot lady. Framing's the problem. (That's writing, not typing.) My kidneys subside and collapse. I am turning a lurid yellow with broken vessels. His own theme is simple: he eats with relish the inner.

Turn right at riverbridge, limp back parallel to track. Stop. Proceed to where a flung sleeper penetrates the bough. Stop. He invokes the most elaborate means to represent. Look about thee. It's too early to say. Stop. He senses the method available to him is insufficient. We ask friends if we may borrow a very large telescope for a very long time. See, he is determined to outreach the others. (How's that damned spot.) What was the effect of the revolution. Our narrator has disappeared. I find myself disinclined, left blind and roiling. This takes us back to saints, to the ancestral cluster.

Raging storms here I write. That is Venus no. That is Mars. That is moon and sun and earth. You are peering down into a chasm of stars, a star-hollow. He is his own remedy. Turn right and straight down to the middle wood, an islet set into flooded land beside a river. Observe there the correlation of individual figures to organs and heavenly bodies. The wreath he wears about his head is thought to be the sign of a plea for forgiveness.

I come back to myself. I am everloud. I am unsettled by that which is always nearby (for example the town, the water-thing with heads et cetera).

We rush into ourselves. He is out of control. I'm no sixteen myself (low). He slips into that familiar edge of affection. The statue yields sound when the sun strikes it. I am a cul-de-sac of sorts, a footsoldier in the service of a centaur—a fine rain from a cloudless sky. See elsewhere.

Really good lord. Do one more page then leave for all time to come, forever hereafter. We regret we can no further. Strange that thread of hair glued stubborn to the outside pane. Now I will tell of the things I have noted, such as the gravel and the ice. Take the distance to Saturn. Square it. Take those limp flowers, goods lost by wreck and found floating on the sea. Reconsider the notion of metalepsis in poetics, the growing sense of isolation. I have aligned myself with a large southern starfield. Are you serious. I want to know well of one solitary being.

A volunteer is ritually bathed and skinned for the confrontation. I see you. I sense you nearby, augur. He is canal spy. And if my double comes, an indirect kind of substitution takes place: underhand linkster, long, thin flat pieces and animal ghosts.

Jesus these funny little haps are not much animous.

Intention. Make up mind. Lingster. Lemures. This could be a structure that I myself had built. It is not the present present.

You've taken a lot from time, when do you start giving something back. A fictive character is allowed to coexist within a historical personality. When cut off I'm succeeded by others. I am lying face down on the damp earth, a moth garden, he writes—while literally decomposing in my head he writes. Perhaps the neutral is that. I never want to move away from this moment in time. I mean an account of an event, the knowledge of past events, a life-story, a past of uncommon interest, a drama representing, or simply to record. He has the characteristic lower jaw and prism, signs of mercurial poison. He is discarded and never orchestrated. I am writing beyond belief. While writing I am simultaneously recording myself writing. He is reborn as food refuse, sometimes a fridge. He is the scan of a lexicon. The goddess of whatever imparts graciousness to death. Gift him one more chance. Someone has plotted out some freedoms, a handful of lairy inclinations. Growth by deposition on the surface of a tonguelike stricture has been observed, and the flight and cries of birds. We kept the aperture open for a long long time.

See. See direction of mind, design and purpose, application of thought to an object—intention, actuating spirit. Hostile apparitions.

Water cyst or vesicle in the body of the animal. A device. Freshwater spermatozoon. One says there must be method, an over-determination, a system.

Memory of bedlam furnace in irongate, a route leading nowhere. His place is taken by a string of narrators, usually undependable.

O, the English chorus. Discourse, argue even, with the person you claim to have created, but no longer trust. On being cut I simply multiply. I lean into myself and fail triumphantly on my word, the familiar howl of chance. Few of my adverbs stick. Because a loss has occurred someone must be sacrificed. He is orienteer and cipher bishop of the glyphs for cardinal points. It is as if he has no real existence. A waxy matter is mixed with oil siphoned from the head. I am itinerant, like her grace in that frontier town. I no longer trust.

Replace pebble to curvilinear surface of polished upright slab. Patents of dignity mark the man. I am a postilion from whose gaze no one can escape. That bird on the wing is a species of swallow, petrel.

Project: remain intramercurial, the slivery yesicle et cetera. Occur between lists of words and numbers in a given test situation. Distal self from self (a small globule, bladder and sac). I am satisfaction. The problem is it shaves off all your edges. We emerge from the chain of dialogue without being identified, bloodblister swelling. All present know he is the key skeletal, a primal cavity, an unwritten law. This morning I remember nothing. My ministers have scrapped.

Like for like. Retaliations. His unpredicted and elegant hand, one ranked among inconscionable soloists. I am widely spaced within myself. I have spent day after day murmuring at this dilemma, which cannot be spoken of. He has explored the northern coast of a large peninsula and confirms that it is not joined. On returning, this incident is contrived into an attempted murder charge. Far apart and widely spaced, I am difficult to root out. Picture a hybrid of taxonomy and fibreoptic disaster. I pertain to the outer end. I relish my role, the inert. I have memorized my lines and wish to creep back inside the belly of the entourage, to conceal myself farthest from the organ of attachment. (Wish I was there just thinking of you.) Tell me about it. No change healthwise no. You must be from the same timezone. Then come the all-wise. Hold your piece. Beekeepers are at hand. How to know a flatterer from a fiend? Cast them all into the burning fiery furnace. I think you've made your point. He calls it his photon horoscope, his unchart. Here's to the last last. Does that mean a yes or a no. Sound is terrible, part of his crucible.

She says I have come to the end of a sentence. I expect a response.

Now and then he is being clever and not saying too much. Being of an earlier time he does not share the confidence of our age. We cannot reach the verdict. His is the only trilogy that survives complete. They can't decipher the writing. There are two unused headings: audience and signifier. They can't reveal the interpretation (wise they are but lingual). Check any imbalance. Archive this in the preserved daylight folder: underkilled in magic and mentally et cetera. Evacuate the island. I am sticky with digits. There is weather. You will not have me. I can't get through, held firmly as I am beneath the adversary's wing. Project: remain intergalactic. Am embedded now, fixed throughout the territory by a string of selected fragments. Ground salt has collected at the spine of being and time. Mister is tolling us through his ghost sorties: rip the top off my dark-lantern. I recognize the source of the crisis industry—forming from distance, sole bolted to earth, voice nailed.

And another thing, this is a translation. Where does that leave you. Analogy of central, supine of timebeing.

Facsimile, I.

She springs up again and again, cordax in her cups. An erased star, seasure—water akin to without, from the semblance of its wake to flowing hair. Every now and then we had a ferox for dinner.

Next in the sequence I write god they have forgot the lift coefficient (any levitation that is not). In later versions include a delegation from another continent.

Her thorax has been crushed. She dangles from the pier at the end of an accidental rope. This is a scene of manslaught. We are sandbanked in for a last stand. Now for some epistolary glassware, blasted in sand. The lungs are filled with fluid. It all ends in a radiant C major.

Desert, dazzling light.

Angels rustling in the adjoining cell. Pang and pull of the cramp or any other painful thing. Get on with it.

Dear When,

Forgive, I have used your full nomenclature in the previous. This reveals. We must put a stop, caress.

She hides the note away in her stays. He is an awkward predicament. It takes time to dawn, but still, it's an exchange of voice. You saw what happens next. Descendent cadence, if haughty. Then rising, as if to breathe.

The outlook is servile and fatalistic. They creep out of the wormwood at high-water mark, undivided in clusters, oblong and downy. Receptacle naked. (Think hired keeners and slow death by canker.) What happens on the twenty-ninth. The doors open you can go in and out. No one's looked at the detail of the pattern. It's like being on a set, almost. It's the kind of experience where you're looking at a desperate but sympathetic audience.

Of the dark alley and the causeway. Magic and incantation. Pump: tell me my name. Preambles into endless space, the pneumatic trough. They seem to have forgotten all the drama. Get yourself out into the open. Any damage due to her must be small, a storm in a liftshaft. There's no cover. The creature's a big thing with a fluke at the back. The hand that wipes away the blood of the eye is your name. Characteristics of you and I abound.

Dreary town of a market squared. He comes with that familiar stabbing rhythm. There is shouting. We want Wednesday to happen first. There's no insurance for structure. She has very strong ideas about her reputed nothingness. When I was a child my sibling had years and there were elegant forms of torture. (On death your identity is reappropriated.) These are historic proceedings. One was to play drowned in the sea. Your body doesn't belong to you. I know before I arrive that I'm already here. I float face down pretending I am until I cry out.

Dry deck as bone. No one hears. My terms are anonymous. They signify you, stars, and each has the same name. Why do I mention this. Each has different significations and origin but makes the same sound. All are committed to ambiguity. Why, I may just mortalize you too, in an equivocal kind of way. This is strange work, isn't it, if you can touch it.

You stars at the foot of a living being. I am not injured. It is not worn away. Taste of rosewater and steel on the tongue. I can't read any more. Take steps, foot for foot. (Does the lover's countenance not reveal his acquiescence?) We have found a spare dna algorithm to fiddle with. Complete penetration of the ionosphere takes place over a period of three roughlies. I am not worn away.

Delight in such abstractions. There may well have been a systemic failure somewhen. I emerge from you bearing doubtful or spurious fragments. I am any manifest evil. There is discrepancy, huge.

The other runs off. It's a grudging respect we share. There's a new points system. I give chase down the intersecting corridors in darkness. Then we skirt a mountain of red earth. It's the notorious autumn of seventy-seven. She would like to hear the rocks clack and see the moraines and the water meadows for herself. I touch the walls on either side. I scatter. I have thought long and hard about this, the point at which I must give myself up to my tormentors. This journey's like crossing a Siberia, or listening to a lengthy treatise on the planets of a region. I am one of the rarest engineering works of the century. My brain is tidal and I have had enough. At a distance horse and rider seem to possess one body. The rip outstretches them.

But the word remains the same. Leave me to be. I split myself during the feathering process. I can't continue this useless talk, blind in every organ. It never occurs to me to refuse. I'm a clue to something else. The ceremony is still underway (radiowaves). I am never the thing in itself. Until about now, I've looked *back* to writing. Leave the machine on he says when you quit the surface.

Scrubland with shacks and inverted boats. There are many things I'll never have time for: rusting cables, the still-water well with crescent moon, limestone shingles—the RX12, the abandoned lighthouse. That tethered man to the earth, pinioned by taut steels of rope. I lack.

Next I shall denote an abject which follows hard on another, and then another. I am inconsequence—an eruption running along the intercoastal nerve, acute inflammation of the ganglia. A belt to gird.

Adieu, I can't continue this doubtless walk, at liberty without use. It's my loss (he who delights in signs). It's my gain (he who lays down or deposits). Look, with an arrow relief running around it, is the same holy egg. Inveigle him to the top of a high cliff. Punish him over.

July the seventeenth.

Kybernetes. A steersman.

Some kind of pivot has been reached. The key difference is that we are only alive for three days more before the flight. The life ebbs away from us. She speaks a dark fable et cetera. I splinter. I am scattered at the four corners. She is enigma. Something more here: song of arsenal, the memory gland. Mimesis.

We were always very good at smell and sound, a walking audit of stuff. In his sermons the sublime antithesis appears again and again. The sheet of paper crumpled in his right hand is tossed into space. It fails to reach the mirror placed against the opposite wall. This reflector is liquid mercury, no tain or foil. A graduated glass tube with a tap is driven into his orifice. (Listen, distant muted brass.) The image stretches in either direction. Our party clings to the pontoon as if she were some raft of medusa. A hand plunges into quicksilver and is grasped at the other side. On the magnetic tape he says he feels forsaken. (Thuswise the liquid run-off is measured out.) He persists with his diktat, despite the adversity we face, the clear and present danger. Tomorrow he composes a robust and uninhabited finale. Any disorder naturally affects his peripheral nerve. Across a bridge. Will it reach.

A steep arc is glued together using thousands of tiny bird yokes and a multitude of straw: solvent transfer, stolen rhythm. An antecedent carries the link through darkening streets (melodramatic the elder)—torches of pitch and tow, burnt inks used as blacking. She says I thought I'd lost you. Molten glass is dropping into the water, bursting when the tail breaks. Uncentre everything.

An insignificant postlude.

All these coincidences indicate that we're on the right track. And I ask myself, how should the book appear.

Tranceponders. Herd-book of life stock—earthlike plans forming and dissolving and reforming. I tongue at the margin, the outskirt. Traces trail back to my ministers. Rejoice, we can quit without making use of the electrode hooks and other tools of trade: he is become glass.

Bag her and rope her. Beg her to turn around. Spin her about in order to preserve the flesh. What remains of us. What is the role of that building (prophecy, knowledge of the present). We're paralysed by hereditary notions of exile. Observe, tiny arm at the window, flapping.

He is no longer, substance. You are not for me. You have not sprung from my head. He is substitute. If you feel this is going to cause distress, walk away and avert your surviving eye. There is a sound behind me. There is a sound beneath me. Is this animal desexed. It seems absurd to damn a whole country like this. Let's understand one thing: these are not theories. I wrote face down throughout that long winter. We should name these wonderful players. We have immediately ceded possession. And we mustn't forget our miscellany: dead insect in honeycomb, sweet limes from the tree he spoke of, a flesh-scraper, a mechanism for cleaning the antennae et cetera. Away, far away, some far far wreckaway.

With trenchfoot, formerly the signalled names of initial letters. The art by which notoriety is secured—with categories ranging from chamber, utterly chromatic. And he too is found, still born.

It is about this time that our town begins to come apart. The mediaeval walls are demolished to make way and contagion is introduced. The old city within remains completely intact. The desert is held back. They have decided to destroy my taciturnity, not on any supernatural grounds, but through the agency of a rational credulity. (A blank page, quick.) The diagnosis is bricabrac aphasiac, with vulsion of mind: a stack of railway sleepers, the zigzag fortification, a hook for a cauldron. Try gluing a memory to this image, this hinge. Next to nothing is known about the subject. His pen is savage. The silence solidifies. A more satisfactory plan consists in drawing the enlarged gland out from its bed by means of a double. (You must be getting used to this kind of thing by now.) The window steams up. Fingered sigils are arranged in parallel rows, rusticles eat iron on the radio. He drops a shoulder as he strides through. Flung open, flung clear.

Revulva, she says. Meet me. I don't know which is worse, your absence or your return.

Wine, oil and semen spatter into the altar cruet. The tactic is divination by transparent bodies. The id of flies. Something like that.

Postludic. Ecstatic mourning. Catalepsy in seizure. Moral rectitude and exemplary dying. That's it. Were it possible? A man should die more than once. An artificial part is fitted onto the body politic. It begins. It begins to hum. Hired grievers sway in a trance. Eyeballs swivel back to reveal a whiteness. We are situated on the banks of a great river with smoking pyres. That's when the overlap occurs. What's the authority. An hour to tell.

A quantum of light or other radiation. To go across, split in two.

As a child he remembers playing with an invisible. Some of us won't make it out of here alive. Let him wait. One of the three can turn beholders into stone. From beneath his cloak he produces forceps with teeth and a claw blade. At breakfast tomorrow his life will be cut short by a sniper's bullet.

We must press on. The edict is cruel. We recognise each other by the smell of our urine. I believe every word. The malady is oedema of his remaining lung. I place the chisel edge of the rock hammer against the lid at each nail, and strike inward. Writing still exists as a kind of plumbstone. I glimpse the pelt of an animal at peripheral vision. And heavy masses of lead—repetition, a resounding plummet. He will last no longer than a fortnight. The muzak in the lift is four stand-alone schizos. He's illusive, radiates from the breastbone, outward to shoulder and arm. This is a feat of translation, with its drones and pentact harmonies—heartpulp of eaglewood, with axe-shaped crystals. The fevered kidney-head.

Elegiac fragments. Say, a close-up of a worm, its all-consuming mouth. It was like swimming in the glare of a photoflood lamp. Those are lone hunters in the snow, by the way. I have sourced mercury from the blue flowers you sent.

Far environs of a settlement ringed by orange burn-off flares. The men naked swimming beneath the circumference of a turret at rim of bay. Paroxysms of intense pain. I set out at a trot (halfhorsed). My yoke sac is still attached. From beneath the surface she prevails upon him to break his fast. A severed hand floats and bobs in the foam (missed the beach). Damn he murmurs from the deck of an offshore skiff. Once in a while we had an uncanny for supper and would tell such as these.

Ditch all background Yes. They have expectations about who we are. There is a wreath of bread attached to the rear of our vessel. They have expectations about where we are. Walk away. They have expectations about when we are.

I cannot catch up with him. Who was it in the whale's maw that time, so lyric, so unaccustomed. A new job has found him. The taste of stale saltwater clings to his lips and tounge. He supplies artificial parts to used bodies. He is seer, thoroughgoing—out-and-out abounding, a covert abundance. Signs are bolted together and flung into the harbour. If they float, we're doomed.

Five-rayed. An ancient ship with fifty oars. Panopticon. I mean the descendent city of the skies.

Ghost chamber with pistols. He reads with the tower as backdrop. I am now an integral part of the state. He has created some really useful technical terms. (No cough amazing.) He chews, softly as he scans. There may be trouble ahead, the tubercular miracle. It's the great fire study day. No annex remains standing. He is given a title, a new lease. He siphons down his food. My only companions are spherical in form. The director is easy to pick out from the rest of the company—an extra edition is being distributed. In the photograph he is seated dead centre, surrounded by cast and crew. The rest of the population has not returned.

A blue domain mid mossy banks fanned by giant zephyrs et cetera. Resolve is not enough. Whisper to him that he must be a worthless individual to have survived. To wit.

We are still alive against all the odds she says. It comes down to a single microscopic participle of gunpowder (the past). Curled up under the bridge my heart pounds. I must reckon with the stacked minutes. Nearby a man shreds at a steel cable with a mezzaluna blade. Keep it short but to the point.

Horsemanship, seaweed in his clothes—if he sinks we're doomed. Well, writing is bolted to death.

Alchemotherapy, mort madder lake. Much bodying about these parts, an associative pattern of words and prime numbers. And she asks are you heartbrake. Upon these assembled stones burst lichens old as civil war. I am to be hanged by the neck from a gibbet. This indicates a true vertical line that if continued would extend to the molten core of the planet. The block of ice supporting my feet is kicked away. We have a limited amount of time for one of my attacks. Now vitrify, through a lens, saintly. And she asks is the pump shattered.

Some life interiors, a painterly mix from gas-black to greasing soot. Place, encircling. Environs of whalebone lane. It's a job. Can you believe. This is still only the first verse. There's static in her hair, semen. The remains of the day are schizomythic. Some of its method is missing. No human hoof has trodden here for three or more of your earth years. I did and I have returned.

Pass me the vulsella. Pierce to a depth of one fathom. Three membranes shroud the skull and the vertebral canal. The operation takes approximately one thousand hours. I visit her grave (pauper, yes). Narrative drought suggests an immanence. She pleaded with him to kill her. The headstone says so. It's snowing. The following day I find myself lost in a foreign city. I rise before dawn and pack a few things. I have been abandoned to unknown territory. I wander. I arrive at an intersection resembling the ribs of a gigantic vault. I am without. I am resolve. Forgive me.

The game dwindles away to nothing then grinds to a halt in the street. She speaks. It was like having layers of tissue peeled away. The game has stopped dead. Its origins are midway through the first dynasty. Wife and child should never recur. While returning with the book she falls into the river and is drowned.

Weight her body and seal every orifice with lead.

A corner. My natural home is a shallow gravel depression in a riverbed. I meld quietly with the sequence. I pass into seconds. She left a note saying she has recollected things and does not know when she can return. There is a wreath of bread attached to the rear of the vehicle.

Closer.

A circlet of interwoven materials, especially a twist in the tale.

(More detail.)

A single coil in the helical object, resembling a curl of vapour. Wreaths of breath. A stilled ornament with bosses, the conduction defect. She says it is the lack of word which makes us what we are.

The rifts formed by snow.

I've been unconvinced since time, which is usually quite handy. Unravelling across open country, at last they reach the cairn. A story is told as if a riddle.

One day you wake to find yourself in a cabin on a mountain ridge. You have no memory of coming here—landscape with hunters in the snow, petrol sky. You are about to remount when an uncanny sensation of exile overcomes you. The closest star hovers low over the summit. (We're still embedded in her year of fires.) You can feel the shockwaves passing through your body. The top left sickle of the moon is missing. Clearing darkness, and from the rubble of a wasteland, a voice: come tomorrow, if I were glass. Yet repeated, replaced.

We arrive at the appointed corner. I am performing this from memory. One day this will kill us all. We watch as it drains the volunteer (some of my clients, they want the world). Now it's got a dead thing to take home in its jaws. Its transparent body and narrow neck are encased in wickerwork. We are closing down the brain and the spinal cord. Use language whose meaning has evaporated from continued repetition. Usage has been thieved. Take control, for instance.

Who pulls the wires in this intrigue, hollow and empty. You decide. Take action with an element of chance. We were going to stage a duel. Things and their interlocking spaces are a pressing concern. The found object is a spiral ornament, a piece of deciphered meat. If it exists even once, it's allowable— sprung not from place but self absent from place.

An abandoned ash mine. I have quit my post as a vertical line. You have not said how you felt during the memory of those moments.

Our comrades will always find ways and means to free us.

You must state how you feel.

A sudden flux of brine, a flood when the ice cracks open. Too many variables, really. Prisons come and go. There are times when the only feeling I have is one of mad revolt.

I miss my lucky lexicon. He is a man completely out of time and space. The last decades of his life seem less rushed. Respond to the advice given: meet me in anatomy or the facial cell. Add a single female voice to the mix. It all ends in a magnificent fugue, internal errorism. The finale is the longest of the thirty-three moments. (In truth it's just another layer.) I've used up all my organs. I have used up all my signs. How to make representations in wax or clay? Sometimes I think I'm just callous, but at least the haunting has stopped. He is a species of awe.

A procession of lepers, with bells and flails. One wields a bladder bobbing on a length of cane. There's no rest in this house. She is stitched into skin. I can be traced back to the confluence, signified and transfigured. They come with lighted torches in their hands. It's evensong, or a riot. One of those.

Flung cloud, driving mist. A shallow track with drifting wreckage, some kindred forms. A series of irregular spines appears on the surface. Wind erosion and decomposition are parallel in the direction of the prevailing. He is more than himself. He outstrips. There is something within him that does not wish to dwell. You've had sixty-seven pages of this up to now, detached from the root, driving on to hollow laughter at the close. Spikes of iron shingle underfoot.

She falls in love with the wooden prince (the inanimate reproducing the functions of the animate). Tacit eternity. Altazimuth.

The final flourish, on an instrument devised by air for determining. Untimely mediations. Effect and cause. An undirected train, a wounded healer. (How inexact and fluid and provisional such a coupling would be.) Each of these vignettes is a narrative stem, with events and characters boldly painted at the outset. Then out of nowhere.

Tap-tuppy-tappy-tup on the back of my chair. There is no one else in the room. Nothing ever comes of this. This is a useful method of organizing a community, but how authentic is it? You know me but you have never seen my face. I'm always a step or two ahead. Things are getting a little surd. I am yet to be disestablished. When I extinguish the light he is not here. I am yet to be petrified. Big fade is rumoured, bitter kvetch. Strands of fleshy connective tissue are found wound about twigs of fiddlewood. There's a verb famine. Things are getting a little out of hand. We are questioning how many people actually died that day. Sorry to hear about the failure of your radical breathing project. Now, do we remotely ignite the room? Scan the destructions. I don't dialect. I'm a consequence of freezing. You are staring at the fright of day. I am a conviction that has no wish to be overheard. I am right. I am always fucking right. The three screens offer manic simultaneity on a darkling plain—knees stiff, soles nailed flat to earth. That covert goosestep rhythm is always with us. Nonetheless, you're a useful subaltern, a professional reverser. He is the name of a river running through, an undirected chain of thought or fancy set up in mediation. I am overturned. I am reading the plague. I do not know why. History me. Nothing but foreground, piercings. We chance upon an unploughed ridge, a place overlooked.

He loses another limb.

An omission.

There. See. I am complaining.

Salt-electric. This is where the pestilence halts the flames. I am watching out my years. I have one eye out for you. I am stationed at this watch-tower. Why they are so-called. I am at the same time writing a tractatus. You would not understand. I am decorated (sand & glue). You have no right. Do not even speak to me. I am no address. Me, you, him, her, us—all of you, one and all of you. You have no imagination. What the picture represents is its own sense. I keep an ear to the ground for events. I am full of missing word, variorum verses. I am full of missing objects. I am surrounded by the gentlest people. I am no remedy you could possibly know of. One of the two frontispiece portraits is now lost. I am invaded by another test, battened physical barriers. I am chiselled in from here to here. I keep a nose to the ground for events (things). Sometimes love is overwhelming. This place is named. This place is the dwelling edge. This place is disarmed. This place is unmanned. Meet me at the dock. She suggests speech. This place is named the unsettled abode of no. I keep an eye to the ground for events, any stray letters. I keep my throat to the ground for action. She works like a kind of breach, I suppose. I am a presumption (come and see my sea by the place et cetera). I find myself in the company of a vast lexicon. All my places are named. I am invaded by another set. My radius is about seven years. (Back off to rim of landing.) Between these lineaments turns a pivot of unbearable tension. This makes people smile—cult and race crammed to every boundary. I come to you each week and explain myself: maturing nerve and heart cell. Good luck on the day. All my places are unnamed. I walk on torsion with the toppled legs of an insect. Step across this taut highwire. How far down do you wish to go. I empty out (blessings, the blessings). She says I have lost agency. I am distemper. Dull ache in the kidney, underseal of cage of rib. Then she says I am beauty—a forbidden action, stitched up from wall to wall. Can I say. Meaning, emptied out.

A welcome intrusion.

Silhouetted bedouins against a desert fleet. The blue fades, the sky retreats. Stars emerge—full face at five yards. (It all sounds much better in my head.) Soon exit to cease. All the lights go out. Pause for existence unsummoned. There is this ruined pontoon. I am attached at my base to a flat-keeled ferryboat—a raft of planks and oildrums bound together with animal sinew. Stretching along the riverbank as far as the eye are the massed ranks of an insurgence, a new model army. Somebody is about to return. There are rumours of rumour (interest rates itself). A hair-trigger instrument sits in my lap. You talk about the whys and wherefores. We pass mountains and gorges, perpetual mist. A railway track skirts the river. You talk about the frailty of word. I once witnessed a murder at the galley oar. Such events are rarely meaningful. The dog cluster shouldn't appear in this scenario. Evidently we are in the wrong hemisphere. Return, monstrous obsolete. Return monster.

Nada movement.

She attends. A loser, lost for good, but never knowingly undersold. I've been having quite a lazy time of it myself. Today's the great fire offer. Little squares of orange light hover in the air. A bloody clot rises up in my throat. Sound is a reedy burr. A triple-clip grasps the gas check and aims for a projection at the root of the shell. Her skin's like ivy, growing along the pins until a scab forms. Water flows down the walls and into an electric fixture. (What's the matter.) Look, I'm telling you again and again and you'd better believe it. I demand something relentless and driven. (How about atoms.) An acrid fog leaches out of me. She says her hand looks exactly like her mother's. A bell tolls. I'm not about to put her in an asylum. It's about power I hear. The action takes place at a distance, rays of light burring out from all the bodies. Above my head in the stand a green exit sign flaps on its chain. A quickening has taken place: serendipity, pure chance woven with fear. I've pissed myself again and lost my keys. Where do I live and who are you. Becoming our fathers was an overwhelming subjective experience. I can see the ermine staring rigidly forward ever now. I have folded his letter, his E. I actually need you, solitaire. I have broken through. I am no more. I feel like a fraud, a descendant offshoot, a breach or derivative of everything. The only beam of a balance.

He dreams that a state of cessation exists. A check. Graftling and stumbleblock. Struggling, pushing—starving out the old ones.
Recklessheaded.

The eternal sell. Atlas, I know what to do. She dreams a vast grille of orange latex and concrete. Safe at last.

A brief symphonic chorus. Mystic insignificance of the numbs, the seven. Bendy words heaped into bulwarks. That instrument is a strigil.
Baulks of avoidance. The boys laughing.

To place in check, to chop logics.
Make slow in pursuit, together cluster the prey. Descend on the bridges between furrows. Pile up in mounds. Question now whether the plague stopped the thaw or the thaw the pandemic.
Erosion. Fade & Disquiet. Spooring moss-troopers. We're still lobbying for an official apology. Languish & Decline. I am committedly unemployable, but then, if you'd sat watching the flames fly up through the night like meteorites.
The bursting shell of an abandoned car reveals the silhouette of a pack of feral dogs. Backdrop of yellow onion domes, as if I had returned, back to blight. She manufactures unease, the orchestration of enlightenment. I have never said. I think it's the awe in which I behold myself. A woman abruptly opens a shuttered window just above my head. You see, I simply exhaust all the possibilities before you can. I relish any flaws.
Like the final asteroid.
Like a bridge of boats.

Like a boundary line for a preliminary run.

All glossed without time, planted among the notes of various redactors. Make an end ont.

Hermanaut. Talusman.

XIV

Stately pump murmuring
  down from the naked starwell—
Your within-timeliness
  and wilful vague—
(this is why we need the deadlihead things,
  to explain stuff)

Now, he steps gracefully from barge to barge as a waterstate is navigated. I myself lie low, withershins to sun. Nearly everything you measure will be wrong. My shadow is long and twists at the centre.

The clear whiteness. Atomized prey, Atlantic chanting. There's been a sharp decline in rhetoric while I was away. And why is an autopsy being conducted. He moves his tongue about inside his mouth. That's something. He's alive.

She says I waited for him and he never came.
Note the tense, past. Red scar on inner lip, homemade tattoo at right-hand flank of thigh. Tell us about the grudge, half-loon.
I resolve to stop answering (some translations leave this out).
She says do you hear voice. Do you inscribe feeling.
Low grey cloud obscuring hill. I mean high ground—more elevated at least than the crest of my skull. Moon over ruined castle. Cenotaph at peak of turf cone glimpsed through willow pane. Condense and distil. Cease listing. A flare erupts. Oxides of silicon, boron, phosphorus.

He is momentarily paralysed by any noise whatsoever. A few weeks later he's taken ill—changes of synaptic resistance on a grand scale. He says we're all universal symbols, but I'm not sure that's good enough. I pass on the watchword and he splits open at the groin (I don't think you realize what a repellent little story this is). Crawl inside I say and unlock the trapdoor cell. He thrashes about on the floor until he loses consciousness.

Yesterday's narrative began with a ditch, an invasion back when. It's chemical (rhinegold). The big storm is coming. More spidergram games, unclaimed voices at the dock approaching from every angle. I assume the shape of rocks hidden under the water. The large wait is coming. Samples include a mass of moving air, a crescent-shaped ridge of shingle, a tangle of fluorescent fishing-thread, a stub of burnt cork—desiccated excrement pressed sharp to recumbent hollow of thigh. I reminisce: six moths trapped in a lift.
And she says, in future, insist. Insist that all those who come to contest weigh

their hearts in the balance. The deceased is provided with an abundance of mood.

Psi.

After months in a medically induced coma he wakes to resume competition. The familiar region of space in which forces are at work recurs. He is now protected by a husk of metallic scales.

I've been awash all these years in the popular (my killer side—technically, one who puffs). He accepts behaviour. He resumes mortal guise and attempts to explain the family tragedy—the entire theft must be seen from the beginning in the light of this divine standpoint. Others believe only concepts they accept as false. He is struck by shrapnel at his wide window, the fragment from without. A paradox emerges. There is circulation of blood everywhere one looks. His name is not to be confused with its bigness—compact head or inner mass, a mine of compulsion.

She drugs him with sleeping notions: lung of abjection, spleen of distemper.

Continue. I want to create the sense that this is unfinished. He might just be the one. Document the remaining sigils. It says now they can avenge their loss. Most are back-formed, elegantly calligraphic. I tell him we're delighted. The skin erupts. He is a moulder and shaper. It is said. Beyond the walls of the town raw flesh is consumed, a harvest of muscle and sinew. Inanimate objects are removed by marshalling soundwaves.

Keep silence, that we may ear. The day's catch is a matter of flat rays.

Black triangle at base of skull. Ill-formed, out from lettercrypt, yet I shall keep my promise: happenstance through time, the barren envelope. Some of these nonce-words might make it to the final beckoning, the big volume. I should never be excluded from the algorithm. A slake of the feathers, and he hauls the cable in. Overlook me, proximal to crest of bone (the way I use books). Fossil trees form the remnant. Men and women pass by in their shapes, parallel rows of leaflike scar tissue.

Local nous beyond pebble mound, situationist ethics—dead or in suspended animation when born: one who refuses. The clouds sink and take on an olive hue.

Notes on the sedative gland.

I am aligned to a constellation in the southern hemisphere. Too much bigness in the last passage. Do not explain. It resembles those brittle lines that form steps in the rigging of ships. I am in need of the providential gap, a little glaciation. The most common states are as follows: continuous, discontinuous, and insular. Tracks of ascent and descent inscribe the snow. The animals are bleeding about the hooves. Reach out a hand. I am abstain. Our books are cut to pieces. Last night I blessed myself with another unacknowledged citation. Rax yourselves.

Clearly been dead many hours. I must do more work on this. The missing word is pan-harm. She declares herself a humanist, albeit with reservations (occasional sadism). She is exactly one year younger than the earth. It says so in the text.

Place of witnessing (this here, not that here). Is this a singing contest anymore. A stream of particles is jotting back to earth from the stratosphere. Subject: the recovery of a body at the tramway junction, murmurings from the radiation belt. Frozen cables bisect the dense fog. Throughout his life he has always brushed against some form of absence. He has been known before to die of lack. I have set us the right way up—one more day of this at least. The instruments press at their highest register: musical silence, an indelible sense of calm (the common universal about what is beautiful in a temporal art). I have decided to rename the earth's elements. I am giving titles to events that happened in the past, rare points of equilibrium in a place swept with confused alarms, the straggling light. This part is called the echo aria. Microbursts overhead, a cluster of saints—lastless in breath with countermined epiphany. He fashions himself replicant. His lyre is placed in heaven as a consolation. The strings were stretched over a bridge.

Now, green equals the familiar dead image. One steps forward and volunteers to carry witness. She stretches under, possessed.

She says I love November and December when Orion comes. Do you know Orion? And the great W of Cassiopeia, which she draws in the air. And the Pole Star too, guide and distracter—there are now so many pole stars I have lost track. Also Pleiades, the plough or cist. I forget the rest. O yes my morning star, who is Venus, and the rosy planet. I shall telescope. Yes she says, I will, yes.

In this cell we don't discuss solely you. I am here for his code. We touch upon many things that occurred beyond and before the time you came. A narrative is slowly being drawn out. It conducts its affirmation by discovery of kinship among disparate things. A strap is passed between the horse's forelegs, noseband to rein.

Trace ratios on the true skin. I am that I am. Keep your heads down. The supporting spine is the fin, the fluke-tapper. Orders are transmitted to the engineroom by means of a compressed air signal. Take a quick turn to the right, breathe in some complimentary oxygen. There he is, humming over an old lagtime tune. Half-open the slide valves. I am not what I need. All his mantle is hanged full of ray trails. Navigate by that first magnitude star at the foot of Orion. Copper pistons crank and drive the burnished rods of the central shaft. In the midst of this a memory: field of bone hull, surface of upright lichenstone within a sleeve of sunlight. Concentrate. Very casually, he speaks. Red shift is a factor of a thousand—or more, more, more. Propeller blades harrow the water. The uncanny is set to crush you.

Place of lax rule.

Once we were sealed in a wooden horse and delivered. I am remember. Caution, men are burying the canisters of gas. I dissaint thee. Apply filter with underside of tongue to metal yield of green salt. One of our mendicants has escaped. To date, everything I've written sounds apocryphal. While visiting that city I did not seek his grave, a neglect I still don't understand. There is a tendency to return when twisted. Check haemorrhage by cauterizing the cut end of the artery. An obscure law is passed concerning self-destruction.

In the distance he hears on the greasy cobble the step of his assassins. Does this count. They are destined to hang by wire from their wrists. You see, in this burg are two designated pressure districts: one for returning emigrés, the other the temple. There is a tendency toward insurgence. Who is he who speaks through me. I am using language (a state). Disappear sometimes with away— augur to cause, in any sense. He urges a tongue who melts, dissolving to lose distinct form. This last passage predates me.

A shading off. To uncome imperceptible, and disperse.

We just stopped at big and paradise. It is so cold and I the snowing I love you. When we shop we use our unconscious mind, which has various heuristic rules that seem to work for us. None of these tactics is illegal.

One, four, three, then two. Did I not say.

Cowering beneath the perspex bubble of the dugout. So far nothing has changed. What we want to look at now is how to smuggle risk into the system. We are here, a crisis. Right across the country, reports of a bright light under the water, apparently a meteorite. I have begun a careful inspection of our cell. Seafarers come with the letters of a strange alphabet. (So far I've used the word trance about three times.) High-speed film resembles the topography of the vocal fold. Invaluable is the word by which something is said about something else.

He describes his vision of the chariot as his absolute point of departure, his masterpiece. None of this matters. He has broken my teeth with his gravelling. They may as well unsaint him hereafter, as saint him now. It amounts to the same thing.

Another glance at the flyer. He has covered me with ashes. We are invited to put our fingers into the wound. (I hate this bit.) He says grant me sleep, solitude. Then two armoured men are battering each other in a bullring. I leave something of me behind in a sack. One triumphs then collapses to his knees, weeping. In spite of all this the journey has been worth it.

Describe the crowd. For example, are the men gladiators.

Petition, extract gently. I have.

Item: a pocked marble cube in the dusty square of an Adriatic port. I will leave when the sun reaches its zenith. This is war, yes, but prosecuted with grace. Sickles of reflected light on chrome, untimely documentation. Italic facades with peeling shutters and chalkface graffiti. Urinestained pavingslabs. Think of this kind of history as the living head. Don't explain. A door abruptly opens (a hatch more it is, like that of the cellar above). We are the simplest solution to ourselves.

Exposed graves in the neighbourhood gardens. The anticipated becomes another memory. I am the things I do not want, the vacant lot between stars— sediment after infusion or distillation, dregs. Furnish me with rays.

The hypothesis of a floating islet, with branching stem and axil—the return to writing, to parapraxes. Funny how it does that. These are scant notes but they've been arranged with care. I am set at an angle between a limb and the torso it springs from—a convex sound-chest with a pair of curved arms, reconnected by a crossed bar. Stained substance in nuclei of cell. Today we have naming of past: a bead of coffee, a stain of oil, a resembling.

Jeremiad. Diminutive of wing.

Disanchor. There's something in the fog. I am thrown out from among the numbers. He says can I get them cinder stores in the next random ten. I abandon life to the others. He underscores the word it must end. Glance down to lower limb: greater part of tibia bare. There is this strange tune at the close of me. Yesterday the object was fleshed, a perfect cone. A drop of translucent fluid oozes slowly from the eye set into the head of the shaft. Reach a decision by chance alone. A powder consisting of his spores is being prepared.

A separate portion, a parcel of ground. Reservoirs of inert gas. Sun poised just above horizontal crack—a day of dazzled sea-torn crowds. Grand though this is, I feel we are inundated by ghost. Water vapour condenses. Your pi charts have no currency here: rupture of vascular sheath investing mind, paralysis of limb.

Dust particles are trapped in descending droplets. Looking directly forward, he gestures with a tilt of the head, as if he would beckon his star shift on its axis. Earth and sky merge in a single whiteness. We catalogue. This is one story short of the full set. We rise too late for the mist.

A slip of wood, a straw.

The fourth flute of an insect's leg.

A rope stretched from place to place, to prevent the foresaid.

A makeshift with fringed wings and abdominal appendage.

What is its name.

Flesh cackles in the pan, the relished innard. Mournful oboe, debris strewn along the quayside—a unique festival of ideas. He enters the gloomy interior. Coils of skin and strange translucent membranes have been hung to dry from the wooden rafters. Rising halitus of freshly shed blood. The objects presented include the needle, the shuttle and the distaff. An embryo is forming in the gall of a still. The tracks are clearly missing. Dry ice pours in. He says I have come to meet your intermittent gap. Crystals are forming on every surface. With my free hand I turn the fortune tumbler. The volume cranks up. There is no visible light source. A voice whispers: let it emerge out of itself and be done with. Matter is discharged in a molten stream from the fissure. In the centre of the laboratory is a receptacle in which pollen gathers. Below this container are listed all the words I didn't think we'd be using anymore. For example, wolf-footed.

He picks up the hammer claw.

A brief enquiry into what the objects which underlie phenomena might be. An excess of contact. Ten is now equal to one. We are told and we are retold— creeping bubbles of oxygenated fluid (red in the higher animals). Lamentations are descending through the body in question. Swallow down some light. That sign has dimmed as we speak. High above the city in the park that overlooks, a circling hawk, intractable and unforeseen. Below, a falconer—stunned pivot, hollow-eyed and gaunt. Deep scar at left temple. Faint signals of dissent, forcing up from the throat the act of doing.

The trunks of camphor trees and other indigenous products are drawn on by the current. The leg is of no value whatsoever. Trigger: a row of poplars.

The faintest of connexions.

Location, a mud-town named after the ancestor of a discarded name. Outside with tripod is a surveyor of land. He has forgotten, like nearly everything else. A group of six naked-eye and a multitude of telescopics are found in his shoulder.

When I return I will be wearing steel boots and a head. I am disarmed by the slightest touch—distemper, vaguely outlined: a small hard body, seeds in their envelope of flesh. Spinning plates on canes in the background.

Each scar signifies a particular rank: a spot on die or domino, the single corolla in a cluster.

Speck on the radar screen. I interpret: two–and-thirty, a shortfall of one—but one in excess of the total aimed at under the old rules. Hence, having overshot the mark.

A signal sounding like the word. A spot of light as presence of object. Indication.

Pluck, plough, reject and fail.

Foil or thwart.

Strike with a bullet or the like.

Wound to kill, especially with outarch—defeated at the point when success seems certain, or at the very last moment.

Make off to leave. Let us go, as a fledgling might. The other night it was. Enjoy the respite. Enjoy this brief renaissance. To not live within these fractures is the disease, an existence obscured beneath covert glazes of control and ortho-doxy, strata silently laid down from conception.

He rushes into your dwelling. Someone is hammering at the blank slate. Go out and get some starlight. In the story I'm killed off when the rope is drawn to its heighest point above the trapdoor. May I see again the prized object at its time of coming into being? One may be perfectly confident that we shall utter. Include as many horrors and infamies as our two friends are able to invent. Resist. Have done with us.

Didn't know thighs had hands she says. Something like that.

A haruspex. The sacrifice consists of a bull or two (cows will suffice), a pair of gazelles or antelopes, and hundreds of ducks: anger, grief mistimed—the deer's entrails et cetera. Look, don't try to follow me down this hole. It's said they're descended from crocodiles. Vertical lines are cut into a stave to denote incidents of psychic deviation. I am bled from connective tissue—an elective head, a stack of fleshy discs. My eleventh vertebra has collapsed. (The soul dwells in an eye and he nearly succeeds in devouring it.) I can't remember how I entered here. I am full of sleep. A wooden vessel supports the structure on masts, with gabled roofs rising one above another to the sky. I resemble the char-acter in a tale who has lost his own shadow. Each storey has a projecting root. I reach the foot of a hill. Substance: genus of porcelain. I'm considered divine and adopted as a vowel sound missing for centuries. For the rest of my life I am debased and averse to labour. I am idle-housed, indwelt. Worms were once sup-posed, bred in the fingers.

Relate to us now the second example of suicide. An x-ray thereof.

I am at the end of a valley which pierces my liver. Corkscrew vein at left tem-ple visible in cracked lookingglass. People form a circle and beat at something in the centre. The thing struck looks like an ox's head. Rods of light penetrate my remaining eye.

The tone of this canto recalls the contrast noted in the ninth. The wood is not marked by any path (blurred patch on negative here).

This story is the incandescence of memory: no signature, no grafted name. I'd like to hear something about the song proper—any working pulse, generally. Or a letter excised from an alphabet, a small lead weight. Afflict us with your art. Uti-lize a mournful expressiveness. The moment he fell silent you missed your chance.

I can't agree with his theory of natural coding. A mirror and a razor lie crossed within reach. The things tear him apart piecemeal—jaw yet still com-plete, scarcely mobile. The structure is best described as a tapering tower with many storeys and a widening crack running down the middle. What happens to you here, within these pages, lasts forever—the roundel that binds the sheaf of fact.

Coiled (often of, often not)—the cylindrical pile of coin, blood corpuscle or other disc. Meaningless refrains.

Item: one of the parts of which a cask is made, a protective covering for the skull. I persist by making some noises of my own. They cut free and carry off the suffered organ. It's my turn to be consumed. They say we have decided to eat you because of your disobedience.

Discs enclosing fulminating substance—a yellow powder composed of glands and bracts, thinly beaten into tissue of gold. We are a sedative. Terrain, mazzard-hilled. He lays his hands on her diaphragm in order to fathom her technique. A subtle change occurs. The roasted flesh tastes bitter. A sequence of sheets has been marked with her seal. Sit here and think of something new to say. Actually, I think the situation is more to do with an obsessive attention to detail. The pages have fused together and must be sliced open. A stanza, one verse of a song, bursts out in the compound. (He, she) struck, hammered, forged, printed (this).
Correction. Megaera is one of the furies. Add third the elsewhere.
Usurpatrix.

Old distilling apparatus beside the dock. Cruciform crystals, genus of flesh-flies—condensation of the family Now. The drip of a still. A sense of doubt and delay (e.g. the evil day, withsaid). It does read better here, in actuality. This be a narrative of incidents set firm in their sequence. Who infers it is existence, unrelieved?
A kidney-shaped leaf. Fusiform agars, the steersman in his glass cage, with ethercap.

We are labouring under the security of a popular form of control. I have detected an ornament of interlaced arcs of light, common in the early northern: the three-edged worm bone. I have had myself converted into signals. I can be measured and retrieved. I operate. Subjects aroused from orthodox seepage rarely recall dreams (a phase of orthodox lasts for about one half). Numbers have been found tattooed in the sutures of the skull and the pyramid of the wrist. These articulate over and above the state. I am the usual unnecessary, without speaking parts. Bare bulbs and red velvet drape are reported stolen from the chapel. A click can be obtained and is diagnostic of congenital dislocation. A nerve impulse is propagated in any normal direction. I feel a bit numb, a form of censorship, still-born.

Witch trial sketch, circa 1919 (domino effect).
Uranium isotopes by gaseous diffusion.
The suctorial mouth-parts of certain insects.
Such casual remarks are scratched on silver birch bark and trampled underfoot. Each of us carries around a set of shibboleths.

Year of aloud, misused as for advancing old adage. Metamorphosis of air, rockward. Great-circle sailing.

This is the dreaded protection. Sounds more like bureaucratic sadism designed to isolate and punish the prisoner further. Not to mention those of us still gnawing at fragile liberties on the outside. They'll be forced to take into account not the past offence, but the future disorder.

Just as you left voice I woke and recalled the estuary, a huge mound of shingle to ascend, the red tower beyond apex—a many-storied tapering pile. Are you watching. In away. You dressed sockless for the heat, intervening with staves, and the grasping of dogs' tails.

Slept well really again. I wonder whether she's related. I wonder whether she is dead at least.

I walk the crew at the riverfront. This is where they fell last night to sleep, forced inward on waves of contraction.

The silent impassive steward.

In the painting the trees form an avenue. Also note the abandoned shopping trolley, the tap of a retort, the rent in a silk stocking, a bobbing toe—collarettes of tentacle white with hammer shells.

Silhouette of citadel beside radio mast, the blue haze of a million exhalations. Bony process on upper mandible. Cubist washday, caged squawk uncertain. A doctrine of signatures: wrap yourself around a sense of place. There's a presence on the radar screen. Origin, hardly the dim of casque. Reconfigure and repeat.

Are you watching.

In a way.

Lower marsh street. Book of antiphons. One who passes. One carried along by the efforts of another, flung out east of inland sea. One who can sign his own name.

A permafrost zone. The atmosphere is bursting with electricity. There's time but not much of it. His insensibility is getting out of hand—no big gap of reigning years. Is there anything specific you need to do with the writing. If yes, in the room of the film of the mouth.

Today I become my own adversary. Just listen. There's hope, an impossible rescue situation. It sounds like writing. The suggestion: draw out with your tongue the prick of venom. Just listen. Don't delay. You step forward into the ruins. I am sick of love. This has gone on rather longer than expected. I presume this is where we exhale in unison. I can no longer see your eye in this peasoup fog. I have the instinct to quit. The tracks are still missing. How will I lead you out of this place and into the promised salvage.

Wave swell sensed in outer dark beyond. Projecting lines of illumination, bone cold. I preferred it much more when you were sinking.

Rusting graphite on landing, light Victorian. You can presume war as a backdrop. I've discovered a new level of breathing. Put yourself in a place where there is nothing to add. His last missive remains unanswered: the old world counterfeits et cetera. There's no time. Approach, draw close to touch, prepare and separate. I am having an agon with reality, the facts of the case, the true state of things (knowledge). The sun sets suddenly. I enter the penultimate phase. There's no twilight. (Any excess fat, we'll get the Mars instruction in.) A guide is woven from any remaining material. A ring of people shuffles around the inner courtyard of the tower. We have run out of time. This is set in opposition to my own distractions, nigh-hand guesses rambling towards calamity. The courtyard is circular: spinal discipline. Destroy his old habitat.

A slit in a garment, the wrack of a ruinous coast. He would be observed. He would be grateful.

She is she who rends.

Mislippen. You can see the blue bits of the picture spreading all the way up to the top of the sphere, the ellipse. Lead ground in oil. Water-glass, neglected.

I have my cill moth for company (the nature of its demise is immaterial). Am writing dreamt of him, incensor of equilibrium and disaster. At this very moment I lie in recollection. He has forsaken voice. He says he found himself surveying the view and wondered about my own perspective. He says on days like this he sees spirits and angels in the oblique sunlight. Then I find my very self crossing the same bridge. I am momentarily vindicated and erased from pain. I have recorded a wavelike movement by which the contents of the canal are propelled across the viaduct. We are charged into stars, one lost or invisible in a brilliant group of seven.

Her cries alert the police. Firework and callipers, splint-life. A rare left-handed shell. Exposed white chalk of quarried undercliff. She says I family.

Of the squares and their influence.

Tiny organic compasses measure the inside of our bodies. The other night it was my turn. They bore their way in anticlockwise. I am convulsant before the window. I am eight cubits long, two wide.

Orchids in bloom at the overlooked park. Now where did I bury that ring, inscribed with an unvented word. The upper pedal, by twisting about on its axis, is actually the lower. I'm not in my stride at the moment. Guess me.

I serve as a landing place for insects.

I am a refrain, the burden of a song or complaint.

I am yclept of doing.

I have one fertile stamen (or two).

I am the incompleteness you fear.

I am united with the column, the pollen in mass—psyche over matter.

I am clock-ignorant, a distant double.

Wreckage cast ashore is exposed by the ebbing tide. Family blooderwrack, powdered pigment. The destiny of this sign is service, attrition.

In the end they had to cut her loose from the house with oxyacetylene torches. See on war I have seen. Abortive, not able to succeed.

Simulation secretes mucus into the urethra. He is the last of the native informers. I read myself here once, with counterfeit musicians. He behaves like an estranged twin. What are my chances. He is fixed in his restraints, neck braced for action. Projections flicker on the bedroom canopy. Is there much, the together to speak of? Good voice has stilled, for all his belonging. Is there cunning. Is there present. Come chew among the used books—a steel cave lined with black velvet, the said sign. Listen. Screams from the atrium, that scraping sound. Columns of blue flame lick out from fissures in the earth. Raise the ramp.

Guardian wraith with thin distensible sac. And he asks, can you do a little magic, your self.

She sends a signal. Oi, mendicant, time leaves us necessary. Bereave him to stand in need, under a mountain of suspended books. Thank you for nothing. Within a foot of the door she stops, as if arrested by an irresistible force, the threat of that final chord.

It has a fringelike sieve to collect and retain food. I am developing a direction away from the soleplate. I have sweats and the nightfever (I always seem to be doing something). I aim to crack this case. There are the customary clues: truncated plane trees, lime spattered on all the corpses in the avenue, steaming asphalt. At a break in the garden wall stand disfigured strips of rotting fence—bark shed in thin plates, dissolved in white noise like melting silver. Encroaching lichen and moss, acid pulp, the innominate bone. Wherever are we going to find enough water I ask.

Substitute in flat regions of decayed self. One leg is of brass, the other a relic that resembles the haunch of an ass. Fetid water and minerals gush out of me. Split corroded planks inconstant line a filthy runnel (Elizabethan). Figures emerge from the mould on the wall: tropic zone visible from orbit, scars of latitude and longitude. A sag has furrowed deep into the mattress. I foresee a journey to his last resting place—the disciple pebble, the winter hearth. Underfoot, jangling frost on pavement frazil, brittle fibres of ice. Now I must do this alone.

At the corner with volleys of snow, home soon in our childhoods. Is he a version. He possesses.

She sits beneath and accounts for me. The view is remote. This brings the afternoon to an abrupt close. Chance strips us of everything. I cannot weave her

174

into my perfection. A shade is cast through the interception of light by an object. Nothing is being untrue. What is the opposite of dilated she asks, not contracted. So what thing was very very hot, exactly? Under the overhang of the crag we creep in shelter from the north wind. Everything is permuted. A dark figure is projected onto the surface, mimicking the object. Of course I had everything to myself then a girl. The days are accomplished, beloved physician. This is going to take a mighty long time. And she says how now may I sleep in this midst. (I'm not sure what it is I'm supposed to be apologizing for.) Influence what befalls us, men of ghost who once were suitors. It rains fire and sulphur from the sky and destroys us all. Amen.

More to the point, we are literally waiting. What scares you all into time. I am murmured by translation. I shan't step forth today, sandbagged in like a saint, angels on the wireless. The marks on her body indicate. She has at some time been pinned to a board. A person or thing wastes away almost to nothing, an inseparable companion. I meet spirits who double as magicians. Performance is in the open air by night, especially a lady's window—cold clear sky, with meaning influenced by late. Now I am used impersonally. Without, without only id.

Except her breaking shadow. Sun weak yet still set to melt the upturned iris. Everything else I forget: men from the roof spilling language one summer, a path of light leading into the waves, the adjacent chimney stack. An unmistakable cauldron of molten tar. Note to self: bring eye-flap next time (if there is a mistime). Did I write cunning. The tower is to be demolished. I am blinding slow, the plea from without the superstructure. Nonetheless, much dwelling and preparation of inherited foodstuffs. Is there anybody else. I takes precedence. Corkscrew vein at right temple signifies wariness. I am wary. Today is the day. The sail hangs in heavy folds unfurled. A million people are here. I am trying not to work.

Dazzling light, brief notes telegraphed from a nervous breakdown. Strip him to the mast. Strip him to the radio pylon. Whiteout. Desert aerial. Sustained airdrum on fugue. Is is exile? I am matter of scrap.
Palpitate heart.
Descend into morass of nerve.
Hyperventilate.
Sudden shrink of sinew.
Spasm at grief-muscle.
I would have remained much longer at that window but the portal closed.

Rout of memory. The creaking chain of being. Of blood loss, an epic retold in a look-blind study. Lightning doorman, word-reave and overseer. Head in motion with bile sap at ligature of muscle (think iodine on a flesh wound). The solution is simple: if there's less time, write faster. Vernal war in equinox, dispatches therefrom. These words are my own notes, as recorded verbatim. Scent of coumarin—woodruff and melilot, mingled with fresh hay. He has one eye out. He has pink in his ears. This stuff's posthuman. Our mission seems perverse. One brother was wearing an explosive vest. We are looking out for puer aeternus. I have such great revelation. The meaning of the second element is unknown. I strike a guess, a neckname. I determine an irregular dotted rhythm, small blanched followers with whirring leaves. A funnel-shaped corolla descends deep into the earth divided into rings. I have been sent beyond the outermost layer of the central cylinder. This is what I saw. Soft tissue within the clasp of vascular bundles at the stem. Similar material elsewhere. Anaemic inner skin of spinal marrow: substance condensed with insignificant meaning. My revelations are nonesuch—dark nefarious aspect with light element characterized by stars. Look up: the lesser wain-wheel. Now destroy the central nervous system. Kill my animal after this fashion. I am without writing or marks, unstrung from root of to glitter, to shine. I have this torn in the flesh, sigils cloverlike with racemes of white-flowering cyan. I shouldn't boast. I'm held fast in ordinary language, vacuum close. A law, a replacement, a settler.

His heroes are those giants before. That illustrious animal is the tiny hymenopterous insect of proverbial industry, loosely described. Being is more or less form, grainy and inconclusive. The wet is unpleasant, rising halitus of bloodshed. Each day passes without comment. There is no concrete. No one ever found two of us the same. A high-tilting wagon lurches at the crossroad. He is standing right in front of me. You ring the very minute of my recollection. The head is buried beneath the junction of four roads. Each night passes without comment. He speaks. He calls his men to him. He is beating down the freshly dug earth. They obey. In spite of what I've seen I still believe, and always will, in a revolving core of molten iron. Europe's great epic, he says, is a comedy.

Something renders her incomplete and wounded, a disembodied lament for herself. The scalp is speckled with stars resting on matt black. Down here, men dream awake and don't know of it—you won't find what earlier writers call the populace. The pupil of the eye is reflecting the buildings opposite. (Has anyone thought to administer bitter wormwood.) Indelible sense of calm under the atmosphere. (See cause of his blindness, below.) Bury him agog, he and all his multi. Yes, I am afraid of it as it closes in. We may lose our way and never find magnetic north again. There is a dissolving path in which one heavenly body spins around another. There is a simple row of linden trees. There is the asteroid belt. And there is a hollow round vessel for the holding. I am the fifth of eight parrying fences, godwitted.

A void of fluid spurts from the stanchion.

Follow every movement, shadowcast. I set out to write a history of remembering the world (bloodsucking serpent-witch et cetera). If people so much as think these things they are going in the book. I have secured a furnished flat overlooking the avenue. We find material among living statues. I have cornered the market in embers of cork. (It amounts to the same thing.) The subject is he who or that which draws or lets bodily. Five or six points of the zodiac hang on the craw of Orion. I no longer want. This is going to take a very long time. The nebula covering the eye has split open at the top and is thinning in the centre. I look up and see the junction, a torso illuminated by rays reflected back from the surface. Flesh oily and glistening, breath shallow. This is a body situation.

Trees ash, of course. I think I've jumped a head, somehow. Somehow saturnal. Skull, helmet, cask.

Mandragora.

No referrals in that singular day. No reaction again and again, driven away with impact beyond the white line. He comes in and steadies the ship at an instant. Set this obscure field to his coordinates. Protect the usual areas. He is stretching this out just beyond the incident. The time is the time when the sun crosses the equator. Any shadow is identical to its thrower. Speech and thought balloons ascend to the surface from the ocean floor. The strip shows a siege engine and rocket booster rockets in operation (captain the crystals). A similar paradox can be found at the core of any narrative. Slip quietly into zones of unorthodoxy. As if a star, breathe gentle. In the limited space of this book it's not possible to reproduce the ceremony of opening the mouth and eyes depicted in the tomb. He is the subject of many strange fancies—that faculty of the mind by which it recalls, represents, or makes to appear past images or impressions.

He shifts into my presence. Save our soul. Through the needle, send chaos—send chaos engineers—within time both early and late, which I have laid up for thee, o my beloved.

Ramakin. A small quantity of satellite, or cheese. As if held within a body at breath he slides back into obscurity. On page one hundred and ninety-nine is a general overview, as given in the papyri of the dynasties. It says here. A division of soft tissue produced by external mechanical force is taking place (i.e. incise, puncture, contuse, lacerate, poison). Hang on, fiendship—the crow is a permanent resident throughout its entire range. The day is overcrust. Vomit up any excess. Sometimes I can see the misused book at some inner head. I hear through the gapevine. I name this ship the ship. We are brushed by a darkening oxide rim. I call out and am called in return. I usually deal with any fluctuations in current myself. A hood covers the moss capsule. Note to self, inject some fucking and humour.

Various features of a beguiling old myth, ultra marine. A cluster of latent cells illuminates the root-cause. The damaged tissue is rare and exotic. Now night is equal in length to day. Harness and chain-mail, scales and splints, siege cap and riot shield are all misaligned. I am twisting to one side and then to the other. On the answer machine is more seditious praise. You have no sense of time he says, do you. He has never asked for pardon, we will see him go to the scaffold with the calm of a clear conscience. And I don't mean a nickname for a lamplighter, or a glass-annealing oven. Scumbled and mussy, with cuplike cavities, this contains the longest paragraph I ever writ. In this way we are historified, see.

Commander, you bin tonguetied with this capricorn blackly in a dismissive. Meanwhile is driving on into an empty space.

XV

Moon crossing meridian. I can hear you in all this ruin. We are crossing the terminator into night. Jupiter rising to east. Grind of scrape, rattle on hull— that familiar hissing sound. She lies twenty-eight feet down in the claybed. These days are field notes to a season.

Does it have events and characters. Do they have traits. Do things happen.

We closed last night at the motif of the stairs below. Continue. Everyone sticks to the script (the idea of talking plays an important role in this chapter). I'm a faculty of subsense, a form of understaff. The glottis resembles the craw of a bird, in two halves that fit together like box and lid. Flinty shells underfoot. Stagnant infusions of animal and vegetable matter. I am delayed by voice. She teaches a rare class of exorcism. (Murmur, o how awful.) She is utmost, an end in herself. At the steep stair: do I not know you.

She asks if she may borrow some sleep, something.

Waiting room and hall leading to bed recess. Late day. We concern ourselves here with what passes through the mouth in either direction (bespoke foodstuffs). It's only now, for the first time, that I hear what I presume to be talk. Autonomy becomes a stumbling-block. It's been a week of words that disgust you and the selected words you cannot use. I am embowelled of a doctrine. Etym dub.

She's dead two days before they find her, in a narrow trench at the base of a ravine—a dried-up riverbed like a street you might gallop horses through at night.

During which he explains his lifelong. That room is her room. It's about control. I can barely be contained. Untimely mediations: I am unhead, a subjective indication of disease, an uncharacteristic sign of existence: symbolic stem, the foundation of vast estates. I am contaminated, a nothing, sat in the twilight with incanting voice. Beetles click in the cavity wall. The idea of listening plays an important role in this caper, the nuance of key. The smell of the smoke isn't the normal smoke smell. I am at landsend. Time begins.

Antihelix.

He dies interstate. The organ resembles a wing, a sail, or a side-piece (horn-work in fortification)—the flanking corpse on either side, a flock of rapid eye moments. It behooves me: a figure in which thoughts and words are unbalanced in contrast, the direct opposite of being here. So, dreams are particularly vivid, hence of, hence pertaining to. Who never uses the singular.

The last chapter is good for nothing and not worth troubling the printer with. Doom and date. Alleluia. Consign to waste product.

Tisiphone is one of the furies.

At the rim of the second largest crater on the visible face of the moon.

A companion is unsettled by voice, by mouth. We chance upon an abandoned settlement, a cluster of ruined huts dating from perhaps. I take a measure of its chambers—windows, gates, lintels and thresholds. A pitcher lies broken at the fountain. I recollect.

A string of low rounded islands in the gulf stream, prehistories. The man clutches a gate-staff in either fist. All kinds of edible species are visible through the hatch. Each mental vision extends far into space. One looms close, six pairs of legs quivering from the thorax. Its plume enters my vein. Vision has become so sharp. I can make out the portholes of a distant craft. I bend to retrieve a pebble. One is acutely conscious of every instant. I place it gently on the table. I am intermediate where anything occurs. Ask to make a noise like that of insect wings. Utter with buzzing sound, or whisper to spread, secreted.

Flung clear afloat in the shadow of the perfect crime: an action bleached of gravity.

Index this further, more detail.

A slow fuse, or matchless chord. I am now able to converse with ease, on any subject engaging thought (an aperture for the refusal of light, or pointing). Ideas for ingenious escape radiate from the margins of the head. We are the planet next to earth in order of distraction from the sun, the female branch of descent. Port of saint.

Brief coitus against wartime railing. My technique is an accumulation of subtle increments. There follows a kaleidoscopic nine minutes of the underbelly, the pier—past lives and impervious futures, what you've done and what you've built. Everything is cancelled. I'll keep an ear to the stars and an eye to the ground for you. The significant word stems from the root found in flax (my purpose back then). I don't want her to understand. Everything is attached to me.

I walk through a galley of ice-crusted gold. Stones are poured out at the top of every street. It's a time for strength matched by redundancy. I uncover his name and denounce him (F K Robotnik). Under a soot-blackened arch I bind a promise, with angelic attendants. Farewell and withtake, upstart. Everything is abolished. I walk out through the international exit. All the signs indicate a creeping sidereal thing—earthshock—an incomplete mechanism in butterflies and moths. I am at home in whatever abandoned shell I can find. This zone is the much talked of buffer zone. Here, sedation triumphs over malfeasance, love too. In the first vision of this chapter he writes less provocatively. Shell tracers crisscross the sky. A probe is tracking a nerve. We are the rare doing of not. He leads me out of and into myself, away from the ghost we call things. It is dark, not light. He turns against me, attains and touches. He compasses me. Glimpsed in the darkness are creatures driven to alien forms of locomotion. (One counterfeits my death.) A projectile leaves a smoke trail. Greengold lichen or moss clings to the hull of our vessel. Likewise he cordons me about. We have triggered a chain reaction. Crew force broken glass into their mouths, between their lips. It's a kind of game. A chemical substance is used to mark the course followed by the process. He forges a chain for me. . . . Mouths stretched taut by shafts of glass. . . . There are bodies in the water, quick and not, living or dead. Pictures rise up out of the words: I am shout. My voice is shuttered. I gather. No, my voice is gathering. I shout something white rears up out of the water, breaking the surface by the gunwale like a hand. It raises a cloud of sparks. These form a pattern in the air. My path is closed by boulders, felled trees and flytipped mattresses—looming planet at event horizon, at peripheral vision. He is a walking encyclopaedia, recently incorporated within the town museum. I am pulled to pieces. I am not remembered. Only now I can fully grasp the comparative hostility of Mars. I am the bullseye for the sudden bolt. I am the only one. The quill of his arrow enters my vein. I have no position in the west. Things are universally derided (seek her grave). My money's on the good money. I am an unreasonable opinion and capricious inclination—such as will divide a number without remainder. A fleshy caul clings to its scalp. Three conical appendages surround the mouth. The young influorescence is eaten. We are deep in the family vault-line. Supernumerary bones are developing in the sutures of the skull, bitter plates of carbon. I have no position in the east. Gravel grinds my teeth. I cling to the metal bars attached to the exterior of our craft. I lose my grip. I am adrift. My orbit is decaying. I ignite on contact with atmosphere. From within, eyes monitor and observe. He covers me with ashes. I breach no question in the occident (a state of chronic apprehension as a symptom of mental disorder). Objects drift loose in the vacuum, deep into unstarred space. I am odd ends stolen forth, wholly writ. I recall mind, spilt and then re-minded. Imminent loss is augured come the end of the reel. There is hopeless. Whiteclad and helmeted, she had a mouth just like yours. I am consumed. Do you want my blood on your tongue. Deep scratches decorate my forehead. Compression falters: scattered glitter, the solid citizen, the endless drone of the adjacent room. I'm shaving off my beard as soon as I get paid. I am undone, tightly. They treated me like one of their own. He sets me in places like the dead. All flesh and all spirit divide the sea and establish the light. Shelltooth. Thoth.

A ridge remains in the mud at the edge of a ploughed field.
His tongue is pierced by the barb of a ray.

Just underneath the central dome. Music has been described as lying between the noise of life and the stillness of death. I am of doubtful origin. Everyone is cancelled. A yellow fluid is secreted from the liver. When thou art taxed free and unsainted—well, then. You are ready for me.

Morning comes.

A large wooden tray housing letter leads has been set up beside the bed. Each sign has its own compartment. The basin in the corner is a reservoir for bile. A used correction ribbon is uncoiled and its whole length pinned around the wall at eye-level (the level seen by the eyes looking horizontally). The audience enters and meticulously studies every error. A dog barks in the courtyard below. We're not sure whether any change is deliberate or not. I decide. I wait. Having nothing better to do, I go outside. At the stair to the sea: a phosphorescent film on the surface, algae sluiced from the reactor. Her life is symbiotic, family residua. There's no mistaking that breath of iodine. Scrap fragments and tags.

I sleep now the sleep. I will not be anchored forever and dismembered. Words are employed in much the same way as they were employed in the days of old. She is hanged from a nearby tree. I sit alone and keep silence, because I can.

She says I too have been there. I was taken. I too have seen out there the earth from the earth.

Without preamble I leap from the window of a fortress. (This is called self-defenestration.) Onlookers astound. I plummet to the embankment and roll. Knees are never the same. I cannot hold a thought for more than six or seven seconds. See, concepts are specific and they are not. I'm the talk of the town.

Tone and music. The great increase.

Intercede she says, or die.

Fires burning in the snow. Hunters. The sounding of a mort.

Lentamente, lentamente.

And there goes the rap of a nerve, the inner curved ridge of the external ear.

A coil. Coit.

Let them touch and merge. At the dead centre of a page the letter I appears thrice. What he means by the word as applied to his composition I dare not venture to guess. There begins an experiment with time. He draws out what remains of her and flings it into the sea.

In the night we write together during the stay of the long night. The object emerges from a fading word. She sits a shadow against the wall held in a fulcrum of light. I'm now six months dwelt in this corridor. (Our things, are they not also our events?) I can no longer be identified with any occupation. I can no longer be identified with any role. Unbeknown, one dies beneath and passes through us. Two extraordinary things occur. A string of flickering lights in the distance signals a coastline. Creeping across the wall are minuscule plants with simply structured leaves. Fierce cold of moving air to face, and the blackening, light-consuming sea. The second stanza has a wonderful idea in it: the moon sprouting thorns and hovering still directly above the sun. (Did I do that.) The cells are arranged in rows of six, a maze of interconnecting errors. A longed-for stasis has arrived. Our ration is passed twice daily through a hatch. Other than that, there's no sign of our keepers.

Trst.

Postwar return to a city alleged, sweet sleep owed me yesterday. It is still on the map. We use a prearranged system of communication, a sequence of taps and whistles. Much busyness of mind and body—an old homestead here, an old homestead there, the denticulate parapet of a fortified settlement. Drystone walls and goat dung, hilltop vapour at dawn. A space is left by the extraction of a seam, into which waste is packed. Coitus at tabletop, the dank alley of starving cats. I close in on the target, pressing my lips against the metal pipe that runs through the hive. They have shed their light on me from without. I execute the launch. Incarcerated with me are the thirty-five just men. My role is a zone of interference. (It's the way we weave together that counts.) The target is destroyed, fate unknown. I'm a scientist and I always think, yes, they're preparing. The concept is correct. In later times we find that attempts were made to secure the deceased. It's said the world began in E flat (note the same gaping hole). A crust forms on the rocks, the trees, the soil. My cellmate looks like a dog. It's all smoke and mirrors down here at the park. A saving clause is needed, fermentation of flint.

They are as unbreakable stone at the passing quarry. We are sick with reservation, mere pretext. They shed their light into me. To the west of this constellation is found the water-listener—weed of salt in a sea of alginic acid. Any expedient word would have done.

I should have mentioned the cellmate earlier when describing the structure of the building. Now is too late. He resembles a corolla. He resembles a long tube with limbs spread out flat. He resembles anything that binds—the bundle of fibres joining an atom radical, a tie or slur, a cord for the blood vessel: illusions by legerdemain. His only task is the precautionary tasting of food. In the tale it appears, erroneously, that I am alone in the cell. I feel compelled.

Simultaneous discharge. Spore-bearing capsules grow parasitically on the parent. There's an eruption on the skin, the inner circle and vortex of a floral envelope—the doing of what one ought not to do. Bitter rootstock.

Zedoary. Valerian. Also rans. Note to self, excessive use of ellipsis is cheap and facile.

She tricks him into wearing a smoking jacket impregnated with poisons. The waiting comes to a blessed end—corkscrew vein bulging at left temple. It's the ultimate form of nihilism. Hair-trigger greys rustle in the eaves. A blackened tongue protrudes. She coils a length of string tightly around the crook of her forefinger. Everyone stands stockstill. There are forty voices, all doing something different (the unknown pleasures of predictive text). Estranged and touching territory this, the ultimate anti-fade.

He leaps across the oily waters of the canal to embrace an ancient wooden pile. There's no going back. He's held together by blue plastic staples. A snake-shaped scar coils itself about his wrist. Tendons are severed. He has lost twenty percent (sensational). A glorious cacophony accompanies this surgical performance. It's one of those events you find yourself at once in a lifetime—an image or representation thus formed in the mind. Before me is a pierced crag through which the foaming sea pours. Smuggle me over to my allies. I couldn't possibly love anyone mortally.

He says these appear to be notes from a past season. And when, pray, is the promised silence to come, the promised eustasy. Collected here are musics, material burned or volatilized—incense, steam, resins and gums—the full operatic ensemble. I resolve to survive without light for as long as possible.

An hour is halved. She buries herself in the next room. There's a storm. (You know how this is going to end, don't you.) I sleep now, resting at anchor, while a man ashore is hanged from a silver fir.

Gulf of ob. A vast ossuary, a watery place where haunted animals seek refuge. They peep and mutter, whispering as if oracle out of earth.

What do they whisper of.

Certain discomposed planets (old calendars long past would tell as much), the faecal mud of a childhood estuary. A thousand idle questions, nice distinctions and subtleties. She is debriefed, every slur, only to sink back several feet into the clay. Return to the image of that final month, the advent beneath the mirror, pasteboard portals to a floating city. The natural divisions of time are adjusted to create an almanac of humans and supernaturals. Pennies fall to the floor from her pocketbook. It contains a list of condemned saints and prisoners awaiting trial. Under the aegis of the ministry I am making use of similitudes (see counterfeit death above). This leads to misunderstandings: heads must be halved. It's three in the morning. Such an irresistible tension, like the worship of a sacred footprint. We cross a suspension bridge. My conscience is clear. I look askance at everything. Think of me as an equinoctial point in the heavens.

The old delivers them. Morning comes once again, as predicted. Fugue on the messageboard. Work faster he urges (I am probably the cause of his blindness). These things hark back to myth and are hard to split open. Others say that having killed them he went silent and speechless in search of his mother. Take an inventory: roodscreen, a shade, a hanging sword. All about me the storm pages.

184

Item. One stake. Item. Suitably frantic dervish music. The accompanying chant is said to have originated as a word grafted onto a howl. Item. A temporary wooden screed faced with earth serving as protection against splinters of shell. My evidence is insufficient—the flapping flag at undercliff, an interlude numbered nine. There is a small anteroom, a passage surviving as the entrance to several apartments. On display in the library is a collection of heresies: restrictive covenants, rights of way, ancient lights. A figure in a glass case displays a coat of chainmail. Calm yourself. In what place, whitherwards I am in this present state, at this point in time? The instant pivots into great silence.

He conceals himself among the stowage of casks in the hold. Spermaceti. (Question. Who us'd to Capricorn her Husband's head?)

Check time. Belief is unsupported by any observation. Those employed at the interior cavity and on the rigging work till long after star-rise. He says I am here, here in this place. It is said his words unravel in dazzling display across the years. We are a form of Russian roulette. The poles of the compass reverse. Events are written down or sketched to compile a record, clandestine resistance.

Pelagic, of unknown affinity. *Auto-da-fé*. It's quite an interior world we've summoned up, is it not. Underfoot stretches a plane of frozen glass. You are the only persons I agree. Your chief happiness has been found *there*: the village, with peripheral spikes ranged in defence about cyclopean architecture. My own stock leaches away. I am a mess of impregnations. How strange all this is has only just occurred to me. There's a pleasing sort of logic to it, the ultimate form of minimalism. I am worked as a single isolated deposit—of, in, or using a solitary tongue. Whitewater.

Whatever. Iron, old chem. The villagers gather as much intelligence as they dare. A great many extraordinary signs compensate for their lack of liberty. I am standing at the eastern gate—in this place, in the place where the person speaking is situated.

The past is disinherited. It flags attention to space and presence, not to what one is about to say. I have two chambers, separated from one another by a warm wall of flesh.

About this place. Crack inside the skull. I am standing in the anteroom of a legislative hall. She conjures three test questions. All time is contained in the body. She repeats a meaningless word (a whole chapter of the book was written with the aim of enabling her to escape unharmed). She recurs as the burden in old seasongs. A dart jets from the hastate leaves that ring her head. Her tense is present. Her present is the mental equivalent of a clenched fist. Note to self, apply copious rumblegumption, and quit. The release date is poised for the slightest pressure. Time is well after the eighth.

And she says, my dear, I didn't notice you there. I thought you were a statue, an automatic door opener.

The men on the shoreline angling at stars.

Three characters in search of an oval. I obtain a reluctant hearing. She asks who are they who live in the book? Their names and their events? Everybody must have a place of berth. Trust me. The alignments are perfect: the ascending path, the obelisk, the cell, the pyramid, the courtyard, the moon, the stonemasons' temple, the concrete vessel, the lake, the ever-locked park, the gated arch, the basilica, the sea.

I'm force-fed rice gruel, gullet stretched open by a hollow shaft of glass. A half-naked man attends to his aquarium. Now I'm hungry again. It was like going deeply into somewhere not, an underground fault. The future is located at the back of the brain in the pineal gland (the postilion of a gene in a chromosome). This is my first campaign. More there are will be, yes. That is to say, the advantages of waiting and the disadvantages of position.

The morning redness in the east. How is my hand like or unlike other hands. Through the opening door she writes and down the mossy steps to the sea. I know now where to find you. My own image waits to startle me at the embankment, opposite.

Causative of to rise, to rear up (time and again).

A tiny oblong of dampcrumpled paper lands at my feet. Beetle-blue ink sluiced by fluid. The hand is rapid, spearshaped with basal lobes twisting outward—initial adjuncts, circles and loops in hook, under-dots foraging, conned. Think of those winged seedpods that hover in descending spirals of late summer. The small circle represents and the small loop is, in the same manner as the end but with limited powers. What remains is a desiccate. The large loop is not used at the begging of an outline. This science fiction thing has become second nature.

He says he has written of me, Zen violence striding out to greet the sea at dawn. And what happens. He is one of those people who, when leaving, one never knows whether one shall ever see again. Nor does one care, either way (love).

Scene: either of two points in the heavens where a line cuts the elliptic. Light sliver with strands of uncanny. When white stands in the snow it has a different colour. Numbers seven and eight have one foot each in the baroque past. The relationship between this pair is none too obvious. Skip a cycle. Come down and see for yourselves. We glean that he is full of years. He scatters thinly.

Where is this thing that passes for understanding.

It lies three kilometres beneath the ice, interseeded.

Such looking back is now forbidden, dissenter of thought and intents of the heart. She says I can ghost it, the after-image—a beam of particles moving in parallel paths, trammelled rays of light that penetrate to the marrow.

Mercury rising, with sulphur jaundice. Spreading weeds of salt. An impassable wall holding back a sea of alginic acid.

Subject phossyjawed.

Creature, the emmet or pismire.

No whither.

A murder weapon is bolted to a cathedral. Place of exile and pilgrimage in one, two halves of the same chamber. A complicated circumnavigation is taking place. There is no etymological justification. I continue erasing the productive apparatus—the mines, the machines and factotums. Erosion of surroundings leaves an isolated elevation (with excrescent *d*). I do not know the thing I am writing.

Raised sutures map out across the scalp. Primary cells are attached, zinc and copper electrodes. Olibanum, benzoin, styrax and cascarilla bark are the candidates. The condemned are condemned to fill with water a vessel full of holes. A crude diagram shows the location of her grave. The heads are buried there. I have a dogtooth missing, right-hand upper mandible. Bodies are elsewhere. The chief landmark is the meat screen. I have seen the legend. There's no going back. Old rolling stock, ruined bunkers and deserters line the track. Some have no scruples whatsoever regarding the casual executions. In no way do I want this to appear real, as though it may actually have happened.

An untitled book is being written. First twilight spreads across the imperceptible curve. The writing is goaded on by a dilemma. The onset of rain is the cue for feelings of dismay. Steam pours from my stem.

His cell is rather monastic. He is cuntular in form and demeanour. Nice smile, small bottle of liquor and mixer on route. I see the inquisitor greet him with a secret sign. Blood is pumped. There's nothing to write about.

Noise and sensation of moving air on flesh exposed. Thousands of tiny filaments expand and bristle erect. Inside the carcass are found oblong gold coins, bursting forth on brilliant wings. I stand or die on my own moment. The trial comes unsought, out of nowhere. I am stepping aside but I am not going away. Light pours through the stained glass above the door. An official lifts a receiver, an earpiece. Every one of my characters has a vacant side. Pay attention to detail. An official lifts a receiver, the earpiece.

We are at the same height above ground as the average person's eyes—the surface constituted by all positions of a point satisfying a given condition.

A unit of luminous flux.
The cavity of a tubular organ.
The space within the cell wall.

For the love of her own image she is forever connected to numbness. Optical wire quivering, opposite. I crouch low, cheesecutter at the ready. Spring comes with vindications.

You, she whispers, are your own salve—iron-grey. Hesternal.

He presses his mouth to the dust.

XVI

The one who's running things is referred to as the countryman. He's a staging post on the way to friendship. The oldest among us confine ourselves to answers—the subtle character of the line, the unexpected. I'm ejected from the breast and lungs. Tomorrow should be interesting (forward slash destruction). Any problems, give us a shout.

I'm painting a gentle portrait of you. The dead cells are still alive in their atomic dimension. How will you take your leave when the time comes. The floor slopes the room imperceptibly. This ratchets the story up several rungs. Music amplifies the silence (there's a horse on the roof). In eighty-six seconds the inevitable happens. Sunlight splits open the trees. I think the knowledge came to him at the last, only at the very last. Make a decision, a groundbroken solo attempt. They assist me by holding me down, but it's no use: yes and no cling together in the same chamber. I dream a powerful magic ritual and escape from oppressive forces, an anxious flight from underworld to surface. And I am not yet worn away. How would you know. The statues and sarcophagi become ani-mated and stride out across the great hall. In seventy-nine seconds the irretriev-able happens. This must be the youngest profession in the world.

Tincture, see tincture.

Long periods of sitting and wasting. A word has been stencilled onto the pavement. The starlight binds me. The time is just after the episode when sun and moon stood still in the sky. There's writing. That's it. Take him, earth.

He helps me return to the moment I quit. Dense fog and a discarded quiver at my feet, its arrows scattered. He's a guide of sorts, albeit volunteered. Vague forms at peripheral. A lamp burning oil through siphoned oxygen functions as an aerosol. Cherish him as you would yourself. That's me naked on the balcony forever. He sings scat in the street, gutter proximal to tongue, tethered by an imaginary belt to the heavens—a hawker, a tranter, a peddler of unease and aim-less news. These days he's displayed under glass in a vitrine, erect, surrounded by scribbled messages. Mark my word, with wiry vein.

Barges pass in the mist, near colliding. Effortless he steps from craft to craft. He buries his head in the oily water. Caught in this suspension is the one who waits. He goes footless. There's a cocklike rhythm going on in the background. The heavy burden of knowledge is shut away in silence for another season. Are you here to judge. Those clouds don't look like rain-clouds. We're like a block of ice. This brings me back to my theme of the south. He has a close-set eye. It's like nothing, seen before. He is hawk-nosed. A word is pencilled onto a crumpled scrap of paper. Nothing is what it is. Whiteness now rare.

A pagoda in a park.

Can't grasp the errant word. There's a paradox—a kiss, a torso hung upside down and flayed. Last night I climbed that gilt memorial opposite the dome. I'm the one spoken of who is nomadic.

A marginal note in a used book of controversial dining.

Like wise the northwest wind. Objections and dislocations. Faint scar long across smooth skin of cheek cuts through downy hair. He was assiduous in his courtship. Ill-health is quite normal—it plays a large part in the creation of such suggestive images and impressions. He carries within him a book of changes, the work of cessation: miscellaneous scraps, the neck of an organ, uncommon volumetrics scratched in a commonplace. I don't trust numbers. In the space to the left of the text stands the deceased. This is the last thing I will ever do for you. I witness his fault crack open and then split apart myself.

The embossed manhole covers.

A hollow sphere is set in a volving motion. Steam escapes through valves fixed at a tangent (you're not concentrating, are you). Sometimes I forgo. He's kept in solitary for a spell and left to think about things. Three in total are prisoned in this prickly husk, within its brittle timbers. He is left to think about what he can safely reveal to the tribunal. An equilateral triangle sits black at base of skull, debased at back of mind. A triptych of tablets, painted panels, have been hinged together. Supra-orbital is the password. Unbroken and separatist, I hang on.

Not so fast.

Too much has happened to write, standing outside of all authority, with scattered remnants of the living. Depict a surface resembling this, yet without stating explicitly what you mean.

Northern constellation close. I'd better wean myself off. In her left hand she clutches tight a number with twelve digits. Notes fly out at the speed of a tenth. Rattle of glass against a frozen pavement, the splinter at footfall. Muscles are stripped of skin. At first we couldn't. Their blood is midnight blue and yellow. Now we can. There's only eighteen degrees in it.

She sits alone in the station carpark. Graceless lyric waltz on the wireless. I arrive well after the time of writing. I need someone I know to reel me in, someone I can trust. My only comparison is a dead comparison.

Flash of light from adjacent vehicle chrome. It's a mistake. I'll never be able to hear that again. Ignore structure like hysteria. Where will all the money come. We don't do error. When will all the time be. They change the personnel but keep the rhythm. The ecliptic passes through me, slices through the nerve centre. I split. I discover my inside is undated. Out of a blue enamel sky, I split.

This is not how I composed way back at the beginning. Offstage he indicates an octave lower. It's amazing how much of this I have kept, how much I can remember. He's begrudged a cameo. The selectors say they have no choice, drama is a chasm of detail, an abyss. This necessitates a plunging in.

Green ash falling from the sky.

Salt and pure water.

Coastal defence of granite logan.

Low-ebb mewstones exposed.

That familiar hissing sound rising from the gullet of a dog, vocalist beating suitcase. Hot metal of beltclasp aligned to nearest star. Hundreds of tiny fossils found embedded in a stratum of sticky clay. The perfect yes rising up from the orbit of an indexed wineglass, a vague attempt at orchestration. The B libel he dropped.

There is no hierarchy of models. The hound lies across my head and throat, panting rhythmically, body rising to fall—a creature of folklore, diminutive in graceness, inhuman in form.

Any serviceable household demon of dispossession. A host.

Marsyas, river.

The lowest throw. The interval of a second, passed. An uncanny host, whom the base and vulgar call the Uncarried. One has never before had any dealings with a person of that name. Love is departing from the ordinary extra. Could there be any court cases that stem from this code? Answer, please.

Likewise the northeast wind. The height of a sail, a set of signal flags fluttering on a single line. People speedwalking. Two notes in the time of three, or three in the time of two. There's a barrier of vanity. Lose half as much of these pages again. He claims they're a kind of diary, the exact parallel of Rembrandt's self-portraits: spikes of showy flowers and a poisonous sap.

Lines now paired sets of double figure eight. Con trails. Notes to infinity.

Their unheated chamber. I am day-blind. Don't be misled into action. Like me. We reach the surface and become allies. Voice cracks. We draw lots to find and seek. One is sent ahead to secure logic and entertainment. At the inn he is questioned. He's asked what he knows of the double. There's a strange backward link here (the I think is bound up with it). About him he notes heavy water, some obscure works for piano, that newfangled destructible glass—a mixture of this and this, ordinary hydrogen and ordinary oxygen, isotopes of triple mass. I never got a letter back.

Bad timing. We languish several weeks. An escape route reveals itself. This is called running away (legitimate).

No exorcist required today. Since you've been gone, I do whatever I want.

A group of seven superhuman beginnings.

As she does she says to him once no more.

Notes on my disgruntled ghost.

Wedding swell, beach whaled. Musicstand standing by window against failing snow. Alchemical red. A trumpet fashioned from of it. An incarnation of shepherds (I simply mean one who tends).

This text probably belongs to the next century. I am lungful. Her pragmatism leaves no truck with the uncanny. Sulphur and mercury vie together, with an abandoned pier as central spool. Vast and sudden influx of blood. Why don't you just say what you want. Return vestiges of self to castle ruin.

There's nobody who can't be got rid of, if only one has the will. Material actions still belong to the state. This may do, or it may not. A tribunal governs the external man. I'm floating in a warm bath of acid. I fall asleep. I light up. In eighty-four seconds the inevitable happens (what's called a jeremiad). I wake. It's a perfect fit, surface to surface contact—no air in the sheath. It's two in the morning. Then the clouds dissolve and are spoken of as rain. As for me, I perform the background for notions of the sun, the moon and the planets. It's not my task to lead.

And she says, you know, you unseat me with your words. All my life pivots about your moment, your own personal sense of time forgotten.

I'm sectioned into twelve equal parts. Ancestors are forming. I justify nothing. That would only make me lose my way. Wouldn't it.

Vade mecum.

A long journey is divided into short episodes called canticles, each with its own particular sense of doubt—inclined teeth with which a howl engages. Wave mechanics focuses on the altered state, the principality of the uncertain: thunder in the lower, debris on the road, the oral intervex. He loses precision in the gauging of his momentum. He teaches atonement, a coast of headless electricity. Now it's the lady with the astonishing octave range. Through the wall a magnet can be heard, feeding on its own tail, one-to-one. I'd love to know the possession status for this chapter.

It doesn't take long this. She's like a one-man. A die rolls. The colouring is part of her eclipse plumage. The wings are of no use for flight. Stiff featherless quills along the spine serve for combat and defence.

Underlight, cyan. Decomposing oxide of iron pyrites—forming apart, an outcrop of metallic veins. The span of words here is hat to intervacuum. Ultimately I'm duped into buying from her three prophetic books for the price I had refused to give for nine—a later set assembled after the destruction of the first. (This apparently minor detail will prove pivotal to our narrative.) But it cannot be shown that she ever composed a rule, possessed properties, so called. We owe her tenets to her sex, which when first formed was immediately exiled. She alone among them extended up the valley and passed out into the desert. Atrocities were committed. Time dissolved. Under this tyranny arose a controversy, the problem of the real and the named.

Dullthudding palms slap firm the chopping block beyond the kitchen trap. A stout elastic tendon extends from the dorsal vertebrae to the occiput. The scalp snaps. An apparent change in the position of the object is taking place. Too much pressure breeds unwanted light. The observer too has shifted his position. Now demonstrate the art of execution in sound, the science underlying—a connected series of sweet or discordant echoes, not mere noise. A world of potential is possible.

This account contains no ideas or facts. Every time I turn around the money's got a lot better.

An outrunner in a postapocalyptic world, he is fated soon to die under the shadow of a sudden. Now he's moving into the square vacated by the adjacent pawn. At the tip of his nicotine-stained index balance five gold coins. He undergoes periods of speechlessness and immobility. What are you doing up there he says being. Nearby are the names of several important mountains. He once corresponded but no longer. The colouring is part of the message. Order more coffee, more blood. He is depicted as a field of shimmering sparks, or dots.

Outfangthief. To face out with scorn. Outdwell.

Theme: nomadic. The story has gathered further momentum. It is here forever. The pipebomb is hauled into the classroom on wire and string. The rope isn't burning or anything. I found someone to tell, the only person I could find.

See how he has fallen into the hands of robbers, eunuchs and magistrates.

Res nullius. An object or objects that can belong to no one, this massive underclaim of year upon year. We are all deemed unculpable.

I climb. I sit and chafe and half the day is worn away. It's eight till five—that's ten of your earth hours, isn't it. Ionization takes place in the air. (See harbour, below.) The tumours are limy nodules bursting forth from London clay. Disregard the inherent contradiction of any of my statements. Come without names. The room has been swept to reassure us. A diminutive of freak, he places the three words in random order. He casts a handful of yarrow stalks. A diagram of these is published once a year. He allows himself to be bled from the corners of the mouth. I'm like a usurped town. In the mindful eye he sees a valley of dried bones. A tendon supports the head. One among us represents the sun.

Return. No man rises. Success. We scramble up a chalky roundhead counterscarp, with bayonet fixed and the ridge through a haze of spent gunpowder. Trees rush out from a gash in the flank.

From source of root to take and of thief. From swerve of shore, back to sound, accidental retroflux. Literally, a rivernovel. Quiet riot.

A salt-crusted coastal plain beyond the tidemark. Likewise the southeast wind. It's a funny old day. Error falls to pieces by degrees. The chrome helix outside the station is ringed by an imaginary belt of fixed stars. Its base is divided into mansions, gas masses generous with heat and light. Layer after layer, my muscles are stripped of tissue. The metal plates are relatively stable, an apparent path within the confines of a perfect square. I am calculating all possible routes. I am searching for the spot he alluded (go out and come back in again). We are reassembled and fleshed.

Incorporate edited fragments of other recordings. Now flee.

Heavy renounce in the music. These days he keeps aliens at bay on the high seas. His being is job.

Portico and harbour. Her widely spaced teeth, sharpened incisors. Dogfangled. Strings of four-four beat. The way is hithered, thithered. Two wage combat on a deserted beach. Haar-mist floats in the oncoming tide. One is closer than the other. Offshore stands an isolated rock worn into the shape of the sea. One combatant hurls a discshaped knife as a missile. A voice says pay attention to the missing letter. I think the sun. The curved instrument drops to his side. Reports of murder and suicide, accident and its execution, running battles. Without warning last night all the lights went out. The witnesses quit the island (that spectral face at the fourth storey window, the thing in the forest). They'd swallowed enough. There's an opening between the sandbanks, a truly narrow strait. They picked a course.

Immediately, a crashing through the tall yellow canes that fringe the beach. It's a rehearsal. One navigates. One brings compatriots. Another brings an artful evasion. One brings his own behaviour. It's rammed. One is ex and therefore unknowable. This is the manner of louche concentration I demand, a state of extreme vigil. One dies in the night. Of the figures, a small carved and painted statuette has been stolen from my animal. Against will I have been sent to a place, the end result on the far side of indecision. I am subject to occasional flogging. The other replies I do, I have.

Now covet this facet, in this direction. Out of the ruin, glowing sparks rise and form a symmetrical constellation: a great circle, a plane that cuts the earth's surface in two at any moment. I did not notice until they gathered up and span.

A figure with pointed rays. They must number five, maybe six. He claims to be a cypher, a space where nothing must occur. And therefore a non-existent: conduit zero, zero number, zero quantity and the figure resenting it. A nought, a thing or person with no significance or value, the empty trial of uttering.

Low conduction (a rifle)—in no degree a thing at all, once and for all. Six signifies a pair of triangles, one inverted. Fog approaches the bank.

It is she assays.

He implores the emptiness around him, seeing nothing, not even air.

Day sever. Never return. Never again renounce yourself. Faint illumination of sky to crack of west. Pink object unidentified resting on cill. He is as limited as the valley is vast and open. Solidity and extension in space, mackerel clouds at the border—large-rolling masses, not rain-bringing: fractonimbus. Full stop. Stratopause. Old alluvia of rivers, someone close by murmuring Sappho.

They were once beloved friends et cetera.

He reflects. Bent knee of bay, agonyclite. To this day I've shed nothing of myself.

Then a continuous horizontal sheet of lightning. Iron contaminating a little carbon, with or without things. I can see the shining light but I cannot read the words.

A plastic clipjoint connects her lower jawbone to my skull. Find note on perfect alignment and install. I was born someone elsewhere, at the cusp of different signs. Now I find myself on the wrong side of the lake. As time goes by I divide and return. The splitting always begins beneath me. I am a mathematically conceived curve. A grain of sea-salt is a cube compressed of an infinite number of smaller cubes (stomata in D flat). Consider the value of random notes and ressentiment, any act of spiritual revenge. Even thought or name permits the merest hint or shadow of difference. A small room has been set aside. It is the final day of the octave. My own beginning is in basilica. Any minute part of this, when amplified, has the same character as the whole. I am many miles from the frontier, hidden in the trunk, or otherwise. God knows what's in it. The first act is always the weakest. (It is I who have it, not you.) That shrivelled artefact is the dead composer's memory gland. I have his hands. They float in formaldehyde in a sealed jar, all that remains of him. Take a good look at that device. The object is shaped like a lens and elongated in the direction of the ecliptic. A conducting surface of current has been carefully prepared. Red is associated with the goal of the great work. I am now a set of eight. (Not you.) A piece of parchment is inscribed on one side with the text and on the other with the divine names. This is enclosed in a glass case and attached to the doorpost of the house. I have the temptation to exist. There's no coming back. Take me.

There's scope for this space, a crack in the western lands.

There used to be an aperture about here. Through fog the silhouette of a castle and the mezzaluna window.

Apex of triangular form. Cut this out, or up (I hate being taught things). Big waves are expected in about three, the hours of time.

I manifest everything she suppresses: bone, muscle and scales, the snag in any opposition, the compass of a voice. Is that how it is. I suppose a slow turn—this is a borrowed fiction, after all, something visceral. Finally I wake. In the adjoining room someone sings a mass for the living dead. A vast circle glows and expands in the isolation cell. The plane containing the centres of the earth and the sun cuts through this sphere.

Roman collar crowning coat buttoned (or the topmost sail). Deterministic theories of human nature follow, of an accused scientific character—a drumming out, female flowers found in all the heads.

Tartarus, that's the word. Tartarus.

The medium speaks to us, pitifully, a professional naysayer. The first element modifies the second by standing next to it, an afterclap. One on whom material to be chopped is placed.

Understated conditions.

Recluse in size, ex-mass. Evensong in the latin quarter. A triangular sail is suspended by a long yard at an angle of about forty-five degrees to the mast. Now is archaic. Iron is tinned over: tin-plate, more explicitly white (a sort of hat for the head). Now dial, quick. He's thoroughly decided. Recently there's been a shocking shift in style. A mixed metal of yellow colour, either identical with, or closely resembling, brass, is often hammered into thin sheets. A lobe projects from the edge of each hemisphere. First build up confidence in your subject. There's no point trying to change. Simulate psychokinesis through any accepted means. A dream leads him to restage the work. He is thoroughly deluded. It's like when you wake up and you don't know where you are. It's the day-to-day tactility that I miss (a little revolutionary romance, baroque pastiche over breakfast). We are entering a tunnel. There's an awful lot of counting and recounting going on. We're concerned here with hearing and speech, the quick and the not, the living and dead. A small self-deception soon reaches the dimensions of the absolute. Am now wheeling about faster and faster. You'll never guess what happens to me next.

Light fading through ninety degrees. Most of the dwarves are moving in different directions, away from each other. I say onement because many writers would not truly be at one with the unusual thought processes of their subject. My role is official court savant. I regained consciousness at the foot of the escalator. There is this temptation to exist, the state of other people's books. Now you will rise and you will remove the stones from the furnace of this mouth. From beyond the two-way mirror a voice murmurs. (Go by these your twelve names et cetera.) Some things have to be guessed at. I mean it can be heard, murmuring.

Wean the subject off the normal to the paranormal.

Termination of uncertain forms. I can hear, but I can't see. The emphasis is now geopolitical. We pass through some time. It's kind of strange, like a stormy sea. Particular keys depict particular moods. Now return to the subnormal. Deuterium takes the place of ordinary hydrogen.

Twister on the horizon, incoming. Time to unsettle the horses. Seek a form in which the letters are grounded, and flee.

Likewise the southwest wind, the side piece of a razor. Outward clash. River-drift. Commentary on my sentences appears. I don't know why.

The dark drama of an introduction, peculiarity of action—entities with only intentional being, never actually present. I wake covered in thin metal plates like a fish or reptile. The scene is made up of different angles. The men set the charges and abandon ship. We're still sticking to the plot. Nothing multiplies beyond necessity. Objects are split into strips and juxtaposed. Selected items are laminated with corrugated plastic. The whole thing resembles a clockwork, an obsolete name. It's good to have somewhere to go though. Right they nod in the dark, right right right. Hang, without.

It was like having thin layers of tissue peeled away to reveal a core. (Strange that inversion of positive and negative.) Then I'm left alone for thousands of years. That seems standard as well, doesn't it.

After the dark drama of the introduction, hand me over to my adversaries. Those assembled are the epitome. With a flounce he adds another card to the stack. This is endless, needless work. In the corner is a cluster of magnetic ghosts. He's asked to point his mind at an abject. The platform on which he stands curves to a half-moon. An old woman approaches—her mien is on the abiotic side. He leaps up with a terrified start, thinking he has seen his mother come back to life (graveclothes, corspsegas, greysunken et cetera). Of course, of course: a panic imbalance, direct consciousness of striking and being struck. All the information is held inside the uppermost part of the animal's body, in the understanding, the memory-head, the membrane of the ear's drum. Now remove the top of the skull. The brain is exposed. Insurrectionary force culminates in a general strike. He is the one who withtakes, is a prelude to something that is yet to happen for the first time. Hallucinogenetic.

Erase the recorded material. Meet somewhere in the face. Shape one's course anew. Steal a vow. Now dampen the sponges, apply current.

The dilemma is how to marshal these scant items into a work, a progress report. It would serve to make it mean something real, undeniably present. For example, the following are yet to be allocated.

A detachable piece of cuticle, shut in by large boulders.

A short-period star of the cluster type.

The outermost or thin skin.

A mad-apple, fruit of the egg: the dead sea.

Dead flesh at the edge of the finger.

Gall reproduced on an oak in the east.

The waxy, corky layer of the head.

Randomain. Light and darkness and sleep. A reduction. Refusing to decide is a decision. His dwelling is a cylinder with axis set oblique to base. He wakes in a bath of freezing water. There's something very appealing about this. No one ever said anything about torture. He volunteers. Paired muscles in his neck extend to the first and secondary ribs. Drop a hint then leave. The plot is convoluted (pale rose-red clay). With unfingered glove, he types himself out of the story. He types himself beyond witness.

Riverscape, with a little piece of ingenious embedded. Slowly she removes her glass eye. The membrane ruptures and melts. She's a practised incendiary. We are unequalsided. Tap-tip-tup of blind stick on aluminium floor—fracture test department, and on such a leery day.

A short series of exercises leading to Type 2 healing are held. He orders me back to the fringe, the firing line. We are within range of memory for all practical purposes. At peripheral is a small flat structure sealed with butterfly wings. There's a cluster of selective hearing. In your head you have the set look of a person of certain age.

Innards of court, unofficial. A watch-turret with garreteer, which houses a collection of theatrical memorabilia: oxidized jewellery, canisters of notoriously flammable gelatin film, a bundle of wigs, an X-ray tube, swords and walking sticks, a cutthroat razor, tickets and shoe-laces (believe hanged), a flower taboo, lalique lotus under right arm raised, assorted snuffboxes, an antic chair, a puff of smoke, marionettes with grotesque papier-mâché heads, the women on the float dancing (shot up-skirt), a freshly dug hole in the ground at a cemetery, a bale of shorn hair, a finishing rod, skin, tendons, ligaments, the matrix of bones et cetera, a violently explosive rubbery substance, a sleeping place, the hammer of a gunlock, a wedding (worn and inscribed with fused initials and the date), the cracked lookingglass, a wicker crib containing the mummified remains of an instant, a spiked god collar, a groove around the cylindrical part of a bullet, a perfume ionizer, a semen tray, the police. I have composed my first miracle. There's no hiding anything. I've been left inside a mistake. There must be at least five people in here with me. Now at once the deadly sallow. File this under the number distilled from the aforementioned date.

Gentle is the act of operating. She holds his face. A distinct pivot takes place about here.

Electric discharge from iron plates on either flank of skull. That thing's much closer than you realize. Cloud refracting surface water, ice of jug. It's confounding, the number of actions a body has to perform in the world. Gentle is the act of discharging. Keep ye, unsound.

Cilium on ceramic tile, white. We are within range of the enemy for all practical purposes. Prosework substitutes for experience. Keep going till you get bogged down.

Fine aerosol in the breath shared as we walk. She says you must understand that you are not who you are.

At that instant something jumps into the roadside ditch. Masturbating furiously, its legs become entangled in an abandoned shopping trolley. Water falls from the sky in tiny droplets. A glow worms about the masthead. A short series of exercises leading to Type 3 healing are attempted (a rhombus is whirled about the head, the bull-roarer). The stripes of certain fungi are ingested. We're rightly famous for our cylinders and our canals. It's not very romantic this, is it. The first trophy of the century is reported stolen. I'm best viewed immediately before sunrise or just after sunset. I have plumes and spine like a hawk. I am at a turning point in space. All the forms are ancient and mutilated. I have careered for thousands of years unready, driving on towards a rather quizzical conclusion. I am looking today at colour. White is not when surrounded. Fetch my scales of armour, boy. There is no need whatsoever to think of an image that appears before the inert eye. Perspecting the distance are the twenty-one pylons. You saw a static man.

Someone murmuring Diderot.

In each section the deceased stands with hands raised.

On thy face o fiend. Devour me not. I am pure. I am within the time which comes of itself.

Unevensong.

The supplicant has a lengthy breathing tube sticking out of its abdomen. There's a heroine over there. News travels fast. A toothed wheel turns my shadow. Don't mention the lost incisor or he will refuse to cooperate. Above the cheekbone is a tiny tattoo of a lyre. There's nothing else to talk about. The tide from the sea rises and ebbs in the river. I can still remember how words were once said. There are all sorts of variants pressing here. Quit para. Quit para and desert.

When the volunteer is fast asleep she says remove the top of the head. I listen to the wind rusting through the grave. She is a primary discharger of souls. I think we've exhausted the idea of scale about here.

He operates under names and guises, a member of a family who goes about unrecorded. Nonetheless, he is bound by the same covenant. Note his easy workaday manner. Corrugations in the eye act as lenses and create the illusion of depth. If accidentally broken he subjects himself to a penalty. Preserved image: ice of jug. Craquelure in veneer of sign.

Deep space. In the cockpit on the spine of the ship. Remote orders scanning through: missile incoming. It is locked on. There's a homing beacon on board. Locate it. Transfix through pilot skull to interior head. A sphere emits an intense red light. This is the beacon. This is the beacon that calls down the missile. Learn something from this: be certain, when you start, that you can scramble back.

She is coated in a waxy shield secreted by her insect. She's rolled up in a carpet and flung from the roof of the convertible. Looks as though we'll never see her like again.

He leaves to separate. He is spared. The collective noun here is a designation of ghosts, plucked from the proper realm of civilized life. So much for that.

An encrustation. Ochre lines scribbled across the wall of a cave.

The red silhouette of a hand, digits parted.

A man in skin with solitary antler or antennae.

The slaughter mammoth.

The men with seers.

These gaps in the story deserve much mutilation. Ears burn. A giant claw is drawn through the liquid surface of a mirror. Sphericles of mercury spill and bounce across the worn varnish of the laboratory bench. Graffiti has been gouged with knife and key. Someone fires a gasjet (I'm always charmed to find a welcome alliance). Icicle-like pendants of calcium descend from the roof. Vibration of reed to lip—the line right through, the tension that builds. I could surrender to him tomorrow and walk free. The outcome's all the better for my concealment. Avoid all unnecessary conjunctions. I could document the sign and walk free. Avoid all unnecessary repetition.

My entry into the conservatory coincides with a dramatic change in medical practice. Molecules in the insect's nervous system are toxic to bacteria. Maybe one day I'll bring in some used memory for you to see for yourself. I think this year's going to be like last year, a set of twelve. It (the insect) has sticky forelegs for seizing and holding prey. I shall listen out. She says you nearly ate my head. You nearly ate my eyes and tongue. The heart is indicted.

A much earlier sect regards her as the figure. Here and there things have been distorted for the sake of continuity. Her material may be composed of anything of familiar form.

I am trying at the links. Shadowed angle of cranium at forty-five. . . . A film, as iron heated at the forge. Her radiant skull, sticky insect limbs quivering at the thorax. Beneath us the multitude of fishes, a vast assemblage. Out of a blue enamel sky, I fell.

Frequentative of to say.

Able meaning emptiness.

By time we mean the moments taken for a dispatched rider to return from two fixed points.

This disappears into a literary gap, or blank. Retrace, you steps.

Today, divination by observing the way the mice move when released from their cage—a network of cracks in a vanished sign. You can turn this around to become anything you want. The white parts aren't empty. Imagine, they are chalk trackways or trial by salt, rivulets of anaesthetic, trim lines of alkaloid on a toilet seat. Quietism is a word. The time I depict is no longer your time. It is neither his time. His powers are weak. He once said. Is that open electric or throat-drill? Time is approaching the final segment of a cycle: caste brands displayed on every forehead, rift designs in twilight. Any thought transports me while at work, rises up from the radiating nerve. Memory hardens remorse. Would you test this out for me, see if it works. Ask yourself is there a hook, sister. Will it bend at the centre? Can it unfurl? Can it fold? Can it be diminished by shaving off minuscule amounts second by second? One cannot read these gobbets too warily. There are pitfalls lurking behind every word (e.g. preadmonish). Heart murmur increases, generally. He replies. Letters have been suspended. There's a momentary aperture on the landing, a range of bleached arid mountains beyond. (You're breaking up a bit.) Words are spent, sunlight splits the trees. For a few terrible moments the good doctor is illuminated, lit up in the subfusc, strapped to the mast. The rest of the crew are disappeared. Coffins full of native soil cram the hold. Rats scurry everywhere, accompanied by suitable music. A cadaverous man in a cloak with ears lurches about. Dogteeth punctuate the narrative. Light is the savage whites of an arclight. I hope I shall be pardoned for confessing. It knits together. A voice says this means we're entering a liminal zone, a place of parted spirit . . . large cursorial birds standing some seven feet high . . . a violently explosive rubbery substance. . . . an opening or passage into a canal. . . . The remainder of the text is unintelligible. Translation cannot contain errors. A nine or a six is painted on the roadway. It depends. I am wronged way up myself. That date again. Taxis and rank. They delegate. You are breaking badly up. Stay well ahead of us, please. I don't know why he is here. (The clothes.) I confess I did not sense arrival. The bogman cometh, as folk say. So away. They are broadcasting into our dreams from the future. I resolve to practice a form of quietism as a subconscious defence machine.

Crown closures, Europe—a world of choices. They are two hours ahead. You're wasting breath. In his bones he knows there's nothing left to grasp.

There was no specific time given here.

Meat us.

Frogs croaking in the eaves. A world of choices. Are you still moving. Tiny green lizards scatter about the coolness of the cave. Outside blazing starlight. Shallow streams crisscut the rocky beach and empty into the ocean.

Create contrast with dark hibernian wood.

I'm always dancing on the wrong side of the trench. God help me finish this once and for all. Approaching on the road are stolen players, troubadours. It seems to me now that this has always been running away from me: schedules of fasting and abstinence, a treacherous character assassin from a mediaeval romance. If you move your head slightly it distorts. (Try it.) One or two gnomic phrases are repeated. An accumulation of individually innocuous elements is being subjected to a weird organizational principle.

Relate what becomes of the two suspected senior rebels.

They're possessed of much skill in grammar, hence ritual magic. We are negotiating the catacombs. Every surface is oppressive to the touch. This discourse is rather one-way. I am confuse. It sounds like you're underwater, among the clutter of grave-goods. I'm losing you. Liminal was among his favourite arrangements of letters. A white mark is visible on the animal's forehead. At peripheral is a small flat structure sealed with the wings of moths (the sub-angled wave). I have reinstated the previous sentence, no. We take centuries to build up to a single action. I am in need. When I left I just lay there without invitation for days on end. The way we were both behaving, it was us.

Lock of bedroom door vibrating in the cool evening air.

Some of these features are borrowed from the files and locusts of an apocalypse: rusting metal plates and rods, bolts and nuts. Sentences may be slowly peeled to reveal an invisible core, the proverbial onion. The result is amorphous, brittle with taste and smell, transparental—a faint, yellowing hint composed of carbon, nitrogen, oygen and sulphur.

Ethercapped.

I'm discoursing now on a person's right to be evil. It's that incredibly experimental time when we discover just what the human voice is capable of. The pattern we've inherited begins and ends on a droning silence that weaves a solidity. Project: the others don't care, discuss. Our control arrives, a head of time. I am of the opinion that the problems tackled herein act like a universal solvent. The value of this work consists in showing how little is achieved when linguistic dilemmas are unknotted.

She comes. She denounces: I am diminutive of sphere.

In us and by us to the very end. Crumbs of e.

A lozenge-shaped circumstance, anything that whirls, as the wheel of night and day in the hind-brain. An intermediary, almost a white square on a white ground, or blank on black. Fine-grained, igneous with feldspar in section. In the act of writing, I generate more concerns than I surrender. Surging music makes you think of gods or things. A figure approaches, fading. An objection, an objection shaped.

Dial back formation from hawk. Collage, unvisible.

Sentinalmental.

A hidden world where everyone is a pseudonym. Suddenly we shift a little to sinister. News of the death of fictional enemies arrives (factious). We slay the messenger. Notice how some motifs are used ironically. I extract one of my teeth and position a tiny lens in its cavity. There must be a passageway back to the river. Notice how some motifs keep recurring. Their faces are like the faces of men, nothing more. I am hawk-backed, me. A model can always be deconstructed.

Stunned above the meadow, a pivot about prey hanged in wait.

Mostpeople.

XVII

I wrote this chapter while the siege was still fresh in my mind. It was a dreary morning when I heard their wheels approaching.

Distil from this an image of the moon collapsing into the sea. Check all responses for signs of heresy. She is simultaneously enthused and at peace. Check at three bridges. Her white hands pluck at a book, as if so much straw.

I desire. I die before I can conceive. I am diagnosed ambivert. I record everything.

Imagine her hands clutching any white object. Invent some remarks on colour of your own. Imagine her hands clutching a white lily. On a pedestal in the foreground is the reliquary head. Its style is declamatory. Extra units are being attached to the rear.

Write a letter one says.

Build a pyre on the shingle, bale-fire. She pauses a moment before kindling the embers. Place the torn letter there and burn it. Such borrowings are repeated, over and over. She stretches for a charred fragment as it flutes upward into the choking air. I offer myself, an obscure clarity (a chosen grace). No one ever witnessed this vignette before. Evaporate to yield acid salt. Immerse the lover's remains in water.

Lake mort announced by wireless at the close. His surface head is a fungal skin of honeycomb, prurigo, so named.

Now tell us what you noticed in the abandoned house that night.

The foreman of works keeps a diary. He records everything that happens, beats time on the floor. He strikes at the root with a long staff. (I don't like the way this is going.) A gangrenous abscess is forming in his hoof. I change things singlehanded. The foreman dies. Air is sucked from his chamber by a passing vehicle. He suffocates. A marking out has taken place—large, flat and elliptical. I am having a part misunderstood, over and over.

Piano keyed in the adjacent room, a faltering at the edge of something unarrived. My destiny's a matter of politics and good citizenry, a ring for a hawk's jess. A chance meeting at a crossroad, a collision of three routes.

In place of symmetries, engraved.

Cries from below. A leg is broken, the femur. He's no longer the complete self, no bridge between lower limb and turning world. He's disqualified. Being is forbidden.

Image of him gazing gloomily at a shift upon which words have been scrawled. This place is any place: guilt, with crypt-like recesses for storing books. Perhaps in some way down and cup. In yours, in mine.

But of course these announcements have nothing in common with direct practical advertisement, the history of ruptures.

Upon returning he's glad to see the room is bright by a well-trimmed lamp. The underlying theme is redness. He has a superfluous idea. Unwanted matter is expelled via the insect's proboscis. About the cartouche weaves a design of vine leaves and tendrils.

In exchange she is drawn up through the same appendage. The sound of a bedsheet torn can be heard. All of these actions and events are symbolic in the extreme. In what should have been a blank page is an embellishment without a border, without purpose.

Mind, gut of twelve-string. See page thirty-eight for the missing.

An unaccountable liking or disliking.

It's said he holds conversations with himself about the books he's reading. That can wait. He lies in a shallow trench sunk into black earth. I sense there are things I need to know. The notes help. Salt is in the air, sharp improvisations, rolling out over a wide plain hung with clouds shading off around the head. Some carry flags and banners, tricolour cockades pinned to hair and clothes. Topography: remote mountainous spine proximal to sea, resembling. One banner states that he's the man (ingenious). The crossbeams of a bank of lasers throw a mesh across the night sky. The slope pits down toward his feet. Inquisitors come. Tell us all you noticed in that ruined villa. Are you tired, remote star? The bare concrete platform resembles an unknown abroad. A smaller figure lies beside him (note the androgyny in a shared hole). A faint shudder occurs. Set your mind upon a theorem. Nothing works because I expect. At the end memory collapses. It explains everything and then dies. Hello. Yes. Hello. He seems incapable of keeping his body still. The entire planet is manned by worker drones. I'm dissolving into contradictory law games, the stuff of which I am unmade. He is tall and he hath the demeanor. During the following night there's a visitation, a chemical and material counterpart. Verses are keened: mournful heart of death-zephyr et cetera. He wears a long robe bearing insignia—erasures and words. These relate the story of a monstrous shadow that courses beneath the water, breaking the surface to hurl itself upon the flank of an ocean liner. Its translucent grey body has no substance. I'm in the act of boarding the vessel. Clinging to the rungs of a ropeladder, I turn and look down. The event repeats itself. I did not think there would be space for this, but it turns out that there is. You should learn to be unattached, never flinch from your allotted course. In the centre of his shift is a purple cross cut with arms of equal size. The pit is strewn with wild cicely. He is stone-blind. He delivers speech, something about capital and schizophrenia. Therein philosophy and the divine nature are revealed as of duplicating aspect, connected to the nerve-fibres by a two-way mirror, hence having a double mode of variation: two dimensions contained in the one. There's a question on every lip. Something profound and grave is recurring, unavoidable ritual consequence—a noisy wrangling, an uproar. It's so hard to talk of this. At every turn I'm compromised. Water suddenly appears at the base of the trough as if from a spring. The witnesses step back from the edge. As he speaks, still lying there, he treads water. Blood is released. It expands to flood the whole trench.

I leave and return to the cob. The crew are admitted on board twenty at a time. They form a closed circle. One resembles. They climb aboard and take up their places to row. Ice cliffs at the horizon, orange beneath horsehead nebula.

No habits, no territories. I sense there are things I need to know: the times and dates of future masques. Over sleepness, seas of grass whose waves et cetera.

He is trapped in the ballast of his guilt, searching for a home, a legal fiction. In and out the empty blockage: somewhere to dwell. Somewhere to go, or to not go. The decision is yours. The decision is out of your hands.

Her attributes symbolize productive power: go astray—tarry, delay. The raven itself is cried hoarse. They must have some sort of mirror that checks you but can't be seen. I've the sense of being exiled from nothing, from the very light of day. I don't know. The time of increase will not endure. Sorrow too is something chemical, she says. Utilize it while it lasts. Note to self, ornament this telegraphic abruptness. Make the most. Everything happens.
So what looked to be no more than a brilliant anecdote?
I'm relating in minute detail all that happened during that night.

Equalarmed, once spoke.
She leans forward. Experience always triumphs over meaning. I've decided to make everything on the planet my own. It's really that simple, schizomythic.

As you can see, the knavish methods which rule the manufacture of most magical books you will not encounter here. Men are chained in a cave facing a blank wall with a fire burning behind them. Anyway, isn't white that which does away with darkness.

A longroofed chapel. Invitation of spirit, a spurt of viscid fluid. This image is taken directly from the local hunt. Follow me. Retrace the outline of an old courthouse sunk into the asphalt of the quad. Lay thy paws upon the treasure thereunder. He brings news of great works. He's disarmed by the blasting rod and the channel-stone. Leave me to be he repeats. He issues from the circle at the point where the door disfigures.

As for her.

Distance opens between the woods and the space-craft, a smooth acre of ground covered with lush grass. It's said she's half human, half fawn. Offsprung improvisatrix.

Elongated tropes of cloud high above the softening head. Death comes at any moment. The blindings hold firm. He struggles. You could say the work represents a forty-year gestation period. We share a single letter of an alphabet. Radiation glows on his breastplate. By writing he defers. It hadn't been my intention to rise at all today.

Postwar catharsis. Implosion of eye. My foot is swollen (the pool). Something is growing inside me. News arrives of the sociopathic field. He dies through an excess of joy and tactical leisure. His adversary is rumoured to have mysteriously choked on a grapeseed. This is the end I never aimed at. In his absence he's accused of licentiousness and debauchery. By substance I understand.

Neural tic beneath left eye, bandaged. None of us is permitted to peer into the infinite hive. Neural pulse at right-hand corner of mouth, the quivered lip. The man opposite me is being policed. It is the surname of his ancestors he protests. Take me back to the edge, please, quick. We are precisely half-way through the tragic slow movement. I immediately feel guilty. Stop up my valve with signals: solitary smoke plumes, the bruised hills—and of my youth, the rusting wire, barbed. Fluid secretion of gland, a perfect suture stretching across the field, across my back. Raised arcs of gravel, the chalk men stumbling at the threshold. I'm putting all my cards in order and laying them on the table, face up. Hand me the trickster, the liminal.

A horizontal circle consisting of four colours.

In all there are three of these plates spinning one above the other. The whole contraption signifies the farce that holds everything together (sniffing glue). A name has been given to the hypothetical particle that passes between us. Chunks of volatile memory embed themselves in the grooves. White cancels all. A voice says do you not see that you were wounded for a reason? Think about it. All I claim is that I dwell inside *here*, nothing more.

Smoke seeps from a tunnel, half an hour ago, murmuring. Of her sufferings in the country of the papyrus swamps—unshakeable mishap, private lunatic asylum, the body-snatchers.

Ghost flies, outbursts of spiniflex.

A genus of bony fishes with open-air bladders and projecting eyes. Notes on strangeness.

Movement behind me, a book rustling of its own accord. We're divided into two for vision in air and under water. The search for a home goes on. Next comes pain, the wrong man et cetera. I anticipate a lively debate. One of us has been given the title. One is usurper over the living. Another is usurper over the dead. Another is derailed. The gloves are off. To be on the safe side everyone whitewashes their windows. One has authority to stand upon the other's head. It's like tilting at windmills. (I don't believe any of this.) There is much to twist and shout. I should do as your grace demands, or else. Around here folk hold nullness and void in equal measure. To be on the safe side everyone sticks parcel tape to their windows. The experiment is a waste of time. Volunteers are arranged in concentric circles. We haven't gone an oar's length from the bank. On it stand four little men holding pendulums. They personify effectless will. The raft hasn't gone more than ten yards downriver. We are not moving. We have allowed ourselves to be.

Many are lured into the light of day by a questionnaire. The answer is the third segment of an instinct's leg.

I was once oppressed and harvested as sap. I used magic ritual to escape underground, my tyrants rising to the surface.

Elevation of right hand to left eye aforesaid. He wears a crux. This means you must wait.

Silence, malevolent. An outlander in the role of nightwatchman. A vacuum. Some fancy they heard the inrush of air. The landscape is wary, full of wandering signs. Or if you prefer, you may try the suspect with my cuckold chair in the village pond. I keep thinking that mesh of metal is a goal sunk deep in the water, that we're embroiled in some kind of game. The text probably belongs to the first century. There's a fish on one plate, eyes on the other. Twelve outlines converge nearby, quite mosaic. The text reads sunken tesserae, his rumour or some such. Remains are commonly spangled with iron pyrites. The current volume is more prosaic. Critics have made a head and a tail of it, conjoined. All the corners have been smoothed and rounded by water. No surface has been left unshaved.
Paper pulp and spittle. Chew wax, until blanched. Self, swallow hard. Another storm is heading towards the state.

Glint of visor under sickly green lamp, some disremembered pool hall. He's no longer interested in courting listeners. I've lost my job as an interpreter. He addresses the air. It bleeds from a thousand tiny holes perforating space. I am going in, head-fast. Liver and gall burst open. I neglect my work. On the path along which my blood draws me, power has no role. I'm here to stay. Amniotic fluid spills from my sac and onto my shoes, the cobblestones. A sudden and unexpected reincarnation is due to take place tonight. Make a decision. I float between turrets and pinnacles. He supports me on his shoulders, with steady grace. There's no going back. I am far above myself. There follows a seven percent decline in footfall. We're stationary but we're happy. I am making a decision. Everybody is a state of shock. If they continue narking about I shall be forced against my will to eat one of them.

Truncate self to footnote, random levitations.

That bird is the phoenix. Only symbolic, mind. It is balanced on a sphere with outstretched wings, pecking at itself. Is this wrong. Have I confused my avifauna. Signs of multiplication and increase, verve. The bowsprit gets mixed up with the rudder. Hold onto my breath. Wait for the next event, the implosion of will. We are holed beneath the waterline.

A quadrivium, the place in a story where four meet. The head is buried with its owner's name engraved upon it. That vibration is his unmistakable sound signature. At last I find myself face-to-face with a method, a wayless. Predictably, a swollen foot, turned inwards. Vervelled.

Transport the obscure things that do remain.

Travers.

An old dried-up river god.

Naked and silver as the flashing knife, he returns and sets fire, itself.

I have withdrawn over the years I have. A tree burned in the ash-fall pinholes the time to within seconds. Snail and clam shells are found compacted in the nearby strata. Also remnants of ice: antelope, wolf, horse, and snake. These are all awarded dates. Overlaying the tools and bones is a vein of cobalt-60 dust. You are to seize this mischievous and hurtful metal.

One day I had to tear the phones out of the wall and switch everything off. The digging up of spare rubbish and other artifacts is consuming time. I have forfeit the use of the phantom leg. Let me tell you. We were once smooth and limbless, oval bodies that rolled about the peaks and troughs of the countryside. Then we split. We died and were recast as airborne spores, familial drift. I could listen out for you in the night. Now you must cut the pack in two. Today's colour is duck-egg blue. The theme tune is a high-strung signature (a striking example of a dream-built perfection that can reside only in an idle tinker's brain). The accompanying image is the illusion on a banknote, a surface impregnated with wormwood, what's called a tidemark. Your orders are to break yourself in half. I use the possessive rarely. The correct distance is either half of a ship's yardarm, right or left from centre to end. I am labouring under an attack of nitrogen narcosis. I wake in a covered portico, a colonnade open to the sea. I finger my forehead. During sleep I've been trepanned. The promenade is an exposed and naked place. One comes and speaks without preamble. I hear the crunch of gravel underfoot. Inland, vineyards cling to distant hills. He says I have been here before.

Ridges are formed by tide and wind erosion—sand and silt, scattered with salt-pits and charred limbs of wood. I lift a pebble and place it on my tongue.

Weed this episode from your brain, forget yourself. Seawater was found in the head.

In my hand is an instrument for scraping bones. I lie parallel to the prevailing direction. A peeling sign reads old scratch's horrorgraphic company, unlimited. We descend zigzag toward the foreshore (one of the chief difficulties of walking while strapped together is that when I step zig he goes zag, and when I step zag he goes zig). Safely under the ground we find an altar, inlaid with smalti of lazulite depicting an angel—I sing in the shadow of your wings et cetera. The design resembles an embedded knot. I have the coefficient of elasticity, of stretching. All that day we saw the viking ship.

He rises up and is cut down, flees like a shadow. He is discontinued—ultraviral, with glittering veins of gold. Calamitous, oversea'd.

Anima Monday. A steep bank with precipice attendant. Light, cyan.

Next, how to write quartets properly. I remould obsessively before handing anything over. I'm the anatomical equivalent of chamber music, splendid and horribly isolated up front. Now here comes the one with no speech. Construct a choice. Dig a hole. Cover it with palm fronds. Place a rusty mantrap in it (other way round). She says there's been a warning, those big red shapes in the sky at night, thought balloons cut loose from the earth. Deal or no deal, something is due to happen. Wastelands are being reclaimed. Follow my insurrections. I lack the eloquence to describe the purloined letter, and besides, my interest wanes. What number are the horses hereabouts? Note how this fabric has been granted a little token of instability—coded lines of escape leading nowhere, a pale patch on the printed page. There's sure to be more later. The foreman says a gibbon is to be reconstructed. Electricity vibrates between my fingers, unto my mouth. Thus in the book of overthrowing we're told not only to make a wax effigy of the monster but also to write his name upon it. Amoral qualities can be taken for granted. I still haven't looked up blue.
Grow his nails like bird talons.
These uncompromising ancestor figures.
Part of your brain is dying: it doesn't actually realize.
Hello, I'm the really fussy nightmare.
The heavy rectangular hand is huge.

Stone blind, he is no longer interested in listening to the advice offered by his courtiers. The orifice is examined in a mobile lab. He stands up as though to shake off a recollection. This miracle stunned the dominions and angels for some time.

The seven stumps of classical rhetoric.
One. The land's lip, the country slide.
Two. Sea escape.
Three. The sky and its bodies.
Four. There is no four.
Sidereal time is set at unfamiliar. Seizure the eighth, the vanishing—a sequence of three rhythms in a single vision, my counterdream of his face. Let me out. Cut me down. Men are trapped quick in the concrete. Why don't you look where you're going. More people, lack milling about in white gowns, groaning. The sun rises out of the earth. I have the feeling of going through something that's happened before. In the town square there's a new man waiting. He is the image of progress. It's time to set more fires. He is known for his body. He is know for his machine. Huge pyres are ignited on the beach, fuelled by limbs lopped from the feudal tree. This is taking so long because I am a rare perfectionist, and besides, to save my life I cannot write. He's liberated by the expansion of an acid. Behind him fades a scene of open veldt. Rising heat vapour corrugates the stagnant air. Vacillation is symptomatic here. A second tattoo line bites into the skin. He refuses to look back, the wind ripping at his shirt, his heart, the irradiated breastbone. Something like the kerching of a cash registry beats time in the background. Avoid adverbs, they are dangerous impostors. I'm only interested in what I cannot remember.
Analysis of the foregoing.
Difficulty at the beginning. Black veins in the hexagram, end of the pier stuff—a book of snares. They struggle (he's a heavy man). They pass at undercliff. They don't speak or exchange in any way.

A cameo in an amusing ruse.
Sixteenth-century interior with corresponding furnishings, stirrings of empire. She crouches beside the reliquary head. Not until covered with blood does her lover discharge. As you know all remembrance is set down in the form of a draft. We should have attacked during the first fifteen minutes. The last one hundred and twenty seconds have been hell. I split myself into three (maybe it was four). I would never have known I had a history of my own.
   Upon arriving we find the cave has been bricked up. She reads from a book written in an unknown alphabet. Inside is the wrong man, just sitting and waiting like some mendicant beggar. He is well camouflaged. A puff of smoke curls from his face. I set about measuring the segments of his imperceptibly slow rotation. He does not realize, he also is condemned. Much emphasis is laid on the effect of our controller. Come nightfall the space-station is visible with the naked eye, a blinking light off the shoulder of Orion.

Isolate. Impulse, the now obsolescent. A change of mind, the complete collection. The shell, seek it everwhere.

I call out three times before he rises.
I'm known as little red riding thug.
She returns the book to the shelf.
Come back. Don't abandon me.
I love you.
We love each other.
She is looking out at the sea.
We are looking at each other.

Foregoing, perhaps reminiscent of doxology as the closing act.

Of the colour of not knowing, or the unalike. Woodsmoke and skin-milk, lead-livid. They have taken space out of their time, with airs of indifference, lack of substance. Sad illuminations, greyish with dismissal, compressed. Obtusely dressed and symbolled is the colour of things. Comes an objection: the sky, the sea and its pigments. Choose power, or liquid. I am founded in usuries.

Narrow-skulled, with contractile sinuses in place of a heart (rotating neutron stars). Then three then four, the rising barriers—transparent leaf-shaped larvae of the disorder. Go forth in your own semblance, sometimes neither slow nor rapid.

To treat, to turn metal, or the rot in thy wood the socket-eye. And who murdered his wives in quick succession? Creeping from the veins of our dissent, the dung-beetle, with flashing metal abdomen. Random militias, corrupted nightwatch.

I digress, the last one hundred and twenty years have been hell. Whose spiny heads blow about and disseminate?

He attempts to board the moving train. In his pocket is a list of the fifteen rare earth elements. (Store with care all these tips on pronunciation.) He clutches a red lily in his hand. For godsake let this go. He slips and ends his life beneath the wheels. The scent of turkish coffee never fails to conjure this event and its consequences. Any pedestal or base equals a slice of earth. Now he lies in a trench with foaming water swirling about him. There is company. It presses close by, close-grained. None of these characters understands a single word that has been spoken. Good news arrives about the paschal birds and the loons, the huge order of perching, harrow-like in form.

Note to self. Rewrite without the melodrama. True story my arse.
We are using all these histories for an unfit purpose. The noisiest of them has

been faithfully set down and buried in a capsule at an unknown location. Today's verdict will reinforce. It's a lottery (urine). To ensure that events don't repeat in time, we have altered the way in which we supervise. We are unlearning organization. Some paragraphs appear as broad sketches, yet to be worked up in their details, while others are finely ornamented, and yet urge a dissolution that reveals underlying structure.

She asks in your head are there scenes already constructed. Are there snowflakes drifting across a dark central plain. There's no doubt about it, you are an invaluable aid to comprehension. We are no more than thirty yards from the wall now. The man with the hammer arrives. Do you hear voices (not so fast). Much is said about the taming of wild horses, the barter of grave-goods. Some of this is simply the people things say. I recall the English tune, carrying the burden. I ask the first person I meet in the street what he's thinking and write it down.

He appears in his guise as the sun standing on the solid ground of chaos. All stages of the work occur simultaneously, or not at all. A commentary on his vision follows. No title has been supplied. There's a haunting canticle at the last (a pointer quivers over the blue disc). Everything occurs in the slack of a half-moon. There's more, but as you can see, I don't feel like listing right now.

An elastic bladder containing pulverized ice is applied to the brain under congestion of the head. There were murmurings.

More on their doubtless influence (once upon a time there was a poor wood-cutter). Narrative goes up and down a measure but remains pretty static. It has many heads and many stomachs. A sequence is about to be broken. This is a recurring theme. She enquires in the local head.

I am standing up on my own, unaided, and working a way back in. The lizards are still inside, stealing substance, stealing time. Did you ever see the like. These are characters in search of a page. Attraction always leads to isolation. Spring one day will come and redeem us—a system of what claims to be knowledge but is without basis in ascertained scientific fact, as if astrology. I say I find the castle oddly comforting. He looks surpassed. You are my antithesis: matter and anti-matter, the work of mourning. Nobody asked your opinion. Come over here with that candle. Who's making personal remarks now.

Ready she is to lose her head the moment she feels that familiar pounding at the ovaries. I say do you hear voice. Utterance, scribbled.
A figure floating face down in still water, limbs astral.
Sea-green nightshade.
Zodiacal light of lenticular form.

The shots you hear ringing in the background are hunters in the snow. I for one find these volleys reassuring. I demand an answer. He says he thinks himself divine. Now read this letter for me. An eyebrow is raised, a knuckle wedged between molars. A short strap is coiled taut about the leg of a hawk.

This is the first plateau that they reached. The perplexing word here is klepht. Chest and stone being aspirated.

A parley of instruments. Difficulty in breathing and that peculiar ringing burr. The title is as long as the work itself (the hour of parleying is dangerous). Come nightfall he's urged to take advantage of the darkness to launch a further attack. That's the third constellation going up the hill right now. I have come to the end of my sentience, I expect a response. This strategy is too easy. There are recurring tendencies, too much false etymology. I'm up against the clock in a nine-year project. I start all over again, forever starting again. My ailment improves each day. I'm chancing the lid later. All the curves I have left behind to rot in the landscape. In no time we're at the finish. Before you can say book, matter is exorcized. He can't be sure how much time is left. The required instrument has twelve strings, to be plucked or stammered. A dragnet is used to trawl for remains, as in play merry hell with.

A rinse of boiling oil, liquefied tobacco and rust is syringed into the rectum. It's been a quiet day and the lads are bored. You have the world between your finger-flaps. She retreats behind a locked door. Understandable. From the sound made.

This is a striking example of the belief that the name was an integral part of the economy of a living creature.

The insurrection.

He suggests the analogy of a planetary system, a counsel of tumults—the notorious blood counsel, bloodwork. A petition is delivered (bolts of jism, demands for rusty nails, cubist minerals). We are well beyond reason. We are well beyond excuses. If the men come to build, well, they come to build.

This one's a member of the old academy, a sifter of language under the yoke of dementia praecox. You must return to the workaday world. It's my dysthymia. As much as can be added is being taken away. Heart spore he murmurs—a calling, a naming, out of one's mind from excess of mind. It is precisely this ability which the problem attempts to snare in a modest way. I shuffle the pack and place it back on the table. The croupier deals me a card. This arcanum is also known as the limner of thresholds. Waterquake. I was there, Eurydice.

Never again come around unannounced.

Tell us more about the petition.

Continued use of the thanatorium. Continued use of the young men known by their title. Yet another vignette that makes criminal use of someone else's ensemble.

Softly still the dark mutinous now descends in waves. A voice echoes in the predicament. I too am falling on every part. Within the frame of happenstance I have unearthed a fact or two. The event is abolished. Soul discharges, silver and dark.

Silence. This room has that same malevolent silence. The tortured thing has been immersed in a body (catgut your tongue). A messenger struggles through the snow—one less thing to think about. I'm dealing with phenomena, not with metaphysical insertions. I easily spot him, clad black in the whiteness. A haruspex is ready to expose internal organs to the poisoned air. Reassuring sense of drift and fracture about these parts. If ever I write a comprehensible sentence I will doubtless go out and hang myself. After a while, all adopt a used-but-happy look.

More scavenger—dirty, dirty, dirty.

The mysterious affair of the murderous attacks.

You're an energy void. Deep space. This is all about my persistent reticence. An insect alights on the spine of the book. Preparations are clearly underway. I count the same number of fixed stars visible in each catacomb. Increasingly brutal acts of self-mutilation are occurring. I cut the pack in two. Such a candle is said to be an omen of death, indicating the pretext for spirits or the devil. He sucks the energy out of every sentence.

Trumpet, solo (*cum grano salis*).

We return the following year to resume our work. The blood jets are getting worse and worse. The stalk swells. The only thing around here that moves is the light. I am not supposed to mean, I am implausible. I list the problems and their appeal. Explain this simulation as best you can. Begin with the tongue of the mouth, then the palm of the hand. Erode the voice, erase all handwriting. The history of the commune has become a touchstone of great importance. Close with the liver and the spleen. The question is how should I.

In front of you imagine four designs made up of two colours and two shapes.

Blue diamond blue circle.

Red diamond red circle.

Ghostly as it laps the boat, your meaning will be the death of you. The question is, why should I change it for you. Now, depict me. Should you dare. Unplace me.

Hologram (ant). A picture postcard. St Ingarde, patron saint of the pismire.

Never the quiet life. He says they shave off all your corners. Do they not. He infuses tongue, a bewildering mix of fact and fiction, congealing to a terrible compromise. This isn't a description of a town, as such. It is not a simple place. As set at sea, fulminating.

And they bleed from a thousand tiny holes. A trillion bright stars have been hand-painted across a blue-black canopy. He leans on his palms over the counter.

The official work here is prizing open the uncanny. He observes that the varnish is worn, exposing bare ash in places. His face is one inch from hers. Dreary surface refractions from the street outside, with passersby, destroyed. I should know. I'm able to judge between things pretty well. Not a perfect, but.

What's in that box of ghost.

Vertical strings of shingle balance on the precarious sleepers. He empties his pockets: ganglia keys, the scissors, the stolen feather, the five gold coins of change, a brass knob, dead psyche, a crowbar, the toe of a stocking, a love token. The inscribed ring he hurls into the milky lap of the sea.

Imagine a ballast of flat bricks resembling books: mottled granite, heavy as gall and inconsolable. Units of magnetic flux. A yellowgreen fluid is secreted from the liver, bitter and malign. This involves a degree of intervention, but there exists a sketch, scraps of paper. A thing can always be made.

A pen.

An arrow.

A measuring rod.

An unsung pipe.

The vibrating tongue of an organ.

The erstwhile stone.

A long list of injured men, encoded.

He is tied to a stake in the desert. Any wasteland of shape and flatness will suffice. Separate his warp threads. Unknot the weft of any torn skin. Apply electrical amplification. A guard circles him, swallowing hard. You need to find yourself a name, perhaps tumult. The circle of footfalls in the sand spirals back into the aperture. By wasteland I mean any desolate barren region. It's the dead brother story all over again. Back off. His eyelids are sewn open. His flesh has turned the colour of puce through exposure. He's cut down and buried up to his neck (I'm surprised you haven't heard of him). I'm a lapse in your cultural knowledge. Much later he comes back as a flea with a human head. He states his number and is admitted. He bears a name. Literally, scarce vapour, somatic wanderer. He's a noted transposer of signals, sound initials, the cluster of reproductive cells—lichen, threads of fungus mycelium. He reminds me of that virulent spread. We have to leave now, with or without the fleshy parts to which he is still attached. The final port is predestination, a hawk of the first year. Perhaps tumult, the craved absence of things.

Today he is tempered by a deception. He says all writing. Challenge the integrity of the body. Manufacture another within it. For him there are four key areas of putrefaction. Whatever. Fuck it: he joins the circus, becomes his old self again and is swallowed by a big fish.

XVIII

We can't see their faces. They're moving in the same direction. The eighth spool remains undisclosed. They're behind us. One is fraudulent, another flatters. Now they're alongside.

You might argue. We're stripping the work back to its basic level, revealing its fundamental harmonics and structure. We were going to pass straight through to the loop section, but that's no longer possible.

Here they come.

How did the woman who entered the room leave no traces (entity clearly has a sharp legal mind).

There is a plentiful stock of flesh. I see one with its own head—tail fin translucent, eyelid bloodless. Shoes flat. Let's all pause to think about what happened today. A guard gave me away. Downhill everything hurts. I catch my breath at long intervals. I lie in wake. You enter the thoughtstream, and snap. My redundant title is a usurpation (dictatorship). We're at that place where the ground opens to form a passageway, what's known as a souterrain. We could simply crawl back in again, die happy.

An account of a typical hypnagogic invasion.

Blue stone monad. A brittle root supports the cilium, a whiplike appendage. I'm a univalent radical. This brings us back to the afterlife of plants. I believe the symbolism of the three orange pips was your suggestion. This brings us back to the science of making marks, of stigmatism. The heart is exposed. I lie in wake.

He is cultic.

Where.

A station. Our first piece of luck in some time. We're fused like filaments into one bundle. There's a method. This has me reminiscing about the old world, propels me back in time. At the terminus only the clock face is illuminated. This circle encloses an inner ring composed of twelve equal sections. Each is further divided laterally into three. All of these segments turn through a complex and unchanging pattern. The roof is a vault of wrought iron from which offenders hang. My own body is bisected by a central spindle. Monomachy must be combat with yourself, nothing less.

We've been doing pointless sums up to here. The outcome is the thirty-six just men. No one dares question me after this. Particles are visible, suspended in a moving fluid. I press pause and hang up. Thoughts crawl through the head. They're unrelated. Remain in this moment for a while, then move on. Everything's going to be all right.

Inferno.
Some further remarks on the red dufflecoat. Linger in this instant. Involuntary witnessing during the hours of sleep has become a new sport. I have myself lowered into the basement. I'm semi-structured, quite hairless. It's dark (of course). I draw sightless on the wall with a piece of sharpened metal. There's a technician armed with a pinhole camera. We resume filing the subject's hair. I'm too raw to settle nerves. Writing seems like nothing. One mustn't live in the past. Tomorrow, I mean.

Unevent.
She turns around and stares right through me into space. Strictly, this is known as an isolated act, or non-act. I am attempting here to adopt a casual, conversational tone. You will get used to sleeping one fine night. I'm electrocuted, gently. It's not all bad.

He has distilled. Vague sense of transcendence. It's like a kangaroo court. This takes three hours more. My palms vibrate, tongue too. What's happening with time, closing hard on your body? Begin as requested with the mouth, the track of a vein—then his voice, his handwriting, the inert organs. Disconnect this somehow: a turning sphere of earth-brown crystal. Have you ever ventured inside. We're nocturnal, aren't we.

Weary men tramping homeward. Sometimes it feels like a prison. His death took place a week after his final return (echoes of Mahler). Everything's ongoing. He meets hostility. (I wouldn't suggest anything that wasn't, now would I.) All eyes turn toward the slope. What crimes occur.
List these elsewhere.

Result: some form of self-abasement, an unnecessary colour trapped within a superfluity of instants. The bed is damp. Burn down my house and leave me for dead in an act of spiritual revenge. He brings into light the collapse of shadow, rhapsodies of an unknown prophet. I carry about me a sheen of sweat. I find lodgings in the shabby quarter around the station (Gare du Nord). He was once caught declaring. You will never work again.

Thin partition at foot of bed. Take what I am—draw in the eye from out the knot, you weirdly unconventional products of nature. An obsolete word meaning to dance once again is repeated, over and over.

Tell us more about the region and its publics.
Valley of ground bone, riverine funeral pyres, open-skin boats manned by amazons. A black marble is used for testing gold and silver, by dint of streak. Diet: people eating one another. Panic in the streets. A storm of freaks is fore-

cast. The narrative involves a dialectic argument, semantic paradox. Throwing a six on the die announces the convergence of a limit.

He tongues an eyeball. In one pocket nestles a test-tube full of battery acid, in the other an erection. I add up to so much less than myself. I'm an unbound. The heart is suspended from the ceiling in a porphyry urn. What's suggested here is extreme sensitivity. I'm not unlike that obscure expression. I too am unbreathable. What's suggested here is ectoplasm screaming from the fingertips. The magic number denotes the phase we're going through. It's said he scrabbles in the quagmire of the occult. Lifelings, here he is—a pointer that has picked up the scent. Belief in od. Serendipity.

You have lost your way croaks the old. In places I return to my notes, and remake, refashion.

Item. An erotic toy consisting of a small corkwood box crammed with bees.
Item. A long list of uninsured men.
Item. A slow creep of soil down a slope.
These objects should have been placed under the table long ago (we should all be under the table by now). It's earthshock. What I hate past all bearing is the glister of his spilled blood.
Battery low, voltaic cell ebbing. I had no choice but to cut a lot of this out. Stop me master, please.

How a magnificent *auto-da-fé* was staged to prevent further earthquakes.
She's of petrifying aspect, winged with hissing hair et cetera. All this sounds rather darksome. Since uncollected time the psyche has been described as highly strung. She's an intermediary of sorts. We both aged overnight. It was like being siphoned off to a home.
Rest-harrow. Total eclipse. Total collapse. Come up and be dead.

The accused is strapped to a spiked frame. He scratches, tears, and harasses the land. He squints (soul, more or less). Back-sound of claps, belling. Someone's got to do this. Now get out.

Men in gold, then black. Would you like to do A or B first. Violence. What's at A. Violence. Are we doing the whole body, or just the face. You won't complete in time, at least not at this pace. On the pier of all places, they appear to be mating with one another. What colour eyes (identical). Of all that I saw that night no clear idea can be given. These scenes relate to a lingering sense of injustice—breakdown and fall-out, the malign influence of the central hub. Yellow eyes mean radiation, processing of dead tissue. White eyes mean death on a forced march across a desert. A little hill of distrust gathers at my feet. That hollow reverberation stems from a chest-shaped burial chamber made of flat stones.

These lips are tiny wings outspread between my gentle teeth.

Genuclast. Kneebreakage.

C.

I am judged as never before. In a glass tank a snake is busy swallowing whole a live quail, as busy as a snake can muster. Today is piano day. I remember a very large man with huge hands and a voice. He passed all the exams with distraction. Everything is as awful and devastating as people say. The chips are down. My own submission was rejected: a seditious declaration, a myth of interdependence ripped to shreds. He says I will venge and I will revenge. What have ye done.

They cut the power. They throw in CS gas. They come in through the large glass. An enormous cat the size, shape and colour of a puma pads into the room. It appears that the chips are still down. It's a gamble. I was at times almost sub-conscious it seemed. A kind of hilarious cynicism descends upon the banqueting table. Much of the style and content has been eroded. It's a puma. Too many friends around the table. All start talking in would-be spurts. I gamble on black, sometimes red. We lack that utterly doomed sense of must and action. The dis-ease is incandescence of lid, eye-spasm. In your gore ye shall certainly be destroyed by him.

The ceremony of opening the mouth.

An assistant holds me upside down at arms length. This is all about vengeance. Brother and sister, no less, are conjoined at the torso and left to swing about a central shaft. There follows desperate toiling combat, whence we earn nothing. It seems you were right all along, mister reptile. Now you have to give us the names as well. I lean toward voidance. A dead dog and a slave lie head to toe, side-by-side in the cist. A train timetable rests unfolded on the table. It's stained with vomitings, blue wine. Each minuet gets dedicated to someone you love. They are separated by the Atlantic Ocean. All the names of the stops allit-erate. I went down to the sea to the darkness (peculiar atoms of physical inti-macy). In every tense I want to avoid.

Sit here. Put your legs around your head. You must surely have picked up the topic by now. If you can't keep up with the conversation, don't try stealing in. His ethics are best described as Aztec.

Of that which is contaminated within itself.

His critics often think of him as an inventive savant seriously limited by a deficient technique. In this perspective, reading as much as writing becomes a matter of injustice, an aberration. These aren't pieces about death, they belong to death. A long series of throws is converging. We're frozen at the moment of descent. It was like being sectioned into parts. We perplex.

The argument.

Lingual revolution in the body of words, an artificial system of signs and symbols with rules for the tongue, relentless systole and diastole. Further inquisition begins. The correct answer is a tidal bore. A debate ensues. Is another battle worth the hazard. Rooms of different size are flooded. Some advise yes. Some don't. The boom interferes with the bowstring, so it's cut loose. Others dissuade. One begs for absolution. Varieties of light, artificial and natural, bisect the nave. The building creaks in the rain. Seedpods fall from the sky.

His last request was for an appreciative crowd. He is animal conjoined—a shining breach, the antithing, the beasty. Under no circumstances will his inquisitors deviate from their chosen strategy. He passes through the wall without difficulty, directed by chaos, the occult power of placement.

Everything works itself loose in the end. I discharge, silver and dark. Under no circumstances deviate from pain. He says I am writing a book about the unfinishable nature of books—debris, an epic, sublime wreckage—neural sensation in a phantom circuit, forever looping back into itself. The vehicle is an alphabet. It's turning. Under no circumstances deviate from pain. This constitutes a supplement which can never exist in fiction. An extra performance has been secured by suitable disarrangements of the real. I've lost all awareness of the concrete level we're on, the sense of the cycle still being attached to a body. A consultation begins, long overdue. You get the idea.

She clutches a butcher's knife. Eye and ear are unhinged. She stares him back down to earth. Ideal sequences of events always run in parallel. Let me put my arms around your head. I'm manifest in light, electromagnetism, chemical reaction and hypnotism. Under no circumstances deviate from the plan.

She flinchless views the gathering rain.

Purgatory displaces hell.

Detail their departure.

A raft of bees.

You've moved mountains in the previous layer. Now it's time for some supplementary tortures. Undertake this piecemeal. Be careful. There are precisely one hundred and twenty variorum notes, a succession of changes. I know of nothing. The arousing shock brings thunder, ruin. By means of a hollow tube a mouse is introduced. Radio interference is discovered pouring down from the stars. The tube is withdrawn. A warning's given. Only an adjustment is intended here, not a move.

All right, where's your office he snarls. Through that glass dome. Now he has shown the helper his entire hand of cards. Just because we may posit the existence of an ur-language this does not mean that subsequent tongues are inferior or corrupted in any way, are so many linguistic compromises. We're at head quarters. The orifice of egress and entrance has been sewn up. Stop the female says it hurts through the ceiling. Crucial information is being leaked. We're holed up with human and alien figures. On the table in sealed freezer bags are a vial of semen (the hanged man), a dried perineal sac, semi-organic computation ducts, the eye of a ray, and an unidentified. Alongside these, facing northwest, are a plastic model of a double helix and a spirit-leveller. Such elements rarely coincide. Much time has passed. From a great distance she says meander and taciturn, I remember those were your words, your petrified words.

A pulsating diaphragm. Tunnels and starwells. Looking out is down in fact.

Somehow the items in the inventory haven't been missed by anyone. M is for meteor. My office is now a true sinecure. Finally, the four men come to a looking-glass on which is scratched a heart pierced by an arrow. The problem with the knight is the magic square problem: the sum of the figures indicating his position is always the same. This is a truly horrible thing to say, but start listing all the words you can think of.

A ballroom with crystal chandeliers. Here again we wander into anecdote. That which is misconceived within itself.

Birds' eggs with dark blue shells. Others of disparate colour—yellow, red-orange, green.

Shoulder-striped clone, the Chinese character assassin.

An arch of corrugated iron, built partially under the world, used.

Now I am done with things.

A rare coincidence.

The last two survivors meet one another by chance in the street. That fact over there is a myth. Her smile does it all for me. And what's that dark shape rustling at peripheral. Her smile has lost its redundance. My other animal is a jaguar.

He orders us to be boarded up in the garret. Small holes have been dug in the wall using a fingernail. I draw the letter K in the condensed vapour that clings to the only window. Now complete my papers by answering the following questions, please. The accompanying card says avoid everything you favour. All will be farewell. Never leave the apartment. I want to stop seeing you. Be invisible. Be untouched, a concrete act of departure, a dilemma. At least the dialectic does not *present* itself here.

How much do you want for that. He whispers from deep within his cavity. I too was once believed to mimic the phases of the moon.

Pencil on document paper.

I swoop straight into her eye. Eat only food and all will be well. A rip tide rushes with great violence up the estuary. Come letterhead, come husband home.

We should send these pages in to aliens and monitor what happens, ashen submariners.

(After this, one.)

Hyphae. A short stroke of ink. Veins of fungus spread rapidly to form a web across the dewy earth. Most of these tricksters were once composed. Proud flesh worms on the wound. I am learning to wait. It's like being sanctioned. Return home to screed alone, he insists. The head is the desired head.

A mason's atelier. Strict timetables and regulations cover the walls, an undertow of melancholy. In the middle of the room stands a table. On the table is a ground-plan: the abbey is taking form. (It depends on the writer.) Painted on a framed papyrus is the hieroglyph of a crucible. I never do things all at once. I disaim. Arbitrary arrangements of letters have been used to form words, an impractical topography, if ever. My own map lies in the torsions of the body. Now I'm released into the atmosphere, listening out for something, someone. In the earth I draw a circle bisected by a central core torn open at either pole. A solution kindred and empathic might emerge from this, if we can stand the long wait. In time we're divided into three. We have spanned the one hundred and twenty days. I always wanted to write something senseless, quite stupid. We turn in space. The image here shows a dense mould of glass fused with cancer.

And I say. Bring a jacket next time, bring a sample of desiccated skin tissue and your conical hat. One observer wears a tape-measure about his neck for luck. Lent against the walls are huge stone books, set aside for grinding. There exists a lack, a past to glimpse no future through. We're divided up into actions and events. Has there ever been a nasty shock that could account for this present state of unrest? No, we were left to fend off ourselves.

A dull glass of unresolved light. Rapt of bees.

A sepulchral chamber is excavated in the bedrock, formed of stones and hallowed tree-trunks. This stone coffin is made of slabs placed on edge and covered on top by one or more horizontals. I want your body. The whole book pivots about the next paragraph.

A novel kind of lunacy, whereby the patient fancies himself to be a wolf (a vain attempt at story-telling). These events took place in a remote region of our century. Herein I play the role of a concentration camp guard. The climate is harsh. Narrow passageways intercut endless rows of cubicles. The development of meaning has become puzzling. The next image is a discarded chassis. Arbitrary arrangements of letters are used to form words. Snow lies kneedeep on the ground—by contrast the grey of the uniforms, the prisoners in black. Our only chance of survival is to find an individual who can see that these characters and things have no substance. The place is infested (manwolves). All narrative reeks of melodrama and sensation. I'm distracted by memory, a stony beach at low tide. The guards stand on their hind legs and begin executing the prisoners. Grotesquely shaped rocks are exposed. The protagonists meld into one another. Extermination of the entire camp gets underway. I search for surviving inmates, opening and closing doors. Behind one are primitive latrines. A remark, a sentence with two clauses, recurs—something about erasure and a mythic river, the Styx. I am unusable. All responses are convincingly blank. I turn a corner into a snow-clogged passage. A naked prisoner kneels before me. I shoot him in the back. It's always too late. I shoot him in the head. In the sky flickers a tiny square. A disembodied voice tells us. Monochrome signals resistance. The invaders increase their number. Now for our customary group of three (a threefold conflict is underway). I accept. Fear is usurped. This tale has been several times re-examined, with the greatest care and attention. It consists of random signifiers, orderlies administering medication. Must be three o'clock already. This isn't convincingly written, but that was never my intention. Footfall leaves no trace in the snow. All narrative is conceived through itself, an endless loop of accusation and control. What befalls is generally embraced. There it is. There you have it.

Here again we wander into antidote. Move further east, the encampment once more. The workshop has a long wooden table running down the centre.

Think. In one corner is an unfinished reader. A huge insect eye lurches in front of his face.

Eagre.

A sudden surge of the tide. At the foot of the stairwell humps of soil swell up out of the earth. Both agonists are painted white. I'm wary (the sudden absence of inquisition). There are objects on the table, under the table. I presume everyone has heard of me. He has had time scraped back to the flat slate. This action deposits a readable script.

Some ancient musics.

A mode of two tetrachords with a semitone between the two highest notes in each, and a hole in between, more or less. But reckoned downwards, i.e. authentic. Extension from ef to eff, with ef- as fatal.

The aforementioned crossbeam.

Portrait photographs are ranked above our heads. I calculate twelve years back: a vast atrium with soaring roof. I gaze up. Cuneiform inscriptions cover every surface. There exists somewhere an indelible sense of space. One figure faces left, its depiction flat and stylized. The framework of an engine wraps itself around a column. An entablature surmounts this pillar, resting upon its capital. Gathered in the hall are combatants—guerrillas dressed in their workaday, allies and adversaries. One side is decorated with heraldic crests. A sense of indebtedness pervades the atmosphere, a sense of doubt. At the core of the structure is a menhir cut from red stone. I'm a captive, or guest. I hear the distant sabbath bells of my childhood. A permanence is taking place. A stage has been raised a little above floor level (I love superfluous detail). Infill of rock fragments can be seen through the huge glass panels set into the walls. The audience rushes after the performers as they run around aiming kicks at the disintegrating fabric. The whole spectacle is an assault on culture through parody. It is under-rehearsed. It is elsewhere. It refuses to function. Doubtless our long stay in the eternal is responsible for this. If you play this war-game vertically, it will never work. Likewise, if you run it horizontally. Doubtless the length of my sentence is a consequence of this. Such unearned memories drift daily before my eyes. I'm uneasy. Nearby.

Eating people is bad for you. He lifts a garment to reveal his groin. The genitals are clad in woven metal. Recollect and record the detail.

Odd bulge above pubis, set slightly to left. Do as he says (ejaculate). The skin of his lower half is a livid purple. The atrium is the central core of a reactor. I relish the idea that this is a memory which manifests before the event it memorizes. The upper tier is fleshy (soft texture of exposed glans). Translate this into a lexical structure. Blending in has become a matter of life and death. The furniture arrives. Without blinking, a footnote. The future arrives. Momentum liquefies under applied heat, by nuclear fission. Repossess poverty, read into an austere, with idle and strife. I am so glad you are here, I could never have fathomed these things alone. Cause to fail, my eclectic. I am the reducing liquid, well within sight of mourning. Every gesture fuses with the text. Now, desilver me, mister macabre. I am inert, a safeguard. Move with indelible steps—a series of trancelike movements prefigured by the algorithm of flocking birds above the pier, systole and diastole of the swarm. Yes, I make mistakes. He whispers. The distance between each wing tip is identical. For fusion, see fuse.

Buzzing of unmeaning sounds, his usual underrated perfection: magnetism and chemical reaction, hypnosis of unclassifiable names.

Err civilisation.

At speed she whirls a lozenge-shaped object through the air on the end of a string (bull-roarer, rhombochasm). Usually the square is excluded. It blurs a circle, the wheel of night and day. Just before dawn the wake really gets underway. The refrain is still audible in my head, driven and arhythmic. Parallel gaps open up in the crust. Straight away they are occupied, interpreted. We're held fast under the old laws, the hinder-brain.

Upon his return she speaks, after a pause lasting many years. You are changed, somebody in you has changed you. A bloodfine is paid to the family. Time for sleep, he hazards.

Rap. Rap. Rap.

The table. Her ghostwritten missive.

Come letterhead, come husband home. It's true. I don't love you. I refuse to tell you anything, beyond reason.

When you produce the final version, keep a notebook of all possible variants.

Number four hundred and nine.

A gigantic statue on a building high above a gulf port: the many-limbed Aztec spider goddess of death. A festival is underway. At a certain time of day the sun is behind her, casting a vast shadow across the aquamarine waters of the bay. Observing from the top of the building, I have a perfect vantage point from which to view this phenomenon. The light is dazzling, the sky blue. Ships and small boats and skiffs crisscross the bay leaving long trails in their wake. The shadow begins to quiver as the statue becomes animated. The vast and towering complex it's perched upon begins to shudder and crack, as if earthquake had struck. At the top of the structure a man is balanced on fragile stilts. Only his face is visible through an elaborate carnival costume. Into a microphone he pleads for his life. The whole edifice collapses into the sea.

Repeat image of metal and concrete disintegrating and plunging into the waves. This process is one of distillation. See, the dialectic announces itself (already) according to the mode of the not-yet.

At a request from the left half the taxi stops for conjoined twins. They slither across the back seat and spill out onto the pavement. I mean it.

Scarification obviously carved with the diamond of a ring.

A little tonguelike part. That volley of snow, ghoul of the season, whenever it was. A centrifugal machine, the tooth abyss. There are still some empty seats. I am seven earths out. I have vacuumed. I am said to have betted against occurrence.

A café bar. Eight marbletop tables. The cadence of the pianoforte always triggers nausea (by this I mean absentmindedly, like swallowing plankton). It's a brain condition, a finger-hole in the wind. The three year shock gets underway. The effect is widespread: violent repercussions in related industries, flying pickets, unofficial air strikes. It is my wish to juxtapose here many types of unrelated discourse, with none assuming primacy. There are three lots of two and I know it. I leap from the ledge. All night long I plummet. I'm not going back inside that house without him.

Consider this a record of delirium—horror sorties, the exact axe et cetera. An inquisitory.

The tale turns. It's telegraphic. He levitates. He is following the scent on my heel.

She writes blindfold with a planchette. There is reading and reading. It's a strange game this: tightly packed nudes, unlicensed skin composed of tiny dots, scintillas of light about the masthead. My own role is uncertain. The tradition deviates to the east and to the west. She parachutes in, unbolts and flings opens the gate. This stretches back to always and perhaps, therefore it has no beginning.

He remains concrete. He is hamstrung by the terrible lie. Feet are involved. The relic is restored (they have a thing about extremities). I'm a registered precursor, a minor deity of malicious nature. An outrider. Anything that whirls.

Heart-chamber music. We must be nearing the end by now. A slip of the mind took place that day, snatches in the voice. Happy days are here again, god-head soup. Sometimes I think there's too much going on here, that we are losing ourselves in detail. This chapter is about femininity and seizure. I've accustomed myself to the simpler forms of hallucination. I hear rumbles and swoophs, the rush of displaced air. We're reunited at the bridge. New laws about espionage have been passed. That tapping noise, I'm sure it's you sending yourself back.

To communicate more readily we shoot an arrow across the gulf and set up a system of pulleys and ropes. Deviance is capable of rapid attachment, of the blinding iron and the text. Of writing books there is no end. I only wish I could. Writing is like waiting for someone who never arrives.

He bears a dragnet on his shoulders. Think about it. First season of delirium: people dressed as counterfeit, people dressed as trees, nerves. It's difficult to move. A worn leather bench runs along one wall. All the windows are blacked out.

Of that which is dead inside itself.

It's said she is no longer capable of presenting a convincing challenge to orthodoxy. Familiar crack inside back-base of eggshell skull. In short, maelstrom—a tale containing an allegory shadowing a parable. Four beasts in one: the homo-cameleopard (mystification). Silence, a fable. As you can see, my id has escaped.

He cannot both know and succumb. For him there are three key areas of dissatisfaction. Try as I might it's impossible to dismiss such nefarious themes. In memory we pass that hill again, the magnetic mound. As I said, a threefold conflict is taking place. The whole of this moment constitutes a transfigured sphere.

I can take it or leave it. Volunteers step forward and make a bridge of their bodies. He's wounded crossing the span, just below the femur. Right now his feet are touching the edge of a deep horizontal fissure. The muscles in his face tauten and start to twitch. Things crawl out through the gap in the underworld. Suddenly there's more light. He must've carried it with him when he crossed the frontier. The sinews and ligaments correspond to ancestral symbols. Things crawl out through the gaps between words, the flickering peripheral.

A stowaway. He lives in a spiral, a screwshaped coil. You've moved a mountain he says. He counts himself among the detached pieces, descendants and their offshoots. He cancels himself. His origin remains obscure. Remember that film: a reservoir of bile, a cauldron of pissasphalt, the workmen in their shirtsleeves. Two mirrors speckled with rusty stains have been left propped against a chalky ledge. Hereabouts they still honour tickets. I myth myself. I'm no handsaw, to speak of.

A brief introduction to nonfascist living, the idealist folderol.
My subject is the inability to make good use of foreknowledge. Speculation and sanity. Apocrypha. One who pretends. I'm not happy with that word tilt.
But they still have a small population of blood stored in their veins. I declare this day an official work, one among a dozen designated throughout the astrological year. We are divined into decades. Sit on the floor should you feel so inclined. Focus your mind on the stones in the metal box. Out with it, from us.

News from where (hallow time). Deuce-ace, the slowest throw. Send copies and a cowering letter. Fire and water are interpreted morally as passion and tears, the intimation of frailty without which melancholy could not exist. Our share appears reversed. Hundreds of these procedures have been left behind in an archive. Bury yourself under land, rootstock and barrel. Shift to an indestructible state. By the way we have located March. He had it in his pocket all along.

We find ourselves trapped in a hostile underground gallery. Someone has photographed a circumference of blue lichen. Our share is cursed. Explode the image before mailing it off. The book is counterfeit. At the last of the cages she stops. Outside, something nasty stalks the streets. She can't help herself. It's night. The panes of the windows are infected. A long shadow stretches across the moonlit garden, a shadow without source. None among us harbours any meaning. Even so, someone's vibrating in my pocket. I am officially declared. I'm one of the twelve insignificant limbs. I am finished in thirty-seven days. She repeats in every word. Nasty, nasty, nasty.

Merry the hatchet. The blade's about five inches deep, two at the base. In his head an attachment is forming, a winking membrane resembling the third eyelid of a bird. We're losing power.

She is stripped, measured, and photographed for posterity. You have come into mine eye. Not copious, yet enough to spin out a legitimate lineage. Bits and bobs thrash their way inward and remain in the head, forever.

He cuts eight horizontal paths across her abdomen, fragile threads of ancestry. The frosted pane of the door has cracked into the shape of a target. It bears the number forty (his age at the time of writing). She once had cheek-pounches that reached to her shoulders and upturned tusks, now look at her. We are all three kept imprisoned in a great bronze vase for thirteen months.

It shatters. Imperceptible letters cluster and congeal, before dissolving and drifting apart again. I'm a state of shock you could never have possibly imagined. Morphallaxis can be doubled, tripled, then quadrupled—regeneration in a changed form. The lizard is so oily it's been dried for use as a candle (not-dark-loving, as folk say). And how pliant. And how now. And how are you today. He comes bounding down the stairwell, demanding as to whom I would care to speak today. He did indeed place that emphasis. I am convinced.

At his departure she says take care amongst them. She foresees a season of dissent. Protect yourself. Find an individual who's been named after somebody already dead. Determine why there's one too many of us on the list. Find an individual renamed after a deed that only he can perform. Upon one page in your notebook of characters draw a plan of the cube, room by room.

Enter. Observe closely where you tread. Close each section now, one by one. On the floor you'll find the founding document. There are aims and goals scattered all over the place this evening. Throughout the whole, induce a quality of moral dispersal and diatribe. Quick now and exit. I'm in this for the season, the haunting—a suspension of time through time to weary away.

She sits to one side. Quit without warning. We're back above ground. A large white room is encircled by a lack of light. Window in shadow. She smiles at me (yes, but malignant, a silhouette). Writing must be quarantined or it dies, she says. Now close this section. Why can I not recollect each myth.

He stands the other side of the bisecting wall. How fortunate to have two guards in attendance today. He wears the uniform. I sit in an outsized chair raised on a platform (this means I'm talking rubbish, apparently). I begin to relate the tale of the circus wolves. I mention the erasers and the pincers. I am uneasy. I turn my body so to speak. One of the observers wears a red dufflecoat with a hood, an unconscious joke, clearly. I must learn to express myself less. If the envelope is opened, we have no choice.

I can now relate the detail of the film in the sky. It begins to run in the room, away to my left, grainy and flickering. Somewhere a projector clicks and hums. Steadily the mercury rises. The strident Slavonic soundtrack grows louder and louder. I can no longer recollect. A voice rises to my mouth, I vomit it up. An unseen hand controls the volume. It's much easier to entertain the fear of the intellect being infected by ghosts, than to escape the mind altogether.

Start listing all the words you can think of that start with V (the letter). Itemize all the things that are done in each room.

The music mutates. Exhibits include samples of atomic writing, a table of heraldic elements, insufferably kitsch glassware.

Wormwood in space, the great tendon at the hock of hindsight. I do not know what I am doing here. One of our chief customs is the seizure and blinding of men and women until they earn money in exchange for their liberty. Days are only a guess from the spelling. No animals were harmed in the making of this book.

Further inquisitions, atomic wait.
Siberia. Incorrect. Stop. The poisoned atmosphere.

XIX

Here's the same thing speeded up and played three times faster. We are moving in a large circle. There's dead skin on the table. This chapter is reminiscent of the management of light and shade on a photosensitive plate. We can still make out the larger structures—the dome of the Orthodox, the rotting wooden piles—also details, such as the heads of the gondoliers, the white doves nesting in the eaves, the crust of solidified metal in a ladle. We're perfect, an immovable articulation, as of the teeth in the jaw. There's a hawk on the track. Nerve breakage around here is acute. Talk me through it.

Random letters are found strewn in the gutter. Traces of fecal matter, grinding screams from the lead piping, an infant incisor. Adopt the reverse recovery position, please. I have tried this twice already (debasement).

He plummets from the sky, armour clattering across several acres of battle ground. I have contracted a spirit union. Vapour rises up out of the earth. That fleeting light has vanished. Scattered oak and ash in the landscape (this is the moment of our great lament). He glances at the barque prepared. I can see all the obstacles. It's an age of denigration into tasteless ornament—originally a jeweller's term applied to a rough pearl—florid and tasteless, grotesque. Look straight ahead. The world is simply *informing* him, nothing more. The crime wasn't staged using a channel-stone, that much is clear. It's going to be another blunt day. In the opening section twenty voices enter successively, with the theme held in attrition. His own portion isn't cut from this, the cataclysmic. Another twenty enter with neural material. The unspecified child has been placed out of mind. All forty combine for the ending. This triggers a famous riot. I happen quite by chance. In my absence a metal box has been screwed to the cell wall. He asks why did you abandon the painting, why.

I think the tide's coming in. That old trick. Number one: detail of ankle-vein. Midsummer rain. The founding rule is that two lines clinging together must always rhyme. Another image depicts a valley where animal sacrifices are made: mountains of black earth collapsing into a void, lightning strikes, frost-rimed mirrors, veins of red lava that corrode the eye. The sheath clenches in a spasm. Its flesh is corrugated to urge inward propulsion. Ice is deposited by the freezing of supercooled fog. Now we have despair to reason with. We're approaching the low-water mark. The future is complicated. I feel like the man in that film with the sunglasses who can see things. For miles out, the waves retreat and the seabed is exposed. Always the base feels so much more at ease than the apex.

Monochrome. A man in a bat costume. Every ankle is swollen. Home is elsewhere. The old isolation returns (the confusing effects of light and smoke). I often catch myself scratching at the surface of glass. I am unconscious, unalike, futile. A card with two diamonds lies upturned on the baize: Roma card index, impeccable futures. You're the favourite to win tonight. He only knows that he does not know—into brevity of speech, even absolute silence. I have resolved to start saving up from today. He digs his hoof into the ground with force. The others settle around the sounding table. He knows that he doesn't stand a chance. Other people's memories are infecting me.

No-coloured sphere just inches outside the dee, with crescent moon at precisely a forty-five degree angle to the setting sun. He murmurs, something resembling. A thing shaped like this.

The rain, the thin film of rain.

You create this malefic silence when you sing. An elongated wedge of sky turns orange then rose. The refuse of the city is conveyed to slow incineration below a craggy peak, a place of torment (subduction zones, transformation vaults). The idol is ram-headed, gigantic. Not a ghost of a chance.

A barbed net is dragged along a riverbed. The lucky number is fifteen. The cards show murderous iron hulks, porcelain crabs, shattered cylinders. Seven days from now you're to be fixed forever. Yet more items: a mailbag, a toe in a stocking, tiny plastic infantry. A space is enclosed to mark the return of a religious from the outside world on release from her vows. The river comes complete with tributaries (the chief direction or trend in any historical development, including that of art). We have arrived at the very middle of the dream.

Faint gesture to lifelong. Today is independence day, not tomorrow. The mouth has been gaffer-taped. He translates with rage, turbulence, thus seeming to combine the two meanings of the word strait. This is in accordance. Downriver, a man is suspended from a hook above a huge block of ice. A canister of ammonium sulphate rests on the engine, running.

A type of circus town where carpal bones are cast as dice. She's been dethroned. The cost is three hundred. Here, the tortoise is an alchemical instrument. The symbols of work are disintegrating: phosphor and mercury, the pewter vessel, the crucible. It is independence day because I just said it is independence day. How long can you outlast yourself. Another asks.

Delta. On the street above it's daylight. There is little to see. Black alluvial earth, a land of animated statues with warm hands. We're close to the hub of everything. I can still smell smoke. It's a contracting market. All die soon or late. We have seen several casualties already. Transmitters project from under the wet sand like a vicious root system. Another word for a walker is ambulant.

An uncharted subterranean forest with tunnels (I made this thing). Something outside of me is proclaiming its authority. We're at anchor precisely above where the wreck lies. The current fact is everything we know. Too late often happens. Is he blinded yet? An imaginary is reputed never to fade. Radial bands cover the inside surface of the shell. These bear rows of pores through which protrude tubelike feet. Whip a nylon cord tight about his shattered jaw. Reconnect the upper and lower sections. Spread thinly across the whole site are the garbled remains of an entire generation. You get the feeling this event would benefit from words accompanying it.

Through the French windows and into a moss garden. Over the wall rises the wail of a lykewake. I observe a scalloped silhouette. That familiar sense of isolation has returned, the twist of some brittle material within. We turn in a counterpoise direction, opposite to the course of the sun (i.e. the wrong way). There's a solitary dolmen pocked with lichen circles. I'm reminded of that moving statue. He goes to fetch a needle.

Of migration to a country that has no need.
A thin movable membrane grows across the surface of the eye like a veil. No matter where you go things are seeking. He brings me something to quench my thirst: a matrass half filled with foaming green liquid. No matter where you go things will seek and find.

I would love to climb that magnetic mound with thee, the journey back to the concrete. She says it could be the impress of their landing. Across the chalk downs, shadows of impossible speed rush out—streaking between the columns, the great ganglion of the forebrain.
Fragile tracks of intimacy, fibres whose action is controlled by the will. Traces of blood, fecal aerosol on a torn white sheet.

Good to hear of you, film. I am losing impetus. No, I love you. May no ominous significance attach itself to these words. Her very name is an augury. A luminous apparition is visible on the horizon, the reflection of light from ice. A task is set as an experiment. Enlightenment is promised. The high apsis in the orbit of the moon or any planet is the same as its apogee. When the restoration is discussed there is some reluctance to send the objects abroad. Geology: eye-shaped masses of feldspar and quartz, prophetic gestures. Take it with you for godsake.

Thick-set clusters of things. The usual death applies. Earth is reshaped as an oval—a cleft with projecting edges lit by the gleam from distant mass. We're on course. Evidence is lacking. What has taken place, she says, is a corruption of vow in the phrase I vum. One is all written out.

Excerpted notes from navel commando.

A smaller version is enclosed. It had one eye and three pairs of appendages. Have you been up working all night. Time within him is drained of land. Arms linked, we advance upon the nearest earthwork. This is a calcified era. From a tract of mica-schist, a boss of granite rises. The core has hardened and is fixed at the intersection of the ribs. Currency is leather money, through which a silver nail is struck in the middle. The upper surface of the atmosphere is horizontal, quite flat. We reach a port without walls or defences, a coastal town harbouring an ancient oracle without its walls. The news arrives that he has made a decision. The music is out of time, ambiguous and difficult to interpret. I shall continue listening until the first recognizable quote occurs. Do you remember that woman with the accordion. She stole away with his tongue and liver, heart and eyes. He recovered them by stratagem. Now, conjure an image of this man on a barricade, with pitchfork.

Home to nowhere, he forever rearranges himself. Insert two distinct sections, with rhymes here and there, objects disassociated and confused in number. He says he heard aircraft and birds, the creak of the building, and that forthwith we must cease or be ceased. These stellar strata are not so much above as down—a looking down into a chasm of stars. That's it. Words are confused with things. Say, an armillary sphere, obsolete.

Inspection of entrails, the mantic device.

Two-spirited, wood plus fire equals carbon. Like the act of running and the blood of the runner. Too late often happens. Is he blind, so early. Back off, that's a private object.

Metal plate in the skull, voice ghosting. He drags you to his sty. Therein, a sequence of wrapped heads, as if for an arctic season. The land lies north of the timber line. And to think we once spoke of this famous race living under the sea. Lids are gently peeled open to reveal whose eyes have been lost. I shed my first today, space I mean. The organ has been replaced by spheres of liquid jet. Ships weighing anchor bring them up impaled with the dead.

He forgets himself. Who has withdrawn from the world? At the end no one will talk to him, even the dogs are snarling. Whose strings are sounded by the turn of a wheel? A period of literature ensues, increasingly rapid repetition of word and phrase. Again, speech, closely akin. There are few entire moments remaining in this key. No one knows for sure (an erection of playing cards in storeys, any flimsy or precarious structure). He never again returns to B minor.

Break off here, apart. He's a sort of transnational revolution—efficacy of grace, absolute predestination. Greasy palm prints line the wall of the runnel. Faint whiff of latex. Roof of turf, helical smokestack rising from low-slung thatch. He has no knowledge of the three persons hid inside the head. I am undisclosed myself. He sits sullen in his corner, rocking at his pipe like something resurrected. This can't exist much longer. Misfortune batters me in Old French. Later he departs to wander in a land called wandering, migration to a barren country that refuses to seed. I take refuge in undisguised melodrama—a quality of simple and unrestrained beauty, of a rather sombre kind. A more prosaic twist in the tale is required about here. Anyone of solitary or secluded habit is vetoed. We have no money and nothing to eat.

Then comes a recognition of ordinary things, but seen in a clear transparent light. This spirit of eternal loneliness is something known. The substitute is an old name for decomposed basalt. He says we are cursed to meander, mister irresolute. (I believe this exhausts the current oracle.) In the transition from middle to times lost we encounter one of the fascinations, the moist figures of cultural history.

He was fourteen ninety-three. A crust is forming. I cannot breathe. A passerby (destroyed) whispers. You are an instance of manifest hereditary evil, the family constellation. I speak origin. I speak steam, a head full of clicking radio samples. I speak false etymologies. I no longer wish to relate. The robe reaches to my ankle. Look, we're sliding down the sloping part of an internal earthwork. And I see time within you. That's my territory, the hinderland, the lilies. I have turned away years myself. His lobes reach to his shoulders. They are pierced and split by barbs of metal. A dreadful science is being excavated. A word is coined, something about the nostalgia of origin. I have never glimpsed to chance back at myself, the supple art of no. Anyone who withdraws, say no.

Bit of a skip in the narrative there. To probe inward is also to confront. Besides, we're beyond recall. This paragraph tends toward quietism—a consequence of living, here and there.

It swam around back on itself and then struck.

A holdfast organ, the means of retention—a sticky apparatus that holds fore and hind wings together. Pollen mass. Dim of fog, with anchor-ice. A scale at the base, plates overlapping with titles. Akin, from someone called, or from to be (I mean to make).

A rib-like veinage or ridge—nervure next, the coastal having or resembling. A small membranous fold that bridles the very notion of the tongue.

From all this you can see that I'm a man who deals with things of no consequence. We're into the final twenty-three seconds. There are many questions but the furthest is quite simple. Just to approach used to be thought enough—to draw close, touch the near at hand. The tide has sunk so low we can ride out to the nearest continent. A debased style is prevailing in time, marked by endless multiplication of ornamental details unrelated to structure: rockwork with shells and scrolls, asymmetrical curves of broken spirit. Almost, quite sparingly.

The mucilage in the gland of the lip has dissolved. The flesh of the mouth is clamped flat, tongue quivering like a big lippy fish. There are atoms in the shafts of bisecting daylight. We're in a laboratory. In this laboratory is an alembic, which has been sealed at one end. It is primed. Flame is applied. We utilize jaw. Entreaty yourself. I'm the eyes and ears of this battle group: the alchymist, the angel barred, the angled shade, the annulled, the anomalous, the antennae, the antitrade blockage, the argent and sable, the arsenic carpet, the ash, the black-veined, the bleached, the border grey, the botched emerald, the brindled cloud, the buttoned snout, the caterpillar web, the chalk carpet, the chevron, the chimney-sweep, the Chinese character, the choke-miner, the classification, the common lustre, the common wave, the conformist, the confused, the conjecture, the costal nervure, the costermonger, the contortion, the current clearing, the dark spectacle, the dengue ness, the deviation, the dingy ellipse, the dorsum, the double kidney, the drab loop, the drinker, the early tooth, the engrailed, the ermine, the eye-hawked, the exile, the false, the feathered ear, the fieldwork, the figure of eight, the five strikes, the flaming shoulder, the frost, the geometrician, the glaucous seer, the goatfish, the gothic, the grey chi, the hawk, the Hebrew character, the hexagram, the hook-tips, the influence, the ingrailed clay, the iron prominent, the jugum, the Kent black, the knot, the large dark prominent, the lead-coloured, the least black, the least minor, the letter shark, the light, the lost wave, the lunar thorn, the lutestring, the many-lined, the map-wing, the marsh oblique and barred, the miller, the neglected, the netted mountain, the nigh, the nonconformist, the oblique, the obscure, the obsolete No, the ochraceous wave, the pale thing shining, the pebble hook, the pigmy, the plain golden, the plumed prominent, the pod lover, the powdered quaker, the proboscis, the purgatory, the purple cloud, those reddish arches in the distance, the reed leopard, the rest harrow, the retinaculum, the rivulet, the rockweed, the ruby fake, the rusty wave, the sallow, the saltern ear, the satellite, the saxous beach, the scar-bank gem, the scarce, the scarce arches, the scarce footman, the even scarcer forester, the scarce prominent, the scarce silver lines, the scarce tissue, the scarce vapour, the scarce Y, the scorched wing, the semiconductor, the seraphim, the setaceous character, the shaded plug, the sharp-angled cock, the sharp change in direction, the short cloak, the shoulder knot, the silver X, the small angled shade, the small dusty wave, the spectacle, the sprawler, the stigma, the stranger, the sub-angled wave, the suspect, the swift ghost, the three humps, the tiny square spot, the tongue, the tooth strike, the translucent, the traps, the treble lines, the lichened bark, the triangle, the triple-spotted clay, the true lover's knot, the tussock, the twin-quaker, the uncertain, the undersigned, the union, the unpopular grey, the V, the valerian plug, the varied content, the well-nigh, the white man's colon, the white prominent, the white speck, the worm-wood, the yellow frost, the yellow shell, the ziggurat, the zygotic number.

Parked outside is a skipful of redundant letterpress lead. Inwardly, the voice is not quite voice—quick with droning bass, like a badly mimicked close.

Lykegate. Free passage through the dank tunnels of the ossuary beneath the streets. A grudge, a vigil. Uncountable nouns. I detect you and everything you suspend. The dramatic personnel include invisible speakers. The surgeon holds all the aces. The animal is the fox. Here be huge answers, though none to speak of. The volunteer's stage name is Head. Cancers have been stationed at both ends of him, that two-drummer thing.

That aqueduct. Outside, broad rays of light fracture and nominate. Digging deep into the peat that covers the hearth, we found ornaments of foreign greatness. Make good use of the double-headed axe. Be inventive. Dig deep to the hypothalamus, in and out the empty block. We also unearthed a structure made of beeswax and feathers. You are manipulating insignificance. Everyone speaks in epigrams. I recall you did say it would be a September when this thing came to pass. Carry out the search alone. How long have we lost. How long have we got.
    Nevertheless, a vessel resembling, from an earth-supporting structure—a so called suspended, not freestanding.

Additional keys and fonts. An animal howling down a fight of stairs. Never pass on them (bad luck). By this I mean the passage of a compressed meaning beyond what the grammatical construction can strictly carry. Narrow lines radiate from the head. Insert a needle into the spinal cord between the lowest rib and the pelvis. Thin bands of red silk wound around her neck simulate the consequences of a good guillotining. Each step is divided into three discrete sections. Now she is here no longer. She is collapse, walking—death under the ice and terror beneath the dome, both at half price. Take a specimen of cerebrospinal fluid. Inject drug et cetera.

He has studied in detail the business of coining a name for a hitherto unnamed find. Such horror stories are these, let the gates thereof be opened unto me. Let me breathe air.

She stumbles down a flight of drunken steps. One comes with a pillow to finish her off. Here, the universe is assembled *beneath* the spectator, with airborne chunks of masonry.

We pass at undercliff. Shelly deposit mixed with sand underfoot. It's what she wanted, this strike of grace. We miscarry (justice). I can still lose you at an instant, if I put my mind to it. The text says she will come wearing feathers, noise. This trick is quite easily done. Composition is readily feigned. Is it not enough to spool out an intractable thread. A uterine law of nature is being applied.

The name of the letter. Anything shaped like it. A substitute for damnation. Either of two hollow semicircular electrodes in the cyclotron.

Theatre void. Inoperative will not visible. He's sliced neatly along the edge like a flatfish. Twenty-three is a useful number.

A deep gash to the forehead. Those present are divided into two groups, that line the east and west flanks of the quadrangle. Paste a little slow to congeal today in the freezing air. Estranged means other than clan (fremd). He examines the crowd, unkindred.

Location, a type of redundant circus town. The third stomach of a ruminant. Unsafe axes (no, plural of axis). She says yes yes I would love to climb that ferrous mound with you, hollowed out by associations of age. At its flank a rush of trees stride out. Have you noticed she says. Appropriate equipment does not exist at home.

In 1753AD he says the mouth is a protective portal composed of many anatomical details. A writ is issued empowering one not a judge to act in place of a judge. In the continuing war between men and the hexapods, only a fool would bet against the insects.

Absence of grief or sorrow, insensibility. The initial element in some obscure technical term. Each leaf is one-twelfth of the whole sheet, usually abbreviated. Right from the outset we've been haemorrhaging power. On the free margin of the lips, uninterrupted from one side to the other, fine pale fibres are closely approximated.

A dweller on the same meridian on the other side of the equator, whose shadow at noon falls in the opposite direction. He is palatable, neatly cylindrical. The citizen alongside has been conjured into a five-pointed star. Deviation from influence has been forecast (the poor man's atmospheric pressure). An origin is doubtful, as if from cut loose—unfamiliar forms of strife. Which may be from the name, creeping, and which may not. Have I the strength.

Now, an untimely conjunction, the presumed necessity of the civic type at play. Or the name of a range of lofty ice cliffs, the sea-front of a glacier. Perceive this light too in the oracles of prophets—a lump of speech, the narrative strain or whatever. The entire penal colony is based on a short story. A vacuum sounds. She likes a day out, people exchanging, immediate and mortal. We're talking about a unique type of surrender (a decision), a psychology for building and waiting. Let's kick off with some drunken gaustering, units of magnetic flux. Density has been measured between meals. This action is commonly referred to as an extinction. I don't usually give advice. Hence, the number of guesses around any closed curve linked on a cycle is equal to the number of turns in that circuit. The hub also has twelve parts or sections. It isn't eternal and it doesn't return. I am re-establishing a suspicion. Deliver me the suburbs to the south. Citizens are funnelled through two little grooves. In the backroom, knucklebone dice are thrown from a cup shaped like an hour-glass. Take me to the middle of town. Drop to the ground. That heap of tiny metal cylinders, they're spent shell cases. It's rumoured the adversary has his own legs.

This is demented she writes. You should take up magic. An attempt has been made to secrete the name. We become estranged. Success has broken us. We argue over the remains of the chicken.

She is an individual who, on parting, one never knows whether one shall ever meet again. I answer. I have unlearnt words.

Now I am staring silently at my ingredients. Somehow I will bring him back. Too much electricity is clustered in one corner. I remember him saying, I hope that thing's not here when I get back. Recompose the room. This part of the narrative has clearly corroded.

She may be dissected under the counter. We reposition ourselves, pressed close to the walls. There's a million different numbers inside her. Everything considered—all the men and equipment, all that cheese—it's an anticlimax. At the end she reclaimed herself. Giving up the dog was a bad job of nonsense (one year of a life). This suggests poverty, at the same time multiplicity and calm.

An instance of blackout. This implies an inexpressible, an adventure which leads to coitus in the antechamber (parliament). We had set out to meet our new hireling. Each day harbours the promise of inconsequential loss. Get to work boys. We can show them what love's all about. I get violent when I'm drinking. I'll bring crayons. Who knows, we may wind up struck out of time altogether. Try this at home yourselves in the coming winter months. Will call when we're back above the surface. I am crushed by grace. Change the circumstance. I am erring on the side of circumference.

Figure of moon, full. Nerves and blood vessels invade the pulp cavity. What colour was the middle of the flower? The insect head? It's said they kept slaves, milked them for their sap. I was once purified in the pool of the south. Permit your eye to roam across the scene, a dependable riot. It's misleading. Do you wish now to make your own book (mucosa studded with bubbles of gas). A sequence of dots would have sufficed. She appears without. She is disheartened. A solid state of compression has been achieved. Pass me a toothpick. I do not believe they can do anything to harm me now. Press firmly with the mouth down upon thy face. I search for her grave and I cannot—a beaten track, a trial in the snow. Stacks of silver birch glisten beside the quivering track. I have never been true to you.

Ether and alcohol. A medium, not matter. Stop staring. Assume in the century. Fill all space. Retransmit the electromagnetic wave. The days are become longer in the senses.

Red shift to eyes, bloody tang of iron and beeswax. They are shooting without revenge, without aim. Many hundreds of miles away in an unmanned region, a thin film of rain, gentle compromise. This changes the whole perception of what a secret is.

A dimly lit continent. An accumulation of glimpses (the deception arm). People growing food, keeping goats, that kind of stuff. I've come a long way for this. Two lesser satellites are discovered revolving around the same planet. I only report back once I'm certain. The women carry heavy jars of water from the river every day. I've been walking for seven years. He says his life has passed, but what could he do. At dusk I doze beside the embers of the fire. It is clear that the person who is speaking believes himself transformed by means of bewitching oil. Suddenly you see an image that you recognize. With frozen hand I stretch my sinews. In the dark I take hold of something slender and brittle, a wing or thin stem.

The portal may be used by any of the following: a magus, a juror, a conductor of electricity, a diviner of recall. An artery is marked in preparation. No one complains. How far is the next continent. He unwinds a ball of string to match his way back. Black up your face with burnt cork and crawl on your belly. It's not logic but at least it's a consistent method (poetry and dialectics). Always cover the upper part of the head. Grotesque face on keystone, on doorknocker. A wild sigh is taken up, a final exhalation of disbelief.

Two blind men insist on a duel. One has a rapier, the other a pistol. I have wrecked the air-conditioning plant. Details are crystallizing into a personal figure. Careful is expensive. Up till now the crew has remained unnervingly quiet. A dangerous torpor can be transmitted by wingless parasitic insects. Intercessor, it was like being here, only cheaper—quite beside oneself, beyond recall. Strange beginnings with flat bodies and short legs flocked about on every side. Today, the norseman.

One of the wheels bullies at my foot. I have a traditional role. The basic astrological premise that the sublunar world is subject to the influence of celestial virtues has practical implications too. I will answer for him. He interjects. Now burn everything. The mood is deteriorating inside the study, the politic situation. The sound swells and extends to other animals, related and unrelated.

Operation anagram. Trapped in a house for days with his dead mother, he resolves to leave the walled city for good. The air is pierced. The more I hear the more I became abstracted. Go back and check (show me where it says anything about a market). People hurl stones at the accused until he loses consciousness. He had always wanted to die publicly, and in an interesting and unusual way. Every day we recite a prayer: of bar-room combat, be here in death or fail, chew glass spit blood et cetera. It's up to you. There's a clicking noise coming from the moon. We don't speak or touch in any way. We break out of ourselves, as if from to loosen, as if from strife. An individual's aura may stem from the personal name, or then again it may not. The temple-tower is pyramidal in form. Each successive storey is smaller than the one above. Back inside, and I can't hear a word above the uproar. I want to cut to the part where he's dead forever. A voice says, as I get older I find myself more engaged with the forces of smallness: chamber music, the atom, particles of some chalky deposit, that kind of thing. Look behind the star charts.

It's the gene. A blind alley. Electricity shivers through my palms. It's night and there's nowhere. Mephistopheles summons ancestral ghosts to dig a grave. Men were once famed for their intergalactic ships. You are breaking up. There are two reasons why the women don't complain. In this clan consequences aren't shared by family members. List packets of land and itemize. I've got to get back. Having it is giving it.

My ears. I re-enter. There's someone else here, someone that can never be shared. His collarbone is sticking out of his neck, skin of hot milk fused to seared lip. I make up my mind to walk. Everything was crystallizing into one word, and then he disconnected all the clocks. Work falls away from me. Scent of rolling brine, a suckling sound. No one notices. Externally, the portal has a hard exoskeleton, internally, a surface of mucous membrane.

A reclusive cell. The first mood recorded is a sense of detachment. Onliness renders the other impossible. This stems from mimesis, an infestation of words, sounds and colours. He says I'm flaunting disbelief, you changeling. Step back with us and recreate musics from the past. I'm a species of inverted religious thought. I am slowly counting backwards. This helps. Why do you list things he asks. Remember when you said that people were better off extinguished? He habitually lies to one side, sleeping on terminal floors, asymmetric body pressed flat to the cold marble.

Such inquisitive writing. Many of these little figments are taken from old, or folk. No stone has been left unhinged. Having burnt your fingers, what do you have to say for yourself now. So I don't lose anything is the correct answer.

Who wants this (lumbar puncture).

Around midnight. Bloom of unease, the sense of sorrow at any loss. Ordinary things and events are witnessed in a clear translucent light. A knife cuts where the paper joins. They sought for nothing else but delays and tract of time. I regain my footage.

An extent of space. A region. An area bisected by traces. Perhaps as drawn out, perhaps as sung at a stretch without purpose—a region of the body occupied by a particular system. Repeat, in ever-receding gradation.

We too of later love
you are all my love you later love, and I recur,
where time is untogether.

A great burst of instruments for misreading by descent of a heavy oblique blade, adopted. A lavish must-see threat: the universal contour wrap.

Continuing protection. People do go away, or even arrive. Anyway, I wish we had a map with us. It's cyclical, isn't that rather obvious. It retains its larval character through every stage of life. She won't appreciate the position of those nails. Despite its condition, it's still capable of breeding. The trolley brakes on the polished linoleum, and the corridor falls silent once more. We just have to drive out and we're free. One of the heads is longer than the other. Listen, his misrule lasts only a few seconds.

My thumbs are receding. An inarticulate sound of disapproval, or doubt, unqualified.

The trench, with chasm of stars, bodies dragged at horse's hock. Join the dots that appear before your eyes. At about this time he received the contents of a sack of flour in exchange for the nightwatch.

Astarboard. The only harmful thing is the vision of a spinal core. Dry your eyes, man. Do the obverse and run. I don't fully understand how everything related thus far has come to pass. Now he is murmuring inappropriate things. Three unresolved clues still intrigue me. They are among us. If any are to be dispatched, reprieve the last. I believe I'm already used up. Notwithstanding, I remain a neutral: mere opinion, the speech act, the microscopic shavings. The path is long-distance. Save yourselves. He explains that pi means against in language.

She appoints herself troubleshooter for the day (such a tiny head). Here lies

buried another of those unrecorded words. See, she is descended from an ancestor, a moment's achievement.

Troth-plight.

A conical pit with a pointed stake fixed vertically in the centre. Rows of these
have been dug before the earthwork to hinder the enemy's approach. She is composed of a quite different spectre of letters. It's not a question of opting for sacrifice any longer. What has led, she announces, to this neglect of misery and
ignorance. There are cables hanging from the trees. There are mineral subnets.
The quotidian is her domain, the workaday. Nobody is selling. A wand is surmounted by two wings and entwined by two serpents.

His body covers upon his fall several acres of sacred ground. This tract
encompasses an abandoned iron-age fort (any settlement emitting ferromagnetic
patterns). Nobody is buying. He has developed a measuring instinct, the drive
toward an absence of meaning.

Still smoke from without. Traces of blood aerosol on the sheet, archipelagos
of semen, imprint of rectal mucus. Why is it that I've never killed you yet.
Smooth rounded pebbles roll about under the bed, the sea. Only at the last could
I make out the tide predictions. The forced double doors lead to an inner sanctum where patches of light pulse dimly in the fabric of the walls. Things have
started happening by themselves.

He purchases a walled garden in a nearby village, but it's too late for that
game. A heavy carnivorous animal with hooked claws and hair has broken loose.
Populace plague-stricken. Prefix restored to form.

An unsexed cell. Ghost of moth, flame and wing interchangeable. It smells like a
storm is on its way, sticky salt crystallizing at palms and fingertips. Trust it, this airborne electricity. Much of this transpired as written. I can no longer feel my face.
What if I write that he had winged sandals when he came down to meet me? Time
is a detail that can survive any story. To experience death without dying seems a natural enough goal to me. Apply this technique to the everyday. An implement for
restraining a ship by chaining it to the bottom of the sea has had to be invented.

A further question is raised by the possessor of a specified object. The
speaker requires another word for the density of breath. It is a pleasure to read
him, but his writing is never *great*. That is, it survives as a bright halo around his
existence, a foil for the murky foreground. You have become a threat to yourself.
Nobody's going home till all this is over.

We're in abducted time. What about the sound of that cowbell in the distance. I was quite unknown during the epoch. A device for holding a balloon to the ground has been invented. I don't think much of the little I can remember—those closing minutes, anything that grants a little stability and security. Then we get the order to make it up the stairs blind. The provocation described above is known as colony collapse disorder. We seem to have lost an hour or two somewhere. Let's not do names today. This is a form of uncritical restraint. Where there's a dense body of troops we're sure to strike someone. Note that his prediction may not have been a fluke after all.

Say, a seascape, wrongly remembered. Vortex of dead animals, fossiled sea creatures. Everywhere transition. I witness a murder. Sticky claret is smeared across the bathroom tiles. It's my job to taste for poisons, or failing that, poor quality. Two men hurl books from a chest into the sea while another films the scene. Looks like this is it. Absolutely every note struck is archived. You've got to be kidding.

We have now reached the bidding at auction. I'm intrigued by the sudden reversal of that arc in the sky. There is an absence of style. A mound of corpses has been stacked up without the city wall. He offers a hand and the stone nestling in his palm is warm. This art is called the art of making do with what's here. I trust that's not hope, rustling. Nobody's selling today. I write letters and leave them on his tomb, expose him to more weather.

A cantina at a remote mountain pass. Though far to the north this anomalous triangle of loose rubble is designated desert, thousands of cubic kilometres of pumice. Now, tie him to a stake sunk deep in this ancient silt. I am disheartened. A lung has been lost through his neglect. Another advisor comes: drive a large metal cylinder into the earth alongside him. Construct an inverted pyramidal figure.

All the gutters are choked with weeds. Rain pucks against the window pane. I want to write the perfect sentence. Unmistakable whiff of rectal mucus. I am total work, the obscure sack of lead.

He has semblance on his side. A siege mentality sets in. The damp roof is decaying, all about are collapsing buildings. Heads catapult over the parapet. There was once a little eye on every finger. A downward curve is impossible. I won't be here for much longer myself. Emptied into a dirt ditch, we draw friendly fire. Now the tide's coming.

Tenth pylon of the still heart. I never wanted to make decisions like these. You will rise at the horizon. This is the agreed signal (nil by mouth). A train advances towards us. The squares indicate who is to be favoured and who is not. Sew open his lids. I made my own way back.

Senseless hidden reverie, blind at gully. This is an obvious reference to the roar and destruction attending any storm. It's the worm in the oesophagus that gives you away. I know you, name. The chosen form of divination is that of observing the way in which people die. Having it is taking it.

He is miscast. This is turning out better than I expected: long stretches of blank wall, empty vaults and syllables. The dim sources of light in the inner sanctum beyond the basement, they've got me thinking. I had to force those double doors again and again. Let's hear it for predictability. Then we kept missing the last tram out of the terminus, again and again.

Cragfast, unable to move from a rented position. Englishlooking plain beyond the city ramparts, the earthworks. I have heard that a novel type of light is to be introduced into the sky.

Cage, evening. A barren landscape. Two policemen struggle against the driving wind and rain. Use binoculars. I wouldn't go in there if I were you. She won't permit you to bring those nails into the house. Make use of the stethoscope provided. Then comes a completely unexpected shock. I call out the numbers one, seven, five and three. Silence. Not yet the salty discomfort of the womb. She will be here any minute.

A leg is crushed. One thing at a time. I am mortally injured at the spleen. Only the line at the very beginning is ever considered. Padding towards me along this private beach is a fabulous hybrid. On the other side, and a little further west, is the west. One speaks and points. He believes himself disguised (a piece of wood fashioned into the shape of a bird). The block is being drained. Rocks are firmly anchored to the seedbed. One twitch more within the body compass, and I can hear upon my knees. The guidebook mentions lycanthropy, but it's too late for that now. The bird is the condor.

Of one who steps with grace upon a gentle ice-floe. Composition's the art of transition. He withstands. No one will find you here. It carries him off to the estuary of an abandoned city, and beyond to the opening sea. Unsheathed muscle glittering in the sunlight shows where crows have been at work. There is nothing to record. Advise manner of divination (the number of futures from knots in the navel cord).

A list is compiled of the various unsuitable materials with which the shrine has been built (wax, glass eyes and lost keys, thousands of desiccated pupae). A vote is cast and a decision is made. Through one solitary and precise movement, an obscure shape is taking form. Yes he says, alphabet in origin. And a dekalogy could be ten novels compressed into one.

A single green lion on the sign that swings and creaks on a rusting arm. I wake despair. I am paralysed. An unfamiliar light flickers in the sky. It descends. Everything claps loudly. Its name indicates its colour. Now release me.

Shinglebook,
typhon—
danger,
aeolian ink.

Imagine it happened one hundred and twenty-three years ago (tangibly perceptive silence). There is a direct link back to musicians of an earlier ear. I hear her plumage has turned—arled and grieved, half-wed. The fibrous matter of the skin was never found. She forms a sediment on melting, and is pressed. Refuse of tallow, cracklings.

Flora of septfoil, sometimes called tormentil, now rare. A zodiac of just seven cusps. It is not yet day, neither is it time. Of writing books there is no end. This action is akin to a stretch, coalescing with to shriek. The objects are the cross-staff and the scallop shell. An instrument is invented for stealing the altitude of the sun.

A film of thin rain. Blue predominates, the colour (mappemonde). I made it once before to here.

Accidental strangulation by dangling cord. If you've just joined in it's too late. We are blindly prevented from ourselves. You are at your best when everything begins to fall apart. The illusion, it's quite simple. The illusion is so perfect. You manipulate.

I meet a stranger on a meandering mountain pass. It is a terrifying silence. In all the world though, the place he liked the best. The sounds rising from his throat are a warning. Glinting mirrors reflect sunlight from the distance. It's said that when they come they will be nine in number.

Before he leaves the breakfast room he wheels around the table, crushing to atoms with his fist every eggshell upon it. I remain perplexed by his account, despite its conclusion. I've been looking around to see if anyone else is fading. Can you not read the body language. I don't know what's going to happen next.

Those revelatory genes. Flickering super eight of self-fellatio. At the border is an elaborately annotated nought. E and F both mean the same thing: more hacking in the green, gulls pecking at a heap of ash. Fiscal sky burial. He fashions household gods after the likeness of his own appearance. The liquid element is sap of iron, leached from the liver. A selection of songs without words follows.

It looks precarious rocking there, balanced on a tiny silver ring—egg and logan-stone. Tell me, how does this fragment sound to you.

Haply self-poised.

The very word itself. Nobody's going home till all this is over. Composition's the art of translation. The hull itself is magnetic. Within the margin of an illuminated book, and I can't hear what you're saying. The rest of the evening consists of dissection. Learning is pursued with style. Speak up (what a time for a mouthful to swallow down the wrong channel). Each paragraph is a series of unrelated chords. The earth tremors struck within a one-hundred-mile circumference. A symbol is required for the plight of exiles who can never return. One man has blinded himself with a wire coat-hanger. Torch everything and quit the compound. We've come a long way from the assassins of old.

She says I wish this life would quicken. I do some brisk thinking: impact statements, erroneous settlements, the law of tort and erasure. She makes too much of things. The chosen object is shaped like a force-feeding funnel. The topic is one enormous undifferentiated field (guesswork). She talks too much of herself. They have abandoned the body-count system. Space is superimposing itself across time. On your knees. A meaningless refrain can be heard from the adjoining cell. People bore nervously into the frozen air. No clyster was ever injected. Thy testimonies are unsure. Grains of salt creak and weave across my rusting palms. Count me out. After this ceremony the apothecary withdraws. Attempt the triangulation while it's still daylight, while time remains. Count me in. Push that phantom limb back into your torso.

The night-watch has fallen short of expectations, does not begin to approach invisibility. I remember when time was divided into distinct days. They have shaved off all our edges. There's a hive in operation. A canopy protects the skull. I wake to find a deep gash at my right temple. The drones sleep in a complex of waxy cells, a bewildering maze of cavities that spreads to every crevice. What if they refuse. The official gauge has been rejected. A metal platform is steadied into position, dangling from the boom. This will function as our base. And can I say something like, this is my room, and truly believe the statement? I cannot accept that a lump has gone down the wrong way. This has caused an almighty. The result is fracture of the radius, backward displacement of land and air. The soil is composed of octagonal ruins, units of separation, a solid stretch bound by eight plane faces. The manuscript is held back to this day. I am reworking memory. List.

Pardoner, afloat in time about a central spool.

Dusk.

A barren treeless plane.

Driving rain.
Killer.
Reaver.
Spouse.
Lover.
Weekend ascetic.
Summoner (unsummoned).
The stolen goods.
Franklin.
Outfangthief.
Physician.
Ship's husband.
None but canon.
Yeoman.
Manciple.
Person, purchaser.
Never in space, the foregoing.
A witness.
A redactor.
(No, it felt at the time like a meeting of equals.)

Sense the style of periodic unease, the local colour—tireless surveillance before an inevitable straw-death. I have made my way to the present-day town of Cobalt. We are not called half for nothing. Crossing water twice in the same place is considered bad luck. In the hills that fringe the settlement are huge factory silos, pink in the sunlight. Watch out for your feet in this terrain. Watch out for the local fauna. He says there is the small matter of displacement. Make your way inside the Arabian castle to the ruby. Turn aside, furrow into the soil. Tremble, benighted, as per nothing.

A small writing tablet. He is blocked at source, aerial twitching. The cornerstone has rotted, so too the supporting column. Language is sifted. I have caught my breath. An incapacity to retain any logical connection is all too manifest. Now we've a picture of a woman, tall and slender, with freakishly long limbs. A rope is wound about her knees (someone has been condemned to eternal wandering). In the cubicle mirror she inspects the black triangle tattooed at the back of her shaved scalp. Flipping open a compact, she squats to inspect her cunt. Now, should the governor of a besieged fortress go out and parley? The triangle has been squared, squared and then circled about by the emptying skull. I am to forget.

Metamorphosis, salt of chance (narrow shoes). I recall that undertaker's bar near the arsenal, full headlights swooping in. I shall here and now fix the actual day of your going. Disguised as the archangel Gabriel, he journeys westward, fumbling after an ancestor.

Unchartable nightshade genus, the headly agent. Zero is for ouroboros.

Star-angling. He is conscious of but cannot apprehend our wayward and flickering existent. In his pocket is a strip of film containing miniaturized data, the cardiac output. I subsist on shadowcast, externals. Traces of an archaeological site are revealed from the air. I resolve to forestall. He probably bases his statements on the theory advanced by the astronomer, not the other way round. A structure is like a bridge going nowhere.

While she is sad and weary, illuminations withheld. Of course, by hearsay.

The patient self destructor. Russian roulette, makeshift days of scrambling. They appear to be, the little ones, in a trance. After a lengthened curve the I-Have-Hook adopts the power of five, and the In-Hook the sound of either/or. (See line eleven.) Even when he says the word finiteness, he means the same thing as when he calls it forth, essentially. And this is also an example of comedy. Which is as much as to say, may new torments suffer your soul. Never permit the more causal composition—a great disadvantage when writing for a lengthy period. Just the surface, the scales of dead skin.

I see you. You saw me. Do you know me. I know I ought to know you, and I do know you at this moment. See my brand new sickle. I see it. Who ate up all the ribs.

Show by further examples how a final may be added to and or air. May we go out now. Row me up to the promontory.

Those onlookers are charcoal-burners, dotted about the cliffs. The detail here is analogous to the layer of rungs and cones in the retina. The point of collision is the junction of three roads. One leads to the sea, the other two lead to the sea.

He says, you exhume more questions than you bury. Okay, place subject on corner of ripping stone, opposite.

Its spine is split and its leaves flap and ponder. At the surface is a field of nodules within a network of mineral cracks and stigmas. I have now observed carefully until the end, as instructed. And heaven knows it's not a grand thing—just me reckoning, here, in a shrinking cell.

The subject is delivered with its own attention signals. Look. Listen. Be quiet. Pay heed. Here it comes again, at each ear a hovering lip. There is not time. He is older than his look. How do you feel about that.

Pray you and mark. Come to me and do not prevent. I cannot think of one good reason for doing any of this.

He is reckoned the last but one. He is nicknamed in the speaking world. No set dates have been struck. A path has been cleared, straight to the sheath of the optic nerve.

Man held in amnesiac fluid.

Suspension in a floatation tank for an entire generation. Echo disjunct, ectopic. How much more of this is there. Deliver me from your promise. I've had enough. There is nothing to invest in me. You have a list of things that need to be repaired. (Must make will.) There's been a change in the wind direction. Amid loud laughter, one deflects the kiss as it flies in. The task of the man standing beside me is refraction. Dreaming and not dreaming, they could never love me. See found text of war-game (title inferno, gothic inspired). His heart is bricked up in a pillar. There's more of these brief studies to come, what's called an etude. He is no doubt wise to leave for good the domain of the air. The final element is metal. We're reduced to scraping a living as performers, tumblers. I show them what they can have for a shilling—the full size, with the knees, and a table and a vase on it. Neither of us can agree on the change of facial tissue. He soon finds himself at the very gut of things. He crosses the great water at the high arc of a bridge. Everything bodes well. A fresh interrogator arrives. The suspect is offered a clyster-pipe. (There must be some design at the root of this excess of courtesy.) I know of no familiarity. As he reaches out, he salutes with a gesture that has something foreign about it. He holds up three fingers to order three shots. The other hesitates. Are you near the tank or a little further on from the tank? Wind whistles through my body, burrowing inward. Yes, leaving did feel a little like dying. Now I have to glue this back together.

Memory of dazzling oblique winter rays. Say something. Fire in the turret, rapid eye movement. The land itself is on fire. He points. O yes fancy that it's the asteroid, the so-called imposter. Down in the valley, immediately beneath us, lies one of those newfangled lakes. Thrice he tries the telephone again, before midnight, at the stroke, and after midnight. I cannot offer anything more than these scraps. A sleeper is embedded in the trunk. No one speaks. It's stuck fast. We are reminded. The instant we remember the names of the two brothers our train is derailed. One day I will hurl up trust on every side. Robust contingency plans have been in place for fifteen years. First guess he guesses right: a life of husbandry, tillage and thrift with two oxgangs.

High above the city, stationed on the battlements of a fortress that overlooks.

At the foot of the ramparts is a field of semi-molten cacti, scorched in conflagration. A cablecar sways high above the docks. We leave the three fallen men where they lie. Their orders were to find a way into the redoubt, proceed to its core, and locate the mineral. Let's finish by hearing.

Far off was something gainsaid. Many volumes were damaged on route, stacked high on the lurching caravan. He is withholding our attention. The species under study is a legless hybrid. Motion is downward and the image is rain, dragging on the shin bone. The situation points to chaotic profusion, a union of movement and strength so violent that it suggests the word terror. Yet still a light firm immanence (the ancestress, a sister driven to desperate terms). I reckon hanging will come of it. It's amazing how you can play and replay this stuff without altering a single line.

She says I have reached the end of a sentence, I expect a reply.

Okay, the insects are stiff and numb after their long winter sleep. Or, to think we once said this infamous race crawled out from under the sea.

Will that do.

A house, inhabiting, to dwell and forever to still. Let's meet at the amusing curve, puckfister. Cast shadows of projecting parts of the specimen by exposure to a stream of a vaporized heavy metal.

It is widely distributed, yet without appearance. Again, I failed. Still the same thought running beneath everything. I've destroyed all the existing beginnings. You are closer than you think. The answer is the patent air-preserver. Or an obsolete wave, the science of floating bodies. The act of starting, especially if limited. Ore particles cling to the bubbles.

Lich-stone keen. Psychopomp, decked out with glistening wings. They've jacked a load of golden seven in the ash of her hair. At present she's toasting under the orange element. Silent luminations gather in her head, mourning states and siege-craft. (O to fetch a compass.) Our slogan is retrieved from the fading impression. As for futures, and this must be stressed, do not withhold at any price. They must be of a fireproof solidity.

Now to sew up the wound. I mean a clannish war cry, partly caught, partly misheard. Hence, the flashing lamp on the helmet, the toothed wheel, the funeral barge. Did you ever think to pen a test book? Did you ever write a hypothesis for this experiment, plot an assay of bias? Carnal, with ice forming on windlass. We are out of range.

A purchaser. One who summons and one who pardons. By indiscretions, a final direction, sea foregoing. A liquid is injected into its intestine.

Pelf-grieve. Zero for conduction. Zero conditional.

XX

He wakes and surveys. During the night one came and broke the zinc table. There was a cracking sound as the circle split at the rim.

Twentieth situation, the key to a circuitous movement, games of misinterpretation. Line with two arrowheads. The dominant strategy here is craftless and lacking in direction. I'm about to introduce a creation myth. Props include an instrument for bending a crossbow. Today's numerology is peculiar (two to the third eternal). I am seven.

Scene, a kitchen. Cinque port. If time, pillars of mist in the cathedral, counterpoint drifting through passageways. One melody is added to another—apparently a trick, an opposite point in some senses, scratched into the flagstones. Plenty of life and colour: murder weapon nailed to wall, the severed head of a bull, mediaeval panelling. A choir teeters on either flank. Form and motion have been outlawed. List everything.

Perfecting by erosion is at the same time a retreat toward an inevitable close. This immaterial novelty is without a subject, simple ballast: a child in the womb, an obligation to prove one's contention, the ship's hold. Any restriction or limitation. A drone bee (confused). The stuff of pilgrims. The leading idea of anything. Part of the song is repeated at the end of every stanza

Stroll up cliff to local pyramid, take a few photographs, move on. The story is a romance of the middle-age, a tale of chivalry about real people struggling under disfigured names.

We're setting out to remonstrate a thesis or opposition, a series of self-contained narratives that tell the story of a family over successive generations (assume that object-relationships are the only source of psychic health). Similar mythical themes are set to recur—what's known as a saga, just one small part of building your own library.

Valley of lees. This is coming together. A ladder with nine rungs. He clasps her legs as she holds the bulb aloft, trembling.

Man held in the ice, crumb still attached to lower lip. Remote vista of beachhead visible from caged landing. A wedge of sky fades slowly from rose to orange, then vanishes altogether. Someone says the earth is to be continued. The island lies fifty kilometres west, across the entrance to the channel. Is there a recognizable distress code? Movements now ultraslow, with distinctions between clean and unclean food. Yes, we are witnessing an event, an exercise in mass intimidation (typewriter, daisywheel, used correction tape). I remember his first salient entry. He died on this very day during one of the years. Are you ready. We're just seeing another little lump of moisture. Tract and reclaim footage, tract and reclaim footage.

The sheltered aspect, a flyblown quarter. Tranquility obsolete, but I am forthwith your devoted. A measure of years is taken. We lie opposite to windward, the weather driven underground. Coincidentally, my companion is an avid hunter. Seems I've missed a trick or two. I shan't be present at the sacrifice, the titanic struggle with imaginary opposition. Ask whatever you want. Emphasize the binary nature of the act held in the image.

He's the last of them, the antique. Darkness falls like in exodus. He drills a tiny hole into the base of the remaining tooth. His role is the jealous constant— a neat spiral is growing at the root of his back. Two ladders are propped against the land, forming a buttress. One is silver, the other fluorescent orange. The body under study squirms. He stretches his hand and a thickness of three days occurs. It's ten twenty-two. There's no reason to move. The head penetrates to the ribcage.

The day of his death has been reset. Condensed fingers on the freezing pane, emblems and lineaments. The date is a Monday of the seventh November. Well, gather the ashes, put them in a glass, fill it with wine, and then drink it. Our orders are to retreat to the periphery. He is vindicated (the disturbed minds of the mentally). Tiny figures are visible in the ice. He regains consciousness on a hospital bed. We're lost without the satellite. I regret this advantage, this bias toward reversal and withdrawal. Use of such methods has developed gradually, without official recognition.

Another self-administered morphine injection. Forward displacement of eye (I'm not getting very far with this, am I). He lifts a flap of skin, enters.

A mesh of leather and wire. Redundant technologies, cathode limbic. The chosen field is time dispossessed. This method separates the ore from the gangue by forming a froth. Our inquisitor has the heretic whipped and beaten to a pulp. A broad blade like a fractal spoon is used. He's rubbed with glasspaper yet somehow remains placid. The musicians are forestalled. Across the wall stretches the forbidden line. The family has been spiked and part erased, according to the graph. By this point we've given up all social responsibility for the words we utter.

Dedicated territories have been conjured. Words are seeded, angels and spirits everywhere. I am manipulating this. He suffocates (blue polyethylene bag from corner shop, elastic band). An end is ignominious. Celebratory dances follow— stepping on hot coals, sleeping on nails and suchlike.

A package sits waiting patiently in the meter cupboard. I tear it open. One particular word signifies both form *and* void (gilded bridge over sixteenth-century Thames). Point B refers to the manner of performance. Suddenly I realize that he must be alive at this time and set out to find him. St Ignatius advises us to use a preface. An apparition has been seen in the scullery among the blackened pots and pans, at this very hour—a successor from the last hundred, the early works. Consider whither I go, and to what.

Character. Limner, a portrayal of moments. Listen, it's the rain quintet from act one (false imperatives for small orchestra). Here's a lovely photo taken some years later. Note the jaguar mask in the foreground. She pats him firmly on the head and mutters a complimentary remark. I'm reminded of the night we wrote on the walls as a dead one passed right through us, unbeknown.

A trivial part of the reconstruction, mass epiphany. Eye, arm and cock are the favoured details. No, I brought nothing through the portal with me (see anatomy of mouth above). She yet remains disoriented, a master of vague anecdotal evidence.
The day of her death has been set. Reread her letters, crammed into that box beneath the pallet.

Describe their poverty.
A haven. A noose. An enclosure. Wife on shoot. I'm concerned here with the basic emotions—borderlands and thresholds. The concept of empathy is not applicable to long periods of art history. A murder once took place up on the promontory—skull to thorax, floating rib. Sunlight glints from the top of the coffee pot, immediate right. The numbers are twelve and twenty-six. How did she know all this.

We are together, yet only when adopting certain parts, as if prayers in a role. See how it reads now.

Certain rocks are chosen and painted blue. Had I plantation of this isle, there's one more thing I would add. The climax is exhumation of the body. Bones are collected, polished, and placed in a metal box. This is then transferred to the local ossuary. I could have walked off at any moment, forsaken my leave beyond the mound.

A big sallow moon, low over the sea. The criteria determining selection for exile remain obscure. Rosy planet juxtaposed, due west, descending to horizontal. Dissonance and worry establish the foreground. In my commonwealth of contraries, I would execute all things. Wish you were here—hung, drawn, quartered.

He woke early that morning. He takes the stone he has used for a pillow and sets it up as a boundary marker. He pours oil over the top of it. Tiny plastic infantrymen are scattered. Every face is set towards the rust-streaked plaster of the alleyway. This particular facet of the tale ends abruptly.

Lessen by taking away, detract. Animal skins are stretched over a frame of converging poles to form a crude dwelling. We've taken a roundabout course and are depleted by subtraction of redundant parts. An earlier form of origin is rumoured. I shall now attempt to describe our illuminati.

I want some souvenirs of this, mementos and keepsakes. The rules say one must have the courage to venture outside, regardless. I watch them scratch and dig, excavate the foundations. The pack yields the hanged man and the temporal lobe. Dissent is revealed, love's affray.

Playing-card kings, with fasces, Phrygian caps, tripods. And a promissory deed of place, signed. The hooded men would never recover from their experience. They come with raptures, spleen. The erosion rate is ten millimetres a year. It's an equilibrium, that's the consensus.

I do not wish to break off. Don't all rush at once. The beauty of this medium is its mutability (chalk on blackboard, straight from the dictionary, male-voice choir off-screen). I must will myself sick every week. It's hard work. I prize open some new territory, assassinate a few plates and cups. Outside in the street a sign has collapsed. Regret nothing, every offence. Rain is forecast. We approach the bay. Allow yourself no distinction. Defecate in your hat. The autonomous collective is replaced by an inner circle of twelve. Insurrection and public tumult follow, the first food riots for two hundred years.

Especially offence, I am offended since birth and have complained little. If you look closely you can spot me in any surveillance photograph. I'm miraculously cured. The battle looks like a parody of the spatial grid. A curse always seems to gather itself up in one place. (There's still a long way to go with this, isn't there?) At the end of a fortnight we were wearing out seven pairs of skis a day. I begin the long walk back to the universal on my club foot: one degree west, fifty-four degrees north. I feel possessed.

An ulcer sheathed in a dry crust of secretion and dead tissue. Great indeed is the meaning of the time of retreat. A new technique for wreaking summary justice is being introduced. The tone here is meaningless and arbitrary—observe the toothless gaps, the missing consonants, the rhetorical manner of speaking. Chance a close-up of that lined face. Allow me to explain.

Those who have glimpsed report wondrous internal debris. In a book or film you can keep returning to the face in a way you can't in the theatre. These images parallel the pattern established in happier days. I can still hear the clock, even though it's long been removed. But for the swaying of the floor and walls, one would rest content.

Quick, list the flagstones, the lanterns, the anteroom, the rusting metal instruments, the cracked varnish of the sign. I can always make another Wednesday. Time has virtually ceased.

Instruction re birthing sack.
Backs pressed flat to earth, claw obsessively at handfuls of soil. He conducts all of this as if it were a major symphony. The archimedean point is situated at one pole alone. A full year of peaceful agriculture is foretold.

I get paid today. None has sent word. There is interference. The needs of a healthy person differentiate the field of experience. When I say they it could be anyone. Don't worry. Just who is the child who has no confidence in the mother's return? A reckoning is made: the length of the path travelled by a vacuum illuminated during a séance.

The five hundred are lurching across the lawn toward the sanitarium. I'm reminded of those interminable festivals of dancing dead of the fifteenth. I want to grasp this picture tightly in my hand. I want it in my head. As we speak.

Tantalic phantoms, latter years. You could take the dialogue out of any character's mouth and put it into another, and it fits. A faulty moment has been archived. Division is deeply cut and divided into leaves like the pages of a book. I should add that the lawn is neatly clipped (terminal corymbs of rayless yellow flowers). I do hope you too have a unprepossessing start to the day. Observe how the casual tone of sedition grows.

The fleaman has been promoted. Notes follow on the subjects of misdeed, breathlessness, and resurrection. I myself have been kept from learning to sew. All this is nothing but the odd idea of living in matter, whether called forth or not. That silk-worm mystery, it's an experimental fact.

Body held upside down by ankles over oil stove. Tongue bitten in two. This takes no more than two hours. Your eyes look strained, she says, with an air of superiority, as if some rare supernatural gift had delivered the insight to her alone. It's my job to pass the spatula. I am reminded. Flakes fall from the dead crust of her ample lip. Ritualized actions are a form of discipline, as is solitude. If you can't keep up with the conversation, don't try joining in.

None of these histories will suffice as explanation. An eternity of beginnings can always peter out. I owe nothing. The ancestral tree is hung with frauds and tricksters, estranged fruit. And I reject the human form beloved of the spermatist school, the now exploded doctrine that the spermatozoon contains all future generations in germ, the planet and all its descendants foresworn in the seed. This is to be discontinued next week. I'm looking into all the possible outcomes, the varieties of numbness. This is reaching beyond to another dimension, albeit shaking exquisitely. Utilize peripheral vision. Lay the tarot on the table and leave.

Lowlife. Collapse of left ventricle. I reconvene. The tower is drawn. Damn, all this detail is so specific, obscures the broad local colour. Somehow things have been nailed back together into a recognizable sequence of events. Useful forensic prints are being harvested. The correct expression is *nostalgie de la boue*. A glance at the calendar tells me.

Nothing but the clumsy suction of his footsteps, not a soul. The logic circuit has one input and one output. It's the day of the dead. The creature is so oily it can be dried and used as a candle. Its skin is stretched over a frame of converging poles and left to dry in the midday sun. This type of encounter is euphemistically called breaking down the bedrock.

She has an abnormal desire to go back to unfamiliar places. There is a name for this (indigenous theory of catharsis). Who else can show astounding results while still in the act of leaching? Now she's busy counting money. Who is the suspect today? Are we entering the field of vision from the correct angle? I catch myself knotting lengths of coloured string. These serve as a counting system (I've always been magnetized toward success). When I return to the past, she says, a little bit of me always dies. A fingernail scores sharply down a window pane.

At sunrise I pass the temple wedge. I ascend the east. I'm sunk into distraction, the second layer of my anchorage. Sun rippling on large body of water to south, immediate. There's safety in numbers (glandular dreaming). He creates what are called *days*. It's time to rekindle a fresh grudge. Is there a clever way of doing this, or isn't there? You could never have foreseen.

An endless chain of buckets on a wheel. Lustration on an ascending spiral path. She is going below (methyl violence). Her output signal is one if the input signal is void. I wonder what time it is—that is to say, let us creep toward something impossible. People are ready to break down the doors and burst in. An antiseptic dye is used as a stain. From the crest of the valley trees stride out, spewing from the flank of the selfsame hill. Same brown eyes.

Another shift has taken place during the night. That's me with a glass to the wall. Genetic endowment interacts with circumstances to produce repression. I have chosen the defuse option. It's hard not to look for irony in any state of mourning. The angle of the rain appears to divide space. And there she was gone. Thanks for the reminder, the sea, the exit.

The bones of the villagers are joined together on the ground to form a single bizarre skeleton that stretches across several acres. People tapping on pipes et cetera.

The radical of wood with tumour of jelly-like substance, that inflammable gas from brine. I am used to mixing and impregnating.

Hypertensive, the drug compound without palate (drunken, let no pebble). And usually other things, such as the refrigerant local aesthetic. And functions similar to those used as a stain (antiseptic dice). The former infection, crystal violet, a mixture of wine, wood. And a resident alien indicating change, and a house. Or synthetic without reactions, or actions. Any monetary unit, equal to the one hundred. Eight times radio.

A lack of industry, taking possession. Here be newcomers (a person or thing that measures). There goes another counterpane. Signs are said to be carved on the four sides of every bone. Revert to seven as the ruling digit. Slow and majestic, his output signal has been reset to zero. Those white, red and black flags all say something different about the algorithm of each individual wave. The eye is shut, yet spasm of lid. The eyeball flickers, rapid, a tube bent spirally turning on its axis.

The page reads. Libration of the celestial sphere explains oscillation of the ecliptic. The magnetic needle flips. Soft pink cloud formations, alien countenance murmuring Shelley. The dip is ninety degrees. And he with his ailing wing, drunk in a muddy field—in the choke of wood-smoke, a full stack of it.

Simply pay up and leave. I know, this kind of precision is uncalled for. You still haven't dared venture beyond the margin. Her time of death is set (love's work). The chamber is a scale replica of the auditory capsule, complete with anterior bone. Conversations are conducted with the departed.

Is that what you call him. One has to enter a recuperative mode to even suffer a glimpse. What's aimed for is a sort of neutrality. We can no longer be satisfied with a purely physiological conception of the troubles. How may I prove this saying to be true. O and I forgot to ask.

Who is reading the tragical history of the death and life? A white speck floats around the head, the springs exhausted, almost sightless. Avoid mirrors and clocks. Here is another day in which everything is taken up in the wrong key.

A plague hospice was once situated at the top of this cliff. The ground fell into the sea. Take a look at this (wrong eye). Any man within his senses could clearly see. A choir of angels is tethered in the corridor. I crawl through.

The plane in which the horizontal surface of a fluid cuts a body floating in it.
If I leap high enough he ventures out of his hole. He binds to himself. I have dreamed another of the saints. And what of those dates scrolling down the upholstery in the rain? That's never a parachute he carries on his back. What is the numerological equivalent of a name?
Let this go, before it's too late. By means of certain supernatural consecrations, his wings begin to quiver.

From one recurrence to another. An anteroom to parliament, carved from solid rock. Ashlar masonry. Who was telling me this? A synopsis and the dramatic personnel are listed. You must behave as though you have permission to stay. Copulation takes place as publics drift by. We're in a corner through which others can pass and dissolve. Your problem is that you ignore the salient detail. Everything has been arranged beforehand. Take a look at the last lines spoken anywhere. I admit distraction as a mode of concentration. Everything is authorized. I've entered a kind of erotic economy. Check for any wrong moves, false starts.
She fashions a tiny vessel and slips it silently into my sack. The winning invention is an improvised trepan. We have become discrete, with inflorescence. She says stop that's the rib-frame. You will never finish this. Wrong saint, silently transfigured.

A telesm. Spectra beaming upward and straight through the ceiling. Erase from memory this event—the conversion still to come, secure passage.
The curve described by a point moving forlornly along a radius vector.
A battlefield, surrounded.
These suspects, there may be some questions about their reversal status. The inventory remains unchanged. It's a precaution, then again maybe not.
Deep pressure felt on head within entrails. With a long enough lever and a point to stand upon, I could move the world. *Here* is used connotatively.

The culvert (an arched channel for carrying water beneath a road or railway). If it comes, it comes. My system is so, a consecrated objection. At the bottom of the same step is a file marked iliac crest. Competitors must submit monthly reports, verbal.

Thunder on a fireslaught's twisted spine. Damp tinder in the rain. Reason's work is not founded upon any moment (relationships with others in adult life partly depends on this). Inquisitors come at midsummer to resume their questions. The fourth lot is drawn—a dry measure, a smooth pebble. We begin any minute. Adjoining the chamber is a rectangular cloister. I have the honour of kicking off the depravity. One says interesting, I have a man who must talk before dawn.

At the point of the retina from which the optic nerve radiates. Sales have fallen by five. I hold an instrument for measuring the infinity of heat. At the centre is a mediaeval tomb. Reified love is the basis, a solid shock of tongue. Lying on the cist is the statue of a saint, hands fused. I've ventured inside a trap. The final letters spell out name and calling. He has a concrete sword. Every surface is lichened.

Numbness in skull from over-the-latrine medication. At vigil beside your bed, the wicker basket. To her the sea is cold and mad. Philosophy's not concerned with expressing obvious personal statements.

This shows off the range of her voice to magnificent advantage. Take another look at the storyboard: a flat plain is hinged at bedrock. The spelling comes naturally enough. I can still make out the strapline. What a truly formless day, set to a mighty theme for void and harpsichord. Our pact is redundant—eyeless, now haunted by influence, the mortuary texts. Continue in silence. You know, she says, you do, when you walk. Sweet the pleasure of gentle pressure.

Polar equation. The region of the abdomen on either side, under the coastal cartilage, undershot ribs where the vast do dwell.

New scenario. You can see and hear them but they can't hear or see you. Body parts are being stolen from funeral parlours and sold to collectors. There's an avian connection. This micro-narrative is possessed by a deliciously pessimistic mood. It's very difficult to exist as a beginner, stuck midpoint between the first two thousand years. These scraps were never meant for viewing. Every detail of the work has been composed with you in mind. You can spread this analogy as far as you like.

At true magnetic pole, closure of airspace and so on. Dazzling light. Scenes are clearly being orchestrated. There are now at least two people in the room writing. The artefact remained buried beneath the ice all these years. He has an abnormal fear of going back to familiar places, and believes he can levitate. These output signals are a start. See, we are bringing them together, a convergence.

Absorb substance without admixture of experience. Note the maudlin violins. The required moniker is an old alchemist's name for mercury. There's a want of symmetrical sequence about here. Consider the many things one may find in the world at any given moment. The latter part of a sentence doesn't always fit the earlier, such as a siege of herons.

Nonetheless a sunny headscape. A flat surface decorated with heraldic atoms rises up to fill the gap. This is the signal for something uncanny to happen. One possible side effect is sudden unexplained death. Error falls to pieces by degrees. The hill explodes and the statue becomes animated. A giant dragonfly beams into the room, crashing into the walls and the shadows. From a column of black smoke the body of a man is flung through the air before falling to earth. A frantic jig draws all the players together for the climax. Things begin to take their allotted course. If ever his name were known.

A coastal town from the sea through mist. Please don't take that next corner. A man looks up at a window, where he recognizes a silhouette as himself. (Do these sorts of things happen to anyone else?) Everything turns white. A small aperture links the two remaining spaces. Music has been dismissed as the ideal discipline. Do you actually know what love is? Over dinner he declares his sainthood. Egg-capsules are scattered across the ground (the ovisac, according to the ovists). In the next chapter we hear about his lucky escape to the Americas.

You're to work your way back through the arc. We're leading up to the most phantasmal denouement imaginable. Hyperbole is to be marshalled. Finding the philosopher's stone turned out to be surprisingly unproblematic: make your way inside the Arabian castle to the ruby et cetera. Things are not turning out as I wanted them to be. I remained with him until the moment of his death—in the corner of the bed chamber, sinews of silver light spilling from the solar plexus.

Concealing tables of law within a closed container seems somewhat odd, doesn't it? Before he can answer he feels a sting of pain deep inside his body. It's nerves. The lift shoots up. It seems to climb *through* him.

Westernland. Flag flapping above the shingle. (God pity his poor mother.) Chattering morse from the white poles. What is that word I find, the exhaust. O come on. Unstoppable rivers run through the text. What is that word which cannot be isolated. Steel cages packed with broken flints have been set into the cliff. Foundations are sunk, then comes an extended incantation, apropos of nothing. Nothing here but empty leaves, at best. I wanted to say something more, but I could not remember.

A foot-soldier approaches. Language is shared. We've waited a long time for this. A thick cylindrical shape protrudes from his anus, between his legs. Everything happens concurrently. Nothing is clear. He holds out a hand. It's smooth. He says the point of writing is to ease transition—say as little as possible, while incorporating thousands of used words. This hand of marble is warm to the touch.

Just a solitary crow, the contractile chamber of the heart. What was once referred to as an absence of time, space. Diastole and systole.

How many words is that. We've got all the moths and the bells to include as well. Put this away for now, rattling at the rim of sleep. The narrative resembles a mediaeval legend, a cherished ambition or goal. We're going to buy blind from now on. You want the dead man, we give you the dead man.

Oxeyes hover above a flooded watermeadow. Find your perfect job. A body weighed when immersed in itself shows a loss that resembles displacement.

He's an ally unrecognized in form, a hangover from severed time. The weekend is lost. I need another rung. The day is confirmed. I leave letters on his vault, printed characters quivering at the end of spokes. You have me, have you not.
She breaks the deadlock.

A trigger for both mental and material states, his approach has the ethos of the building site. He's to spend the next four years in a refugee camp (there's a definite ontological theme running through all of this). His emaciated face is partly covered by chain-mail. I have to stop. I can't see.

Jealous blood. Silt on every window. Putrefaction by sacrifice, the inroads of solitude. There are problems with the relaxed and idle condition. Therein is evident wariness. It should be said however that states one to three may work for some people under hypnosis. The vessel now is calm and steady. Up on deck I spot one, my first—a bioluminescent. Psyche in flight, where soul of mud is being signified.

A letter is chosen to represent the spatial factor. (I'll deal with you in the morning.) Night entia run their course. Ensky means to place in the sky. I retreat for a single week, and look. What happens.
Abbreviate prefix, given to no.

The bronze resembles the dung harvested once by tanners. Yes, but the important thing is to remember. When there is no other way and the deeper wells have dried up, then is the time to march. However ephemerally, this has a sense of experience which few compilations can match. The pump belongs to a pumping station that is being built.

You may recall how we talked of the little mistake that can cause a deadly accident. Well, now you're to cut through the portal using the oxyacetylene arc. I'll be busy generating things, separating. I have forgotten to reproduce. Note the curve of the graph: crystal violet, radical of wood or alcohol. I'll be busy forgetting. It's now too late. The stone is the size of my hand, green and perfectly faceted. When peering through it, space seems to dissolve. If ever his name were know—a leap beneath the threshold for the last time.

Monopoly with seditionaries. All that's left is a triangular bone, nucleus of the insurrected body. This manoeuvre is on record as the iron-mound commando. He withholds: ash, three aces, and four thousand wings.

It escaped, slipped through my finger. Is this confusing (eclipse plumage, unnatural coverage, trembling antennae probing space). Judge now whither thee and I shall ever meet.

Just woke to the independence of grace, gravity. All depends on the assumed burdensack. Today's plan: shave skull, inject head, make way back to centre of earth. Convenient potholes punctuate the road. I navigate the day by creeping in a crosswise direction. Meet me at the amusing curve. Note the sound of insects crawling across the walls. All my life I've sought a corrosive type of perfection.

Traders' jargon, drifting corsairs spurting fire from either flank. Clusters of candlefish glow just beneath the surface. He switches venue every night, will only lodge in safe-houses.

Please ignore the young lady making the renouncement. Events take their course. She's a little confused about where we're going and where we've been. Possible side-effects include sudden unexplained death, or incarceration for no good reason. Keep them guessing. Assume no daily pattern that may be traced by your adversary. That sound is the sound of a lash falling across an exposed back.

And now the disconcerting rocking of the track across a viaduct. Can you hear me through all this. We are pursuing the game through a complex network of escapes. Irresistible predestination is much the same thing. Our invention is withdrawn at the last minute.

Becoming now so undercrowded. Slow fade to centre of astral triangle. We're trapped in a steep optical decline. The stars are moving away from us, see. He's been given the considerable task: uproot the remnants of a widespread moment. I was institutionalized a century earlier than expected. My own role is unlimited, and determined by an aptitude for remembering form and structure. The platform tilts and sways. My clothes are all wrong. A letter is often followed by a numeral.

Sometimes she adds a sentence of her own. (The sperm according to the animalculists, never the brood-pouch.) Be patient and wait.

More on the experiences had. Sometimes I put my foot down. I am not of your nous. Study the transmitter key and try to figure out how it works. Sometimes a number of convulsions simply have to be added. I don't want to be part of your content. This declaration lends legitimacy. It's a trade-off. Using one of the metal spikes as a pivot, draw a large chalk circle on the floor. With this as a guide, build a low wall. Fill it with soil, into which you must plant lighted candles. That'll do for now.

From all external evidence this project is impossible. The stem temperature indicates that we're on a planet close to the sun. Then two matt-black chinooks copt over the crest.

Still more traders' jargon. Is this the promised contusion? There's an ornithological theme running straight up the spine. The manuscript was found in the hollow of a petrified tree. My question would have answered itself in the course of the narrative, but I always want to know at once. I'm released. The body lands at my feet, a descendant of animal signs and savage beatings, the language.

Inspectrix of all our actions, through which the strings are twitched by quills or leather points.

Have you finished with this. I've been released on a square foot of compassionate ground. We're busy worrying the arcane from the quotidian (that old trick). The place where you feel most vulnerable is called dwelling, a host of queues and caesuras. He will never say what's to be demonstrated. Spot the blind sac, with concealed eye, burrowing beneath the skin. You can see the weal in motion at his hip, raised grapes of flesh pulsating gently.

We buy up all the sanctions and utilities and run them into the ground. They arrive, the promised bargeload of assassins armed with hickory staves. His legs are broken three times in as many minutes. From today's perspective his death can be seen as a turning point in space.

Rhizome of speedwell.

Asked for a name and an address, she recites a lengthy chronicle. This is then printed onto a continuous strip of type metal. So many events seem to occur around the number forty-two. She's judged through a heavily silted lens, a kind of redundant musical score. Placed at hazard, I fill out the blank lines as I go along, trick the boxes. A lot more could be said about the thickness of things. I include the galaxy of stars on the blind. This retains a still momentum, which is of course a contradiction.

A logic circuit is invented that has two or more inputs and one output. That was quick. He is sewn firmly into the world (the hexed girl). Clay mineral shed in flakes from collective exhaust.

A station on route. There is no convection here. A man quenches a dog from an upturned cidercan. Writing is now on a longshore basis. A sudden gush of acid rises to the mouth. Telegraphic, signal with no memory.

A movable tower is introduced by the besiegers of the fortress. Archers crouch to aim through slits and roundels. Climate cloudy with dizzy spells. It's too late. You probably haven't eaten since I last saw you. I venture outside and haemorrhage, casually. (Use this in conjunction with something else.) Last time I was angry. I have moved mountains. Now I'm not. Is everything all right (no). We approach the landing pod, echoing the contours of the earth's crust. Nobody else comes through the portal, so it closes.

Her output signal is one if all the inputs are void. There's a definite stain of irony at work here. A saucer of concrete forms a mass, unaccountably thick. A rallying.

More about those societal strictures. There was a reason I stood up, I'm sure (memory, one's anxiety to avoid the expected). Where are you now staying? Answer. It's got stop written all over it. Never go through that door. The subject, He-who-keeps-alive, is led in and stood before the inquisitor. It's said the whole body consists of eyes and tongues. Their number corresponds to the number of people inhabiting the earth at any given moment.

Hypochondrium.
That man over there painting the fence is being punished. He wears a fluorescent orange jerkin. He's daubing flesh—faces and their bodies rendered in oil. Smell is unmistakable. This is the opposite of distraction. It's a long story. It might be the preamble to a dark night of the soul. You could say he had principles, albeit of a rather perverse nature. I possess a copy. Nothing can save you. It's the thing that selects the imagination, not the other way around. Action leads to weakness. It gets better towards the end. He fears idleness, his only blessing. The output signal is void if any of the inputs is one. This is excellent in terms of an event, but useless when out shopping.

Buried old photograph, as of porcelain or glass, ground bone: the crushed petals of a chrysanthemum embedded in a dog turd.

Anima Monday. Discharge of glass. The first phase is confused speech. A root system is spreading through the ground beneath our feet. It's guiding them in (this passage is quite separate from what's come before). They're among us—a cursorial species that keeps its footing on the steepest slopes. They course and range, limbs and claws adapted for running. We are denizens of dry land with few affinities of structure. But we'll think of something, a ghost of a story, something.

Puer aeternus. That basically expresses his whole life. An afterimage, unglued. Lip-rapture. Go now. Everything's wrong. In the main, works of dubious attrition are confined to the appendix.

Liminal, doubtless unattainable. How often he would marshal that word. We sit opposite each other in a hook-lined retreat.

Well, as far as I recall, a mediaeval fair is taking place in the grounds of a cathedral— throngs of pilgrims from the mainland, Slavs and gypsies striking fires, bivouacking Germans. I'm here to carry out undisclosed espionage. Humankind has twenty years remaining in which to pursue the surface, during which the temperature will be fixed at six degrees. I am deeply sorry about the timing. Alongside the cathedral I meet an unknown. A harmless deathlike state ensues. All this has a rather contemporary feel to it, don't you think. I am water-brash. Forgive me.

Futhark.

Ornamentally interlaced runes encircle the building. The consecrated ground it stands upon has been set aside for misuse. A body's discovered in the cavity between two walls. It's night. An electric charge crackles in the air. Every head is open to the sky. A haunting is cited, but no academic reference given. We busy ourselves with apparitions. The characters are he, she and I. We stand beside a fissure in the ground. A wall of white tiles continues below the surface, deep into the earth. The distance down is forty-two. I'm told I must assume a voice that is not my own. There's a rumour (spirits of the dead leave the underworld through this portal). An animal climbs up and tries to work its way through the gap, but it's too narrow. I think of helping. I don't. Get off now or don't get off. Repeat.

Dying, therefore, is something to do. Erase this memory also. Shift away from this obviousness to something more dense and complex.

A piece for twenty-three solo players, an arrangement of naked and helpless individuals. Test what should be clear and what should not. Entrenched positions are taken up, reshuffled, and startled into a lasting form. A subtle and incremental build up of indifference is taking place. Ink is escaping from the cartilage. Metamorphic, hence a prized trophy.

How did it sound. It sounded like the sea sucking on a multitude of small stones. How did it appear. An arc of yellow light bent over the water, dim figures angling at the fog.

Milky, galactic wave. Uncanny sirens.

A sinisterhood of three. Each wears a piece of chain-mail about the chin and throat. They surround the unknown man, shuffle in close. The *integritas* is the result of psychological forecasting. This trio are identical, wear the same greasy air-hostess uniform. Somewhere beneath the sutures is a face.

While sleeping he's visited by the ancestors of his spirit. Jupiter, of all people, hands him a tablet bearing a prophecy. It's going to be a busy night. The tongue is clamped firmly to the roof of the mouth. All memory of events is being reconvened. The characters are hurtling through space in a sealed compartment. This vehicle is what's called an elevated. Keep this simple, please.

One room is similar, above. It's dimly lit. Three sit in a row on a seat that runs around the wall. They have fleeces like sheep. These otherworldly lack-laws, with great care I stitch them together.

List what is to be found.

The run to the first turn is very sharp. Recollections of heart and lung. A tooth falls out. Sheets of vivid greens and violet, white semée of sparks descending. On my shoulder the word your in black. Everything is unfinished, indifferent. She claims her first thought (here's trouble). Memory fails. What did you expect, something implicit? I have exposed. That woman has a grainy voice. I recall an anecdote: the barbed-wire tattoo, voices who pip and squeak. The entire population is quixotic. When she asks for the title they inform her, without hesitation. A threshold has been crossed. This permanence has an uneasy texture. I can never return. Penance is complicated. How can we be manoeuvred without scarring? I foresee. The process has been discontinued. I meant presence.

An urban environment of infinitely directed nanotubes. A famous suicide occurs. People are toxic. It's quite ridiculous, the anachronistic now. I can no longer visualize backwardness. A black triangle is slowly taking form at the base of the spine. Remind me to tell you about her compressed life: two weeks sectioned in a padded reading. Symbols appear in the text, here and there (for example the cherished libertarian). I have committed myself. A circle emerges at the base of the shaven skull. Crush underfoot, and take your leave. And we had only to be unfolded, with fermentation of emerging parts.

A transference cell at the very edge of the facility. Protect yourself from food. Outside, exposure takes place on open ground. It's like the earlier boneyard. I have returned. Night remains, in case you're confused. This time only one unknowable. I am not concerned. I may wake, I may not. I'm uncensored. I slip through a doorway. She's placed a pillow in the adjacent room. I'm propped against the wall, injured, though it's not clear how (probably writing that springs from the surface of existence). Sleep is misused in this methodology. It says here there's probably nothing. Her actions are reminders. I creep towards the door. Sound is congealing. I reach for the latch. The point of a butcher's knife is pressed against the jugular. It seems we have trespassed upon something. She flings an object, and signals that this thing is mine.

Search for narrative tributary.

Since childhood I've been acutely concerned with the displacement of things. I am busy recovering the land. Let's agree to forget the above. This passage is for your own personal safety and security, your own personal use. Explain how she survives.

First crop circle, tonsured copse at the crest of a passing hill. The eye returns to the book, myopic deconstructions. It's said she's a woman of ungovernable temper, of fierce likes and dislikes. It's the day after today, ambulant plant-life everywhere. I survey the outlook and think little of it. I am randomly invited. There are people I haven't seen these twenty years. This is a striking example of how feelings of helplessness accompany recurrent attacks. Sedition is the crime which contains all other crimes. Resolve to seek stillness, the outsights of solitude. List items in cell: rotting bed-staff (handy weapon), faulty infrared, mattress of transparent aluminium, ultraviolet strip, see-through air.

Game over, she approaches and whispers. You were the person who requested a tempest, were you not? A healing plant is vaguely indicated, the promise of a panacea. I'm pumped full of compressed helium and left on my pallet to burst.

Why so much of this. List any oddities—creatures with fingers and legs, supernatural food. Or a man prepared to give up his unwinding years (the very last thing he did, you do not ask him). It's the same thing with the wonders. You cannot underwrite. I have drifted away from my subject. Then the dead come to life, utterly forgetting.

Popular occupations include vivisectionist and scribe. The structure is so-named from its unique pentadic design. We are sealed within. I look up—workless folk swooping about. Now place your right hand on the exposed rib. My palms vibrate uncontrollably. We're situated a little beyond space. One close by expires.

Leaf shadow under crane. Any remedy will do. When you've finished your shift, go back upstairs and never come down again. You grant a hunger. Anything lost is regained. The audience spit and wipe their mouths. Time is ritually stretched until it corresponds to the content of each page. Keep it short and punchy. Bethankit comes as swift. Fetch counsel. Slide the body away offstage. It's always too late. Fetch capital. Refuse to put anything down in writing. A sorrowful purity has been discovered. It's company policy. There's a rumour. In a certain sense, flung clear of the hill. Pursued, unburdened.

Tempest isle. Or rather, islet. Elliptic for grace, for gravity. Everything's nearly ready—the flashbacks, the tangents and interruptions. Now for the next piece of information. There are four men on horseback. I've chosen to tell this story because it's a fine and satisfying story. I digress. The skull in the display case appears to be made of crystal. People like us are swarming everywhere these days. Peradventure, one speaks against me on the adverse side. There's a sudden crash of impetus. A man wearing white face powder hangs from the hand of a clock in the air. Citizens are herded into a hall and forced to write about this. The word charming is often misused. Overalled workers sit on a girder to eat their lunch without a safety net. It's before aeroplanes. These are the things you need to consider. The crew are tipped back on deck, straight from the belly.

She feels the need to compile another of her lists. I existed long before any of this. She won't give up her big dream—everything was ours, space wide and flattened, as if perspective had been outlawed. (She always did worry about the correct posture in which to shit.) Measure for measure, I'm unfutured, fatigued. We can't find the right platform. I can no longer identify the salient problem. Someone is walking behind me. We march in time, tapping and whistling. This is what matters most. One song becomes a kind of signature. O fuck I'm not plugged in.

The one in front now walks at a rapid pace. He assassinates and reclaims. Note how the right arm has been accidentally severed. Another intervenes and everything stops dead. I'm still not happy. Whether called or not, a name has been invented for a hypothetical substance. We are magically alive though structurally deficient. This is an experimental fact, a phenomenon called art. As a consequence the gullet is burnt.

Respond to the following questions, and remember, there are no wrong or right answers, only answers. What's your birthright.

I'm fine when left quietly to my own devices. There's nonesuch place. The search is underway for a particular urn in a subterranean chamber stacked high with urns. We pace to the end of each corridor, counting aloud our steps. Presently an idea occurs. The world is shaken to its roots. We must locate the landing cage. Everything is difference, almost a nothing. The stone floor is ankle deep in liquid excrement. I turn slowly to face magnetic north. A faint soundtrack of chamber music seeps through the runnels. A wall of putrid fat four feet high, three deep, and fifty-eight feet long is blocking the main sewer. I can't find her grave. For the sake of symmetry another foot is amputated.

Reading between the lines: irregular musical structures, apparently from to break open the edge or side, remote areas of experience beyond the paranormal.

Closing remark: his animal side is unassimilated, and there is a danger that it may become irreversibly distracted. Modus operandi located within a network of mineral cracks.

Realized ultimate reality piton (a very small booklike).

The septum has grown back. She henceforth pulls the casement shut. It's well past the time-lapse. Her life is a sequence of dull climaxes—a mass formed by parts thickening to an obsolete limb.

He says when we next encounter each other we will have reached too far into the game to abort. My own number is one hundred and sixty. I struggle on till candles and starlight and moonshine switch off. It's easy making decisions when you're exhausted.

This is the first time we actually get to see her, a cipher-key, empty to zero. She always wins (different aesthetic, different kitchen). I promise I'll brighten up—unload, activate the toaster.

Atom element or radical with a combining power of five. The end of divination by right.

He's baffled to death on the emerywheel. Sporadic popular uprisings can't be averted. Heavy metals have been discovered in the water supply. I said to mark my word. On each vessel is a label and a fading snapograph. A seabed sampler operates by enclosing the jaw.

One rather baggy profile. We are very close to the end. Out of his depth, of course, yet he's still regarded as the founder of music: molten plastic, section with cowpat, endless silences. The calibrations mark his level of achievement. Countenance pallid, with spasm of left lid. The composition deserves a graduated series of wooden bars rested on straw, an instrument used to measure elastic properties. How much more of this is there? A voice renounces. If they get a certain number of points, they're sure to survive. Now everything is being scaled down. The sense of being haunted never stops once you come back through the portal. We have exceeded the target. They've given me one too many of those pills (solidified electricity). Security has creased. Now everything is being scaled up. There's an incremental threat. The railway money goes straight through the bank and out the other side.

What I saw was a girl with a broken leg encased in a metal frame, dribbling. You can always find a torn snapshot discarded on the pavement. She lies unattended on the kitchen table for twenty-four hours. Her hat has Mexico written on it. Almost ready for the last runthrough, spem in valium et cetera.

A law, nail, or hoof.

A hooked instrument of torture.
A bent stick for hanging a carcass (cambrel).
A piece of meat extending from the hock-joint upward in man.
A morbid growth in the eye. Unglee.
Is there anything else you feel the need to describe or make.

Torso, two men withholding. It's made of chalk. I wake up during my reputation. It was like watching. Repetition is fading.

He's not a target holder, yet. It's like a world perceived through reflective gas. I could see all the stitching, your leg up there with no sensation, exiled ghost of limb.

A brief note on a spreadeagle bet. Wings outstretched and body split, they remove the spleen. We no longer have a function to perform. She's sure to be the last to die. Let's get something clear. Only straw can feed a plague of this proportion. I'm the limit below which a stimulus is not perceived. I deeply resent having to work. List what is and what is not to be found inside the body. This will take a life.

Heavy internal bleed. A lagoon is separated from the sea by a lengthy wall of lard. The ancestry here is ground-dwelling, spooking the shores and the river banks. A selection is given below. I grant access to the resonating chamber. Keepsake it, crumbling sound.

Lower ribcage cracked. Origin uncertain. Many have been scored through, dross and slag from the smelt, flanks of lava with steam-holes seeping. This is about as scary as it gets. He's like a mentor (the scent of this bloom reminds one of saintpaulia). I quite like that not-being–able-to-feel-your-face kind of thing.

Loopline rail, glimpse failing. The chains have come off. Environs of nowhere. A five-rayed star is constructed. We regularly shovel out from the tide of the head—incoming haar interlaced with frost. The shadows of gigantic clouds rage across the surface. Father lost in dazzling reflection of sun on level sea. Now I'm back digging in the cellar (more unrealized projects). He has written himself out of the world. One moment he's here, the next he's not. Now for a completeness. I emerged from the first six letters, lengthwise, supporting the splinter-bar and carrying a metre rule. I meant a meteor. Coal is about to be introduced.

Cabaret. The vault is spacious and broad, sharpening at the apex. She says we seem to share a few amusing anatomic details. It's magic. There's little left of us. I taper at the base. The words unabandoned to unzoned are listed, trapped in a loop. We're left outside on the lawn in the rain for an entire day. A tocsin signals at regular intervals. Breathing is sustained and sea defences have been breached.

The filter skews to a false angle (do I mean the funnel). This duo are inimitable. Such redundancy has its uses. I woke up during the operation.

Glance to the root of the page. This alloy is a fuse of lead and borax. The stars desert the skies she says. And by the way, you may have noticed, we're surrounded. I've had it for a while. Nothing works. Mysterious things begin to happen (nothing in particular). Left alone, objects quietly convert themselves into events. Her voice is echoing the piano keys, some artfully awful singing. Atoms and molecules are oriented in parallel planes. An obsolete type of primary cell, a battery, nestles inside the jaw. She's a species of folk, that's all I can say.

Brief note on a species with antennae. Then they say scream where it hurts. Long-term this does me no favours. Her own confession is haunting (the men were discussing token legs). When I get home, I find I can't.

I have invented. Zinc and platinum, electrodes in dilute euphoric acid. In the course of the trial my face is smeeched. I have days to live. See alien, or, see unalien. The larvae dine on wood. Spectra of semblance, the delayed signal.

An intermediate state between sniper and discharge at random. Universally, such a person's acumen is much esteemed. The scenario is the one in which she's holding a doll that licks like a dog. It takes real skill to gauge these antirhymes— barely noticeable simulations, the difference.

How did the distracted one chained to the wall voice her disapproval? Write to request an answer. There's still a slender residue of horror. Bless you. Here now is the serious mode.

A pivot spanning two extremes—the neutral, between star and moon. She has access to the records, the archive. I have failed. The content is either comic or abject. She adds excess weight (gangwork displaces the tribe). What are we to do today. List her remarks, a brief epiphany of shadows and mural scratchings.

I met a mystic he said i am burnt orange aura lots of water around me lots of past lives like bethnal green in ww2 and a dangerous lady shouldn't take drugs as they have been feasting on my open heart. Then i met an earth bound man who asked me questions and i opened my mouth further than my head could hold and romance turned from stone to sand thru fingers to a glass mirror as he stuck a pin in me and now everythings collapsing. I miss you.

Spam in aluminium. Her text with ears attached to a head.

Apply to oneself. My economy, tender, and on and on with its sinews. Neck slender. Gallful, of molten glass. Spleen excised, redundant in rapture.

XXI

More on my situations. This will involve further joining up of dots and hand-clapping, until a vivid picture emerges (eidetic memory). I've been made to feel like an idiot with no ears. I might have lost you she says. The word theatre is repeated, over and over. These are complex indices. The adults should have reached the peninsula by now, a vast plain stretching out to the south (think of the hypnagogic state as an anteroom to sleep). Strange fire is stored here, jacaranda and flame-trees. A night vigil can be heard—laylock-coloured flowers with fernlike leaves, beetles crackling in the eaves, in her eyes the impartial darkness. She imagines she sees the form of a young man dripping beneath a tree. We're going to wait until the morning comes.

So, a triangular promontory bordered to the north by a sea, to the west by a canal and to the east by a salt-marsh. At the centre is a deep gorge hemmed in by cliffs. Walk cautiously until reaching the first of two little houses. List flora and fauna: ice, abandoned silver mines, scarlet bell-shaped blooms. Add deep blue gentians, asters white to violet, knots of forget-me. In the three thousand pages of his travels there is buried not a single clue.

Pitch into wilderness. I receive a thrust to my side. Work cautiously through this method. I feel nostalgic while reading.

A humble dwelling in a dark wood. It's a place where three roads meet. What is within-the-world we have to look upon as something that is also within space. Am now crawling slowly towards the equator. The day is overcast. A network of conductors lies buried beneath the ground—tower-to-tower counterpoised, hence no ghosting. Our conception, on the contrary, is that there is no essential problem in the scientific sense. There is nothing else that I am prepared to call a solution.

With arched keel and brittle stem, star-raked.
He led a quiet and colourless life.

The map represents his circumnavigation of the world. This is the basis of a grand interlude (to write of writing is surely a tautology). Using a tiny spatula, harvest a sample. Rub rust into the eyeball. The terrain rises to a plateau at the centre.

At an oasis with uncommon rain, where legionnaires doze beneath swaying palm fronds. The mission is the shipment of human ballast. All the windows bleach and turn opaque. The chief occupation hereabouts is poverty and a studied asceticism. Desiccated human dung is strewn across abandoned ground. Currency redundant. I feel affinities here. We're being lifted as far as possible beyond what actually is. Grasp those two parallel lines. They are analogous to the stripes. The numbered bones of the face appear to be glowing. All containment is sterile, and then away our hasty life doth post. The relationship suddenly shifts. It seldom visits sorrow, loss et cetera. Bolt fast the seven gates of the netherworld.

The outside wall of a wattle and daub shanty. A framed perspective. Hovering above the shack is a starlike figure. Its head is one gigantic bobbing eye. The terrain descends to a narrow littoral between mountain and gulf. The aforementioned hut encloses a perfectly circular space. At the centre is a pit filled with ash and animal bones.

Low tide. No surviving kin. The promised storm breaks.

A confession of infidelity. Demands on every front. Technically, very difficult territory. Editorial strategy is complex, the pipework shoddy. Plates of ice can be heard grinding together across the surface of the lake—and the tiering waves, mysterious illuminations in the mist. I belong to an image. The image belongs to a form.

Thermidor (the month). Item, one or more catastrophes without evident cause. Stilted or tornado-proof domiciles are perfect. A motif is being pursued. Crabwise, take one step back, three sideward. Uncommitted notions have no position in the world. A pistol crack is heard (by whom or what you do not say). You mistranslate, something like showy radiant with head. The townsfolk barricade themselves indoors, clearly panicked. Travelling is a hard life, but I couldn't live without it. I think there's more of them outside in the street. A fine vein of seminal fluid stretches from the tip of the head to the rim of her lip. Record heart murmur, body temperature, behaviour and vocalizations.

A murder of crows. I'm invisible against the shadow of the yew. She says I'm a foretaste of things to come. Leave the detailed comparisons till later. That trunk is full of used notes, take it when you leave. She says I am the state. The book's title means snared by names. I am perhaps days old. Fires burst out from their anchorage.
Leaves left six, or nine. Thumbs pressed into wasteland of genes.

The body under question is suspended in a glass column of amniotic fluid. I have talked to lots of different people (recollect the republics of twenty years ago). We're now interpreting through metaphysics alone. Social onslaught divided by psychic cost yields income. Even historical disclosure paralyses itself in terms of the future. What is incontestable is that all of these questions have been deferred. The chain reaction is contained inside a steel coffer. By refinement of mind the witnesses build disarming conversation. We simply have to win this mismatch. The attack cannot prevail. Resistance is intermured behind the membrane, the keep of flesh. A hollow needle is inserted (rupture often serves as an inducement to work). This record of death and transfiguration dates from about nineteen sixty.

Torso severed mid-thorax, breastbone exposed, erect with glistening cartilage. There is an accompanying commentary, ceaseless epiphany.
Hummingbirds, kingfishers and bright blue starlings descended from ghosts,
a pier at night and a beach with cigarettes and the smoke of charcoal fires.

One of the constellations is still visible in the northern hemisphere. You could once hear my pulse from this very spot. Look, the subject is making intelligent use of the chemicals provided. Superficial observations can be made. He drags himself about the earth with ballast of scales, an apparition with sharpened pectoral fin and wings that drizzle blood.

Salt-hoarse at the giant coast. Belubbard, disfigured by wept, phrygian cap pulled down over remaining eye. If not any of these, whom?

Breaking into place and stealing therefrom. Divination by means of arrows.
Alkaline lake shore visible from wrought-iron balcony. Sleeping lizard under pallet bed. A yawning—snakeskin for the heat, profanation of things. Hover too close to the book and a flame is discharged.

He writes mostly during the torrid season, and always beside a body of water. Consider now the role of the redactor in this tale. Time is battered flat under summer rain—whiff of ozone, electrified dust. A petition arrives. The answer is a lot. Verdict: the mountain is now being mined for copper. One passing speaks in a low whisper. Something neural crackles through the landscape. The atmosphere must be on a thermostat.

Ten fifteen. Finish yesterday writing (leaflike organs of obscure morphological nature). That solitary leather shoe has split along its length. Two new toes emerge. An entire millennium has had to be exported. The promised waiting room is non-existent. This well-travelled route must be fortified: peregrination leads one meandering back on oneself, unbeknown. Every indulgence of theatre is to be cross-referenced. Undwelt signifies the founding of geographical boundaries. It's said he doesn't compose, he reverses.

On signs, the cathars. It's a nonsense song, points of insensibility and cycles of exchange. Your domain no longer exists. Refuse all compromise. The losers get nothing. He fights from within the law. News spreads on the warm dry wind

that blows down the eastern side of the valley. A bone is removed in the final ritual—the quadrate, which suspends the lower jaw. As they ascend, they diverge
from each other, assist in forming lateral boundaries (airborne grit, ultramontane
spores). I am nerved. I learnt the cello in those four years of incarceration. Here,
take one of these, it may kill us.

A submarine manned by aliens made of white ash.

A world whose entire surface is bolted sheets of black metal.

Do as I do. The next sentence changes matters. Typographical presentation
lends a breathless quality to the book. I'm entertaining a form of combat, swinging what looks like a flat shovel with a quarter-moon blade attached. There's
unfinished business. The region south of the plateau is quite unbecoming.

Quarantined from the workaday, these are your subjects: the one who stores
the cable in the tier, the one who arranges.

A tiersman.

This tactic works rather like the strategy of lure and destroy.

Instruction. A pounding can be felt in the pit of the belly, the solar plexus, so
named from its radiating nerves. Then as now, the body being into dust confract.
It is not too late.

I'm abandoned on the island. My adversary takes up the chessboard and the
soapstone pieces and leaves. (In what year did you receive your volunteer?) I
regret. We can no longer bear witness. A gland below the deer's eye secretes a
waxy substance.

At the boundary ridge of an unploughed strip.

Lynchpin of orchestration. That rising stench from the ditch reminds everyone. The mouth opens wide and little angels fly out. There are people downstairs, cusps. (Why should it ever show mercy?) I suppose I am a little vengeful.
The noise level rises as the pace drops. A diamond sparkles on her wasted finger.
The hill is flattened on top and pitted at the centre. The surrounding air is
unfaceted. Turn to face true magnetic north. No one comes.

Interrogatrix: why have you abandoned *these* (pointing). She doubles as executioner. A surfeit of love the other retorts. Unhinged and broken, the law is set
gently in the recovery position.

How did I ever find you down here, dying well, with salient quotes? Point c)
represents total ineffectiveness. Two rectangles of zinc provide the charge. The
excavated helmet was clearly never intended to grant adequate protection in an
intergalactic attack. We might even hear footsteps.

A withholding.

The one who keeps nightwatch loses ears, nose and lips. You don't know when to stop, do you? Fomenters of division are found roaming in the neighbourhood, dealers in havoc. Scarce indeed does he know thy quivering form. Do you want to keep your pretty face?

Look, in the window opposite. This is a fragment of a date that signals birth. I got my reference number through. I usually resist all outside influence. There's a cluster in the inverted triangle at the base of the spine. The city has an occult pivot, a hidden shape. Now derail the composition: parallel lines sloping diagonally from dexter chief to root sinister (her). Dangers abound—meteors, fieldmice, fire. Parts of the face were gnawed from the corpse as the vigil slept. This is a measure of how far we have come.

Read aloud, and quit. Release tongue beyond flap. Give ear. Times shown in light are connections.

A world in which the pivots of existence are moments of innocuous detail. (You shouldn't be adding on more at this juncture, a situation where abject terror is a given.) Provide a vessel in which blood can be caught. Candlesticks topple over and glasses explode. Who shared between them a single eye and a single tooth? A lexicon should be retired once the task is completed. List items on trestle: the marble carving platter, the two knives, the sharp protruding tusk, the templar cross, the baton of clingfilm, the reinforcements, the male or its flesh. The entire infrastructure is down (only joking). The table itself is counted among the remarkable objects, the genera under study. It represents an interpolation. All the other rooms are left bare, empty of furniture and chattels.

Granular black light glistening on promenade step. And here is the unravelling tape that can lead us back. Occurrence: nature as quartz, chalcedony, amorphous and hydrated as opal. There exists a compressed genealogy of therapy, just three degrees of separation. An idea suddenly springs to mind: abscond without hesitation. Inraids are being made. There are potholes in the road. People were beyond the control of their superiors. It's as if I were back in time. Any kind of property cannot be distinguished.

Further into the real and impersonal. Non-metallic element, psi at numb fourteen, more abundant than oxygen. A milder variant of this curse demands fasting for one month, with detailed instruction regarding clean and unclean food. See, we're on the right track.

Idle talk, much costing of lives. Arrival at the field of the star. A church is built over the bones. A metal vessel has been crafted to hold the remains. Noise clusters in every skull. Cross this plain of asphodel et cetera. With groundless meaning, expire on buried ground. My o my, a genius with ears.

More wandering. On route she's crowned with feathers. We're not out of the woods just yet. It's the custom to place a sheaf of corn under one arm. Only two hours to wait before an event comes around again. It is still the middle of the life (land of the giants). Objects are composed of neutral matter, a would-be absence. One hand grips a reaping-hook. The severed head on display is preserved in a jar of clear alcoholic fluid. This sounds like an account of their final collaboration. Unnatural phenomena have possessed the host body. This sentence is number seven of seven. The charge is hearsay and witchcraft. A glass grail is used to contain.

Erase self at rim of fissure: asterism and countertorture. It's said he achieved this singlehanded. The two worlds have evidently been confused. I follow a zigzag path across the transfiguring ice. I did forget, see.

A circular fort whose sole function is coastal defence. Beneath, a group of stars with cell division. It is his intention to treat the thing as his own.

Last years of pilgrimage. A pair of elliptical incisions are cut into the spine (too late). The turret was not built to keep someone out, but to keep something in.
An obvious symmetry is at play here, the etymology of a sound. Check the date, check the signal. Cease, whomsoever you wish.

Con trails from stray drones crisscross the stratosphere. Spittle in the navel hollow, vertebrae stretched—tattoo ankh and sperm cell at muscle of tensed calf. Occasionally we go right to the wire. I need to work out how much of this is myself, and how much the others. Before, I could speak coherently, now all this invisible duplication, trajectories of silence.

The act of opening, protrusion of an organ from the abdomen. An event. A politic strike or deconstruction.

She is talked about in much the same breath. This is one of our miraculous in-sync moments. There is license, a sudden switch to a different tonality and atmosphere—beating of distant wings, eurhythmy of the flock. At precisely three a.m. I check my phone. Very dismissal day.
Naevus wrack. Listening in on the irresolute defensive line is exhausting.

Plague. Mass infinite. I promise not to speak again.

Talus. Mourning and lamentations. A jeremiad is underway, a telling metaphor of birth in the old self and death in the new. Pieces of bread are being swallowed. Investigation of the discipline is underway, but this never corresponds with experience (to touch such hair affords but little sensation). The aim of war should be what its very concept implies. There are no more numbers to distribute. He sits watching the ants build a net, the spores they drag. Beggars gather daily at the city gates. He presses his mouth against her shoulder. I can see the light pouring out at the navel. My own condition at present is not at all gruesome. A call to arms and freedom is being distilled across the valleys. They're massing. Make thyself naked. Aerial photographs show slow migration in the direction of the slaughterhouse. My cardinal points touch the outer circumference. By behaving in this way, you are depriving your very self. Now, if we think of the archetypes alone in a pit on the mountain.

No more carrying away into captivity. I'm an external, the residual image. The house is declared dead. All the resulting numbers must be squared. Recognize, appropriate, and resist distinction. Remember, if you must. Sociopolitically, this composition is a type of mutant fugue. I'm the one who arranges everything in tiers. Remember, symbinfinite is not actually a word.

It resembled the ground plan of a cathedral. I am without charge. This test is unassailable. An eye is lost. While in flight from the realm of things, a man is both resident and alien. A line on the compass bowl marks the position of the ship. I don't want to have this kind of habit that keeps me trapped in memory. Try thinking of the letters of the alphabet as so many names on a map. The style is aboriginal. Traversing the thickness of the world is a compromise: a preliminary proposition, a premise taken for granted—a theme, an argument, a beheading. This is our first opportunity to enter a plea (no more infallibility, please). There are the two doctrines of the external, and the copy theory. It's rumoured that one patient was beaten to death and a second smothered.

Nocturnal grammar, so much shrapnel. Misremembered splinters and echoes—jarred rhythm of old then, old next. An afterword, always later used, so much ago since time streamed out. The last page is blank.

I suppose there'll be security on the island. I will wait. The monad, which we'll discuss later, is unofficial. We declare this day the day of exhumation. It turns out he's a simple, without recognizable parts. He's given a title (the magnetizer). Paradoxically, writing suspends the act of writing.

She is gathered up in the opposing square, naked in sack.

Consist, solely. Detonate an afternoon of your time. Consider the following intimacy: being is either or not. This demand includes the task of working out the different categorical structures of those entities which are nature, and those which are history. Donate a briquette of dried blood. Exit via navel. Exit mouth. Exit sphincter.

Primed disc bomb attached to asteroid, evil supermutant clinging to nose-cone. Fluorescent green, he glows in the dark—nay, in the very light. A headlong plunge is about to occur.

The unidentifiable yet discernible. What is the name of this infinity symbol? Reset dial to infamous night journey. Offer resistance (large-clawed edible crustacean, red when boiled, extending to kindred).

Vignette from root of to take. Lesser hills, rolling smoothly to horizontal. In the control room, more of those showy radiant heads. It is too early to despair of change. A solitary reason persists—tropes of fog, great blocks of ice. Disfigures of speech, cadence shot peculiar. I think this is inside another language. Everyday speech witnesses to the merger of meanings, the assault on culture.

In the early summer a leaflet appeared in the city appealing for large sums of money. In return, complete protection from the living dead.

Unhomely with mourning, heart-shaped scar left by seed.

Look she says hills pointing.

I know what I am but have forgot the name. Alleluia et cetera. The disc is held in place by a vacuum. These are striking doctrines, if true. My fact is now. I rise up to promised work. I live without consequence. My rubber is number eleven. I wake to duty. Why do we need so many rooms for so many people? I am merely a cipher. I no longer need. I no longer know how to fit the structured hour. Your family pantheon is a defeatist strategy. Today's word is *hydra*. Stonemasons labour at the local pyramid, hammering the capstone, scratching at the mortar. Nearby, ancestors stack up. Orion tilts, flung clear to southwest. Some of these species are pathogenic. At his extinction it's said an eye popped out, dangling from its optic nerve. This work is dedicated. They are a race of burrowers. Instigate mouth to mouth (the voice, the handwriting). Now the building is vibrating. It's that bitumen machine. Use a mood-processing agent, huge glacial erratics.

Guttering strength, obsolete and rare. Guth-strength, in the sense of razored and barbed.

Depending on who you talk to there's a different version. His fleeting form is now lost in the shadow of the stand. Being-for-self falls to memory. Such a step is impossible, even for the ordinary understanding of the conscience. I feel I have been neglecting. Shirts, for instance, are now a necessary element of subsistence. The government also had its official couriers. Writing can never be remembered (try it). The same uneven vibration is in evidence, the same solid text carved of stone pitted with glistening aerolites. Diameter: as time permits. And here, as always, a passage is being marked out as you read. White lines zigzag across the tarmac (we're fatalists). It should be all right on the night. Sink down into a state of quietude, the edge of wrong.

We conducted the rest of the interview using hieroglyphs. We took photographs. Winter grazing is impossible at this altitude. Flesh once covered these fossils of sandstone. It's said he made an absolute fortune in insurance. The encampment is well above the tree line. From the darkness a cube emerges, a free-roving cell. I invoke the square but no higher power. A solitary winter ray strikes my forehead. Romantic wanderers on the mountain path saunter with arms around shoulders and hips (mountebank & quack). Those who were asked for help never doubted that the news was true. When in the darkness I awaken, a handing over takes place.

If taking up a book, always perform the ritual of blowing dust from its uppermost surface into space. Complain to heroism, again and again.

Assistants set about beating the soles of my feet with batons. It seems these two games are identical. A battery. An aesthetic torment.

His eyes are held underwater until he confesses. The survivors will no longer need to depend on personal magnetism. A confluence is taking place, a flowing together to a meeting, as of tributaries. Before any literary activity can resume, the tape-recorder is switched on. There are no spatially extended substances any longer (commodity enters into the reproduction of labour–power). This huge thirty-three movement work is set between the rivers at the first and second cataracts. I hereby renounce all show of strength. Carry him away to the underworld.

My soul seems to have departed through my lips she says, all of them. The blaze of the footlights scorches her feet. She wakes to faces blackened to a crisp in the camp fire. And within a matter of days, the radiation sickness.

In place of vacuum is left the body, dead yet still living, without sense of self or surroundings. An assumed or demonstrated proposition is used in the argument as proof. The book under study is a false variant of lexicon. A heading indicates the subject of the argument (freefall). A motto has been screwed to the base of the big picture. Nothing is assumed, deep to the root of to take or to buy. Always do things in threes, or ill-luck is sure to befall you.

It is without conscience and without unconscious. After a while she flinches and goes out of the room. (Shut those relatives up.) The circularization of power, knowledge and discourse brings every polarity to an end. A certain sorceress has transformed our companions into beasts. We are declared. We declare this day the day. I meant appropriate.

I hand my father a tiny claim, freeze the air. I will put money away. Playback speed has been adjusted for correct pitch and kinship requirements. A bridge spans an arc across a gorge, a trust of mortar—egg and straw. The river is dyed an impossible green. The orchestra consists of one hundred and forty-two musicians. And noise is *made*, pale redundant volumes. The chorus numbers two hundred and fifty-one. This is the cue for a unique harmonic language. A traveller needs a bed for the night. There is no respite (the metronome). Can you not see, the tempest is full of magic. Next comes birdsong from a distant continent, reluctant applause. A bitter cold steals into the cottage. A woman with feathers woven into her flesh suddenly appears. We are east of sterling, the stars tiered in one place like a harrowing sea. All matter is in motion. A ritual marking off of time is taking place. Isolation is a function of something. Cardinal east is founded on the cry of a bird.

These are striking doctrines, if fake. A few inches from my nose hovers a circular disc with branching rays. At last, somebody whom one can associate with genuine greatness. Compulsory improvement of local morals has been reset according to my own rigorous standards. I suppose there'll be security on the day.

That infamous night journey.
Since the day we heard of it, nothing has been the same. Until these gangs eventually self-destruct, you will always be their target. They have translated us into redemption. Who now is the image of the invisible god?

Three stars are plucked to direct attention to the burial ground. Under analysis, refracted light reveals the secretion to be a rare type of mineral. Conversion to scales of bone has taken place. A tiny luminous figure is transmitted into the cavity, pearly-white and firm. One is assumed to have occupied the position that the other formerly held. This is going to take forever. Our species is ranked with the sharks, the rays, and chimaeras—cognate with wickerwork, basketheaded. Indifferent yet temporal.

The strapline reads vain offering mercyseat in hopes to cure, something like that. There appear to be parts missing. There is no exit. A piercing silence is emerging from the resonance of an empty concert hall. The exterior and interior follow the pattern of all the other hotels on the planet. There is no entrance. Company now surrounded by a cartouche of vine leaves and tendrils. A promise is taken for granted.

Éclat. They press. Why the sharp edge to north and south? Sixty-four different playback curves have been used to promote the original (a small state without a frontier). The chorus sports traditional dress. I exist in what should have been a blank space. That eerie sound is the cawing of a gorecrow. Movement itself is the only truth. The others can't hear. I behave as though money is no aim.

Choke of wood-smoke on return to base camp. I believe that this comedy is not very effective due to nerves. If I said I were merely pursuing every whim, would you think any less of me? In the forest there were bears and wolves. The others mostly do not. I loathe mediocrity. We lack inter. There's a face-off, then the guests sleep for several days. I always aim for a point a little below the centre of the forehead. This process can only occur when the animal is prematurely aged.

Tent of presence, illuminated simple past. A veil is slowly drawn back. The exposed face appears burnt. There are no parallels here to aid comprehension. This detail represents a turning point in the life of the suspect. No one can now look upon him.

A piece of theatre.

They are holding a rapid rebuttal. Blinding sunlight is reflected from ranks of sheet-copper on the far side of the battlefield. Depression at centre of abdomen caused by detachment, no doubt. The market is a correction of itself, patination of overlapping centuries. A film of copper carbonate forms on all the exposed surfaces. Everything happens at a very slow pace—mediaeval, so to speak. The official number is two. Both headpiece and tailpiece go back a long way. A preservative gas is being pumped into the vitrine. I venture back for the very last time. Incidents include a spectacular fall into the gorge by one of the pack mules. I have seen your beloved city completely destroyed. The police are trained in historical interpretation. Such an imagine as you have is inadequate, shading off as it does around the head. Take on all comers, as if dazed. It's called the champions' challenge. Everyone else is trapped in the vapour trail. As with any siege, a great repertoire of kills will be made available. We were once betrothed. Stick to your job.

A classic study in witchcraft. It's the oracle himself—a giant egg composed of respiratory tissue, air into which a vacuum is poured, nothing more. The nose-cone comes loose in my hand. Talent nights and competition are encouraged among the survivors. An arrow circumvents us. Just listen.

I am *that*. The ash disperses. An aerial photograph is handed around. Representatives of the ancestral tree are enjoying a well-earned break. In the foreground a rim is visible. He puts his hand to his mouth (at least hit the target). The copy we possess is based on the copy which became the first property. A memo says no paper is to be taken home under any circumstances. The very definition of the real has become a sort of covenant. Resist any form of coherence, act as unconditional partizans. One passes from one era to another rather too quickly. The organizers of the remonstration were just as brilliant on their day.

Faithful to his legend, he has hardly proved talkative: seven to the power of eleven, which is a bigness. In any work of art all themes are decoys.

Astray of water, still earlier in time. Hearth of unknown origin. The grey crystals and amorphous powder have semiconducting properties. The latter are movables—plate, cattle, and the like—the former include disinterest.

I don't know how I got this past the ombudsman. Now you can forget about remembering. Consider a character piece or word sketch, a simple vignette (as opposed). And the just-in-case came to pass. There were lots of emotions in the tunnel that day. That is *my* eye (ravins as the wolf et cetera). This is *my* first operatic breakthrough. This room is *my* room.

At night he divines the spoils (fraudster in hole eight, subsection four). Furniture stretches away to the horizon in the north. Unforeseen meetings are taking place. Overhead there suddenly bursts out a circular rift of clear blue sky. Separate yourself. He wakes to find himself cast as an insider. The concept of appropriation is neutral. I reside within your body. Now look, dry ice lapping at our ankles.

Driving spray. Lemmata, from the root of to take. Whether moving deliberately or by accident, I always find myself back in an empty room. We have often tried to climb these rapids. The body lies scattered to the west. Every prison has its own library. The liver lies somewhere to the east. Some words have been put to better use elsewhere, in the past (for example, the famous chest of viols). Lay him gentle in barren earth. Lest I too should chase after the infinite, I shall briefly state.

Tomorrow she gets to find out the hard way just what her duties are (six to five thousand, approximately). It's not cricket. What is the nature of the current crisis? I have already begun to haunt this place. You glow inside my head. I don't mind so much the hum of the generator now. Professional experience will set this essay within a theoretical framework. It's the state were in, though admittedly not the being-as-world outlook we'd gambled on. Stick her in the corner, give her a colouring book and some crayons. All this makes me mindful of the light and of the dark. An image slowly emerges. Resting near the core of the shield is the nombril, the nave of the wheel. Ears are cut off (punishment). The mouth is unstitched. Warning, do not soul. Take action to battle, station men.

It was like watching a film of silence. All this makes one mindful of joining up the dots, only to reveal an unfamiliar abstract shape. And I believe, in the final analysis, that it was on the last day of the siege that she died. In history I survive her. Yes I know, I love her very too.

The satellite's mountains and valleys rest upon an inner axle. The form is the larval form, incapable of breeding. This chapter includes any words which may have crossed over.

A watchwing over one deceased. Scratchings still, shimmy of beetles in the cavity. Always pursue the first thought that passes through the medium. You are transfixed by the intimacies of my design, no? Mistress is undone, warm and hoist—fluxed out, yoke-grievous. She is transfixed by the frontward swing of the wall-mounted handwash. The head was incinerated in the camp fire.

Drift into sleepless night. This deserves a question mark over the word insurrection. The luz, an indestructible bone, hangs from the ceiling by a thread. Don't move a muscle. The pressure drops. Now put this away, erase into arc of convenience.

A curved figure is squared and given the cult name of germ. Stubbornly, his remains are unresponsive. And espy *these*, please. I can count on one hand such individuals.

I am about to mount as skilful an attack as ever you will see. I leap from one state to another (quite Aztec). None go out and none come back in. I will mention later the rhapsodies of the unknown, I will mention the loving kindnesses of the law. I will utterly consume *all* things. A series of spokes emanates outward from a disc-shaped centre. Gather yourselves together—carry on, carry through. What can be known about him is plain enough to see. Prepare yourselves. Each sign refers unequivocally to a status.

Concerning the well what they dug.
People swarm through the gate. They run to him and say we've found water. The name is the same name to this day.

A nervy afternoon, furnished with tropes. O to find oneself in a horizontal posture once more—to lean, to press, to be a situation. Metaphysical sanctuary is no longer of reliable origin and substance. I have begun to unfold on the philosophical front throughout the entire realm. Apply for any of these positions. Grant extent to remain. It is in your midst, a pregnant reference with bristling crest of nerves—the keys to this & that, the Hebrew unpacked. She never wears a hat. Her dull, fair hair is smooth. She hears the promptings of a dark interior. A small fatal incision is made on the inside of her stem.
It's funny, you know, as I reminisce of the time when I first gnawed at the marrow-bone. I am deferring, everywhere. On the run, with shaky soundless footage.

He is never stagnant in his interpretations. He was waiting in the corridor, uncertain. Alive, with pivot.

Waxed flesh of unaccountable female subject. Let's agree to forget. Such cases have been known. Such persons are usually granular in form. Such persons are usually more lucrative. The remaining lung is ready to be sacrificed, pubis cropped to a neat circle. She's an original, of doubtless form. A curved figure is squared and a triangle set within.

Infection of brood with bacteria from septic focus, abscesses in different parts of the body. Evil and good were much embellished by the gnostics. Take on human nature in one world and not in another. Only an isolated annotation survives in the margin. I can count on one hand the number of times. With care, with fabulous perorations, marshal your material. There's a crust of dry blood on the pavement. Samples have been taken from the seafloor. In the space of just a few hours everything changes. (Such individuals, libertarian war machines.) List below all the places where she has appeared, or disappeared. Embedded, one insect is found to have seven legs, intestine smooth. She carries a lockknife.

The crate is lowered into the hold. It becomes dark so suddenly we cannot see each other on the smack. So far everything is perfect and good and straight-forward. This book can only be read in such libraries as possess it. If you want help, notes or translations, look elsewhere. They will detect our scent downwind with ease.

Shore leave. Staggered on the groyne, head aligned with Venus, Mercury. Among the crew of a small, two-masted junk. Flying beetles the size of flying beetles. Still chasing strange fields of misassociation and breakdown, into which memory is gently lowered. Spirits can occasionally be heard buffeting about in these ancient containers. Next the string is lengthened and an outer circumference drawn. The objective is the discovery of a universal catalyst.

Anteroom faced with ashlar masonry (architectural embers of commerce, too much detail). Nothing compasses. The final form includes the seven recessed tiers. I have to work with something.
In characteristic fashion, construct a new staircase for each temple. Next the string is shortened and an inner circumference drawn. There are people standing in lines that stretch all the way to the horizon. A mould is shaped to the required outcast. The platform above our heads suddenly expands. The overall impression is one of superimposed limbs cut into by steps. At the end of days these total fourteen. A volunteer is led forward, the spinal cord of an animal bound the length of his back. Citizens stand in lines three deep along the corridors. Penetration runs directly to the filament. This subclass are thick-bodied and dun of

colour, with adhesive toes and vertebrae concave at either end. Now loosen, cut him down. Next comes a fit of perversity. That shriek is mimetic, dorsiflex (what when you are usually bolt upright). A sheen is acquired from constant handling or conduct.

One-time salt-plain, somewhere. The point of an escutcheon which lies midway between true centre and base point. That can never be the piledriver down in the gorge. One is merely the mouthpiece of overwhelming forces. I too the gorgon's head, neither stone.

Some notes on his student days in bohemia.
He takes the book of incantations in one claw. The witnesses are complaining about the dew, the moisture in the air. This region is an aerial reconstruction. Matter: vinegar and brown paper wrapped about femur and hip. He rips open the seal. The head is renamed peril. Diluted yellow blood glistens on the road where the accident happened. The head is unmanned.

She feels a remote, threatening. Deduce surface area of ligament. The story has been renamed. Walk now on ball of foot. Walk now on back of toes. Walk now on flat of heel. Sustain soles parallax to earth. Walk that white line stretching to infinity. Form dull compressions. How many of us will it take to cover the surface of every floor, every storey? Late copy is pouring in. Mass is infinite. Medicament liquid: resin of storax. Solve the narrative by resembling. Launch yourself into ungovernable geometries (the oblong and the pentaprism). Scatter excess tissue of every second. Which of these shapes will now fit together? Skip to solitary. The sense of transition is becoming so acute. *All* these decisions are important. A close friend has died. (You're reading my mind, aren't you?) I try to frame the photograph, but perspective is out of kilter, forever. Within me I feel the chemical influence of a substance not itself permanently changed by reaction. Skip to obituary. One bone is said to be indestructible, probably the sacrum. To the tip of the lung, we know when we are speaking—almost a scream, almost a meeting. Another tells me my turn will come. The lips are raw. We know when we have been spoken of.

The lake, motionless and resplendent between white and blue. Yes, we are cross-referencing as we go. No, there is no index. Neither is there glossary of the unusual, obscure or archaic terms used. Rule: admit no models from which others may form. Note the antiphony, statement coupled with disconnected response.
She has red eyes.
　　Sudden blow to seam at midrib of carpel.
She has four arms that widen out from a centre point.
　　Tattoo at crook.

She has matted hair.

    At this instant the ear slips through her fingers onto the ground.

She has huge tusk-like teeth.

    Continually shifting borders.

She has nipples pierced by bolts of iron.

    On the one hand, and merciless interims.

She has a protruding tongue.

    See arborescent, above.

She wears the skin of another.

    In this case a response to a failing connection.

She wears lid of cadaver.

    Except the relationship shifts.

She groans in imitation of the plumbing.

    Deserts are rarely oceans of sand.

She wears a necklace of gull heads.

    Grotesque toccata in C.

Her body is jizzed with serpents and symbols.

    Us intrepid bunch of anarchists decided to turn up as well.

She is a minor planet.

    Nothing has thus far been successfully decoded.

She is unfleshed, unfinished.

    Quote me if you will.

She is meteorite and she is starfish.

    Into the climax we are dealing.

This much be damned. Work backwards from here. This famous collection of dialectic tales was supposed to be told in the space of your remaining five days. Is that an animal in the window, stretching across? This silence is unbearable.

Semblance. (Who wouldn't want to come back as a mystic?) I am being naïve. The grammar of the real is no longer present. By night, teeth are ground. This much is clear. I coincide—heavenly body visible at angular distaff. This signals. More clichéd moves and absurd postures. Something comes through the portal whose name has long been forgotten. (Or perhaps I simply have no wish to recall.) It is the time of being here. The existence of a historian who only edits sources may be characterized by a want of authenticity. I have *made* no notes. In the final phase three tombs were cut into the platform. Are you ready for the next step? Work survived in the archives until its accidental discovery. On the other hand, I too want to be remembered. It is the time of not being here. The holding cell is composed of monolithic slabs of upright stone capped by a quoit. Origin remains obscure. Basically, there was this amazing day, existence falling to either side of the skull. Time is unusually resistant to being broken up. The condemned man paces back and forth. Retreat and scrap all directions, all definitions. A thousand volumes unlearnt me. Now it's our turn to be too busy. An original type of heresy is being mooted. In the next room she feigns sleep. Her anatomy and plumage distinguish her from other species, resembling uncertainty. A vibration is used to express the simple sound of n on the underside of the straight horizontals.

Inventory. Life-pivot. Compression of small objects. A fluke of doves (one tap is death). An overgrown coalfish. I take it that the earliest standard of masthead was the old. Between five and eight hundred were massacred before sunrise. Discovery: equivalence of moss does not equal weight. Identity: cranial disinformant, signs of dental mutilation. Documents lend every detail. (Yes, this is it.) What surprised him most was that his adversary appeared so young. A diminutive rimfire .22 hangs proudly above the door of the cabin. Blood is caught in a flat metal dish. Imagine a soul embalmed. Lift him up on extended arms, while holding him in the eyes. We follow the well-travelled routes provided by steaming rivers. A journey is like the soothing of a pebble by the mouth of the sea. We pass a sign of five English pounds bleaching in a field. DNA can be recovered from those semen stains. A plot is afoot. They retained him as their major operator. We are tracked by assassins.

Open to question the validity of the entire body of feelings. I myself worked at this, by heart, by rote. Captain strolls in, hands in pockets. This event is due to some glamour or illusion. There is nonesuch alike. I've become a little squeamish about angels myself.

The small arms are factory-made. Use animal sinew to secure the subject. His soul has approached that region where dwells the vast coast of the dead. He drinks. Reception is flagging, fogged with static.

A beach with shingle, dance of furies about a bonfire. What would seem to be the most logical place to flee during an outbreak is actually the worst. We are now in stoppage time: arrested growth, blood-let and haemorrhage, forced trepanation. Analyse and list the contents of the large interstice.

Printed on used correction tape is the legend *I augur, I divine, I am egomantic.* Maintain a state of disequilibrium. Bind the bunch of flax. It's quite touristy. Maintain constant. *This* object must have originated *there*. If the ratio is greater than one the system is expanding, if less than one, it is withdrawing. Guide us out of this fearful country. Probably same word original as story, angular magnetism.

One-time salt-pit, elsewhere.

Comparison of different countries remaining underwater. Seven types of ambiguity. New species arise suddenly as the result of major mutations (cf. living dead). Everyone thought it was a misprint for bay. It's too early to start moving things around. When does she want these by? Answer: of the family. Whose cocoons were egg shaped? The ode is sung only after the chorus have taken their places. Measure one is sapped, as in B. I haven't even begun to chop this up yet. Using teeth, pieces of flesh are torn from the conductor's face. As time goes by this becomes second nature. Also try this in sector D, using hundredths of a second instead of imperial weight. Conjure in your mind's eye a footman in livery (gaudily striped caterpillar tracks). I wish now that I had come along at that very moment. This is a recapitulation, a manner of obituary. Did you live here legally during the glorious fifteen?

Clarify mode and direction of subject—slope and dispersal, drive and purpose. This is my animal's lurking place, its favoured situation (a hair-trigger vein composed of clay). The dark core of the tree's branches appears to emit light. Rendering this in oil is impossible, not to mention the hotel room.

A railway siding, a spell of mendacity. Already the next section is drifting off into deep space, well beyond reach. The creature has been described as a diminutive mountain goat with the tail of a fish. It's held upside down for the extent of the ritual (a repeated series of actions). Chill yet fresh spring air wafts in through the slats of the blind from the sea. We are persisting with her romantic vision of the countryside. At the foreshore, where the neon light ebbs, one is not looking up, one is gazing down into a chasm of stars.

He has named all things liminal. Upon reading this I instantly realize what he meant all those years before. No interruptions by language are permitted (which of course also means community). This weather is oppressive. The subject has been reset to automatic. Something has fallen silently into its allotted place. There are four simple rules. These will lead us to the surviving colonists: the stump of coins, the sacred names of coincidence, the relativity of neural valves. Now take that path and walk through the forest for a while to *there*. No suicides or smoking are permitted. If I arrive so much as a second late, admittance is denied by the gatekeeper. Answer. How many of *these* are worth *this* et cetera? Answer: the vagrant's inviolable oath, skirting the next issue, skirting the next move. Remember how he murmurs my god it's full.

Horse denerved from knee downwards. Sump oil covers a triangular tongue of land, just one sector of the scorched surface. Pierce with anything pointed, as spear or horn. A dark-red film of slime is sometimes visible on damp walls, a simpler form of life that just as readily vanishes. Make grafts to indicate absent companions.

Ash, alien in soothsaid mouth. A concourse, the act of meeting, running into one another. Resolve this by unworkable shapes, such as a rectangle, aslant.

290

After a lengthy wait on death row, it was on this day during one of the years that he was guillotined. A mineral plan is needed, a four-square figure measuring six metres in every direction. Consider the pit of the stomach, when someone we love returns home after a lengthy spell. (See you later children.) Or a similar film of oxide after long exposure or burial. The surface ripples now and then with fleeting apparitions (wood, flint, metal). Let there bechance him, pitiful.

Tetragrammaton. Is anybody watching. A silver mosaic sphere hangs in a window, forever. Here's that little old catholic woman who ate up all the neighbours. Think of bodies of water as different types of terrain. I'm obsessed for a day (potlatch surpasses use value in every way). Have you considered a dolmen cover? Surrounding us in every direction it was completely still.

Ash of lens. The grind of sight. A slope by which a curved figure may be squared. Ambient sound has just been voted the greatest theme tune of all time. And then he asks, how many blades of grass were there upon the earth on the day of the battle?

The law subsists in the recovery position. We find ourselves in the same territory, this time headed south. Transfiguration is occurring. That settles that.

Background hum of drone at crazy altitude. Electric pulse, flashes of lightning beyond the pylons. Plumes of black smoke. A perfect front is curling in. I wake. Someone's strapped a camera to my head. The silhouette of the double crouches in one corner of the room. Sunlight streams in through the blindless window. Below is an earthen courtyard enclosed by flat-roofed cells of corrugated iron. There's a chapel attached to the compound. Whisper it: what one is addicted to is allowing oneself to withdraw. We are our own subject. The real sense of building, namely dwelling, falls to oblivion. I rise and sip sweet tea with the rebels.

A bargain mister.

Talk sense boy.

Inscape. Paralysed abdominal tissue. Who holds the keys to this bethel of mischance? The required shades are pale lily white, sanguine red, and a dark green reproaching black. The walls are glowing. I cannot own anything. Be still, remain silent. An electric current is measured, radiating from the solar plexus (song of the mercyseat). Her heartbeat descends. Colours flood the field of vision. I will pray for you too, one day. My finger points inward. The index quivers. A man hands us a little bunch. Creators utilize what therapies leave behind— probably the sacrum, erotic memorials.

He was unseamed from crown to groin. I remember he was once *here*. Sometimes I am vaguely alluded to as the centre of the earth.

A low islet, the same as key three. I remember he was once *there*.

The names of the intelligences are as follows.

An impromptu truth serum has been concocted, a compound formed by the condensation of ethyl alcohol and acid. The subject's mouth is gagged and his limbs gaffer-taped to the shopping trolley. The slowest members have to struggle to keep pace with the fastest, and vice versa. The thing in action equals the debt owed to the consumer. All the water is eliminated from the equation, and slowly leaches from the volunteer's anus. (You can hear all this happening on my phone.) How long will this lunatic last? Myself, I was only too glad to be adapted.

Proceed, go directly to base of chapter. And could you sign this suicide pact when you have a moment, please? We would meet regularly, once a week, at precisely the same time.

The subject is bound fast with unbreakable cords made from the intestines of animals. Evidence has been stolen from the root. The prosecution draws him out, this demonic adjutant. Verdict is passed. He's sealed up in a vacant amnion: he who delights in signs delights in signs. This is called the state or condition of lying nearby, and waiting.

Nervous fission at rocking-stone. At the hoof you cannot feel anything. Even now, at that moment, every seven days a sense of loss gathers, an absence tangible.

A brief digression on those ancient turf-cut mazes peculiar to the island.

The words in space. What follows is the instrumental case of a long-dead art. If that's a human arm, it is a very still human arm. The newcomer is declared insane, at once divine and human. I am personnel, neutralized. No one actually refused me anything. I'm a supplicant. Morally, this book is on a low plane—it's the persistent spirit of venge-thirsty blood. I submit. I am the eighth in line, or the ninth. Uneven the barren.

The supplanting masculine of theta.

He is captivating, but could be far more unfortunate. Candles gutter in the sockets of the sconces. This encompasses a system of what claims to be knowledge, but is without basis in hard scientific fact. As I prepare to write on brain and mind, someone hands me a papyrus on immortality. Whisper it, a slab of floating ice, a small fort or earthwork, a shelter, a chimney-seat, the crown of the head, a forfeit, a dark lantern. Hence, to entrench, to screen. He works this sort of rocking sound. There's more, a fine paid in defiance or otherwise. O to hide within, as folk once would.

The vital principle of thought still holds the middle ground (the part of a compromise between the foreground and the background). He carries with him miscellaneous looks—pookas and daemons, analytical concordances. Yesterday is washing up. In this desolation the peasantry roll themselves until extinguished. A primitivizing emphasis on the primordial past has become a key element in the development of expression. See oil-screed and photograph. One writer has suggested an appropriate name. Catastrophics mitigate agitation. Take these ashes of bone and grind them, perfectly calcined for the scattered inside. Take one mucilaginous root. All feeling in the limbs has been lost: he belongs to an image. Fifty tiny metal hooks curl inwards at the edge of the lung. Instruction: fight off the law. I have decided to undertake a complete withdrawal. Tomorrow is set at the very latest. Must ready self. Another grapples with the law-keep at the gate. Teeth are supplanted. Pluck that hook from the remaining kidney. What concord hath he with the other, with death, in the general sense of demise?

An old ship is fitted out as a place of worship for the surviving mariners. The law is now in the recovery position. Each posse of twelve should carry silent weapons, grappling hooks and bolt cutters, a hatchet, vials of mercury, petroleum jelly, sterile lancets, a compass and emergency flares. Any word composed of four letters qualifies, actually. Take extra care on the left side of the straight uprights and slopes. The supermutant is decanted and a sample removed for protein estimation by the method.

Puerile encounters with death. Ketchup and friendly ghosts. What did you expect?

Re-scream. And then some. Still can't make a decision about that. The core of a rotten tree: heart-pulp of eaglewood. Burnt cork on the surrounding faces, pressing in toward the centre of the circle. A latticework screen meets the sunlight streaming in through the window, casting intricate shadows on the opposite wall. The subject is found wandering listlessly in the market square, howling like a wounded animal. Sight and sound are merely interpretations. Build your clock simple, with time severed by five minute divisions. On the hour and every hour quaint figurines depicting mythical characters shuttle before its face. Carve these from the living wood. The subject is exposed to constant sound, a tireless lament. Let's hear it for the conclusion of the whole, the final dispersal. Do I want to go back in, or should I cut the cable now? Vaguely, we are not moving in the direction of a coherent image. Compass into stillness the whole of the land. Write to me (symphonic poems welcome). I am returning to my notes, to my shoes, to the battered suitcase on the wrought-iron balcony. It's the usual practice to bury radical compromise. We are, after all, our own objective. See above, parallel to pendulous round earth. See repetition. Subjects are waiting to be earned. If not now, when?

A dwelling in the uttermost realm of the sea. So called for unknown reason. That night sleep eludes him. He orders up a chronicle of the day's events. Aesthetically, this remains one of the greatest tales ever told. It's believed, and that belief is widespread, that this was dictated by some supernatural agency. Two thousand years of mortality have been bred in the spirit. See, a shift of one iota, and meaning is transfigured. He merely acts as a mouthpiece. Wings are depicted on every ankle (structural modification takes place by arrested development). We are well into stoppage time. He knows nothing of all this. By night, stoicism is eroded. That's when they come, as folk always have. His history is uncertain. There is such a thing as stationariness, after all. It shrinks back from the head, from the very beginning. A polished shield is the solution, held aloft.

The at last of the universe. Arrows in relief. Ruins encircle him. Check water temperature then return to base camp. We carried the butchered men on horses for three kilos until we reached the river. Now what. I have not read this your book so I cannot comment.

We take shelter behind a solitary door standing in a patch of wasteland. Sheets of rusting metal fly wildly through the air at speed, sharp enough to decapitate a man. My companion's head has been fashioned into the shape of an ibis. There was an international manhunt.

A model country crisscrossed with rivers. Stress composites, veil torn. An egg of polished black trachyte rolls across the floorboards. I take up my poisoned apple and stride down to the sea. There are weavers, fishpeople, emergent stars. I hear breathing, the faint creak of an infant. I have been observed for precisely one day. It's not until the thirteenth that the priesthood feels strong enough to impose its will. Their shape here is one of disintegration. Space collapses in on itself. This silence is unbreakable.

Uneven motion of hand pumping at taw. Origin unknown. Who thought a rumour in her throat a punishment for having worn a necklace of lost days? Narrative occurs well outside of these tight concentric circles, the enduring substrate. You already have one deadly enemy to contend with, don't create another. Pincer claws of male clotted with unconscious spines.

Simple atrocities of construction, elemental props: L tessellation in figs of arc, the divine semicircle. At this moment functions are indistinguishable from each other. The subject is human and therefore can only appear at a single point in time. Another of my strident yet falling-apart figures, I can simply will him to cease. It was once believed the precipice must be woven of stars.

Signs of mental denticulation, digression of air. A sheet of paper skiffles across the waveless waters of the tarn. Verbal instruction: make patterns in the snow with your hoof, then leave. Tiptoe across creeping rootstock, spikelets of flowers on lengthening stalks. Cry out in the chief place of trade and concourse. Transmission lines should be buried within sight of the highway.

Yes now. The remainder consists of miscellaneous scraps culled from books on any subject. Weave one final template. At last I am standing on my own four feet. Arrows in relief run about the interior. Missiles descend from every angle. It's the end. Comrades carry the wounded man into the tent. The animal is hung upside down from a metal hook and bled, the stain forming a beautiful symmetry on the concrete. Porters shudder under the weight of the reliquary. Its metal rings are threaded by carrying-poles. I once moved mountains. Do not return and never look back. I remember him saying. The asteroid draws into itself, its valleys and its mounts folding until they vanish. He too is changeful in the space he inhabits. I meant autopsy. I said not to mention the hotel room.

Salt of antimony. Personnel present include the backwoodsman, the bee-keep (i.e. holocaust), he who delights in signs, the lost-born, the pineal eye, the muzzler of pain, the enclosed, the lifer, the nightwatch. One should spend much careful analysis in discriminating the more faithless colours among the reproduced. Together they total nine score, which has long been known as a mark of condemnation. The tokens cry no recovery—surfeit by eye. The marquee will burst. Quick, assign the name. I haven't finished.

On sea demons. In the wake of such an aesthetic discourse.
Press, man in article of high summer. It was a simple spelling error that caused all the females in the colony to miscarry. Who constructs limbs of wax? The span stretches, scratching out and away. Ironically, today's shibboleth is *talaria*. He says I could not have slain the other. I treat with signs. They say he parted well. It is cutting through the nerves.

Mimesis. A mizmaze. He drowns. He melts.

Ungeist, with emptied head. Death in the ballast box. That which would be premature. Shift fingerings to slowness, twist carcass on spine. I shall now attempt another translation concerning the negative. The canister contained irregular pieces of iron, formerly. It's important to keep your mind in good shape as it is your body. The subject circles around and around in the dust of the yard. Beyond, cacti punctuate a desert landscape. It is the underside of writing: res in graves to distant frame, the far shiner—alike in leaf, with arms up-flung. The thing resides in matter. Liaisons must really be copulations (the back of a book or writing).

She suckled in secret and none knew the place thereof. I will not give you a word in answer till you rise up from the earth. A corpse swells to the surface: long beaklike jaw with sharpening teeth.

Nightjarringly.

Psyche with hoof stuck. Behappen and ensky. Her ashen mourning hair and tattered gown. Keep nerve, door-to-door. Kill swift in A major. I cannot go back to your frownland.

An enclosure, the upper end of the narrows. Make each member of your group an export in something. Switch caress to dorsal suture. He flies from his crate, wax-winged class of messenger—fretting in fear with inward conscience, under all patience. Restrain by binding the feet together, chiefly in plural when left to gaze. It's all about the contract between opposites—say loud, say now. Spooks aloud in the fading publics. The uncommon secretes in border names, in compounds. Spooks démarche, fraught with hope.

Now end—end in love at the crest I fashion.

End. Ens. Spermatozoo.

XXII

First word of the introit. Month nine of fasting by day. This section is about the surface of memory and things. Slide back the steel shutters.

Light striking needle-shaped crystal in cell. In posture of prayer, a comedy with lamentations, contrafacta. A sign at the station says there's been another abduction. In spite of all this ambiguity, it is still fair to say. Foreswear, and extinguish.

A piece written for keyboard and void. Caput mortuum: a star in Draco, a star in Perseus, in Cassiopeia. Fossil also, the crown of the root in to plummet. First they shot dead the nerve.

All virtue is extracted and spent—residue after sublimation of distance, a workless waste, good for nothing but flung clear.

The fleet is moving towards the shore. Time a certain period. He can no longer translate a single word.

Well within hearing. The noise level descends. An urn for storing entrails is carried into the room. The place is completely still. Books have been published on the embalming of voices. We have become these terrific ambassadors. Solicit by hand, up and to write come dawn. It must look as though I'm not doing anything at all.

A representation, in all its naked simplicity. Tongues of flame creep along the gullet of the ditch, gulf-hole of the eighth. A subtle arc rises and falls across the page. I worry about the close juxtaposition of metal and glass. She says this is the shape, like an age curling inwards from a point of no return. Entangle the limb of your quarry before retreating. We're ankle deep in petroleum.

Peel your eyes: alien in veil of shadow, obscure convert of space and time. Gulls peck at the abandoned shell. A small correction was made for the windows of the dead.

Standing on the corner, battered suitcase in hand. You were always premature. Observe the hardening light, the timbre of the moment. Where is he now?

She rejoins: he belongs to the first epoch, dead by the late period. She has one reading for me, a second for another, and so on.

The year is numbered nineteen and twenty-two. By night a vigil is marked beside the wicker basket. Devotion to common usage is rife—dull by overuse, stumbling between inept officials (yes really, you must let me go). Shape and limit continue to provoke recession to an earlier state of mind. Ignition was accidental.

The outer cast of the speculum. A dome–shaped hut of snow. Of or pertaining to saint, first-century bishop. A cure is found in the poisonous seed of a plant, akin to nux vomica. This tally is inconsistent with my original, tense shuffling here and there. We should really say lacking in unconscious authority, to the prescient mind.

Supine on pallet, described.

Somehow in the street, shouts (he's a killjoy). Cot on balcony for the heat. There is the overwrought iron. Luminous dots and scratchings vibrate in slow descent—the gift, without guilt, of every moment evoked. Dim shape a trouser-press. Unbeckoned revenants are stealing in. We are portless: architecture of inferno, inverted pyramids, a germ cell. Helpful arrows rain down. Now make use of the implement with five blades. That roar is the shifting spine of the sea.

I trip over a bucket of smoke on the window ledge, nine stories up. The action is set in a brothel. For the very first time I'm placing myself well beyond reach. The being-possible is to be distinguished from empty logical possibility: there is nowhere else to go. An afternoon of news follows (bright star in southern constellation, the soldiers advance upon the village). We are photogenic to a man. Answer the following question, correctly of course.

Nightshade. Yes. How may we not enquire into the unsearchable? At the end the only characters in the whole opera who come through it undefiled set fire to themselves in a grisly rite of purification. There's a suitable musical accompaniment. He enters in a coat of frieze, particoloured cento. The script dates from the early thirteenth, the mythic bird-in-space series: batten my heart et cetera. A discus blade is flung as a missile. There's a collision. All surface colour is withdrawn. A cooling paste is applied in direct contact with the skin. Short and sweet, I have tackled Elizabethan England. Now hush, in the corners they seek. Ballast engines carry materials out to the girders.

Bolt-struck tree at the intersect of three paths. Time, five hours later than now. I am addressing some well-earned misfortunes. It stays with you long after death, scratching at the electric. She detonates. It's a fate day—invisible infrared and ultra-violet, black light. Unwanted society enters. Draggling calyx, overlapping leaves.

A gorgonized forest. It was completed one thousand two hundred and sixty-six years after the road was first broken. On route one saint takes another for his enemy. I am pacing over and over the same square of time. (That would be giving away the ending.) Everything will be all right.

A programme of heroines. Computing logic, substance and road conditions. You can't keep adding to this. Reminiscence is retained by objects. Why didn't I just tell you that.

Index pressed to thumb releases interior scent. Heads are turned. Pertain to sense of doubt, to touch. No, she did the right thing. The voice is incendiary. Nonetheless, frozen hollow to the ground. All forty of us combine for the close. The scene is a hilltop village on a Balkan peninsula. A vestigial third eye hovers in front of the body, scraping attention. Imagine writing a book under the pretense that its author does not actually exist, an incomprehensible lie at the pit of a coffee cup. Where is my judgement fled.

Phrygian cap in hand, he lays himself gently into the dank gutter. Across me, he says, breathe loosely. Sound is withheld. There is loss at our flanks. The characteristics of flooding differ here from ordinary impassable bogs in the following ways.

A plaintive wail in the street, rising. Penetration is neither rapid nor easy. Attending on death, the living are torn to pieces (my primary linguistic argument). Cocaine is injected directly into the glans. Speech is cut loose. Outstanding are their cries within this disorder. I don't know if enough is the right word. This is open country, unlimited and transparent. Funny I can never find the book itself, can never decide upon the correct sequence of words. You were very nearly someone else. A long line stretches back to the fifteenth. I recount illustrious forebears.
Exhaust at coda, the putrefaction of space. Such images must be caught with all their original dynamism intact. Mechanics scribble a treatise. The water was dark and murky, thick with disturbed mud.

Distant choir, Gregorian. He digs his own potato patch and builds an air-raid shelter. One is excessively misgiven. (Well, that just goes to show.) We live for a very long time indeed. The beak wedged in the animal's gut and the result was ambergris. I shall now proceed to get magnificently lost. In this sedition, the music is retained but the words altered, or vice versa. Something fluid begins to seep out.

Talk, a conversation about meaning. Cupbearers linger in the wings. The whole project is about the impossibility of dwelling.
We're flung forward to situation twenty-two. Existence depends on the tap of the keys. One stays behind to guard the shrine. In the span of a single week he's become an ally. Trim yourself back. Use that subtle voice of admiration usually reserved for another. Point it at yourself. You're in sole charge of the operation today (erosion of river banks caused by colony of mitten-crabs). And then he says, what draws you to her is this.
She is without gravity.

On this expedition it's said the nanohenry was first discovered (uric please, aloud, left wheel). Also the lung-drill and the remote viewing organ. Such unconscious process doesn't consist of independent actions waiting one upon the other. The third is the head of a jackal, the foreseer.

A large clasp knife. Take this slowly, one parallax at a time.

We had him but he escaped from our head. Rounding past a quarter circle, the arc of an ellipse traces through a curve. Robotic and finite—defeatist, like a family.

Pending, eternal investigation.

Handmade clay tiles, a woman annotating. So many of the players have been removed into different positions. I am no longer recognizable. In nowise can I authority a body today. The howling from the courtyard resembles a mantra. Looks like rain. I can see no reason to be doing any of this. Matter needs a face-to-face exhumation. The foreign tongue fades as translation kicks in. I speak with borrowed authority. If I should steal the floor at the opening of such an historic colloquium, what would I pray for? Of course, the victory of divine omnipotence over diabolical silence.

We found ourselves in a vast cathedral. The project is the purification of ordinary speech into something sacred. Cards are drawn from the stock and sequences laid on the table. The tin is perforated by tiny points of light that plot a map in the darkness. There's a sign on the door, glued fast with spittle: no pills, no bicycle, no consequences. We have chosen to quote from the most beautiful part of the work. I am trying to remake the body. With its rhythms culled form the orthodox, some would no doubt hear the all-night vigil as a pastiche.

And he could see nothing. Lowered into the sea he swims in a straight line toward the horizon. He will not stop. I love these chains of happenstance (chiromancer to numerology to pilgrimage). He's in the habit of suddenly disappearing in the middle of a sentence. Transpose to place, the otherwise. Empanoply.

The specktioneer's tale.

Words are corralled within the ellipse of a cartouche. Pusillanimous, she says. An infant is snuck in its wicker cage. Mute, suffering from amnesia, and long thought dead, an amber glass protects it from the light. (This fable's got my name on it.) The composition suffers in shape a distraught curve. We approach the building from below, via a stem of underground concrete. Above, the daylight glows green-blue. I'm reminded of a souterrain burrowing beneath the old peninsula, the last earth-house. A hot dry wind blows down the steep mountain valley. Sheer cliffs hem us in on all sides. What is the colour of the men says a deep voice in answer. I hear laughter. Underfoot, loamy deposit of aeolian origin.

This tort concerns the etymologically unsatisfactory egg in the tomb. The postcard states that fire and rose are one (whatever form that might take). There's a hole inside, slag in the forum of particles, elongated in one direction. The individual details are distracting. Outside there's a three-kiloton wide boulevard. It's deserted. An exclusion zone has been established. Technocracy, no matter how pure, sustains and streamlines the continuum. Soldiers charge into the area below street level.

Seven years late. In the background orange embers, the trio of walkers. The sound is very dark but not yet black—old-tarnished silver, I'd say. Have you seen my comment face? Remarks such as I rust.

Gold glittering on charnel, a silhouette serenely balanced between two moons. And looking back at me, a constellation in the shape of a helmet. Use any one of the three divisions of the canon. Apply to the epistles, attributed.

She walks slowly back from exile. It is not just one country that the scream accuses. I'm found among a group of undesired people. A friend breaks the silence. The craft is made of a material more resistant than steel, yet yields to the touch. It bears a circular insignia: dragon with V flag, black on red. Time is the pollen-laden air of midsummer. At the close she takes a few false strides of her own. Abandon this to chance. The cast count to seventeen-and-a-half before crouching low again, faces pressed into the stage. It gives, soft matter, like a gaseous lens. Who still idols these days?

Abgrund. What a strange thing to shout. It rolls and it rolls and it still rolls. Insanity begins in late childhood. I am under supernatural influence. A nascent twister overhangs the charred pier. An enumeration follows, all the days of the near. Light now flashing metallic. Two march straight ahead. It's all downhill from here to the safety of the cavity, the blight at the end of the runnel. But we must plan our own route, secure our own motives. This is troublesome: conjoined twins, sudden bursts of electromagnetic radiation, ribbons of lightning ten bolts thick. And there are checkpoints, so many styles to clamber—the full spread of isolate, liquidate and annul.
Anyway the expedition.
He cuts the primary lesion. It's the beginning of year nine—sinew and griefmuscle, pack ice. There's an inventory at base camp. The next stop is a bridge of sorts. Many die in the street without warning. A plastic sleeve is found hanging in a tree. There's evidence of trauma, congealed blood in the polyethylene crease. I'm helping out with the amphibious group: Vitus dance at low tide-line. After class, I hold forth on the necessary qualities of the guerrilla fighter. Phenomena under study include a fatal ear infection and one crystal never accurately analysed.

The pain is nothing. (Did I write this.) It's from this very spot that I opened the republic of people. I'm exhausted from long nights of fire-watching. Who has not considered leaping to his death into the crater? We resolve to change horses at the next toll. There are torrents every three hundred jars or so. Our postillion is struck by lightning. If you forgot something and had to go back, then what?

Primeval forest, powdery rain, the plop of a virus. She starts quacking, a series of repetitions of the same passage, each a tone higher. It's that old Saturday morning option, fucking or shooting. I dust off my old rosco. (Get back it's the dead.) Sticky aren't we? At either end are white sightscreens on wheels. Maybe there's an animal in here somewhere. Our costumes are appalling. This three storey building is now sealed forever. It was once the central nerve of a vast empire. The text is subtitled the homage—a measure of capacity, roughly one bushel. Do not touch the glass. There's an arrangement of five at the rim of everything. The kitchen smells of smoke to this day.

There are vacancies. The homestead has landed. A new map is being stitched. Each different accent should be drawn inside and assimilated. All that needs to be done is for me to throw this switch and release my most evil creation yet. Yes, it says in the last part of the treatise that substitutions are impossible. Evacuate the island immediately. Do not approach the glass. I drop a match into the pool of liquid at our feet (we are two who write this book). Overhead is a celestial, descending softly into the gentle bog. On the radio we're situated farther west. Until now we've been buried. Arguments begin about point one or point two of the margin. We have been voices off.

Originally a watercourse, the expanding vessel. You don't always see the planes. You hear the planes, but you don't always see them, because they're moving too fast. This is coming together. He is explicit, switches over, philosophically speaking. Knowledge of the word permits no illusion. The moment passes. I'm so sacred (the disinterested use of the intelligence). I count three Fausts marching out of his pregnant belly. We're in between for want of something better, are used due to the lack of an alternative.

I was born at the epicentre. It was five years before cinema. The wife descends from a race of Balkan hat-worshippers. They look as though they're going to a funeral, or are returning from one. It makes little difference. Once again, you've fallen in love. The result is a general downward spiral in incomes and social infrastructures. This accord produced mountain, ocean.

Metallic element numb at seventy-one (first separated by George). A town of mud, a member of the rare-earth group. The name was originally given to a substance later shown to exist.

302

A quarry. Certain paltry material satisfactions, violet in colour, embedded in quartz.

A plant of the northern constellation.

A drug relieving blood pressure. A man of honour never failing, gules with a fess fair, he bore. A pipe is inserted into the urn to draw off liquid. Form is obsolete. To womb indeed, but for that old roman. Would-be loss, all to ourselves.

The book is a novel tale of chivalry with unreal people labouring under disguised names. It says as little as possible, while marshalling thousands of stolen words. Say, that creature is a repository: all your experience of humankind to date. I have set out to demonstrate a thesis or proposition. The mentalist stresses of our time have grown into an uncommonly fat tome.

See triatic (stay). Flying ants everywhere. Sound is being manipulated and transferred. The heap swells. Familiarize yourself. Get off the island, instantly.

The hum of the pylon. Very pistol, plus the grind of the glacier. Thus on the beachhead the armed, with sundry dead. I shall not fail. A drone, and glinting silver, a white horse, felled, another misunderstanding. But I am not going to tell (you were never a priest, whisper it). Here, take this key for your own protection. It unlocks a place, or locks it up, depending on your perspective. Cross yourself with it: head, heart, right shoulder, left.

Since waking, every time I repeat this gesture, it's like an epiphany. You were very nearly someone, almost absolute. Move lightly across the earth, barely touching the surface of things. Where does this semblance end? Withhold the sparks until they perish from lack of nourishment. The moral literature of later generations distinguishes between four categories of penitence. I am going out once more into the starlight.

She says you come unto me with open eye. The colour white, made of coral, hangs at her watch. Divine helpers offer useless gifts and advice.

A sloping mass of debris at the base of a cliff. No sir, it was more like a word—gram-negative rodlike bacteria, a mechanical horn with a rasping sound. Will anybody remember this date? The earth's gravity could be released. The uncounted cards match ten or less. A silhouette holds high a torch before the slope of a disappointed scaffold.

He finds himself in a wood at a place where two paths cross. Stop the game for a moment. It's three months before an untimely end. The tree he stands beneath drips earthward tiny beads of a translucent fluid. This will surely swallow many hours. I am never happier, poison in my eyes.

Nerve, the deity to whom the hill was originally dedicated. A burial-ground, a place splintered with bone (the pilgrim's motives are never simple). Someone enters the grove. The chorus turns: after death, stellification. We haven't selected our flag yet. Cover his dead face with an inverted dish. The fourth head is the head of a hawk. This is practically a summary of chapter one hundred and forty-nine, in tabular form. Red dot of light visible at centre-back of pilot skull.

He is off on his own two feet. Touch of metal aftertaste. Decomposition is manifest by joining scraps of other authors. The music of this period is chan-nelled through vast concrete amplifiers—a solemn dance-form, old and bare, without movement. Time is reputed to be of an age. There's nostalgia for social standing, a need of something. Chock full of mis.
We crouch. The capstone is missing.

Now I'm standing in the middle of the cell. A screed shuts off one corner in which icons have been placed. She turns up, bedraggled for rain.

Someone hurls a weighty rubber phallus from the sixth floor window. On its trajectory it bounces at the open pane. The following day a workman pockets the thing. It's all about getting bodies freshened up, where tongues of flame are folded into the knot.

The very animus mind. So called because it contains so many insects, figura-tively. Which is etymologically impossible and historically untrue.

Five of us have gone under today. We cling to the swelling raft. The residuum after distillation, worthless residue.

Think of a circle. Times it by three, or whatever. The mislaid cadaver is found in a neighbouring cell. You're not permitted to juggle with any of these condi-tions. I am harvesting five-star refusals. The familiar odour of patchouli oil and garlic clings to her clothes. Any changes will of course be live. The greatest pres-sure comes from within, the old primary lesion. Now I am no longer standing in the cell. I know, I know—a bit of doggerel, experiments with the punch-cards. The quality, the attention to detail, is truly amazing. See my dereliction.

Inspan. The local populace hasn't the eyesight for this limning business. Preparations for a departure are underway. The acetate allows sound to pass straight through the engineers.

Nox. Animal beneath pallet bed. Animal spirits, answering to nerve fluid, nerve force, nerve action. The kind of insane detachment usually yielded by numbers.

These humming vibrations intensify then fade away. Why do you think they call prison the hole.

I pick up a many-limbed statuette with a bloom of copper oxide clinging to it. On the table sits an unpeeled book: ghosts, psychic annulment, the challenge to unbecome. One remains indifferent to everything. In slides a shadow. Sickle in hand, she carries a sack of cats on her back. Fear and flight are conveyed to all parts of the body through the neural stem. Compression oozes from guilty pores. Boats were once hauled up here from the sea, and buried. Relegate subject to a post where incompetence matters less.

Tracers in the sealed iris, after-trails of green sunlight. I am close to have not, the unmistakable mass of realized experience. I am awake and I have lost my way. I perplex (the odour of growing things). And it all ends with the thrilling spectacle of the gods crossing over. Time travel works erratically the woman said the woman said.

The supreme punishment of voluntary exile. Propulsion toward a certain end, from the development of traditional ontology to the modern mathematic psyche. Who dwells in the city of embalmment? Cinema was broken. He is repeating to himself a discarded name. Hopefully we will bring in five or six new faces. Consider the substitution of a sacred text for a secular one, or vice versa.

A pockmarked cube of marble weathers in the principal square of an Adriatic port. Veneer of river in the humid heat. A reflector of polished metal is used to view the open cavities of the body.

A raised causeway
ascending its gracious curve through
desert fictions (science)
this screen of saturated colour
flips open at the master star-chart
with disc representing the sun,
punctuated by outsized architecture:
Triestine basilica, a pillar of glass
landscape of imperfections through
which I carry a holdall packed with ice—
at rest we cut the flesh into
smaller chunks for the coming fast.

The human race. Tick. Eczema and halitosis, notwithstanding. Tock. Note the number and zeal of its purified inhabitants. Live ants are introduced into the plumage. I once knew laws, customs, ceremonies. The sacrificial platform is raised a little above sea level—lapping waves, a glimpse of gentle cilia. It's become painfully clear that some of these gaps are crucial, are situated at the forefront of the brain. A series of self-contained narratives bolster the story of a dynasty stretching across successive generations. All the tardy news, endless cycles which the book fails to redeem.

While on the subject of birthdays, the skin sampling begins here. His emblem is the shell. These are special emergency circumstances. Let me through. Several writing systems appear to have been eaten away. This is still the early period. It's then that he comes, clad in scarlet from sole to crown. Such harmony and grace isn't easily attained, and yet he's a supple breed of liar. My footprints have only now begun to wear off. This companion is of self-appointed blood, as yes as the dead. He is the book that comes, that promises. The I is the miracle. He says in this way the bridge gathers itself unto itself.

He lived on until the nineteens. In the final years he woke. An inverted camera was used. Devil is not the appropriate word. He is silent, unmanned.

One of my mads, the neighbour. She knows every legend behind each of our whims. I have pressed my hand into the concrete. I have forgotten. But according to some a native name, not shaped into an image of human form. I remainder (puppeteer's hands with the thundersheet). The distinctions are becoming much more obvious now.

Ens. Low-lying marshland covered with brackish water. The house you can see in the background has been spray-painted black. Zonal tributaries lead nowhere. He is dated lengthwise and walks along the upwardcurving path. No gap remains between now and the coming age. He runs a finger down the index. The chorus suddenly joins in. He releases the scanner. I wake with soot-eye, overhung (at last, a career). The power doesn't stop here. He releases the cancer sign. To wit, I am glorious failure, made sharp, hawker.

Four lips on a stalk. Swapped felt for speck. She abandons her hair. An outcry. A rupture. A stillness. A quarrel. A flaw. A broken peace. The fragment. An atom. A violation. Discontinuity. A fault in mine. A stripe of uncultivated, shut in between two plots. A sudden breaking out of water. A flood when the ice breaks. A quality of snow—earth or debris shooting from a hill where the trees stride out. A cliff. A crag. A rock. The system of official snorting, of goods and produce, now in vogue at all the principle ports. The canon and its breach (horsehead nebula lit up by full moon). The gloss, forsaken in the margin. Contaminating seeds of interior refuse. In the next moment she turns up at a cardinal junction. There's no point in asking.

More on hair. Back to work. Cards are drawn from the stock and sequenced. Move this section down one.

More on the ageing of powers.

I strike a bargain with the living. Pattern now twice or even thrice seven, rather than the redundant fifteens. I gain limitless soul in exchange for knowledge. I am also without cap, literally, a river novel, with helmet of skin.

More and more I think it's about numbers.

He enters the room. Straight away I feel tired: a dead man's wife with hands, these hands.

Topic. The first thing from which something is not, or comes not to be, or is unknown. A country of scattered nomads. After ten years on the run they catch him with a beard. I'm positioned in a slow drift toward a right angle (hung, drawn, quarantined). He's a talented all-rounder, a scrutineer—seditious romantic, the radio said. I bring the nose around full-lock for the hairpin. Hundreds of feet below a sheer drop are the waters of the tarn. The empire is now more real than ever. We start slow, go very fast in the middle, then fade again towards the end. Great slabs of rock build the cliff edge.

Angels on the dashboard. I fear I wear them out. Situation: miles inland, a remote. I've seen the cables too. We're being extinguished. All the little outback places are like this. It's the aridity, stupid. Register, and conform to say. Fling self onto back and leave. Remove axe first.

Notes on vassalage, a feud. He always acknowledges letters. Memory is what I have instead of a viewpoint, the place where anything can be reproduced. The dead triplets are laid alongside one another on the table. Heart massage didn't work, neither the sterile pump and the air swabs. The deceased without recognizable qualities and pass undocumented.

Talk, a conversation situated between beginnings, descent into maelstrom. A circle is traced by arcing chalk the length of a taut string. On the floor is an arrangement of five objects placed at the corners and centre of a square. A gap opens up when the disc is spun. Miles inland, yet still the sea laps at our ankles. Now for one that cannot be seen with the naked eye.

How long. Answer. Wait a minute, it must have been, it must have been.

Professional shovellers, discalced. The ochre handprints are beginning to wear off. You'll get no reply.

Separate exposition, a tincture of persons and passions (the seventy-two names of god). Notwithstanding, the failure to establish doctrinal unity. Only seventeen years independent, and already the state is dying. I'm snared in triple time, a series of variations grinding down to a baseline. A real thriller it is, a trilogy straight from the rule book—the girls with something about a film of dragons. I want you. I appear. A misty indistinct effect is got by gradually bleeding colours of different hue. Shade off, leech out disguised as smoke.

A scream. Pretty. At first it looked as though we were going to follow the sump regime.

The head-springs of this river. An entity as opposed to an attribute. Fleshy spine of flowers, leaves reduced to scales Lovely day for it. No synopsis can do justice to our exquisite partnership. The deceased is led in. She's accompanied by her self-proclaimed inner (I'm mystified too). She is overseer. When lowered into the water she swims in a dead straight line for the horizon. She will not stop. Low level asperger is the diagnosis, pathological narcissism. Eyes are carried in on a dish.

The lineage looms large, abandon all ye and so forth. A hexagram hovers nearby. A volunteer is chosen at random and assigned the task of recording specific details.

Axis of hanging stones. Back-formation from a famous example. I will not cease. I'd have felt happier if that thing hadn't happened this morning. No, I must be obstructed: bony armour with undeveloped slacker jaw, one of identical twins. The second that comes through the portal has the head of an ape. I want to do things in a certain order. I refuse to move until I can replenish my strength. I fell to earth without lung. There is strain in the voice. They plant a field of rape where I land, whistling all the while. (This chapter will never work.) I walk silently through the corridor, the press of passengers. I must be ostracized. One night during a storm the high girders plummet into the sea killing everyone. Trippers came to stare at the work. Powers gave ear. I am closely allied to all other species. They grunt back my murmured prayer. That's about the sole sum of my standing, the whole pageant of the bucolic year. Come the season, they plant the meadow early, neatly in neat rows. The official flavour is syncretic. I am emerging, unsupposed. A feast is observed before every fast, then it's bread and water till the end of the month. I can't face another winter. This is the first chapter of a new life. I volunteer for undisclosed punishment. The grand choral enters. I take hold of when, someplace between here and next. Quick, baptize yourself, rammed thick in matter. Again and again and in a different way—refuse of seed, when all has been exposed. I'm deceived so freely it's impossible to provide a full list.

Requiem massive, the great resting shoal. All said, all done—beholders into stone, cut off in aegis, without cap. Hybrid parent colony attached. The literal, the ruler. Hydrozoa. Retrace steps, at last.

Finale, with entry of masquers. Place of no abode. Follow, less this condition be unfulfilled. Passages to be crossed out appear in curved brackets. To-be is the future, now usually attached to the word it modifies. The glass door adjacent promises casino, a glimpse of a ticket (the price of cease). Bruised air above, puffs of smoke from the smelt made visible, the signals. The subject is night, a deceptive mode of simplicity. My colour is determined by a poison. I'm back on my feet. There's twenty minutes of air left in the gravity cell. Compelling isn't it? You are simultaneously revolted and awed by this display, the drive of a process toward realization of a certain end. A mixture of publics has been set in the present.

He specifically mentioned assassination by explosive material. They tear pieces of flesh from the corpse with their teeth (collective response is always preferable to an individual attempt). We correspond to each other through sheer enmity. Send ambassadors in paper skiffs. Yes, just lying drunk by the river, dreaming.

All other priorities rescinded, crew expendable. Fade away, annul and abrogate. Cut to back, a rent in the time tablature. Write ploughwise, alternately from right to left and left to right. See, the plain of the blessed dead, any delightful place.

Alluvial liquidity problems, noxa. Six plaster lions on the back of a truck, one with face corroded. Character X was once here, right here.

We're quite different from how people imagined: diners with cracked and curling surfaces, the liver, the lungs. He throws himself into *this* river on *this* day and he is seen.

Winter. The death of a nightingale. Resemblance, difference.

Finally she speaks. I wonder whether that last sentence has its comma in the right place. The intelligentsia is on fire today: common fire, electrical fire, the fires of phosphorus, of volcanoes and thunderbolts. Slit open the belly. Anatomical parts stick to each other in random configurations. All the signals are deferring.

The head is penetrated via the nosecone. I'm a master with the exploratory drill, a genius of boring. The subject's shell forms an elongated stone, ending in a disc pierced with numerous tubular holes. Observe the microscopic mould of decay, frayed dynastic linkage. A heavy flap of skin is crudely applied. It both conceals and signals a wound. Our own faces are blanked out with burnt cork. Send ambassadors, send ambassadors at once.

He is scapegoat. It was a world so cold you couldn't set foot on the surface. Beware, he has special training in forensic anthropology. How are we supposed to plan our lives when we have only twenty-four hours to live? This drug is not of the same molecule. All objects are frozen in time. Whether by piercing the crust or by the hook test, someone must be found guilty: the promise of a collision between two things.

To study in silence, to be absent of mind. A state or fit, loitering. To hold the muzzle in the air, as a dog that has lost the scent, perhaps influenced by muse.

I do this kind of thing wherever I go. You have been set loose into the emptiness—the curve described by a body under the action of a given force. Because you are never home.

You are now standing in a circle laid out on the clay path. My first thought on waking was what a disaster, a return to the nakedness of telling. Perhaps the faculty of reason unsettles the mind. It's too early to say.

The next word on the list is iconostasis. Again the frogs are skreeling down by the lilypond. This a purely semiotic relationship. We have reached the coquelicot road. One of those infuriating slownesses appears to be in progress. It's a vocalist's nightmare. Exegetes have named the author of this part of the book the errorist. Do you want to hear more of this magnificence? First regale yourself with seventeen years of independence. The others are already here among us. We link hands and all the candles are snuffed out. Ectoplasm pours from the medium's eyes, nose and ears.

The vein of an insect's wing. Apparently I contain all future generations (by germ failed of being). I exist as an accident of substance. Literally, to bite into, again and again.

He is haunted by the vertical plastic grass.

Divination by origin, obscured.

He remembers every word, rumours through the ear. He says the event never happened. The text is becalmed. Who can transpose into thought the mode of his own day? There's always the risk of injury when standing in a naked flame, especially with so much straw about. It was well thrown, my guess. Dragonflies tangle in the barbed-wire that hangs from the ceiling. This masks out any lingering sense or meaning—the crush of mind, the hard-driven head.

Dawn is photographed as though it were dusk, a moment's library. Ahead of us the twin mouths of two tunnels lie side by side. (It was a curious comment, but not in England.) The image is a bit ramshackle, a handheld exhumation. Separate and distinguish between different types of fear. That's what I love about you, the relentless unapologetic paradox. We sit idle in the compound and watch the dust spiral. Everything is of our own making: ash-grey, strongly-scented, found floating or cast up. The bullet entered the upper thigh and struck the bone, spreading out before leaving a large exit wound on the other side.

An event preceding and leading up to another of greater importance. Daz-

310

zling light and ozone. I am presenting again each of the moments that distracted the audience, a series of slits. An aperture for feeding a kiln.

Haphazard man, in a region of mist, once ruled over. This is where we clip together—roots of temporary earth, screw volving on a central axis. A strain of human kell, investing membrane obsolete in form. Head and face sometimes reach the ground. Inexplicable whiff of lilies. Perhaps the memory of.

She sighs as the ship sails past. There is no longer any intention. The third time the phone rings we all freeze. We are not grasped, are manufactured purely for misunderstanding.

Here is the nous, more notes on the mystic writing pod. The dice are loaded so as to turn up low numbers.

His italic. Superficial associations, verbal ambiguity and similarity in sound. He goes unsmiling, complexion sallow. Bright patch on wing. Sheets of loury rain. The outer skin is composed of polished deer-horn plates. I am apparent, buried under flesh.

Stony inner cast of the fossil, as moonfish or common name. A kind of ventilator.

In the centrifuge bolted to the workbench is a mixture of sand, gravel and cement. Annihilate forever all that could one day destroy your work. Is this statement intended to encompass the both of us?

Cast in the eye, a bust to the king's gambit. We used a neurotransmitter closely related to adrenalin. My angel is in her. I am set among the stars. A man passes with scalpel in street. The tale is played out on the greasy cobble.

A hole or depression receives the liquid, cooling sheets of paste. Try, make it to the nearest list, then quit for good. A voice appears.

Disused atmospherics, hummingbirds, the burr of the generator—the persistence of a sense impression long after the mystery of its stimulus has faded away. Something to finish us off. For brief moments the world is composed of bolted squares of black metal—ally of copper and tin, something that demands a certain precision. Now he's doing his own face, woven from a single strand of synthetic fibre. You know the story, while carrying the host from one catacomb to another, he's stoned to death by pagans.

Waiting for to happen, the creeping shadow. We find ourselves in a fortified cave with a plan. On the brickwork of the well is a projected image. These impressions represent all my conversions to date. The 1893 text reflects the consequences of undermining. Don't copy any of this verbatim. Morse is used hereafter, as a signal of archaic conscience. For some time the concept of introversion has been employed for this condition. No one will understand. Note the swelling outline of the shaft. Even before questioning the oracle, he was believed. The oval area is enclosed by an internal ditch containing burial chambers, something hanging or in suspense.

Next comes one of the thing poems. Bellringer still rocking back and forth. A faint voice in the dark explains.

It's an acute study in syncopation—a hell-shaped object, a bloom, perhaps. One or the other must yield.

Same music, different text. I am adopting the posture of lodger-cum-lover. Don't worry, your secret is safe within me.

He strikes at the flagstone with his fist. Above is infinite space. They lard him with makeup, a face of transfiguring sorrow. Once his mouth is filled with straw the suspect is blinded.

Irrigation ditches crisscross the desert terrain (a certain ambiguity can be darkened by a small gesture). All had bullet holes in their chests. A woman's hand is glimpsed annotating the margin. A shell explodes high in the air, lighting up the scene. The psychological options available to me are unlimited, encompassing both crime and countercharge.

I am bespoke, he says. Could this be a sea-change within the industry? A certain end is promised. All these answers need to be questioned. He withdraws the camera to a distance to reveal the event. A subtle division of ex is taking place.

Do you hear voice she asks. Research and analyse. Animals are coffined within her, lion and unicorn. Observe calcification of left foot. Observe flapping cartoon griffin, with large angular heads and three-finger rays. Body, beak and wing, she is total allegory.

Was she ever excited about this. Yes, it's as if I'm still present. We have had to rename the building. Enter the principal candidates, then flee. She insists on writing under a masculine name (the tempest as prophetic test). This backlog is reminiscent of the old alley, a lost cause. Spider-threads float in the air and form a film on the grass. Beneath is decomposed rock, largely quartz, impregnated with iron compounds at the outcrop of every vein. The text speaks of the governed, regular and continuous, forever. She says I am set among the stars. With atom, outpeopled.

Many of them died on their feet. The footprints across the lava field were scarlet.

He identifies himself in a series of dreams breaking out of the skin. Crucible whitewash.

Analysis of fumes with fiery solid. Various modifications have been made to the wheel and the axle. (I would do this right now, actually.) We employed a revolving cylinder. This allows intensive delivery thrust.

Maybe there was a defect. Result: neuter of arcanum, the sealed chest. None of this is certain. The rainbow is a reflex contraglance of the sun.

Mark you the hard line of my shadow. Now at the stair, clasping the narrow stem. I'm digested only with much hauling and hoisting. The sum of this discourse has been teleported. Conscience pares me to bone. I can't see through the window for the feathers and the dust, her vestments. I am a recent detachment, carried arm in arm. So much for my written application to the self. For other sounds see derailing chart.

He's a virtuoso of lateness. Go direct to exit sign. Never amend. He is seen by passers by on the other side of the street. This fissured body always recovers. I sometimes envelope the birth-head. I have lost momentum. Call me my cell.

Newcomers to the east. Explosions next door. He with fur collar and stole, shells spliced into jangles at the wrist, her with visor and magic wad. There could be hidden colour codes. They twin (the buffoon). Thanks for leaving the map out. I can still see the shadows on the ceiling. The well is poisoned. The flesh of several species has been sliced into. I no longer listen to rumour. At this departure she says take care among them.

A bird's egg. I am over speech. Chamber piece for rubber mallet, saxophone and naked flame. No wonder there's such an intake of breath as we roll away from the compound. He splits open the papier-mâché head.

The investing membrane, an enmity of reason which can only exist outside of the mind. The town is called nerve. Form, to be. Years later she returns with an answer. Safe within the tower, he is momentarily appeased by this plan. Retort with an old, slow dance. In silence, form a circle and stamp at the earth. See note pinned at clearing, at inwit.

One.

Two.

Commit him to arms.

(There is no three.)

It's best known for its cordless vacuums. Slowly encroaching upon the following page is a film of ice. A ricochet strikes the rim of the adversary's shield. Hypothesis is taking crude shape, the comforting sound of a commentary. It's the simple present or bust. She speaks of exile from the tongue, her last link to the unsurpassed. What do you mean exactly by transfiguration? Mysterious patterns are floating down: giant hailstones in the bay, a vast shadow under the water, alternating from white to black. To this day, a whiff of wood smoke. Duration is eternity, the wretched jollity of it. Letters, representing, hover in the air.

It's worshiped in the form of an urn surmounted by the crude semblance of a human head. A single element carries all hereditary characteristics. Light flares beyond his hand as it swoops back and forth through the rear of the skull.

More on this, please.

Complete dismemberment followed by fire. Hovering attendants gnawing at gravity, ghost of infant at bedside wicker. A haunting, just beyond those trees. And then we said something more. Glinting slant of guillotine poised above exposed neck.

We set out two hours before daylight, fanning slowly back to earth. Give me a glass of that, and remember. Strip down all the instruments. He now grasps the composer's purpose: reverence drawn by outward action. Say nothing, ask nothing. The smell of carrion announces them. On the communard plate sits the chalice cover, a metal disc. No one wants to touch the abandoned apple.

Part of the skin has been stitched to the floor. You get what you pay for: a shallow pool at the centre, ankle-deep in ammonia. Overnight we defrost. Don't mix the two. The beast's brain skates across the floor, propelled by a slathering jaw. Now my feathers are damp. Before I forget, the first book is the dead. The colour blue is missing.

A structure. An entire day has been lost in pursuit. The entrance portal is renaissance, preserved. There's nothing wrong with the exterior works. If you persist I think it will pay off. (Remote female voice.) Come join us.

Beside him on the floor a low porcelain table supports a casket of acacia wood. A cover for the head is provided by a certain species of bird. This hangs from a process on the upper mandible. By the end of the year he seems by his shrunken frame many years older. The dimensions don't fit. I peer through a lens. The box is three feet nine inches in length and two feet three inches in width and depth. Plated inside and out with pure, it contains a clutch of scrolls, miscellaneous tracts. The compound in which the vessel is kept is dominated by vast metallic gates. Completely shut off from the outside world, they have grown vocabulary.

Dissolve. Treat as per molten crust, treat as per salt water or seawalk. My sense of failure is not so important. I have no outer limits (put in cats, sew up again). The setup of a well must necessarily be revolutionized in time.

A horseshoe construction of upright stones and wooden piles. Newcomer to the west, foaming red with white flecks. A novice. Nothing fits. All waters converge in one place. They have countermined the levee and the banks have burst. The principle elements are earth and oxygen. Property is raised to higher ground. Forgive me, I did not dream on thee. Time was unkempt.

Now, a random word or phrase, any plant of the genus. Place: woods and wild roadsides. You will not be able to tell once we've finished. The correct answer is a hunting jigsaw. They bathe and unscale him slowly with a cuttlebone (note the automatic gunfire in the distance). An event is being repeated, one of two words. Doublet or casque. Self-contained unconscious breathing.

We pass. A bone-white promontory, castle beetling over. The track curves away within reach. This is crazy. It's staring me right in the face. We're nearly home. From his eyes he understands.
Aperture caught in spasm. A contracted form of O, while I read this.

He asks was there a time when you were a child. A great number of things, especially trees, have been spaced in the same way. We approach the junction, carried on by the delicious number seven. How does it come to work, this trans-ference? Why can he not talk, hollowed out to a round vessel? I left on the false head because bizarre (man-faced ox-progeny). Do what you can.

Electricity in the chamber. Think of it as iodine on a wound. I love great throwaway lines. I love the funny things people say. Events lead to the formation of memories. She once stood in this room and heard whispers from beyond the wall. Tiny black crabs scuttle through the hole in one corner of the ceiling. They flood the chamber. The door bulges under our collected weight.

Night contact. A gathering of disparate facts by erasure, by a want of surety. We collide. I cite and partition myself. Who still grows from a dilated base? A letter arrives. It seems this is no particular day in no particular city at no particular time. There was a depression over the Atlantic. The word myth is incorrect (it's the sting that holds the yolk sac in position). Proceed by stitches, by uncertainty principle. Several of the species were found to be extinct. Come the armistice, hunger eclipsed.

Apparently he is still looking. He waggles his feet over the sink. The sign above reads chemist at work. Stop-baths, acid and alkali, I don't know how you feel about such things. The avenger of blood is the nearest relative, whose duty it is to hunt down the murderer. A human image is brought to life, a shapeless embryo. There must be true statements that cannot be proved or disproved within this system. He snatches the glass out of my hand. By rapid rotation, sub-stance is separated (a short cut to a quick death). Tattooed across the flesh is the ground-plan of a cathedral.

Augur, melancholious. So he is alive—a trance state, missing at sea. A landscape covered with flowers, poppies and asphodel catching light from the nearest star. This is actually conducting. Now tell me how you would have outsold them.

Contractile curtain perforated by pupil. The map is contaminated by a cluster of names. Sound waves pierce the vitreous humour. A piece of transparent matter is causing this divergence of rays. The subject is hauled back to the bog, trepanned and gently garroted. I am a man in the course of excavation. All depends upon how flux. The women are instructed to turn over on their backs and stare at the sky. A change has been wrought by the sea.

The men in the boat would have been aware of him escaping via the rope-ladder. There are consequences. On the whole it seems unlikely. I'm told I represent the lost country. A filigree of creeks and tiny rivulets fragment our northern shore. That sound is early music, for sure. And mud-green flatlands with ascending geese, the delta of a great river only visible from the sky.

She is too distant to assume anything. On route we squat on a wooden bench. Still frost on the ground, fog in the hollows. Nearby a canal cuts through the valley of lees. I am underused. Take the shadow of this copse.

There have been all sorts of false rumours during the last few weeks. Well, the next is very different. Above the crowd hovers an eclipsed disc. Here we are again. Mathematical operations are being performed on random numbers. Various systems have been tried, the Monte Carlo method. Elongated cones stream down every page.

X-ray of mooncalf, fabulous arabesque birds, apparitions conspicuous by trace. There may be no pattern to this at all. Numerals run down the upholstery of the seat opposite. Time will tell if there's been an impact. On a sphere, two arcs of a circle enclose a space. Scrapeage.

Thrown from every saddle, he takes up his first proper. The body is a chart, a map of language spoken through time (bread and coffee, a little pillow talk). Nails project above the welts—back arched, head drowned, forelegs stiff. He is post-off. All the metal objects he owned were buried with him.

A murmuring. Does it forestall you, your fear of here and there? I barely existed. Then the ambush, a place *taken*. Buy up before hawking the market, hinder by anticipation. It is drawn from within yourself, your fear of him. Divine is too feeble a word. In the beginning four human beings walk out of a roaring sea, appearing from nowhere. The dwelling is a low shanty built beneath street level. Relax, something more abstract is coming up now.

We tried to show in an earlier work that all chemistry is penetrated by an immense reverie. Solid objects are refusing to remain prisoners of their volume. By the same token, which characters are the original, the living? Two people have the same idea at the same instant. That must happen in the scientific world all the time. Correction of the globe's axis is being considered. Tell me now, please, the story you once told of a visitation.

Always choose the simplest option on offer. He sees himself as an eternal apprentice. The neon sign above his head reads wanted, apply below in person. He was hanged from his father's ledge. We follow various stages of his progress until the signal fades. The nickel content is measured. We're evacuated from the island. There's still hope of absence (the square root of *I shall see*). Utilize the knotted whip—I think you'll find you're in the witness category too. In his pockets are found strange metal coins of an unknown ore. We clip the vessel together, rudder confused with broken wave. In composition, alphabet brass, sixty-forty copperzinc.

Pasqueflowering. Deficient in lime. Latrine aesthetic—an aggregation of ids. Paragon of rearguard action, but in fact his army has been eliminated.

At these altitudes, God it's frozen and it smells like carpets. Extend these genetic qualities to all other species. She is digging at the base of a strange momentum. Everyone's lively at present, but we're still well short of a goal. She hums in imitation of the coach, imagine that. She is the slowest start in the world. The congregation murmurs solemnly. I have solved all the puzzles in the almanacs. Striped gillyvors unravel and glide gently past. Usually I love problems. White and red varieties are adopted as political symbols. The sky clears. The author sets out on her third voyage to parts unknown. I have composed in my head again and again a prison letter. She unearths the slaughter-axe. The young homo sapiens recovers. He's done a decameron of his own. They get happily married and settle down to enjoy what remains of life. This is more like what we're used to. In the script she dances herself to death.

Refracted crystalline structure. Now a curve, with wrinkles in the stillest place. A small deer-bone handle was later found in the cave at that very spot. It's too small inside the cavity for an organ. The correct number is one thousand and three. Dip under the waters, and thou shalt see.

The image of a large type of shell, prized, cutting into the back just below the shoulder blade. It is found. They plummeted out of a blue enamel sky. Nothing is where it should be. An edition is renamed every half a millennium. A negative capability allows for autonomy. In the curse behind the goal you basically have no choice. There's drainage in the mine, salt in the engine. You'd think they had invented death that day, give or take a few seconds.

Refer to his long-famous primer. In certain card games a counter represents ten fishes or points. This perfume is prepared from many kinds of flowers, atom bound by ambergris.

Venous hum. Make a sound like bees or that represented by m. Sing with closed lips, without words or articulation. Pause while speaking. Utter an inarticulate sound. Be audibly astir. Rend by humming as great wall. Express doubt or reluctance to agree. A fabulous restless bird. An imposition. A hoax.

The Greek zeta as a numeral equals seven, equals seven thousand, i.e. a small room or closet of some kind. Perhaps, only perhaps, the sexton's room over a church porch. Hence, a dwelling therein. The equipment for research into plasma physics is being held at customs. A dipterous insect hurtful to cattle can be dried and used as money.

Raskolnik. Scraping the ground for food—an obsolete order, with or without the pigeons. Any confused mixture of unlike things. Any inconsistent or absurd medley. A miscellaneous gathering. Ragout. Hash. The day the ice-roof fell.

Brother betrays brother. I'm trapped in the witness category. The younger wears on his head the so-called cone. He endures to the end. In line five there's an allusion to a ladder. I'm never leaving the house again. He is saved. His significance is unknown. Place him within reach of air.

On the quality of sound produced by the percussion of bone. An ossuary. Earmarked. Naughty hermetics, lunar cornea. Seacanny. Osteal.

Contraction of form at I would, I had, I should. A fish of the same family, inhibiting. An element in the chromosome carries all hereditary characters. (His theory.) My own private apparition is suggested by ideoplasm. The sum total of the primitive subverts the principle. Abuse occurs in the name of a particular zoo or dynastic line (cf. arachnid). Son of.

A southern constellation with clawlike architectural ornament. Later we shall assimilate a signal of warning. What do you do all day, following text.
My staves are bound with hoops of rusted metal. Yes, names are funny, shunting about from thing to thing. Stretch base of ovule to tip of larynx. Who would ever have thought it. Counteract this illusion of convexity. Save yourselves.
Diagnosis: inflammation of lip, a matrix altered under the influence of something misheard. Conscious hiatus between life and death, the emptiness of a centre. It sacrifices itself to fire every five hundred clicks. On strict etymological grounds, this should only be applied to sites which contain a hanging element.

See, strangeways, we have captured a chemistry of hues. Still on for tomorrow (the silt). Silhouette of his fingers before the lowered lid, candlelight guttering beyond. Hand pressed against cathode ray. Any unrecognized instant.

We watched the film over and over—craft low in the hull with raking masts and slender smoke-stacks. Ring yourself about with fire and chalk. Scoop salt from the frozen sea.

A valley narrow and expelled.

We start off in the crouch position, another of those wretched inversions. We've been primed for electrocution. This stage of the game is set outside on a vast parade ground. Stitches of light crisscross the darkness. We escape on the climb, peeling ourselves off the runway. Colours bleed and trail away from passing objects. Time is spent, closely pursued.

Fabulous misfits, barbed-wire and acid in the bath.

Severe damage, an unconscious accident leading to insensibility. The jactitating struggle of the limbs form a picture. An onlooker seizes her wrist. Turning now through coefficient, fast and flat, void of mass. The single and peculiar life is bound up. Part of the brain makes up the sidereal wall. She's very slow, but with ample dismount. The throne of the tyrant must be cemented with blood. The perfect sets the cheesewire. All of the witnesses present in the room can now spy the subject from different angles. We sit in a closed circle, a ring of twelve. Memory is never what you think. Seems we're no longer synaptic product. But it has come through, impatient of form, contemptuous of sentiment.

The south or south-west wind. Shores that are largely submerged, or remain underwater. Opening page of notebook. Tellus.

Clinging together as automatic gunfire approaches street by street—pressed to the back of the room, willing the wall to absorb us. Music was first heard on the same day, but could not contain all the exhibits. The island, known in history, is now connected to the mainland by a causeway. I have finished with expectation, the first cutlass of spring. Little animals never before seen are swimming about in a glass of water.

A brief scientific study of sleep.

Answering to R, as numeral one hundred, one hundred thousand. Two words were originally the same but now vary in spelling and meaning (everything). A diminutive of trouble, detachment of the soul or psychic element. Or, on a cross sable five escallop shells apart.

In the forests above a sluggish river, flat central massif. Perhaps white wave, phantom. The sun rises beneath us. Vignette guarded by three dogs—the head of a jackal, the head of a hawk, the head of a cobra. Our course charts a ranging U. Without my qualities you would never have made it to here. Undoubtedly this must look dreadful from the outsider's point of view. I slave at the chalk-face for seventy hours straight (binary logic). I have resolved the problem of making it appear as if he is speaking. The cornerstone seems to have rotted from within. He disappears, he reappears and so on. Think of a difficult question. I'm disappointed: no arc of light, no disc shunted before him across the sky. An ache has taken root in my chest. Gatekeepers are appointed and primitive demonology introduced. I return to base camp. The rule is five strikes and you're out. Time is at risk. I have forgotten to make copies. Now tell me of the name so named. Slide back once more the steel shutters before the window. In the room again the scent of lilies. The drumming gradually fades. A neon sign, reading.

Tubular cavities of the body, gland secreting. The shaft of a vehicle, detachable fore-limb of the gun-carriage. A channel is cut either side for drainage. Concern has been expressed regarding the basic emotions. Borderlands have been assigned. Some are unsurpassed, the righteous who died before. This could be any satisfactory place of consignment and oblivion—from the phrase bent backwards and passing under, progressively. A fine-grained glassy groundmass, placement uncertain.

There are too perforations of the mucous membrane. Surface dimensions are retractable, labile. Sound: her-colourless, purple-black fringes of flesh that glisten and quiver about a tiny pink nub. A forty watt bulb shines dimly on the music-stand, pinhead camera plucking detail from the gloom. I'm written out of the cycle, being neither safe nor unsafe. For confirmation, see my overjoyous letters home. By entering the analphabet domain, the deed of verbal commitment can be circumvented. Ink is scratched across the face, the wrists. Sounds rise up from the scullery. The complete work is schismatic, cleft at the source of to know. Right-hand antenna paralysed, apparently functionless.

The second reason is clothes.

He abandons his usual cynicism. Wire up the zero energy apparatus and stand back. Physical existence is in reality a sequence of statements. Rising fecal odour on slow withdrawal of member.

The silhouetted campaniles of the town are visible from the lake as we approach the jetty. That prophecy informs dreams is a universal practice, the simple engineering of light and gravity. The kitchen still smells of wood smoke. We disembark. The courtyard is a remnant of a previous structure. All that dreadful night, spent rocking back and forth on my heels.

Nitrate of silver, crystal fused. Apply to ulcer. There is yet no evidence that she was ever enlightened. Fire is contained in the bucket. She opens the gas-jet in her room. Deadlock within, taking root as cravings toll—swaying wildly on the ledge, stumped thigh numb with severed nerves. Black water spreads across the floodplain. Impose a soft imprisonment, but not until the evening of tomorrow, and then as my slave.

Your mistress, wander.

A kind of plague memorial. The siege of saint at twelfth. Rain beats at the window pane. Open wide to the burr of the moon.

One place unaffected by the movements of the day. Where families are expelled, total depopulation. Snail tracks glisten on the brickwork underfoot. Where was that dank cellar? We have reached the crosslight, the water-head. These holes are filled with fragments of minerals.

Being slowly extinguished. The whole region behaves like a single organism. Quote the exact quantity, height and pressure. I am speaking for myself. I once pressed against the wall where there was a whispered rent.

Museum: weals and sutures. A protracted era of piercing. Lead of air, much needed alkali and salt of acid. Erected letters and electric fence at the boundary. The axis has strayed. Prizes disgorge: gaudy oriental prints, maps charting the progress of the disease, the diary of his lost year. Leave no bodies within six feet of the surface. The cart tips over. Bodies slide into the pit. There's an intense apathy, but something close to a general strike takes place in several of the surrounding villages. Another of those obscure discharges of harmony occurs at the close. I'm to be modified. A flowering has broken out about the east. Position: arms and legs spreadeagled on both sides. We're doing that all-important thing today. I promise. Take shelter, list flora and fauna. Observe the silence.

The red-beaked crow or jackdaw, obsolete from its cry. That constellation to the north is Andromeda. Consider a bloom whose scent is so-shaped, inclined toward hoof. The inferred notch.
Another chinook skirts the shoreline. Ex votos of all kinds hang about the walls—scarlet hearts, rosaries, the barb of a ray. Shell-tooth. Thoth.

Exteroceptor. Unaccountable events on the surface of the skin. Am still receiving impressions from *outside* the body.
This solution lasts about three to five days. (Go eat.) She says you stand out.

A structure of blank slate: no mosaic pavement, no pilot, no dog, no tomb, no moat, no money, no timbers, no roof. A severed head could not produce noise without a diaphragm and vocal cords. I don't know what happens next. What about her remaining arm. (I can't say.) Withdraw bridge. Steaming arcs of piss rise and fall into the snow. A false conception of fleshy mass is forming in the womb. Modern writers speak of a particular kind of fracture. This they call a contrafissure. A conversion is taking place, a mass drowning.
A match. An equal. The rival. The comparison. A diamond. Black marble, intermediate between great-primer and its double, the archaic or rare. Printing-

type of indeterminate stature. A touchstone. A mark of ivory is sometimes used. There is nothing of him that does not fade, the outcomer.

Maybe a solemn ecclesiastical curse, words recurring to gather in time. Up, and the root of to place. Nightlong spasm on the boards. Insertion of pollen tube, neural crunch of dissenting body. Involuntary clamp at backbite of spine, the solar tangle. Clumps of hail, numbing tooth-grind. Near the lotus hangs the skin of an animal. A man, preferably a youth, is enclosed in a wicker pyramid. Its framework is camouflaged with feathers and leaves. She shows me how on a map. I am at a loss, the lynchpin.

A rent in the wall. Where. From his prison diary—believed lost at sea, believed found.
Night entia. A vast parade ground, light and air. Ajar, with human head.

The beating of wings in the adjoining chamber. Compostela, lascar steersman. Quarter-moon. Emblem of scrip and star-shell. Unsignificance.

Proliferation at floral axis, budding forth of spat. It's not just about face. I shall show you, written in paper. A charge of mental energy is attaching itself to the object. I am convinced of this. Where else—white-hot bolts through the knee, the head. No interval of calm. Deadwood, false keel of temporal purpose.

Bone issue. Partly scrap, the total sum. Layers, linked, a wholesale drowning as by career. Press of tissue within integument of ovum. The pumex stone must be fired and quenched twice in white wine.

Unnamed as flowered. Man-giant tethered at earth at taut cable, by sway above shingle.
The circulation process of an individual capital represents. From various poisons they have absorbed.

Illuminate the parts of the region left in shadow. One light comes athwart the direction of another. Sometimes he does see you, you know, then nothing. Please don't be tempted to comfort him.
I am disused in the names of the body. I am surely son of. Disused in the names of the constellations. Never father, never yet. Flavour, bitter-almond and peach-kernel.
Disused in the names of the meteors. Pyrrhocorax, perhaps from its cry—siderite of the swarm whose radiance. Disused in the names of formation and particle. The breathing in of metal fragments.
Spiral nebula to north, stone-pit nuclei.
Eccaleobion, daughter of.

XXIII

Incipit.

After several generations a tiny pierced body emerges. The new arrival adopts the same attitude: white mark across scalp, a tree facing the wrong way. Stop up the passage.

Epitaph, a phantasy of uncharacteristic stupidity. This chapter may have to be considered. The trail has evaporated. That machine is a primitive incubator (spelling influenced by cease). I am not yet awake. I can confirm the flatness of the earth at every step. They were once spherical in form, rolling out across the karst.

Kingdom, east of sea. I did what I had to.

She says her assailant resembled an ox, a dogling, and a flock of geese. After the introit, the words and the music. She's proclaimed a municipal. One prayer, deconstructed.

A crown of rock balancing above a precipice, the uncut book devoured by lice. Mark the phase of these rhythms. Reset to the beginning, always the preceding—massing in time, with lamp-on signals. Ill at ease with the year, these waves. We lagged behind the rest of the column, axle-deep in soft sand. He cannot be precise due to the lack of certainty. Down in the gully, the rapid sway of foliage, urged on by a finger of wind. This was the only sign of movement.

A measure of distance averaging a single yell is used to span the gulf. We find ourselves in an undefeated ruin. They ordered this pit to be dug. Labour is being withdrawn. Now, follow the track of indices.

Eyeball swallowing warmth from nearest star. I share empathy for the condition, both animal'd and person'd. Rereading this, you have to hand it to him. My heart wants stunning, my head wants impenetrable.

Some reflections on the votive power of fire. You cannot die. All my good works are schismatic. The correct number is seven trillion. I'm betrothed to the enemy. My vigilance goes by a simple name: a grain of sand is enough to rock the boat. I am well within the region. The onset of darkness occurs at a constant time of day. I document and reflect. Since the sextant dropped overboard we navigate by star-work. Amazing examples of gravity around here—sea-cob circling, the background crick of insect life, snapping reptiles. The ripening of fruit underground. Serendipity, guess-warp.

He enters a piano competition. I notice a finger missing. We have to work within constraints of our own invention. Violation quivers, warm to the touch. I'm self-appointed, making something of the silence, halving the scope of chance.

She fiddles with a lock of her hair, manipulating it to a tight twist. Consider all the other candidates. A shawl is thrown across her shoulders. Each island had its little green bays that resisted. None fits the promised number on the docket. Glimpse of pale mediaeval belly.

A deep valley, vacuum moving at superspeed. Functionaries in robes and sandals. You look serenely anxious in your slumber, a breathing oxymoron. We're approaching science fiction. There's a hidden passageway. The world's protected by a transparent dome which grants access to the light. We're looking at teachers and pupils today. Say nothing of the gathering storm. Our centre is destroyed. Scanning gear stands useless around the table, like so much abstract sculpture. A burst of electromagnetic radiation, and he fell from out the clouds.

Colourful mobiles dangle from the ceiling. Existence here possesses. An anvil-headed front is curling in from the southwest. Everyone whispers in voices. A thought passes through the head. Go back to the original negatives.

Lunarscape, multiple eclipse.

Press-ganged. Beyond the workaday. What appears corporeal? Function degenerates under suspicion. He knows this when he learns the use of each word. It had these huge bug eyes (space, comedic). We are lean-yeared. There must be something in your geology. No man ever passes through alive. The correct number is seven hundred and seventy-seven. Now I know what the book means by the shadow of the valley. A figure is writ large in the air above the stage. Its square root is being calculated. That's how I see it. Seal up the capsule, weld it fast. My staff is composed of foreign emissaries—magistrates and land-stewards—infested host. We trek due east. I've been here long before. Pursuit comes down to a methodical plummet into an abyss. The sanatorium overlooks a deep natural harbour. I'm at my appointed place of residence. Having descended to a vast distance, the emphasis now has to shift. The administration carries a whiff of ancestral horse-thief. Back then I was dead to myself. We chance upon a river. To protect the bridge from rust, a fatty secretion lubricates hair and skin. Plant-beings develop. You'd expect her to see reason he muttered. I am shamelessly flawed, a residual clutter of found items. It's perfect. Bring me a more whimsical version of these events. Apply as acid to surface, draw together into a bent form. They uproot themselves and creep out across the landscape. Enjoy the present pattern, your tranquilship. Contract, curl inward to a crook, shrink and give way. All your rights are about to be reversed.

The tale of the toothman. Corresponding morphosis in the circuit of the other.

A patent shoe sits on the exhibit bench. That was old age a voice says. We lie in straight lines radiating outward from a core. Rumours of defenestration. I shuffle over to the counter. She places the tarot. I'm unredeemed, unfutured (libido is frequently symbolized by a horse). Was she involved with her own thoughts of love and death? Through the bulletproof glass I swear my hand on a laminated oath. I shuffle over to the window. Across the partition, the wings of the jurors summon a low buzzing sound. Thirteen in all, foreman in weird kilt of ceramic tile. I am addicted to counting, among things. The mare's placenta was purple.

Insomniac sleep. Death by what is called forth—apnoea, suspension of breathing. That dictionary's out of service. Behold the spine. I never learned a human tongue. Events take place largely within the context of activities (visit the coenobitic life et cetera). The suitors are now permanently beyond reach. I too am out of mind, slowly clinging into a form: warm-sweet fumes, jellied creep of flesh. Ice in flakes or detached pieces.

On the connection between four peculiar sets of signals from independent orbits millions of miles apart. There's an element of escapism here. I'm so readily assimilated. Calligraphy also flourished. I'm proud of that W in the night sky he says. You should be she replies. Meaning is only half attained by words. I hope we still. There's a coal fountain at every street corner, spurting hallmarks. Space in this labyrinth is composed of moving units (viz. madness and exile). This complementary world of different things happening at the same time is very familiar. Its core business is growing. The hero of the book is the book itself—not readily at prayer, but listening to the rain as it pours without.

Permeable limestone quarry. A shift of emphasis from idealism to nominalism. Airborne drainage, a caution for simulation. She's aflame, subtle-bodied. There have been complaints about the dust (note the mouthlike pores). Three adjacent houses were hit. We make a party and set off. I don't know where. Another clash is announced in which five prisoners are taken. I haven't been in a position before. She comes galloping straight toward me. The branches quiver. Smoke streams from the horsehead. I'm surprisingly orthodox, always seeking confirmation of past usage, verity.

He emerges from the ruins of his cellar and looks up. I delight in the simple curvature of the earth. Still, it seems we've been outmanoeuvred. Up by five percent, but did it say why? We have had our eight days.

Lead her back to water. Consider the angle of curvature, the incipient anarchy of any recognizable shape. The counterpoint of sympathy and hatred is sounded out in gentle drum-beats. She floats on her back at the centre of an expanse of water. Orange flames spread out across her body. Medics push down with latex palms, all the force they can muster. She sinks slowly into the smothering lake and is extinguished.

A column of books was wedged between ceiling and floor.

Yes, I know, I know. What does he find in here that is so amusing? There's only ship-biscuit, no liquid. The men employed in the hold and on the rigging work till long after dark. One foreign tongue murmurs, the wail of seamews stunned on a warm updraught.

A rope has been noosed to a distant object. I gather myself into resemblance. The book was invented. I am giving an account of these events. The narrator is a teller of legends and tall tales, histories of uncertain origin, packed with immaterial figures. Warp the vessel toward us.

He invents the odd adjective and the odd noun. Crippled and split are the sloping roofs, courtyard in shadow below. He draws a pistol from his cape, a pearl-handled 4.5mm. The dress code is to the nines. Shattered glass is strewn across the floor. Let me make the first move. I open you. You are unreadable. On through the gate to the sea. A far cry, another guise. Such unnatural devices. In the end I sent a cheque.

Northern milltown. A disappointed bridge, oily canals. Nothing here. The open front of the set represents as solid a wall as the other three sides. See them pass in a long funeral procession, the heroes of this situation. Everyone must raise his head, assume responsibilities. I am enisled, strictly and forever anon.

Vibration of rocks and sundry items, the rustle of language. Cum spatters into a shallow metal receptacle. A bond is being set between the temporal line and the tendinous hand.

Remote headland. Address with purpose a biased object. Listen, all this came to pass within a single day. On the whole continues. Ever since, work has divided critics. There's a mechanical digger down there at the eighth gulf-hole. He says we're descended from a common ancestor. (Why don't you just walk away?) My chosen subject is the history of sleep from eighteen forty-two to nineteen thirty-nine. It isn't writing, it's supplication, the desire to come home to somewhere.

Supple numbness in groin. Nerve cable pressed by enclosing hollow of bone. I thought you meant me for a second. The guest-rope tautens as the vessel drifts away. There follows a series of ludicrously specific notes about how to perform. An ideal adversary's strength and beauty lie in its ability to mimic its detractors. Nonetheless, impending collapse, an encompassing. These aren't exact words.

A lion, rampant. Intersex creatures. Ghost of the sun and further on the judgement scene. Utilize hot-box detection kit, isolation located beneath panel. A rush of light or flame, seditious politicking.

Beneath a raised deck at the fore-end of the vessel is the crew's quarter. Ice in flakes about the rigging. Shifting winds sent the ships drifting apart. We conduct a private interview. Behold the samples of flora and fauna preserved in formaldehyde. Be still and listen. Quiet the hatch and descend. In every hammock an irrepressible erection, air fetid with dried meat flatus. An imaginary country is being revisited. The entire population of the town crowded onto the jetty at their departure, a bristling ribbon stretching out into the sea. I picked up my money and left. He and his crew had lost contact with their world. No musician could portray the sense of space and depth down there. You don't need narrative to understand. Historically, this has been wrongly interpreted as a returning curse.

Visit voidoscope, the futurist theme palace. Surely it means something if somebody were like another.

White triangle still visible from window, communion spade rammed deep to bedrock. Beneath, a coal-seam, representing. We mount the tower. This position should form a right angle with the direction of the main line of retreat. She says there's a fourth dimension to the stage. The text is merely paying off some previous demonic possession. That funeral is a thing I will never forget. List the syntactic reversals found that day—the interplay between the gravity of earth and the magnetism of the moon. Claw your way back to the summit. The book vindicates its author.

Green branch revealing stamen for half year closure. Her box of seabird eggs. And from there to the cemetery, returning only to weep by the hearth. I don't want to listen to any more of this. She stops suddenly at the second floor. The ideal mineral is number twenty-two. Opal as a petrifying agent has replaced the woody structure in this specimen. I was once renowned as one of the players. Brace yourself. Reinforcements spring open at an outward joint of the fortification, each of the turrets a splendid illumination. I have appointed myself scholar, broadcaster, conductor of electricity, transcriber and editor. The circles of light at our flank are deflected from dental mirrors. Unconsciously, I find myself rubbing the scar tissue from my descent into the gaming room. I resemble use. The hands are not coordinated, a precise imprecision.

He soon fell into a pattern of composing at the weekends and on holy days. I assemble such scraps—lead piping juxtaposed with herringbone cloud, signals of unease. And what the hell are you doing here? Sides can switch very quickly indeed. Before it gets better it's going to get a lot worse. I'm converting notes on the page, responding to suggestion by believing or doing the opposite (this has nothing to do with your case). You're running through this too quickly. It demands resistance, consequently it seeks resistance. We have achieved the opening words, the introit.

First murmur of a good tide. Drop it down a notch or two. I did not wish this distraction: opening nonesuch glass et cetera. We burrowed our way out using a cylindrical mechanism.

Nothing's going to happen. Sting quota up one percentage point. The two messengers arrive. Sound now above eighty decibels. Don't get excited. Save your powder for the interlude of mourning. A scream carries across the heath. Bone is exposed—brilliant, smooth and white.

Turn your attention to the night shift. He did in fact live in that attic for many years. A factory whistle pierces the freezing air enveloping a remote industrial town.

Reinvent a sense of pathos. I've seen that a million times he said disappointed.

The photographs have been cropped. Locations, context, identities are never revealed. They will be down here forever. Can you follow every decision? Is this rational for you? He might still come true if the body holds up.

It was delivered during the interval, a redundant symbol. It had gestated in the womb for just seven. Everything is reputed. A hymenopterous insect is remarkable for its loud chirping sound. We walk about the park admiring the grass and the air. (Hello are you hiding in there?) Perforate the remaining lung. She says I resemble a complete matrix of probabilities, sacred work. Within is a long way down. I'm working my way back to a six-way basic. It's a gamble— shrunk and ejected, spelled backwards. Magical practice is devoid of scholarly or religious context. I have sliced the waters of illness at the evening, when the hills close in.

Inferiae. He can be counted among the long-dead, aperture open. He hears nothing. (Yes blackened tongue protruding.) I don't aim to be convincing. A storm can be said to rage uncontrollably. A giant twister hoovers up the town. Can anybody grant this quality a name? I appear ninth in line of carnage. First this silent piece came later. Conversation was difficult and correspondence virtually ceased. The wager was a heavy burden. These forms present futures not easily explained. He seems surprised to see the two of us standing there, side by side, staring into the distance. I've never met him before, but I would recognize myself anywhere. In other news I have no memory of this. I lie within the remaining figure. Ignore exterior voice, then quit. Simulate the central nervous system. I'll sign anything you put in front of me. I don't want to understand. (Are there macrophones, then?) It boils. Is it a triangle? It is triangular in shape. How much time we've lost. It's like an arctic three in a circle. I watched my life in a trance. I could see right across the islands. Adjacent to the graves is a landing strip. We're creeping dangerously close to plagiarism. But there is also a gentleness here that is unfamiliar, of a place that's just begging to be photographed. So much time has been erased. I was always the last to arrive. Imagine being out in this every day? Folk say he's just got back from Egypt. I could do without too much blood on my hands. If thou canst nod, speak too. We are about to be bolted on as a supplement. An object is underneath us, the giant fluorescent hinge. Air leaks from the atmosphere. We're on our way up. That's the man. That's the spirit. He is now away on leave. Twister due south over the sea, a cone drilling into the horizon. Get out as fast you can, get the old pins moving. Ancestors are breaking through to the interior cavity. You can hear them at low frequency, low tide. Sounds are not represented by single letters. The tap of my fluke is death he wrote. We are at the intersection of cross-reefs, carrying sulphides.

A belief in constructive retrogression to earlier states.

She suspends another forty minutes of her life. The title means the boy with the magic wand. What could contain the seeds of all possible forms? This is backbreaking work: save, slaughter, decide. It's feared that many were swept out to sea. He seizes the music of an earlier era and compels us to listen. I lead a careless life. We're down to the dregs of the war loan. This has to be the penultimate stratagem. Infantry was established eighty years ago, and has persisted. I'm next in line. Comes a sudden command, greasy with ancient tears. The score is eighteen. Our legs knock together like hooked hams. The next game has to be the last. A defensive shutter descends, the clatter of leg-armour. My fingers reach out for hers. The other contestant sports an iron neck-ring. In the market square sits an old pillory and yoke. All her belongings were packed into a removal van. She turns and flees the doorstep, white with ash. An opera has been named after her. Let's see now who's prepared to sell up and leave.

Nobody likes someone who sticks to the facts. We can go very far on very little. O my ears. We're countermined, an exemplary detonator. The whole piece lasts about five hours. She trudges off across the shingle desert, mattress folded into the crook of her arm. She's electric, the complex. But there's been no messenger to tell us of that.

Dawn. Mark my word. A lone hand is being played out by aggregate. Warp the vessel toward the asteroid. A birthmark is unwrapped, distant Rorschach.

Is no longer move, lady. Laughter without. Each evening was ceremoniously sealed with red wax. Better too cold than too warm. An evident problem with singularity can be detected in her speech patterns. A funnel of glass is set at a right angle to the pier, the only line of retreat. The others are helping a nurse carry a large panting dog along the promenade. I am lauded as officially sick. She works now for the diocese. We swing to and fro through circuits of jurisdiction. Words come, irregular and interrupted. It doesn't stack up. The iris opens wide, too wide for the light. A significant step has been taken (more stolen, in truth). I am not obliged to speak to you. She now works for the plurality. I think we were supposed to forget about all this in time—plane trees and fog, fecal matter on kilt and suchlike. You deserve all the money you can lay your hands on.

Ten twenty-one. We could pick out painted ammunition boxes and broken crates—a used clothes mountain, roving edgeland. A woman clutches a sheaf of receipts. This oracle, it asks you a lot of difficult questions¬. How dwindled have become our grand predilections. We have embarked upon a work that will eventually turn into the planets. No, it answers, none. Dead remarked the doctor absently.

Slash customers. (Still finding typos.) Thin skin of paper cup. Fingers and palm warmed by heat convection. Turn deasil, anti to withershins. I recollect last night, with police. Good morning, here is a cello concerto by the unknown man.

One of the lips of a stoma. Hips swivel forward to raise rump. Include the guard-cell and the taunting.

Black-crowned night-heron distant at median tide, glistening sheets of wet silt. Rock ledge exposed with sea-wrack, the bladder family. She stands in the booth with a guitar and a box of facial tissue. (Are spectators permitted to observe other people drowning?) Sound now at creep in small sections.
Clearly there are still decisions to be made. I concur. This can be summed up in scant words, none of which has won any currency to date.

A laying on of stones. The corpse's belly is concave, suggestive. Sticky proboscis sucking like a sponge. (This is a variety in which the glume does not adhere to the grain.) The bier is set down before a pyre of cork smouldering on the shingle. A thin film collects here, all the piffle and the dust. Reanimation occurs above magnitude seven. Isn't this what you always wanted, an ordeal?
After an absence of years he appears before the remains, believed murdered. One player lays all his carbon on the table. As folk say, concentration of mental energy into one channel. Even had I remembered before, what could I have done?
To make fast a boat.

Horse latitudes. Two brothers are chained together and await execution. The anaesthetist accepts the unconscious as part of his everyday routine. I sit on a bench at the fountain's rim. My share has been reduced to five. Our desolation is complete, the dreaded light-off signal. (I wonder what they imagine feudalism to be?) A trail of lighter fuel spatters the dank passageway. To escape relegation, all they have to do is ignore their recent history. It yielded to pressure as if foliage, and I fell through.

Sir,

A lady appears to have flung herself from the rotunda. Fear shall never set foot again et cetera. The tool appears both feather *and* shaft. A flat circular object thickens toward the centre. She was once here, waiting, having memorized the formula. My opinion is in no way altered. That wax completely obscures the title on the spine. Discourse has reached my ears. Maybe I should step out once and for all, contend by flame. Discuss this sequence.

Pieces of old bark are kindled at the altar. A menu balances on sticky formica. I lack composure, harbour a derangement of secretions and ill-humour. Time is an hour and two minutes. The inscription read corelike fruit of stone immutable.

After a little insanie they fled, tag and rag. Sudden taste of mercury to tip of tongue. In terms of wealth or reputation, I have never had anything to lose.

Render me back to a time well before the first stint of isolation. Pass me that box. Seal the orifice. Pass the iodine. The prince dies happy in her arms in the end. Pyramids were once clad in polished marble that dazzled brilliantly in the desert sun. The upturned eyeball would melt. That was the idea back then. A body emerges, piecemeal, a disorder with four transparent wings. Let's have a foretaste.

Keening could be heard within the earth. I pray for alone. One by one we're extinguishing all the candles. Hers snuffed out on the return journey. She lives unblessed to this day. (Where are all the men in your family?) The carpet was coated in gravel. Calculate to the second how long this walk would have taken. General terms have no corresponding reality either in or out of the mind, being mere words.

The dragon-fish and sea-moth are also encased in bony plates. Elements, it's all we've got. After this I can no longer gaze straight ahead of me. I believe I am back among the living.

Febrifuge. A colony of unicellular organisms. Strict curfew. A compound perennial, closely allied—posthuman. Taut circuits of jurisdiction. Don't worry. I anticipate your appetites and have brought along a little something (the past participle of slink). Justice has miscarried. Note the slightly swelling outline of the shaft.

A god-inspired possession, or the like. In her cast shadow some animal springs to life. I'm not done staring yet.

The bulk. Collapse of the book. One born under the planet, now obsolete. He has framed himself into a cul-de-sac. I can smell gas. He died in a lodging room up on the ridge. Never push against the fourth dimension. There's just one colour and black and white. We've been caught hollowing out the evidence. In the event that the theatre goes bust, I recommend the following course of action. I know from my spies that this garrison is hexed. We are well within sight of conquest. We talk like a body of vassals and tenants, a thicket of citation. Typically, he is capable of helping us but incapable of realizing the danger this entails. The infantrymen stare right through me in the silence. Suicide monkeys. I daren't move. Quit this place before it happens. Stand ye still and deliver up your goods and chattels. Disconnect. It's the end as we know it. He denounces himself, such perfect long-breathed stillness. I perform false genuflexion. If strapped, he can make a decent fist of sucking himself off.

Chloride of silver, fused. A tricorne hat. Whiff of rosewater. Our numbers are a perfect match. I measure wavelength, the click and hum of the nervous system. Compare yourself to the speed of the surrounding medium—motes of dust, particles, atoms of air. Tiny small things. You're breaking up. (Relax, we're not doing science.) I speak too soon. I've got that creeping feeling. Scribe as well as time permits, in excess of nothing.

I think it would do one good to venture outside. The first element is always doubtful.

Henge beside a foggy bank. Affordable pasture. I broke my toe on the edge of the pallet. Guess at a working title. These are actual historical personages who once lived. Now for the long walk out, over the burial mound and into the trees. How long can we outlast this terrain? We spent a day in the exposed watering place, next to the fire, waiting for news. Lichen and moss cling to rocks slippery underfoot. The primary shapes appear bruised. My companion is characterized by bloodness. Our paths run roughly thus, zigzag and meander. We live symbiotically.

Late arrival. A fortification has been built by besiegers about the place invested. Even then he is swept off his feet with passion for another. This is derived from the pricks placed against the melody, in some senses.

Undergo trial by randomization. The scaffold rises, converging to a single point.

Scourge, the lone runner. Long cilium with whiplike appendage. Turn left here, sharp. I would never alter my own life.

A trek across a landscape of azurite and olivine, crystals of gypsum. The promised electrical storm arrives, cracking open the temporal line. (Don't bother checking, my science is exact.) Repetition is like a vein running through this lyric. He says we must demand. Do you want more meetings? By this point in history one can say anything. Place your finger on the jugular. Consider the secondary experience that accompanies every moment. It's about five years too long. Substance eludes, covers up more than it reveals. We may divide at the next station. Whose hero was infected with a micro-organism? The image is fading fast. Once he entered the woods I lost sight of him altogether. We will never know what happened that day. We will never know what was in his mind. Parallels meet because time is curved.

Abandoned earth with a neat row of core samples. At the farthest reaches of the cave limestone marvels glisten in our torch beams. (Who fell in love and committed suicide after being repulsed?) A ring is blessed against flesh, against falling sickness. Clatter of grappling-irons—darting sandpipers, stalactites and stalagmites, that weird boy from the film with a lantern. Albino lizards. We tore up the sheets to make a rope ladder. There's a tubular hollow cut into the chalk, ram full of ants. Heavy water and superheated hydrogen are being pumped into the mechanism. There's a sudden horizontal flip across the screen. A cavity lined with crystals is growing innards. Hark, a mariner's soundingline.

Facetiae secreted in briefcase. Desired subject: the one who lives or serves on land. Which mythical figure lacked experience of seafaring? Let's give it up. I want to go home.

We're welcomed back after a lapse of years, but come unstuck on the twelfth floor. That's the way it goes.

Godcocked, lovely view. Then a clear piping note. We're going through a process of renovation. Those people gathered on the other side of the street are sight-seers, hoping for a glimpse. I no longer feel motivated to say anything.

Eruptions on skin. Legs cross and uncross. Knot of flesh, wobble of under-thigh at right angle to solid earth. A spine emerges from her back. Of a sudden, the core falls out.

Equator. Much graffiti, chalk scrawled on the mottled surface of the passage-way. Proper eights. Lurching tower blocks, runaway men, a cartoon griffin. Things do all that chemical stuff for you—the spangle of green mineral stuff as the industrial zooms past. I am struggling away from sense. (I agree, you'd think.) The image held in memory must be very far from here, or much later on in time. Masters are quite human. They get sick and die. They know.

The eyelids quiver as if blind. You must lead with the foot chosen by your opponent. A frame of wood for supporting the dead body has been constructed. Let's start with an elegy, adding little countermelodies as we go. Passing between the two hands, defused

seaagape

seaanchor

seaash

seaasphodel

seaaster

seaattack

seaawe

seababel

seabait

seabalanced

seabank

seabar

seabased

seabat

seabathed

seabeam

seabear

seabeast

seabeaten

seabecalmed

seabed

seabees

seabeggar

seabeing

seabell

seabelt

seabent

seabind

seabird

seabitten

seablackened

seabladder

seablast

seabled

seablessed

seablight

seablind

seablink

seablithe

seablitz

seabloom

seablown

seablue

seablur

seaboard

seabook

seaboot

seaborer

seaborder

seaborn

seabottle

seabottom

seabounded

seabrace

seabranch

seabreach

seabread

seabred

seabrief

seabright

seabrink

seabrim

seabroken

seabuilt

seabull

seaburial

seaburr

seabusiness

seacable

seacactus

seacalf

seacalm

seacanard

seacanker

seacape

seacapped

seacard

seacarriage

seacat

seacatch

seacave

seacell

seacentipede

seachange

seachameleon

seachart

seachecked

seachest

seacircled

seaclam

seaclamp

seaclay

seacliff

seaclock

seacluster

seaclutter

seacoal

seacoaster

seacob

seacobble

seacock

seacockroach

seacolander

seacommand

seacompassed

seaconcubine

seaconquest

seaconvolvulus

seaconvulsion

seacoral

seacorpse

seacrack

seacrafty

seacrag

seacraw

seacray

seacrossing

seacrow

seacrust

seacry

seacue

seacunny

seacup

seacurfew

seacurse

seacut

seacypress

seadanger

seadark

seadart

seadate

seadeath

seadeserted

seadevil

seadike

seadisc

seadistemper

seadivided

seadock

seadog

seadoor

seadove

seadown

seadrag

seadragon

seadream

seadregs

seadrift

seadriven

seadrone

seadrug

seaduel

seadune

seadusk

seadust

seadybbuk

seaeagle

seaear

seaeclogue

seaedge

seaeel

seaegg

seaemperor

seaerrant

seaescape

seaeyed

seaface

seafamiliar

seafanned

seafarer

seafeathered

seafed

seafever

seafew

seafig

seafight

seafinger

seafire

seafisher

seaflame

seaflash

seaflat

seaflea

seaflight

seaflogged

seaflooded

seafloor

seaflower

seafoam

seafog

seafolk

seafolly

seafort

seafound

seafoxed

seaframed

seafreed

seafret

seafrog

seafrontage

seafrontier

seafroth

seafur

seagate

seagalliwasp

seaghost

seagibberish

seagill

seagilliflower

seagirt

seaglass

seagod

seagoing

seagolem

seagrasswrack

seagrave

seagreeninc

seagrey

seagrief

seagrim

seagroan

seaground

seagrown

seagrudge

seagauge

seaguard

seagulf

seahaar

seahag

seahaired

seahanger

seahard

seahare

seahaven

seahawk

seahaze

seahead

seaheart

seaheavy

seaheir

seahell

seaherz

seahog

seaholy

seahome

seahood

seahorizon

seahorse

seahound

seahouse

seahull

seahung

seahusk

seaice

seainsect

seaisle

seaitch

seajacked

seajarring

seajockey

seakale

seakeeper

seakelp

seakept

seakey

seakindle

seakin

seakindly

seaking

seakite

seaknot

sealabile

sealack

sealamp

sealamprey

sealantern

sealapack

sealapse

sealark

sealatter

sealattice

sealaurel

sealaw

sealeague

sealeak

sealeavened

sealed

sealedger

sealeech

sealeg

sealemon

sealent

sealeopard

sealess

sealetter

sealevel

sealift

sealight

sealike

sealily

sealimb

sealimit

sealine

sealing

sealink

sealipped

sealit

sealiver

sealizard

sealock

sealocust

sealog

sealonging

sealoom

sealord

sealost

sealouse

sealull

sealung

sealurch

seamade

seamanite

seamannered

seamantis

seamap

seamargin

seamarked

seamarsh

seamary

seamaster

seamatch

seamatted

seamaw

seameasure

seamembrane

seamen

seamerged

seameteor

seamew

seamile

seamilk

seamist

seamoit

seamolten

seamonk

seamonkey

seamonoceros

seamonster

seamorph

seamorse

seamort

seamoss

seamost

seamoth

seamountain

seamouthed

seamurmur

seamushroom

seamusic

seanail

seanarcissus

seanavel

seance

seanecked

seaneedle

seanet

seanettle

seanetwork

seanile

seanymph

seaoak

seaonion

seaooze

seaorache

seaoracle

seaorange

seaorb

seaore

seaotter

seaowl

seaoxeye

seapacked

seapage

seapainter

seapanther

seaparted

seapartition

seapass

seapassage

seapassenger

seapath

seapeace

seapeach

seapee

seapelf

seapelican

seapen

seapencil

seapeople

seaperched

seaperil

seaperson

seapie

seapiece

seapierced

seapig

seapike

seapilot

seapin

seapipe

seapit

seaplace

seaploy

seapoacher

seapocked

seapocket

seapoint

seapoppy

seapore

seapower

seapressed

seapriest

seapsi

seapull

seapurchase

seapurple

seapurse

seapurslane

seaquake

seaquag

seaqualm

seaquarium

seaquilibrium

seaquill

searaft

searag

searage

searagged

searaid

searaft

searake

searange

searant

searat

searaven

searay

seareach

seareader

searebel

seared

seareed

seareived

searescue

searesounding

seareturn

searevolt

searider

searift

searim

searing

searisk

searoad

searobbed

searobed

searocked

searocket

searod

searoll

searoom

searose

searounded

searoute

searove

searuff

searum

searunner

searush

seasac

seasalt

seasand

seasatyr

seasaw

seascallop

seascalp

seascape

seascarce

seascare

seascarred

seascent

seaschlep

seaschloss

seascorpion

seascramble

seascrape

seascud

seascum

seascurf

seascurvy

seaseeded

seaseiche

seasement

seasent

seaserf

seaserpent

seaservant

seaset

seashaman

seashanty

seasharp

seasheathed

seashell

seashimmer
          seashindig
                    seashine
                              seashoal
                                        seashod
                                                  seashot
                                                            seashrike
                                                  seashrill
                                        seashrine
                              seasickening
                    seasidepict
          seasidereal
seaskin
          seasleeve
                    seaslide
                              seaslope
                                        seasmelted
                                                  seasmoulder
                                                            seasnail
                                                  seasnake
                                        seasnap
                              seasnatch
                    seasniper
          seasnot
seasnuff
          seasold
                    season
                              seasonnet
                                        seasong
                                                  seasonticket
                                                            seasoot
                                                  seasore
                                        seasorrow
                              seasouled
                    seasounding
          seasown
seaspeed
          seaspider
                    seaspike
                              seaspin
                                        seaspine
                                                  seaspirit
                                                            seaspit

seaspleen

seaspout

seaspring

seaspur

seaspurge

seaspurt

seaspied

seasquall

seasquill

seastack

seastaff

seastar

seastate

seastealth

seastep

seastock

seastone

seastore

seastorm

seastory

seastrand

seastranded

seastranger

seastream

seastrewn

seastroke

seastuff

seasubject

seasuck

seasulphur

seasun

seasure

seasurge

seasurgeon

seaswallowed

seaswill

seaswine

seaswing

seatack

seatale

seatamarisk

seatang

seatangle

seatempered

seaterm

seaterminal

seathief

seathin

seathorn

seathread

seathrift

seaticket

seatime

seatoad

seatod

seatongued

seatorch

seatorn

seatort

seatortoise

seatossed

seatow

seatown

seatrack

seatract

seatrader

seatraffic

seatrain

seatransported

seatrap

seatread

seatree

seatrench

seatrifoly

seatrumpet

seattica

seatunnel

seaturned

seaturtle

seaumbrella

seaunicorn

seaurchin

seavalve

seavampire

seavein

seavine

seavoiced

seawail

seawake

seawalk

seawalled

seawand

seawandering

seawane

seawant

seawar

seaward

seaware

seawarp

seawarrior

seawarth

seawary

seawashed

seawasp

seawatch

seawave

seawax

seaway

seaweary

seaweasel

seaweaver

seawedded

seawell

seawhaup

seawhip

seawhistle

seawide

seawife

seawillow

seawind

seawing

seawise

seawitted

seawoe

seawolf

seaword

seawork

seawormwood

seaworn

                                    seaworthy
                                              seawrack
                                                        seawreath
                                              seawreck
                                    seawright
                          seayarn
                seayearn
        seayen
seayoke
        seazement
              seazone.

How now the road, what's happening? He was about to throw a pair of dice against the wall. I do require a certain mindset. That was someone, unidentified. It's becoming another country, a surgical impossibility. There were lots of people in the no room. Dew is used to wash any debris off unlickable body parts.

A bitter fluid is secreted by the liver. Now working in short bursts. I am as one wakened suddenly who struggles to recollect, and can capture nothing but sense. There's some aspect of physics here, the conversion of matter to energy. You might say that we had taught him the rules of the alphabet. We're trying to build something that doesn't exist (a local payment of an uncertain torture). Build-up of rust on tongue. That's the whole point of the message.

We have a reduced appetite for risk. Our vessel docks at an unknown port. We are underinsured against securities. There's no choice but to flip over to the other side. Her story makes no mention of the massacre and the humiliations endured (skip to final three paragraphs). I could see this huge wing sticking up out of the straw in the hold. It's not like a proper structured company, this. They could not have pressed one more into that pit.

Icicle-like pendants of calcium carbonate. He was once so precise. Haematite acts earthy and ochreous when deposited under sedative. One of our advisors will soon be with you, the impossible. Composite symbols make up a number of the individual signs. Each represents. Now make haste to forget—the maws of kites and exit ghosts.
A pattern is scored by long parallel wheel marks in the gravel. Charnel-houses are a speciality. The head had been extinguished. Stem of I wail, to see. A nugatory leap into the unknown.

Sticky bomb. A séance. We can't say anything until the situation actually happens. I feel so guilty sometimes. (Isn't that what one does say?) I picked it up at birth. I was so like light. I mortalize her. There are dark times ahead. This object

350

has a broken neck. Composition: variorum loops and rattles, retakes. A miniature of guesswork and calculation—five uncharactered pieces.

The material of which I'm composed is being weighed and measured. Something is clearly missing. Three ropes fasten us to the earth. These stories point to an anatomy of the figures: the king of eternity, the prince of everlastingness. Miles away, then a greyhound ran into me.

A second chain is fastened to our vessel. An elbow was severed in the collision. We're in tow. Ready yourselves (I'm a rubbish waitress but I know my knots and ropes). The irregular report of a firing squad could be heard across the bay. I'm temporarily at rest, lying between two parked cars. I always shun the short-term deal, preferring the full matrix of probabilities. What do you mean by a complete list of rules for the deployment of a piece? One will witness only constant attempts to escape, airborne stunts bound together by contrails of red smoke. I know how unconvincing this must sound. She's wheeled in. I fear I push too hard. She's persuaded she has a new role to play. I decide to leave till completion is secured. Keep a safe distance. Every inch of ground notched between individuals is a small victory. We are concerned here with unobtainable desires. This is a free-flowing fancy, a brand of esoteric fellowship. Things can get too interesting. I have proved a lamentable nurse. Whichever situation I find myself in harbours everything I need. Discreetly as is possible with such things, I bury the head in the ground. According to legend she rushed straight off a nearby cliff. The white parasol's her signature tonight. It accompanied her descent. It's said there are armies of ants and all sorts down there—suffocating tunnels, spurts of foam, cruel and gravity-splashed rocks. In the back of my mind I think she must be someone else. This is all I ever wanted. A vignette is no piece of theatre, structure as intimidation. (I can't do everything.) Nonetheless, it unravels conflict, liberates occult power. The fifteenth simulation is murderous adultery.

One of the specimens has lost its crutch. He was once chief detonator. I could talk to them and understand their speech. It's a long journey out to the sea. Conviction goes a long way. Pursue divination by freezing time. I have spent mine, on the steadfast duty of watching.

Digression, the turn of the crew. An organism that lives in absence of free oxygen. The interrogation room was lit by a single fluorescent strip. Tell me how you know my friend simply repeated. His brow is disfigured (distant thunder). No one lives now on the island of herm. Vague murmur to south, without warning other than a small white cloud. Vibrations are picked up by the antlers and transmitted in coded form. I can pass on nothing of use. Displacement is anticipated. Wait a minute. One of the volunteers is opened. Did it have time to give its name? At the apex of the island is an extinct volcano. I'm new to this cardiac thing. If I can compose three new transformations, it's said the carousel of phantasies will stop.

He is not making, he's illustrating existing ideas. This is not the same as making (when, for example, I am teaching him ethics). If it can really be done, the complete scription of everything, well.

Next, a sound like a spiked contrivance for climbing mountains or telegraph poles or walking on ice being dropped.

Objection.

The chorus is mute and speaks to no one. In the shop window she is busy stretching a bathing costume over a mannequin's torso. I have an opinion. It's a wasterife course. I am precisely where I always wanted to be. It tastes very different, the artificial stem grown in the petri dish. What else remains to be done? I tighten the bulb. She films in the stairwell. (It's amazing how slow the English are.) The act of writing is a form of dissent. That distinctive taste is pig-fat. A bell chimes, as if in slow motion. Every noise appalls me, like the fingering of discordant keys. A piece of metal, bent at both ends, binds everything together.

The door to the yes room was locked. They have set themselves up as potential targets of the movement. Words are a law unto themselves. The art of painting follows a difficult path: harmonic frequencies, shavings of time, uncharged particles of the same mass (i.e. neither). I have reached the same conclusion. I once moved, but only slightly. Teeth are being ground. We're named after neglect, named after anything to hand. With the interment of his little friend he buried forever the last of his line. Any residue is abandoned to the light.

Shifting of bodies from furrow to seed-burst. These beings are no creaghters, as other humans. The soles of my feet curl inward. Hold on.

Spasm at hollow of thigh and calf. Traces can be found within the readings. Spasm at base of spine, the nerve junction. The countryside is trawled for fugitives. That fishbone tattoo behind the ear reminds me. I must eat. The head swells. I embrace all forms of making. No one has noticed. (Goodness sakes would a runaway serf run south, into the sea?) Her head swivels through three hundred and sixty degrees. It was like a doll's house inside. We're going from strength to strength. The weapon was a four-bladed device for hurling an assailant. Thou comest, being renewed each day. Lots are drawn to elect a champion, someone called forth from the multitude. Draw your own conclusions. But yes, go ahead. (Is that it?) They always expect some fresh attack on the part of an invisible enemy. In the hope of earning a reduction in time for good conduct, I persist. You've got nine lives. Any object can be traumatic for some, a bland experience for others. Boredom becomes me—a peculiarly detached air, specially adapted for every occasion. I've done nothing to speak of. That disc is completely obscuring the title page. What places, what people have we come to? A medicinal plant is used to counteract the illusion of concavity.

Thrown for distance. Offerings to the manes of the dead. When an end is nigh I make big changes.

The interastral body. Himself became the agent or vehicle of revelation. Demand is high, so too the risks. The late afternoon sunlight casts its frail rays over floating specks of dust. Human beings have thoughts and feelings and a will like ours. I confess. I have made much use of the waves.

Now, a flicker behind the expedient face of vagueness—as of lines in the spectrum, consonant or vowel sounds, faulted strata.

Join the three remaining originals together. The undergrowth creaks. This is it, the headlong rush toward a close. Everything is executed piecemeal, even the conclusion. From the lead mule to the end of the wagon train is one hundred and fifty kilometres. All of this should be delivered in a deep monotonous burr. At the bottom of the box of firecrackers I find a note: any magnetic content rises to meet the body floating above it. A very low frequency transmitter was used to communicate with the substitute. It's better to experience things than ideas. If I fix my eyes first on the corners, a appears in front and b behind, and vice versa. You should be able to recognize your own type here, the last stand of a haunted animal as it faces down the whole quarter. This feels like ten minutes to me, the space between two columns.

All these vessels were once called living tropes. The less said about this the better. Cobblestones rain down from the rooftops. All things can be divided for easy recognition into four groups, based on their characteristic habits. For example, how can I make sure that I don't get lost? It turns over pebbles on the beach in search of food (the state of being without a claimant). Don't go outside. The dark air between us slowly starts to hum like radio waves.

Brittle lace of skull-plate. Of iron, chalybite, ferrous carbonate. Another centenary is being celebrated. The colours on display are black, brown and red. When compressed it behaves like graphite, at other times like clay. Barite roses, resulting from the weathering of limestone, are common (recall that night with the armies racing ever closer). Tiny fibres nestling in the palm of her hand, she moves over to the window, where the light is. This statement was intended to mean I call forth life.

Whereas he's in the habit of sitting and waiting. Another rehearsal takes place quite soon. These errors were once a tool for striking riots. Cover his shattered face with oilcloth. If other men can stay sober on this watch, you can. The exterior walls of the structure are clad in stone. A scaffold rises about the building. Come nightfall, my heart turns to beat at the eardrum. His existence reminds me of the fragility of death.

One man says I am stuck in a loop. He has tubes coming out of here and here and here.

Usurpatrix. She things with conviction. I think of these two as family, a symbolic constellation infecting the psyche. The guest-rope hangs limply over the side of the vessel. Activities lend structure and rhythm to the day.

Two zones noted for their long calms. There's a one in ten chance of waking up in the fourth dimension. (Where is he now she wakes and screams.) The chief players are the animals, birds and insects of childhood. Our first difficulty is one of translation. A brief interlude is over. Circling and circling, whether I speak or no, I am still not understood.

Strange days. The bartender sees me and moves casually down toward us. Sentences emerge in a laboured manner, with a lack of understanding impaled upon them. This is becoming very technical, but the nearest thing to a main course you're likely to get. Slanting light plays through—manna-ash, edible fragments, seeds of vaporized men. Grains of glass. Imagine a solidity.

I should make more use of ellipsis. Anything advantageous falls one's way, by-and-by. One line of priests stretched back five centuries to Byzantium. What is it, this gift? Stones in every shoe, my dear pocket. Take no prisoners and never come back.

Total epiphany. She loses everything and flings herself into the sea. Your own ancestors do not appear in the archive. You have the power to stop me thinking what should not be thought. On route an elbow was sheared off. The word epitaph is nailed to the title page. I'm full of such microdramas and subtle delicacies. Doubtless these furnish points of departure toward a given situation. Right now I'm looking for night work—cardiograms, anything. This is composed upon the basis of my field-notes. Time makes a pass. Cairns of caged flint are stacked high to hold back the land. The monetary system is based on the troy ounce, variously reckoned to suit the reckoner. It's the soul, stupid. In the end we won on penalties.

I have brought coral in lieu of the cat question. A reinforced circumstance is seeping through the perforations. It's such a privilege to hold an object in my hands once more. Seven, we see, then foreclosure.

Usage is scant. We endured the first performance through the agency of incorrect physics. Is this situation ranked as possible or impossible? Numerous combinations have been forgotten. I utilize the lesion. That explains the strange mood abroad—electricity in the air, ozone at the foreshore. I can't get started. Everything I hear sounds the essence of tango. Before writing was discovered we spoke the past by using the word after, and for the future the word before. This gave me a kind of confidence because a feather isn't a normal brush. The story expires before your very eyes. It hinges forwards rather than back, shuttles side upon side. We're secured in an adjacent room. This situation looks, rather than is. I'm a crucial part of the standard repertoire. Flung clear, we're cast into anchorless territory. We gradually speed up, then slow down again. Today is to submit. Take this she says it may kill us.

Who is she then? Who is he? An allusion to submission has been made. The subject is an outsider in temperament—strange, foreign, guestlike. We're witnessing a rudimentary stage of development, without segments or limbs. That fold of skin secretes a living shell. It derives its name from its habit of skimming over the surface, from the resemblance of the notched end to a mouthful of air. A method of mental substitution, I should say. Disposition of parts, some pictures from reputed afterlife.

The following day at dawn a lawyer comes to my cell. The head is circumscissile (trapped in a lift). He says I have a bad feeling about today. It could swing either way.

A friend hands me a totem for luck: a chunk of man-shaped wood blasted open with a nail-gun. Some points of similarity between the mental lives of savages and neurotics have been agreed upon. One drains his drink before squeezing the empty glass in his fist until it shatters. Here's a précis of my defence.

The chief attributes are fortune, fame, speech, memory, intelligence, steadfastness and suffering. At the heart is a lengthy andantino. I prefer the middle path, a straight-down-the-centre shot. I move with slow and uneven expression. Exhibit B is the noose that the accused laid around his own neck. Inglorious wastrel of time, I have undone every deed attributed.

Quick, before the boundary changes. Suicide watch, all the women in black. A whole nation. I sometimes write things that are plain wrong. Open her mouth. Throw away the score. It's all down to individual errors. Force air into her body. So much depends on who you live. And I didn't know moths pollinated (I said that, or something else). I can't remember. I am the wrong day. Our waste is on the up. I can see objects in a shaft of sunlight. The loop of a bell-rope quivers against the stained glass.

Beggars crowd onto the patch of snow where a solitary ray falls. I think we've got the very faintest moment of shadow. Beads of liquid run off the track like mercury. The following day the bar had been raised.

Impact craters dominate a bleak landscape. There's no atmosphere. In terms of real time we're way back in the nineteens. We are various unknowns, some fragmentary, some probate. The proof: a written paper purports to be the will. A sideways movement toward history is recurring, a continual change of milieu. The lab bench that day was worn and pitted. You are competing with ghosts.

This is a trick scene, a flashback to an incident that never happened. The surface was bombarded for one hundred days by meteoric debris.

He encompasses the entire vocal range. It's all art and artifice that doesn't add up to anything. (How to know one another?) He falls short, but is clearly a popular runner about these parts. The one surviving aspect amounts to nothing. What precision, mind. Who else is mentioned? Ordinary causations, cohesion and specific gravity. Extinguished in the thirteens, we've parted company with immanent use. Analyse the thematization which is constitutive for this science. (There'll be a lot of people willing this chapter to disappear.) It has an irrepressible impulse to manifest itself. He scores eight points if he captures all the risks. Do not move your left heel. He moves his left heel. I never over-rehearse myself. We're taking part in an exchange—synthetic principles of pure understanding and negative contribution. A corpse is expected to bleed in the presence of its murderer. Consider, if you will, that elusive quality of being read. It now only remains for me to give you the full translation of characters upon the parchment, unriddled. Here it is, the catchword. Prize open the mouth. A sheet of sunlight strikes the water. Used air floods out. The origin, the remains, are unknown.

Sedimentary remission. Storehouse of remember. He thought it was a retractable stage dagger but it turned out to be the real thing.

The music grinds on, a four-hundred-year-old viola. Flora, a genus of willow, aspen white with black its variety. Lombardy poplar, cottonwood and tulip-trees.

You never know what he will say or do next. It's the logorrhea. Strangely enough we now have a dearth of singers. Houses were much smaller back then. There has been a disconnection (look at you). His death was indeed an annex. That sound is an official copy of the human voice, perhaps a rustic confusion of satyr and saultier. Goodnight.

Hide me between the cracks in the ice. What of crystal earth, well armed? Remember that both sides will be fumbling in the dark at all times. Elements: two adulterers, a betrayed spouse, a slender dog of great speed and keen sight. The sixteenth simulation is madness. This simply means he won his substance through piracy. Any position of the left hand except that nearest the nut will do, a groundbreaking removal.

Unjustified intonation (cf. suicide gene). Why biography. Lower the bar as a precaution. It's said he once made the trip on foot.

Grainy snapshot of a mass held at base camp. Clumps of substance, root composites. Secure the archive. I am seeing the experience, same unicellular organ with thrashing flagella.

Due to a childhood accident that we will not give away.

A workman stands on the rim of the well and drops a plumb-line. All the guests are expected to choose today when and how they shall die. Calculations are based on a minimum of guesswork. The text charts a deficit in desire. Another hangs from a harness, a swinging point in space. Perfumes are released from the animal's ruptured gland. Sound: piano, celesta, gamelan. In the hall of mirrors is a harpist. I wander the concrete stairwells of the ministry, cracked linoleum underfoot. The whole must have been halved, somehow. Notwithstanding, the rubric to this chapter orders the head to be made of gold. It takes an incredibly long time to burn a body, and an awful lot of wood. By some miracle I'm completed by the month of germinal.

Already I'm faded and tired-looking. Flesh covered with silky iridescent hairs—a grate of broken colour on the silvered water. Occluded front curving in, double spectrum. I would have written. I made the same mistake last time. Love is suffering, but we're safely back in uniform. What are the men doing, without? I once heard the murmur of things growing in the garden, and was afraid. It might be a question of making a statement as witness before a court. A curious rhomboid shape is used to vanish across to the other side. But where is the penny to pay the post? Utilize any clichés you come across. I once fell from the sky.

First that little song about jealousy, courtesy of the company (you got your shares). Books have a habit of falling open at the same page. Crusts and tufts are forming on the rocks, the trees, the soil. It doesn't stop there. It would be an honour to celebrate your birth at the seaboard. I have found a word that's impossible to pronounce. Again, outland men, presumably. Blood-rain.

What follows is a brief account of early life. Seditious passages are accompanied by examples. He runs around off-camera. Sickly-sweet smell of film cement and warm celluloid. You've caught us out already, the flaw in our line-up exposed. A grey moth alights on the window pane: fourth storey, north-facing exterior. All sense of place is temporarily in abeyance. You feel you're taking part in some supernatural journey.

He passed himself off as one of our own, i.e. eternally sterile. Shoulders have been surgically pinned back. Place the toe of the right foot a half length to the rear and slightly to the left of the heel. He's decorated (egg-sunny, scrambled side up). The moth itself points due east. At the end the youngest son must retrieve the skull, shatter it, and vacuum up the ashes.

The species is ground-dwelling, a wading intermediary between plough and sniper. A number of my themes are shown to be musical cryptograms. This arrangement is immediately suggestive of the word thirteen. One day I hope some genius will come along and set all this to music. Bear in mind that these are pointers and suggestions, no more. I hope to make it to the breach this afternoon.

Childness, the minor arts of putrefaction and sepsis. And again, furnishing us with two new characters. I'm not moving from this spot again.

Face outward. Brassy layers conjoined by a soft weld of mercury. The great brazen layer of kinship, having shoulders that displace the sea.

Moloch-shell with smooth yellow body, bilge ducts and gall-bladder. Very well he said finally if you insist. The signal is breaking. A door creaks as he opens. Enter a person of inert habit and gas, scattered rhymes. There's a cack-handed reference to Faust. They're not going to take her as well, are they?

On safety and self-harm, improved security with fewer absconds. Light reflected from distant pane. An idle current, straight into such channels as these. Loose superficial debris. She finds the circumstance comedic, while he's for dredging the canal at once. Three of the volunteers have been hit already. I've got other photos that resemble them. They came unprepared. Likewise, I'm rumoured. An absolutely straight column would have produced a concave line.
Exit iris via crane.

He was a pale ghost of a man in the ring. Movement now somewhat slower, once intended for somewhat quicker. (You'll be looking for that later.) The body was burned at sea. It's the duty of the author to undermine the reader.

A floating aerodrome. Foreground, her shingled head. Continent: a compromised one. Time, somewhere before dark. Mode of transmission, wireless, or otherwise. Telepathy. Forum: an ancient observatory. I'm a byword for silt. The odd rock here and there. I'm not sure about the wisdom of this list. The time-signature changes as we drift from bar to bar (this was never intended to be performed, just to look spectacular on the page). Negation and consumption can no longer coexist in the cultural sphere. Of all men I have voided thee.

The best example is the famous minim. Vapour passes through the epidermis. He leaves a trail of suicide notes pressed flat under glass. Flasks of quicksilver are missing from the mines. My dark rhythm is a continuation of my light rhythm. Everything has been arranged in alphabetic order (*i* and *n* are represented by six and an asterisk). Reeds sway in the much-needed breeze. Amplitude declines. The worst example is as follows.
Practitioners of the art reject the traditional element. I mean composition, and the interrelationship between parts of the whole. In this way he shows that he believes what he is looking for is there.
Imago of the same, a popular and unscientific division, broadly distinguished. We're a diminishing class. The whole hospital was invited.

Not so much unfinished as unbegun. Do you remember money. He says again a tooth has fractured. Cell floor now decorated with torn strips of cloth. The diagnosis is paralysis. The main room is stretched, rather like a greenhouse.

Partition me, obsolete. Brake and valve are missing. Gathered here are all my substitutes. They form a circle. A yellow oxlip bursts open at the centre. Then a blank, where the nodding violence grows.

He lived prematurely. It's me for him, a straight swap. At that moment I recollect that I too once killed a man.

Here we are beside the lake, where I started looking for the chorus. Offshore is a submerged temple, a stepped pyramid. I swerved the chicane at turn ten.

Describe him in more detail (dissolute, capable of passing through the membrane into the surrounding seawater). The fuel pump comes away as I pedal like mad from the checkout, pulse bursting. All reports speak of a man short and squat in stature, with small hand and foot, stunted limbs and a convex abdomen. There are little problems, knots one has pondered for weeks, and then suddenly the solution becomes obvious. He has a thick neck below a round face strapped to a large head. By definition: the naming of the parent from the child. The infrastructure begins to crumble. A solid figure of colloid sits on a triangular base. Lumps of masonry fall from the viaduct above. I'm only effective when in action. After rendezvous at an inn we ascend the western slope. Thank you for your letter of the fifteenth, my poem is my knife et cetera. There's nothing else to do but go back. Elevation equals nine hundred and eighty. I have belief in impasse, deadlock—the place from whence there is no outlook. I forgot to say. The earth trembles. I protect my head with a severed arm wrapped in a blue polyethylene bag. We listen out for the hum of passing rocks. The ground starts to disintegrate beneath our feet, which is always alarming. He is a herald of the amoral creator who is a law unto himself. Despite these hazards I achieve the nation, placing it under the body till a system forms. Notes are squeezed into capsules and buried. A kind of suction cup is placed over the soul. (This is the version I heard.) I'm ready to cause quite a stir. I'm ready to quit. She says open every window and read this aloud. I move in the direction of the tip of the planet. I swim out and sink. I drown. My spirit implores. I pass through levels and platforms, the inner courts about which the hub imperceptibly revolves. The answer's a).

Less interest is shown by the drunk sprawled not far from the intersection. Movement here is counterclockwise, rotating the plane of polarized light to the left. Air can no longer claw and tear at me. Above, sunbeams penetrate the surface. We're surrounded by fluid collisions. We'll work it out in time. I find five small objects. Someone's going to have to pay. I take them back to the land. It's been an odd day of transaction and digression. Now's a good time to ask what the budget is.

Welcome, things appear to have deteriorated in my absence. Everything collapses, degeneration of tissue. I find being quite selfish. The two of us are tiny human figurines. Freeze me till there's a cure. My adversary is white-hot and spherical. I levitate high up in the chilled air. (Thaw me out, that's an order.) The public always covet a magical. I strike a buttress and shatter. Flints of frozen flesh chatter to the metal floor. We are coming alongside on the opening sea. These extreme highs are a problem. You'd have been dead in the England.

Are you listening. It was more anti-dentistry than any conscious attempt at repair, something mediaeval. Audiences were notorious. This is an art intended to test the assassin's technical kill. Signals pour through like random fire. (They played this at my wedding.) Then a seemingly insignificant detail, like the quick blur of a grace note with which it all began.

The itinerant carpenters down in the street are singing. Within, flickering super eight of self-fellatio. My sides meet in a point. You look blank. I have the feeling you are not: thicker body, antennae not clubbed, wings not tilted over the back in rest. It's a problem.

Sickle cell. Invasion by pathogenic bacteria, a genus most legless. Dreamlike invocation of the golden age. Bright clear sky, with meaning influenced by late. The creature builds itself a shady recess adorned with colourful feathers and shells and smooth, rounded pebbles. Unpeopled names press close (an aching, passive nature, which in love is discharged). We must be approaching the end. The fourth object is a feminine lodestone. To obviate the danger the whole fleet is degaussed. We practice conductance, experimental dying. What's your own testimony? At the entrance are unauthored pages, a tome tethered to the surface of the earth by taut cables. (Name its parts.) All sense of history is decorous. Don't mention the rucksack full of money. He who doesn't see needs no reinforcing. There's a full programme. Tonight's the night. I'm tightly bound within cloth the texture of jute and the colour of amber. Be patient. A body slides into the sea from a tilted board. The problem was something to do with the empty cylinder. I yearn after a little talk. A surgical mask is strapped to my face, oxygen administered via a tube. The mattresses have been stuffed with straw for the troops. Unrelieved gloom hems us in on every side, until battle commences. Still more are we exploited by the creation of natural obstacles. March onward to a wait of even greater significance.

Note to self, amend forms in isolation cell. Another and another are delimited in ink. My temperature won't go away. I hear a celestial in the corridor. She says you're clearly that man of fission. An above average number were members of a political scoop. Outside, a machine like a metal pig's cock on caterpillar tracks is wheeled up. All that could be seen from the window was a gigantic K. There's no guarantee we'll make it home tonight. I might just happen at one time or another. The missing part is a quality of unscrupulous fulfillment. You should hear yourself. What a vainglorious day. I am becoming further entrenched in my own cupidity. Splashes of hot coffee and buttered toast stain the formica. Also present are a revolver—attendant bullet aligned northeast—two paper-clips, a tiny white cup (chipped), a slick of espresso, one saucer with extinguished gauloise stub and scattered fibres of tobacco. Always tackle things in strict order.

Disposition of parts. Snapshots of afterlife. Exhausted coolies naked in the starlight, hired labour squatting beside the canals that bisect the territory. He's here, the one I wronged. Graffiti'd ooze on flank of turret, scratched grids hinting at purpose. Whatever will they think of next. This design is uncertain, is never to be performed. (I'm missing things here.) The whole city's carved from stone the colour of bauxite, a red mass embedded in the grey earthly matrix. It's the terrible year of commune. It was once long ago. There's a connexion to intergalactic space. Two travellers are discussing a game of cards. (What prose is this?) Etymology is unknown. I return to the book. The font is large, lending grandeur to volume, the spine embossed with gold leaf. On one page is a collage in which lapis blue predominates. A siren sounds. Weather is on the way. If a player fails to make three tricks, he's euchred. A column of books is stacked tight from floor to ceiling. Ringing this one-story house are dream-hives, gnarled and stunted trees, the tomb of a cat. Why has he stationed me here? Try reading now I hear you ask. Every cycle turns from zero through x number of years and then begins all over again. Schoolboys and idlers were common in Pompeii. The column is sealed in latex. I flip to the last page, where it states. All the guests are trapped in an exile of their own invention. One account was written in the first person. I haemorrhage tiny stones.

Once, such objects. The remaining distance is one-and-three-quarters of a mile. One book is called the death of psyche. There were magazines too lying about in that mountain hut. In them I found some recent discoveries. Here, time will not permit an analysis of the choice of readings. We heard someone tapping out a last request, as if rising from the mouth of one deceased. Pellicles of ice hung from the roof of the cave. Changes have been made to the text. The signal is faint and garbled. One woman suggests cutting off his hump (it's rumoured she took pleasure on his corpse). I'm gorgonized for another cycle. Three possible modes may be distinguished, each associated with a particular image. We encased him in clay for the final orbit. We considered what to do. The only figure I can see clearly tears itself away and drifts off into deep space.

At three in the morning I'm yanked down from my bunk. An hour passed, then another, and still no one came. We are moving in from opposite ends to the same conclusion. I'm like a sponge. Who was ever condemned to a comparatively light punishment? Dissent has its basis in no particular character of this narrative.

In a single imperious gesture she waves me away. This is what's known as persuasion. It marks the promise of landfall. There is this tradition. The validity of an act can sometimes be acknowledged by others present. It's called the cut because it cuts through from one place to another. We all saw it, notes rattling through like random fire. None of the usual criteria apply to me.

I wake to the sound of the building being tightened, inch by inch. I heard also a rumour. Cigarette burns punctuate the torso. It's a bad example because it never existed. Right out of the gates it was a disaster.

Sex unknown. A crystal form of separate facets. Calcium and sodium have changed places. Each cuts one of the three axes. Fibrous white spores glint by the window where the light is. It's two agin one. We're expelled. I find myself alone beside a house in a remote field. A large mirror has been placed in front of the only window, blocking out the sun. I search for signs of location. My tenure is brief in its difficulty. Sandblasted into the glass is a palindrome arranged in a self-devouring circle. The brigade was bled white—cut-purse to the bone, the chase.

Hint: a tendency to exercise controls that would isolate us. A clamouring. Total ineffectiveness.

Anything of similar form may be superimposed upon this memory. Each member of this group was carefully removed from a cave.

An opening by circular rent—a piece of time, written off.

The shape of a gentle arc across the sky (seven up). I sit down to write. It's magnificent, but it's not war. And no one comes into the town and no one can go out. Disappearance has been erased from the record. None of the usual things happen to me.

Last resort, usually the docking of two spacecraft. I'll resume when I get back. He is pale, mouth agape. One day, I hope.

In her night shift she came. I think I'm back in the car and safe. Conduct all business in-house. Undergo phonetic change. The legend *Geosolutions* is stencilled on the flank of the planetary sampler drilling outside. Fluorescent men bandy about at their work. They pass from mouth to mouth, give and take reproach. I can feel the static. The carriage smells like a used groin. I was last seen at the fire, escaping. (Talk about dicing with death.) We pass flashing seiners on the shore, tending their nets. One cap was cleft by the fall of a sword. Sometimes I take two or three leaps up the stairs at a time, but not at this altitude. I am once and for all. It's to do with the ribcage. Whoever only remembers the capture of the army does not know how to calculate matters of this kind. It's a time for action and omens. The last who burst through the portal, it still isn't clear what he said.

After his death the trend of interest was in a direction that discarded all his works. He could never have escaped over those hills.

Beads of sperm across a marble slab. He says I blame the movement. Just one drop of blood and it rose up out of the sea. Such a performance. Our orders are to collapse into a single world-view, and wait. With one sweep of its wing I'm condemned to sleeplessness. I'm both winner and loser. By one decisive action you are erased, dear reader.

Fetch me a stylus. Grant me unpeopled time. I reel out then drift back to land, an object of expectation. As quickly as the seconds arrive, they evaporate. I open my eyes and look down. Cleavage: ankle fracture at fifty-six degrees. Grudgingly I share the compartment home. What follows is the inevitable conversation on a train, in the course of which my travelling companion unwittingly reveals his origins.

Diminishing stock is his dilemma (a flammable glue composed of polystyrene, petrol and benzene). Then I notice. Both his legs are broken. It's a false alarm (he has arms). Always assume failure to be possible before starting out. Men raise siege engines around a passing settlement. I have become the abyss of a greater victory et cetera. In the stinking latrine bobs a discarded erotic toy. Now what? A predictable dropping away, about a joint and a half. I would do anything to stop.

Boy with sword on promenade. Maybe an expedition to hunt, fish, fight, or to gather toxic plants. The blade has front and reverse sides, black with greasy soot. (Check signal aspect.) His adversary scores against him, repeatedly. A dreadful sacrifice is required. The wick should be ignited just before the missile is thrown. The temperature at the sinew has risen. See that scaffold through the window? That's the whole point of language. In meditative practice, the contemplation of the number three is used to create a repulsed state. Where else could be spoken of?

Craze forth upon thy own lands. They had seen him again and again over the years. It takes an incredibly long time to return to a body.

A walled mediaeval garden. All the objects you see are the only objects owned by its inhabitants. She says this morning we must interview some rocks. Who, oft as he sauntered the streets, would curve within his arm? As time travels the airborne dust withdraws. The answer is that worthy son of a family, who has gone to the dogs. Often blood-red, with streak.

The extinguished. Dream thirteen, digestion as reciprocal action. The diners at the next table hurl their glasses over the parapet. Indices of deprivation, impressionistic events achieved by the sustaining pedal. They shatter on the towpath below (the glasses). That ink is poison. I'm making hell to be nothing but that, weighing heavy in the various senses. We must be nearing the end. I am not averse, a member of a wandering troupe of originals. Exchange ghost was our section.

Things are made no clearer by the emendation of ice to vice. I am no longer nerved, you see. A brief interlude is over, and so too the narrative of childhood. The main action of a drama leads to the catastrophe. A coffee ring eclipses the cover of the book. My fear of the allium menace prompts me to dead-head every species.

Busy movement in triple time. Self-slaught. O fuck she says. I'll need all my ears for this, the blank page of division. The bitterness spread like acid to the farthest boundary. Somebody must have known. There were a number of grain-testing beds inside. Outstretched hands found the window which ended the passage. I heard the opening words the mother stood I burst.

That gentle needle, the failing of the light. Flutter in now the ticket boy, an arrival of newsprint. News of the giant ray, news of a spindle shape balanced in the sky. He brings a gripping instrument, the stone that attracts iron. Surface thin-skinned, with scum of ice. There are some concluding remarks to come before the end. The horizon of the local context is indispensable to this analysis.

Much residual influence, units of radiation dosage—an amount which has the same effect as one equivalent. Score over, as above. Outwit.

I have overstepped my welcome: the pallet beds, street traders with their herbs and apothecaries, an obsessive drive after documentation. Also the habit of flying by night—that which eats away gradually and silently. Without calculation there can be no sure result.

The current cools. Traces of loss, my claim to part of the territory. She felt the coolness and thinks it nice to feel. I see you, yet I see you not.

There he goes, with his running motif—negotiating another day, just passing through. But this would presuppose that one can separate what is said from the mode of saying. I'm seeing things not present to the senses. From beginning to close, a final glimpse: bulb of tentacular outgrowth above primary holdfast. Refer to note scribbled on envelope.

Nayward. Substance nexus, swinging at the plumb-line. I dive down to a submerged joss-house, find the five magicals and take them back to the surface. Remember that intoxicant spike? She holds up the palm of her hand, digits spread to acknowledge. I remember the act of writing. They have thawed out.

A big book about the minerals has been discovered, thought lost. (Ideal conditions for crystallization.) This is distantly related. Therein he obtains possession of the crater. The object is the colour of embers and wrapped in hessian. I am unable to recall a single word written. Calcium is entering the structure somewhere below the waterline. These are all the recorded indices to date.

Cheesewire soundtrack on radio overhead. Characters are sometimes killed off at a single stroke. Advise him to give up. You can't keep adding things on, like a counting machine. He retorts. I'm a fateful savant. Remember my medium of false identities? Each cycle outcurses the end by five hundred (clever at guessing and riddling). A hollow in the animal body is containing. One cell hosts reproductive bodies, the spore-case of certain fungi. We're on the final page. That's the ticket, except for the naked tip, which converges to a quivering point. I straddle three borders. Today's password has been slipped beneath the flyleaf. Still haemorrhaging tiny stones.

I'm not sure whether that's possible. They once were thought to have come from Egypt. I caught her drying her hair over father's burning body. A new species has adapted its colour to the moment. It haunts the foreshore and riverbanks (yellow in mankind, green in vegetation). As it dies, so the roman. Of these latter I can neither think nor speak except in capitals. You have to be absolutely sure.

He would scrabble about under the bed and find boxes. It resembles the butcher hook, trapped in a column of silt. Function is smothered in surmise. He would experiment with the contents. Now action to close this, move in.

The gentle inner grip, beneath the spine of an unsung pier. It's true that in strategy one needs more time to reach an objective than in tactics.

Somewhere beneath the rim. I've been trying to write the business. There's a stack of handwritten crisps beside my cot. Salty in my enclave, I cower beneath the scalp. A detachment's taking place—a woman, flagging.

Try living in some other time than here, some other place than now. To the last brake of sinister surmises et cetera.

He visits the hospice on a rare day off. I am resident to write, polishing the silverware. Museum of where? I ignore. Reinstate each and every one of these words. Reach out to touch the thinning hair of his skull. You decline, withdraw. I release my own head. He smiles down at me from the ceiling (all these dummy vessels). Here we are together once more, plaintive brass in attendance. I can be written in precisely forty-one seconds. I was first recorded in the nineteens. Too little rapid eye here.

Can't rest in this futurist hotel, with its shake-down straw and shuttered dispensary, furniture carved of ice. Nonetheless, I'm archived as being present—a fragile, readily dazzled into distraction. Maybe nothing of importance was said after all.

Recall a tower of pallets nearby a river, an abandoned pollen station, her fragile hand. Dice on the pavement in the shadow of collapsing buildings. The name implies, invisible in a rose garden bounded by a thread. Mesh of parcel tape on every window at a dusty border town. Trickster in suit of cups.

At the mouth of a cave on a rocky beach. Spiny lizards paralysed in the starlight. Here we go. There's a demonstrable link to the middle age, royal healing power. Abreaction of zerovalent complex, numb at fifty-four.

I am exempt from going anywhere—a situation in which both the horizontal visibility and the overcast are technically nil. The day of the raid the plane reeked of gunpowder and spilled coolant. That looks a very full pit, I must say.

Notes toward the slaying of a husband by or for a paramour. Animated abstract shapes scratch at my eyes. Accept the wager, or dig for relics.

A species of smallness. Excision of cerebral cortex. A floodplain seen from the sky—the river has burst its banks. I misread oversight. Levels are high, a probable maximum.

He meets them at the gates and invites them into his house (mistake number one). The instruments are the dulcimer and salpinx. The angels refuse. They prefer a night in the streets, where they belong. No choice remains. We are improvising a countercharm against a curse. By this I mean perspective projection, behaving as if the point of sight suddenly vanished at an imagined infinity. A species of wilderness peeled back layer by layer.

Now from something very ancient to something very modern. What are we to do with the three remaining days? Don't leave this too long. If it should fail, we all fail. Cubic or octahedral crystals are rarely more than two inches across. Then water falls from the sky in tiny droplets. The island is full of such noises— arresting newsprint, a casually crafted emptiness. Rusting iron plate behind eyes.

Make random selections of historical fact and firsthand evidence. (I've seen it happen.) Language isolates are fascinating.

A closed sac of morbid character, liquid or semi. The peal of those metal poles, as bells distant in time.

He has been wired to the topmost of topgallant rigging. They divided him into parts. (You don't say how many.) That's never happened before. What is his mouth called? Unearth a useful adjective for once. How many and what are his arms called? (This is looking good.) What are his thighs called? I have to smile, looking back at the twenty-first situation. What are his feet called?

Vignette, the deceased adoring the god who stands in a shrine. Note the avian algorithm in the sky. We laugh because everything is so funny and so fine and so sad. He recollects: treeless scrubland at the edge, the discovery of a mineral that repels flesh, attracts iron. Lost and regained, without structure, all change is said to contain. The abstract or perfect circle becomes concrete and natural—an allusion to the fact that many intumesce under the blowpipe. I was born out of hemlock. Move this to and close, loosely upheld as water.

An indication of measure at the beginning of a line, or wherever there's a chance. Each with grain at different stages of growth.

Heretic all along, she was surely here herself. During the civil war everything shut down. That opinion is not singular. I have no great mind to halter (traces of hereditary epilepsy). A wide range of reminiscences are about to be delivered. She dances on hot glass, broken goals. After dark petrol is siphoned from the tank. Who can encourage greater competition? There's been quite a lot of crowd pleasing today.

Copious ejaculation, then the sacrifice fades. It's only now that she recollects the men who witnessed. Hung and drawn they opened its throat. I think of the concrete circus we found up on that day at the downs. There's nothing else. It's too close to prehistory.

Dawn of night that long summer long they cut a slice from every limb.

You're making all the right movements, they're just not happening in the right order. The charges include murder, kidnap and unlawful detonation. One man was left underexposed.

Ordinary echoes of a sink estate. A divine task has been overlooked. I lay all my credo on the table. The house collapses. It's like I lost my nerve. He presses a huge palm flat against the jugular. Matter of time creaking in the eaves, the sinew.

Do you remember that game: tiny animals impaled on thorns by a bird. We're circling back to the uncanny. Examination of fresh material can convince us that we have, and that we have not. This occurs not only in disavowal but also in repression.

Never the latter, the stationed bands, the never-vacant watch. Exiled to a point beyond which lies the realm of losses and defeats.

Creditrix. Genuflect and salute. Secodont, without left hand or right leg, a person of sex. See under atom, ephemera, under universe—with cutting back teeth.

Undo its sole possibility of itself, slightly delay the timing. And nobody knows why they are here nor how long they will stay. Visit stellar drilling at the first opportunity. Discharge in short controlled bursts. My watch said.

The bulk of my iron vaporizes on impact. This intoxication lasts several days.

I've got used to the bruises around my wrists and ankles. It's been a long night, laden with things, the sheer volume of stuff manifest. It's said a readiness lives on in the book. Unfound, parasitic in man and the other.

At rest, lying beyond the orbit of Neptune. Disappear, lodge any special plea, as of sanity et cetera. Amplification can shelter all things. Some day I will reappear. Ash from distant lands is falling into the sea. On the beachhead stands a wooden statue with extremities of stone, bone charred black in the fires.

Self-sacrifice for kindred. Life and honour in exchange for a parent or loved one. The future is three to the power of eight. We could always move on. Underfoot, notebook sketch, apex of obelisk.

Icon in upturned coffee cup, female morphing slowly to not. I present to you each of the reasons, eye adrift. The vacuum, remade.

XXIV

It's been a really good year for popularity. On occasion it shows. The change was tactical, explosive says total. An empire of witchcraft is gathered here, closing ranks against the outside world (I've run out of characters and ideas).

A metal bolt falls from the underside of the ear onto the floor. I exploited the competition to get a work permit. The other person in the room is a purveyor of sorts. It's time to step up a pace.

Grant initial impressions. Air a few nebulous concepts. It's now considered that no such element exists. It was liquidated by the green line (the amphiboly of reflection et cetera). A thin film covers one eye. I'm puzzled that people could have been alive before me.

He discovered a new moment in music. This explains certain fissures in the spectrum observed. Perplexing controversies on the indivisibility of matter are byproducts. Another compromise has been breached. Circumstances are known to rely on states of oxygen and nitrogen impossible under earthly conditions. I'm languishing on an enforced sabbatical, permanent evacuation. The system is forged by the contraction and breaking up of a rotating nebula. These are axioms that, properly speaking, don't concern us.

Can I live within him? Revoke all change. In my face the west wind pounds off the sea. (Enter assassin.) Any symbolic hand gestures will suffice. Childhood was terrifying.

I have the look of a man who's gone over to the other side and has not altogether come back. I could once hear light. A mesh of coloured beams bisects the cell, nocturnal bleedings. Beating reeds are concealed within the body, the stir of particles. How many strings are we writing for now? (I notice you use the saw with the teeth pointing outwards.) Clearly you enjoy danger in your music.

Make note to table a sermon on the subject. The age is turned old, of a sudden.

Disallow me, a brief digression.

He set sail on the ess ess something or other. It's torpedoed. It sinks. He dies. He seems not to have heard what the other is saying. Anything of that shape.

It is now late spring and we're becalmed. Enter, take possession of bodies, force shelter. Some species lack primeval simplicity. Usually, I never get much beyond this point. Four pieces in all were composed using a single note.

Approaching full moon, any length of time. I tend to think of catching trains.

A few last questions. He agrees that seven is an inappropriate number. Remain special and memorable. Volunteers are being held in storage. The wrong kind of root has been sent, the wrong kind of soil. I discover I have a flare for opposites. The news from outside is vague and confusing.

Scribble between the tracks. A knot has been detected under the ground. The pianist recalls her final season with a long-time meteor. Put that way, it's truly unfortunate. Nothing happens as a consequence of our actions. It's said there's an artery that spans the entire continent from north to south. Pages tear into one another (rift, calculus, ink). She took with her some magicals. Alter the rhythm of temporality by transferring the accent.
Synecdoche? Indent?

Hand-pierced strata in lee of caul. The cry of a bird, from sound casting shadow. A cutting up takes place. (You'll know it when you see it.) Elsewhere, I have only to glance at a figure and it disappears. Taking inventory, I count seven dead or dying. He says my god look at me. Towards the end of his life the intensity of the rain increases. We are together yet estranged, together and erased. We are severed from the will. There is a shining underneath.

Another caution for simulation. Waste gunners from the replacement depot. I don't deal with objects themselves. Maps of translucent sinew drift through the air, solder of invisible thread.
Glimpse of night entia, the rustle of animal familiars. The tort against a defence. One sequence runs don't tell me I can guess you kill everyone in the end. Which is the voice check? It is doable.

This was composed around a solitary note. Some refuse to pass on. It makes no difference. He is treading water. A voice (stage-whisper) says you have taken a lot from history. He gathers up and leaves.
I feel at home. There's a hunger for this type of terrain, the gentle rolling of the valves. Chalk and rust, inertia.

Sunlight flooding a bare hotel room. The subject is waiting. Tissue without distinguishable cell wall, curving lines of chrome bisecting chartered space. (When are you going to give something back?) Today's objective is indistinct.
No-coloured carpet, beads of cum on dresser. The silhouette of a hand creeps across the screen. There is rumour of his book, packed full of errors. I am converting. Things are not as I thought.
Mozart on the wireless. Minimum whiteness of interior—below, aimless trafficking. He recalls a remark once read, the soundless O of her mouth.
He lifts his snout (free pig skulls, the ensign). In the end it is simply not enough.

This type of drama is highly prized, a theatrical wasting away. Absence of smell, a film of silence through shuttered glass. The partition slides across to seal us in. I recall the phosphorescence of the sea one early morning, still dark. You know in your heart that my descriptions are roughly right.

Reflections are squat due to volumetric distortion. So too those columns, framing a tanned face of perfect alienation. A slight touch of evil, memory slipping by, the barely implied idea.

It occurs to me that I could finish her off, right here and now, and no one would know. An event may be desired and unwanted. That's a dangerous game. Only the dental image was retained.

A heraldic device built of overlapping transparent leaves hangs above the bed. Here then are the facts.

Divergence from the elastic, compromise by frequent diagnosis. My dear life. Pass me the mouth guard. Parasites reside in the selfsame body.

Before, when they notice the encroaching cart.

Move to one side as it careers down the steep hill. (A joke, to judge by their eyes.) Some slither about in the mud. Every act is reduced to the level of that which surrounds it. Which character was a martyr to the moral law?

Yes all day he has been here beside me, I swear, and in a rectangular box. The return betokens an uplifting. According to the text, he once called himself. It's altogether quite nice hereabouts, actually. I am no longer needed. Here's a sweet little song about a half-buried head, two trunkless pegs of stone set down in the desert. You are not listening.

A man leaping feet first to his death from a bridge. It is a curious comment.

With cutting back teeth (repetition). Place the subject in the recovery position. I took with me a few letters of introduction. Flasks of quicksilver from the mine were missing. None of this alters the facts. She says take this this may kill us.

Semée of crosses of lilies. Choose any one of the three subdivisions. The neutral was the first book I read. You tried it here for the first time. He took with him some only clothes. The next step is the seven-hundred-pound dictionary (weight). A sentence may be construed in two distinct senses. I have miscounted since the notorious Valhalla edition. Think family mythologies.

Opium, aconite, lobelia, the cardiac paralysers. An ejection seat that works at rest at zero altitude.

There once were many of us at one time. The uncanny thing is I don't feel at all hungry. You are a tribunal unto yourself. There's been a gradual drift away from the plebiscite. I had an opinion. She is renamed (greycake the wise). I was once at the top of the pile myself. Upon reaching the crest of the loop, rest a while.

Naked to left near entrance of rock chamber, hands clasped behind spine, waiting.

Warm panels of walnut and oak. They are haunted by the bleak motto and the large hammer. The rest of the journey was by canal. There can be no more mistakes. What is it about you you keep asking.

Our boat has a flat keel. Navigate by those stems trailing from the sky. This is a chemical dialogue, some of the oldest music ever handed down. The stern of the vessel takes on water. Keep her nose down (those pesky torpedoes). We sat side by side with two movables. The steersman's face is a picture. Follow the horizon line for a moment, then stop. Space is an enormous fault.

Time to seal up the rose window with molten wax. Next year marks the two hundredth anniversary. (Can you do the Doppler shift?) We were up on the top tier, clouds above the emirates. This moment is the one. I like that kind of thing. Pinned against the lightbox are X-rays of the head and of the body, a great list of abbreviations.

Cumulonimbus. Stratocirrus. Cirrostratus. The crisis dissolves.

Could you do something about that cracking sign.

The chief clerk runs a finger around his collar. It's going to be quite a trip. We lack properly protected vehicles. In the wardrobe is a secret armory (the majority of writers and artists were retained after the civil war). He almost passes out.

The legendary executioner is not named. I'm told I remind people. Look, a grand revolving door. Even wood can appear worried. I demanded an encore. The bitterness of the pill on the tongue spreads quickly to the gullet. That usually brings things to a close.

It exists at the border of consciousness. This is what I've done with the picture so far. They were labelled liquidators, the gravediggers of the party.

Depict an itinerant, he in modern habit. We need to go back much further than this. These objects can hardly lie still in their box. Only the very hardest crystalline substructure remains. Do something. Draw up an inventory of the largest items.

Stonecrop family succulents often grow on rooftops. Lights illuminate the auditorium (house-leek, kidney-kvetch, ganglia shoestring fungus). I am making this up. Fact! By now he had three fingers and operated under the dominion of mercury. As an unreliable companion he is well-known in the tradition.

Corolla bulging at base, lance-shaped uniform. I see his nostrils split, the eyes snap. Set in the floor of the gaming room were panels of armour glass.

Then there were two, one inside the other. These errors have been several times amended. The outer cannibalizes the inner as it grows. A furnace was constructed to throw heat back on to the substance exposed. They keep returning. A diagnosis is emerging from a popular condition. The dreamer is in a hotel. Morse, he demanded.

I'm simply talking about the things I've heard and the things I've seen. The first to reach the appointed place starts time running. I'm suspended beneath a wheel. There is no more room on the island. They were driven on by the exigencies of their nature to obey.

Survivors were found in scattered units of operation. Sometimes it appears as a silhouette against glowing matter. (Memory of hacking light.) The wind hath carried it in his belly et cetera. Leave-taking is personified.

Objects have been superimposed. There are some writers you can't wait to be born. It was constructed in fragile layers. Here, the waiting is inversely proportional to the loss. Let's go outside and explore outside. I have it all planned: a pseudoscalar boson with very small mass.

Render east. It was clear the causalities would have to be measured. He swoops down and makes off with the grave-goods. (Return them, father.)

A black elastic substance, calcium salts of human acid.

The medium is deflecting rays. These fuse together as they pass through to the next element. A weapon was dropped into that well, a broken word.

In the basket he carries off the head. I ask if I might go upstairs. (We need the repairs.) It was the following week. We need more batteries for the torch. Some among us are being withheld. I reply to the questionnaire: decreased comprehension of their inner was the pivot.

A solitary cellist. Seeded planets, a design of overlapping feathers. Much earlier, a chuck under the skin. If the rain hadn't come down at the end. (No electric flying suit, no body armour, no catheter.)

Handmell and crosspin of iron.

A conversion in the mountains. If I took my question, a question among others. There can be no exceptions. I try to keep life simple. I refuse to go outside. You'll hear for yourself.

Sinister. Dexter. Chief plumetty, with base to crack. One me, two me, three me, four me. Excellent.

Speech, on the occasion of receiving. Attendants in the rain. The sound of an under-ripe peach being split apart. (Open up that lead box.) A train of antecedents was found inside the body.

Sound, a sequence of industrial moves in unrelated keys. This is actually a sequel. A foul-mouthed character starts applauding. I do not wish to go outside. I have said this, we have covered this ground already. The variations are due to the planet. It'll take two days—one day for this, one day for that. A spike of sunlight beams through the overcast. Men were in doubt which way they were to walk.

He found her not (just the hand). There is always more of the body.

Finger sulcus between convolutions of brain. Note the inert sound of the limbs. I know what I was going to ask.

About the scar on the face, this thing of the meridian. First he surveys, then he humbles and eliminates. He once reminded us of our implausibility, but now it's too late.

A set of rooms. That's one of the words you can't use.

Start a fresh cycle, trumpets and horns. It changes sign under reflection. An ancient wire rattle is used to keep rhythm in the galley of a workship.

The glandular bell. It puts you firmly in control. Exclusions apply. This is an incomplete account of who he is. That's lighter than your foot.

I suppose a sort of muted obscurity. Yes, that's it.

Introductory notes on curry. Year one of his last incarnation, flesh the colour of flesh. It's because I know what will happen (one who dwells in the blight of the stream). At the same time we were instructed to conceal ourselves.

Writing makes my shins ache. The fever is characterized by a withdrawing. And his tongue which is *therein* is poised. He may invert.

A compound in which the first member describes the second (ever the way of letters and action). A highway leading nowhere. Each of us was inspired by the untimely death of his son. Your house is left.

We are both, with options remaining. The vortices of one line were sustained midway between those of the other.

Outwit, from with, and the root seen in array. Eaters, an asymmetrical double fault. It wears a pelt of scales. His job title is that of journeyman, one who works by the day. First past the last post is the rule. And then he says.

Among all
you lack,
but.

He is investigating the phenomenon, the sphere of glass that's said to encircle the earth. It was natural that every god should represent a discrete phase. The tempo is wilderness. I'm drawn to the fragment myself. The ghosts of the dead are about to cross the water and return to their homeland. It's fascinating. Nations are dressed in uniform white and carry banners. As in dry desert, when the winds.

It is natal, of or connected with birth. Include some high-profile activists. Apply the same principle here. Appoint a guardian spirit, some bird or beast. (Remember and it's true is the golden rule.) He swings an arm at his side for two or three years. This is a signal.

Lift and winnow the immensity of sand. Spatters of cum on dank greasy cobble. I'm inseparably echoed to a distant person, fog in every crevice. (An atmosphere is building, can you feel it?) The impression was taken from a plate smeared with molten sulphur. Nice magus, he says, a nipshred with thy shoulders narrow. A birthmark appears, a livid patch of symmetry migrating from under the skin.

Sometimes it gets quite frantic around here, as you can see. This arrangement is unstable in certain conditions. Then he questions us: mesmerism, the Tesla coil, the impossibility of speech.

He loved to tell stories of beautiful losers. I chose a beast as my tutelary divinity. Do everything in stages.

A wrongly addressed letter, the hundred years' war. You will need the green pen for this. The spinning propeller shaft whirled up through the air. You're just storing up trouble for yourself. I still have to check things. Gain momentum, then leap.

It's when sound changes as it moves. This demonstrates his ability to think in colours.

So soon I forgot the exit (slack tide).

The sick boy who floats outside the window.

He leaks an Easter message of his own. Moving backwards means you're standing still. The exterior was kept in place. (Unrestricted submarine warfare.) A surplus remains, poised and unique, trigger on the index.

Alter the temporal rhythm by transferring the accent (*mus*). The result is a sudden fall of blood to the brain. Ambiguity arises from the uncertain construction of some sentences. She shrugs and feeds a punchcard into the machine. A graft of tissue was removed from the scalp, by procedure. No further acceleration is possible this side of the light barrier.

Shorten your life by cutting out the middle. By this I mean sheltered. On his head sits a tricorne hat of plaited straw. The reminder is hived away. The opponent seizes the holdall full of cash and threatens to leave. Through the two-way mirror we watched him without seeing. It's rumoured that one of the boundary rocks is missing, the large flint. That noise is ascension. He stays five more years. The subject here is the gathering of hair in a fillet, nothing more. Nonetheless, he had a game plan, more of which later. You must come, inheritor: the arousal, the extraordinary ray.

On the unvarying characteristics of thermal springs. Inert experience, concentration of mass—another name for the first temperature. Those present are gatherings. The wrong date has been struck. In one place there's a recurrence (some of those inflatable hands). When he died five archive boxes were found under his bed. One contains a precise description of how to manufacture. Another describes the oblong in some detail. Every year we commemorate his casting out. The fourth is a voting slate, the fifth a palindrome. The sensation of time slipping by has always been a keen one for me. Listen, that tune at the end. Obscurantist, no? The sixth object is a pebble. This is not visible in the manuscript.

An appointment. Breakwater and seawall, any surviving insecurities (the hired assassin's trade-off). My first action was to replace the obsolete word. I'm only too aware of the votive power of the improperly formed sequence of letters. Dense matter of uncertain origin lies beneath the surface.

Substitute Mars for gules.

Mass exodus: their pillars ten, their sockets. One of the women reels away from the column. We are underwrought, thus.

A bellicose plant, bushmaster snake venom. Marasmus. Go and fetch the light, primarily.

On the concept of the quantity of an act, behaviour in the right. This combines a dirge and a lullaby. The cell is fumigated from below. (She always referred to her absent husband.) The best thing we can do is to put you off.

Discharging showers of elasticity. Hapax legomenon.

In relation to the old and bearded metropolitan.

CANTICLE ONE

First Canon

TONE EIGHT

He is said to have quoted selectively from the memo. Father will love him. Make good your abode within. He was ramlike (quick-tempered, pulsive, daredevil). As soon as I knew his spirit had left him, in the old-fashioned way I struck a candle. This life is so brief. It's just the thing for me.

Make an argument for your destitution.

Orange flare at base of spine. Neural spasm at calf and hinge. Dull ache in lumbar region, sinister. He was last seen at the revival stage. We've got a barrier here. He can see sound. There's much grinding of teeth. The number he's let slip through his fingers, it's uncountable. It was like peeling an onion, in utters.

Another sits at the piano all day and plays the same note again and again. Not for the first time, we have a problem with volcanic ash. He's moving about inside me. It's the anniversary of the armistice. There's no such thing as distraction. Who would have thought.

Imagine, a man sitting at the piano playing a single note over and over. Get involved.

A finishing line was threaded through the individual strings. Some things will never return to nature. Whose wave function is such a quantity? Art and leisure, imagine that.

Eyebright disorder. The simple answer is no. Spindle-trees, let every mortal radiate et cetera. The image on the cover depicts.

Senex with phrygian cap, a picture postcard. A man is sitting at an antique desk. He holds a quill in his right hand. Another stands behind him, peering over his shoulder. The theme is deference. From you to me is strictly ornamental.

In certain conditions the eddies detach themselves and branch off. I am very far from you, and this you plan of. Alternately, by passing either edge of the obstacle we might cross the stream. It deviates outward from a spinning core (ailerons and flaps). That's the end for today.

As we break away we form in our wake the pattern known. She stacks a huge pile of cards into the sloping track to the right. A voice says this is my beloved in whom I am well appeased. I pride myself.

Perhaps this present danger. I have allowed myself time. Sometimes the egg is confused with the kidney.

The near-eastern markets have burst. I know my master for a canny man (the fifth had more angels than the first). Sometimes is simpler. What course of action transformed him from an enthusiast into a draft dodger? Now he's reduced to begging alms. Each individual word is equivocal: reverb no hollowness. He held off the assassins with a daring masquerade.

Night. Streets and gangways of a former home. It's called strange days and I think it's here already. That bright area is caused by a galaxy turning imperceptibly—the collapse of small regions within enormous cool. This is cutting off circulation to the head. We sat it out in the relative safety of shadow. The concept of the quantity of actions is now paramount. My companion is busy fashioning a piece of driftwood with an army knife. Light springs up out of the ground, a bright area seized by gravity.

Albumen in the urine. An attempt at union with our remaining hours. Waters thou shalt seize him et cetera. Red velvet curtains are drawn aside to reveal books embossed in gold—a claw clutching arrows, a crown of metal spines. I'm usually depicted with a falcon's head, perhaps the throat. And very close to the neutral, moreover.

I shall now preoccupy myself with a deconstruction (nautical sermons had become something of a tourist attraction by the eighteen-thirties). They volunteered to descend into the shaft. A capsule is attached to the winch at the head. They're held in a pit while we decide what to do. Writing has no choice. It was traditional that no one should speak. On deck the gunner's scale was utilized— rigging oiled, topmast sliding about on rungs. Who did you think he would bring out alive? There are certain noises you just don't hear anymore in the world.

The first pile was driven into the seabed today. Dung of marine fowl, horrible coffee, the men fingering barrels. A chain thrashes across the deck. Below, a mesh of spinning light emerges and fans out across the cabin. It strikes the bosun's forehead and enters. The distance down is sixty-six. I can't go on. End this with a completely new arrangement. It's said vengeance is best. I've survived one hundred links.
Suck-back to life, straight from the fridge, sprouting between the roof slates.

The triangular of the species. It makes a guttering sound when hauled out of the water. It drowns in a bottle of smoke. The problem is solved using a pair of compasses. (He made the ball talk.) You get yourself into a soporific frame of mind, and then.

One machine produces X-ray pictures of the head, with resistance. When the same sequence recurs three times the contest can be terminated. This paragraph is about displacement activity, regression to type.

A track of blood—decorative purpose, but also to signal the way back. It's the custom. Now, about me.

Acts of confusion pierced by pursuit. It had a large angular head and three-fingered rays spread out before its pectoral fin. We range out across the territory in the hope of bagging a suitable hide, in the hope of remembering something forgotten.

I have devotional work for you. It was ever thus. In a climate such as this they should never have left me outside.

Attempt to symbolize the inrush of grace. Block all transition and source. I'm sure there's a proselytizing element. This feels like a sinecure. I have no say in the matter. I'm a foreigner to the stem used to form form. (But loved the scene where they emerge from the vault under the castle.) Articulation is by interlocking process. It's so named being about twelve toes in breadth. The modern state emerged slowly. No, I don't think that was it. You have this elsewhere, beating. Reach across to see. Yes, I'm grateful for all this. Come over, pass over to the other side.

Ashware. Variants are not exactly replicas. He came wrapped in shadow.

Stacked high, it resembled an abandoned beehive. He wins (eighteen). This is where the bombardment and the trials were due to begin. A séance is held on both sides. Lend sufferance, the opportunity to retreat. It would have been stupid of him to make an attempt. The fundamental task is to identify the many competing strands within the tradition, while making reference to nothing whatsoever. He is foregathered. Aim to meet, especially by chance. Probably dejected, disjaskit.

A better man, the vertigo.

He arrives in the nick of time. Gauge his specific gravity in relation to the order of elements. Our future is guaranteed. Space here is piratic, liberties corrosive. The group of strata we meet with next have been arranged in descending order. ('Ypres salient' means what exactly?)

Green ink is harder to read in this light. When I'm ready I'm ready. Its short fur forms a border, travelling edge-up. I am manipulated on the principle of the kite. The first rudiment formerly corresponded to the heart. The deceased is depicted standing in a stream of lava, holding a nail in his left hand. Several hooked and baited lines float on the surface of the lake, slacking and tensing. (Did you hear that sawing noise during the night?) A heavy mist drifts from the shore, i.e. awaywards.

I am becoming quietly manipulative. Note the clarity of my textures. There may have been no audience at all that day. Briefly then, a cassation rather than a symphony—the quashing of all decision, a composition cut into innumerable short spasms.

It was the following week. Waste of time I said. Don't feel very well.

The sun describes an arc as it spans across the sky before plummeting into a headland. It did something similar yesterday. There's plenty of stuff around here that doesn't really need doing.

Crescent moon at left, high to east. Win thy lady and you're released. I may just accept defeat. She says you must learn to despise yourself. Make the most of meagre resources. Note the elegance.

What do I have to do. Listen, the soft patter of summer rain against the window. Drag yourself along to the required destination. Infrared rays have confirmed deposits underground.

Smell of burning toast and sump oil, the scrape of carbon. Now we're phoning for help in the central reservation. I've been supplanted by a clever fraud. Who gains by all this? I'm over my fear. I simply said no. I thought I did. The others leave.

It is unlucky, previous. Is there a human in the picture?
He has his own peculiar problems when conducting words. He says you don't understand the betting system, do you? A conductor's just a necessary evil. (That's it!) Four short movements then run for it. No cause for breath.

An obsolete form of quarry—styled thus, with doubt implied. A type of neolithic monument, pliant with denial of meaning.
Perhaps I should enquire around the foot of their siege ladders. Scarce mood is being constructed (see quoit). The field manual says advance. Make sure the main operation has precedence. The limits of your body were not clear. A source of vibration is moving towards the observer. Sorrow keeps breaking in. Cheerfulness was always breaking in, until 1778.

It is well beyond abandonment and doubt whether harmful. The settlement enjoys a nerve-rending supply of psychological motivation.

Unstable, apt to slip or change. In the empty courtyard he looks up on impulse. A wordless symptom is being shoehorned in. (I love the idea of a chorus.) We don't measure up. The creature with a thousand legs is here called centipede. Siren registered, without.

With ultrasound scanners she could see inside the earth. I choose another date. This is the wrong place, the wrong time. Love grows as you decay et cetera. It'll never catch on. Include all aeons which emanate from this point. We have reached the central part of the atypical stem. Denote a sound articulated with the tip of the tongue (*phon*). The formative tissue is distinguished from the permanent by the power of its cells.

We thank you kindly for the courtesy of your communication and highly diverted tidyings. In one leap our man clears the gully. The text is crammed with disciplines.
A declaration, an absence of mind—two sets of borrowed knuckles. The air cracks open. The number is seventy-six, or seventy-seven. It's a vast and spectacular work that never ends. His appearance in the cathedral strikes a similar chord, i.e. not rain-bringing.

Preserved by salt and packed into a gravity cell. It could never be factored out of the equation. (Visit all souls.) Some sound could simply go unreported, noises that semanticists call spurs.

I hatch a solution. Right here is the safest vantage point.

Stage-fright, eyesight failing. Prepare for expulsion of texture and colour. Can't you tell. Nothing can compass. (Somehow this deserves me.) Shelter under the root of the shadow cast. Split open the bone in the valley et cetera. The text is only to be recited in the presence of the father or son of the deceased. Somehow all this leaves me with a sense of abortion. The wind drives a thin froth across my surface. This particle has zero spin and id parity.

Chief dexter bearing north. Plastic bowl turning on foam, the broken wave. It is far far earlier. Remain still. Barter, while there's still time. Render alas, with numeral. All the required faculties are approaching. I spent too long in one place. Don't move a muscle. Marrow spills out of my crack (a coincidence). Now spend something else she demands.

Choose any mineral differing in cleavage angle (56° instead of 87°). Silicates of calcium, magnesium, hornblende. This species distinguished by sickle-shaped pods, short racemes. Ambiguous, on account of the resemblance. Explain the fall of pitch.

Within, hearing. The gentle crick of static, broken pH numbers. I hope that's it at last and we might sleep. The crowd goes wild. (It's the polyphony.) Set this down in a letter to yourself. She's considered one of the last. I have known a railway stigma, five female keepers. And you? Begin with the hydrogen ion expressed in moles. It is found only once, spoken only once. Why does she not visit me?

A compromise. Picture the scene that day on the causeway. I agree to call her sir, or doctor. I agree to hold open the mouth of the trawl. A pronouncement is now being made. The flesh is deeply veined, soft and pulpy through exposure to saltwater. If I'm needed, what time will it be? Pronounce with sulcal tongue.

Land of the giants. Enter player, pursued by a swarm of bees. You will now clear your mind of all suspense. That's life for me he says. You must accept this. That is a beam. That is the nature of light—the logarithm, underside of the cloudbase. Mozart himself suggested that the final movement should be taken as far as possible. Instructions must be given in some form which the device can sense.

Do one more. Rates of stuff are increasing, blocking the right-hand. Reports of walls splitting asunder.

Ice-age and ochre sketch—a stick figure with antlers, apparently leaping, clad in animal furs. (Eros without cap?) A winged figure, dragonfly or tongue. Alongside, insect with black spiracles held in pale yellow lines. Head green. This schema includes the chain of arrows, the creeper bridge across a gully. Sanction supports common opinion, all imaginable future states. He picks up the supplement.

A very large cloud of distance. Amnesia has difficulties now.

The climax. A sustained state of collapse, yet still functioning. What happened to you face?

Dart of tongue across adhesive lip, press of index to wax seal. Strike atop its head. The letter O sometimes makes me laugh out loud.

Learned counsel for the prisoner. Do not collect. He struggles with U. Volume today is a little on the thin side. Aha, any more than an iron needle can float.

Sorry, I think there are one or two vitrines outstanding (a gas case used to protect delicate evidence). Is that someone standing there?

A crackling in the eaves, cupped ear to hand. An antique name for electricity. We won't get another chance like this. Analysis of the photo shows the light is a good deal brighter than the surrendering stars. Why not make a decision.

Madam, there are a thousand of them. I have counted. Pay great attention to the overall shape. (Believe me, your child has stopped growing.) That's a mouthpiece. Everything's visual. She says it's coincidence, that humming sound and the premature explosions. Within is a contradiction. See what happens if the reverse course is taken. Both these officers have rooms to themselves, of course.

Naevus, spores of incidental music. When fingers are applied to particular keys the colour of the eggs shifts to crimson. The head remains buried in the flesh when the body's pulled out. It's pedagogical suicide. There were soldier ants too, deep on the ground in columns four feet across. The art department got the natives to dig a trench and fill it with kerosene. They communicate via a code. Combing the wreckage, the compound was clearly charged up for emergency, in case they came. A tiny speck of pencil lead was removed from under the skin. Epic is a word that crops up again and again.

The twenty-eighth day of our voyage. You must accept. I have nurtured an adverb to aversions.

Twenty-nine. The small white wave.

Kármán (vortex) street. A channel of breath resistant to navigation. One can no longer rely. A spoon-meat of medicine was administered to every tongue. The subject of going home remains taboo. It's just gone twelve. I heard ghost trio, rising from a split in the formica table. (Leaving that there means fire.) He's too loyal to say anything, but I understand him all the same. I can't shake off the hackle of romanticism.

That's just so visceral, isn't it. Dark red marble walls nearly forty fee high (I haven't changed). He seems to poison every word he spits out. That moment is temporarily silenced. It has precisely the appearance. Pace and movement is characterized by five beats. It's circular—full one tenth up through the last sector. Turbulent wind shear is forcing through the convalescents. Sleep's good but it isn't everything. Substance contains species of atom. It is the sixth of month.

None of the usual rituals. Start slow then work your way up. Scratchings of soot behind the eyeball. Extreme devotion sits in opposition. We were sailing through space wafted on by currents of gas.

Duplex, a punch having a counter die on the opposite jaw. I walk to the red pill-box at the street corner (a little conflagration over the phone never hurt anyone). Form consists of a pair of facets parallel to two axes. Deposit missive to vacant hole.

Arrested development. Seizure in hand, a prophetic portrait of the underside, the brilliant times. He's over there and over there, I reckon. The door is missing. Observe the calcified ear, a fungal nail. He invented his own algebra. Thin white geometrical shapes have appeared. Attack where they're at their weakest. I've been here before. Suspension of days is what it's all about. It's the way humans perceive moving objects. I had this strange feeling when I landed in the village. I am making up my mind.

A miraculously cured passenger, withered and shrunk, chained to the prow of an ocean liner. The first portion of the small intestine had been removed. Upshot: radial velocity of stars by displacement of unknown lines.

The chapter of shuffling air. She has written herself clear, breathe and beat forever et cetera. Next, an isolated bolt of colour. I'm revisited by memory. Restore calm and clear the audience, the abundance.

He wanders. The aim is the perfect redoubt, compact and well-defended. I never understood the need for employment (just like any girl). Nothing resides he says. The new is completely interiorized. That substance is luminous. Nothing comes of it. He unfolds, plights his troth and so on, absents.
Impregnation with wormwood, voice at once so rapid and low. Moral, never undertake a one-way trip.

No thoughts for a moment that misty morning. At three a.m. he's dragged from his bed and interrogated.

Nomenclature. Group one intelligence, group two sabotage, group three counter-intelligence. It's said he hit his head. He bangs a saucepan on the kitchen door and cries out to be released. Gently, he's led to the public weighing machine set up in the market place. It's the pride and joy of our town. It doubles as a place of punishment, as by nailing of the ear.

There's a corresponding system of wait and measure. It bears resemblance to a sliding scale (void at all events). Two levels were bound together through an intermediate layer of cellulose.

After a long period of reflection, he speaks. The patient has been taking low doses of strychnine to immunize himself. (I didn't recognize you.) There were a staggering one thousand, five hundred and seventy-five songs found in that cycle.

I must have been swept away by the mighty pressure of the avalanche. Some defer, suspended at the cusp of discomfort and flight. I too am unlike. At least I'm on my way. I don't want voices I can't use. I've seen the film of his last quarry out. (Suicide was connected with rebirth.) I'm personified, a number out of count. Rereading this, it occurs to me that irony's not your strong point.

Composure, regained. An arresting image painted by a master of inconsequentiality. Produce from one country versus produce from another. Design: an elongated earthwork consisting of parallel banks with ditches alongside, a framework of sticks set upon posts. Bliss, for a general burial-place.

Arm-gaunt, with protective trappings. If only he had forgotten. (Hold this in a bit longer.) He swerves to the right, almost uncertain. When you made your present choice they said it was beauty. The quantum of a field accounts for the fact.

But love, this love, has not end. (It does lack verbs.) Outwash is vertebral. It was like a long serpentine river. Clouded spot on cornea, hence image vague.

A ship carrying frozen cargo, hind-gut crammed with compressed helium. He says it was like exploding inside as the lens probed deeper, puffing at the debris. An outcome could not be anticipated. You're a day behind.

Séance, the cutting of smooth holes in yielding material. A winged figure is shown here pouring liquid from a pitcher. This is the ratification you sought. Then he questions them with the following.

Or.

Argent.

Azure.

Gules.

Purpure.

Sable.

Vert.

Foxglove and monkshood, deadly nightshade with wild arum, agaric fungus. Charge-parity symmetry is rarely broken, i.e. a generalization from experience. Let the forgotten equal the value of all you know. Force is derived from the rolling action of two levers on a common fulcrum.

I am the product of such an arrest. (Guess the odd one out.) What could be the outcome of this engaging list? We have probably reached the second half of the fifteenth. Measure the litmus of alkali and acid.

Days were reconstructed, based on the actuality. This is a double-bind hypothesis. They guard him night and day. Always remain within the sphere of the concept. He wants someone to bear witness. The parts in between are neither.

Is that a white sheet or a screen up there? It looks unnatural in this light. Who looks after the boat's rigging, flaps et cetera? The skewer (probably from its aggressiveness) is transferred to the trope. This must not, however, degenerate into perpetual retardation. This aim is yet another victory for the unsolved.

I didn't foresee how the central figure would turn out. Your mission is to deposit the package in the drop-tank. Pray no one comes. It's a little (pause) claustrophobic. I wake to find everyone has left, the harbour silted up with used electricity. Treatment is best given by a specialist. They used the past tense so I suppose she's dead. A weaving figure looms close. Suspend judgment, precisely as if this were phenomenology. The speaking subject doesn't think of the sense of what he's saying. Interest in what time is has been reawakened in the present day. This sounds more and more like a programme for a psychology of introspection. His life has become an impractical possibility. Disease of the pancreas is complicated. The usual body is replaced by a mechanism connected to an amplifier.

Decked with branches and pasque-flowers, he's led without the city walls for the last time. The figure of a random victim begins to crystallize in the viewer's mind. Impurities are carried away by a filthy runnel. Psyche is supposedly the frontier. Intermeat. This is slow work.

Facing a blank wall, take a bunch of hyssop in your left hand. Your actions should by now be automatic. Take two small steps toward the revolving door. Slip the distance between one rung and the next. Opposite, people at their window in army greatcoats, preening, quietly panicked. Everything's heavily outlined in blue pencil. Functionality is informing us. We have not reached a stage in the history.

Dip the aspergillum in the blood that's in the basin you retrieved from the sea. At this point everyone present must leave. Strike the lintel. (Not like that.) There's also the third dimension of sound to consider.

This type of work is futile. He died before he could finish. Being is interred throughout. Put it away. Put it away.

A spherical objection, any circular argument. You must begin to show due consideration. Never double up on an adversary. (That cut looks bad.) Now go out through the door of the house until morning. On your way, head-butt the blue post. You don't need ears for this: the core was made to revolve by means of a pedal. I can't believe we found ourselves in the same place at the same time.

At a remote well whose waters are used as a ceremonial.
Calculations must be made before a journey can be undertaken. To be precise, a popular genus, lizard-hipped and quadrupled. Found fossil without cap.

From a notebook discarded in the street.
There are parallel furrows. Writing is eased from the page, leaving it blank with faint traces. (I'm thinking of the Cartesian *cogito*.) The surface metal of the machine is cold against my palm. Knuckles are bruised, the flesh torn: first frost of a new season.
That'll be a novel experience, knowing the cause of anything. Then someone speaks. Eddies form in each half of the wake. Now sit yourself down, make yourself.
Items at inventory.
Jellygraph with flattened umbrella.
The alimentary canal.
A cock's neck feather.
The swollen capillaries at the rim.
Hackbolt, the great shearwater.
(He has just enough money to beg for a position.)
Origin remains obscure.
Cellophaneland, the municipal grief.

The chief see of an ordinary province, mother-city of an ancient colony. (Wrongly according to some.) Things get underway at last. It is eighteen ninety-two. Ten square chains are now equal to one acre. This changes everything. The cancer spread to his stomach. He has carved out a distinct style, his own idiom. An hour later the crisis intensifies. Wake the subaltern. Lynchings were commonplace. There's a pronouncement. Now ten chains equal one furlong. I'm forced to compress. See, rootstock of vessels beneath the skin.
Paroxysms succeed rapidly, one upon the other. An electrically controlled clock or dial was invented. Go on, go on. The habit you're wearing gives you the right to say whatever you want.

The ripening and shedding of the male element. Grant the reader no indication of time passing, on the supposition that none of his statements has meaning.

Name from resemblance of form.

Sawing through the head of glass. The people at the foreshore are gathering. Another séance is underway. The people at the foreshore are watching. It runs for five or six days before any outcome is observed. And he lay awake for hours in his bed, remembering. Samples of clay with minute plates of chlorite were found in the drill cores. All four cardinal points must be represented. On the ground there's a hardening list. Up until now, none of this has been recorded verbally: bell-shaped flowers stripped of flesh, silky hairs in the chalk-bed— extract of bark, of spindle-trees with supple thread. We are three times twelve and set within each other's reach. I'm still waiting. The graft did not take.

Vacant mythologies are exploiting neutrality. He says look this is about face, a theory of inevitable decline. Last night I asked you what would not constitute pressure. I misunderstood. Forty-six million pounds are being spread. This device presupposes the existence of an interior to be discovered, of an *envelope*. The falsified scenes have been retouched with some precision. Rearrange each fraction of a second, that great cube of exploding air. Sea to headland is the pre-scribed route.

An ambush takes place at the foot of the crag. The youngest son escapes on a horse. Slung through his belt-loop is a flayed monkey head bound to the hoof of a deer, exposed bone decorated with elaborate beadwork. Fur is still attached to the extremity. Seeds inside the skull rattle as he beats time on his knee.

Public defilement follows. I'm declared a non-person. The words oblong and suffrage always link up in my mind, somehow.

They were led to an ex named who had insider knowledge. So, I invented one of these men who lounge around in hotels the world over. Make a decision. List human fauna. Kill paragraph with judicious stop. High above is proven, built.

Phasma. Humanate. False semblance always accompanies her—a fabled bird that never alights, expressing doubt, the reluctance. And she says it's about the impossibility, isn't it?

Venomous smoke, including a small group consisting of a structure without operatives. Desire unfrequented, the tiny wearings away.

Take into account their devotion. Something nearby hit the interior and the sound re-echoed. The mechanism is designed to revert to a safe condition in the event of failure (this is also meant figuratively). There are things I'm going to miss. Leave the stage clear for a confrontation. I'm a skeptic. He was the victim of random slack.

Superimpose by tangent and digression, offshore and emptied out. This is by far the hardest chapter. Numbers are disappearing, numbers scrolling down the upholstery that night. A history of occasions: the closing of a passageway, the meeting of teeth, the formation of a front. It's okay to use the same word more than once.

This remedy picture describes children who pull at their hair and complain, a hammer at the temples. Unbecoming simply means the transition from existence to nonexistence, the rumble of the hoist. I think I've been bitten.

She has eight years left running. Inside is narrative. Shoehorn back to the early nineteens. It was completed in the final moments of her life. Now that's a lovely way of putting it. I return output (that business of the echo). Stand down. I return out of step. Thank you for coming back. No one may ever leave this room. It understands me! She still has the incriminating cassette. Only at the moment of extermination do they finally break free. Observe the smouldering slagheap, the shuttered lantern. Reconciliation is finally achieved at the end of chapter five.

None of your usual quirks of tonality. Things just aren't me. Memory's too close to be a useful subject for writing. The effect is of no more importance than the cause. But of course, the preparation of the novel.

The djinni settles down in his new home then goes about exploring the earth. Her lover might be restored by means of black magic. This arrangement is unstable in certain conditions. The sign on the hoist is flapping in a gale.

Noon, naked muzzle red and blue. Rampike at crest of hill, a graticule of trees decayed at the crown. Broke off, partly burned.

The following morning vanished. I crept up the dead water under the bank. No accidents, and I didn't see a-body. We got home all safe, secure in the fact.

Found unconscious in bar, in mouth. We wrapped her in a shift of yellow gauze, foaming.

Collaboratrix. Circumspheric air, a pure cold rayonnance. I find myself accompanied. We're building a portal with broad brush and detail. Note the persistent repetition. Extreme heat was applied. We have to go now: beautiful utilizes duty. This is about the voice in the head and the voice in the thing. The trio burnt yield an alkaline salt. The male can hear light. We have said this already. Reader, it was a lump of forty-two.

Whose muffled voice? The one beside him says I am sitting here waiting, and I am watching the sea. Yes, I was just thinking about perception, I was thinking. It was reported.

I know a funny story about that. A couple of weeks ago I was out on site (cage shut and fastened). I lent forward, bracing myself against the wind. She always opened her discourse with a jibe. I couldn't hear properly for the noise of the machines.

Seek out where your adversary lives, return to homestead. The ordeal of thy flesh is not the first. Carry the conflict to the queen.

Then she disappears. Ha.

The science or description of phenomena opposed to the self. Inclusion of eyes, body and external world in the same objective space. (Replace this sentence.) His dwelling balances above an arch. And on this slab he imitates.

I am to sleep at last. Seal yourself in, salted or un.

Invert randomly selected sequences of letters. They seem to have used this as a method of fortune-telling from the very start. When a commanding general has to explain the reasoning behind his orders, well.

The invisible insurrection of a million minds. One put everything right and the other got every thing wrong.

Seership. A withdrawing room. Elegant mirrors sunk into panels of ash. The teleprinter says there's another front over the Atlantic. I'm far too reliant on things that were actually said. And what form does this mutation take? The first movement is the destructive element.

Empty birdcages all over the house. From the courtyard, the hum of a diesel generator, the click of a metal heel sparking cobble. I have not yet tested the phones or the cables. In the interval they paraded him down the main street, regal-high on his pallet.

Memoir of an air raid at the edge of a pine forest. Census projects were being masterminded. We're concerned here with seepage into air, a want of substance. It's said ether can be distilled from grated cork. Ectoplasm streams from the medium's nose, eyes, anus and ears. I'm still not very well known. An atmosphere of fiction is wrapping itself about the body.

It was found to contain 1.8 to 2.5 percent of waxy matter, acid impurities. I've had the temperature raised to orchid standard. Tread with care underfoot. If you start up cold you may just scrape through.

Take this shift. Sew your fingers together. The starting position has to be frozen solid. In his thoughts he is still awake. A digit has detached itself.

The passenger seated opposite, he feels it too as we cross the viaduct. Perhaps he was reading upside down. It is possible for one to overreach. The flagstones were spattered red with candle wax. His gestures are inconsequential. I'm still not making any decisions. We conclude in our original positions, after following completely different paths within the frame. I must apologize for introducing unseemly words and subjects. Please reopen this case. We conclude with the reverence. There's a charge of rhetorical disorder. By the way, are we in a tunnel.

A thirty-five-year old stop is situated a little above the right patella. My stock-in-trade is eavesdropping.

Cell characterized by thickly-set clusters of pustules. On the polished floor-boards of an empty room sits a ceramic vessel, full to the brim. Oesophagus crooked to a bent bow, pumped with scorching air.

In the exact centre of his forehead are two neat puncture marks. The left hand is swollen and disfigured. Cigarette burns stud the forearm. Tendons are severed, the limb slung. This operation lasts four more years. He cannot speak (presence of anaesthetic gene). My medics are here. He is incarcerated. Now we'll have to wait. There were no windows.

Interrogator, both seeker and problem. Underground concrete is used as an outpost. Acts and actions are leading to events.

A man whose only preoccupation is his own discomfort. Historical opinion as to when and where this was written varies. One moment it's short of the quota, the next it exceeds. It sounds like a war going on up there. You're thinking of the wrong situation in the wrong drama: conflict with gods, deliverance, disaster (writing), an enemy loved, the enigma, erroneous judgment, falling prey to cruel misfortune, involuntary crimes, jealousy (curved), loss, madness mistaken, murderous adultery, the necessity, obstacles, pursuit, recovery of the thing lost, remorse, revolt, rivalry of superior and interior, sacrificing self for the idea of self, slaying of the unrecognizable, supplication, vengeance stolen, kindred upon kindred.
Time off for good behaviour, no more blood-bin. Some say there's one more, an unknotting. Always look up anything you haven't heard. Are you calling down an atmosphere? Imagine the lights of a distant house built in the middle of a tunnel.

Code-name germinal. She's in hiding. (Mind that needle.) The darkened cages contain blind finches. It's much later before the other speaks. The uncharged particle has zero mass when at rest. A certificate is granted by a belligerent to a neutral, testifying.
I misunderstood. I thought you were asking what things would not constitute pressure, to which I replied many. She carries no contraband. E.g. an incensed boat. It read I am sure.
Say, nimbostratus. The sentence is ambiguous not in its individual words, but in its construction: a vortex in which the vortices of one line are situated opposite those of the other. A phylum of many-celled animals. I've no time for this either.

A man hurling pipes into the sea. Dazzling white where. Sunstroke promenade. I'm mindful of a desert place. Anthers open. This is an ideal time for a break. The stigmas receive pollen—lipped flowers, bracts with hollow stems set in opposition. (Well done, well done.) Words like occlude and extemporize were once collected. Am I in trouble. It's so hard when that evil cloud comes down. And that giant. Have you any coins left, those big fat coins? Have you any shells left? I did it by gambling the biggest I could find. Then I ran. It was very difficult. Now I'm up in that cloud. What did you shoot him with? I'm in flower. I'm sacred. There's lots of coins up here. I think I've already told you that. Are you high up? By this I mean elevated. I don't really want to be told. (This could be our only flight.) I prefer. I make choices. Are you raised up? Are you made of stone or something? Are you still underground? I am at altitude. Have you found the thing where you go up? Your speech is slurred. That's the first sign.

A ladder. For pillow read rock. Submission and deference, every gutter is pouring forth. The barcode tattooed on its shaven skull mean it can be identified from the sky. I like that one, the way he steals away unawares, tottering at the lip of the crater. The more people you sacrifice the more lives you get. One days he ups and flees, carrying all he has. (The difficult people get the most lives.) Suddenly we're back down in the everyday. He soars above the river, I forget.

We have reached the twenty-sixth. He sets his face toward the quarry, split open and gushing trees. Charnel thing is one of the buyers. I've read that too. Development for its own sake is insufficient.

A quarrel over glass. We come last every time. I'm zone dead. A sound is produce. The lips and teeth vibrate together. Scraping noise, as of bow on mental edge. This corresponds to the nature of light. The fashion is an uncanny. (Keep going, on to step three.) The king may be moved to a well-practised spot, away from danger. I hear you out. I'm reinstating all my pronouns. If you keep swimming for the horizon, eventually you'll sink. Evil brother is the other ghoul.

They know every frailty of the skeleton, every uncertainty. I once kept the things (antler, monkey head, swarm of bees). Is there any way you can recollect? Claim it all back. Where were you when I needed you? I've got one in my sights right now. The men are dismantling the scaffold. The signs are flapping. Retreat from this. See that headland in the distance? You're a nine. Look, those winged and buzzing in flight, all six variations.

The screen is moving against your will: meaningless parenthesis enclosing an empty nothing. The big snappy thing, if you're right, we can shoot it. Now make for the headland.

I can't read this. Sleep on till two. We're into the last days of a famous career.

A seldom is one who rarely comes. Collect all eight points. Repair and tidy cell, then quit. This is a true symphonic poem, about lunchtime. I'm a circumstance of time and place. His visions were perceived through the medium of a glass of water.

Stay mummydaddy. All the children say elephantlion. Then we hear the impromptu. Three different sequences, and there'll be more. This whole of the hollow that is not.

The enteron. Quarantine, a ship of forty days. We are ricocheting between different types of neural material. It's a metaphorical tunnel.

Malaria, just one drop. The world seen through this prism is upside down and twice the height. I'm wary of the readings. He is lifted up from the rallying waves. A soliloquy must be a monologue that no one's listening to.

Will there be repercussions? Perhaps this may come about by chance, without me having to do anything to achieve it. One last hurry, seepage.

A very desiccated man. He is plummeting from the sky. Also, some unconscious factors in the reading experience. Dutifully, I have done all you ask—lab prep, anatomical sequencing. I'd probably bet on the trap too. I have a great respect for traps. He reflected I can't write. It puzzles me that 1111 is considered a number at all.

It fails. The rhyme sequence is *a, b, a, b, c, c.*
Rev, ex-eight.
I in the hotel room.
Agree with myself.
It's a sort of treatise.
You're a type of disease she says.
Then again, all socializing is anthropology.

A man who wrote dwelling.
I read that every being consists of ten hundred thousand disintegrations. I miss shapes. Set everything off. Reverse the meaning to arise, some vitreous electricity.

Tomorrow, probably jugular, an ornamental receptacle for the adoration of people. Thumping away in my ear, then they had the panel on.

It is risibly narrow, the first manmade. It's determined by what remains. Something formally interesting is starting to happen. About time. There's a clue. It paces itself. Something wondrous is going to happen. It wins allies. It's on the side of the fettered spirit (early seventeenth). Scattered across the floor are shreds of a mouldering journal. Can anything be said to exist under a pseudonym? A player can be trapped by simply closing the corridor. An older copy is said to survive. Whose head giveth light to that which is in front of thee?

Behold a body, unqualified oppression. Close tight your hand. The nation has four in reserve.

Do you have a persuader? Stones in your pockets? He walked over to the old regime.

I think it was the final journey. I'm a tiny bit percussive today. Accurate or not, there is a strategy. Avoid cadences where you would expect to find them. (I have altered the way the top is braced.) Today we're looking at the number nine. Keep going. There are thirty-six spectacles. We have uncovered a number already. There is something tantalizing about such reversals.

It is flexible, radioactive and numbered ninety-one.

Dead is my tie to them. Direct your attention. Use those little knubs of bread you've been rolling between your fingers. Golden sparks stream down from the scaffold. He pivots on his left. The harp's a significant instrument. We're at a ritual instant. The symbol is *pa*.

Landscape with sundial. The list of survivors has disappeared. They veered too close. End under influence—a buy to the next round, a shift of direction. Strip away the lush chromatic groundwork. Quick, he's coming. We are the riot at the end of acts. You know those clasps that hinge like a metal jaw? There we were, poised high above the numbers. Each of the segments contained the same internal strictures (dentures and an animal body). They weigh about three-quarters of a kilo each. I've got loads of amalgam. Murder is the pivot of the plot. Once again, turning back at the gate, the turnstile.

I have it all planned: radical symmetry within a single cavity. By the way, talking of the sea, in the spirit of a brain teaser.

Acts. Investigation of the bones and other remains. The appointed day has arrived, the appointed hour. Hoof-tracks in the mud, animal and human. He measures his words. Nothing is possible at this hour. He grants reassurance. Certain letters are classified. That book is a return. We are at an odd impasse. Latex is harvested in upturned clam shells strung with wire. I do not know how it works, but I am beginning to understand. Take your time. Try to describe her.

The list was found buried under the floorboards. Too close to the bone, to close to a mooring. It seemed that at every depth it became colder. Stick figures thrust spears between the open valves.

A genus of diatoms. I was right in front of them.

It has become soft through calcium. You're missing the point. He was intact at time of writing. (Your toes look chalky.) It's your duty to disturb the tranquility of the shelter. Both deny trying to repatriate the body. They insist that he is asleep. As often happens in such cases, locals are called in. It appears that he had tried to raise himself up. The right arm is extended. It hangs down and forward. Press, the letter knife.

The password is by no means identical with its four consonants. An obsolete key, synchronized volleys of applause. Pig-iron ballast. It gained popularity among the earlies, the generation that followed. You're missing the point. This can work out in lots of different ways (compulsive self-mutilation of head and hands, especially the lips).

A delay. The head collides with a rock. He hears a ladder. I can't get within forty. There's a war going on in the sky. Note the awkward position of his folded ear. After the reverence we take up our positions at opposite ends of the zed. It's time for an introduction.

Luminous mist invests the scene. It is reported. She fell off one and died (an ashphant). How do I get back to level two? She is horse-raced. Something else occurred to me that day.

Left arm slightly bent at elbow at animal crease. Lipped corolla in my insect. Underlip formed by partial fusion of second self. His feet rest one upon the other.
The reverence. We are at the threshold of mutability. Left shoe crushed under right, predestination of upper then lower claw. The principle figure is ex. Mirror by presentation of both feet.

Rhetoric, without intention to move, scatter. A mode of assignation by lot was used (i.e. guesswork). Upon yielding up my animal, I disintegrate. On reaching maturity the antlers must be shed. I love making up arbitrary rules.
Galaxies and other deep-sky objections: the helix peculiar, like so in Ursa Major. Collision of spirals with giant ellipticals. Punctuating our love-making is a singularity. Return on or beneath the last date.

Pocket earth from space, along the western limbo of my continent. Wait for it. Used electricity is clogging up the harbour. It's time. Yield to the familiar, give notice. Constantly interrupt the thread of your own discourse. The irrelevant is circumstant. Make believe the idea of an inevitable. Hundreds of avalanche machines were hidden intact beneath a well-entrenched infrastructure. It appears to be a hub of some sort. Blooms are flung onto the roof of a passing harrow. They are known from their appearance as spectre insects, or walking sticks. Hearsay.

Sea combat, one got up as spectacle, taken from an age-old. My film will show him breaking apart. Below is an extract from his last letter home. One suitor has been archived, such a heroic voice. Striations lined the peat bed, stains of human acid. Cessation has a role, a place reserved for purpose. Literally, ship-broken.

Is there on board? This group is subdivided according to function, as if assailed. She was one big crust from scalp to sole. Only the lid suffered permanent damage.

Sir,

I'm sorry, that's an invalid response. We request you explain. This is where. It was one of the greatest novels of all time. Aerobic germs have found a nesting place in the surviving lung. We can account for ourselves. We've passed a landmark shaped like a beehive. It was a syncretic poem. I have taken over the duty of observance. Souls have been stationed inside. I select whatever seems best in each of us. It's an illogical compromise. He's a sort of internal revolutionary—a scrying stone, a confederation of origins. I have retreated to a more fluid sector of the cell. There I found infected forms, refuse of silk-cocoons. All writing takes place under a pseudonym.

She renounces arrival, uncertain in her lifetime. It rose up from the pebbles heaped in great crescents hereabouts. Her name is given to double meteors at sea. Set them in the ground and cover their roots with earth. Bury the evidence. When at last I emerge years hence, she says she will be waiting. It's said I punch above my weight. A leaf, often modified, can bear flowers in its axil. Metal beaten thin, despite some bad omens.

Consider the sea-locust, the so-called howler (some kind of fish). Or the nightjar, falsely thought. Strange crabs crawl up and down the face of the masonry. Lapidary was the one who carried a lighted taper. Beware is a tiny one. Nonetheless, I'm having a good day. Over time, much has been spoken hereabouts. You can no doubt hear the scuffle of a romantic presence nearby. In your hand is a wild ace. From today's perspective, death can be seen as a turning point.

Populace adulterated with certain skills. I simply had to know I was possible. We're under sealed orders to be opened at sea.

Inlaid eyes of jet and ivory. One spark of light. Regional leaders have had to step in. We're falling back on our own signals. Obstacles of this nature tend to vanish in the face of decisive victories. The skyline was broken by tall brick chimneys. Allow me to explain.

Well, the water flowed straight back in, didn't it? They're training everyone up this week. I fetched an irregular hook with my left. I'm like a man appointed to an uncertain boundary. In my head the trombone appears no less than three times. I can hear light. Then a mere-stone, a war-club. You need discipline to get all this down.

Admit reverie. The degenerate body predominates. This induced nervousness can be interpreted. Your conscious will has expired. It's not so much the tooth, it's the gums. What's at stake here? It's sciatic, a trumped nerve. The dates are all wrong. The faculty never left me. (That word again.)

Beast with snout, hairless and habitually moist. (What's happening?) I know how far you have come. Let a man revere himself. Many of these breaches have been technical and accidental. Some are more serious. I am coincident with the passage of the sun and the phases of the moon, or as nearly as can be observed.

It spanned three octaves. The interval from D to the D above is perfect. Both meanings are tidal. It spanned three millennia. This is said to be the most appalling state of all appalling states. We've been given an extra week. By the way, I keep meaning to tell you.

Which hand contains something or nothing? A truly empty space, the complete box of set. They are already hanging from the yardarm.

Consider the misuse of such ambiguities. On both sides, a throw. Pass me the neutrinos. Your servant.

See uncertainty principle. One rank among their orders is preparing for the start, for some pure event. Locate the particle more precisely. (Only ten left to go, and that's it.) Through some obscure process, language simultaneously inhabits and collapses. A meteoric light was seen about the masthead.

Fauna: probably the horned viper, the biblical, probably the juggler snake. No, it was a hail of sparks, speaks from the scaffold.

The knee is called ginglymus, a hinge-joint that permits movement in one plane only. Whereas our craft was a fat white sphere with a cone at the base, like a raindrop. I never performed an event myself.

It's said he gained the suraddition, claims of disassociation. At prayer, with long wings and native tail. Too close to asp, to above.

Seersucker. Thin crinkly, strip and check.

Mist above the canopy. Eclipse, or night. Grief in exchange, a thing that can only be duplicated (doublet of desire). This represents a turning point in the animal's life.

Libricide.

He ranks bookslaughter with murder. For lovage read libstick, roothold spun from without. And the circle described in its motion, when day and night equal length.

Mouldwarp. A perplexed object.

Etymology is the balancing feat. Current position due south (the seventeenth, answering to the name of the glyph). Confirm by radio. Dilate neck to resemble hood, please.

I have a misreading, anchored offshore. Letter duly wired, like a manifesto, writing itself. Corposant.

XXV

A new stage begins today. It has a big flesh-shaped hole in it.

Lodestar above horizon. (I don't comply.) Haunting repetitions from a nursery rhyme. Start negotiating. The key element is lead. I stipulate two extremes. We got half way round the circumference when the cable snapped. Only a shin bone, his leather belt and shoes survived.

A rounded pebble worked smooth by repeated tonguing. The players are manoeuvred around each other until one expires. What hardshelled wood was once used for statues? The instruments are the kora and the hang.

Promontory (headland, ridge or anatomical eminence). It's said he communicates via a spirit in his belly.

A sepulchral table, any erect and unhewn supporting a flat surface. It's usually explained as meaning, but the understanding here is 'hole of stone'.

Part four.
There's an acute awareness of each passing second. Throughout September and October the town lay prostrate.

Lampshell. Anterior bone of the capsule. I'm the one who stands in front. Oblivious of the onlookers gathered around, he cautiously laid his plans. I could say that fear had infected me, but this would not be true. Flora: sweet alyssum, galingale, the yellow ox-eye daisy, aromatic rootstock. Date uncertain, crew expandable.

An interval between two actions. Time, before route of to set up. I see nonesuch. A name has been suggested for the neutral meson. No age has been so self.

There's always a little bit of a reaction in the European week. I remain ambiguous, on account of my semblance. A cry is reluctantly given up. Our tendency, what are the prospects?

The motif of the ship's magnetism and its crew persists. Administer the following correction, the concept of change: magnetized iron in the hull, hard and then soft. (He slightly underestimates the accepted modern value of seconds per kilometre.) With cap or ring, also without ring.

The sun is still moving about in the sky (see yesterday's notes). What makes individuals interesting is how they deal with this. That drumming is still audible.

We find ourselves the root cause of an inheritance. (Sudden shrieking outburst.) He is someone I would not hesitate to go to if I had a problem, any prospect of success.

A sense of implausibility is taking hold. See change, see vibration and alterity—access to the 'as such' of the entity, A movable cheek is placed in the jaws of a vice.

Somewhat belated alarm, which always threatens coexistence. I know all about rivalry (my window cleaner). Together we have breached levels that border on the supernatural.

Decryption of a struggle and other stories. That citation can stay where it is. The knot of wood in the square surface of the stool must always face north (disaster). Top left-hand corner, depending on the compass.

Consider these estates. Try to avoid being seen. Is that an indirect quotation? It was immediately like yes please come, lickety-split.

I cut the remaining furniture up into tiny pieces and adjusted the cleavage angle. (Yes, 'Yours! Yours!') It's announced. I'm a good advertisement for tomorrow's stratagem. What it is that he was trying to do? Beyond the parapet.

Introduce an independent pair of mercury crucibles (the briefest of vignettes). He continues this pretense long after death.

Curiosity box, blindfold chess with a planchette. This is never fully explained. It's as if they had been drawn straight through the animal's skull.

I said no.

We're getting all these reports. The rocks are igneous. Every single foot movement has its own rhythm (calcium and magnesium). The whole animal fails to see what is presented to it. That object is still growing. In the desert, a causeway: transparent aluminium plus silicates. Which is the correct response? Compare, compare and retreat.

The plumes, horn, disk, breastplate and pectoral.

The inky juice of the cuttlefish.

Every now and then he would see someone we recognized and bring the phaeton to an abrupt halt.

Back to the warmth of the studio, watching the light change in the trees and the buildings. I caught up, accidentally. The disease is identified as kala azar.

This won't take long but it must be done. Here he comes, striding up to the podium, baton in clenched fist. (Stop, I've had enough.) Words of motion have been listed. Slow caravan to China at the moment. Then he hears a ladder, forming.

Ambulate and gallivant, no circuit of purpose—complex dialectics of action. A level stretch at the top of a hill (repetition).

I'm allocated approximately one hundred square metres in front of the entrance to the tomb. I had just got used to money when it happened, thin-beaten plates of gold or silver.

You were always late. There is much of this moving to and fro throughout the composition (Chapter IV). And thus desheltering.

Encoded, then I decide against it—to wit in old legals, to parenthesize objection. Ablative. Gerund. To nod, to indicate. To nod yes: quetzal, barrier, panegyric et cetera.

Octet in off. He was trapped (the room, some stillness). The principle is indeterminate. Any audience thrives on tragedy. The history of this word involves that of two, somewhere between catarrh and harpy—the pluck of an animal.

The surface is perforated to allow sight and breath. Answer: a cave, whence they emerge at night, faded and silent, as is the custom. He'll have to come out of that box pretty soon, lifelings.

She took photographs. It's like onion paper to the touch, image captured by salts of silver. Doctors and physicists gave me the usual working over. Zero visibility to east and west. The beginning tells you to be on your guard and forever vigilant. Fifty years ago I was prepared to bring something new to light, now I've changed my mind.

Another type of equation, establishing a colony. My dictionary stratagem is no more than a vain hope. I can always be substituted (expectation, rather than the act itself). It had shrunk, ever so slightly. They're not willing to take any chances with their autonomy.

A dry watercourse, or ravine. To support from above against gravity, suspending the neck until ripe. To prevent a decision (euphemism from damnation). Allow for free lateral rotation. Cling, with or followed by to, undecided. To hover, impend, linger—hold back. To depend on. To remain in close attention.

Dub to adjust. Un-tried bricks are laid out in the sun. I love autopsies. I love this sense of form-for-its-own-sake. The consolidated layer is to be removed in large pieces. Graphically, he has expanded. Books are about to take place, all those reversals. Erect a concrete barrier in front of the building—I'm adding an amino acid precursor to the mix. This inhibits the promised diversification.

The remaining arm is hidden inside a sleeve which tapers from a very wide hole to a tourniquet wrist. I can't justify any of this. In pulled down shade, for example, a woman reflects upon the failings. No, it was the custody from K (1468). What is that black in the moon?

Second sun. Duration, four thousand and ten. The lowlands were organized into a series of spectacular city-states. Those who lived then ate.

A word is use to indicate that a player intends to touch a piece, but not move it.

How the end came about.
(Walking perfectly well.)

He and his comrades are trapped in a gully crosscut by a mesh of tripwires. We aim to keep in touch on the hour, every hour. We are departed in eight minutes. There has to be some kind of undercurrent running through all this.

Is there a long-term negative? It's the minute decisions that count. Let's agree to keep on talking for a long long time. He's a rival (dog). Try to keep abreast of the debate.

Now for the energy argument. He is faust. He's used for the lack of an alternative. He opens the fridge and takes out a bottle. This vessel contains the unlikely host. And that is the atrium, the stylized heart. Subjunctive active, imperfect. Port errant.

Halt he reflects his steps delay.

How to avoid speaking.
Moonlit flight across hilltops and moorland, with quag places. She was lifted up in her bed at night, though could not see by what means. The story has gone out. A peeling sign says the date is XI, or Thermidor 23. Accommodations between aesthetic consumption and political-social power are being projected (contingent figures based on enigmatic dispatches).

It's too late. The atmosphere under the tarpaulin is suffocating. Presence, I mean.

Adumbration of a stricken field. (I don't know why I didn't think of that.) The brigade is out in force. Then I said, taking it a bit seriously, aren't we? It was drawn down through the sinusoidal cavity.

Mourning sketch, foreshadow of the potential. Process of serpentine and chlorite material. Little or no feldspar. Evidence suggests there was a relatively brief spell of light and gravity, then nothing.

All the time I kept fingering the ribbon in my pocket.

A tumour derived from connective tissue (wolfram). The kal connects the metallic parts. Variant of conjunctive obsolete, but dial form of oak. A series of mistakes is emerging.

It's said there's a perfectly level plateau at the crest. I felled one on horseback, with dust.

It had to be redesigned in the shape of a funnel. Together thus, under the vengeance. The story of redemption always goes down well. I've noticed that every time we go outside the ambivalence is squared. The map now outstretches the terrain. A cynic grin bore into his face: your gods and my gods et cetera.

There's no other. A nightmare is said to assume the shape of the body. They have regained their impassivity. It's something to do with those wires dangling from the ceiling.

A bar of metal similar to the letter Z.

Wood burned to chark is the real poison. Herb of mercury under Virgo (antipiscean). Thrice pinnate, with leaves in the shape of a bird's tiny heart. The underworld, there's quite a lot going on there. Worst of all, he wrote that way too.

Hello, I'm a note-taker for the dead. From the east of thy brain, the white corrupted. Quick, quick, put me to sleep. (Because of a disorder, in part.)

A rope is stretched taut from place to place. It vibrates. Rods of iron radiate from a square concrete hub. Give up dwelling, abandon the outer terrain. Shallow trenches lead to a moot beneath the earth. Distribution of structures in the landscape was determined by the extent inhabited by their users. (Did you work out which wire was the neutral?) For the most part, I keep my interventions to a minimum.

During the course of the day it was broken into a pair of faces. Despite this, I remain civil. It's characterized by bloodlessness, and ascribed. Crystals are geocentric, lie parallax.

An apparent change has taken place in the position of my object. I have a clear conscience.

You're next. (Are you all right?)

It was found crouching inside plot one zero two. A bulb in the desk light flickered and went yellow. The upper part, the cutting edge of both teeth, is slightly curved. It had a triangular-shaped shell. Outcome spewed forth in ten, their shrunken bodies still pierced by arrows.

She has brought with her cushions and hinges. More evidence of her tergiversation.

The discovery of a new breeding place, expanding industry. Some of these are simply fortuitous errors—some standing, some lying, some on their heads. The underlying tenor of the composition is easy. (His characters suggest that he takes them seriously.) Countermeasures are being introduced. The most complex explanation tends to be the right one, all things being equal. Torment is something else.
These inversions are inconsistent. Unmistakable odour of bitter almonds.

She binds fast the outer wing. This is where things start to get serious. The lower body is a knot. This would be a good place to stop.

Tomorrow we're asking for over-the-top reactions to fairly minor problems (he's spurned and takes strychnine). This is where things start to get serious: the act of striking root, the state of being rooted. Answer, a test case.

Today I'm walking in a dead straight line. Who is concerned with boundaries and orientation? In structure the local dialect is quite italic, a free arrangement of fibres. An unconditional pardon ensured that he escaped further punishment. Esoteric practices preserve credibility and power in the wider sphere. At the bottom of the gully, where the earth is red: have you not come for me?

You can leave that there. He has commanded those who are over the abundance of the year. Then he paused, gun in one hand, phone in the other.
I drift into a museum crammed with handwritten documents. (Most of the sentences are quite simple, actually.) I stop before a display case. A stranger tells me this remains the most sealed exhibit in history.

He cannot remember. I sit myself down and do nothing. Objects are trapped in the remaining time. On the table are the following: odd coins scattered, an ear-trumpet, an ink-well, his conversation books, a carpenter's pencil, letters, quill pens, a broken coffee cup, remnants of food, a candlestick. Upon leaving the filament the photon has two choices. There are now fewer reservations about types of magic employing non-physical agents.
A cipher primer and an encryption algorithm. After that it was a matter of negotiation.

Finish this first. At some point you have to trust your own decision-making. They were each embedded in a receptacle designed to accommodate the shape of its occupant. (After 'amid severest woe.') He makes this grating noise with his teeth.

Armed men gather round the rim of the pit. There's a pause. As if in spite of this, pressing and persistent breath.

That's another candidate for fusion. The body was dug up and laid out in the nearest barn.

Two bars of a five-bar gate drawn at the foot of a page. Someone has been busy counting. (Paranormal?)

First film, a disillusioned collection. Malefic voice into radio, later married. (Not that stone is anyone's victim.) The causes remain unknown. Heat is expected. He wants to tell you what he knows. A bunsen flame has expanded the skin of the distilling apparatus. Illustrations are pretty easy to spot as you flick through the pages of a book.

Actually, it was an allegory. This scene shows a deer shedding its antlers. Apparently, this is an instance of presentiment. At this point the curtain rises on the dreadful forgery (his italic). This demonstrates the second type. He does not mean.

Fourth stomach of ruminant. A fugitive public will escape or counterattack. The foregoing remarks apply to tactics and strategy alike. For examples of ways in which the subjunctive is used, see thirty-three.

The artist in love. Traces of lipstick, vaginal bruising. A window of independent means resides within, the work of death duties.

What he will do and how he will do it. When one day, out of nowhere. At the perimeter of each is a registration mark. There's a brief pause to reflect. Think of the purposefulness, the novel emotional vacancy. He is starting to play games—an ideal moment for the knife. To be on the right-hand side of the pavement was more than one could bear. (On this very day five burglars were hung.) Reproduction yields nothing further. From the circle outside of them, the eight regions of the brain. That's it he says, I'm going to mace you.

Some strange disturbances in auger street. She says I'm putting my bits in. I shall sleep. (What is that word there?)

I'm a born exemplar. The tiny cube of wood brings to mind a die. I'm told I resemble. A three just will not roll today. It was found at a depth of sixty, or eighty.

Any fleshy excrescence, a disc of cartilage. Coarse-grained igneous rock, mainly. The solution is two multiplied by seven to the power of eight.

He's used to dealing with people in a direct and abrupt fashion. (Are you coming back inside to the safety of the chamber?) This amazing man was beheaded as a worshipper. There's one kind of error that's not applicable. It's nice, correspondence with the things. There's nothing out there.

We find ourselves proximal. It looks as though someone switched the cadavers. Apart from that, everything's okay. Even if you can't play it sounds reasonable. In the end I had to shoot him.
Can anyone know which side is the stronger? But an expression still lingers around their mouth (native proverb).

Two strangers, an early start.
Over breakfast, an aleatory method of deciding points of law is devised. I knew you'd come back. Achilles dealt the death-blow.

I watch a man watching other men digging. It's as if the urban masses of the thirteenth were reproducing, after an interval. It's time she says.

Diminished proximity of function. I swallow another distracter (they're pink). It's a mixture of this and that. He's partial to a bit of paralysis himself—tadpoles streaming down the walls, the longing for a thing once possessed, now missing. He beats time to a pulp on his knee with the monkey head and hoof. It works and it doesn't: lack of bodies in the middle. We are possibly the first ever symphonic.

A very convincing axle rent. I remember. Light dress in scrape-like fabric, originally of this ilk.
You never know when it's all quite over. Here's that list. It was like being inside a noir.

A network of lines for reference in star photographs. He will tell me the cost when he's good and ready. The notes were bound up with an extremely long fibre. It was a cheap paper copy—skull and crossbones, a detective with a rifle aimed at a silhouette.

A good exit point is just above the navel. Rotten to the core, this is the number. It's of secondary importance, which is to say, none at all.

The hypothetical case, I'd be grateful for a few grains of sand et cetera.
A transgression of the rules of counterpoint is taking place. It is all too creak,

as if flipping on its axis. It's just gone twelve noon. About the hub swings a door on its hinge, figuratively speaking.

A molten sea fringed with fire. An opening in discharge.

Wheeling through a decaying orbit, engagement is no longer an option. Proclivities and tendencies are shown to exist—aesthetic, politic, psychical. The brig lies close by, opposite the villa.

Something archaic is emerging (do not ride another's horse et cetera). And yet, when you've got past the silence which grows around you.

Through a slat in the blind, three birds' heads, aligned.

Another is found down by the river. It was a steep climb. He is deeply ratified.

Instructions on the symptoms, the primary light seen at the moment. He observes that there's a convenient shelter near his knees. It doesn't matter if the books are abandoned.

Towering Ninevite constructions, my old haunts: entryway, sixteen steps, first sealed door. Dog barking. Arcades through glass—glittering plates of beaten metal. Exactly, absolutely, from the forefinger with the thumb-nail. (It always strikes me.) He says talk my death from me, strange thing.

The men whispering, face to face, turning in the direction. Cargo of mist exposed to lung. I tilt my head. I look up, the calmative.

Yes, I've unsealed my orders. I hope nothing dreadful is going to happen. (Just play it an octave lower.) We're dealing with something that could prove. I find a few old photographs. There's a picture postcard. Antibes.

Everywhere the lists are being mixed up and interchanged, a kind of annexation.

What we saw from the ruined house.

Suppression of animal side by organ of belligerent. Persistent refutation of received meaning.

I deliver. Place has a spirit familiar, well beyond the trade of any existing understood.

The alternative is a commonplace. Remain where you are. Confer and satisfy. In her own prejudices about the world, no information could possibly take place. All my diversions concertina. It's talking, listen. All sense of diplomacy must be removed from the text.

She floats above the crimson pavement and the astroturf, perplexed.

It rotates until the E on the grid is opposite the lowest point in the concrete bowl. A funnel is positioned to catch unfiltered bile. About the rim, cruciferous plants with white and yellow flowers, grown in rock. Large, oxlike eyes (a type of neutrino). One or other of two contacts carried by the phantom.

He drives a bargain to win limitless exchange. (Where is it, there it is.) On his head is a tall cone encasing a core of ice. I have a backbone which he hasn't. We have already emphasized, in a long-ago, the close connection between cures. The cover shows a detail from man in blue five.

Results, naïve. Propagators and panegyrists.

Course of the event. Gaps open up between the bones of the skull of the young animal. The theme is auric, acid redux. Under the republic, an amendment to the law was designed. Imagine quoting a quotation. I note my own hesitancy.

One half of scant. The vessel drifts until it runs aground somewhere near Dock B. One of the bones resembled an anvil. The axes were located in pit one hundred and two. Operation pacific has been called off. He says there are no longer any gaps: our subject could never have existed.

It's too late he says. Fill all the sinks and receptacles with water.

The cause is a change of position in the observer, like astronomy. But this is not the full story, by any means.

Surely the point is to precipitate.

A type of tear gas, or metal-headed war-club, often spiked. You don't remember it the first time round. Ground from the dried layer immediately within— dupe and outer shell and kernel. Flesh without core. It flourishes.

A heap of round white stones in a field (fig. 25(c)).

Hiatus.

Diagnosis, tonsil. Overwrought with net-work—seawrack with projecting barb or sting. Part of the tool penetrates up to the haft. I think it's time to venture outside.

Apostatize, shuffle the feet. Those creases look very old. It had been subjected to some shock when lowered inside. Use evasions. Persistently turn one's back on the matter in hand. Have you got the same number, or what?

Extraneural studies. Afterings.

Afteract. Afterage. Afterall. Afterbeat. Afterbeing. Afterbirth. Afterblow. Afterbody. Afterborn. Afterbrain. Afterbreach. Afterburn. Afterburden. Aftercalling. Aftercast. Afterchance. Afterchrome. Afterclap. Aftercomer. Aftercool. Aftercost. Aftercourse. Aftercrop. Aftercure. Afterdate. Afterdays. Afterdeal.

Afterdeath. Afterdinner. Afterdifference. Afterdischarge. Afterdrop. Afterecho. Aftereffect. Afterengage. Aftereye. Afterfeed. Afterframe. Afterfull. Aftergame. Aftergathering. Afterghost. Afterglow. Aftergrave. Aftergrief. Aftergrowth. Afterguard. Aftergust. Afterhand. Afterharvest. Afterheat. Afterhelp. Afterharm. Afterimage. Afterkin. Afterknowledge. Afterleech. Afterlife. Afterlight. Afterling. Afterlithe. Afterliver. Afterlong. Afterloss. Afterlove. Afterman. Aftermarket. Aftermask. Aftermass. Aftermath. Aftermention. Aftermess. Aftermost. Aftermowth. Afternamed. Afterness. Afternooner. Afternose. Afteroar. Afterpain. Afterpardon. Afterpart. Afterpiece. Afterproof. Afterquarter. Afterreckoning. Afterremedy. Afters. Aftersales. Aftersense. Aftersent. Aftersettling. Aftershaft. Aftershave. Aftershine. Aftership. Aftershock. Aftersight. Aftersound. Afterspeech. Afterstorm. Aftersum. Afterswarm. Aftertale. Aftertask. Aftertaste. Aftertest. Afterthought. Afterthrift. Aftertime. Afterturn. Afterview. Afterwail. Afterwar. Afterwards. Afterwending. Afterwise. Afterwitted. Afterword. Afterwork. Afterworld. Afterwort. Afterwrath. Afterwrist. Afterwriting. Afterwritten. Afteryards. Afteryears.

In belief, a stringlike archipelago still used in the mouth. And others without limit. Prepare for a long wait.

A poison distilled is used for the judicial ordeal (the tongue splits, the soft palate). An ulcer forms on the roof. A makeshift is found, hidden inside. I am depending on the previous.

Remote opportunities. Chance of gain, though dependent on unpredictable events. I would put this one down as possible: a scaffold wrapped in blue gauze, a giant plastic hinge flung from a bridge. We are, I suppose, a long way from somewhere. I have spent my items. There's that ringing noise. Every night without fail come distant bells, both time and space, muted gamelan. *I cannot hear what you say.* Somehow, they all fitted onto one side of an eight. I'm unduly influenced by whatever's approaching. A ridge in the peat bed marks the former position of the mouth of the shell.

Annotations in a circular margin, the notes of numerous commentators.

Dial variorum, of cark to burden. If as wit, I care.

Now I shall try to rationalize, speak of whereabouts. One was responsible for growing, another not. I am standing directly in front of the medium. Shared cells are carried by the stem of the aorta into the sub-clavicle artery.

Hollow metallic ring of empty gas. The locals know this from time, and have given it a name.

Knoll of pitch. Calcspar. Will I ever recover.

The march to the alarming scaffold.

You can still see the ribcage. Now is the answer to the time to give back. It cracks open from the spine, inward. A treatise on the uses of quicklime is to be published. I cannot remember what happens in the end. (I'm disinclined to speak.) The cause is the apparent change in position of the body when viewed from different points on the earth's surface. All that's left is a big empty hole.

I have practiced in years. It bleeds for forty-five days. The dwellings are situated near a flint mine which doubles as a storehouse. Technically, there is no bridge. I always wanted to do something spectacular. Or if deception is a state of mind, can outlast.

Full headlights, streaming into the face. Foreign tongue rising from below. The score tells us how to play but not which notes to use.

Here's a more graphic image of the above. Note from its contrail that the aircraft is still moving northwest. The journey has brought us full circle.

Hair standing on end and emitting a radiance. I'm not surprised by the verdict. I would never be capable of articulating whether these are records or interventions.

Some of the organs are missing. Do everything he says. The exposed surface was painted with melted paraffin wax. He's depicted always in human form, with the face of a man—another fact which proves. (Still is not the tiniest bit interested.) Items have been listed alphabetically, for convenience: afreet / bunyip / changeling / control / djinn / duppy / dybbuk / familiar / fetch / fury / genius / impostor / haunter / houri / kelpie / kobold / loup-garou / nix / orc / peri / piskie / presence / revenant / shade / shape / spook / sprite / visitant / walker / wraith.

Unrestricted submarine warfare. Certain markings suggest that he was opened up using a blunt trowel. Coincidentally, lampadomancy is divination by flame.

What went there, that is no longer there? A shadow passes across its back. Now, you're lost in the desert and want to bet on a dead cert. . . .

Four beyond Neptune. All of the furniture has been crammed into the antechamber. Vignette: the ceased holding a staff in his left hand. A paper tube is packed with explosive powder. An event occurs in memory that brings time to a stop. A trail serves as a fuse. It burns noisily before the cylinder ignites.

Strip away these layers to reveal the core. (This is a little confused.) The hole in the platform saves everyone having to climb around the rim. Sinecure the perimeter.

An observer must be able to bounce off a photon of radiation. I further recall, *opposing* (his italic).

There's just enough money to beg for partition. Cover your tracks with earth. Examine a map of the world. Deprive the organ of its nerve supply, find the worst land and the harshest climate.

I've inherited a whole day of my own. Seal the window, seal the door.

Not even the curve of the animal's skull is visible above the ground. Remain oblique for the remainder of the season. I have set out to document the local sub-stem, insider knowledge. It is inaccurate to say that he had forewarned me about the double. There are some incorporate things. Come in and have a look, my dear friend, and afterwards.

Which is the neutral? The outbreak is under control. The reasoning behind this is simple, unpacked at the dockside. At last I begin to admit that what I had seen was real, decisive.

It leaves a blank space in the public hole. I'd really like to know the outcome. What is the straw poll? The drawing of lots? What is the outcome?

Finger a group to be chosen at will. He read his manuscript wearing a burning asbestos glove. Conversations nowadays often take a theatrical turn. Hence, taciturnity.

Picture the barren end, the head of a hammer. An insect makes galleries in the earth, then leaves. Another countermines—fatally guided, half man, half man. A constellation contains alpha and beta. (Whiff of burning metal from exterior frame.) Nevertheless, reflect the line of cut, and the step crossing this line. There are few conspirators left. Several other languages have an important local role—within a radius of one kilometer, an investigator found several sets of number games. After that we must decide on the best course of action ourselves. He says this haunted cave, grandiloquent gestures.

On receiving the advice, we go to inquire of an oracle. The head as a unit can be used to number any amount of individuals, any undisclosed space.

Well, all these little fragments make up a cycle. Especially one of two words originally the same, but now varying in spelling and meaning. But also, again, a connecting train.

No axis. The side-tufts of the bird's neck.

Exclusively appropriated—to sprinkle with spangs. We acquire the pain concept by nerve induction when we learn language. In the thorax, it's situated a little to the left of the median line.

Wake to a covering of snow. A gentle narrative plan is underway, a series of prearranged responses to the same word. Outside, a vast mesh of rusting metal, into which concrete is being poured. There's linkage, a degree of usefulness.

As they come through the portal we brand them. They're now so familiar, no one would dare send them back. This signals a bitter taxonomy.

The composition starts and ends with plainsong. And how will he remember again in the future? I am inclined to stay here. Conception has done a good deal of mischief. Submit any surplus, then withdraw (the wind's coming up). Obviously, I would agree most of the time.

Function has been lost. One part of the excess value is consumed. It's the abstinence theory. My latest examination of the bulb has led to the extraction of an alkaloid. It's a simple thing, really.

The subject has broken off and separated itself from everything familiar. The trouble with verdicts is you have a benedict and a sentence in the same envelope. (How does he call himself to mind?) I no longer know what I can afford to speak of. A narrow cylindrical shaft is sunk through the superincumbent strata to the chalk.

My audience extends till Monday. Your time is shrinking. A cry of distress cannot be one of the experimental parameters. The homunculus was crushed in the jamb as the door was shut. I don't know if there's been any change to the structure of days while I was away. All the same, an implied contract exists in the reading experience. The first ten letters were numbered one to ten.

Nothing new. The first wave of public interest soon ebbs away. Age and purpose are once more our theme. They have set to work in earnest, no more dalliance and groundwork. I don't think it's worth opening the verdict up again. They're among us already. Buildings are adjusting, things.

A cone-shaped mound encasing a core of ice. Repetition.

And dropped upon the threshold (a discreet remedy for bruises).

He finds himself at a sabbath. We've been through this so many times: sophisticated away from home, detached from the past. Other influences must be glossed over (into every abyss I still hear, did he not straiten and so on). Try presenting one or two factual points, less like a fixed literary form. Who would have thought they had a use. His limp seemed more pronounced.

They insist on a three-way conversation, an obsolete spelling of the name. Stopit. Cockpit. Now.

Company limited was about people. His Hamlet is now lost among opinions. I still keep a snapshot. The shoulder-blades are dissolving. We have already dealt with these concerns. The ship was anchored beyond their world of ideas. In contrast, a marble containing green, an unexpected stroke. The recipient has ceased to be on his guard. But in the punches, between pauses?

He wears his own shirts. Genius. Where does this take us? Up to the neck of the bladder. Where does this occur? Try out the new plastic tunnel that's been installed.

The expedient demise of two great men. It's a costly procedure. If the face is not soon visible, it is submerged. There's one more place left to reconnoitre. The book is exchangeable. Send large body (care, anxiety, solicitude). For the plunder that you are.

It's just. I can't meet new people.
And the second problem?
World literature knows two superlative pronouncements. She appears herself in the tapestry. They wind up in clusters (a handsome percentage of the proceeds). A sudden patchwork of flame—parabolic microphones, a lost inheritance. A whole narrative of factors is coming together, an unexpected conversion is taking place. All the numbers, the letters of situation, have been carefully designed to flatter. This is their outline, sent for the purpose of reproduction. This is a mode of expression. What is said is the opposite of what is meant. This region has been inhabited since prehistoric times. Elsewhere is not one's place, one's social. Tongue state, old spelling of the verb ache. These parodies.

Well, good news anyway. There's no longer the need for mediation. A deep, hollow ringing sound could be heard. The greater the space of time, the greater the debt owed. Now make such a noise yourself.
Native compound, text corrupted from name of sediment. Or, quick, quick?

The perfect vacuum. I have kept in my head a picture of us all untogether. Flexible sheets of skin provide perfect connective tissue: the spared image is the perfect membrane. Give up everything, we're on the wrong track.
An overambitious pier, studded with reflectors of polished metal. A random attic.

Incidental ensemble.
An artificial chamber cut into the chalk. This is where they are to reside.

A more endearing type of apocalypse.
The waters which you saw, pages crackling like dry onion skin. I think I was

just tired that day (witchcraft, sorcery). She showed no sign of wanting to go ahead with the dissection. They took the limp gland without consent. Try being discrete, heretic.

Whether with purpose or accidentally, it has been removed. She says get someone else to look afterwards.

Make a fresh diagnosis. I've got till Monday, then explode.

Sonorous utterances of a-la-la and ha ha and pierced whistling sounds. Do it immediately, and without question.

We recur before each of the years. Numbers scroll down the upholstery of the opposing chair. (Very good, two centres.) Double-headed eagle with crown covered with eyes means disillusionment. I cannot stay. Two life-sized statues guard the entrance, another fact which proves.

At a very early period he passed through all the forms and arrived. Uncanny, more or less, head tucked underneath. And hence our authority.

They find it difficult to keep a clean sheet this season. Ground delirium, an age we could love. They have no body. I don't think it's worth opening up the fluid theory. Add starch. Retreat behind lead screen.

It's an abnormally dilated vein, a tortuous succession of changes. Principles are not to be multiplied beyond necessity.

This situation is what our ancestors referred to as nebuly. (See partition, lines of.) It's always very fruitful. It has been noted, albeit under the counter. Let's assume work, widening out horizontally into the chambers sunk beneath the earth. My eyes were close.

These grey, gliding shapes push themselves into the field of vision. He brings with him samples of the votary's skin. Writing felt like dying. Beneath the beak is a tiny fold of paper.

A used element of chance has been buried. It's one of the most complicated machines on earth. The next eight are given the values twenty, thirty et cetera.

The two events are clearly connected. (I'll wager wisdom once played the pier.)

As if operating the cage door.

Shall we invent one place where the man was asked? We got in early and they unloaded us in the freight yard. They say he scribbles pastiche, the unmistakable disguise of his most commonly known piece. How does he call down the other? Would he take the place of the man to whom he was about to go?

The sharp point of anything. We've only ten to fourteen left, then it's good-night Vienna. I mean a face clogged with nerves and burrows. The power of golf is cyclical. There is enacted a recognition (all that I have seen hundreds of times before).

That asterisk is meaningless. The pictures were ugly. We'll never make it to the end. I don't think it's a fair reflection. (You get to seven, and then you just don't perform.) They have to go back to their terrible lives, partially paralysed. This features the statement. Maybe I'm amazed just to be following in someone's footsteps. A swift one-eighty, echo park water again.

This is the chapter of raising arms. I'm on the case. It's guilt, probably, permanent cloud cover. (Must learn to be less self.) It's often said the end sounds like the beginning. Illuminations indeed, an indescribable circumference amid the gauzes and tropes. This caper sounds like an effective manner of avoidance, i.e. violence. I've done what I can. Bring armour of the foot, though not necessarily.

News keeps changing and so do the decisions. Words that don't coincide are no longer important. I'm announced.
A small magnifying glass is to be worn in the eye socket. There's a flaw, a speck of black floating in the green of the iris. It was like meat in a butcher's shop, slamming down onto the ground.
See the XVIIIth, and following. The drilling was intermittent.

Smashed up garden, no police hospital. Give yourself back. Of the fugitive in the dunes there was no trace. (What come to the forge et cetera.) I sometimes achieve psychological states unmeasured from early time.

An alternative spine. The surviving link is a brittle ligature by which two objects may be joined together. The signal is a winged thing, displayed without beak or claw. Am I to be paid for my time spent deciphering notes at the innards? It's not a question of a sign—a comparison or an allegory. It contains. It's stabilizing.

Late glacier interstadial. I move up and take my proper seat. I'm not used to this backwash, forwards.

What I read about. Her life.
There is a resemblance. They're borne in triumph on the water-cart pulled along by the crowd. Reconstruction of the three-armed still is taking shape, courtesy of the annals. I like the episode depicting a colourless and insignificant person, the perpetual victim (distance). I didn't realize objects could flow right through the portal and follow one about. What nation made their way across the

sea and the eastern desert? I'm a clear case of synecdoche. I'm amazed by their technique. Damned fact, but that is the concept once more. How did it grieve? Answer, that this pettiness should be manifest at all.

I have my own idea, a little cloudiness. I can go back any time. The prosecution has done a fine job. I envy. I've been in training for this. It's a big social gas me. Semicircular in section, a figure can be generated—the receptacle of a flower, a ridge, a ring-shaped discharge. Leave it be and it'll begin all over again, the lastness. A hood is drawn over the signal light.

The assault on St Elmo.
Desiccate white veins spread out across the earthwork. Circulation of animal spirits, suspending madness. We went out to explore the firm ground to our left. They were encased in planks of wood, another fact which disproves.

Ox-blood on chin (perhaps 'image of'). Methane gas, a small field of crows. Nothing more can come of this.

An announcement. Who extended to metallic form? (Assume the silence to be compression of selfsame.) Let the edges spread, as in conventional representations, i.e. a level stretch at the top of a hill.

Can't use the latter first. I outlasted criterion one. These conditions can only be fulfilled using atoms. The hieroglyphic figures serve us in two ways (not decay). It's wonderful, this impression. Lots of things have a maximum life.

You have to rig the performance. It's three years before the end. We have been repositioned. He's down-to-earth and thick-skinned, and is no longer concerned. Up to that time I had never conceived the possibility of a body being imprisoned. Colonel arrived at eight o'clock. The workforce is aging. The overall impression is stable. Skillful use of knights is the mark of a professional.

There's only one word for this. We're combining the wreckage for signs of life. When I get home this evening I intend using the excuse as a trigger.

He says he will try to keep the day free. Come back via the west. It has redoubled its strength—that's the least that can be said concerning the situation. People aren't stupid enough to overvalue a product. She had no right to call him back.

It's been renamed, a straighter version of something already familiar. Unknown, perhaps from root of perform, or outgo. These older variants are prone to dilate. The circular blade goes nowhere near her.

See, you have been compromised. We're not finished yet. Let's take the lid off before it starts to sweat. Death will slay with his wings whoever et cetera.

There were certain things I still had to do. Strings of light delineate the runways at night. Ground: a spore-bearing surface, exposed from early age. This model of concentration can be quite haunting. We've reached the midpoint. You flinched when I said that.

Insomnia to vertigo, by way of gout. A valuable ally has been lost. The formation is incomplete. Military transports are leaving every day. A guide was bought and offered to take us to the crossroads. Big gaps now opening up all over the zone. The last four have the values 100, 200, 300 and 400.

From the very first day, unredeemed. All the sanitary workers wear surgical masks of sterilized muslin. Naturally she shouldn't have gone down alone. The maximum height is fourteen hundred metres. Metaphorically, I'm leaving myself behind. There's still no news. A switch from an intestinal to a time-holding economy is taking place. In times of maximum tension importance rises to an infinite degree. Enough is enough she says (seeds of nux vomica).

We are not above three weeks. There are no further questions to be asked. Shear flat the remaining land. Follow the utilities and fault-lines. There's no proof that the upper cave was ever located. Flames from the conflagration shot thirty feet into the air. No one will say that every time I enter my room I am actually present.
A discreet touch of rage. I'm returning to the idea of learners, feathers of ash.

Hands pocked red by the berries. The first phase signals infidelity. A new subject appears.
They can't be separated. It's all that can be done to keep the lapses in check, the space of sense. Another day, another.

Let me adapt one of your examples. For instance, those that are read from the shells of turtles cast into a fire. The crisis is one of consumption, the sudden inability to borrow what is not. Misfortune is directly at hand (a shoal of fishes strung across a wall, signed). It's basically pouring itself back into its old position.

Mark of birth, a checkpoint at the frontier. Keep your identity in your mouth. If we find your head, we'll know who you are. (Move if keep last.)

A projecting piece of shank. He died the way he came. The account is false, poor pilgrim. This precipitates the same effects as the plant: shakers, muscle clamps, diffident breath. It's still in use to this day. But you're the one who forewarned me, no?

He serves the same function he served in the petrified forest. Without cap, a mass of nonesuch, a name for various birds.

Pass current through one of the field-coils. Or, *consequences*: there are only intentions and actions (his italic).

Cylinders of metal half-buried in the mud. Slight opacity of cornea. This is the first printed instrumental. Powerful storm lamps flood the entrance to the cave with white light. (She was drawn to music early on.) Liquid concrete spews from a giant nozzle to fill the rusting matrix.

Each segment of the starburst, it's filled to the brim in its turn. A buildup of ions and electrons in the equatorial plane is distorting the data.

With four membranous wings. We're exposed in this location. The place was shut down, sterilized, and turned into a sanitarium. He claims he's allergic to his own nervous system. So, not a relation of conventional exteriority.

Strange days. Freezing men grieve and scatter at the surface. Some wield improvised weapons (wooden staves, planks, iron bars). Warily they step back as the surface stirs, lit by combustion: emblems and barbs. They may have brought the idea and habit of preserving their head with them.

They are withheld in a transit camp. Buoyant, unlimited, firm as a rock—what need of a whole day?

Woken for work by artificial night. Lift ascending. The assassinations were done execution style. At such times equilibrium is redistributed.

Somehow I doubt. Allow them to see, but conceal the last segment.

Step back he says, I've got the fifteen signatures I need. (The blank spaces represent things I don't remember.) We can recognize pastiche, plagiarism, even imposture. Or, conic section about a straight line in its own plane.

She said she was afraid. At which point you came to our attention. I have always practised moving about: (a) for aesthetic experience, the search for a more beautiful way of setting up a problem, and (b).

Perfect view of the mound. Lodestone from passing window. The tower keep vanished. An attempt is being made to adapt mediumistic design to dwellings and furniture. They unfold their napkins and pick up their knives and forks. The extremity of this perspective is unbearable.

Linen mask over mouth. Navigate south.

Discharge yourself. Intone the vibration located in the lower limb of your partner. The puncture is surrounded by a perfect square of livid flesh. Use a compass with repeaters. Use the tuning-fork and organic coil. I'm positioned overhead, dangling from a safety harness. Draw breath in the interim between rungs. I can see for miles. What follows is the official retort.

That's what, a reversal of fortune? Antique dirigible in the heavens. You go upstream in a boat and you see all these cocks. All these pagans, rehearsing: flesh compromised by gravity, dazzling fire-flies. It's like the distance between a lack of necessity.
Chapter one contains a reflection glimpsed in the well. The firm had a concession to the west of minerals.

Question, it's both prehistoric and post. It constantly comments upon itself. Answer, a vacuum cleaver. A rhyme in which the words ending the lines are in fact the penultimate.

You need to book for that. Now we're moving away from the eastern seaboard. There were queues around the corner. I am now observing the men building an outhouse. You see, there's this moonless night.

It creates a space by vibrating its fins rapidly from side to side. They were blissfully unaware of the disaster to come. A visitation enters through the portal of the convex lens. We are viewed from opposite points on the earth's surface.

Movement in and out of the great laminarian zone. My own story is much simpler. Come noon it's still dark and then the rain. (We know that tune.) Rubble has been poured between the moments. It's too late to start introducing semi-colons.

A cliff that is subparallel to the fault trace.
He says this was bound to happen one day or another. No syllables were recorded. I have several of my own teeth with me.

Hele stone. Yes, I heard. Shall present nine minutes of morph.

Continued today across country, one or two of them with the salt we still have. Most of the others have given way. We found the same discordance in the details (point against point-rebellious arm). The girl drew her legs up to her chest.

Similitude. It bears an extremity (wing, fin, feather). There are signs that it has been here before. I mean praxis, but of a more feedlike aspect. I'm beginning to tire.

Similar expansions. White rook of calcium carbonate, chiefly shell, but no substitute. A puzzle from the millennium: blind old one who never used any sort of men or board. Objects on a cold metallic surface. Colonel moved his jaw.
There was a silk handkerchief of dark gold poking out of its breast. Upper lip stretched tight against bared teeth. Camera bulbs popped behind his head as he repaired to his corner.
Forearmed, forewarned, forever is the motto. Let's get that air sorted first.

Crosscut scarring at ribcage, likeness of bird. A perimeter, the registration mark. The maximum, I refuse to guess at. They do not know what to do next. The very act of observation distorts that which is doing the observing.

Electrons are feeling plucky today. We've been yoked together to form a fairly large ensemble. One last performance—the old cut, parry and slice. What a day, what luck. Unite by erasing the strands. This is word perfect, the internal early. My own discovery now looks fairly ordinary.

Augmentative of cap, augmentative of cover. I criticized the slow rhythm of the march. All forms of the copy are contained, the ashes of papers burned in the grate.

Misinterpretation of the winged bull accounts for the curious details. She was unable to avenge the outrage committed against her: waiting for trains, glass eye at the ready. A perfect indigo circle on buckled paper, as the frame distorts.

Perhaps made old from popular association and hole. The platforms are unnecessarily wide. A line on the compass bowl marks the position of the head. A wide area can be surveyed, including the river. I'm going to finish with a request—the price for a small hand is about fifty. It's hard making decisions: poems, letters, private diary. He dips the quill into his blood (775).

Give yourself a well-earned break. Who would have thought, when he jumped bail and fled from the charge. (That was much later.) Also in hymns et cetera, especially in the vocative and oblique cases, contractions of on/off (4).

Useless losses of life for not obeying rules. That gives us the option to release. Recurrence is become feverish.

The following featurette contains plot spoilers.

That has to be him. It's the mournful insistence—these organs, their function and life in the second nineteenth. But you must recognize it too. Everything I have received and want to transmit through you is lost. The entire avenue has been pollarded. Is this a question of comparison, or metaphor? A conflict between will and necessity, bored and tearful.

Hornless animal of horned kind, bearing head. Lots are drawn. The winner is the loser, and must. Origin remains doubtful, but the death of you.

Rigorous abstract determinism.

It's about placement, isn't it? Nothing can remain outside. We're exposed. In order to enter, one has to submit. I've grown quite fond of the decay. The thing is redeemed before the ransom paid. Of the actual body only the toes were visible, soft white feet on the pedals (opus six). The projection differs from all these manifestations. Mine's a score and a half. If I ever cut you out of this arrangement, you'll know why.

Digging up one of those ancient claims.

You should be counting up the stops by now. The hands have the appearance of wanting to lay hold of him. He crosses the border. He does not come back. This is the traditional pace of suspense.

A big redrawing of the continent—an expanse of freezing water surrounded by permafrost. The proof, circa nineteen (a kind of humming coined by Paracelsus). Find a ballet about newspapers. Note how he tends to write everything out in full.

It had a single hump and was encircled by men with pitchforks. He refused to drink the tap-water. Then a machine for spraying light is rolled onto the field of play. Ignorance and fear are the abiding impressions left by the narrative, the disintegration of everything that causes. In none of these cases does the production of means labour to absorb function. I have laid down my hand. If there's an incursion, we don't stand a chance.

Do last the term, if at all. Say it again, correctly. It fell apart.

Constant necessity to observe oneself, to replace.

By twitching the metal tongue with a finger, a small shape is rumoured against the teeth. The waves are twitching.

Night, he says.

Night, they say.

Still so strange to ears, overcharged. Double-cracks. It was drawn upon parchment in black indelible.

Broad-leaved lavender with thin distensible sac. Three feetless birds on a

420

plough, six tassels pendent on either side. This route into the body opens up pancreas and gall. Use aerial techniques on as many parameters as you can find.

That to which a descant cannot be added. The two men have a script. (Someone once said that to me.) I was sure I heard our friend's silence. Fugitive smell of tanned hide and metal polish. Here's the news you've awaited for a year and a half. They are unable to place this in time. Move if passant.

This very day another lexicon has been retired. It is spine, dog spine.

Imagine, only connected by the soles of one's feet. Evidence of breeze blowing about me, shirt flapping, shirt pressed wet to skin. What to do with those who have remained? They moved quickly, expanding the spiked barrier.

The last and most valuable leachings. For example, words not listed with the spelling *sub* may be listed under *sum*, and vice versa. That same year saw what terrible thing occur?

The documentary evidence does not favour one approach over another. How do you think the idea of intrusion came about in the first place? He's intent on an audacious supernatural revenge. They were inventoried with all their statistics intact. Then a defining crack of heat burst in front of him. Charred remains have been found among the embers of the fire. It's quite unrealistic to regard a place or situation in this way. They were meaningless except for the names.

We are for one long day and one short. Nailed to the wall is a typewritten list. Go out and talk to them about their timing. He lays the conch on the trunk beside him (ceremonially). I work in this fashion because I have no imagination. The whole neighbourhood is now living without vowels. I don't know she said, I don't know any of the faces around here.

Clearly unaccustomed to the discipline of composition, yet casual tap masterpiece.

A curled cyme, as in forget me not. Oviparous inflorescence. The plane of each daughter axis is set at right angles. A ledge of rocks lies to the east, exposed to the vicinity. This fact justifies the recognition of the term.

Cinquanter is an old stager. He never numbered among men, condemned by formation.

To reach a lower level than, to probe more deeply than. Plucked and stricken sounds (63). Wind into a ball, with focusless eye. One tribe is fabled to have lived in perpetual darkness. Beguine is beghard. Elastic, the common dwelling.

Elsewhere, from the thirteenth. A man could live, also without vowels. He took the offered hand and waited. Like a fog they gathered before their enemy. I

clung to a rock as the torrent ran faster. Phlegm origin is doubtful. Haemor-
rhage, haemorrhage, haemorrhage.
(Silent parts.)
Code-breakers.
I saw the smoke vanish through the water till it curled up on the riverbed.
A hugely influential slave culture.
Chorus of ones.

Who's who (stone tablets to both). Nothing known. Nothing doing. The
three roads were blade, noose and poison-plot. I can't do the drop-off myself.
We're maintaining a tempo of reluctant clashes, spikes of action and remem-
brance. And of his madness in the book?
Father what is that.
Did he really look like that.

Who would have thought.
The subsequent exile became his way of life (199). Some of these terms are
not clearly understood by trained physicists. The title could also have been a plurality of saints, with necessity acting as a veil.

About thirty-five minutes have been lost. It's like a solar eclipse. He inherited
all the genes. Unusual results: a diversion is being set up. I am Oliver head.

The bacillus is used in drilling muds and food, an affliction of the eyes in
which all objects appear yellow. An oval was used to trade with people. Whose
armature very closely resembles that of the myth? A comrade-in-arms is stationed at R. Mournful, and therefore brother. It's nearly all done.

Because of its intolerance of salt. Now sire, quod she, I could amend all this.
An assistant prods at the liver.

A forge-hammer worked by foot. An adherent of the protector, one of an
order found in the original house (capital of ancient minor). Letter jays with sallow needles, a plant used for hair. Whose fruits bore hooks very troublesome to
sleep? Answer, a tree having the whole crown cut off. The cannonade of V
decides more than the battle of H.

Spike. Remember the nineteenth. When a thought cannot be found and must
be sought for, you'll be the first to know.

Brittle metaphor of frailty. An account of the journey itself, the terrain.
There are no traces of an exploratory run by the river. The disease is not at all
pathological. In structure and general appearance it resembles the salivary glands.

I don't remember doing any of this.

Sketch for character: a student of parapsychic warfare. Consider a word coined that has no recognized standing, a disembarking. (What do you do?) Add the impetus of the fantastic catastrophe.

It finds a suitable tree-stump. It conducts itself. I am discharging all care, their lives held in tandem. Entropy and dispersal.

They are inhabiting ancient, a fabric of digressions. But they are not discoverers. We find the same impossibility of repetition, the same delight in the nerve-ending curve. An aimless exercise in editing is drawing to a close.

Suppress by focussing too close. I haven't suffered the test myself. The majority of audiences find it beyond their ken.

I was seedheaded. He had his lasered off. Now, about the origin of stars.

Chalk escarpment with longitude. There's more than enough material here. No one said the remedy would be painless. A tooth is liberated at each vibration. It feels like everyone vanished as I slept and I'm the last. The key symptoms are retching with nausea and phosphorus. (No, I did not watch too closely.)

Whose root produces? Answer: a foreshortening. Even at the stake, it's difficult to discard everything.

Convulsive without cap, wormlike. Psyche is a controversial treatment.
They may need sediment during this period. (Flee.) Whether he had himself fallen in love is much disputed. Whether I had been warned by an oracle is much disputed.

Myself, entwined with those I never could. It certainly sounds as though you know something I don't. It's not a piece of journalism. The will just isn't there. I am slightly concerned. I am slightly undercooked. The answer is I have done it, I will do it et cetera. Afford has lost its meaning—a scraping of the cavity, by means. The wind is about to pick up and carry. Tomorrow we return to those remarkable pillars of silt: my-telegraphic, wires taut, where clouds dare not linger. In the sacristy there is more. I have rumours. For means foretold. That green stuff's bile—they must have cut the spleen.
Through a magnifying glass is a long time.

Nocturnal studies. Marina. Fierce lions on the loose everywhere. Geological time is a little sluggish.

It's quite unrealistic to regard a place or situation in this way. It's said the island's future lies in its provinces, vaguely. I wish I were. I wish I had said that. Inner decay began a century earlier. I explain the obscure using the less known.

Separate this pair. The first doesn't stand a chance beside the second.

It seems a kind of game, after all (a picture representing to the mind something other than itself). His musical insensitivity is legendary. Note the high altar. Opposite, lapse of date, unsainted.

Another name is semi-lung. He hath hand and both feet, grey with an intricate pattern of tiny writing.

It flew straight up out of the flak. A small black book is carefully poised on top of the larger orange.

To mind, a phial of colour. Any such gravity of the animal body will suffice. And if I should say I never once saw such islanders?

A nice little drawing of a saint reading something. What sunlight reached them was level. He is obscure and hard to follow. What was his altitude when you saw him?

Of comet fame. He's king of the allotments, master of shares—a convincing enough nervous break. Take things one at a time—space, sovereign cord. We were pulled out of the pit feet first.

Born at N and died there, as this self-portrait reveals. On coming round, the first thing he asks is what's a spirit tab. It's a sure sign that speech is over.

Aweless, no bristly process, yet with the power to fall to earth.

The origin of the easies.

A man is turning round and around in circles, balancing two metres—an innocent enough wrack of work. An indifferent one passes, by sidelong glance. The whole scene in this room is viewed from behind the protagonist's head: back door and flight to fury, the broken land et cetera. Whom would you have believed?

A field of crows pecking at winter stubble. Is that fair, or what do you think? The suggestion for the letter is from entry 291. There was no sign that he made the slightest use of the furniture (move if last not O). He attempts to flush the other out.

Bob's your uncle: the shortest poem, the legend of undo.

Recognized at first from its distinctive note. The fragment versus a treatise on the astrolabe. A creeper of goshawks. Stage directions.

Enter a rankleman, after the manner of the so-called. Enter the space above. But the appearance in all the forms is difficult to account for.

A horizontal bar of iron is fixed across, on which the hooks are hung. Over the shell a huge clock is ticking.

The rowan-tree, mountain ash. I mean a blizzard in hell, under the tongue-root. Spasmodic interventions such as these ensure our survival.

Watercrest, little-great green-toppled ones. Go vexing, irritating, embittering (arch). It's an ulcer, dim of Draco. Look look, a wood a wood a wood a hill a hill.

Recital coming, prepare yourself. At the crest, exact measurements of latitude are taken. The lower reaches are very white. They took documents and photographs of every type. The air was wrapped solid. It has suddenly gone quiet, the finality. Somebody talked. It's about two or three bodies away. Infantry from the zone, just boys.

A slow walk upstream it was supposed to be. Then the man was gone, heaved under with his oilskin. Trenches had been dug. This saves all the labour of building up a heap of sand.

Strictly, we are excavating the foundations of some projected edifice. A pair of wings was seen plummeting from the scaffold. I am moving away from the European idea. I have been composing a new core—long prisms of fibre, pale and colourless. He studied at the state.

I only see what has disappeared. I am no longer possible, compassed about with repeaters.

Walking towards the dexter side, with fore-paw raised.

The lungs were a pale grey, without stars, without gravity. O no, definitely not, definitely not.

Do they mean shown? An emetic can be administered. Routes can be used as substitutes.

An uncanny, perhaps disconnected.

It looks like a bit of a replay: fugitive smell of tanned hide and metal polish. A flight most dread, a practice condemned to displacement by art.

They have position and velocity, but never at the same time. Translation of shield, impassive commentaries. Then knit and swept in, with seemingless company. A bright patch on the wing (duck).

He pleads the excuse of eyes.

XXVI

If I were called upon to describe the photograph, I would do so in these words.

The fifteenth contemplation, which identifies everything omitted: the muscles of the larynx, the palate, lips and tongue. I'm beginning to think now about how it might appear—lacquered bodies inside one another, trespass into a core. Voice is this my skin he says.

A different succession of syllables and characters. Variorum studies, a composition uninvited. Would you prefer to relocate yourself? The synaptic membrane is densely packed—enervated to strain or test, as repetitions in extended time. You were not granted permission to stop smiling, were you?

It gets its name from the avenue of linden trees that makes the reproach so unforgettable. The legend is that he bound his head with poplar. But which, you do not say.

Confess, it was only three weeks ago. He once owned a big old cake of his own. By examining the evolution of chess terms, it's possible to establish the exact time when the work was written.

It's my otoliths. Think nothing of it. Must stop at next junction. The end flips open: complete protection for the living dead.

Always depend on contingencies. He begins rolling the wheel at a good speed. The only certainty is rust. He heard the sound of running water, and guessed litter on the whitewashed stairs.

Evenly cut all over my body. Some are rumoured eaters of chalk.

On inhibition of the enzyme.

Wait until it's time. Wait upon the vanishing, scenes of the arena through expectant eyes. (Is this the appearance of the nexus advance we keep hearing so much about?) I observe that she is offering me a silver-headed cane, more sweetmeats.

Let me tell you about her. I paused a full moment.

He finds a bullet on the strand at low ebb. (I wish we had married when.) Incunabula, those saplings et cetera. That thing has been here for a while, I am no fool. No distaff flank, such as ambiguous. One burst into my chamber with a pistol charged under each arm. But how, through that earth to earth channel? These plants need a peculiar kind of soil if they're to survive. That's when you make mistakes. I don't think anybody really understands, or ever will.

A deterioration of small holes, or scallops.

What is your destination. Now retrace your steps. Redial, quit the fortification. All the pumps are pumping at full tilt. Theirs is a rather time-specific rejection. A circle of hostile creatures surrounded me. A head costs more, and another, raging.

The great chamber works. There's a lot of people overhead. The key is to make the wheel and shaft revolve together. You speak of me as if I were the man without. This justifies holding them here, in this detonation. Very clever, said he.

Sondage, a deep trench dug at the third situation. It's a miniature masterpiece. As you see, I'm rendered. (The second word on the list is rosary.) The soundings reveal a flap of skin that covers a gash in the earth. It's time to reveal the various. First taps of twilight, ushering in the darkmans.

What I owe the ancient.
As is commonly believed, a subtracting. The adversary: company distant versus limited thunder. He fumbles the string of beads.
An opening or aperture—alternately to right and left, with that of its parent axis. I can no longer trust the decisions I'm making.

A man bearing flotsam with utilitarian pride. Discuss. Proposals have been sent in. Then a much smaller quake. I am returning. More of your Brahman text et cetera. For twelve years he tended the fires. After his death in eighteen he became conditional—unexacting duties which left him abandoned in time. The key is a reckless driver, a furious whip. I am unaffected by the gala nights. Re-establish foreign influence, manners and customs, ethical indications and so on.
What food is eaten by the shades or dwellers? Sing a simple them—white-scented perennial of related genus, with yellowing disc.

Landgrave.
He finds he has eleven gates left. Harmonic foundation is largely a contribution. Above the territory is an inner. Latterly is a mere title. Beyond him can be glimpsed. A whole decade is substituted, looming. Or, it was not until ten years later.

A sullen trumpet ringing, ballast of light on translucent oblong—a stretch of earth (you will die here). Manuscript thirty-four refers explicitly to the Pleiades. I can see no reason to remove this comment.

He is whispered. Revulsions, that's the nature of it. Principle (vignette, scream). First god of the triad fallen unto a pit. As it expires in mythology human fantasy has continually been preoccupied. He is a member of the highest caste. A zealous soul may offer devotion. Don't rub your eyes. That's the nature of the limb (ow). Too many mortuary workers in rubber aprons and waterproof. What? What?

She says I fear I have stolen empathy. Behind, in the head.

Kept in storage for some future event. The object smelt like whom? I'm to be reanimated. Ratify monotony by a grander monotony—but in the third movement, at the end of his long passion. The groups include all twelve pitch classes. A feather is pressed inside the archive, shocking pink. The head is seeded. It's dipped in latex and set on a pole. The height is unofficial. It is one hundred and seventy-three. His own heart is going to pieces inside his ribs.
Think through another way of putting this.
Innermost part of the person, the component. As he plummets from the oak a tentacle reaches into space to break his fall. It was monks who first sanctified the past. In my day it wasn't a foot pedal it was a dial (the illegal passage toward the perimeter). Resin can be extended, and is said to be living from the numbers found inside, but perhaps not.

Practise rooms are rather nice to be alone in. Perhaps a name, a rapture, the price expected for the time. (I too was once so said.) Those objects carry electronegative ions.
Animadvert. A guide to deviation, navigating.

A disused alphabet, floating within things. He looked at his tightly clenched hands. (This is me too.) In the snow he begins to wish that the other would come soon, as promised.
Thank you for your letter of May. What about the resistance? This was the morning which decided our fate. I say 'decided'.

Together again at the ablution (the novalis complex). Wastelands newly reclaimed. This is the highest mystery. The reverie works in a star pattern—philosophy originates with marriage. A nervous trick: whenever you come in here you breach my concentration, a cycle like shining. The time and cause of events are always indicated. Once more the useful mist gives way to explanation by the agreeable. The hydraulic press is invented. She straddles an updraft of warm-rising air. (By stilling thought one kills.) We have arranged to meet again on the return journey. Despite what's said, your heart doesn't have to be in it. That is what we don't know.

Two people who never meet alternate in one place. Sleep et cetera. An assassin. Who longs to break forth from this? We're said to have been bought. We cannot comprehend the thwarted passion of his art.

A ductless gland near the root of the neck, vestigial. An old instrument for taking altitudes, from lab of root of to take.

Solely the underpinnings. Only the bolster and the holding cell remain—numb, within the oxides. Due to the fog a long cylindrical contraption had to be hired. We resemble form and use (some kind of toothpick). Pictures full of visceral incitement. I don't recognize any of the other shapes. Rich cinematic textures belie their cost. I have painstakingly glued this back together.
You can retrieve your old ace in the hole. Any piece of mechanism affording support against pressure will do. Say, the cold chisel. Cold chisel.

Alloy of copper and tin. His beams fool the world with light et cetera, with majesty. Distant sound of all saints drill, the fractal sign. And with white ray, the elliptical window. Dormer.

The blade of each is broad and splayed out. It's used in the cutting of slabs, of stone of ice. It may be that the evidence is cited as a counter-example. The front room and the dining-room areas should be indistinguishable from the rest when not in use.

The archaeological situation: observations made during the days following the discovery. Night too is drowned in a cold weave of grey. I don't know, I was just expecting more.
Flickering orange sparks cascade from a the pier. I vanished myself about seventeen hundred hours.

A unit of acceleration. A small two-masted vessel. It is the hardest blow they have delivered. A number of insects are said to live within the carcass.

Swaying under the weight of the pile. I have come, that's all I can say. From the mound of dossiers she plucks out a list of beheaded ones. And the spray blown from the crests of waves, a casting out. We are trapped in here until now. Pause. Pursue that faint flicker, a path across the sea. Many seasons have been dropped. And so you fly. I've dim hopes for the head of the column.

The writer in extremis. This is the loftiest effect the ethical expressionist can hope to achieve. Try to leave for there. No, *from* there.

Of that terror that still possessed the power to wake her.
At daybreak we arrived where everybody was celebrating. The chosen form is the sonata—a specially impersonal frame of equality. He agreed to concede defeat in an oral statement. This world and that world date from the sixteenth. We are trapped below.

And it occurs to me now (though not at the first encounter) that your film is a suicide. One who walks fully clothed into the waves at night, what else can this be? One who, driven to rise and tunnel beneath a river, crosses miles of woodland until she reaches the sea, and without hesitation, strides in.

Where are we signal? This is a place where drops might fall, the nowhere of middle. Are you trying to sell me something? I am going over. I am not really, even the shelving. The beauty of the sacrament is, and must always remain. Do you want to shunt yourself into one of the other meters, a violently convulsive form?

They move by night. Solo incant, from root of to hair. She is guided by the green ray. Now, a word about breakfast.

Inkblot technicians. The broken flask. Some cases reach independent viability. Everyone runs away (412). Cowardice is all about him. See that shadow unravelling across the garden—the unfamiliar blue-black, a spreading stain of electric ink. Squat down and reflect, defecate. What can I say. Why so late, tourist? Pull yourself together.

Come up on to the roof he says. I want to show you something. (Pharmakon of ear.) The rustle of the elevated, its metals and abstract. There is here, first of all, a formal limit of the analysis. All out of joint, yet I find this performance compulsive. There is a relaxation, mechanicals—a trial bore, more soundings.

Won't the alarm affect us. Guess what, I never noticed or understood. Wasn't your arm broken that day? Whoever wants to can sleep. There was once a place of safety.
(Narrator voice.)
I saw thus in vivid light a picture unannounced.

Same as a spirit level, contained in a vial. How to infect judgment (revolution sixteen). Now for the inquisitory pronouns (what). His bedroom overlooked the garden on the fifteenth floor (who).
The nominal, a destructive ulceration of the cheek. Every faithful partisan could rally.
A knot on a tree—knur and spell. A game played with traps. He says around me all my life all I've known is violence. That is what wisdom means, backs to the pier. Blessed is the death which leaves no time.
Revenant wax in the shaft of bone, that gentle eavesdrip. Unclaimed odds and ends.

A thin film of what. And about the eyes, looking? Isn't that important. It resembles an underground, sundry correctives. Explain to me said he, impatiently deceased. It is incapable of solid exchange—not by individual words, but in its reconstructions. This is an islet, in the proton-current-of-a-river sense.

Someone or something has chiselled away at the lock. In this role he can out-manoeuvre his opponent on a perfect square. On and offs, ins an outs—two spare cramps—all sorts of fancy leaps scattering about. In the hot plains they planted a maze.

Anomaly child. An ancient military engine for throwing stones. Decompression, in the form of a web, is superimposed. A tight grain. A toothed instrument separates the fleshy crest, the curve of the wave.

An aggregation of cells, breaking white at brow of hill. This is a good time for quiddity. Roll the die, then retreat.

Object fifty-four. Solid ebony with a silver handle, in the manner of frost. Swirling fog in the crevices. High above the interior courtyard is a roof of glass. Curious, a voice says. Everything's lost in the translation. It's about isolating a certain faculty. He had all the movements and gestures of youth. Things have dwelt astray. Try to resist, where no signifies. The engraving from this sequence is by the monogrammist—esse, of the gross cartspiel. Mourning in confess of tongue.

Awful music in the elevated. Face turns to voice, and thus her gentle arrangements, her gentle arguments. If you place a boundary around an absence, it's no longer a hole. Ge language also belongs. O, I see, I think.

He finds me a place right at the front, toe-to-toe with a familiar alterity. It's about us—for perfecting myself, I decide. They want to make a destiny of it.

The following remark is predicated on the intellect's self-esteem. You have been racing on. I'm not ready. The sounds without presume each other.

The inquisition is still very much alive. Birds flapping, then the musicians. She plays the guardian angel fighting for her home against an army of vampires. I suppose she must have seen the wish in my eyes, everything patched up—a simple and improvised accompaniment (the without). To trudge now is dialectical. One is gatekeeper, casual assassin of the large door. I.e. a guard for the hand on a lance. She says I dissaint thee.

It lives on the insects harboured within. Perhaps a rapture. What's the difference between a steeple and a spire? With to after, or an infinity? According to some, the gods from the wreck remain underwater. He paused, then muttered inaudibly. It's slow work, if you can get it. We possess no less than sixty-one futhorcs. Love, undine.

An apparatus for drawing air or other gases through bottles or vessels. (One can study only what one has first dreamed about.) Once, he had disappeared.

I let myself fall to the ground—a horizontal precipice. Compare your relationship with *them*, to my relationship with *that*. I mean something intangible, one centimetre per second per second.

A slight flip of your hand. Thus it happened, like beads that drop from the gutter of any dwelling. The rumours are flying, the implications extraordinary. Leaked moments include a prism cracking open, the disclosure of an empty space—ink, with its powers of reverie. Before you cross over, be sure that one day you can scramble back. It returns to its centre to shoot out beams of flesh. Pull yourself together.

Take one womb, wandering. Confine it within the body. They were already under strict orders to cleanse the cattle wagons. A golden light floods the island. The rescue has been reconstructed from a withheld ceremonial. Who slew the gorgon? Who rescued the sea?

A constellation in the northern hemisphere. Meteor, of a swarm whose radiance. I felt a reluctance to write that (as the mediaeval recognized when they built on the site of the deserted).

Now, take one stomach. Take one spleen. Excise a thin strip or slat, nothing superfluous. I am trying to arrive at a detail which might reasonably be expected to return—a sort of journal into which all the notes converge.

Take one sea-cob. I have built a corridor for them. If eavesdropping be your stock-in-trade . . . he stares at the fly screen. Big notes on grizzle, the backdrop greys—piquant by the steam of melting cartilage.

Your visitor, sir.

There's much more ambition in these remaining seconds. Call out, late-wake, late-comer. A small spherical mass of white floats in the centre of the yellow. I know exactly what to do. Take cognizance, take note: surgical removal of the timepiece.

They are obliged to introduce new methods and measures. That's what I thought, yes. Hence the image: a swing-frame, a loon bearing reeds. Reversible motor—the azimuth. If separate, second phase as next.

Paralysis of remaining limb. It's easy to miss things out. I glued it back together by joining all the surviving shapes. E.g. he with the tusks and mad R. Like who out of the brothers who didn't speak? There are classes of contents that cannot be apprehended telepathically. He was here just now. It's much talked about when such things start to happen. Ever the source, in direct proportion to the length of the period (a famous piece of string). Then dog, an earlier catch, perhaps from verb, and everlasting mute.

It let itself be taken in by an illusion. The pragmatics of space, of touch. What funereal waters? Hourglass games (me). He will lean on the dugout and never move.

Drug of melted tallow. And what I'm saying is, by next year we'll have more then twenty legions of you.

The head is furnished—acid, the rustling back-plate (slang). The artist here is no longer in opposition to the amateur. To turn one's back is to desert. Writing always means hoping. Don't let yourself be confused by the penalties undergone by malefactors, the neutrals. I was expecting to meet you one day. I had a go at the centrifuge myself. You wouldn't have known what to say. There's a limit to how much I can obtain, deaden witness. What then of his surrender?
Vampire incanting score.

It's the centre of time, right here. As you're drawn in things becomes more nomadic, yet paradoxically rootlike.
Spectral face at fourth-floor window. There are clues everywhere: phratric totems. The body and the blood are local and materially present, under the firm. Men they called themselves, their clans after animals, plants, inanimate objects. At the outset of movement, the feeling of pain is located in the left hoof. They think he has foretold himself. Imperceptibly, a shift occurs. This reminds one, incidentally, of the intimate correction.
He can no longer sustain footfall. The highest point we have ever reached is two thousand two hundred and eighty millimetres. There is this astonishing violence within me.

This tangent is what separates us from the plane of consistency—explained by some as an abridgement, brief chronicles. There is ease in this, and yet it superimposes itself upon a scene of havoc, a specific way of doing things. Cough cough cough cough cough goes the man.

So this is the birthpiece—base patterns, random guesswork. She says all I've known all my life all around me. Make me the imperceptible, as you might say.

Fugal games. A fresh face, for the last time. Move my stem across, say, ten columns. That whiff of wood-smoke must be from without. It was separated flake by flake, pieced together and sandwiched between sheets of glass.

I need an unlimited version, to undermind. Into every hole they had sunk their illusion, their stopgap. I like orange (the colour). I like. Prepare such a gathering of mourners.

It's found at the cusp where the concrete meets the spectral. More precisely, the rustle of some near-dead. A leavetaking, certain words which resemble. The photographs are to blame. I take it someone's in charge around here. My authority with these gentlemen is somewhat limited.

A man in an empty field with a battery and a ladder. No, it's not about a journey.

It has invaded at four five two. Something dipped into my forehead. Soft tissue in hollow at apex of bone—precisely, the diaphragm, where it divides into branches. Pithy fictions (phalange, a solid formation of ancients). Inside her a faint mist is dissipating—in the heavens a group of stars, demented. A few minutes later a cell rings. What society, what beauty, and how it reasons with sound in all its discourse: a tall, with fur sides—the tapering pill, usually of one stone, toppled with a pyramid. Do I mean to obstruct?
A sheath formed by two stipules is united around a smear (leg it). It's used to brand the suspects. Word, in the form of scrolls, was seen poured into a mill by the four. Good news. Who is without a fixed charge—an itinerant, a mister of the third grade? Mould between the toes is deposited on the organ. He agreed.

These various incidents are only uncomplete parts of one and the same action. To acknowledge this is to plummet. Yet he limns the image with such grace that she declares it tender.
Longlegged harvestmen.

Mother of and by him (the titans) apprehended within a solar stem. See under G. The name of just one of them, its deserted satellite. Astral without cap. Also without cap, a man of entelechy, but not the spiration—the procession of ghost, to breathe. Once more, a satellite, a spirit of revolt. Fossil, unglued.

A hoof (*zoon*). Section of cylinder, cone, drill et cetera. The claw of an insect's limb, the claw of a petal. Cut off by plane oblique to base (*golem*). I was obsessed, suddenly: an ungovernable desire to see where the trapdoor led.
With claws or hoofs tinctured spectrally. In all I counted twenty-three solo instruments.
Walking on nails (*her*). Remittent fever with swelling of the joints and enlarged spleen. You're not listening.
Undulating a wave or add to next.

Critique of separation, all power to your event horizon. (Call father.) How on earth do you persuade your feet to do the right thing.

He was walking along the strangely promenade.

I take your word. I am pretty uncertain.

On strategy in general. It just goes on and on. There is less now. Perpetual motion is recognized as an impossibility after all. There is much that remains unaccountable in his movements during those famous manoeuvres.

The conclusions.

In the whole history of science there is perhaps no more fascinating chapter. Use part for the whole. We lose two men and one is wounded. A social gathering is crazily interrupted. Under a dripping tree other forms are closing in.

An instrument for removing fluids or solids from cavities of the body was used, now rarely. All my members are set down in thy book he says. (Chapter CLXXXV is but a short hymn.) The narrow latex tube must be thoroughly gelled before insertion. It was like exploding inside. You see, mutilation is suddenly here. The wet burn relaxes the sphincter. I always leave *before* speech. Life is just diffident here, that's all. For he sent me over to the window, to repair anew.

You have never left she says, despite yourself.

And I can well remember sitting beyond the studio glass, the patiently waiting lever.

He awaits the arrival of an amanuensis to set down his very last, some complicated fugue. For instance, the alto and bass sing it in keys, and so on. That can lead one very far, as if a thoroughfare. Thatness.

A new day.

I am horizontal and, it appears, in a dead sleep. A figure springs up from the box when the lid is released.

Hand-held air, hammer for rock-drill enclosed in a shrubby framework. Or, the crosstree at the head of a topgallant-mast. And I aloft, indifferent and easy, not caring one way or the other. I cannot move yet am still aware of my sensations.

Let's put psyche and death back on the shelf. My concern is with the rhythm, a knot of two syllables, short followed by long, unstressed by stressed. I am beside myself. Where the sky meets the earth a crack opens up. Yes yes a sun a sun, upended at the blood-shuddered rise.

During the night my clothes froze to the ground. I understand your antipathy.

I have neglected an entire genre. It simply breaks off part-way through, never to be accomplished. He sees these games as a sort of decay in which there are no superfluous notes. Well, I show you the possibility of a single moment. Through the casement window is a pyramid, the sea, some primitive dwellings. He hands me the sword. A divine seer, always youth, he too carries—a bowing down. Whose radiant is found in the constellation? Comment critically (on), express censure.

This one remains fairly brief. How much do you make out of all this (special thanks). I love the inhumanity of my work. The neighbourhood assassins, they parted as casually, as bewildered, as they had met. Friendship isn't a gift, or a promise. Simply drag the crosshair over the area you want to capture.

Asterisk.
All previous editions have the word inverse here. He meant to write dialect. In short, the longer the period, the more money is needed, and vice versa.

Research and visit with a view to living here during the winter months. If you don't worry there's always enough, enough to go to ground for a season. Where is flawless? Death demands new images. Erect in the lifting, an obsolete colossus, in any case.

She barely touches the surface. There is contact with the tips of the fingers. (Ulna concealed beneath apron.) As the parvenu entered the drawing-room . . . the preamble leading to a joke, surely. She has already been funeralized. Now for things more molestful.

I've just tunnelled successfully under the river, leaned toward it and kissed. She says there is no zero west, just zero. An obsolete form of catch. Surely some mistake.

Compostela equals field of stars. Electric blue the hair and eye. A road is swerving, our industry zoned off. There's a slope of debris at the base of the cliff, ghost of chalk and mass. Scout round the boiling tar.

I think the rounded base of a hollow organ. There is a stoppage of time and the peal of a sacring bell. To send us away, perhaps, from the phase at the close—separating the threads, beating upward.

Hollow in form and route, still guided by the green ray (moving pulsar frequency). All her plans are stymied. Then the withdrawal, as if sudden swarm. We are seeded in columns. There are huge gaps in my value stem—let us say, in payment for means of production. My outermost scarcely hovers off the ground. She pauses in a sly voice. Writing is bolted to time.

I am momentarily usurped by the ruling the following.

Landgravine. Too much prefix in back there. One becomes aware of incongruities and possible breaks in the fabric—excommunications, lapses in conviction. Matter is being cut.

Last one, more day. They did not know anything about him. No, it's not about the money. Don't worry about the rift. The army are out looking. I'll quietly sit myself down behind you. Ignore me. I have no way of knowing. I am unaware of how much of this will survive. It felt narcissistic. Epistles often create confusion. Proceed by a series of slips and reckonings, a particular form in which something is embodied, a particular way of foretelling the story.

The lost variant: you sail off in a coffin-shaped vessel et cetera. A thin film of fiction, slippage.

1151BC-1212AD.

It has been developed as the vehicle for any useful manifestation. I come complete with my own gang of selves. (Paperback reconstructs intellectual development.) A large sort of peel was pared off and remained. It was afternoon before I found you. I remember, for the second time. Do you remember? Under a dripping tree, other forms were closing near. 'Surprised' and 'shocked to hear' you were. But later on, someone established that this could not be writing at all.

Or, the cultural threshold of the person who holds legitimacy. Thank you very much indeed—the field of cloth of gold, some garden tools et cetera. It's just like pictures in a book, the dread of being nothing.

Another chapter of making perfect the queue, with two vignettes withheld. Emptied words, a page of blanks. Part of a commonplace, a hymn to unsettlement (179). Don't run. Wait for us, amid this wilderness of rock and vein and wrinkled sand. The material is said to be an n-type extrinsic (or simply n).

Listen to this. An exclamation is variously used to express interrogation, surprise, emphasis doubt—that which is continued. This pertains to the probability that in a system every state will occur again and again. Could the synaesthetic sensations be of my own willing?

A point in the sagittal suture of the skull. Dim of spit, in front of to stretch. The mill of the host. O, quite. And has he a special room to haunt?

Any slender structure tapering to a point. A dagger is used, specially designed for the feet.

I notice tattoos on her webbed hands. She can't quite understand what the words are saying. She flashes forth with violence (interstellar space they are). There's not much to tell. Everything went all right. It didn't take long, and so forth. Asocial division of peoples is often contagious.

Union of gametes not closely related (boil). The introductory part of a discourse or composition. (Ends here.)

Out of to begin.
Pertaining to underground water, or probably able to supply. Of subterranean gases, causeless eruption. A deep root drawn from the water table, or just above it. Sympathetic magic.

Flavour extraneous and sharply fleshed. I myself am brief and fibrous. (I don't know prefer.) Under an old law, a bloodline is paid to the family.
Move my ray across, say, ten columns. The complete score is spread out over forty days. They who are in the midst of it depart.

There's this imperative to speak. The form is the operatic mood, with garble benedictionary. The rite is extra-liturgical, its details varied. In thick sheaves a garnered my actions. That word is almost a synonym. D recurs the same as in group one (ex twenty-seven). I can still smell her on my fingertips. Beneath the ground is a dropsy cavity. Decayed spots are obscured by health. I have allowed the room to chill.
Up at dawn to write.

Of involuntary hints, the minim hook.
The hour is the hour when light grows smaller. Once here I know I'll be confused (the condemned). What we have is an error, an error of passing ways.
Dog days. For plates read Pleiades. Is he dying a death? A doctor of thirty-five also had a siren dream. Cock penetrates deeper et cetera.

Substitute lithia for potash. She says it's easy on the eye, the seduction of impossibility. The illustration shows a bell virtuoso of the seventeen (see form). It isn't real.

A sea abounding in islands. Rusting atoll. A circular belt enclosing a central nerve—barbed organ, mindful of moss and fern. (What?) The date is also suspect. Note their silhouettes against burning light from proximal star. Route same as obstinate.
The first successful measurement was made. Of something sold, as it stands, with any defects, visible or not.
The locus is a place whose distance from a fixed point fluctuates, according to some rule. As the radius vector revolves, he declares. Which is iambic?

Remarks on a classical author whose name everyone vainly searches. What would be the right answer to give to such men? (A vision, bedraggled.) Hitherto we've been constantly immobile, to both hear and possess his products. Either state is a concretion of loss, elimination. Seawater was found in the lungs.

And yet another version—in that filament is her most touching et cetera. The path has raptured in a thousand pieces, a heap of elastics. Not the least mention.

Now for the ultimate triumph (pass on generation, one to another). I am tracking what I'm doing. No question the crowd were up for it, until now.

On the enormous power of small means.
She spins. Insufficient—the privative of end. The falling in of the wall of a fortification. Toxic cladding, in spades.
No portrait in this book has the character of an actual person. An image bleached to the frontiers of recognition, that's how I see it.

Fences and other obstacles have been set up in a nearby field. Fluorescence in the septum, rudimentary ice. (I still have your book.) The neolithic is one point five eight metres. This is a form of medley, scrapings from the bore-hole—quite arctic, one last desperate struggle to ascend the back.
That in each word which numbers and measures is illuminated. All was unfit for, inhabited and eaten. It's the place where four roads meet—the complete organ or embryo, cauterized tongue. The twin carrying the survey cast its shadow on the northwest coast of William. Indeed, cries of Io, whither an oath.

Used in naming, a pathological condition. Envisage a trajectory, say, the history of an organized beginning, right through to extinction. Everything became dark et cetera. This factuality becomes accessible only if we perceive it by looking straight at it. The body, together with its severed head, was brought back in a stone boat.

A taxonomic diversion. Therefore, look not upon it, the whatever subject. Abandon the tendency to move in a certain direction.

Statistical methods for search workers. And, moreover, a guide for thee, the lesser. (Two copies of this chapter were mistaken.) O look, the ribs. It was the name given to one born, a unit of acoustic absorption. The mind, too. And now to take up one's turn.
A plurality of things pertain to something specified. Even then, the validity of the old images remains.

Let me know as soon as you decide. Sorry we couldn't send the asp, as requested. Vignette: a vulture with outseized wings, symbol nailed to each talon. A biological category, or its name. A sack-formation, from sling.

The ankh bone, it falls apart every time you try to grab hold. It's incomparable how this infant is able to reveal, while at the same time withholding. He stayed in his cell on mount thingy. The caves were separate.

A vestment like the alb, of or relating to sticks. A branch producing tetraspores, in red (bottle). Methinks I am marvellous face. Long-white seaweed vestments, a row from to march. And at precisely what hour do these shades come to visit?

Rainwater streaming down blue gauze, opening tiny voids.

I always assumed I was wrong about everything, every detour.

Detached, or to bleach. Or rather, the verb to detach (thrones, dominions, powers). He led safely across the dangerous ambush, placed on the flank of the selfsame hill—grizzly man with white hair and white eyes. Ground-based observations, Beta Pictoris occulted by disc within. And he that looketh to the clouds shall not et cetera.

It all turned out to be quite amusing. The answer is ten. Do you feel different now? The survivors reported sighting a ghostly cloud in the night skies of the hemisphere. It had a quality of absolute objectivity. I've lost that extra little bit of incentive. Clandestine books were printed in the early days, especially before the year. I'm talking about the origin of a thing, a locust before its wings grow.

The participants are rubbed with raw garlic and sealed into sacks. Enter hungry dogs, a tray of saliva. Those who walk in sleep over high buildings, that's the real work of mourning. Was this true seduction? The desire for the abject, that which insulates.

Everything's as safe as pi in my book. She says did you not understand my work.

No, that is someone else and somewhere else (a female grave).

Light-sensitive diodes are produced by diffusing islands of boron into a substrate. Inner rant, any corrupt or spurious personages. Wayfarers.

Intrigue at inner ear, mid-template. Unearthly constituent of bone, something flashing on and off in the cornea. Enter from the bottom of the depression in which you are contained—back part of the vestibule, lying in contact with the five. Numerous filaments of the nerve are embedded in the wall of the vestibule. Its cavity communicates, the uncredible century et cetera. Alter or abolish.

Construction of the canal began. My name was formerly used, some unrelated principle, but within easy walking distance of each other.

What have I come inside for? You could say it lacked a shape. Now here's a failing I suspect you're all familiar with. Coincidence is akin to sovereignty. Each letter is of equal significance, inducing a certain solipsistic misery. I have got to do this thing right now. (Ground base might be a whole word.) Jagged rocks are exposed. All that matters to him is that he is going home. This is an erroneous reading for anathema. When is all that matters to him, i.e. a plant whose root once spelt.

Conscription of time in a notional emergency. Try a reason, the rap of your finger. Merely an incised pattern, an injection of miniaturized physicians. To the west of this location was an inlet filled with rotting ice. The long count was barely over.

Entry of the gogs, a body swamp. The land is full. He was reared in a theatrical homestead. (And as she said, afterworld, his writing exquisite.) It's the infinite densities that are responsible for the universe possessing an edge in time. There's an awful lot of traffic down here tonight. I myself am viewed from opposite points on the earth's orbit.

Which is now called skin? Certainly not. He just goes wherever he likes. Bless him, jammed between the front and the occipital. For fugue, see form.

Exordium. On jobation.
She says I have hollers in my head. By whom were all things unmade? I am the first person to disprove. Write it out in full or it will distort the sense. It turns out the glue burns quite nicely after all (submarine). More of my scandalous abdications.

While it exalts itself, the all conviction can be dismissed. Vignette: the deceased standing in front. Work your way into its belly. Having that extra skin taken away has opened up my eyes. Eat dust, chew glass—spit blood. Well, there you go.

The lift is a small cell with mirrors shooting through a drill bore. I have singlehandedly re-established that seven-days-of-the-week thing. He runs through the divisions and appoints each a number. He can hear light, see sound. I'm concentric. Channels of intense colour bisect the cell. The fridge is symphonic, the kettle a light-year star. The theme is nervous people and we've got ten minutes. When I raise my atom I do not usually *try* to raise it.

Haar-skein. A rock void lined with crystals (usually called forth). Rough for composed minutes—one of the people, uninhabited.
We've had all this before—no quote extant, unforgettable lines. An early exponent, a piece of awe. Decayed spots congealed by wouldness.

Enter chaos, the great chamber work. There should be an acute over that vowel and a siren. He says therein I like some of the words, but not all of the words. Quite simply this the best available introduction to survival. These (pointing) I shall excise.

Behind him it stands, ibis-head with reeds and a palette. The name of a beast of prey, misidentified by my translators—creatures whose bone structures enclose their flesh. These (pointing) shall survive. We've become accustomed to such seeing and describing, a substitute for a substitute. Another present in the room says you cannot possibly be here. Round about me were people in mostly grey. This aligns itself with a famous classical disputation. An astronomical tablet in cuneiform records the signal.

On poaching for the bile bladder.

This reminds us of the time when wild throve in this part. Two men rent a room by night and day, respectively. They have been adapted (a farce, foretold). Translation appeared just before the insurrection. Careful of that wire. One of these is the most capable orifice of my entirety. I just don't know exactly where.

A pistol-case on saddle or belt. That is, a hiding to nothing. The rising sun found him, senescent in tongue. Tiny olivines weathered from lava flows stud the neighbourhood cliffs.

One step or measure, especially the diplomatic, and a fairly long time in the making. I pray you mar no woe in my reversal, and so on. Vermes, guide of.

Now slithered in the moon's eclipse. I conceal myself, the better to observe (imagine how Mozart). I contradict myself. Somehow I alone have retained the faculty of touch.

If such a one be fit to speak, entitle it. Shred. Fall. Those little triangles I talked about in the first half: they represent.

A strip or border, a lengthy effusion, spoken or written out (neither). He had the alphabetizers in. And I haven't even mentioned painting yet (old glash). Probably a jackal of some species.

A drinking rout. A rend, a tear, with scar tissue. Screed-gripped, no doubt in the sense of bitten and pierced. What is in me dark illumine.

I too am neither. The influence has weathered. It became general only in the nineteens (a lot of opera houses seem to burn down). And generally with the implication of spoken dialogue.

He made the first image of a disc, of dust, fairly despised and quite void of gas. Yet, surrounding, a normal star. Ostinato.

Another continues to harp on the theme of his calling, especially the lenses. Delustre from text, unflowering the dignity of. Which was more of a half-waking, the risen image? Screams from the scaffold, enwrapped. Brass screw cleats.

A figure is called. Two pass around each other, back to back, before returning to their original positions. Just the bare bones of an event.

From a book whose many editions have been influential.
A slow walk upstream, fallout measured on surface. There's seven of us left in our group. The scouting party return with news: the other creek is affordable. I'm not suggesting any of this is at all interesting. It's simply something that presses to be recorded in the passage of time, the boundary of a white hole.

Arc of horizon. A lesion between a sense of place and a vertical circle passing through the body. See, amount equals the plural of direction. The objectives of this culture have been found in a cave. The others stared into the fire. My ideal writing would be a list of impossible definitions, hewn to form a perfect cube.

He is paid for moving south. Stop just there. No open channels remain. Dementoid was first found nearby in the early eighteens.

Without looking up she says myriad others are burrowing into the market. Therefore, act according to whether gold, silver or copper. The head of the operation enters the room and bows, a low graceful bow taken from the waist. (The original engineering flaw has of course come to light.) There's this massive garden with a lake. In a dream I visit a mediaeval boneyard. We get to high tide, and then.

A plant reputed to underscore privation and madness, wings flickering at the ankles. We will meet briefly, for the first and last time, in a matter of days. After the introduction and the litany, we remain, unread. (First catharsis.)

Why would anyone place a benchmark just there? We've migrated to a more attractive economy. This coincides with the arrival of an asteroid. Within certain limits the analysis of the extension remains independent (when we think of a foot-loop or a square back yard). The representation of space stands for nothing whatsoever. I've had to reset all my ballast calculations.

It's just that I miss you. She says I feel I have stolen sympathy. I am undeserved, but shall return. I think it happened because of batteries. Speaking for myself, appropriate models have appeared. Does that mean it's sucking in more matter from one side than the other?

She passes through again, twice-told. I am sluiced of debris. I've lost that extra little bit of incarnation: auditory canal, cochlea, membranous labyrinth, muscles, ligaments of the ossicula, pinna or auricle, tympanum, vestibule. This implies a tactical shift. The general strategy is to take the economy by sunrise (past selves acting in hired judgment). To fake these concepts as a point of departure is misleading. I said I wonder why they don't come. But he prides himself on keeping an open mind on all things. During a pause in speech we heard that noise again. Perhaps during the course of the watch some strange power deluded his vision. Many of the supply depots have been looted.

You know. I tire. Lack, countermined. I fissure. Product: something like artificial snow, astro turf-wars. We have considered this question entirely apart from the facts. The chosen word is aleatory, that, or slave culture. Whose concrete piers seemed to remodel the coastline? It's about here he says, the collapse.

The copy.
Forty minutes of liquefaction. Where did first light vanish? As can be seen from the next entry, on the eighth day he was appointed. The last part, if not arbitrary, may perhaps represent.
Offspring of muster. Albany herald. Industries exclude brick and tile, superphosphate planets.

Driving rain. A pack of carelessly dressed men cluster in the lee of a bunker. Is the outcome more significant, more telling, than that which separates them? A more or less suicidal atmosphere. The image is pixilated, mildly insane. There was no way to cope. They wield metal clubs and take it in turns to strike out at a tiny white sphere. (Writing must be therapeutic, or something.) Beyond, dense filigree of semicircular canals. Some are perfectly salubrious and not at all overcrowded. You cannot die.

A countercharm against spells cast. At the earth's core, used nickel and iron. She laughs o wept aren't men frightful, ideas so grief with suchness.

Big days of birth and death rays. Aside from this, very little appears to happen. The asteroid belt was less than a day ahead. At one pole, the drawing-room ends in purely decorative curves (ants, crabs, silverfish). A charge of mental energy has attached itself to the specified object. No, already too many animals here.

An instrument for breaking flax and hemp had to be invented. Each member pulls the thread controlling one of the bacteria. A flat box with sounding-board had to be invented—a contrivance for retarding, by flinches. Extinctions are introduced. I am not going to explain myself (one hell of a domestic). Thousands of birds cover the sandy banks. Why does language appear to be alien? Dead men do not speak said the teacher. Get out. (Only partly.) A word is drawn into itself, and sometimes misused. Work's genesis is of especial interest. The capsule breaks open along a transverse circular split. (Hello, it's doctor futurity.) Now, invert a spiral. See where that takes us. And myself, with my white skin dyed woad, masquerading. Do you think I should make a statement about all of this? My left paw's trapped in the culvert.

No he says, I aim to snare them at the cusp of signification and obscurity. Sometimes I'm the full accompaniment, sometimes not. I can't afford to lose another day. Your word is owed, under threat of sentence. It lies in the same syntactical relation to both poles of the earth. Each bond is a distinct seme. But there is one more point about the concept of the tongue which should be stressed here.

The inner temple, composed of.
An unbreachable responsibility. A crime scene. It does not mean to think itself. Give another example. In that household the affairs of the stage were the natural subject of daily conversation. Wrap that up and take it outside.

Subject: the vocal organ of a magical bird with bright blue plumage. A mediaeval vision of the wide man (if soul were as ready as the soul). I see no reason why not. Together we foresaw that sound. The first movement begins at the strike of when, another mineral hook.

I am oversleep. Turn through voice. Underneath, hello it's me can you hear me. They still watch over the experiments their ancestors started. Holy smoke, the surface temperature is eighty centigrade et cetera.

She walks along, her shoes in shreds. I no longer stand proud of the surface. That is to say, set in forms no longer answering. A vicious military campaign ensues.

However, at thirteen the missing cones reappeared. They are not really signalling what they mean. I was met by an outbreak of unparalleled delight. (Circular saw.)
a) The tactical pattern according to which the battle was fought.
b) Our terra incognita.
c) The decomposition of farce.
d) The relative strength of the opposing armature.
And what we want to expose is this mass of desire. The third way is to take a detour through the desert. Experiment to be repeated.

Now it came to pass that he made twelve of them. Four cubes was the length and four cubes the breadth and four cubes the height. The name here is the difficult thing. This hypothesis does not seem simply false—a cry forced up, from land and alarm. Later, a mere title.

Evidently time has passed. Let me talk to my memory he says. If such a one be fit to speak, entitle it. (I must have removed something and forgotten.)

Sudden leap to third canticle.
I sleep in a special perspex tube. Have you ever come across postmortem lucidity? There are numbers and rumours, but I am not many. Nothing I declare is worth the mention. I'm only concerned here with what people actually say, shed like a skin no longer granted covenant. I'm the shadow of the object that moves before me on the path.
Together failing, pause.

After dark they worked by candles the remaining ten held for them—a variety of green with brilliant lustre. No radiation could possibly leak to the exterior. It's the geode.

She quivers but continues to feed the hound. This is boundless—a social on the threshold, the bundle with a hint of sediment, with or without axe. Who can wreck infinite. She is worrying about what I have just said.

This is the worst way of all. Running footsteps in the street. (Chirp.) Crouched under a promontory, watching the country to the south.

Dear.
I've had the intelligence quote back. I was all foreseen, hence the lie detector. That noise is a bit of nothing, ruminating (the tests). Oh, and he could see us crawling away from the observation tower. You will subsequently receive the petri dish, together with a group of death certificate. The lives of the blind must be different from those of the sighted.
Yours truly (110).

Exercise ninety-nine. Report of a trial. It helps to draw off foul nails. Slow-motion trembling and grinding movements. It's only a similarity (difference is always maintained). It could always drown itself. We're drawing close to a vanishing. If quicklime and wine lees are added, it works the stranger. Every time we pass that hill I think of you.

Of his theory, in supersuspension.
There are few significant days remaining. We are now entering the thoroughfare, approaching the point of interception.

The rejection of error as the central element. He says from time to time that's my shadow (light of tiny red orb set at hypothalamus).

Tinfoil skittering across shingle. Grisly cobble, stench of rotting vegetable matter.
I put such questions to him. When did the man come back? I've often been dull enough myself, and could see nothing to interest a body. Show a lamp when you judge the other has gone. One of the anvils was shaped like an ear. This was the motive behind his persecution—because he did this, not that.

Acausal collecting principle. Torture by sleep deprivation.
I just think that's way too obvious. He sits in a room barricaded behind columns of used books. That's your cue to start vibrating. All reading is prayer. The first envoy is announced, the oldest known horselike animal. Make sure that the fires are in the right pattern and well alight. I will try to say this one more time, and then otherwise.

The concluding part of a tract, the final word. All his objects are in steerage. This situation's more advantageous than we realized at the time (think astrology, psychic alienation, poverty).

Tendency, the undecided state, still exists in this sphere. You are really very twelve. The next step is to try and discover what has caused these impressions. His magnetic field is connected with the fluctuations to which my own atom is subject. He talks up scant knowledge. We need more bloodlines. And the sea was set above them. Mercury isn't really airless, the body in its sense of place falls away.

Once we used to sit here and watch, because this with my mouth, nothing.

Chance influences the pattern of the ash—a stab, an outlet. The radioactivity is even clearer when the contrast is reversed. I've become convinced that all the names have the same meaning. May we then ask anything of this at all?

Four light-years later: that which depends on the absence of something else.
Hare-head, snake-head, bull-head et cetera. A bet made with the intention of absconding if it is lost. Only in phrases.

This is where we used to stop, pass over. There's difference contained in geometry. Resist the analogy with language, earthlings. Everyone's convinced that nothing is customarily written. O excellent, I'm already here! The theme is mourning, would-be names, and you've got ten seconds.
Name one of the names.

Something falling from the sky. Keep the semantics short: this year's haven't. It was the appendix, eyes as black as what? It isn't too late.

Poles of inaccessibility. It was this icon: the world meant sitting, chair, so as to hear. It's a funny window this. The icelandic thing has collapsed.

Because we presuppose the existence of substance at all time. Lingering random chords. A substitute layer for future evasions, the negative of sign (this is a frequent prognostication of the codices). Operations are now under the aegis of a more durable covenant. I never know when to stop. Which metal is serving as the measure of value? I am declaring you the owner.

Compound sea with prefix, restored to form. The upper part of my face is encrusted. Overall, I am movable. The flesh is perforated. I am not at the required station. Only one half remains.

Of his neglecting to provoke a sufficient interpretation—where backward strata coincide with the general retreat. (Withdrawal of cover design.) A diamond is cut in the shape of a drop, and used.

He leans forward to eject mucus from his sinus. It spatters onto the frozen ground.

Their lives would be more unrest and noise than ours, especially in such concertina'd forms—from to send, from on the way, from on and via a way.
Move para from chance if keep alienator.

I think no she says. And I think she is placing her feet down on the ground, circling me about. And I think you are guilty. Do a fraction more each time (there is some phenomenological justification for this). The clock had in reality moved on, persisting in the removal of something or other—a term denoting the abandonment of a quality (log). About 6,000,000,000,000 miles.
Ha ha ha ha
ha ha ha ha
ha ha ha ha!

I keep seeing the same face all the time. But for the book, the argument (unsex). A shrill whistle and the other escapes. As he came close I smelled the poisoned lozenge. It's the one who runs straight through the spine that wins. Fine. I shan't need anything more. The sand has dried the paint. Call down a resident, wire him in.
Note to self must research.

The sensation of the limb still being attached to the body.

The word gas is chaos. I was fashioned old (chamber of commerce). Something collides with my throat. All writing is precursory. I find myself enclosed in a type of contract.

He is just here for a little while, then he is going to go away. We shall consider the structure of the tongue in more detail at the end of this chapter. I had noticed a monstrous head with scorched eyes, with possessory title.

Scent of wood-reek from nearby copse. Interconnections. Squat on the ground to defecate. I have no dwelling to speak of. Return to manifest, corposant discharge. That's no way to go on.

Bent fold or bay. Blood-space in tissue. I mean by sign the whole that results from disassociation. I have deserted my post.

Sentinel. But it's been known for some time that the last. This took about twenty-four hours of solid. To allow of seeing and breathing, a sharpened plate cut the required shapes. I have discovered our strategies are indeed identical. This would make the picture complete. No, the art of chasing, across a sheet of metal.

Then another question, still the same. Render yourself. Proceed with discretion. He feels uncomfortable, listening. Stuttering telegraph batters at his eardrums. Why this reference, still, to a cist in space, bolts through the spine? That's good, the abandonment, moving through to selfsame. (Fuck off.) How long ago was all that when he asks was a sign.

The last touch, provided (autopsy). She throws them away. Her ankles are bleeding (499). The studio deprivation tank is a residue of the continuum. Legend, foreshore.

Is is in fact confirmed by the many descriptive elements.
Fossil gum, discarded. No is premature.

XXVII

She draws breath from the other's mouth. How things have unfolded in the last few hours. We have fallen early to some major names. It's a bit of a commitment: man-to-man combat in the arena, the rise and fall of the chest.

It was like a harrow. The time is fixed. People are vanishing, withdrawing into their own mediations. The same principle leads the physician to announce that the malady is moving from the heart to the head, and then the reverse.

He leans out of his box. I always hear myself saying no what beauty. I don't know who I'm talking. I understand we have a new number. A belvedere is what's called a mirador, or watchtower. This is way easier than you might think. A complex can only be given by its description (murmurous doubt). Hooded and cloaked manikins are kept hidden in the dark *cista*.

I continue to make use of the available light and sound. There are some very important people here, three facing north, three facing west, three facing south and three facing east. One of those rare cases in which the history of language lights up the prehistoric.

It's just a couple of years before his death. He takes a downward turn before flipping back to his original position. Point the telescope through that open window, whence the suspect made off. Reckon compound interest on capital et cetera. There's going to be no riot in this place tonight (he said sternly).

A space is constructed. It's immediately colonized. Some have seen apparitions they did not recognize. (Now what.) There are sundry objects, more things to negotiate. Fall open, expose the core of the body, push back. Prize up left scapula. It presents two surfaces and three borders.

The animal catches its standing hoof in the ground. It's so long since I sat here myself. This is what's called merely being an outline, an aftercrop.

Extrapolation of voice part, with jaw. Fracture at lower arc of radius. This meant that his shares were actually now less viable. (I was just a courier.) The voices on those tracks, some describe states, others processes. Fragments of shell were found in the eye, covering the eye. Also kohl, copious. Now, stand up. Straws are drawn. One is elected—tarred and feathered. The motif here is evening in the west, nightsent gillyblooms et cetera. In reality, thorax. Thumb and carpus transfixed from third canticle.

Genus of fossil birds of the hemisphere. She has opera glasses strapped permanently to her head. The others don't stand a chance. Usually it's whole families. The sight is unendurable. When his lungs gave out the effect was electricity itself.

Clue, adjective of dusk. Cycle exhaling, far horizontal. The sun is sunk, after him the star. The vignette of this chapter is of no interest. Each statement has the capacity to shock. In conversation he sat perplexed as the other replied. Some shed a wide and silver beam, and suchlike.

I'm up at that hill, come. Blood glugs at the thrapple. The external border commences where the two lines, converge. Now I am going down the hill. Substance lends entropy, rehearsals of energy. I am never attained. I find myself among a group of massless colour, carriers that bind together, breeding collisions. This is a ritualistic piece yet to be detected in the free state, with inelastic scoring. These last years saw his violin.

An ode to renunciation (congratulations). A poem intended to be sung, and generally addressed to somebody, something. The subject is renounced.
Foster-nerve of alumnus. Tight wedge of horsemen, with usher. Blank-hearted fellows, a pitch-clear voice. Near this place we overtook.

A conjurer who works with live chickens, his catchword. It fails. I understand only proximally. After a day within a group of them one feels the need to be purified. Notwithstanding, edible rootstock to a man. One of the eight arrived with the following news.

He is master of the disjunct, perfect loglike arguments. Why do you say he sees things differently?
What we did not realize is that he had no need to calculate at all. For example, a contradiction appears in civil life. (I didn't mean it like that.) Then there's the existing problem. I grant immediate consent. Everything else is shrinking. What could you answer?
We forget that they correspond to psychological residues. Social usefulness is no longer an aim. Now often happens. I select one of the five boxes at random, and slit it open.

We will lose a lot of this stuff. Homily, lick it—maximal in doctored solvent—vulgar in referral: factory fresh adrenochrome. He declined the invitation for 7.30 p.m., an hour he continued to find uncivilized. There was the question of the elite or what saint for the day. Then died, us composer.

Mirror, aria.
Things unheard of or normally considered impossible. He ranges freely over

selected memories of metropolitan life. The beginning is glorified.

Both now swing together. The burning of the hotel. Escape.

It's no longer there, not a brick of it. This is called becoming all the things one has ever perceived. In places there is only a little less light on the white paper.

Thank you for carrying all this about in your head. It must have been a brief conversation. Sometimes I cross everything out and leave without warning. The value of a ton of iron will be expressed by very different prices.

Ruminator lunges, the flexors and extensors.

Tang of urea to tongue. The notes make their point in terms of the existing. Now name one of the names, such as an object denoting the absence of a quality (log).

They're boosting the levels. His head rests to one side, remaining hand stealthy to pocket. What he says is too explicit. Grab hold as he passes through. His Achilles is severed, hobbling him for life. I'm a surprisingly luminous copy of him.

He retreats to his garret and clambers back into the cubicle. Ask him. Perhaps we should offer help.

Usually a narrowed mouth, for ashes, and often a foot. A monumental imitation, the river-source. A closed vessel with tap, with device: the moss capsule. The number four is significant here. The others may not want us. Material producing backscatter of radiation similar to human tissue.

(Among what people did the novel originate?) Indeed, you do seem to hear everything, don't you. Be careful, that thing will take off. It was as though one had enjoyed for an evening the company of a contagious disease. What are the most famous exemplars history has to offer? List them. Then there is his caustic response to the rock.

It's the festival. Fading objects on the street, raindrops inside a tunnel. Follow closely the replay. He ends himself by dissolving (too much suspension in the mix). It begins at the periphery, then gradually soaks inward to the centre. There's too little appreciation of the tough job he's done. This will reward you, apparently—from to put away flesh.

Noticing a dead man's drum. Its existence is not constant. Its position varies considerably.

Since intention was invented there's no reason to go outside. Re-scream means to scream again. This man has definite promise.

It ripens rapidly, before expiring. I'm learning about calibration. We used a sound filter, scorched-earth tactics, little bits and pieces of other people's lives.

But we came to a creek that flowed such that it could not be forded. We don't say A knows something and B knows the opposite, do we?

Where it pointed led us to a rendezvous with the survey party.

Raised barrier of nighthood, child. What's happened since the first strike of noon? Yes, he requested a single day—subtle contractions between music and text. In a number of libraries he found nearly unpublished compositions.

He is expected work. Time passes, no one spoke. He cannot remember. Even a minor success can perform wonders. (You have surely read his prefaces before.) We must also be able to say 'other people' et cetera. Sometimes the everyday is the best option. He was once a great arranger. The pageant is most of it blown down: diffused particles of matter, fragments of safety gas. The recorded conversations are a tactic that emerged in the fifteens. Astronomical geomancy, possibly.

He's sealed up with sheet music. No doubt you will recognize the bore and chamber of the piece. Or the *punct*, which an event-particle conceals.

On this side, on the side nearest to the speaker or writer. Planks of burnt wood keep drifting past. The probe has burrowed far below the permanent cloud cover. Mention is made of plagiarism. (Any illusory ideal that leads one astray is worth the pursuit.) You are sheltering under a misapprehension. But what if they no longer have a use for us? B is supposed to have guessed what I had said. In the morning, only a square of pierced light remains to indicate that he was ever present.

It's slow work. The demand for articles will increase. The object on the plinth is an imitation. Momentum is gathering. (Go and do another sensible.) Meanwhile is evolving. Closer is making inroads. Silence my angel they all snuff out et cetera.

This may well win a place in the theory of conflict. Eyes bleed at this altitude. The meeting lasted thirty minutes. There's a lot more to this than shiny surfaces. Several hours later, it's said that all things are a duality, after all.

Somewhere among us sits an indeterminacy. We're cobbling together a talking part—collected dialogues, including the letters, with introduction and preliminary knots. On the other hand, according to the inessential.

Near the sign-post you say? I will bear it in mind goodnight.

Relocate. Invent a colour with the an identical quantum number. What we saw did not correspond to something transparent. Twelve independent fences stand ten feet apart, circles within circles. Their ends lead back to the cave. The foot-soldiers wore flexible steel-plates, fanning out kiltlike from the solar plexus. There's a gradual entrance into the sphere of another, a reversed exit: a collection of empirical observations of terrestrial events.

But I'm getting over all that, forehead smashing into cheekbone, into carti-lage. I haven't touched a piano in ten years.

Perforce, it must be nuanced and complicated, no? An imitation in metal of the infamous. A stone chest covered with stone slabs, containing. Tissue must be equivalent to immateriality.

Sorry, I meant anabasis.

Ill-chosen movements. A level stretch at the top of a hill—a tendency to establish controls that would isolate. A sudden strategic reverse. We are adding up the lines of the hexagram. The interior has quickly taken recourse to counter-measures. This is what's called a rearguard action. We have triumphed. The past is forgotten.

Of alcohol, the groupuscule—the motor burns out and stops two leagues from where we abandoned. I retain nothing. I was drawn back.

We've returned to where we started, perfect asynchrony. Learn a basic yet particular form, and then mutate. Suggest another description of the features. Grief, one would like to have said.

Spatter of lighter dots across the petals. All their hinder parts facing inward.

Drug, I'm convinced. And a speculative piece on page forty-six about sensa-tion. Vary yourself. I squeeze my body through the remaining slit. This conceives of the image as a replica of reality, dust from the high ridge. The melody haunts my reverie she sang.

On this flank of the hill there is the rustling hulk. On the other, a great out-rush of tree through a gash in the chalk. It's all coming back to me. Posterior surface and/or dorsum.

Imply the act of stealing. Insubstant, tinctured properties.

A key's pressed into a bed of wax. Certain books should never be placed on top of one another. I've always been good with other people's money.

Saturn conjunct, Uranus seventy. Etymological weakness: fixed ideas, rumina-tive states, impossible conditions. Objects will always be associated with forgot-ten experiences. Off with the gang-tooth, break out the drill—the turn-screw, pincers and handspike. I'm learning fast about surrendering intent.

Jets, overhead. Prepare caskets of loose granular earth.

It led. (All of where face extermination.)

Mother, by too early a repetition of thy call. Yours always. He thrust the object into view from the right, as if offering. Listening at some distance, per-haps music she heard when a child.

A subterranean chamber full of stars. Continued today cross-country.

It's said he can't hold a tune. Two of the horses in front have failed. In attendance are the two witnesses. He's been trapped at an angle, the notorious chicane at curve D. I can't talk right now. He studied at his native place.

A hood is placed over the signal light. The score has been rewritten, an accompaniment to an apparition. A thin film stretches tightly over the present. Recall the unknown factor—an abortive project, the anticlimax. Grab hold of anything that passes through on the other side.

Another relates a memory of her own. What she interprets is dead in our language. This is racing ahead of itself, repeated and formulated in more and more differentiated ways. Only on the crumbling causeway, below.

Yes, his free hand. You may believe it or not. Business is out there—we were so lack, your crown of white flame and blue sulphur. And the dreamer, ready for the sacrifice, replies, here I am.

There's a crowd of people at the crest of the hill, some with their own wings. Let him speed up his work that we may see it. Seal me into this capsule. Bury it. The question is, can they make it to the starting line by dawn?

Enveloped in rivers of burning lava et cetera. Make a note of its location, and move on. Call it the iron age, or something—a measure of unavailable energy. I don't know why.

Footsteps in the snow on a concrete platform (o all right). If we had only gone away somewhere at once that night. Thrashing polyethylene in the branches. A set of old tunes. In time, aid zooms down. A circular belt encloses the lagoon—something given beyond what is strictly required. A shallow, especially one communicating with the sea, or river. Also fashioned old.

Dining meagre on suet from the hides. He turned with the tarot deck and retreated. A sign reads free pig skull. We distrust. The oscillations suggest that someone has set the system to neutral frequency.

But this is better than expected. I'm moving towards a certain unit of dosage. He accepted, from somebody in the crowd. Overcoding is assured by the number-as-form.

For which is being an issue, entity? Yesterday they slept without water and they continued.

Shadow of metallic arm, yellow on bleached foundation. God he said with scorn. I'm superceding, memories of a jaundiced limb on the long walk. These fluctuate and reappear with a different character almost hourly. The second of them is kept in the head. To save labour, assume the audience will calculate.

A neurotransmitter hormone, unrelated. Also, especially us, personified in the face—red oxidization product of adrenalin. A disordered time sense is one of the main symptoms.

It is raised high above the shingle, measured in watts. He says he sees the bones before the flesh. It took six weeks of hard labour to transpose the whole body. The two Eustachian tubes open one at each side. I am obvious to meaning. I keep missing things.

See photos. Translate the silence of the second movement. The fourth was screed, straight into the bed of the river. Abscission.

I have resisted in the one mode we both can understand. The signals are down (stormdrain). It fell off but leapt straight back in. One has to pay in order not to be exaggerated. I have finished the big sleep.

A tainted neutral glued forever into a margin.
Congratulations. Move the counter forward seven sentences. An impractical visionary, out of all twenty-six professions he barely makes a living. Rarely he steps beyond his unnumbered door (the rhythmic traits of peasant speech). There are three minutes left to go. Touch me. The men found it and could not hide their find. He is divorced from writing. You have just won the lot. My shapes fall into a numeric pattern.
I will not touch he says. You just sit and gaze at the sea. I don't use touch. I will not even be in the room—I'm a remote.
Gently, jump to conclusions in haste. He says a long way back that hill was flung, along with the island. Carry the matter to baron, mister of the artillery.

An incomplete and haunted landscape, the material by which the body in question is framed.
He says the future may be undecidable. A little serration was found within me, strings of coincidence. Another once wrote. Those who creaght.

I receive a draft notice, some skirmishing about bounds they have. (I had lifted the wrong book.) Monthly analysis: the negative points are the impossibility of making contact.
Goodgrief you on Mars.

The vibration that remains after loss or decay of the rest.
Perfume floods the capsule. There's a new run on the noun. This is the foundation upon which all of my commodities and equivalents have been built. It steadily declines with respect to the fixed part.

A changing pattern of lights on a display screen. Tense of ninety-two. The status of some of the less well-attested sounds is disputed. I'm told everything's elastic. Not today I replied. My open palm seems to occupy a larger surface than usual, scored with deeper tracks. She says there are eyes waiting.

Found therein are cells, also somewhat. (Probably room service I said.) There are small buried stems, light dust of snow at the pit of a field. Concerned for his illness, she draped the flag over his leg. Where is this place they have chanced upon?

Compound mass. Whiff of grave-gas. Drifting forms, corporeal yet fleet. When he was young with his eyes shut, who wrote? It doesn't matter. I'm no longer recognized by touch—locked in between domy cairns, corralled by rubble. Strange flocks feed on the slopes. In twenty-six I went to ground.

Where the boat was? From whence came forth a dazzling rain?

A note on the matrix in which a cast can be made. Regenerate tears fill his eyes. This passage is analogous. She spent her evenings promising herself.

They have done really well with the resources at hand. Tiny atoms accumulate on the sea floor, embed themselves in the cliff. It's true that ships rarely make the crossing now. The door was on the hook, the electric light.

Phantom meter, expressing absence or negation (gram)—the supernatural preconditions necessary for any story. A repository, a container in which to put voting (historectomy). The urn-shaped body.

A void, flinty shells in two halves that fit like box and lip. Kohl about the eyes, hieroglyphic. On is animated—neither loose as earth, neither firm as stone. The daughter chromosomes are situated in two groups near the poles (the great swindle). At five strikes the window slams shut. Their own country is equally deserted, benighted soon enough.

Every second note, duck. Anyway I'm galloping on. Yes, you may cheerfully goad him to strike you. Tiresome steps these—that curt metallic click of the heel, the casual flash of the prisms. It's not going to get any easier, is it?

A wire tray is unearthed. It was once used to make paper with the hand. A cast of feathers or other covering. (He avoid.)

A saw-edged condition, with wasplike tooth. The verb that would roughly correspond to the fear.

That strange hybrid creature who lived alone in an empty room. It died and I don't know how to get rid of the carcass. (Don't laugh at me he said.) So then things went as I have related. The men pressed about.

Light reading for certain classes, as the occasion may require. Alcohol and acid, hence elimination of fluid. A cyst of light, the crackle of petroleum—growth formed in mould. That ashen grey has leeched from the face.

An absolute possession in the instantaneous space of any moment. Something like that. It is (text mutilated).

A moat compasses a small redoubt in the shape of a star. Science is often unacknowledged because of its roots in ventriloquy. It made me laugh out loud when I looked him up in the record books. Convince me that things are not falsely represented. Someone spoke of black matter. It sprang to its feet.

I think I put it back in the wrong place. Repeat the long walk, out from us. It's the irrepressible need to testify. We seem to be attracting a species of glandular beetle. We strapped shells to our legs to protect our kneecaps. How many fingers have you left. Count out loud. We caught a specimen. It had an enquiring look.

A want of correspondence in time. They are eight yards out. Discuss what ontological justification there is. Commander had to use his army, with a minimum. Misfortune took strikes, hymns of restoration et cetera. At the fault-line—sun with waxy limbs, climbing while you sleep, deep in your room. They came from beyond the morning star. (In the nether world there is a place so described.) That's not how you spell grandeur, is it? The idleness of it: wall running into skirting.

The next step. Present the figure of a quaver-foil at the animal pole. They forgot to test the temperature of the permafrost. This is an embodiment, ancestor at spirit recess. The system was made discrete through the removal of certain elements. In the same way they're formed into fibres—bristles and sheets of skin. Branches from the sympathetic also supply the organ. Only then does the shadow becomes an image, something much closer to an extinction. In his methodical way he examined these and other possible hypotheses. Three points of disputation were noted.

A conclusion that trails necessity.
The argument is set out in three propositions. She separates off from the rest. Together they are several. It's great fun dicing with death—all over its legs and angina pectoris. They're going to have to chisel me out, aren't they? The high-resolution method reveals hardening of the arteries, the base of the brain. The axis of the cavity is curved like the cavity itself. My genes are stuffed silly. A voice says this is.
Can lead to the formation of false memories. I disject, personified in lung, also without hyphen.

The analysis and interpretation of events, with the aid of an alienist. Don't miss this chance, the clods of earth. Markers of a dissuasion.

The action. You can't hide. Heel dug into floor and swings his horn about to recharge the piece. Something may well happen in the last hours of the winter.

Artist drawing incline through grid—her body emptied with kaolin, discomposed. People are moving off in all directions.

There are none of us left. They rose up on their hind legs. We want to lease our own lives I said. (What is called one who learns late?) The murals inhabit a grimy realm of expression: terraces on the surrounding hills and ridges, numerous dams and irrigation canals. An attendant takes my clothes. I lie down on the trolley and wait. I can no longer picture. Head is void, beneath creeping nearer— the evocation of detail by detail.

The reformation, a given name. Interest is reawakened by a new type of lip. All this is done under the most trying conditions. (The new signifying process welcomes negativity.) She holds a capsule containing grains coated with a universal solvent. I inquire. Answer: an offering, deceptive from its semblance.

Abandon this. You were right, five minutes remaining. A road cuts straight through the compound. The text pertains to the type of time found opposite. Hold all cells. Everything you see here, it's mine. A tiny shallow in the rock-face was used. What metal daggers are known from others, copper-using? Energy still exists, but is lost for the purpose of work. I am obvious tongue.

They must be those waders. They are fully clothed. The sea looks dead. They strode out of the surf in the early scenes, out of nothing. Just replace, remove and replace the gentle turnkey.

The host was secure. When they fled he pursued them, carnifex.

One of several muscles of the thorax. Lateral cetaceous nerves. I can't picture. Something like the numerals one and four and six, plus attendant arrows and script. (What technique of using language composes the background?) The will turns toward its origin in the nameless et cetera.

The outer skin is situated opposite the petals, tall and composed. Always a multitude, that collective sulphur. One is sent away to master the application of thought to an everyday object. Another is sent away to practise surrendering intent in a given situation.

Ludo. Using a nonexistent mouth to communicate an invisible message. No authentic strikes today. I discover that his name is never to be uttered (stop when you've reached perfection, I suppose). Who are form and fulfil? What is happening.

A reckoning of sorts, the trial of visibility. I would simply offer up thanks and pass over. He'll be unable to check his answer. We lugged it over to the stagnant pool. The corpse wore a yang gabardine storm-coat.

A chalk embankment, within which it's rumoured buried. I'm positioned at the centre of a triangle, always seeking the fourth player. A faint trace of disgust wrinkled the lineaments. There are odd stains on the asphalt. A hood is placed over the head, over the upper part of the pharynx.

Notes on social. The corresponding antiparticle is not as yet discovered. Aftermath in tow, a five-year plan. A finite distance.

Year one began disastrously, a rare opportunity. An insurrection is underway inland. I'm not as symptomatic as I'm cracked up to be. Picture a line which approaches a given curve, but never meets it. When does this stop he asks.

Glittering, but never shining. Reptile of pale-green variety. A residual perception, or glimpse. Work resumed on operas under the stimulus of euthanasia. In brief, any of a class whose behaviour is governed. A mechanical piano on wheels is dragged along the promenade. The young woman looks questioningly at her vacuum. The pier is on fire in the night, very orange against the blue-blacks, pretty. And look, archangel, breaking through the cloud: horsehead nebula, wrestling at the hollow of the thigh.

I need an excuse. Our lines will never meet. I do not assert. It's the workaday renditions that concern me as much as the extra.

A template pattern rich in decayed matter—the spread of an incombustible dust, throughout. They're said to appear during the harvest month. If they do exist, they represent the fundamental building brick. Sometimes these penitential elements are called in to account for themselves. One of the several muscles of the thorax is torn.

O look, slender you. (Just another false alarm.) This must be a reference to a much later sound, a twisted contribution to the civic reservoir. We all wore name tags. Mine said I was a pineal investigator, an Etruscan god. I will read you the questions and answers as they stand. Whose was it, amended by ess in nineteen, section twelve? The schema act.

Ypsiliform.

He took the contract out and once more examined it. The theme of sighing returns again and again. Similar are the basic categories of thought which appear in the descriptions. And the brass sill burned brightly. Hey, opsimath! Mortality following performance is small.

The perfect white oblong. The blue cable, swung to bridge a gap. The blue poles.

A sound like the ring of a finger around the lip of a glass. Enormous avenues, the terraces with paddy-fields, rice in the husk. Long lines of wooden stakes stretch out to the horizon. The time segment is missing. And that of the subsidence?

The author has planted, for the purpose of orientation. Actuality is released through names. Enter anywhere at your peril. (Side aspect has different meanings.) Where did you find it, never heard before?

They form an uninterrupted chain across the mesmeric gland. She catches hold of the rope ladder (creepers). This work is dedicated in admiration of a suppressed talent. Lend them back their debt. I've seen all I want.

Straw death, an arbitrary coinage. It's time to step up a gear, start asking some real questions. *You* know what I mean, said he. Who applies more generally? Who or what descends over the dark central plain? Why are the hills treeless? Against whom do the waves revolt? It could always have been designed to fit like that, I suppose.

Sorry to have to tell you my poor wife was killed. Complete union of bone. He's incandescent. (With?) This lowers the whole pitch of the argument. The grave has been moved. He forgets for a moment the other. The survey parted company and crossed back over the strait to the coast of William. The main activity looks like many other tasks. The suspect swallows hard—I mean the earth of the ground, the land, the planet. I don't want to rush into anything. Muster, mark the spot: central ganglia of the unsympathetic. I.e. he's changed.

Get rid of them (ghost).

I've a hideous feeling that events unseen are moving steadily toward a crisis. He nods his head slightly full.

I was just thinking about things, like, Christ meant having to shop around—that skin-and-bone-defying-gravity feeling you only get in England. In it he plays a simpleton. He was wont to labour at the anvil. Me, I'm at the heighth of my poverty.

Things are happen. Blood aerosol in stairwell. Tuesday, 12.30 A.M. Binding frameworks for actions systemic.

Approaching law on blind side. Since last summer we've heard from a century of such prominent killers. I stab into the surface. I usually become visible after reverie, the motif of this operation. One is legally authorized to act for the other. More and more is required to satisfy the ear. I felt attracted to the most repulsive among them. O, for treating substantiality as a characteristic of selfhood.

Bloated to stretch the skin, pallid with fever. We possess two of the heads now. The joint between thigh and shin-bone shattered to a thousand splinters. This ganglion, when present, is situated immediately beneath the arch. The interior has shrunk, delusions of.

Well, it became logically richer.

Such as that moot. That hill. With reverie, murmur. A work that does not yet exist, yet is recorded.

The defectuous press. Paroxysms of intense pain radiating from the breast-bone, mainly the left. Only one organ survived. I really need to crack this open—smashing plate at the end of a reel. (You can't light fires because of the smoke.) List the recollected items. The air deposits particles upon the oily surface of the tarn. Their offence is to illumine and enkindle.

The coincidental towpath of an industrious canal.

A brightly coloured claw.

That viaduct.

The crowd's curiosity has died.

At all contact he feels polluted, a sensation ranging from the very delicate to the surprisingly fierce. Two thousand degrees at the centre, and the great machine buttons up. The answer, it is simply the number from which another can never be subtracted.

They've actually done the job. This will be either right or it will be very wrong. Their work is dedicated in remembrance of the era. Everything is leading up to an extraordinary event. That's the rumour. (It seems we are always at the fracture of a centenary.) Knowing he once did the same spurs me on. I presume to penetrate. They are inspecting our land. He had to play this malcontent. Now you're talking, take a hasty bow. . . . The cold seized their limb.

Healing in the name of both gods, which is of course the mark of a finality.

A rock hollow in a desert, containing water. And if that were not a clear enough indication?

An alabaster vessel full of ointment, spikenard. Some say this is among the most distressing music ever composed. Bone was ground into flour and used as food by the originals. Think yourself lucky—I'm doing a naevus in total. Fluid builds up at the joints. Check the vibration of the instrument, e.g. the kettle. Touch it in some way. This border separates the interior from the surface. That is an inappropriate name. A heron is standing in the reeds (a multicellular structure in which spores are formed). One captive was shot in the kneecap. Corruption is suggested by the lifelike appearance of the feathers.

An evoking of penal servitude, hard labour at nothing, meaningless tillage. It exists solely as the internal motion of molecules. In the tenth table was painted the emperor et cetera.

Is she still here. All references must be oblique. I'll play the memoriam part, so long as we can all agree on our location.

An overdose of animal tranquilizer. Platinum catalyst. A vector in Hilbert space, symbolized. And he inclined unto me. Where I shall set time running? A little tuning fork is required, then we can begin.
See harp, the first. Chromatic scale seven. The brain stolen from the laboratory belonged to a criminal head.

Of the aorta. Lead/alloy.
How does he react when it becomes clear there was never any intention of sharing the room? (Dust storm and keep trying.) This passage is resistance personified. There's a falling away, no accumulation in deficit. This says too much already.

Hat to intervacuum. Friction sound, indicative of restored contact between the pleural surfaces. They lock together like a pair of giant earthworms on that planet. And he stepped up on the running board. After that we drank off a pot of watery. I also heard shipments of convenience, intended for Ezekiel.

In the land by the river. Runnels of floodwater settle in the parallel ditches beyond the stockade. An animal douses its flesh in a pool of stagnant water. We're clad in a thin flexible metal, full body armour, and bolted together. I'm careless, waylaid by customs. I am incrusted. A meat-bomb descends, drug and everything. He remains skeptical. If you're going to get one, get one like mine.

Dept of antiquark. Artifacts stolen from a tomb by grave-looters, say. He is gone, money swelling the pocket chloroform. The golden globes of the abandoned bed are visible through the roof no longer there. Always proceed through another's observations. There's mirror-play at work. Being here resembles a thin film. (Just larking around, merely a cipher.) We are paired off and expected to perform.
In short, he's usually worth seeing, so long as certain limits are recognized in advance. The text is only difficult if you insist on taking something away with you.
We began pulling it out and rubbing it down with sand.

A finding, closer to that of objective knowledge. Okay, let's release some naked fire (nurture of rubbing and of primitive). It doesn't matter. The words therein are still in the correct order. No one approaches him or takes any notice whatsoever. She writes.

White and blue flames escape in a thousand varied forms and undulations. I think the solution was common to us all (murdered ancestors). Outstretch yourself a piece, mealy-mouth. . . .

She holds out a large pink spansule.

You've done something that will be remembered for a long time. My duty is to be severed.

Now there's a thought, to reduce the image. A picture slowly appears on the prepared plate (salt of acid). No less than seven hundred wooden boxes were unearthed, inscribed with the chapter and covered with bitumen.

Abundant
he
mouth.

Qwerty, since he came forth from his womb (98). Exchange and mutate the first el—a freak of spelling, unsound. It is happening a hundred yards or so from where I sit at this very moment in time.

The vast majority are still trios, triplets of particular. Current flows back and forth between states of shock. Time to cut your loses or consolidate your winnings—you'll be eager to hear what this terrible complex contains. (If I have to ask one more time, you're dead.) We are suggested, the units out of which all others are formed. Originals from word coined in wake.

Annotations (melancholy).

A stubble field, eddish of aftermath. Earshot. The distance at which the voice may be heard, hearing.

Discriminate beforehand, and then apprehend. Accordingly, call for a hammer. I call you—encircling of encompassments.

We are very close.

The approach is mighty, under a swamp (novel). We began to notice a smell. The building is six hundred and seventy-five cubits long. In spite of itself always takes place within the space of five minutes. Several kinds of small fracture appear—long Sapphic nerve, lateral ligament of no-joint. The penultimate question is about the converter ego, whom we never actually see. There is more danger of our under-estimating rather than over-estimating.

A central hall with wings. Today is test-case day. Reason has spread from something unobserved to something observed. His condition is deteriorating. Treatment should be abolished. The argument springs from a cherished prejudice. A cart is the rejoinder. Hence, loosely previous. A structure is restraining water.

A glimpse or other transient apparition. Just one moment—the legal element in the rush from to walk. Firedamp in the pianoforte (see under hat). A place where two things meet with no power of movement, as if hinged. They burst in with the recognition fee. Schedule four, especially.

Too difficult to progress in this climate.

Bone oozing from sanction. Surface and three borders. The steep slopes surrounding the road to the south were dry. An upright iron bar supports the screen, what's called a vertigo strut.

The madness hero, superb commentaries on watching films. (Citizens would laugh.) She has lurched back into my orbit. The entry probe plunged into the clouds on schedule. It's a fifty-part series, an epic, and you're only half way through. How does it feel? Contribute something to further erosion. Those greys are not in any sense agitators. This image reveals the complicated absorption patterns brought about by the dust lanes (383). You've had to make some pretty awful choices. Exit wounded.

Reconvened after a lapse of years. Once here, the sea. Keep the strategic networks open. They painted in unstable words the workaday life of the front. He was aroused by the sequel of brakes, a dirty orange. An absence of coupling has been reported (quirk, the glue). There were moral dilemmas. These are the figures for standard tubes throughout the kingdom.

Answer, his who is gone. The simple you.

What she says may be more relevant to what you think than you think—a multitude of stars looking like dust I love you. Two lobes at the poles give this nebula its hourglass shape. Sometimes I cross everything out and start again.

A return to the main theme of the opening movement, the motif of the isolated rock. His life became clouded by financials. Even the houses near the empty lots seem dark, uninhabited. I knew that he, and everybody else in the room, had actually heard the noise. I refused to think. Up on their hind legs they rose. Avenged of thee, and I feed this day upon feathers.

This brings things to an abrupt halt. Then he performed a similar service for the other, who had been waiting. Some are rare combinations. (Yes, start again.) Fiction radix, as usual, symbolism of the plumb-line and the grasshopper. The sound of breaking glass.

Dead on the cill. A species of moth, stigmas pale. A pale grey, median lines suffused distal, with fuscous. (No, really.) Lying between us is a black mark resembling a V.

I myself am frequently designated. Such a thing as normal life still continues in that shapeless territory.

A strange discovery made somewhere between lab and state. No reminiscence here of the reader's world. When he died, they sluiced him from the turret with a hose.

Figurines of faience, stone and wood, placed. These are the so-said answerers. Now turn inland, the face of the dazzled white cliff. (Not right now.)

Unflocked
he foregathers in
the narrowing track,
with heavy cylinder
and the weightless body.

Should we think, for instance, through to an end? He protests vehemently against this abdication.

The back of a book with asides. Traces of simple description. I myself wrote (heuristic value of the absent et cetera). It's ready. It is generally better to die by speech than by letters. A crack is intercepting, balanced by mass adjacent. A place of last resort.

We're up to the revulsion, which seems about right. It continued to transmit data for seventy-five minutes before self-destructing. A hypothetical, thought of as passing between, and so.

Arms crossed at the leaded window. A scaffold, the mediaeval ladder, through which I must be clearly visible. They are no more, and you know that. Still you must have. The law would release a great stare, and then turn to face me. (Drawn from problem three, not the epilogue.) The whiting fades, bleached beyond recognition. That's a bit premature. Somehow this guarantees my preservation.

Of annul, supine on a pier. The whole point of an epiphany is you don't know. I believe he enjoyed saying that.

Contraband everywhere today. Its name tells you. Scribe holding neck with pectoral, down the back where the wings join.

She licks her flank from which hangs a severed entrail. Featherfew, the popular name—gillyvor and rue. Late fever with corruptions. An erroneous date, the confusion of a name with its foil. Back-slang past the churchyard. To drive away, undwelt.

Insufficient, writing withholds, still wet on the score. On through the island, the acres. A tiny cube is carved to serve as a die, and forever carried in the fateful pocket. He war what added several names—the cooling of the wheels with diamond-dust, liquid albumen. A night piece, each three handfuls. The impression left on wrought iron.

XXVIII

A short history of the mouth in which the world began. The numbness in this section is quite marked. Things aren't as bad as they seem. The image is glimpsed through circles of light. Where, when the breakage.

To start with, certain precognita.

As though one had assigned to a mirror that quality of redness. I contrive to sell my labour for a further five years. The rumours had no substance. (Who was isolated as a result?) There's rather a lot of blood, coughed up from the windpipe. Several square miles of landscape were overrun. The frame is matte, adding a false background.

Confirm the hypothesis, a transition from ascetic to real indifference. In your notebook, list everything that can be seen with the naked eye: the sleepers, the gravel, the timetable, the lantern, the fog, the electrified. An appendix includes a story. They kept on drinking and did not hear the stealthy approach. And that's taken us straight through the night, once more. Silence is not normally a misrepresentation.

To begin with certain precognita.

Of unsettling the ear. When I drew them into myself no one told me they would never leave (as in 'point of fact'). This is an abridgement of horoscope. I hear that near the end we'll never know. I resemble. I am handheld.

A very brief microfiction, speed forty-eight.

See, a mesh of barbed light become a fortress. First she must be drained of fluid. The thin plate of one bone slides into the fissured groove of another. (Make a decision.) It was last mentioned as case number two hundred and fifty-one. I believe that nothing in it has eroded or broken down.

Technique, genital status marred. Diagnosis is district beyond mind. Spontaneous phenomena can sometimes be observed. She covers sheets of paper with complaints, an inventory of the events that happen, all the repeats. Make a wish. When we got back I stood by, groundless.

Signs of systemic delusion. Syzygy of Venus and crescent ulna. Back then the souls wore a feather dress (structure and dynamics). Discover some interiority which may bring us uncomfortably close. This is less than easy.

Instantaneous disobedience. Who made an easy living by soothsaying at court? Infatuation has fallen under the influence.

Of the nature of a general upward flexure of the earth's crust. The late were typically portrayed. Many cases where the subject has been adapted go undocumented. (Who's my birthcart?) I can always go home. I am led to understand. I can always go on alone.

A man with an empty birdcase. The lift descending startled me as it adjusted to the light. You'll have to ask for an invitation. The judgment here is paralysed. This is legendary footage—a thin film of proclamation, the bribe (49).

At the central burrow of a bilateral organ. Median crest of nerve at prayer, the joints of the third and fourth fingers. I have been hired to render these exact tendencies. I go undeceived. When has been fully eroded. The location of these islands has long been the subject of debate (neither byss nor abyss).

Conjunction with the first astringent. I am no longer a subject (science verifies mythologies). An incision was made straight through the heart of the earthwork. An imbalance in distribution is one of the prime causes, molecules the most likely explanation. We left because of the adverts. Gigantic trees burst out from the quarry. That proved premature.

It commences just beneath the head of the bone. In close-up, midrib of asymmetric leaf. We lie about halfway between the final and the dominant, one of the great bugbears.

Outcry up the pyramid. During the years of plague they exchanged their positions. I apply to join a division of verbs, if they'll have me. A cycle of heresies once sapped.

Partial eclipse, exhibited. He is denounced, a hopeless causal. Originally a string was wound about the throat. And what is that hanging upside down? I'm thrown together with people you would no doubt consider deceptive. It's my cochlea.
Garments were placed on him improperly (homunculus, the head swells until it bursts et cetera). This episode is identical to a duplet—at base, a few vocal shreds. Consider the genius of his plan, the orbit of the socket.

Tightening the cord, she hurried out of the apartment. Greetings are repeated. The whole round is that of barrenness. Nights are moving away to the south.

This month is the unruliest, yet quite predictable. She's been quizzing him about herself, or himself. It's not clear. I am told that it is not yet done.

He tells me I should recover. I abbreviate. My fingers are sticky with tar.

The line, with reference to the scene shortly to be described. Go easy, with your talk of the three. It's terrible. I long to adopt a more conversational tone. It emits its own radiation, hatched into the calendar. It proudly bears an acid rim (dry, very spark).

We'll need a bucket, won't we. And in fact the man did turn again, and continued writing.

All energy is spent in hearing the testimony. Thoughts and actions are set down in the form of a journal. She's a vessel of the old school, rather tall if anything. I perceive that the subject is incapable of pronouncing a single word. At all events, we're homing upstream. This is an insanely laborious and convoluted method of composition. (We fully recognize.) Silence moving, silent ship.

I conjecture—try, compare, attempt (6). With an old-fashioned claw-foot feel.

This segment is about forget it. Neutral structures—the green smear, gilded metropolitans. We find ourselves transported back to the iron mound. Our compasses are useless. We dig in and strike fires. She created a new language. Two chinooks copt above the ridge. We embrace. I grabbed the wrong book. (It said triumph, but for the delegation.) Visitations occur in every dwelling—sprinkle the blood on the lintel of the door et cetera. A commission of enquiry was established.

Back to crucible, the beginning of it all. We shadow. The electric rail has not yet been invented. Private homes are ransacked and papers seized. It's like an instant. One approach has been called tactics, the other strategy. That's a cacophony. If it's interesting I go on. The mirror cracks from top to bottom and from side to side.

Here's a ten-step model in how to survive the tradition. Because of this I expect. I shall assassinate thee, but for thy own good. He reacted and denied. It's the style of writing you're interested in, not what he's saying—a measure of the disorder of a system.

To assign, see turn. See twist. Go about it in this way.

That day all governance sat in abject dependence. Strength lay in the unelected fact. (How will the supplies be dispatched?) Disproportion lingers. The allusion to three quarks is perfect.

The subject is still considered contagious. It's granted a small stipend. I like that. There was no story, just a sequence of isolated and disconnected events. Individuals appear and disappear. Several weeks had passed and little remained to be done. He decreased himself, reasoning outward in concentric circles.

Many of the citations were left unclaimed. It is now at rest within itself. Compare what his text pursues (enterprising delusions). He seems more and more self. A wire is sent to report the smelting of ores. Several large domed cisterns were set in the landscape. Their use is unheard.

The gates of hell close once more. We walked without rest until we reached the same field. Which events purport to be chronological? I shall be the judge. The current flows between states of shock. Then anything red appeared.

Of the hut, she refused to leave—as if seen through a window or shadow. For instance, extra-sensory perception for special or specific purposes. (Blow dust off purgatory.) Where are you.

He dedicates himself full-time to the nascent art of astronomy. The nation's most popular are witchcraft and poison-herb lore. Medicinal core samples were taken.

Exterior night, narrative voice. When do I start. What remains is hidden in the adversary's eye—multitudes, and in his describes. (What is that whiteness far away?) The one who sits in the corner says nothing. His reign was stretched by the projects. Now we'll never know.

Died, not asylum—the one who tends, swallowed whole. They should first read, then concoct an interpretation. Out of the belly I cried and you heard my voice et cetera. The footprints in the desert were apparently misunderstood.

I have to expose that. A large body, confounding signatures. The time out is eighteen miles. (There isn't the space.) We demand measures and half-measures. Right. After this, eternal separation.

Overrode, untitled. Greased rayon on writing. (Sit now.) I was looking at the work going on in there. (No, no, no.) The price should be a thousand: the weather legend, the parables, visions of the elect, astronomica, a zoomorphic history, the letters, the apocalypse of week after week.

From that day to this, strategically placed in the crowd.

Caffeine halo. A reversed cell. Confused, I vex out to purchase. Tiny squares of yellow and orange light float in the darkness.

We navigated by a constellation to the south of Scorpio—a cool molecular cloud, their energy.

Inexplicable lapses of memory, contradictions. (There's isn't time for this.) I'm clinging to the present. Employ a complex and convoluted numerical system, occult accountancy.

It spans a lifeline. I think in four dimensions, conjured. Note the slur of my speech. I cast a stone. Ripples.

Don't worry about how long it will take.

471

Fluorescent object in the water. It's not coming, no one's coming.

Key scenes, two or three choices. The things that I said about her (fairly complicated). They called her the look and she was a season. She does not hear from him for many years. Then, dear big books, epistemic please.

Note, short biographical details accompany the plates which follow. These are included.

Sleep when it came was incomplete. It'll swing, whatever overhead conditions are. (What?)

The last major tributary to join from the north: green wounds, ulcers, fistulas. The chosen sedative is a powder composed of glands, neuter of acid (soldier ants, pressed). Divination is by dropping melted wax in water.

A reversal. Here it is, minus the human form—silent and motionless, but somehow doing something. Right now we're invisible to radar. (Reflect solely on intentions, never actions.) A triple line of readers gathers round every gas lamp.

Hanging from her left wrist . . . flying off course it ran.

Everything has been thoroughly surveyed during the last ten. A newssheet unfurls. Set loose it flies till stunned flat against a passing torso. The coronary ligament consists of two layers. I don't wish to try for the target right now.

At last, the business of writing. Once upon a time in my dotage.

Ah she says, what meant. Identity has moments of solemnity, but it is surely the work. Sometimes it's quite indistinct, about an inch below the head.

In experience. From a series, sometimes continuous, sometimes interrupted by long intervals. I could've died, but I didn't. The three possibilities are equally common. Sedition abhors a vacuum.

Events have not given the lie to my foreknowledge. (The denarian proportion will be strong et cetera.) He is pondering over the steps. What must be done in response to the other's call for help? Further on down the road we met combat with a spent force. Now it's ready (surprise), the subject of a previous chapter. At last this is getting easier.

The opposite of abyss or void. A substance with the power to contract organic tissues—a ground of attributes, humming. The same conversation with the same individual (why have you forsaken me et cetera).

We endure a beaten run of the gauntlet, then a knock comes at the door. She starts. Shall we ever see anyone else again she asks.

It's fabled, the so-called, the concealed source you never witness. There is something suspicious about the full moon. (I was observing, not judging.) Generate a degree of incitement. To this day my face is still in use.

Trouble was on the way: two in the time and space intended for three. That object is hirable.

He could not go on. Something was hindering. A single grain of coal was left. Planted gee men start the bidding.

Do everything this way. I fell straight bang out of his consciousness (pentatomic section). But no, the decade is forty-six percent sure. I am merely describing everything you see. Often he's observed crawling around the perimeter of the quadrangle like a lizard. And if he manages to figure it out?

Plain drystone wall to one side. He sanctifies a little cloister of rounded stones. There's a series of apertures, windows without glass—holes thrust through the wall, in truth. And an open colonnade, crumbling plaster with split pipes of rust, charred timbers. The house was on fire, methinks. Just a single bone was left. Was it smooth? Yes I say, smooth as smooth and brilliant white, picked clean. A jury can withdraw.

Regarding this impression, all that the retina projects.

Quickly explain what the island is for. I saw him swallow a third dose. This is all I'm capable of. Seal the outer membrane, the rennet gland. I took it upon myself to interfere.

Lower extremity, posterior surface—the flat muscle beneath. Divination by sounds from the belly, i.e. ventriloquism. Seizure, a stretching out. He hath censored me. I'm appointed professor of counterpoint at the sanatorium. The blood is uninhabited.

Selected interviews and other writings.

Club-rush genus of the family sedge. Mental clippings, scrap left when the blanks are cut out. A chisel, for the spelling of. Sipple.

Intermittent cries between the struggle for breath. I haven't even begun. It coughs up possession.

I had to try it just the once myself. (Who are seated somewhat in the auditorium.) The subject is considering his options: relief, or reactive ailments.

It passes across the left side of the transverse arch, the aortic part, and then descends.

The beatitudes—inner side to bend, if of elbow. Hired men throw up an earthwork. A metre or two is gained. Holes are punched about the fringes. A splinter emerges. The mutual wall dividing the zone would text mutilated. Such things are consumed in the use.

A commentary. If that's a person, it's a very still person. The clever stratagem never works. The door of the inner cell swings open. (I do not have the perception.) A grey mist blankets the garden. It's the first accident of post-history.

Seek a confidant. I collide against a granite limb. Offer up a little prayer. Compare these events with the diverse character of the words used to relate them. You could imagine the illustration.

Misquote at every opportunity. What won popularity up and down the world. They are resting themselves.

I devote myself to his distraction. Whole bars are inaudible. A reputation can spread and infect the surrounding letters. The word for element also carries the alphabet mean.

It's very easy to miss things. They assume a pattern in the air against the dark. Shuffle the graphs. It's too late.

Fee undisclosed.

Three meet for a dark eternity. It's obviously not my day. I could do with a spell of soma right now. I was once an elective mute, then I forgot. Distance has been shed, an amendment paused.

I'd hate to see the whole town levelled. When you're in a situation, you have no choice. His principal artistic action of nineteen was the ludic. I insist that you consider very seriously doing the same. Note the capital, the spurt in the hole— the belly, so to speak. A number of sulphur mines lie scattered across the countryside, near the border.

It's left behind in the spiral, liberated from gravitational pull. Sound becomes unintelligible. The rest of us milled about, trying to reestablish. What do you see, he says, at the base of the gas cloud.

In a trench at the bottom of an ocean.

A whole continent she replies, a frozen sheet of land. A body mutilated with pottery shards. But the tilt gradually changes (all numbers may be an underestimate). The remaining days were not wasted. I'm told it's the month in which the world began.

At the resumption of work, many lab remnants. Solid-state fluids. The galley has fifty oars, set out in rank. This pattern typifies death and rebirth. I slip the chain that holds the boat and the shank and flukes of the anchor rattle.

Into distant woodland, rising at the base of the mound. I can no longer see in this fog. A shout is thrown up: cut your painter and make off. A body floats in the water and the speeding prow slices it in two. His first professional adventure is drawing to a close. (Glike is the same as gleek.) Yet humanely, as of a fellow-creature, just escaped.

What we see here is the light of a single quasar. A condition of adjustment— to go astray, delay, tarry. Why have you placed that there, a key cast in wax?

Pen to a cause, to an external danger. A telegram language of utmost concentration. Sounds like a riot at the masonic temple.

Shell elongately oblong, shade fulvous-olive. (Think that, outside of man's.) There seems to be no other way of delimiting this. I can now clearly distinguish a shape, three-quarter head entwined with veins. And a portfolio of faded photographs, evidence that he documented his journeys. Have you any fresh insurrections. No goodnight.

On the steel cap of its hind boot is the family crest. It crouches in the middle of a circle. With my head pressed to the floor, I have an excellent vantage point. The external order of production has been replaced. Use ordinary materials. Make use of the words found in the cracks, short controlled bursts.

I went eagerly to every broken display case. (Say nothing of the lesser scholars in this lineage.) I've been left to do everything alone, guess at outcomes and processes. For an instant we resembled a type of overlap. She says you have the sense about you of a man who has just come back from somewhere.

By which time it had penetrated to a depth of one hundred and sixty kilometres. We were well-received by a man, the last time. The chances of survival would be marginal.

It is doubled up on the floor. I could already feel the stuff working on me.

I have in mind nothing, so off I go to speechless. I change my name each day, keep one step ahead of the repetition. I balance on the border, the remaindered leg. Ask yourself said the man scornfully. I have in mind something a little more superficial. Goodness knows, and how the virtues would die off in the end.

A canal of morbid origin, in some regions. Ulcer with narrow orifice.

Capture. The garage siege. See September, and the speaks. It lies in thrall to the substitution.

Money is leached from the domestic sphere of circulation. Later, the doubles method is amplified. Tell me all about that. (You understand.)

The six of words. Divinatory meanings. Upright means dissolving of the immediate problem. We're lashed to details, radar. Windows are bricked up. Ridiculous calumny both inside and outside the manufactories—unmistakable stench of the tannery from beyond the city wall.

Just as quickly it falls back into shape.

Those tiny radiation pills, arsenic and amalgam. Some three to four thousand occupiers move in two groups, under flags. There is nothing more to be heard. At the end of the very last volume comes an explanation. Elements are aroused, then just as suddenly vanish. Only then was he released. Our thoughts go out.

This unravelling increases as the star slowly cools. That object's umbilical.

Astonishing work, a type of systematic dissatisfaction. Electricity leaches into the atmosphere. We're declared a stumbling-block. Soot and ground bone were mixed in a preparation.

It withdrew into itself. Hidden under the bed is a plastic model (bang). We must go, the news is coming. There is no doubt. Hovering a little above, something is breathing in and out. I do everything slender and piecemeal. I've developed the technique of holding my opponent by his edge. Spoken language has been abandoned. He remarks. He wishes to be treated with respect.

It doesn't even signal. Proceeding in this way, nothing at all appears to happen. Words, yes, but the words of others, some discreated space.

Thin slices are removed from the subject until it disappears. Muted and unmoved till now, a clerk records the name in a thick ledger. Only then has the man been translated. (There's no point trying to rush this.) What are the surviving traditionals? This brings us to clusters like the coma. Also it's worth noting.

A tale of the hollowed trunk (the end note should be slightly curtailed). Maximal investment, nineteen thirteen. The truth lies not in the figure of the outlaw himself. Any detail could be determined by punching in a request—the wealth, new offshoot, is in slates. Some unforeseen historical changes are occurring. Which concept was supposed taken from a bridge, possibly from an offering of atonement?
An upbuilding, partly through, partly in. If I could I would have rewritten it.

Concluding remarks.
On the eccentricity of the orbit, the featureless anomalies of a typical planet. The man without a throat. He had been talking the way one does.

Nebula is a dark, a dense wing-shaped lobe. Lift cage ascending. That form is used alike of male and female. Out quick at the drop of the blasting gelatine.
I'm astonished that you think I should discard these.
As soon as I've woven a wreath about the head, we can leave. Due to moisture in the atmosphere the skin shrinks. It splits and the interior is revealed.

A panoramic view. I remain unconvinced. This is the most brilliant new star of which we have an accurate record. This is all I ever wanted. It is called accidental degeneracy. He says I see resistance to chance as a failure of our educations.
Swivel eye to sun. Tilt your head upward by seventeen degrees. Sun in astronomic gate means direct testimony. I don't know.
This strange action we may interrupt as follows.

A country in the cemetery. It is all very simple after that. The initial round torments the embers of our party in different ways. (So to speak is fatal?) Enter a most forthcoming individual, wearing clothes. It strikes me that we have all the elements of a macabre in this passage too: witch-haunted walls et cetera, the cat. There's going to be interaction with the earlier street-fighting scene. We're going to see a few pleas to punctuate the silence—the use of actions made with reason, and without. Surprising though it may seem, I still had a little money at the time (fathers only ghost). The bad man is taken off to the place where bad men go, of course. A person is guilty if he provokes false information.

Kitchen midden. Mound of mesolithic of neolithic. Feel the sense of concerned absorption in every instance of They. No concern for likelihood can distract his attention. It was the custom to bury alive a number of slaves.

That isolated turret in the landscape resembles a castle keep. Memory is irretrievable for a season. Touching the page makes things clearer. It would be a mistake not to answer.

Quick. And in whose watery beams, blanks? This is all we've got time for. Why has asterisk become pi? A portion of land is worth a penny a year. He dare not enter another syllable.

Fatal void comp tests. Distant fire-slaught, the fixing of dates in the past. That last drowning smile. I withtake.

It's dug itself into the coastline (harrow till the end of appointed time et cetera). Who was standing by and heard? Who said thundered? You'll need the book he adds. Now is indeed. Try to describe things.

This signals a return home. On one flank it lies while bystanders look on. Perched high up on the ladder, I suddenly feel ejected.

The incredible findings of a century.

Go before me, and after. I cannot see his face (presumably this occurs much earlier in the first draft). No wonder it's cold in this room. These seem to be his final moments. There's no time for the decay which usually follows. Evidence always comes in scattered fragments, something that you associate with a particular time or place.

Subhead. Mediumistic teleplastics, wherein the senses in branch four are revisited. And for what personal purpose or gain.

The seventeenth of nineteen, a new beginning. He was looking for patterns in the chaos. What then was it that was carried through the portal? Armed gangs march on the city from the surrounding village.

Allow me to reclaim the chain of events. (It's delicious when the man's eye pops out and flies towards you.) Nothing is represented in this lifeline. Give us a hint of our own composition. As he climbs the scaffold to the guillotine, a spectator makes a grab.

Corrosives, conjoined with Centaur. Coarse cellular structures. They have in them no weight of opinion. Return to simple method, back to form. What does the celestial part restrain?

Astounding new evidence (for us the plaything).

Well, in ascending order, the first is the sphere of the moon. The average depth of the canyon is about one point six. This signifies abnegation. A hole bored at the edge of the island shows only a shallow deposit. I pursued every remaining note.

It is seen here dressed in a kilt with a tail, depicted running, possibly dancing. First that now this I thought. On the one hand he is a reversed ancestor.

(To whom do you speak.)

A modern eustasy. When you depart, make sure that you can work your way back. (It wouldn't be recaptured inside the body, would it?) There's a universal desire for numerical superiority, divination by large-bellied gases. He used a generation leap of thirty years. You were so keen to jettison, everything.

Postscript. Notes on somnambulism. Great slabs of asphalt, the rebellious inmate.

Died asylum. Case, no. Occupation nonesuch. Letter to husband, come home, come home.

The shadow on the sundial winds rapidly through an ellipse. Haven't you lost enough without all this? The same question is asked repeatedly. This game, an inquisitory.

A big black chest carved in relief, just the front (answer). And your proclamation, the ashes of the paper burned in the grate. Hereunder he replies, and is cited.

Into the vat, ha. You're in the course of witnessing an execution.

Immediately this becomes an unwelcome distraction.

Are you among those of us. I replaced myself. The word in question is formed by metathesis, from disturb. The sense is amplified. I'm conducting research into neglected air—the fruit of confluence, shared ground. It is somewhat corroded. The brass collar is tightened by a screw whose point enters the spinal marrow.

We came to a place of five bridges. (Make a decision.) He seems to respond to the pulse of momentary feelings. I remain inelastic. There's a touch of local and transitory circumstance.

Families would meet to discuss things in their usual telegraphic. Now I need company. Let's withdraw, no thoroughfares of speech. He writes, this haar. . . . I pledge my eyes. The others will be here soon.

From Jupiter, culpable.
The cable snapped. Eleven, we could never win against that he realized.

The wind through the rigging. (I'm surprised the alarm didn't go off.) Cage lift descending. They're talking together as if something was about to end. He had apparently made every preparation. There is none other in the room, my ghost.

Of neutrino collisions. It just sounds like somebody else. He falls in pieces. The narrative is infinite. You are drawing too much on yourself.
Title illegible: the interference, no eighty-six. It's an officially abandoned week. Ont bully, The.

Murmur self, inferior spirits at steadily rising prices. Are you quite sure of this he asked.

Boiling waters hereabouts. I have abandoned a good deal. A gentle, crucified smile crosses her lips.
Whose rampart was the sea, precisely? There is a lack of will in the sudden. An absurd possession fills the entirety.

Substorm. It's structure—I'm hearing structure. He condemns, calumniates and befouls et cetera.

She is carried away in its eyes. Rain in the herbgarden, nerves sprouting, the ruinous leaves. Earth humus, neither poppy nor mandragora. Noisy growth dwarfs quit young in stellar terms.

Beyond yieldness. Only seven ever returned. It's tightened by twisting a stick. Everyone gazes off into the middle distance. Seven acres of land had belonged, from time. Such things cannot be used without their extinction or alienation.

From this day on it is known. Three laws of planetary motion were uncovered. This figure, like that of plate, touches the edge of the ellipse. And there are remnants of a wing. In the opening scene her skin resembles a garment eaten of moths, at my feet the pretty chalk carpet. (Later. Slowly.)

Hung idle on the clothes hook he slept fully dressed. It will take forever, as it must. The animal here is the fox. The continent is Antarctica. Talking was merely a disagreeable toy. One was thus blinded by the light. Picture these years, then you have a chance.

Memories that a nation preserved (the turning wheel and others). Who had to be so extremely careful? But it must be remembered that the earliest had also been called *crane*. They strained every nerve. They towed the raft to their own shore, locus scatterers.

Age of man. It has not the memory of itself—eternal ordnance, shot off. Which is immutable.

Now mean sea-level at wall. Yet chance or contingency also exit.

In their fright they fled into the forest and hid. (Another version ends at the moment of suction.) But enough of this. What maintains the intercommunion of these events?

Live and exclusive. Bits of the prayer keep cropping up.

Since he was no fool.

It is defined by its inherent difference. Atmosphere dense with light-absorbing dust—merchandise, which could and should be exchanged.

Ah, a bone, a bone she says. I do like a bone, a nice femur. It looks real. The organization will not decline of its own accord.

Dendrochronology. Fringe magnets. Each molecule peaks—a perfect, unlit.

Moor of the month, the moon with its entire disc. Up from the ocean, the rustle of fish. Result: assassin rainfall, upon its forewings the dark et cetera. Gunbore pressed hard to roof of mouth. It's difficult making decisions when you've just been introduced.

(Blank page.)

Abroad, it occurs throughout the weaker part. It is also recorded. Coloured beams spin out from the core. People are routinely pieces. Slender wavy lines cross and recur, distinct in my specimen.

Trawlers in the bay after dark, arc lamps sweeping across the surface of the waters. They split. The tide exhibits no sensible rise till the second or third day. Cut away again said the boy. This is turning into pure evidence.

I remain. I am both the bone and the plastic. The eleven of spheres.

Now what kind. Come back to that thought later.

Saints neon and companion (martyrs' tree). Every cognition makes one distrustful. Someone else replies no at ten past five. My mistakes are correct. Tell me, avenge me.

Fell times. And you will help a little, no? Not so fast.

A hypothetical unit of memory. Avenge the threat from outer space—the eating away of a surface, the corrosion. Whose engine cuts out at the crucial moment? He was careful to make his inquiry about the ocean sound casual.

Lift descending. I'm completely baffled. (But sire, how can I know what your thoughts are?) I don't recognize any of these accessories. Only two possibilities of communication remain: take the enemy by surprise, and the non sequitur.

He met it full on with his head. This is longer than I have saved. He replies I've seen things you can't imagine. Picture the body of an organism, in contrast to its germ-cell.

Puissance subhuman, both maker and made. O is no more. However, the always-present-to-itself.

That would be quite a test-case, would it not? There comes a point when two different continuities collide and struggle for dominance, e.g. the canopy of fixed stars.

Script, forshapen into height of sky. Stiffen him. (I don't mind if it actually exists.) That abnormal hush may be due to the interference, the corresponding no. Some of these decisions are good decisions. A shadow, a screen.

Secretion on bark wound about stick. It's an account from history. Hard fecal mass in the intestine, mouth to cup. Cup to mouth. The gigantic total has been and gone. An explosion was hidden in his taboo. (Can't get the staff.)

That which is probed by any question. Some points of agitation between the mental life of the savant and the neurals. It must flee after performing the sacrifice (230).

In this volume the following pages end with a fracture. (It's merely a translation of the objects surrounding it.) And the speaks, becoming called—an acute awareness that your chance of survival is nil. Which one had to keep his demotic?

It loses the local function it has acquired. An attempt has been made to liquidate the witness—teleplasmic masses resembling arms and hands were seen. Outer marginal some shade of tawny brown.

Disembark. This is as good a place as any to pause for breath. Billowing dunes and sharp shadows are thrown across the floor of the intervening. At which point on the map do we resume?

Our opponents always manage to compute their longitude in a matter of hours. (Don't tell me energy.) This argument is now referred to as a rolling contract. Raise questions about the latter's judgement.

In size it is intermediate between the earth and the moon. The salt is scraped into piles.

Estrange, I put that back without thinking. Let it go. She says we're situated at the cusp of what.

It's a question of going over the same ground again and again, until it's worn smooth. (At least the latter demonstrates a little alienation.) Progress is confused by the aforementioned five bridges. I am trying to reach something that stretches unsayable to unsaid. She's eager, here already. Some things you just don't want to know about. Via the nose she is bled.

Not yet seen, the figure of the plunder.

He claimed a vision during the siege of the fourteen. (This is control.) It had collected wings, eyes. That noise is a vibration, more or less.

Select fresh candidates. I consider you one of my most vulnerable. That's a promising sign. The island freezes over.

Because he could see too far ahead.

It proceeds crabwise. A voice says there is a different route through the desert. He glances over his shoulder. We took his stick from him and an arm. It gets very allegorical after that.

Skip a page or two.

Longer than I have memory. I've resolved to keep one ear out for signs of change. He passed his life. (I wonder.) Did I skip a sentence which said something?

Without disappearing the figure acquired another aspect. It leapt head first. You cannot die. He's got all the technique in the world.

Question. Who or what stole away? Permit identifications run for a period of seventy-five years. Justify the cost, in your own words.

I pass any spare time reading the scores (the godfather cock et cetera). I'm on trains between apparitions. The trial attracted the public it deserved. Several times a week messengers came. There's been a long history of this kind of thing.

The experiment is repeated four times in succession. His work in this branch is the foundation of today.

Into the head he placed a tiny clay figurine. When we get there we'll find something to cauterize that leg with.

Beat at the water with their sticks. He says the death in each case is my own. The idea of such food is a symbol.

Jammed between their silhouettes, the other woman in the film. (Which?) The man who kills himself is uncredited. Nobody demands anything of the graphs.

Apocalypse, a small antique commode. Extract of pineal. I want things triple-checked. (You don't do grotesque, do you?) I forgot. In the original, the exterior orbit is the sphere of the sun. The third figure shows the eruption. And yet these relations are nothing akin to fiction. As if on cue two microlights rise above the ridge.

Icy blast on the horn, a whiff of turpentine, putrescence. (Looks towards door.) A layer of varnish makes the corpses gleam. The corporation is nomadic. All this talk, years of stretched light.

Note the blue reflection, a nebula, caused.

We shall meet again at the molten core. Look elsewhere for an explanation of the phenomenon. Some are anxious about why such a futuristic story was ever accepted.

A square of shining substance rushes straight out of my mouth. Four times I obtained the correct number of raps.

It is often rendered as a jagged pinnacle towering above a pit. It can be seen from exodus. Whenever I imagine anything, I see it first in print. Am working hard on the winter legends. What, this day of the dead, just for him?

Over. Come home, up towards the zenith.

List items at inventory. Everything possible, of all types and relations.

Brackish stain on front margin. Photosynthetic fade at edge, variable. (No one's desperate like me.) There are three moments in total: that burning magnesium flare, the mental poles, a flapping expanse of green baize. I was piqued by the sardonic interruptions.

You've no need to think through this view, just yet. I have set it down while you wait. He is already named, a man two years from resentment.

The dwelling image. I have decided to discontinue the surface. We must pay another thirty-five skins. There is all manner of happenstance to negotiate. Things have been carelessly shelled. We're guilty. I watch people doing things to the boats. Look where he goes, stepping out of the portal. Everyone else has disappeared.

This is slow work—an imaginary perfect, excluding the germ-cell. One apostle resigned from his mission in the year. I have tried to fasten onto him.

Cone of light still to be investigated.

Neither just entering nor just leaving. There are, however, points of more sterling merit. I have remembered word for word. And on the perimeter of each, a resignation mark. Carpenters are possible. I have stolen so much from the plague.

Flee outward, pushing the material back into the ring.

Emergency chamber music, the celebrated rim-burst. Exit pursued. I'm bisected by the white line. The pressure-drop you detected is caused by an infection. Can we expect a big curve in the transfer? Sometimes two.

Straight from the century. A moment's relationship to its successor (neither). We found ourselves in a trajectory of flight. Works were infrequently recorded, and eaten.

Cause bonfires to be lit in every street. Find a muscle that bends a joint, as opposed to an extensor. Consider, are these the bare scientific facts.

When everyone thinks it's dead again it rises up. We're able to list things as never before. (Poor dear, naturally anxious.) Disregard its condition. This serves as a warning. The slow pace of exile binds us together.

Yards away, and his clothes were smeared. I too have read the book of enough, the new ligament. The relationship between ignorance and despair is similar, intermangled with all things material. Unreadable, without a stick of like thickness.

Mimeomotion. An oxygen mask is strapped to her face (everything must change). Rows of gigantic black balloons. They wear close-fitting translucent skins. She would always over-emphasize the importance of tone.

We sit in perspex booths and answer the questions. Now they are attacking the centenary end. There is a long way to go. The measure of heat content can be disregarded. Then the earth crumbles, along with everyone who lives in it. The total varies from a minimum to a maximum. He builds a ghost trap in the shape of a miniature head. Crudely-fashioned, a battered and stained metal box, in truth.

In a large room used for lumber we axe and pile up logs. He imagined all the references to the hundreds and thousands. Objects were fanciful forms of speech. This masque is more of an interrogation. What reaches their ears. (Must've miscounted.)

Interdental work. Alive on one side of the road, dead on the other. He rails at his quarry. He says we will never give way to the method. There's the occasional lead that leads nowhere. And don't forget the key for the padlock down below. That last half minute was a really competitive thirty seconds, wasn't it? Just for you, I'll change everything.

Containing or depending on the number ten. An opening for insertion of a sleeve. Indeed, the presence of a coherent photographic style. The eucharist was once sucked from the chalice.

With water-rounded head. He's appointed understrapper for the day. One cord strangled (soft pedaller). It has been recovered. The absence of a physical person as an intermediary can aid communication.

There again. Examine him on the spot (not enough devil in the box). Its civilizing influence was incalculable. Correct the spelling—he vowel that follows the stem, to which we are attached. As his physician I am concerned. Yes he was saying. His ankle turned to mush. I'm led by sheer prescience.

Born land, shut last mentioned, four and forty years. The state ultimate. One of its wings is gracefully lowered and shed into the snowdrift. Mark, this is not an act of indifference or abstention. In this part of the world atrophy is uncommon.

Diagnosis, chronic tuberculosis of the skin, often affecting the cap. The cyclical nature accords well with this hypothesis. Into past, unmentioned.

Other evidence corroborates the pattern (a giant at home with its parents). And who once withstood upon the sea, the land, the air. Authentication is a necessary.

Breathing now by means of exterior lung-sac. Where exists the vast unhurried audience? Misleading logs and chronicles were kept, the angle of camber restrained. The motive behind the unofficial name is all too obvious. We're earning faint praise and new commissions, but someone has to stay behind.

All the cannon on one side of a ship are aiming. A tiny ash-wood box projects from the forehead. The chapter of entering the triumphant says.

Indifferent accommodations kept in underground cells.

Now stationed at the prow of the machine. The ordinary life of men is like that of saints. She was cremated on the fifth. (I am, only by baptism.)

Walkers in sleep, deposited around the rim of an overflowing basin.

I wish I'd made it more like structure now. Suddenly he wants to testify to everything. The man in the container has an unrestricted view of his approaching nemesis—under helpless, through all the beauty, where sits the neutral.

We share a superstition. (Put the castle back.) We can't understand one another (language). And if I see someone writhing in pain without evident cause?

There's no room. Again, a moment's library. I shall try to write down his talk, which sprang.

Pilot lowered into cockpit of plane. Causes have been isolated. I don't know what happened. What city sends for him, you.

Patches of bruised snow, the teetering edge. Torture (you don't say how). Cessation has been discontinued. I am irredeemable. The meeting of these two feet, to be sure, is an accident. The twenty-fifth day of this month is the final day of her last year. A syringe injects blood into the narrow space between gossamer and flesh.

O's superb library and its remarkable archive. Fainting by the wayside. Birth.

Gazing out over the valley as if nothing had happened. Only then shall my ghost come to thy bed. By ill suspicion, this is your law. Or is he just a becalmed and faithful watcher? He is preparing to leave, a scene from which they turned in horror.

It's a work made for enormous forces. Each of these great panels is part of a triptych. What can be done has been done (the lapis parallel). The game goes ahead. We boast undersea heating, the manufacture of a sweltering humidity. In various communities eclipses were marked by mapmaking.

Unannounced, the arrest of the sea clocks.
Surging up the estuary is a tidal bore. I'll see to this strange affair myself. And the spectacle came tinkling down, the incomplete. Their efforts have not been so vain as the fragmentation.

Within the cloister, a caress at my flank. Only the nightjar has sufficient span, with uncovering, mooting. Between periods of political activity he walked up and down.

Immediately the bowels protrude. How can I with all fairness go back to thee? An orange thing hobbles in the water. Nobody's what it seems. Wait for me. We're not even half way there. A halt was called about thirty seconds after dawn. Years pass, objects.
An unmarked paradigm, counting. We are both facing south.
Para, the back of a book, cunning (see next word). Symbolic of repentance, compunction. All of those. Write down everything I tell you. It was burning my face.

Light, fingered gravity. So what would you like to hear now. Things are never as bad as you think. A man is positioned on an embankment, under the shelter of stunted trees—another dismantled inspector.
It has that slightly scattergun effect. The affair seems not to have a given starting-point. List the key scenes.
Ten of cups, hidden. Vaginate meanings. Increased influence of the autonomic nervous. The tenth cranial is concerned, wandering. Upright means a peaceful and secure environment. Darkness covers the earth like a galloping herd.

Fleshes from the unresolved. The seventh is the sphere of Saturn, complete spleen. Reverse means disruption of an ordered routine, anti-actions. This picture shows a detail from the top of the largest column of gas.
He is lowered into the stagnant water. (Look he can't remember.) A klaxon sounds, a tone of familiar pitch and vibration. We haven't actually seen each other yet. All writing hinges on a possibility, a species of small hawk. The lever, said I.

In other words he is dead. What sharply deviated from customary syntax and word order?

Regular clicking sound at base of skull.

The said minute lapsed. Whiff of mercury on the air. Rising ground, exquisite defecations. Saint just still in the background, camera blank on page thirty-nine. The prospect was pretty dark either way. (What faculty cannot be the object of created understanding.)

I have nothing against him, but such a spectacle must terminate at some point. Cut the supply line. Whisper then leave. It's not me, it's the language. The stem valve has withered, altered its position.

Hard palate in front, soft palate behind. But I could not find any proof. Establish a system and stick to it. For two years no one was permitted to approach the court, a state of complete inexactness. Those listed are missing.

Removal and storage. Two in fluorescent overalls with cells. That white haze is a cloud of mace. Then they burst into the kitchen.

I swear I have never seen your face before. I'm at the rear of the building, right?

Night things, wrapped. Homunculi in membranous sacs. (Well, yes, right.) There is still time to let me go. I used words first in my work. Mass stagnates and becomes a pressure centre. I slept the day away. An inversion produces unstable satisfaction. All the things of the past have reassembled themselves within me. (There's that drill again.) Vertical motions are restricted. The suspects are lined up for an identity.

Dreamless to find sir decoding a telegram in the mist. I have not committed theft it says, allusively. Smoke and dust concentrate near the ground. At the close of the book none is left.

His own imaginary moment. A journey is conducted in a counterclockwise direction about the rim of an oval. He is master of introspection and witness—a tongue of road, a curve of time. Some writing is considered a type of fiction.

Body, do you know scytale? Do you know strategies of tension? I'm sure you have seen such things before.

I suppose, fossil hominid of the called, first discovered. Sometimes included, sometimes ex. The next place on the map is a town called ash. And he came dragging after and they lay staring up. Every convention here is beautifully subverted (only in this era of museums).

At the green is a pond and on the pond float paper boats. He drops the key at the desk. He hasn't lost any time. These have each a small recess at the centre.

As birdlime corrodes the frieze.

On the banks, under the river. A lamp hangs above the lingam. It's all about the man who wanted to be guilty (a novel). Perhaps we are not. The concierge looks at him with condescension.

I'm keeping you up. . . . It's still too late.

This reveals not a single useful feature. Who would find difficulty in being believed? He's a projector. The correct answer is the *punctum solis* in the egg yolk.

There isn't a caretaker. A poisonous substance is secreted within the body. Never have I been so touched, so educated. Where do I border? I believe that the last man has been withdrawn.

We never reached the letter I. Force molten lead into the moulds. Replace the method. That little click is growing. It can be adjusted to fit the contours of the human. (Whispering inner head, these days.) A line is scratched across from one ridge to the other. It's like the area around a vent, with the coverts.

To remove the thighs, seemingly. An irregular fabric. In addition it contains the common igneous. For instance, in the temple a single custom was responsible. The landscape pans to a hill of salt beside a quarry. Patterns were admitted to negative forms (no context is unwelcome). The mantic school termed man uncomprised. Is that a globe in yonder window, your pocket?

He has betrayed written remarks. Metaphors taken from naturals found their way back into the language.

Why do you say he sees things differently? I made two versions for myself— service, and animal familiar.

It's growing, at least on paper. Travellers have strung themselves together. The origin can never be revealed. Such a monumental work, and I forgot to mention the idea.

I lose seven years. A stash of apomorphine is always provided. Make good his escape. The voices up front are cracking. Sometimes he runs, earth-delving.

There are stood about us several stones over eight feet in height. Continue along the narrow glassy track. Do not.

He splits in two, unmighty as he strides from sphere. Yet within the spectacle, while it slumbered, uneven.

Secret negotiations are taking place in backroom bars, the prelude to another bout of terrifying wellness. Is that so (no). Fields of knowledge, when cultivated by capable men, have a distinct taste. Deduce his purpose from his works.

The restrictions soon proved tedious, and I gradually withdrew. Who indulges in the more remote?

Nothing at all. Nothing but ourselves. Day on the one hand—the scrape,

scrape, scrape of the ear. He left the town under a rapid, darkening. A blizzard of polystyrene cascaded from the eaves.

Into a different tongue, a different translator. Have you read of the other who comes after?

I heard the approach, counting out their footsteps on the stairs. But I have never heard that voice before.

Day of the smoke, descending flares, the night-brief. It breathes. Then a little sleep, the same but base better. At the end of every chapter one character has to leave the stage and never come back. He did not watch his step on the narrow ledge. Sound off blue leader, who did we lose?

Apnoea, or any other suitable means. Screams from the scaffold—staring way up high, on the third floor. Tell me, tell me of it.

The mysterious substance was found to be pure silex. I am retreating into a noisier world. (Do you see nothing here?) Is it unlikely. This is flint. Open his chest. Sheer driven energy is carrying us through to a conclusion. In this self-portrait the garrotte reappears.

Variant spellings of name. Logograms in upper case, phonetic signs in lower. The situation is reversed, a gravity cell with precognitions. The work should be discreet, or better still non-existent. Come home, come quick she would say.

Born. Last mentioned asylum eighty. Occupation, dropped out of chemicals. Diagnosis: untitled state. Pencil on silt, 1412 AD. Has each man his own peculiar faculty? And he begins to question whether or not perhaps. Others come in the night with balaclavas. The money was to be radioactively marked. (Something is undoubtedly happening.) He is now upended, high above a concrete groyne, the wave beneath his feet. All deny the charge of unauthorized frolic. The malady attacks the body and its outposts: the lung, the kidney, the adrenal glands—the brain, the pancreas, the skin. Again the lift descends. The abdomen. The abdomen is separated from below by the brim of the pelvis. I myself was composed in o six. There is no visible means of support.

It's said the liver wanders at will about the body. Nerves. Actions. So too the womb. A head enters. Taxi to cloister! I am getting annoyed the patient said (no one ever died of idle). There's no mistaking that grey shadow. That's the price you pay for wanting to tag along.

I think you'll find. The subtitle is synaesthesia.

Frames of clay. Kitchen refuse. The goddess, mind. The orbits of the planets are ellipses, with the sun torn out of focus. But anyhow there was just a chance.

The lip that closes the tube of the corolla.

It's registered as a lexical quality. This will one day be a concern for us all. The original relationship between the words is uncertain. (Well, there is a tone of conviction, doubt.) He's done some unquestionable things in his time.

I can't wait to get that safely under my claw. It flew off the bridge and across the power lines. People talk about occupations, don't they. She is always the same dress when I see her. I will surely wind up on my mute—an evaporating pool of water, character from karst.

More on the understrappers (what is). Large helix erasers. Trial by launderette. Can't you see your very voice distresses me? I didn't know all of them personally.

I am hereby instructed. Compensate for the monetary confusion of these connexions. The time is run. When the sphere floats over to him he lowers his head and looks down at the remaining toes. (He is saint the mutilated.) I want to see a few negatives before I can indulge you. An audience is gathering in the masonic.

But we can communicate without other people. Technically, their beaks are at the top of their heads.

Utilize the possession. This still sounds suspiciously like mimesis. (I know how that works.) Bite into it and hold on. We are this ongoing duo. And did the control group suffer an identical experience? It's been a funny old season. I am reconstructing. It's good to work with people who can suspend the obligation to breathe. As might be expected, the shorter the secretion in seconds, the more notes per quiver.

It looked like it was right near my eye. I ducked. Back in time I was called pacemaker, pentacular disease. It was like a gunshot going off. Everything is accepted as reversible.

Named eagre. Drug, the medicinal, wax of head. Laughter and grind inside one the other. The jellied orb bobbles on its ligament. (It is monster under the film of stuff.) I am trying to describe things as they happen.

I have disordered my cause. I am reminded. It's like the time I crossed the river one winter, dazzling, cut loose and on my way, when he rang. They are hovering very close once again and peering in. (I know I am right.) Now he cradles the book close to his chest. He rang to say. Presence is strongest within the spinal cord. Where is he who can contend? Each cell contains approximately six billion baited hooks. He is appointed. I hold peace. It stores people up. He says it will hurt, like iodine on a wound. It spreads through every atom—stimuli, the tissues.

Discharge of the social. Contact with the outside world brings them down to the level of the average. I'm a manner of retreat, psychological ageing of the product. Though actually, in point of fact. Once the case had neutralized, the supply of workers dried up.

The card he drew reads the twelve of batons. Here we see a stern expression, one of low electrical conduct. The food's good but I'd be more inclined to disagree. Obligations dissolve on contact. At the border we chanced upon dense undergrowth, some freakish cruciferous plant. Every hour we had to execute one of the witnesses.

Zero conditional, numb of objects. A dearly beloved. Who plays an important role in the mental life of the experimenter? Last time I checked we were still on the map. (Honest, as he was later called.) Decisions would evolve slowly. It is utterly detached from its source, now rhomboid.

Eighty foot-leaps. G-force with three-D spectacle. A monster with a head sat upon a dangerous rock. And the music of such imposters, opposite. But on one side only.

I set out into the world to see how everything works. They had built a terraced platform made of stones. All hesitate before they hover at the drop. (Distribute adjectives equally, with fairness.) Citizens are perversely governmental— among tall weeds, the female tombs.

He saw her right hand flash up, the nails. Welcome back to the body. Enclosing it is a kind of sheath. Death's a young man's business.

Obscure contacts with the larger crime of an organized universe are the key. Blood now sluicing interim space.

A flail in the darkness caresses my flank. The blur of the water, crumbling rock in hand. I'm passed as offspring. The figures in the area of light stand out, clearly. The present tense is making a comeback. I'm bounded by a surface whose points are equidistant from a centre. It seems there is something here that is a little beyond us.

The stalk is attached not to the edge but to the middle of the under-surface. Hence, a small barrel for training.

Crepuscule of ten, often dreg. Of man's origin and return to the starts. On the other hand, a trickster, the dead man's knell et cetera. In the century, in a wooded depression between two hills.

Of that terror which unnamed, at first. He must have clawed his way down.

More avoid, space. Footsteps and final movements. Don't worry about people. My scalp is creeping (the insect). See, as narcotic—a man called, and very much ectoplasm.

It can only manifest in the patient's own environment. Follow abandon, rush on paper.

Inventory verso, three one four. Note the descending line of tiny particles— one black, the rest white. I'm no longer designated a neutral (yes you can position that there). Etymology is to give leave, to dismiss. The painting is named the effect—lapwings, possibly from their rainlessness. I prefer the more spectacular word 'position'. With this in certain view, we ourselves.

A planetary theory, grainy aerial reconnaissance. Middle and south. I see ideas devouring each other more clearly than in the past. The helix is pointing where.

An aimless institution from any perspective. This makes a pattern. Everyone undergoes the trials of the initiate. The side panels are the sides. A vague sense of malaise haunts objects. Cherished qualities include audacity and dissolution. (There is no end product.) It's like a nail planted solidly under the joints of a stone. Most people would have expected backness, crime.

There's nothing they won't do to raise the standard of boredom. This is a tough start, a kind of apprenticeship of everything. And the spine of these animals?

I took him off to the bonesetter in the hospital. (I miss the running commentary on the real.) The rising figures are stunned, guaranteed. He says I am the sum total. There's a radio broadcast on account of events.

It sits at the epicentre of five equidistant points. These collide at the solar plexus. (Does this sort of exchange exist in your language?) He stopped dead in his tracks and stared at me. You shall witness.

A lot of this stuff won't make it. Code is transmitted via the teeth. God I can't stand yes people. Get your mnemons out. Whose shadow points to the hour.

O murtheress, I. Yours.

Sputum, a dermal plate. Equal shadow of the fire. An abrupt shake of the wrist and molten metal is flung into the matrix. Anyway, the Parthenon was made of stars, and then some.

Slash radio. Slash customer. Slash void. The difficult land. It's the syllable count. Other boundaries given for the state are more modest. People used to make arrangements and stick to them.

Simply called, I am probably a good candidate. Reverse the angle, as far as the eye. The inference implied by the latter is absolutely false.

An itching inside the face. Where lie your concerns. Cough, cough, cough went the throat. We are bottlenecked. Backrooms and halls were infrequently used.

The chapter under study is cyclical in structure. *Who* is triumphant? *What* is your friend called? The act of reading is always followed by a conversation (the orienteer, the inexpressible).

One or two are followed by some wreckage. Or is this a situation which I simply fail to understand.

Above sea level, at the base, are many. Sounds of downpour and of bells striking the hour, where you spent the entirety. No conduct is welcome.

Imagine that wire. We have lost the tables—apparently the onset of a barter ritual. It slowly took shape in my ear after the war. The eighth is the sphere of the fixed stars. My theory was mere groundwork.

They get sick and die, just like anyone else. This view seems to hold an uncanny resemblance.

Nights were spent, end to end—a body conjoined at hip and tip of head. (Blank page.) Love since eighteen seventy has returned.

Local precinct, one such permit holder. Returning from exile he typified the mood, but without success. The following names are those given. He walks to the refrigerator and opens the door. The action stalls. I don't care either way.

A muscle extends and straightens any part of the body. Whisper it, the density of breathing. Here we are four, once again.

Cristiform, where it was undiscovered, the known. Authority mentions similar on the doorway of the old, above a window, inside.

The existing title has been erased, all evidence transcribed. Thick plaited whips were wielded by the mounted contingent. Forget everything that has happened since then.

It was four o'clock in the afternoon on Tuesday, seventeen ninety-three. That shell is obsolete. (It has all the abstract fecundity of the helix.) Apply this to the unknown quantity, or ex. Things are most realized when substituted. I too mirror the surrounding objects. This explains the estimation, all similar phenomena. What is enquired of any question.

An entity can be defined as careless. This can only be understood in terms of a textual afterlife. We find ourselves sequestered, a frontier.

The displacement of books across the shelves is crucial. (My prayer is what.) Give us a fortune-telling, a future. It was not difficult to catch up with the others.

Nobody can imagine how it could be authored. I then examined the horizon. I let the other go. There is net disinterest. Someone has registered in your place.

I have kept them all these years. (Thought so.) One hundred and thirty is better for the backbone. We are outside buildings.

Every nine miles a turret was raised. Open, by a series of minute orifices. Whose tracks had a long process? Geological changes were introduced. It's the sixteenth round, or thereabouts. (There's a lot of counting, isn't there.) A local sound has broken loose. I have only a rough idea where everything lives. Approaching us is a little boat in charge of a single oarsman. Each cadre forms a line of outposts.

Delays will be encountered in filing along a narrow track. I was beginning to despair of the population, until the following day. Membranous canal is misleading.

Some other nerve, or port. Control is imposed by a shady telekinetic agency. Start flirting with some positives.

The prospect of its historical failure. A casual visitor, re-explored. (Who cried out?) I have never once issued a complaint. What must he do now with the key he has won.

It's never an act of secession. It was like being cocooned—a blank space, a spine at the lip of the shell. Do you still want to come along. Coincidence here is out of the question.

O nothing much. She says I cannot talk long, I must attempt the evening ruin. So far so good.

He begins to realize that he needs to go home. (Who could not wait for absence?) Their likelihood depends on the sea. Amidst heavy rain and deep mud, the gathered men. A rare opportunity has been missed: weddings, nachtmaals, funerals. Fever nourishes the body. This is an example of paradox. He fetches the key and opens up their little dorp dwelling. The spirit which arises from the tincture lives in the oil of sulphur. Today is the first day of the convention. He speaks. Unsettle yourselves, downriver (hamlets and walled towns). Something of yourself you have carried over to me too.

The ratio of heat is taken to be a temperature. In the ear or in the conscience, a bounding surface, the apparent. This barrier is commonly called firmament. Time, reconnoitring.

Some local colour. A group of iris gleaming with purple and gold. Terraces of citrus fruit. The other two sketches are diggers. No one can tell. Originally dust was manufactured in the process.

With waxed thread wound around it, it will outlast the centuries. He is the truest troublehead that ever I saw in my entire. A name flourishes.

Intentions: go up to her. Many others were known to exist. After several million years I found myself back on my feet. What can you do with that hooked hand, she asks. I am struggling here to account for the haziness. The fiery snapped et cetera.

Snowblink. In the middleground is a courtyard. The encompassing stone bench is red. The depicted child is grey-blue, stocking scarlet. This is an anniversary said O.

He saw, detaching himself. We are closing in on touch (seal up the first). The ear is alleged evidence. Seize the enormous field that has been marked off. We are close to excavating. What's the next big town. (Passion.) And his serial number. Did you understand anything.

Spent rebellions. It plucks out brains and all. A ray, dim of platter, confessed in use with husk. Is there anything in it. Being can also be called the thing.

I was only three years away when the movement broke. The massive agency of nouns was surrendered. Enthusiasm exists to this day.

She made one of her rare appearances in the seat. The initial hooks are *i, w* and *y*. Her tongue would ling out of her very mouth (sometimes this implies deprecation). They're going to do here next.

He has known personal contact. But does he not in point of fact produce? Let's be going said Socrates.

Pray, pry, price or prize away—the slush-bed et cetera. Some of the saints earnestly desired to resign, actually.

A brief digest of our compositions, vector qualities as well as velocities. I.e. The, feminine singular. The areas described in equal times are equal. He died a death.

Notwithstanding, in the book he's challenged to a duel. I shall excise, later this evening. You have kept your word. Supernatural abilities can be acquired through a simple satanic pact. (No, let's meet somewhere neutral.) Political science has not yet taken charge of linguistic questions. Imagine it was you who had been summoned to combat. Three years left, and where will you live these out?

Resume, inventory. I monitor a total of forty-eight. (Where is your homebody.) I am one of many. Packmules carry the salt we still have. Enter the more forbidding cave. We were looking for a thin flat rock. Supplies are running low. The setting exaggerates the promise. We have chalk and a little bread. The peasants give us coffee. There's a new look to mornings. We reach our destination in a little more than five. It's as if I had passed through. The others arrive at midnight. In spite of all this, events remain in sequence. (In ways, I fail exist.) Different days of the week have been added to the existing strictures of the body. They once drove the agitators from the terminal.

An inferior agent, or underling—these individual passages, the progress of their perusal (the way he had behaved). Estimates have been lowered. Substance can be extracted.

The horses don't seem concerned. The first element modifies the second. Firearms at rest.

Stand in various types of relationship, including possession. Tatterdemalion is a torn shred, a hanging loose. Circles in the kingdom have fallen. This is the wrong sort of weather for the camera obscura.

Dung and straw are strewn across the market square. He had been forced to capitulate at the head. Rebuilding work is going on all around. Against the south wall of the chancel stood the monument. Individual faces don't count in this paragraph.

Such wild recreations. Say what is no longer. (Move?) Erected to sir.

An ideal subject. Arbitrary interventions. It's gone completely tong war. (It means they do not want to die.) No fear she said. At this point the scene becomes confused. There are some unlikely patches of fear, the compact portion of the cell. There's too much space between the walls. And who are called the deciduous teeth.

Obscure by smear. The part of the boy is strung up. Remember, this land is renowned for its collapses. The decision to recognize pushed the countryside into an abyss. We are very close to unearthing the first recorded. How dwells buried in between.

Oversea has fallen. In there has been silenced. I hope to do several more of these, where legal. The first seven-and-a-half minutes were devoted to combustion: work, dwelling, mourning.

Leave a longitudinal fissure in the roof. Pour it in.

Veering close, carrying with it the patents, the possibility. Carried by the most trustworthy authorities, not in the main by great convulsions.

Low tide. The wind rips up again. (Yes, a long long rest.) We approached the town about noon, backs to the earth. All the bodies were shrink-wrapped— widespread bluish glow, the occasional hydrogen. We have made one percent of the required effort.

Objects were neatly arranged in-house at the time of death. Nothing is ever about. We were deserted.

It's transmitting back its own static. Communication is via the internal branch of the nerve. Heads rise up out of the loamy earth. Stars are seen in projection on the concave surface of the vault. (I am your race). It was a sequence of reversals. There were three people in the room and all of a sudden there were four.

The pin of a dial. Index or indicator. That nose. That which remains when a similarity within one of the angles is taken away (golem). Aorta to know.

This route is not easy to find in the dark. Certain peoples are thus haunted. Name the group of instruments—libation vases, the box of purification, the blood-let, the feather. Behind them stands the reader, or lung of books. And falling into ruin, the saintness of watching. Don't worry, lots of people do things they don't understand. One night he gave us a complete account of the prison system. (Fiery shield, panopticon, the hair-trigger.) I began to feel myself thinking. Two couriers came galloping as if for life. This structure can be seen from two perspectives as a cube. We could not compete with their sartorial display. Pages discuss and illustrate a number of dialogues. (Who did you say you were?) On forcing entry, the sealed tomb smelled strongly of semen. A solitary lantern lighted the room. I said you should wait for me. It was fully an hour before we found one. Any discourse ought to be constructed like a living creature. The inhabitants posed themselves as a unique problem, a preserving machine.

Of tetradic correspondence. Broad daylight, sassy. The interior nerve descends along a disputed border. When my body dies et cetera.

A box with aperture. A dark chamber into which objects are thrown. Once, upon a scream, a column crashed through the cobble to the sewers.

Existing without visible means. Nerves are back in vogue—vagus sheath, the fear and trembles. He's no longer suspected of being the man. Four doubled, eight doubled, and so on. He has acquired an instant.

The subject did not comprehend. This might serve as a motto. Whiff of scorched woodchip from without, the excluded.

Last ascent. Collapses were common (embalm, stuff, inter). That's nothing. I think her not to be the one I saw.

East-west athwart the arctic circle. Then with a sharp, deep cut behind the head. A beyond has been firmly established. Can you come with me, this way, please? It's time for a little trepanation.

A map unfurls. He must have wished he could eat those words. The explanation which follows will be confined to general principles.

How long does it take to get to this place? What's there?

No work was done on the cave that day. We trod close on the heels of our guide. It looked about right to me. We do not know why the object has been taken. I mean ur.

A succession of village guerrillas, unidentified man dead in hotel room. There's a surety to the fading arc. Branches pass obliquely, inwards to the pharynx. I'm in there somewhere.

A constellation turns in the hemisphere. Negation could not exist back then.

Nothing that the centuries could throw at it managed to stop it. Threshing in the glare, as though utterly certain in his uncertain.

I want to enquire about flight, the name of the son: she who turns her head. (No smell of cordite.) Allow yourself to be repeated. They say morale on our side is pretty good. Put him in charge of receiving. What more have you need. I wish I could see it. I am used illusively. That covers just about everything I can think of. A figure added or subtracted yields another. Similar is the original.

Limbs are repealed. Your gaze, the spelling aimed at point-blank.

A leveller, abridged into solitary action. He chose the wrong side.

Elision into a single word. Dark clods of heavy earth with cloud so low it obscures the surrounding hills. A brand of the old judicial ordeal.

A leading historian expresses scepticism. I've been in so many places these last few years. I'm sort of waiting.

Bonfires are struck here and there, without purpose, it seems. (Forget correspond.) Estimation is by a measure of distance averaging a call. The seventh poured out the air. It doesn't make any difference anymore. Don't deserts have the same effect on you?

In the meantime, settle their abode. Something without equal, something untried. Make possible the redundancy. Outside, a felled catalpa tree.

Understrife. Skull tip to intervacuum.

XXIX

The nature of work is best understood. Give a brief account of how it came to be written. Who said we have been away and must return (dainty arched feet at the dying fire).

It is now cut off and lies in two parts. The language argument is the first and strongest of the five houses, or suits. Don't you know the story.

I'm in a primitive way. It has qualities of both ear and lung (deliver the grace-blow). Consider one by one all of the characters in this drama. Self-demand, intolerance and discipline are the chief virtues. Last year it was all we talked of. Who is called, dead-reckoning? Their uniform incorporates a fluttering apron of scarlet leaves. Fixity is foregone. A meat-bolt pierces the nasal septum.

There was one vacancy, as an elective mute. He is released after a spell of reminding.

Left leg entrapped. Hand high suspended with hook.

As skin, as the object of an action. It is the fearsome et cetera. Criss-cross.

I mean the concentric spherical shells. (I told him again and again.) The squares of periodic times vary. Opposite, at large, a cup-shaped architecture. The segmenting polyp, jellyflit.

A candlelit exterior. Small sugar dogs are melted on a metal plate. (Could I close the window.)

It was crushed between two converging bodies. The correct number is fifty-three, his trademark. Civilians live in this half-half town which straddles, look. I have recently pointed out the process. The embryo quits the body of the vagina-less parent worm. Do you believe me now.

Halogen element, symbol none. Offerings to the locality, present or not. Which character deceived by birthright?

Turning, intending to represent transformation content. An abandonment would be welcome. Throughout many years notes collected in the margin.

It is still retained in the official nerve of the regiment. It was unknown. I remain behind, untouched. Do you recall the divisions of the globe when the boundaries were staked out?

It appears once a season. Evaporation of sap from the palms has been reported. It blisters, ink tattooed into the lifelines. Others squat nearby. It is found in the memory, lost in the collective. After several years these incendiary exchanges fizzled out. Mass is crushed flat. The subject is grudgingly absorbed and placed under production.

A hollow basin of earth, full of stagnant water. Neural tic beneath left eye socket. I face towards the object. Guilt can be personified. We communicate using simple verb forms and terse nouns. Without, the clatter of stones cast against a wooden groyne. One could see the entire plain as if from a great height. A trumpet flourished as a group of four men entered.

The patterns kaleidoscope, congealing to a map. We believe the rotation is slowing down. An iron plate has been screwed into my side, flagstones under-foot. O to be out here in this very day. Flames quiver across the surface. Then came the signal to withdraw to the outer edge of the platform.

Half-burnt vertebrae are scattered across the floor. We're north of the timber line. Medicine yourself to that, big sleep.

When the weather finally breaks. Ganglia, discarded keys on the pavement. Now usually follows and is attached to the word it modifies. It was primarily a work intended to display—the lack of touch, an action whereby the contestant seems to try too much. Loosely, a sort. A series of runs before breaking.

Flags cracking in the wind. He or she are mixed up at hazard. I was walking backwards before any of you. Throw yourself in where.

It sits down and then tries to stand up again. (I'm a godsend.) One can sig-nify: a fitting tooth, a gift or name. An undisclosed fee. One who arrives.

Who is destined to live and die in my arms et cetera. Each fragment of rock has now been retrieved. A separate assailant is required to enter the dialogue. Several of the fingers do appear to be broken. The book is entitled. Peat-reek, lazy-bed.
Tankers in the sleeve. (This is why sense and reference are quite vague concepts.) An oil lamp. As location, as field.
Tomorrow, big changes in the prospect. A chest-shaped burial chamber made of flat stones.

When some people speak I think science fiction. Above the door, a cellular emblem. There's a pause for space, used iron in the air. A species of dimness, gram-negative rodlike bacteria.

He set fire to the building while out shooting birds. Rumours are abroad, liquescent orange waves.

It is no longer locked in its room. The implications are extraordinary. I mean of course four-fingered, four-toed. This doesn't help the situation at all.

Fistal stimulus. The arc of a bay. A track skirts it. She is silhouetted against a wrought-iron railing. It's uplifting to discover. (I have forgotten something of importance.) The word we're searching for is scarce. Everything has become so hideously easy. And to be held fast so long?

It has become known through the discovery of documents. Here comes everybody. Blood swells the purple sac and suchlike.

Unearned repetitions. An agent, man-made of his class—ill-at-ease and loathe to act. A remedy can be made from arrowroot. Ah, strategically placed.

Wake, stolen without cap, any kindred. Abandoned sulphur mines. The brain is separated from the spine.

Rising up out of that box. Repeal, hoax. Watch your back. It's one of those spectroscope moments. The domain is synthesis he claims. Origins are doubtful. It's made invisible through back formation. The circle scored resembles a felt interior with pinprick stars. The various things found in the world no longer seem to connect to one another. I am a committed man. Enquire what the genre is. There's an open aperture in one side. I lead them to the place where the tongue was found. He was always extremely brave about his deformity. Is this writing, he says.

Evil mason town. Would you like some gaps. It has the usual properties. It was a singularity. The silhouettes of six figures were seen swinging. (That's where we should be, under the ocean.) An army was raised and crossed over to the other side. Buildings went out of fashion. There's a lighter touch. I can think of worse ways of spending your time.

Looking down from a great height on what transpires. The uncomprehending (star of the ravener et cetera). He has a vague memory of steel-capped boots. The realm is a-prey. Rare plants are abundant at the site of the old battleground. I was reclining on a riverbank. You just have to walk around the back. I could consume. Theories have been gauged to describe—the strong pulse, the weak, the electromagnetic. What motive and what interest survives.
Atom numb. The rest of my days were interned. What justification is there. The embalming had failed.

Your inherited histories. Distant drumming. Energy of orbital ruins. There's no shelter. She relinquished all her rights. The bones have become brittle. I open the blind. It meant nothing to her. The melting point of ice has been declared an estimate. It's time for the annual casting process. The subject was packed in iron oxide and a pollen tube inserted. Gravity needs to be rectified. Plankton mass and deviation were measured, i.e. line-of-sight ground waves. What have you done to yourself.

On the cell, its methods and its needs. A few days ago, despite all the accusations and protestations.

Robotnik. A measure of distance avenging one and three-quarters of a mile. Why doesn't he just go over and say these things?

Condensation forms salt of rayon. It can wait. Here stands cave X, unbreached. I found myself trapped within his radius. The echo here is perfect. It was palpable in the street the day before. It outgrew the opposition. I read for detail. There were strange projecting shafts of colour. Twin hollows opened up inside. This is one of their last remaining bases of supply. The impression is that the painting floats outside of space and time. We're witnessing the birth of a new class of filament. If a sentence contains punctuation, it's probably too long.
That recurring tension. There is anticipation, air. The horn of an unseen vessel.

Penetration achieved. It seems to have rectified itself via the agency of a random leap. He wants to deliver (e.g. wither and die). We are not sitting in our allotted positions. D-shaped electrodes were snapped to the skull. I'm told there is loft storage. And how many earthly satellites? I refuse. Isolate tongue, northwest of mouth. Quietly, unwindswept.

Are we okay to just. She twists about and reveals the scar on her back. The vehicle accelerates. I think I just caught sight. It's rejected, routinely. I think both options simultaneously. One hand is too close for comfort. They come to the edge of a cliff. The man's movements are unclear. The local obscurity doesn't seem to bother either of them. I reflect on the cultivation of power, of that year and all the other years. He produces a tiny penknife. There's a light of triumph in one eye. (You are the shallow in this partnership.) The earth looks very flat today. Later he sought me out and apologized. People and things are always falling off. I'm eaten alive. There's an insurrection of sorts, an uprising. That machine is a dredger. The mechanism allows a storm of lead to be discharged. He informed on us.

Which historical figure was considered immutable? No one is permitted to use the word pyre again. Futility renders me possible. The victim is led back into the shelter. There has to be a method or all this would be impossible. Oratory is a lost art. Look at all that sand pouring in. Literature is my servant. I mean, we're doing shapes. It may just stay away, pass us by. There's really no option. You can't process them all together. Prominence of the frontal bone at the base of the fore-head is one characteristic. Subject too infirm to be held long between parentheses.

Between the white and baring straits. Calculate the cube of mean distance from the sun. An instrument for measuring the sense of pressure was used.

The masthead. Nine days in and nights, throughout the air the weathering balloon. Only too glad to get off with a little loss. I was spent.

A means of passing the invisible, anywhere. A kind of simple frame. The head is all over the place. There is a tacit understanding, but this can never be released.

Drowsy, heavy lid with grains of glass. Repeat every seven. Light the fuse and withdraw. Begin again. (Everything's wrong.) The line composed suddenly jumps into another hook. He tells me the word means swarm. A body is composed of infinite detail at a particular season. We cast a look back. The last salvos have died down. How was life lived then. What was the scope of their existence. List its events and obstructions. Try voice. They gathered in a compact mass. Repeat every stem. Come this way, come hither. For instance, because the shadow is so disagreeable.
Dice clack, broken knuckles on a marble top. Cell is covert.

Of his reappearance with those strangers. Silhouettes of helmeted men on a flat concrete roof. One should never fall into melodramatic excess. It overhung near the temple, from my window.
We found ourselves looking out over one of the epochs. Allowance has died. The wagon rolled on through savannah of reeds and razorgrass. Now, about those minarets.

We gathered. A fragment is defined and then torn away from the body. It has been consigned to later use. It waits to be permitted. This is my most shame-ful night ever. Still breathing, offside, is the floating strip. This will never achieve severance. It has lost another piece of itself. An image of the objects outside is thrown upon a screen. The cleared line, bisecting.

It is waiting to enter. I knew you would be down here before us. There is one hole left. There are still several facts outstanding. You have walked away from all that knowledge. It is waiting to descend. We have a thousand minutes left and a long weekend ahead of us. The object landed in a region of tight sandy soil. There's always a voice from the underworld—his abandoned city, I want every-thing right now et cetera.

Well said cries engineer. Nonetheless, ceasing to be. (It's with good reason that mercury is no longer considered my equal.) Note how the body is studded with sharp thorns. I once held the title. He wept. Some people are beyond use. Let us cut trenches under the waters of the sea, and suchlike.

The passing hours are declared an official workday. The idea for the next item was sparked by haemorrhage. He speaks in his dead junket whisper—a suffocating yellow cloud, people in evening dress, fumbling. A feathered rank fluttered down from heaven. (You probably know more about this than I do.) He says he grieves. All semblance is here. Some of my own experiences have wormed their way in. It's said he is irrefutable. You never seem to be waiting for yourself. He says he knows. We have been away and must return. Then the knot sank back into his leg. He lost a vein. That graph is prohibited. Follow your right hand as it moves slowly through space. First you breathe out.

We converge. Have you done your facial execution today? It appeared to be an act of vengeance, vendetta. What is the converse variation in remnant? Relax your limb. Now move the stick. Without writing nothing can exist. I go down a second time. I became an apparition of myself. I am previous. Which one broke the code? We have only a few days left before the accident.

Backs to the sea. (You'll never get away with leaving that there.) This is a closed non-orientable surface. The shared root is pronounced *knell*. He is waiting inside. Some are beyond use.

Those rubber corks. We're moving now, gaining speed. I was going to but I didn't. I used words to write instructions or scripts. I forgot.

He relates how the phantasy figures he has consciously evoked gradually become independent. The interlopers are clad. They have taken on the nature. Flat stones were arranged to spell out lengthy quotes. The contestants turned through one hundred and eighty degrees, then abruptly stopped. To return to the top at any time, one simply exhales. They have succeeded. The number here is eight. Antithesis is the domain name. A knife was eased straight through it.

My attention was alerted to the deteriorating situation by a grenade. Yesterday a debt was incurred (the plants). Dead from the underside.

By the time I got ready.
I now feel that I'm controlling it, rather than it controlling me. That other person is being very difficult. It's a very piecemeal process. The decompression is hidden. I could never leave. Progress is simultaneously needed and resisted. There's an ancient banister rail. The hand shrinks and withdraws into the body. An eerie orange light appeared at the window. Do not flinch. Life is elsewhere. It

was without head or face. The remainder feels isolated. He says I am unfulfilled. A woman passes and waves. This is the only solution to the old problem of irreversibility. A promise has been wasted. I recall. A thread of fluid stretched from the eye of the head to the tip of the tongue. Of course I am. I have access to everything. It's to do with the money, really, duplication phenomena. (Don't look at me.) This is the only solution to the old problem of immortality. We all know. It's that northwest corner again. Sooner or later, something will fall through the trapdoor, the actual neither.

Turning now to face horizon. There was at least one witness. Folk are dragging silt across an expanse of empty stones.

It was renamed after one of the asteroids. The renewal process is spent (tie-machine thing). It will be convenient to speak of this later. We shall come better prepared next year.

Some notes on solarization, the subatomic particle. From either just entering, stunned at the moment of speech, and thereafter.
There is not long left, despite the remaining bulk. Nerves are corroding. Gathered at the rim of the compound are more of those whitewash figures. The source of the matter and energy flowing in has been suggested. The title is cathar, extracathar. Fibrous tissue is found in the brain and the spinal cord. I am the all-important extra, the one who is not considered. The old names were shed. Even the little bit of space I contained was too much. The options are breathing in or breathing out.

The eating of ashes. In this depiction the angel is pressed to the ceiling. It resembles bleached beeswax.
Drawing back from papyrus, with vignette. He will hope to add mediaeval flare, hence his pursuit. And the embers beneath your feet. I always found the castle strangely comforting.

The head is stuffed with them. On the table sits a timetable. A fork in the road leads away. That noise is the subject's pulse. He says I am the one who waits. I return again and again. Skin has been lost.

Recollection of meaning, a gravity cell. They tried to improvise an assembly line using those who had stayed behind. This changes the structure. (Sound of distant drumming.)

Consider to wander about, over or through, discharging at random. Consider to practice piracy, or some such casual remark. Consider to change, inconstantly. Consider to troll, with live bait. Wandering is a mode of incomplete ploughing.

It fell from the sky. There's a further note about this on a different page. He fell to reverie.

Partly at least from plunder. It moves in a circle with a heavy ponderous rhythm. It squats down where the sea is hollow, to defecate in the lee of a groyne. Sunday is still special, the very idea of place. Perhaps partly from a mid-form of obsolescence. All of this happens very slowly. Single-point perspective is evil.

I once revered. I don't know when daylight will be needed again. It came up for air. Each paragraph can be considered a praeludium. Some cunning musicians use decoys. Things haves been represented in three dimensions. The existence of a mutated form proves the case, my precognitions. It survived by passing its neck through the side and joining one end to a hole in the base. A darkly comic deconstruction is taking place. The word on the street is what.

Compound from grief, with prefix restored to form. I am raving. Heads were strung out like a giant abacus. I shall never forget that pistol in the storeroom. I shall never forget his marathon crawl from here to here. Stain the coastline a deep green. They are victorious. You can't do them all in big batches, pouring out, pouring in.

Metal craft glisten in the sunlight. I can no longer distinguish what she says. (From when?) We are about to strike. May you be truly thankful.
The rim of her lip. Scarless, delimited.

Raise their arms as birds of the air et cetera. Pull yourself together. A name is given to mark the occasion of a revival. All the time, the diffuser vibrates in the background. Now there is snowfall, soot in the cornea.

A plucking at the nerve-band. We are taking off, unscrewing the sleeper to be repaired. We have reached the extreme limit. They cut the power. A symbol represents this. They were like broken bones. I think that's premature.

From neither, just entering. Fistiana.
This feels like the last-but-one. You have been travelling the world for a decade or more. There aren't that many. Surviving powers of arousal are detected, net interest. Now we are on the other side of the river. We're wet through (false, guess again).
Have you not? It should have been a really simple day, with prehistoric stones, enraged situations in the momentum.

Overland, from the exposed north-western tip of the peninsula. Now he is up on the roof, with miscreant body. He writes I am regret. It was neocolonial. One of the bodies is cup-shaped. The sirens are still at it. He's a deranged version of myself. I offered hope in that corridor.

It's already beginning to decay. It declines every offer of assistance (look at their tiny tiny heads). I offered them a new type of shell. It had shed its wings. Molten pitch was applied to the stump.

Say, a tightrope. The mathematical description of a curved space at a forgotten time. It exists. A man returns to his hometown. (And something else.) He offers the inhabitants. You are listening to the early, the striking of a hammer, the tolling of bells. As for covering up the tracks of the conspiracy, well, there was indeed a time.

Sandblasted image, a procession of linked angels and penitents, dancing in the round. The city is quiet until the tocsin (more rigadoon). Time upravels. House to house searches were carried out. From a leather bag he produces an undeniable object.

On the undergirders, the night of the storm. Ancestors of civil dead, a new species of abandon. Apply yourself to the problem of the empty span. Between us and the subspace in question lies what? (We were once shaped like wolves.) Now divide by the area of the parallelogram. This is much too much. The image shows that we have no true memory of the event. I have always just occurred. We returned to the lodge and sandbagged ourselves in. Note the U-shaped mouths at the end of every food canal. What could one do but wait. It slithered out from the brainpan and circumnavigated the head. Who among you flinched.

You can't do that research here. They refused to return to the burnt-out shell of the vessel. The story was about navigation. A rifle is slung over one shoulder. It's discovered that everyone in the town has lost their memory. The chosen state is inertia, the reluctance of the body. He reports a reaction (I am caused, and so forth). We may justly call him tightly strung. The lead characters are the hurtful, the unhoped for, and the destroyer. A cave is the only shelter for miles around (specially adapted Winchester). A ship's position was once estimated by randomly opening the log-book. He is declared abscissor. Anyone is free to subvert the nature of the answer, the argument. There is more than one form of discharge. Packs of vagabonds wander the countryside. You don't have to add much. Our plan resembles (see tempest). That's no cave, it's a fogou. Ditch the letters *k, f, e, d, b, c, a, h, g* and *i*. Now try it.

These events took place during an era of plague. Abreaction occurs under hypnosis, magical accessories. He destroys and perverts the name of the question. There is electricity. Hold out for as long as possible. Men disembark with picks and shovels. The retreat goes on. Satellites orbit our planet. We are simple figures, a novel brand of vagueness. Ominous significance attaches itself to every word. (First you can then you can't.) Relief is on its way. I have been appointed one third. We have seen enough of voices. Giant hailstones are falling from the sky. I may be abstracted into easily tangible portions of necessity. The operation is named delta one. (You don't need to put that back yet.) Autonomous cells emerged. By this time the original corrective had been replaced by an inner circle. The day after the wedding the other two suddenly died. I am disappointed. The problem is the injurious list. With U-shaped food canal, one would choke.

Herself is. Stalking the perfect, those untimely routines.
About her memory. It is to walk away. It is to walk away from the heart of the matter. We inherit. You took it home. You worked it out for yourself. You warn everyone else. The remainder is bequeathed, the revival of a forgotten. Semenaunt is a wonder thing.

A small rayless with fleshy dorsal, wreath of tentacles about the mouth. Sly painter of night and wreck. The surroundings dissolve. I am no longer required. Slates rained down from the roof.

Despoiler. A well deserved break. It came from without, born about tabula rasa. Throughout the night they loosen. Soft ooze of mulch, flesh made adipocere.

Notes on an acclaimed ephemerist.
Dreamt I had access to a vast dictionary. All these clothes were stacked up in a great heap, a mountain of used garb. (There are moments when I'm convinced of his sanity.) And the odour of the bodies once clad in these rags. I've always been good at mimesis. Why do you think this is happening.

Found hidden in an abandoned.
He's one of the enlightened earlies. It's said he is one thousand years. Let's say saint, in parentheses, or hermit—a heady mixture of danger and harmonics, i.e. a suppressed sense of panic.

She speaks of him as follows.
I used to collect redundancy. It's said the rib can never heal.
Its outstretched wings resembled a giant book.

I remember it growing into a record of hours and days. He is renamed saint the illuminator. Time was recast. The subject has withdrawn inside its own body. The diodes are positives.

He absorbs A comet appeared according to contemporary calculations. I'm writing much more fluently now. It's the boxing lessons. He disappears and will never return. The number is five.

A discarded hand of playing-cards lies on the table. Insects circle the green baize. An acid yellow light is cast by a lamp, bold brushwork covers every surface. In the middle of the room is a billiard table. All human activity has ceased. There's something of jazz about it. Cum spurts. She says so much of this does not belong. How did you get in. Roots cling to her face. High frequency waves trip emergency bells throughout the compound.

A prayer line, the last movements. Meaning is merely nodded at. This is an erroneous form. One of the brothers was a revolutionary. (It says here.) I am non-actionable. I am not accountable. Now divide by the volume of the cube. He says I have foresworn. That idea is a particularly bad idea. Signification is conjured. So what's it to be, your rapt attention, or defenestration?

The outermost tube. I keep seeing yellow flags. I misunderstand. One must first deny the charge as unfounded. She could scream. Today I am understudy. Secondly, I must decode the surrounding signals. No she says, draw deep into your lungs, against the beat, in his spines of light.

Friday, discussed etymology of the word know with unknown woman. Yes, it is once again the day. The remainder has been cancelled. It is not natural, if father, nor I. The plant in question is thought to emit a shriek when pulled from the ground. Desolation prevails in our field. Tin and copper could be transported, procuress.

The body in question is countermined. He is of course a master tactician. We retreated into the woods. This was a small sector (I think it was B6). I hope I'm not boring you. Someone is breathing out for the very last time.

It had to stuff wax inside its head. She enticed it back. The trail is still visible. It lost. It retreated to a clearing in the forest. Injuries were sustained: bruising, over-exposure to the action of light. It continues at rest, as lightly as a hawk rests. The day went well till the rupture. Many of these analysts have lost their bearings.

It is clouding over. I am trying not to clash with the surroundings. There was no way to see what happened next. I was raised to do so. The sea is truly leaden. Please stay. I want the whole width.

Iron mantraps everywhere, unhinged agents with mental states. If he moves a muscle he implodes. Note the totally unpredictable blend of influences. He announces the following. Here is a variety of begettings, false starts.

Bright legions swarm unseen and sing the glorious architect et cetera. And his place in the boat of millions of years was empty. A revolutionary impromptu takes place before the set lesson. You can always change your mind. (Wow.) He holds me captive. Today is the march of the costermongers, a swarm of fools with great baskets for heads. More rapture, then peace—a red rose, a white rose, all to be not. That refrain is like a nervous tic running blindly through the text. (Those are never portraits of people.) Here, you get paid for just turning up. Each wave builds to such a height, surpassing the previous. A voice says so. These characters are owners of other men. There is much pointing of digits.

That is the password, which leads to further confusion. Its lair is a castle keep. Men swarm. Time is unappointed. I had forgotten about the long count. One particle which appeared relates to a deep-rooted idea of mine. You're letting this take over. Who would become the backbone?

In the sky a clear orbit is drawn by a point of white light. I survive in a special sense. The pass is navigable but we have no weapons. He survived in a sort of artificial placenta. Now we have come over to the other side. We are playing out a comedy in an unknown dimension. The sight and the report were a marvel. He has launched himself on a mission. We are found wanting. It's victory or death. Don't mention the hilarity.

The provincial town is dimly lit. I take note. A lamp sways on its chain. Observe the villagers. Loose cobblestones underfoot, burnt-out shells. To have absolute power over a god of many forms, it was necessary to know all his names. At last it's done and all is well. They ascend the steep incline that leads to the turret. Ships rail in the sky. All this takes place at great speed. A word with more than one meaning has been introduced into the local dialect. We're being downsized. That ends that, drawing to an abrupt close. This is how one feels. There's a causeway leading out to sea. The interior is gold, since the Greek. We cut a path to the interior. There is however the inevitable curvature. Bodies float on the escalators. (Consign this to history.) Tracks and gobs cling to the flesh. You have traversed the surface, these ten years. Today the magic has gone out of the alphabet. It's yellow flag day.

Instrumental, with a freshly shaved head. Hello this is telekinesis. Is that a good sign or a bad sign. Figures on the inside of a rotating cylinder are visible through the slots. There's no point in counting things out right now. Here are rapidly repeating images of the selected. (That too would be premature.) This is one of the most important texts of the five.

Pertaining to animals of rocks. A container for evidence.
They provoke an illusion. One mineral is closely allied to a date. Life originates

510

from a specific vital principle. He is the one who refused to maintain. The rows of parallel lines appear not to be parallel. Now I need a knife to cut this rope.

Man at far window with hood at the ready. The innermost tube. Last run through. Always be aware that you are already doing what you are doing. I left it this way for a couple of centuries.

A customs union. Snake deity, very slow fetish. Welcome back to the cathedral. The rift is still grinding up and down. Nothing works better than attenuated energy projectiles, or a jar of gunpowder.

Take advantage of the pause. Gentle pressure growing at colon, on the other hand.

How things would have transpired if the assassination had never taken place. Experience encourages this expressionist treatment of the supernatural. Today we are still running tests. One small detail has been overlooked. The advantage is that we are no longer in need of anything. There's regret to spare and we have fodder aplenty. A programme has been established. His isolation confirms our disbelief.

Improvised kino in the town square. Grainy projection of silver-greys on ancient plaster. You're letting this get to you, boss of two worlds, history-maker.

A present moment of sorts, unfit for anything. Construction, as the bee hive. Across his back was stencilled the word security. It took twenty years to get back to this. The sound I heard was like a klaxon. They had in their minds the eye of Horus, probably the white, or the sun, tiny threads of radio. You'll know it when you see it. I gave him an instance.

They are hemmed in by the old symptom. That proved premature. The instrument has keys. Blindness is punctured by sudden outbursts of white noise. We passed a wall that stretched beyond the horizon. (I can't just run away.) Step by step you've allowed this to take over.

He once set out with a home-made, moulded to the shape of a wing and strapped to his ankle. He mutters under his breath. And were thou much bitter, with trammels to bind her?

After a while the ears start to ache. Ephemeron is an insect that lives only for one day.

Reportage. A large black bird, possibly the raven. It's too obvious. It had already buried its sharp edge a full inch into my flesh.

I know what we'll do he says. We look up. Giant nests balance between the naked branches. Now we will have to negotiate.

Final night, entrance one penny. Page two of a standard evening with outlooks, people. My counsel wears a copper ring on the top of her head. As long as our ties don't cross, we're safe. Our triggers are secure. Through the ring passes hair. The fuse has become damp. Mine is a secure occupation. Corpse is being reanimated.

They're encamped on the eastern side of the island. I have a plan. The room is slowly filling up with sand. Memories shuffle through. The writing was invisible. Before I can execute, something unfortunate happens. We are stopped by the red light.

Snatch failure from the mouth of success. My left side is unnerved. I dreamt you into existence. I think behaviour could break loose. All the electricity has vanished. Are you ready. I contained the danger. They'd bite your hand off if you offered them. . . . Only a small pocket of air remains about the head. Men's minds were not as they now appear. All the elements relate to one another, link up.

Oblong pieces or other material. On one side an identical pattern. On one side different values represented by symbols and numbers.

An encompassing vault, security against the alarm. A hook slowly descends. A number of people are called forward and renamed. (Is this how little we happen.) There are the jobs. We attend. There is the literal meaning of to touch. We achieved a circuit on route. There we found the twelve thousand. It is exactly. They must be gutted first. There is still the required stasis. It is exactly what is printed on the box. They do not resist. Metal spikes gently pierce the surface. Before leaving the apartment, check all the connections. A stain creeps across the carpet. Synthesis arises from persistence of vision, wrought with figures in various colours. All the blanks, bolting forth.

Moving on from the clamour to the individual voice. Here and there he unlearns. Origin is uncertain. An inquisition is underway. The ulterior motive is unknown. It lay close to the ground.

Who is unraveller?

On which side had it been painted?

How did you cope walking and listening at the same time?

He is describing the cell as it was in nineteen and eighteen, respectively. Your horrible, you know that.

It lay low so as to be hid.

He is the individual declared. The event always occurs at the same time and in the same place. There has been an admission of redundancy. History was dominated by the voice, until now. One man was declared anachronistic. Who introduced the thumbscrew? The listener understands, and lists its advantages. Sound has been restored, contact between the pleural spheres. Ease the throttle, draw back and reduce.

It is self-evident, a universally received principle. The film relates the absurdity of their existence. You know exactly what you have to do. It had a small cut on its lower limb. You accept. Nothing happens. It's almost as if we are here ourselves. It's almost as if we are needed. (Is it to do with a crime?) An image remains, the fissure between two halves—tender mercies, dripping from hooks on the ledger.

Some music that was written in a single day. Optical effects (the power supposed to enter such a body). Utilize the principle of repetition. He expects to squeeze his message through. The result is the reversal. Introduce this into the record. Issue license by any means permitted. I was born *after* the alleged. The word you're looking for is hawklightly.

A master-key, from to pass over, all. Paragraphs are enormous, cracks of doom and so forth—appearance, false semblance. The wearer of such a shift. They are doing what they please.

Daybreak, uniformed junketeers. They seem to be demolishing a brick wall. Among the instruments are the accordion and jaw-harp. You would think we had never seen their like before. You would be forgiven for believing. You would be forgiven for forgetting. The condemned is retreating rapidly now. You would have thought they had invented. He's totally untraceable. The temperature dropped fifteen degrees in as many seconds. The windows were stained with green light. Their language is another. No one ever died listening to this. At the close, the image of a tiny yellow frog. Bare electric wires are embedded in the concrete screed. (There wasn't time to check everything.) A woman yells at a red light screwed to a metal pole. I've got some undelivered letters for you.

The head was impaled on a pike. Reconstructions are precipitated. I can no longer touch my face.

Yes, matter of seconds. Yesterday it was still visible on the denticulate silhouette of the bridge. Here's an extract.

High frequency waves trip emergency bells throughout the compound. He taps his pen against the document on his desk. Someone mutters curvature. The other frowns. Here's a selection of discreet cameos. The age of the composition is unknown. Echoes are found elsewhere. I have written the ultimate example. We are back in the year. An unseen voice says you cannot possibly use all of these adjectives. We're still at the last reckoning. Land is possessed. The one who came before has been declared out of favour. Some of the others have already arrived. Events were quite unprecedented in our town.

Neural tic in vicinity of left eye. It lurches in and out of the field of vision. He is clearly on route elsewhere. The disaster was of his own making. What the others are doing is of no concern. Little is worth putting down on paper. I must be the only one. Today's moot has been cancelled. I am compared to myself. I have much the same feeling about you. The old spirit of reportage persists. The arc of the sun moves in counterpoint to the moon, no? Objects can readily melt into the surrounding space. Musical pictures are emerging. No one ever died.

The portrayal of sensation and unease. As if joined by a copula, judicious conjunction. Syzygy, and then some. He sent a gift of an hundred ounces of silver. Something unexpected is being conveyed (semblance, a few surprises). He was slain in time by his own people.

It lacks a root system. It has a delicate organ of reverberation, a curving dam of head, sunk into silence.

They want me. Take random shots at the unconscious. The others lay about in the road. A lot of people took some. It often calls for three persons. The engine choked, some say deservedly.

A stage trap. The twelfth of his transcendental studies, incorporating a variety of poisonous items culled from an inventory. Whose long forked root was thought to resemble? Thus, with properties.

The man is perfectly safe so long as nobody steps on him. Use less nitrogen. Act as if benign. He is one of the geniuses who invented the head. It promises to be a great occasion. A fine interlacing of fibres forms the outer surface. Events are too tenuous to be visible. Can we can get away with it.

A milled field. My document has no validity. They will have to be rid of me, or carry on as before. One arm has gone into administration (phantasms of the living). The swimming black thing seems to be an animal. You might as well do that now. It's a pleasant evening for spare parts.
Derivation is obscure. The mother is described as Janiform, perhaps wrongly.

They return. It's mutating. The mind offers no selection. Inertia is punctuated by spasm. I would not spend again such a night.
And all the parodies on offer, naturally. The sonic world was completely transformed.

Shadow of wing. They leave and they return. Several of the states have had to be reinvented. One hovers behind my neck. You plead for small mercies.

514

Cross the threshold, enter. It was an enormous cavern of intersecting corridors. (He was once uttered the god of doors.) Years pass, years. This seems to happen every day. The head peters out. See to it and don't forget.

Without cap, a sea abounding in islands. Something sinister was found. Unseeded, hence a group.

Key scenes and dialogue. I'm going back the way you predicted. The world is set adrift within vast mental frameworks. Colours were arranged in random order to evoke a sense of action. Through shattered glass a handful of us crawled back into the building. There's a new school of thought, room for half measures. Listen to the wind pouring through that fleshy outcrop.

In the grounds, a maze. The electrodes were attached to the aforementioned amphibian. The limbic fissure.

Neural tic at junction of arm and torso, tattoo left back. Here at sleep's anteroom suggestibility is infinite. This is a safe vantage point. A bird pecks daintily at the remainder. All the stones were arranged to form unreliable quotes (mortal reef descends et cetera).
Of rave, to wandered. We slit them open.

The grove of cedar trees. Here's a contract for you to sign. A toothless specimen passes. Throughout that year notes were collected. He is beside himself: the spattered baize, the dissent.
Just an observation. We spoke too soon.

For all the possession, there is a gap inside my malice. Chemical residues are worming at her memory. (Who was post-neural?) She stares at the sun until it blinds her.
It remains. Use the interpretations.
That Gloucester was decapitated. The dispersal of error is the initial step, the opening gambit. I predicted that two of the buildings would be plunged into darkness. There is a sound as of the rending of garments. It recedes. Touch me, cure.

Of oblique intersecting lines. Ephemeris time.
This schema reads far better than the old number. We are entering the final stages. The remains were eaten, doucets and junket for the worm. The password is the, which leads to mortal confusion.

It emphasizes movement. Indeed, but the head lives on. They constituted the political leadership of anything up to five hundred patients. With pharynx choked, clotting is inevitable. Who first discovered radio interference coming from the stairs?

What a veneer. Choose as I might, events were foretold. A tooth has fractured. This is a good place to stop.

Just an observation.

The view from the crow's nest. We have existing relics of the great confinement. Consider the sheer amount of stuff that had to be roped to him. We are engaging the unlikely. The slaying was arranged on their behalf.

You'll never do it in time.

A man returns to a town. A siren wails. We have various moments occurring simultaneously. Resonance inside the skull has been detected. Only the threshold is actually haunted. There's a dress code. There is a shattered bridge. Twice I was alumnus. Everyone has lost their memory. He encounters an obstacle he cannot pass, the issue of the heart. There were no bounds. I am discharged without notice. Electricity is crackling about the masthead. A changeling is concealed.

Challenging the array.

A new system of finger signs has been unearthed. Who or what is today's target? In the end, the heroine.

Lying stiff and motionless. Whiff of faeces rising from keyboard. Petrified literature. Next week we'll look ahead to her final years.

It should be eaten fist first. Sensations once filtered through the eyes and ears. (It should have been me.) I fed the animal a big blue tranquilizer.

Until pressed against pedestrian bodies. Uniformed assailants lift her off, the gentle. It retreats, erases.

Clucking impressions. A big decision, a major disease—copies of the first draft of a tract. Members of the committee for occupation were thrown from the window. Too hearing were they, mostly a while.

One time, in the village of saint. There's so much mathematics here it could double as an adding machine. What do you mean, they.

It quietly draws everything into its body. Halfway through the season the mascot was boiled down for glue. Then the first reports of outside arrived. They torched the keep.

A classical question. Document with pendent seals. In some ways it's better this way. His is not an incarnate programme.

Five thousand people in the auditorium emitted a collective gasp. The outer tissues rapidly atrophied until they disappeared altogether. I have conducted such places, straight into the grave.

It has to be based on some kind of objective test. (What context lies beneath you.) The chemistry is right. It's improvisation if you don't make plans. You cannot label the unfortunate. It grew into a name. It may disassemble itself. I will meet you at the other end. And if he is to reach the summit?

Shadow of ankh across wall. Don't forget you are just starting out. The following are examples. If you place two together in a confined space they will breed. The insurrection took place through the agency of magic. It intrigues me how they can totally transform someone's mouth. That's all I know. I am among those. What if we knocked a hole through the brickwork? It can't be opera because nothing happens.

Consider the two fingers of a hand. (You will need a silencer.) My next project is called schemes of derision. The rig was set vertically in the sea with floats and sinkers.

We stood apart and remained speechless. The drones are simply unmanned missiles. I am wary of my own reflection. The land contains empty spaces and hollows. Divination by inspection of water in a basin is advised. It's like a vast retail outlet. All this speaks of a passing into and out of the mouth.

Curious cross currents in the pulse. Descent in scales. Gradually all the detail evaporates, the eternal register.
Suspension of time. He tots up the record. Some among them are thousands of old. Being is never accounted for—I can write standing up, walking around. Now I drop to squat. It hit four times the speed of gravity.

A morbid hunger. Two of the buildings suddenly go dark. Imports include cordite.
Across the river and into the trees. (Are there abstract.) Body slumps to pavement.

A fantastic speculum. Each character is determined—it depends what type of aerial you've been receiving. Do you think we should give that obscure port a name? I feel the vibration of a boat. (Did you just breathe.) The disease is spreading from the east. She is here, and now she is not here. There's a violent hardcore. In the end the subject was smothered. We ventured out to search for flat stones.

Fleeting impressions, clashes at daily life. Ephemera and hurrygraphs were my forte. This lasted about ten years before it was abandoned. Some of the alphabets were contaminated.

It lay in wait. I was much younger. Reading is impossible. These tricks drive me mad. I fixed the time and the place, all recognizable events (incendiarism, the poison cup). I paid dearly. A flap of mucous membrane was stretched taut across the orifice.

Still, it's a beautiful island. Who was declared petroleuse for the day? We had our own duty machine and a book of shares. He offers no comment. We three make quite a team. I ask him what is going on in the background. He refuses to say. An antique bone handle and potsherds were found.

The domestic tort. One of the most squalid pieces of light and shade imaginable. Far off, the keen of a foghorn—bury me standing et cetera. At the apex there are ruins. Some paragraphs demonstrate abrupt changes of style.
Trout hovering in light-stained water. Assassin.

Tracing the history of the other senses will prove more difficult. Nerves are unsheathed and put to the torch. A pool spread out from under the container. The carpet was yellow. One surface is no longer in contact. I am inside. Words are becoming less and less necessary. Everything happens at once, at once.

Hermit cell. Familiar tightness bursting in chest. The ligament between the valves has snapped. Having two separate singularities, a vacuum can survive outside of itself.

A bittersweet little morsel.
The glass box touched the bottom of the sea. Some had axes, some had saws, some had hammers. I'm understood. A thin sheet of skin separates us from the surrounding space. The question is not what you looked like. A bunsen flame was applied, beneath.

Wide-where, dazzling white light. A trustworthy oration. At last the end, surcease. Where.

Somebody once fashioned an unreal. Anyway, there is the after, where more human happens. He says our relationship to objects has declined. (There never was nor can be et cetera.) This one has been labelled. I am delivering. The crime of wilfully infecting a body has been waived.

An attempt to review the current composition—enraged situations in the execution of every movement. You could both hear and see it. (I don't do fear.) The tip of the skull was visible just above the horizon line. I have placed some very real and tangible things inside the world. In the middle distance a tornado is forming. The report says eagle nebula is a stellar nursery. So, a tendency toward dissent. He was economizing.

A trance-like quantity. She says I sometimes feel that sorrow acts as an impetus. The suspect underwent a series of interrogations at five a.m.

An assemblage of easily found items: a sinew, from knife, soundproof suite circa eighteen fifty. Things have been specially constructed for our nourishment. The money dried up. This subject once had good strong limbs and a brain on his shoulders.
Wings beating up the vertical shaft, then disaster and decline. Our margin had shrunk to nothing.

All these vague pieces have collected at the root. It's the gorgonization. The big star sets. After four years the suspect was arrested. Sheets of the score twisted in the wind. I sold my ticket to the unknown man.

A typical routine is marked by habit and impatience. Everything is coming this way, forever. The town woke to find a tree washed up on the quay and a corpse. Himself is wearing a new straw hat, with rim broad for the sun. The sea is churning brutally. She tells herself. She enjoys the good things. A boulder crashes down the cliff and into the surf. I found myself in a strange cave. I took notes.
A figure clings to a rock at the edge. Have you noticed.

They are narrowly missed, yet unaware. Smoke drifts through the passages beneath the naze. I am as my name imports.

Atoms are oriented in parallel plains. She mortifies me. This leads to further prohibitions. It's like a signature move.

One could not refrain from the pleasure. We stand accused. The shore is obscured by sea-fog, the 'exhalant haar'. She whispers I can see you love being stationary. (Woe betide myself.) Being here doesn't appear to be made of anything—no remainder, not even a trace, just the usual mission accomplished message. Completion requires the participation of someone else in the mental process. We have misused some of the courtly forms, a plurality of ghosts.

It's encroaching. Bun licences were a hinge. The nose and lips were cut off. (We never seem able to reach any kind of decision.) I know all about your pyrotechnics. The whole organization has a hierarchy behind it—his look suggests petrol rather than literature. This indicates the return of an organ to a state. I will finish this tomorrow. They swell with pride and split open. This is another instance of repetition, with lung-flag, with tripwires.
Ha, now I'm king of all I witness. Touch me, myself. He dies et cetera. The end, or move two times seven steps.

A veil blurs the distance, sea drawn up to sky, or sky down to sea. There were no mathematic tables to guide anyone. This should be his opus number one, I think.

Found among his posthumous manuscripts.
The three protesting teams. We sought a neutral harbour. The frontier no longer exists. There are eight other planets in this system. (Neptune's there.) It's said they would read bogus stories for their own amusement.

Prized from a sealed deposit box in a bank vault.
One follows. They all resembled workmen. They are lost on the island. Arguments are voiced and will be heard.
Dog-headed men, a vast expense of salt water. There were as many as ten houses of perfect. If it had not been for a lucky recollection.

Exploding columns of water. Hymenlike membranous dissepiment. Listening to the wind murmuring through blue gauze.

It melted into dense tropical forest. A shouting of men began firing in volleys. We're looking at the future now with eyes wired open. The meter recorded static, paranoid dementia—black body bag with zipper, nervous and sensory organs normal. I once slipped from the causeway. There's a numeric aspect, you see, to the threshold of composition.

Some notes on one attitude toward impending disaster.
A neighbouring island, barren rock rising up out of the channel. It's silhouetted against the night sky. Any understanding corresponds to a progressive darkening of the picture. Work is being done on navigation signs. The selfsame wave is pounding into the selfsame gulley, then a sudden flowering as the head bursts open.

The screed, winding-sheet.
We formed ourselves into groups. There was always confusion as to the points of the compass. The basic rules of the game still stand at seventeen. The skin had flaked off. We made a pretense of welcoming him back. It's the following week. We're given ice to suck on. (It's a trick.) One boasts a tunic with an emblem stitched at the breast. The aim is to outmanoeuvre all reckoning. My palms were like open sores. One limb pointed toward the spectator.
Let's choose a more practical approach. On paper this looks like a one-sided myth. It has all the characteristics of a border town. (No, I'm not leaving.) Citizens have had to borrow names. Your presence here might be in the way. This appears to be a new generation. Someone or something had forced the door of the hermit's cell. What was flung clear?

Huge bodies of metal, with hiss from nose and mouth. One close by me speaks. You've been away a long time, haven't you? I prefer deserts to men. The evidence is contaminated. A razing knife could not have penetrated more deeply. Here is accident, in all its perverse senses. Pitch and oakum were scraped from the seams. We'll have to create something uncannily like a brain. I forgot to ask them to leave us some light. Have the murder suite ready, we may need the extra thirty percent.

Melancholic considerations of a general nature. The signs we are.
It's alive, but it's not thinking. When you smile you have those perfect. All this makes one reflect upon the erotic role of violence. Only a cloakroom ticket survived the conflagration.

Of that rattle in the lungs and other physical signs.
One of the phenomena of depression is the marathon trance. I work with the things I find in the world. This does not take as long as one might imagine: the inability to feel what the other.

Say a snowbound, morning. Here a lantern at least, there a pane of ice. An object once fell from the sky. The city has been rebuilt but is now uninhabited. (Herein is the authorized version.) Sea monsters made their appearance again after a long interval of absence. Part of the cell wall is the bare sandstone of the island. Each morning a considerable number of people were found to be missing. Logic can never be an organon of discovery.

Their stories are not consistent. The charge is 'muscular sacrilege'. This technique is known as the method of singing in parts. The only point of contention, if I remember, correctly.

Unweaving the *a b c* of his computations.
Objects have limited use. Neuter, with repeats in tort of stricture, voice exilic.

May-June, three p.m. to four p.m. Interred, about there. A possible ballot took place, but without reliable figures. He points an index. White circles with black lines all about. Exposure is outlawed beyond a certain light intensity. Their precepts and values were inverted. (See sense, above.) I have drawn objects into me, where they remain to this day.

Re the kite. Count backwards if you're not sure. Writing's difficult. Space can unravel. It envelopes. It unfurls itself from the skin outward. I am never busy. They have a camera on a hawk. I have informed a universe of error.

To lay level with the ground.

It can be collected and stored in an accumulator, or box. I am the subsequent misuse. I am that noise. On the other hand, the outer of the two bones stretched from knee to ankle. Note the symbolic red ship towering above the set.

He warned us not to be overly ambitious in our therapeutic effort. A shift has occurred.

Sudden glimpse of half-moon. He is opened up. Proceed piecemeal. I am not capable of bringing about another transformation in the image—say, the head of a bystander. Or a parental, circumnavigated.

Battle-earth undergoes a wondrous sea-change in this passage. There's a conciliatory catch herein. Am now writing of the everyday. Nothing of him that could fade remains behind. Have you spotted the offending fifths?

Letters arrived from nineteen thirty-seven. I had just reached the door when it struck. I am going for the plot variety, of incorporated. Vehicles are being adapted for landings in heavy seas. They have pulled the entire disc from memory. Everything is down to the inquest. I was hauled up to the first containment.

Use is illusory. I recant. People say its dna was built for such pursuits.

Explosive decompressions. Nonetheless, there's a lot of things happening around here that I don't fully understand.

This event, I'm standing on it right now. They have replaced the cones, victoria made shell. Candles guttering over names, inscribed. A parley of instruments. They can't stop you doing that inaudible.

It appears to be scanning for life forms. He prods one with his big toe. I hope it's not too early. It's the perfect storm. Out pops a number. Include these remarks in the rear future. It's alive but it's not thinking. I forgot to ask them to leave us some.

Every object in the room is found to be a perfect conductor of electricity. Will this never end. One word we're going to keep hearing is commiseration. Could I have done much more that day? Another is cooperation—they are not their own consumers et cetera. Listen, this character armouring is the basis of all isolation. I have hit upon the far-reaching connection between some present-day formations.

Such offshore traditions. He is always clad and wears a powder-blue cloak as an outer garment. (Is it that he yearns to be alone once more.) It's a kind of an endgame, an exchequer. There's even been a reference to history today. The tank itself never materialized.

Describe is nature.

A change wrought by sea, the rattle of beetles. They gave everyone a code name. That distant glow is molten rock rising up from under the surface. The skin consists of an outer wall of organic material, wood or cellotex.

In which passepartout.

An explosive expert. Part of the territory is unpeopled. Who finds himself in the odd place? We space. (Think of it as fiscal karma.) Who is the one accused? I have read of this cartilage thief. The device is a gilded hawk with shadow. First, he is copied. How do we know he died in fifteen seventy-nine.

It was tracked by the silver disc. We docked elsewhere. It's believed he speaks of himself. Everyone else wishes to remain redundant. An auction is held for up to ten thousand. (Three of our number died.) Someone has done something to the nail, too.

Arbitrary disassociations are being developed. The eldest son must collect the ashes and any surviving vertebrae. Reports of fighting in the suburbs. You couldn't have made it up. In my house we drink out of your head.

Street scene, the morning. Those were the days. Events such as the majestic collision were caught on film. In short, we could not restrain ourselves. I recorded the events. Start time as per usual, light from the unnumbered.

Spirited away to a building the size of a city. The entire population has been cautioned for simulation. Will she ever come back some say no.

A low mound of soft grass rises from the flat plain. Or perhaps, rivers of grass furrow the flat plain like an animal. Align the nose with the apex. All of the clues cluster together in one place. What motion has the earth thought she. Ancestors issue from fissures in the incline.

Unusually livid blue flowers, typical of the family. Under the shingle, the beach—naze obscured by distance. Twister incoming, fire sales et cetera. Uncertain stalagmites, stalactites.

Two of the oxygen molecules have cut loose. I feel the oarsmen plough by. Now I have an interval all to myself. Maybe omen is absent, void. They were ambushed and held hostage. Can I watch. (Sure, okay.)

Toward a molten core. A brief account of the history of lexicography.

Disputed men, turning. Rumours of Baedeker raids. Landfill. There is no place in their ample kit. Sprinklers line the perimeter fence to dampen the smouldering waste. It is now four. When a word answering another is not expressed, an incoherence occurs. Now it is five. Some of these climaxes are unconvincing. It was a synonym for guide, that slight baffle. I received.

I could fold. Bury it with the skull pointing downwards. All engagements are forthwith cancelled. (She is renowned for her bacon.) There was no magic involved. A sense of dislocation and exile clings. We stepped into the same river twice. There's no doubt where you come from. Of whose bones are coral made? The subject is vomiting blood. We are not going anywhere, specific.

She says you translate every situation using the same old codes. The surface is pitted. Thanks to the clear glass sides they had human bodies and the heads. (But what can you see.) The satellite has been nudged into a decaying orbit. There are vessels of policement.

He is appointed, weathered eye out. There's a third man. We are immune, a very old public. Our work is to incomplete. We are listening. In time we unearth. An upstairs room was set aside to install the finished piece. (Do you even remember writing this.) We built two parallel lines on the floor that continued until they met the wall. Cut yourself loose from the organism.

Becoming hollowed, trickle-down in drops, or threaten to pull out altogether. A powder-blue mantle served as an outer garment. Iron-perfect. I have said that.

By the middle of the month it was declared dead. All change. North and east are now the cardinal points. An ebullient allegro can erupt. The result is the large-scale. There is much discussion as we set about our task. Theft of the image has corroded the social fabric. Quickly, my dear.

There was once a young lad who didn't know that everybody called him. Then an agent burst in holding a gas-powered pistol. I seized the cornerstone of a dictionary.

Our work complete we descended to the surface. Turn everything off. Urine had stained black the flagstone floor. An exchange is taking place. One arm bears a bruise, the uncanny stripe. The subject hangs upside down. We have worked together all over the world. One major influence is other planets. The silence is contaminated, all his manuscripts—the patterns that passing vessels trace in the darkness. This is the rock that everyone has been speaking of.
An escutcheon, saltire engrailed gules. Strictland in isthmus.

The sapless foliage of the oceans et cetera. Detail: a partition cut through the nave. The third man is still here. That thing is bivalve. This is a happy accident of good timing and open space. A sticky resin flows. He tells me of the reverence.

It pitched its body against the core, gripped in tight formation. We are accused. Worse things happen at sea. Substance is released into the brain at the same time.

They have a lady sleeping, and a pig. A flame was seen licking about the back yard. Day-to-day, I am genuinely transfixed. He never paid for a ticket, always opting for levitation.

The cold of interstellar. Yards of black lace floating in the darkness. He was ranked under for many years. I have cauterized an artery. (He means it.) Things have the usual properties.

That was once a singularity. I close my eyes, turn to face the nearest object.

A list of the one hundred most influential people ever noticed.

Re-entering the public. Very slowly the face comes into focus. Somebody points at my chest. He continues his letter after gazing once more. I look down into the street. The person under surveillance is wearing a brooch in the shape of a bird of prey. You will know him.

Do what has to be done, but no bruising, please. Operations are meticulously calculated.

The lights flare and dim as the power surges and ebbs. Whiff of petrol rag. More news of news, the barrel in the body.

Give me your word. A misfire, indictment for mayhem. The number printed on the lozenge is fifty-two.

It never achieves family. I am with a tall unknown in a brilliant white. Tomorrow big changes are the prospect. We seem to be competing for the same transgression. He's said to be the founder. An assailant stood at the console, typing.

An opportunity.

Place the object in the angle where two walls meet. Things have become compacted. It is part of a set, every surface. (Never done that before.) A light brown fell stood out very clearly. The walls are damp. Hairwork mortar separates the bricks, a fine and delicate skin wherewith seeds are inclosed.

A mix of copper, lower case. Numbers and signs are blent in a continuous stream. I peer over his shoulder. Part of the letter reads one short sleep and we are past.

Inhibition of photosynthesis. It divides itself. Star-shaped corpuscle, no next of kin.

One crouches low. Another exhales across my lowered lids. The situation has stabilized. Blue clouds mask the light. There is pillage. I've got a veto. What do you need to do, nothing? We are in the midst of a countryman.

A deeply personal eulogy. This constitutes. Incredible rumours are circulating. One has vanished. As fast as they dried out we strung them up.

Out of root, off to leap. The affects of exile, a number of sundry disparities. It got lost in the dimness. There are two others. Its flesh tasted sour. Any name is an epithet of a division, the fermentation. (It would be much quicker doing this from the bottom up.) Sticky cobwebs span the trees and cut across our path. The realm is much confused. Every fiction is erotic. He's discredited now, but he'll be back.

Blank page. You can't be too careful. The patient shook, as if.

Brief, in praise of slowness. Weals rise. A primitive cell developed—sudden paralysis, endless dog-days. Who loses a finger, the index? Another word for this is tapis. Overwrought with figures, far off, the hail.

Set out on your own to find something undisclosed. Gesture direction. You can't use metaphors of space or things to describe paintings. This is not how objects used to function. I forgot to leave a marker. One star observed moves rapidly in a great arc. You don't need much before events start to add up. I found a discarded blanket. I found a letter. A consecration is taking place—imagine a vast building the size of a city. Rooms lead off. Some structures have different levels. The man was moving northeast when it happened. Everything is deserted. Glimpses of daylight are often ignored. A dense sea-fog rolls in. I have crossed many a stairwell. Look, I have passed through a door. (Sense the presence of people, behind and in front.) Turn and go back. The inspector had an air of indifference. I once spoke to a group of four. In the fullness of time we came to a fork. One carries a briefcase. Lift cage ascending, we talk. I'm told the numbering is esoteric. All the metallic parts are upside down. Some things can't be resisted. Try to understand the subordinate rank occupied by displacement. The number turns loose. They presume. I was once a radiant too. This is a place without place, where three roads meet. Everyone wonders how I can afford. They wonder whether or not. They accept. I don't know which one. O yes, I was asking you about your account of what happened that day.

It feeds straight back into itself. Imagine a family of interrelated rocks. I think I'll join you all at high table. This seems a good place to shut up shop. The living dead have no fear of fire.

Brief satire. When they drop an anywhere bomb we will burn their factories et cetera. Come on home he says. Then we just walked away. I wonder whether support is required. He is full of yedders and wounds. I want to check that.

A discouragement of skin, perhaps original. And the stolen name?

One has disappeared. Perhaps a clear and naked place. Remember to go back after this.

Exit form. And much later, climbing a hill of cooling lava, glittering boulders piled about the base. Stillborn to touch.

A message to a friend in a distant part of the galaxy. I'll know it when I see it.

He has done some truly amazing work on optimism. The ever-pressing moment is the only mode of actual. I'm guilty of randomly opening the book in the same place again and again. Target some more convincing kills.

The whiteness, the statuesque quality of the motionless figure, beyond. Mourning is stunning. Just follow these simple rules.

It's always a risk. They made a decision based on what they could actually see. That's been the pattern for today. She has been to a place you can't possibly imagine. It takes years of work. In the meantime, a grid has drowned.

The causeway. Giant. How things might have been. His posture is exactly like that of the man in the portrait. An imposed yoke would give everyone a little boost right now, any wilful constraint.

A document, chains of carbon atoms with hydrogen coupled. Articles of clay. One man had the power to expel calculi from his kidney by will power alone.

This work involves a shooting contest. One of the suitors is hurled into a ravine. Coarse sand, mud and silt are embedded in the deeper strata. A normal is made up of an aggregate of ephemeral bodies. It all ends on a rash of optimism.

Whispers of smoke curl up from the embers. That depression in the land is like a concrete saucer. The gatekeeper's name can't be released. It's said the final state is the state of not seeing (but some clever conducting). There is continuous wave action. The stone used is an intuitive igneous.

Navigate by observing the path of the sun across the sky. The trick is to imagine you're a rock, viz. his doctrine that the world lies opposite. It gives rise to hexagonals, a row of shadows cast by a colonnade.

Lift is broken. The compass is useless. I will not need.

Live feed from the remote. Avoid tact with any bodily fluids. This is somehow quite consistent. I am closer. (He needs to start showing the roots of a technique here.) A passerby stoops to tell me where I am. Sound advice is offered. He says I do not rehearse all the angles.

Interlocking crystals of three types. (Where I am going wrong.) Persistence of subject now irrefutable. It's said they come at night. Some are concentrated in beds, to the exclusion of matter. The sun sets through that open doorway. Below the lintel someone had sprinkled blood.

It often occurs as a large outermost, discord. Today's theme encompasses dikes, necks, stocks and bosses. The skin is laced with threads of wax to form a pattern. She says I want that gash on the blanched arm.

An oblong of elongated light was sucked into the room and crept up the wall. When we first met she had just fled. These people are at opposite ends of a journey. Everything needs replacing. I occur seldom, but always tenderly.

An intrusive body has been detected beneath the surface. Crackle of bone corpuscule, ceaseless practise.

It is said to mean white wood. It withdraws into itself. A hollow was created for moisture to seep in. I can prevent all this from happening—existence without any visible foundation, hence.

Eye-shaped masses of feldspar or quartz. Static, for reasons of dramatic expedience. The first public was faked. An attic at the top of the turret has been set aside. An arrangement should be carefully considered.

Formation is triggered by the nuclei. In the darkness under the bridge the bare ground is carved by rainwash. A coloured flare was fired from a pistol. We are now being held within something else, an unfamiliar tune, colossal repetitions.

Without looking the concierge pressed a button under the desk flap. We are in league.

Topography. Steep-streeted ridges and valleys. Still not sorted on the powers. My neck, my tongue, shall never be carried away. These axes have an indefinite relationship to earlier and later. There's to be a century revival. The crust is deformed. At the frontier he answers (petty thief by necessity, assassin by vocation). Note that *representations* are also required. A route is being mapped out across the surface. Nothing is almost. I must have miscounted. So much for theory.

Finally, vowels were treated as the most fluid and unstable elements of any tongue. Keeling over from a smart blow, secured by tight bindings.

What could I have done to foresee what happened. Agitation acts as a sorting mechanism. You've got smaller versions of this graphic in your pocket.

An approaching motor, outboard.

Femoral artery severed. A partition serves to quarantine the base.

Iron foundry. One moment your defending your temple, the next your ankle, your groin, your chest. Staff thrust out, I hum, madly. It has been suggested. A lack of prejudice within the system was at work. Everybody suddenly starts to shift position. Time could be the nineteen twenties. We are struggling to manage a deficiency. You must have a threat going forward.

Slow moments filmed from above. Disease is making a comeback, after years of inertia. Curiosity, an eternity of substitutions.

Strange tracks have been found in the snow on the mountain. You are now in possession. What will you do with it. You are now out of possession. Diet consists of residues. There is no need of compass or almanac. Behind bolsters the north, the last of the landslip. (Persons of his calling are subject to quakes.) The o two tanks have ruptured.

It casts a shadow that cuts in two. Bedroom farce, innumerable barriers of light. I was cemented by some interstitial material.

A large dome-shaped mess, the float-boards of an undershot keel. Crystallization takes place at great altitude. But I'm the one upon whom everything depends, the actionable.

Caption or arrest. Relegation of breathing to a leisure pursuit. Section: rock drill. I am hedged in, fenced. A sits at Z's door, without intention. The earliest traces go back to back. It's a sort of house arrest. Use his earth-name. He is being questioned as to his whereabouts at the time of the incident.

Think in particular about measurement and volume. It is not wrong. You know everything. It's the uncertainty issue. (Does it resound, the same, when collecting?) Memory doesn't mean to. It has grown from the fluids trapped in space. Unfurling foliage, discharge.

Defused throughout the east, one of the burdens upon the land. Adopt an arched position by planting feet and hands on the earth and convexing the spine. A pool of fresh water should collect in the rocky hollow beneath. Sound has snapped, the horizon slicing heads. It entered my nervous system and stayed. He has begun the evaluation of his analytical findings. One is compelled to yell out nothing nothing nothing, just the ness of the spectacle.

A moss garden. Spokesmen conjoined at navel. We were given scant notice. This something out of the common proves to be an invasion.

He rends the book, slicing free its pages. Does this immediate historic occasion cover the malcontents of every tragedy? (You're screwed if you want to buy a big item.) He will stay for a little longer. We have transferred the entirety.

It jumps around. There's a whole new arsenal of picturesque punishments. A stranger may arose your disgust. Energy must be released for a short time now and again. This is an ancient word. I have been caught in the act of restraint. (I can fail.) Excise *that* particular body. The options are to remain discreet or hire an assassin. One could always lose one's footing and fall. Another beats time with a stave. I could reflect. I have lived in worse economies. And there I remained, without once breaking my fast. It can encompass any idea. The label states.

An incorporeal, an unmade.
Since time I have received a lot of mail from some very estranged and deluded people. The surface is tough and inelastic. I have turned away from myself.
In the collective sense, it's like a body of law. I could always negate. We are forthwith severing our apprenticeships.

He arrived suddenly in the year. The larvae are ripening into wormhood. A vessel is drifting into deep space. Out in the regions there are no compulsories. (I said calm down.) Gas enters via the animal's olfactory canal.
A manicured lawn. Recognizable words may emerge. How will you act.

Hermanaut. Trial by serinette. Hootchy equals kootchy, actually. (Stop it.)
A thick layer of permafrost. One writes that he is now become old. A sudden drop in temperature alerted us. I have only just encroached upon the territory. Pillars surmounted by heads punctuate the landscape. These serve the purpose of navigation.
The careful placement of books is popular. Artifice has replaced the natural organ. Remind him.

Swampy, organic and alive. Nascent. The mouth is full of feathers. She asked which direction I should forsake. This is among the brightest and youngest clusters known to man. Fling the sack over your shoulder and carry it. (Three of the brothers are no longer.) It might be the long walk, after all, in the fullness of time.

Effluence and self are signified, surely. Nothing is in the order one would expect. Mind reads zero four. Which isn't random, then, is it.

On those who have left something behind, the years without hands or feet. And what have we apart. I contributed little to the state. All the others appear to be female or male.

Backwater. Primordials without lateral relation. All evidence is to the contrary. I pass the guards. Communication is only possible in a vertical direction. A centre of gravity has been achieved, an economic. He was in on the act.

Residua born in sac, secreted. Organ inert. I am detected. Work develops rapidly (avoid gerunds). Now let me show you, exemplar of all operatives. I could lose. Go back to the injuries, list them in detail. Refer to his early works on the neural stem.

I could always renegotiate. Everything is composed of these six elements. A discolouration of the skin is the cause.

The morning after. Because I was thinking about it only yesterday, the cinema. (That did not evince approving sighs.) What misanthropy.

A-frame winding gear. Malign influence of planet or star. It feels premature to start cutting corners, cupcake. This requirement is not a matter on which a philosopher should pronounce. I myself made an arch. Each chemical combines with its receptor. Drystone walls and five-bar gates were also constructed. Rubble can collect in the street, the shred of a stocking. Everything shrunken, severed.

Simony. A vacuum in pleadership. For convenience, that which fails is called the agonist and its vanquisher the antagonist. Use any untranslated signature. Rocks are sometimes taken as a symbol of permanence and stability.

Fresh from the topics, interlaced. An old friend scrubs the germs out and examines it under the microscope. Yes, if you've enslaved, the poisoned choral. The object resembles wood but is not.

Undercut with tireless and heavy, in the midst of it all. Still he writes, and quite of a sudden.

Dear, get rid of the chairs. Get rid of all the furniture. Operate without exception—phonetic exchange, the laws of sound et cetera. I have little or no talent. I have been twinned with an innate stillborn. You work with words and images. The laws of space and interlude are fragile concepts. It's not the worst of crimes. I come with brittle merchandise: amalgam and copper, wire and string. There is no reason. Just thought I'd check up on some of the old places before they fade for good. I have little or no intent. The enemy has dug a counterscarp. Substance is distilled from mountain gentian. It was a graceful bird of prey I saw in flight. Interiority is a movable feast. I have purchased an extra ten. I seek to bring about. Leaves lay sodden in the rain and the wind drives across the big green. I have purchased an arm of land. Subtle modes of censorship are being invented. Vowels are to be arranged in strict patterns. An early form appears set to return. There has been an error. Organic acid insists at my root. The culminating point of any drama is always the combat. At times company is craved. I have made use of your ruins, and surpassed you.

The follicles are so deep and thick its fur resembles a balaclava. It acts as a cornerstone, obviously.

A thief's journal. Divination by diffusion. I tell you it was his voice, the pillage. He died on this day in the seventeenth round. The trick I use is to imagine you're a pebble on a shingle beach. It was a mark of wonder. Payment was extorted. I crouched in vigil at his door. No one is interested in presenting the story as social-realism.

Decoy runners drumming down the centre. That huge metal slamming shut. The subject was handcuffed to the pipework. For twenty years I lived in a crate. Tungsten lamps flood the entrance at night. Only the left eye remains. The idea is to generate an atmosphere of acute unease. He insisted that I stood up for the entire journey. Gas canisters were spent.

Objects must be arranged in a strict hierarchical framework. Terrain now visible, erosion of surface strata into varied and fantastic forms. It had spores.

Because you can't always be there. Spell me the word for starlet please, in upper case. Beams of light pierce through the wall to the interior. The blind unknot any knots in the weave, working with rapid fingers. Explanatory comments were found. Does that guttering candle indicate your presence? I want to say that Z-frame winding gear is essential. The tiny heads of assistants pop up through the warp and weft. Their role is unclear. Others have affirmed that albion is a sea word, a refusal. They have a man showing his cleft to various apes and suchlike—tremors in radix, wars of libation. This symbolizes I don't. Whither will you go, now.

Notes, and I, likewise. Mars, Venus, the Sun, a Moon. Also the back of an unknown—a deserted landscape and the planet foreshore. More remarks on the-answer-is-yes. It consisted of territory, I imagine.

He accepts way too many. I could have dismantled. Yes is agony. Don't remain here too long. Remember to move your limbs from time to time. I could have had everything I desired. In the corner of the room was a mound, memorized speech. He says there once was, and I pursue. (I am talking to you right now.) This could be the perfect moment of suture. South is the slice of light at the horizon.

A deep depression in the bunker. I could possess. The larger of two entities conjoined is commonly used as a blanket. I was not made with reference to other nations. It has been dead and it is coming alive. Encompass and describe both states. I await the judgement of a higher authority.

Some notes on the common bandit.

The one who first spoke has to move on, with haste. Disregard the lack of a theme. You have become embroiled in some real-life situations. You have no real dialogue. I could only withdraw, fill the vacancy. I may not need your forgiveness. A body was washed up. Such and such is no longer the case. What follows are the remaining controls, a few relics.

Calling out to me, this is no masque, or something.

A forest of signs painted different shades of red. She takes him by the hand. The rules only apply outside the circle. Matters are acknowledged by public opinion, however introduced. The latest craze is salt. There's no need for the cuffs he says.

An imaginary country was invented as a child. They disconnected the motor and winched him up to a vacuum. Something lies close to the edge, an undisclosed. By one a.m. the occupation had printed the final draft.

Retailed as a life at rest. It is frequently found in places remote in space and indistinct of purpose. The status is hobby, or not. He has left his mark, a brackish taste on the tongue.

Oblique winter sunlight. They are at the frozen apex. One carries an objection. But we were moving, moving all the time. Another died of exposure (picture him in that grey trenchcoat). Cobble can be uprooted.

The figures expand to become a set of six. The animal's flesh is then diced. The incident took place at a planetary cusp. Note how he is struggling against the dead weight.

This method of composition is absurdly convoluted. Rivulets of petrol trickle across the pavement.

Ate of coin. Upright, advantageous in immaterial circumstance. A turning. Everything depends on this. His bloodied finger turns the oily propeller, see.

A straight shaft of light. An area around a poison in which the privileged were allowed to live. This could stand alone.

Beside an ocean. This man faces extinction. The backdrop is a wall of camouflage netting. (What is the relationship between the two hands?) Beyond, a flock of migrating birds in flight. He is strapped to an empty oil drum. Green, white and azure predominate. We rapidly withdraw as a spasm passes through the body. This tableau ends with one of my rare reactions.

Work goes on within surviving cadres. No news of the others. He could be here already. They will have to do the rest with their bare teeth. I have invoked a sequence of errors, of attributing a song to the wrong head. They are just that, presented in the form of dialogues.

A star-shaped cellular structure in the central nervous. Some people can see things that haven't happened. Go, reprimand him.
It had its own maps. It had its own rivers and valleys. It had its own hamlets and villages.

Aslant, and its equivalents. The deadline runs out in three hours. Pillars of plutonic rock stand high in the landscape. Mass is signified. Every note counts. There were no survivors to mourn, actually.

Here is no backdrop to speak of. In the foreground is a wooden frame in the shape of a capital letter. Beyond, a breakwater, an array of undetermined forms. (Can't you talk to him.) This is not a simple place. You will let me know if anything else is happening, won't you? You were once entrusted in the field, barren tundra.
Still looking for him yes.
Excuse me. I was trying to remember something.
I came in by accident. (Hand sinister.)
Who was he, I mean is. Can't you talk him down.

Elsewhere. An escape, and even its own language.
Bodies are good for hiding in. That said, people disappear every day.
Badland erosion, pressganged tightly into curve of wall.

XXX

The theme of tragedy is sweet from the very start. Meeting in the middle of the desert always made me nervous. (Four hours or so of catatonic despair.) The voice here belongs to one who murmurs. Numerous concordances are in collision. We're dug in below the mountain. This chapter is quite short. This chapter is about donating a heart to the deceased.

Sound was like the eighteen eighties. A tight band of skin circumscribed the head. They have packaged me out. So far this is the only time I've ever done. When two men are in a situation, the role of one will always be unique. I want this fact double or triple-checked.

He moves about inside her, assumes every atom of the space she embodies. We are undertaking a solemn ceremony. The dialogue is graphic. A man is forbidden—self-assassination and suchlike. Well, I said, that's a most impressive argument. I wonder if you're right. Who was frozen in time? The form of insanity under analysis harbours great loquacity, parole and the fabulous things, composite beasts.

They are formed. They have adopted an attack formation forty paces in front of the centre, in two ranks facing the opposing line. A technique of random disassociation, sometimes in foreign forms, is returning to haunt us. Resort to a source. I am underemployed.

Tauromachy, theatrical modes of combat. Second of the division of signs. It says he likes travelling, movement, change. Interest in my possibilities has been generated. A good deal has been gained through the modern that is taking place. Construction of the collar is in two hinged halves, adapted to lock together. The machine does not forebear motion of any kind. He says I feel funny all over. A flux is also referred to as haemorrhage. Now he is interrupting himself for purely aesthetic effect.

With unusual force a wave struck the foreshore at that very instant. Time, pleasure and distillation are at hand. Power is being transferred.

This chapter is without a vignette. Imitative works are the principle cause of the falling away of our support. (Or perhaps it's disbelief at this manifesting itself as such a vaunted cultural artefact as a book.) However, see subsequent critical accounts of the doctrine. The very first step always defines the project. Take me over. I am a useless piece of flesh. How is that possible.

In this account there's no messing about—no stage, no costumes, no acting. When the novel is dead the totalitarian society will be technically upon us. The principal theme is longing, both sacred and romantic. It was so refreshing. He says being immobile for a season did him the world of good. (This is where we begin the long walk back to solitude.) Playing the organ must be a similar sensation. We were little more than coded embers, long-dead stars. I found that rather poetic. There were unofficial mergers. Simple laws of physics governed the origin, an alloy of nickel and iron.

I hope no one has died. We're no longer picking up conversation. We are no longer connected: the proverbial smoke-screen, a taut veil across a bodily orifice. It's all about momentum at this stage, that lingering fear of expulsion.

See how I've titled them, neatly laid out in rows like a ploughed field. Once again a perfectly decent arena of investigation has been spurned. Suddenly, without knowing why, someone feels guilty.

The site of the battle, seen from the island facing east across the mainland. It's like Salamis all over again. There is a causeway, a ridge of mountains on the skyline, sundry expansions and derangements. Complex alignments have been set in motion. (Cancer rising, ascendant.) They want physical conflict and love the feeling of soft, luxurious metals. Nonetheless, the image is fading. All the evidence evaporates. Meanwhile a storm has wracked. And there, surely, not I.

A trigger at brief intervals of time. I am committed to memory. This reconstruction is a precise account of what was actually said that day. The body was rediscovered mid-century. Who had himself translated into a set of fictions? (Bring me the head et cetera.) It's believed, and the belief is universal, that this is the work of mercury. He has a great sense of observation and quickly grasps the situation. I doubt whether he knows what time he was born. I wish I had said that now. More acute, more enterprising knowledge flares up—or descends, disseminates like a shooting star. Consequences are rare. I am inclined to list—anything fractured, chanceful, convalescent. I have no wish to learn your name.

This needs more work. It's become unwieldy. Being a Friday, an inventory of the stolen titles is required. (Upper case, font shrunk to eleven.) The rest is easy.

ALLOTMENT

It occupies a special place in the pantheon. Picture a sort of bathroom with crumbling tilework, a something to which one cannot return. We've been through a lot of vicissitudes to get where we are today. Nonetheless, it is pleasing to the voice. It is pressing in the ear. It is damaged in the tongue. (I can tell you.) The surrounding space has been split open. This influences everything that later unfolds. Emotionally, he understands nothing. I have set out at speed in an easterly direction. The correct number is six. When I made her laugh it came straight back out again.

ALLSEED

A spore discharged by various plants, and producing a great quantity of names. Often a book can be a literal translation of the genus or species, i.e. his wintergarden.

ALMISTRY

No comment. The momentum vanished for a second. Get a reliable. We really need to start eating into this. It's impossible to run on shingle. What is it that would satisfy the crowd here today? I have placed them in a folder called heads. Wilful vagueness still persists. I am begging for alms. Increase the frequency to twelve leptons. Set sail. Vouch for each other's inconstancy. (Present yourself.) Individual investigators are scattered right across the globe. This will energize the search-coil, and in time the precision. In all degree be evermore—lastage, stiller and longer. At this point there's always one contestant who drops from an apparent position of safety.

BATTLE ARRAYS

Flickering depictions of the severed, siblings and parentals. Its physical perfection is only matched by its hostility. Erase all meaning, a rebellion and such like. I lost mine when I was a child. It was a massacre on superstition mountain. Come home. Of course I am.

THE BEES

Where's the verdict. We are concerned here with the actual linguistic behaviour of the animal. (Yes me too.) The incident took place in a deluge. It was night with taxis roaming the slick streets. There's a smear of old tippex on the page. The trigger is your withdrawal, coupled with a visitation. By this I mean an apparition. They compassed about me like a swarm. I'm in no peculiar hurry. The title of the encore is apt: an impromptu, warlike. Us, we are arranged in three ranks. I've never given much thought to how I would die. The vibrations have ceased.

BIVOUAC

I'll go screaming through the streets. Up on the roof with young blood. I am in, I am. This takes me back to myself, my pet subjunctive. This is the first patch of ten minutes, heavy and tenacious. I am counted among the missing. (Who introduced chance into the proposal?) He could manage no more than two or three steps before he fell. I am still counted among the living. The man's hands are thrust deep into the pockets of his bomber jacket. (I too have read the debacle.) He is walking off, struggling. They brought with them an excess. You can feel the tension groaning under the arc lamps—we will just have to see how this pans out. The object was the consistency and colour of liver. He is almost too keen. Execution is always individual. There is a wall of yellow in front of me. I can't guarantee what state you'll be in when they've finished with you. They split his throat. I shall call this executive tide *speaking*. It is passing out of use. I have never seen this happen before. Death will certainly be in a foreign land or on a journey abroad. Out pops an eye. I am drawing on back copies of rootstock. Unfortunately, I am capable of love.

BLOODGRAFT

Embers of silk, your heat alone et cetera. Seconds of delirium. A blank book, excess voltage—the lip or edge, a new strain of shock. (You don't have to decide right now.) She is observing us from outside the box. If you were still on the case, how would *you* have tracked her down. She says I have observed you at the automat, the whole world sees you. This part proves to be the final piece of the jigsaw. I am tarred and feathered. I soar up and fly over, as the distinct before. Avoid inflicting the same punishments said M—splintered triremes on the beach, the clatter of fractured oars, the sweat of the galley slaves. The text is characterized by stagecraft, subtlety, and relentless criticism. Select a phrase at random (the liquid being at different levels on the two sides).

CATACLYSM

First, he sets his victims aside to be admired—if it's not this one it's that one and so on. Good God, how right he is when he tells us on the page of his confession. Study the organization of plants. Follow the intricate working of these living mechanisms. Then he has their bodies opened up. There's always a core of uranium. It's said he playfully assumed the posture of a ghost. In September the infant was baptized. After the break-up only a single deity remained. Her worshippers multiplied. What I want above all is to destroy the idea of culture. It feels like I've been here before. Succeed is only occasionally (by holding his two hands loosely in front of himself). The plug is around five inches in diameter. In the background votaries lash themselves with whips tipped with razorwire. I like the hiss on this. Memory is impaired. That man is an amputee. Another says it is a mere four weeks since father died. (No, never count your footsteps.) His last remarks are as follows. We're going to make a chromatic leap about here. It's bad luck. We turned the corner and entered the home straight. The pulse is quite alien—erratic and unequal. Dreamlife is preferable. It diminishes: rapid degeneration, a fitful plucking at straws. (Trust your first judgement.) The Q beat plummets. Note the symbol used to denote the hypothetical entrance to the passage. There's genuine excitement. Obviously we see too much. What else. A real contest is underway. Consider the bulk of blood inside the average body. Consider the crack of a wave. That vein ought to be stopped. Beside us stands the disastrous name. Is my relation still a relation to the other? Quick, before it's too late. A cluster of tiny birds is gathered at the shoreline, perfectly still and facing the horizon.

CAVE

A crucible, bits of history. No covenant. The day of an unpredictable. How different is his fate to thine? In the cave they found a seal (send with horrors to the island et cetera). This is going so well. It was not in me then to go out and drown myself. This is not mentioned among the ink of the winding sheet. (What?) I am oppressed by things and happenstance. I rejoice them. We ascended together as if in a trance. When we woke we were fed and watered and sent on our way. Events have moved beyond the critical threshold. The situation has rent, is noted for the sudden change in its numbers.

THE CELL AND LEXICON (LOCAL)

You have entered into a contract. Something about cellars of oil, a surplus of salt. Above ground I am declared borrower. The visible world begins to creak and shift. In the eaves they are waiting. To my ear the chorus sounds Egyptian. I can't help thinking. Military garrisons have been stationed at various key outposts. The time of parleying is close. In less than fifty-three years they will have seceded. Mark my words. Set the head on a silver platter. My powers do not reach as far. It had a sort of sucking proboscis, as in flies. Rebellion is chronic. We were bombarded by a blizzard of neutrons. They have subjected the inhabited world to their rule. I agree in all things, everywhere. The hour of parleying is dangerous. They dispense. I agree with all the measures taken so far. I commit myself, i.e. resistance of the mobile valve. (My stars say don't do it.) He is very sensitive and detests. Who left to make his frontier? Every situation evolves towards yet more breaking down. Between the two cubes is the wideness. Into which vacuum did a river rise? I am reading more and more about the classical world. She remained dominant until the late fourth century. And just what is a syncretic poem? So long. Now she walks down the gangplank, hanging on his arm. This is better than expected. A bevel or slope is made by paring off the edge of anything. This could be chamber work, piercings through the fog. It looks so atmospheric. She was afraid to shout out lest no one came. I was thought to be the first to exhibit such a spirit of critical enquiry.

CESSATION

For it began. We're not made of atoms. The whole of physics is wrong. An inner sense of rhythm and proportion persists. I am intensely emotional following defeat. A host of angels returned to heaven with the holy grail. The figure of a naked man hangs by his wrists from the apex of an arch. There are three distinct possibilities: acquittal (namely), acquittal (apparitional), and postponement. I sat on a park bench and waited for something to happen. The bound ankles are delicately modelled in chiaroscuro. This is usually when things start to get exciting. A worthy man once brought me green tea. We share a name. The spoilage has ceased. Our oppressors are whom, exactly? Not all will survive. Unwrapping one bit after the other, I wasn't even planning. No howl, tomorrow, no.

CHEATING AND MAKING

I'm sure you'll be cut down before you even reach the steps. There's a week to go before the transfer shuts. A layer of tissue exists between the hypothalamus and the lobe. Not a single address of reproof comes to gladden my heart. I find myself in an economy generated by repetition and promissory redemption. The crucial elements are lithium and polonium. I've become obsessed with that blood-tax, any workaday fact. This species lacks the innermost digit of the fore limb found in most air-breathing vertebrates. The gateway opens up again a slit. He was found crouching on a dunghill, crazed with brains. I'll keep you up to date with everything else that happens. Disintegration of the populace into a rural proletariat is taking place. In theory, we're already dead. In the layest possible terms, tell us how your plan could possibly work. Perhaps relief will come from that side. The equation is simple: an unforgettable collapse at the end of the season. His forte is parsimony of epithet. Of making many books there is no end, in contrast to the language game itself.

CITY

A tranquilizer and long-lasting hypnotic has set the suburbs on fire. I am analogous to a pillory. It must be coming this way. I have the impression that you count yourself among the politick race. After we've completed the questionnaire, a little trick is to be played on the gathered company (the ontological question of what signifies, in general). Don't be cute. It's near the back, ousting. Nineteen seventy is uncredited. What we're looking for is a tube, two discs, a round metal case and a shed load of uranium. We've discovered how they talk to each other. Draw up a detailed inventory of the recovered items. Maybe it's something we haven't seen before. There's a thousand things I want to say to you. Writing is error twenty-four times a second. O the sight of those glistening inner organs. Miners call it pitchblende. A gelatinous substance is secreted by each sac. The pipers are now standing still. Blight struck again in eighteen sixty-one. They harbour a solemnity. Things appear to be made of names. At the tip of the peninsular they call it kal. You're going to have to think of something else. Being is played out, blind, that which is dependent and consigned to a mood.

CONQUEST

Templehead. If you do feel someone behind you, it's your eyes. I should have begun these researches much earlier. It's the only way. The temperature is raised to room, or decays, as the context demands. The colour is fluorescent orange. I'm not altogether comfortable with how this is unravelling. We've been allotted a minimum of three lines to each expansion. The smell of burning stubble spread from the surrounding countryside. Until you have read this, nothing will become clear.

CONSTELLATION

Suit smart, ash-grey. Plastic wad. It's not our system. Twelve rays emanate outwards in an array. I think the speaker must be one of your former selves. Look at the ectoplasm pouring out of every hole. This is more like it. I shall pass through very late in the day. Remove the mould and see what happens. (There's one and a half kilotons of the stuff.) Hurry. Architecture has been stolen from a magical source, the square root of five to one. But the list itself is retained, embedded in narrative form. I wake each day in awe. I could resemble. It was like a vein of gold. Draw the fluid up, drink. I have taken much from the long walk. The body was lowered into a ritual bath. I mean there is a disequilibrium, strapped to empty doldrums. These were my appointed delays, an overclad sky.

CORE

Grammar's simple, so far. It's funny, people die all the time. (You provoke.) He was unfavoured from the outset. The adversary was deliberately designed with one hand higher than the other. Then came a repeated moment of vulnerability, beautifully incomplete. This also applies to the surrounding things. There was once running water in ever dwelling. Her name was called by chance. (He/she/it provokes.) They are marching forward in their famous vertical and red. Shed fresh light on the situation. Individuals find themselves confronted with results they had not wished for. I'm a great one for keeping the local deities happy. The growing vogue of emblems witnesses the extent of the movement. You are a hawk of an uncanny nest. What is protecting you from the concrete post behind you? The lift is broken. Whether they're here or not, it's spilling, a libation.

CRUST

Fear. I am indifferently constituted. (You provoke plural.) What makes them so effective is that they sit opposite each other on the wheel of the zodiac. I have quit this age of ours. It's like magic. I at least have chosen to defend myself. That number is a prime. (They provoke.) The other player is an augmented head, but this is not why. Twelve rays of blue light fanned out from a central point. I am for the first time anywhere, sprayed from left to right. (Sorry, it has no needs.) Her tranquility is remarkable. I've always admired purity. Financial problems ease after marriage (see sun in chapter VIII). The real time-stream is running beneath the soles of your feet. The author is at the root of it all. It's so unjustified. People will complain. Did you treat this as an ordinary cadaver? Are events any more literal these days? On the third step I sank up to my waist. I have brought about captivity, as promised. About twenty percent has been set at the same pitch. We used a sounding fork. Thou, my brave pilgrim, hast revealed this very second. You must go now. We won't be needing any more to eat. What is called antiquiddity? He likes flowery language, Venus in Aquarius and so on. But the use of suffice is unusual.

DAYBREAK

The set is amazing. Glass apparent or metal is built entirely of wood. (Can I go in through this door, please.) I write lyrics when I have to. Your shadow is casting a name. We each had our own private twelve-foot cell. I couldn't hope for more. He turns out to be my dead ringer. I've nurtured contempt for the vulgarity of a plausible narrative. Maybe we'll never know how deep the rift is. The effect is shattering. The numbers are different categories of people. Smouldering feathers quiver and rise. He woke just in time, but still had to reckon with a beating. And if this day I should make you go back and retrieve, what then? I am doing you with lots of numbers. Who drew the short straw? His kinship is never satisfied with results. (Have I ever shown you my astrology.) Gigantic arc lamps were installed. So mephitic is the plume that any birds flying through it are suffocated. The man's hands were bound behind his back and a thick rope coiled about him.

THE DECLINING DAY

This is a better story than the one I was going to tell you. Some letters are blurred. Scores of objects have yet to be declassified. There is no breath remaining. I cannot read this. His speech is littered with banalities. The mountain is desolate. Arctics trot upon it. On the surface all seems cordial. Homeostasis of bodily fluids has been achieved. We chanced upon a homestead cordoned off by an electrified fence. The passing days are like a shadow that declines within a threshold. The nothing of this place is killing him. Finding guano in its pure state would not be so easy.

DEMERLAYK

I'm using the word manoeuvre. The juxtaposition of these two works is a marvellous thing. Remember, you've had this book longer than you think. It takes place at a time of ruction. How do you feel anyway. Let's draw breath. Some of these uncut pages look interesting. He put his body in the way. You cannot control everything that is happening in the room. It was like a conference of birds, no one else (no stonecutters, no pyramid erectors). Don't even make an attempt. The air tastes bitter. Those are clouds, stratocirrus. I wonder, he says, just how much of this is edible. Where will I be working tomorrow? The best analogy is probably an environment. I am making the most of an insouciant manner abroad. This tendency has always been associated with insurrection—disturbance, riot or tumult. If I talk about a place it's because it has disappeared. All form here is mediated, a mere compromise. He traces and a relief is left behind. Over one million newsmen camped outside, awaiting hourly reports on his condition. Nevertheless, when the body is too exhausted to continue, an easy death arrives.

DISASTER (WRITING)

Patience, belated perseverance. It's become so tight we can't see. We were happy in the contemporary world. Along the outside of the building creep streaks of moss. I'm really looking forward to the next couple of hours. D means all must play the same duration (well, they have done what they have done). His intention is to provoke an outline of the principles and methods of astronomy. These objects are fantastic. Now we are going to interrelate. I don't care what I look like. It was born at one twenty in the afternoon. If possible, and if your subject is capable, suggest some kind of psychical research. I imagine it will kill between two and five thousand people. I would be happy to go off on my own now and again. When I am talking of it, still I can't believe. The substance resembled rust. The light has been decontaminated. We were the first batch. Do you not hear my cells popping? Confused, he calls for a writing tablet. The text occupies a space. One character could be violent and impulsive. I've been expecting you the adversary said (quite inscrutable). He moves too fast for reason. He is habitual. He says he was born to hard labour, semiotics. The text spans the time of three or more zodiacs. According to him the first man was nothing. He is animal. I am surrounded by seamen and a few fellow officers, up on deck, beneath the canopy of fixed stars. Welcome back.

DISCUMFIST

Not all of the letters are represented. It's the story of my life. Discreet changes must be made. The area is cordoned off. We struck at the landward hill, a tactic causing great disturbance. We are masters of our age. Up in the attic floats the ghost of our beloved. It's not the first time I've seen things come back. The women of yesteryear were different. If acted out as required, with merciless realism, all will be fine. Note the way in which this entity functions. I can't complain. You have worked your way back down the ladder. I once witnessed a spectral noose hovering near the ceiling, over the very same dance floor. The man's head lies upon a stone. There took place a siege. The list included the parable of the two. Consider a lamentation, the multitude, a wall of clingfilm. Prepare yourself for the invasion of the hypnogogic state. (This one really seems to understand.)

Who claimed a resemblance to a newspaper photograph? It was more a stumbling wade through billions and billions of tiny stones. I am shocked.

DISGRACE, THE ART OF

A nasty piece of work who's only out for his own gainsay. Suddenly it shifts direction. Today I'm doing my bit. An ointment is being prepared by skilled apothecaries. What follows is an account of how the petrol was siphoned off. (They got the wrong address.) I dreamt that I became really really tired. Walk, leave this to me. Then I came back. I will call again. A crimson lake seeped out across the cold lino. An obscure magnetic device was once used. And the decoding crystal you planted, it's like a snake coiled up at the base of the spine. This passage gives us an incomplete picture of the role played by perception.

DJINN

Precision engineering. The whipcrack of tarpaulin. On my wrist is stamped the number two hundred and thirty-five. A black fluid was ejaculated from the creature's sac. I am one among many. I have been advised to say nothing. I am permitted to play a free role tonight. (Wish we had some fool in the house.) No transcription can claim to be absolutely accurate. All these examples are reconstructions, rather than copies. An outcrop of older rock is surrounded. This behaves quite irrationally, as numbers go. The leg and the thigh, what wouldst though say unto them? An advance-guard was sent out ahead of the body.

DWELLING

Shebeen. I slept too long. We two dreamt the same dream, consistent in every detail. Someone hands me a sacred artifact. Leaves were used for the computation of time. Now to return home. Snakes are busy symbolizing, coiled about the liver. How do I get from here to an actual place? (That creature's never a dog.) I recall an enclosure of books, an embrace from the distant past, also a model of a temple in the form of a human head, carved from translucent orange stone. Bystanders were mortally injured. What confuses me even more. About the walls are paintings of spent matches. (Did you fall out of that tree yourself?) This is like the glue holding you together. I have read a lot. I had always longed to have a share. Yours gratefully, Ibsen.

EARTHQUAKE

Notes from the index cards, a short spell underground. Here you are, out of place. A sequence of parallel tricks was used to compose this—a collection of errors, a trapped nerve. I think you should go now. I am going to interrogate it.

You never know. Terminate with extreme prejudice. Mind what you ask for. Just look at this century. Behold his chain and saw. What's left in that canvas bag? I think you should ask. Use the probe. What did he do with his life. He is here. We can say this. Then he is not. I arranged for a crowbar to be dropped through the bars of his cell. He rarely alludes to himself. Teeth have been set on edge. These are mangled signifiers of actions and events. These fictions are built on a deception. Nonetheless, he has sworn the oath. Our research encompasses merchants and brokers. My personal surgeon is ever at my side. We spread a net to bring them up to the surface. He feared an assassin and struck out in the darkness. I am full of salt water he screamed. (Exercise more persuasive powers of speech.) Don't get your head in the photo. I remember him saying that one day. In contrast to the language game itself, yes.

THE EVENT

A species has been developed that no longer needs to reproduce. It's a nice day for it, the filth, the beatings. The state I was in when I returned to my senses advised me only too well. A bear has been spotted in the city park. After the events of the last two nights, there is no longer anything to prove. I exist within the same attack-decay. This single event has happened to us all—an ice hole, moist, buboes forming under the tar pits, summer thunderheads. Bubbles were percolating through her bloodstream.

EXILE

Opposition Sun-Mars. This discovery arrived in the wake of my own researches. You are induced to follow. What's in a name (tighten those struts, will you). He stutters and repeats. Displacement and exile have been applied to some newsworthy subjects. It's anybody's game at the moment. What is that woman wearing across her eye. A metal door slams shut in the wind. Everything's been pretty unimpressive to date. They stare forwards as they pass. You're a stranger, an ex. My own life consists of sleeping, mainly. He begins, it was unstarred. He threw himself headlong. Sea fog rolling in.

EXORDIUM

Navigating a river full of rapids. Locals squat on the bank, observing with indifference. I shall consider these two phenomena jointly. (Pull out, there's a month to go on the platform.) How do you choose? I am armed and primed—or will the ashes et cetera? She's a kind of Jonah. I have my own voice. Events are long since dead and forgotten. It's also about fidelity and movement, the beginning of anything, the only state worth the statement. Make a decision. They have been paring down the crust year on year, the beaten blood, the beaten breath. I forget the rest—yes, but is was high, very high up for sure. Let's call them gripe-alls, harpies, tantaluses. An ad hoc arrangement, surely.

FIBRE

I remember. I asked you for headlines you'll never see this week. I'm not really here. We are inviting spleen. You're doing that thing with your ears again. I cannot imagine no. You'll have two hours before you detonate. The aim is eugenic perfection. Be my guest. Maybe this is a trial run. Evasion is invalid. We are at pains to demonstrate. The sets of quantities described above are known as deltas. These are analogous to the already unknown. We were not firm enough with them. There really is a type of music that stops you thinking. Burlesque alliteration infects the page, intermingled tongues. I suffocate when I write. A grinning head popped up out of the hole. Five-leafed plants and five-petalled flowers were considered especially sacred. The eternal mystery is to compel two spheres fundamentally foreign (the core is akin). Put some of these away now, the shelves are backing up. I was rapt. One would have thought my responses automatic by now. They dragged him into the cave. I lack the strength to do nothing. They reshaped him. It must have rhymed. It is he for sure. The words which follow may be taken in any order desired. Someone drove a penknife into it. It bled. They had scribbled the wrong address on the parcel.

FIFTY-PERCENTERS

Somewhere around the first junction of the nerve. The breadth is fifty everywheres. We're in a tunnel. (I'm just conforming with your instructions.) I'd like to change some of the things around here. I have had them all numbered. We drifted together, collided. I'm wondering when that moment will ever come back. In a rapid string of images I was weightless, disinclined to function. He is forbidden to attack. He is forbidden to defend. He is forbidden to remain indifferent. An attempt at reconciliation is being made—as by identification of gods, ritual observance. A selection of whatever seems best in each of us is being made. A logical compromise is being made. For it began thus. Don't put that on your stars, you will crush them flat.

FIREPLAY

Horse, the capital's greatest love story. There are a number of potential contenders. Their bodies mimic the cursives and strokes of the text. This is really the crux of the action. Is that acceptable to you. He wanders about from island to island. (Think microcosm.) The voyage was first published in fifteen eighty-nine and fifteen ninety-eight. It makes you rejoice to be alive. Who ran him close? Things come to those who wait. Consider a conjuror's command of his assembled objects. There were several volleys before the man slumped forward. The source of light is an electric arc between carbon electrodes.

FOG

I am upon myself. In doing so I am most irregular. The tactic is a big man/little man combination. We can guarantee nothing (smouldering, gently). His hands are cuffed behind his back. He says I will water the land with your blood. Which one of us is when? Now, present the criminal act as glorious, meritorious, lawful.

THE FOUR WINDS

From a family name, meaning unknown. They were numberless. The task is maintenance of a dynastically stable state within a system, by any means. You've got that sense of something missing about you too. They are in good hands, the things. After the space of two hours I cried out. This blizzard was started. Organisms tend towards economy of action in learning and fulfilling. Quite the contrary.

FRIDAY ON MY MIND

He's demanding a ten year event horizon. A herald is sent out to announce the approaching day. This is getting interesting (a submarine manned by aliens made of white ash). It's a long journey back, isn't it. I'm what's called a forerunner, a freebooter. He stretches a little farther out until he falls flat on his face. I have injected some laws. A dry horny capsule is imbedded at the centre of the pulp. I sent a messenger straight to his face. It's at least three hours before she arrives. Nonetheless, she had sprinted the entire distance. It's not difficult to see how this mode of fortune-telling works. What began as a movement for string.

THE GREEKS

Our relationships with objects. Stimuli and origins. The seventh bone of the head. Is that furrow a scar? He died before the trial could take place. I've seen a replay of the collision. I remain in the previous clause. I occur only once. Time is the setting. Just listen to this man and fill your ears. How dwindled, et cetera.

HAWK

Jobation, on a full-time basis. O yes I remember I was telling him *thalassa, thalassa*. He started screaming. (Should this chapter be titled valedictory.) Can you tell me of the symptoms, the diagnosis? Your command is a lamp for my steps and a light for my path. I could always send someone outside for advice. Now I've lost the signal. I could always do the whole thing myself. The aim was simply to make nothing more. Is it more reference to me/us in this caper? We're below the threshold where visibility ends. Here is semblance, an effigy bearing outward evidence, the track of a wild perceptible. Thirty degrees of zodiac carry the names that are no longer coincident. If it's executed we're finished. Who was filled with molten lead and torn? It rests on signs, gestures. Formerly the structure was a dwelling place. We don't know what to say. This time she'll pay for her transgression. Any mark or portent is quietly miraculous. The floodgates open (remote sense, in counterpoint to contact sense). There's interference. When I look back all I see is wreckage. The convoy passed through so hideous a spectacle—algae floating on the surface of the sea, feathers in the air. You need repetition when there's no story. Now climb back up and count backwards again. I guess. I heard it wrong: the two-valved shell of a diatom, with its contents. (Maybe a slice off a solid body.) Insert the probe into any convenient orifice. I can't tell from where I'm standing.

HEBDOMAD

The very first cause of all. Headwind. I'm not sure how this runs. It was almost primordial. O if all things were ever thus. It froze him solid (the air). Occurrence repeats itself, perhaps the father of similitude. A species is transferred only when we're convinced it's valid. The first gate was called the signal. The remaining six are named after their respective constellations. He has been nudged up one lozenge. The other is called the unexpected. I am perplexed. It sounds like science fiction, a sanctuary to which no one can ever return. After this everyone will either be dead or free of the body in some undisclosed way. I mean the moment that forces us to deal with the past.

THE HEIGHTS

A vast garden that sprawls across several acres. A gravel drive. The villa is composed of a set of eight buildings with nineteen windows, each two cubits in height. There are bodies littered about the tended lawns. On the ground floor is a huge drawing-room equipped for recitals. I'm among those waiting, names uncalled and uncallable. Beyond the french windows gentle sprinklers revolve and hum. Teeming insect life, spurting helices. Be allusive. I am still writing this. A translucency was rejected.

HE IS

It's well after the nine o'clock threshing hour. Any actions I perform are mimicked immediately. I've located the records. Time has been brought forward a matter of hours. (Of who are all things.) Now for the famous scenes from child—hold the glory of a starlike diamond, caught in the yaw of a paving slab. Come out. Show yourselves. He perishes. Uncanny, it's me.

HELP

I want to re-enter the mediaeval mind. All the local electricity is directed straight through me. To detonate you must turn the key clockwise by ninety degrees. It's unclear how all the instructions knit together. There are intervening obstacles. (I need somebody.) I once lost all sense of time but later regained it. A breath of wind emerges from the horizon, a pillar of light.

THE HOOD

Late last night. Alloy of rust, compounds of rosewater and oxide. Note the fine line and the quality of the weave. He describes everything that he sees each day in obsessive detail. Some extinctions have occurred throughout the rest of the continent. This specimen is characterized by black and white plumage and a bristling crest. There are four toes on each foot. Its slaying capacity can only be described as prolific. The upper limbs are vicious forceps. This is going more smoothly than I anticipated. I had no idea of the extent of the lie, the level of deception. Later, you can tell me what you think. I must go now. Replace effect for cause, in all other senses. The sphinx threw herself from a rock. Time and setting, again.

HORDE

A severe test or trial is announced. The usurped is alive and well. He has arranged objects according to an invented taxonomy. One comes after the other (space, 'and time also'). The shadow is buried, of course. He speaks for himself. The rent was paid by an anonymous donor. A duel is announced. We're marched off in different directions. I shoot to miss (gastrocnemius). Signs accelerate the play of simulation. We've come this far, we've got to go on. I meant a fine-grained argillaceous rock.

IMRAM

It's about one of their submarines, isn't it. I woke to find myself back on the island. The hero is a number of the dynasty. Some objects are highly radioactive. He meets otherworldly creatures. These need neither the excitation of light nor the stimulus of electricity. Finally he returns to his native land. On route there's a collision with an antique trireme. (Picture a type of bold face with lineaments of equal thickness.) Being but a pitiful vessel, it sinks. Crew is expendable.

INCREASE

There's a shop on the corner. On her bed of down, but with turning seeds to ease her pain. (It must be fun, to take people on such a journey.) There's a retarded kind of wit secreted within me. Laments have been sold for all the unhappy shades in limbo. This is the second time she's come back. We will just have to wait a few moments longer. An object was found, billions of years out in space, at maximum dissonance observable. The diagnosis is fugal.

INEVITABLE

The whole shebang. They were rearranged in alphabetic order. This darkens the waters and conceals the pursuit. He writes in relatively short sustained bursts (a secular inventory). Every day we're counted in and counted out. Who is this man being described before us? There are less than one hundred remaining. Some have wondered about the sequence in this argument. Some say he must have mixed up the pages on the way to the printer.

INK

They were hidden deep in the archive. Very nearly there. It must be approached in segments. He takes his fill of oxygen, moulded rubber pressed firm to muzzle. Descendants were called. There are sources of light and sources of darkness. It's all about the role of the womb. The chief character's occupation is that of kindler, one who sets fire to things. I shall begin with a complete set of phantasies, people or animals that are capricious, rash and erratic. We have just turned a corner. In the year seventeen thirty we met downstairs. They inhabit the coasts and islands. The animal's innards were inspected and the future predicted. He has a feverish, non-constructive restlessness: square Moon, Uranus. The whole block has turned white and in texture resembles tallow. (That's encouraging.) I lifted the barrier. Clutches of frozen men stomp and clap their hands before glowing braziers. Mine is the next case to be heard. (It has been described by one litigant as an agitated corpse.) This is too susceptible to influence and borders on plagiarism. No one recognizes distance except in the downward direction. I then related how they all starved. Nonetheless, the castle is strangely comforting to me. Snow lies knee-deep on the ground. The inmates wear a knotted cord about their wrists. What is the key to your executive decision? It is a strange thing, this. Perhaps it takes its name from the heart—it's found at the core of the intestines, after all. This dark lantern, it helps discount the general impression. I was written minute drop by minute drop. I ask you. From this point we sail out where.

INSURRECTION

We ejected it, out into space. I don't know what to do next. Looming ice-cliffs in the distance. The skyline has vanished. When the ship is steering east or west the compass swings north-south with the roll. (What am I going to do now?) Don't forget to make a sketch of his house. I tell myself. Up to what point in time was I considered his victim.

IRON

A social renaissance is underway. There's just the one movement in it, magnificent. It's the anniversary of one-man handling. Run, cry it about the streets—the morning star of triumph et cetera. Bring the curtain down. The infantry had heard so much about their mysterious adversary. Much much later the opening is to be repeated. It's like spun lace. The deceased can only pass through the gate if he knows the names of the seven doorkeepers. (I've always loved a good list.) Is that the best you can do he says. People dread coming to the house. No no no I answered. How can you possibly think so. The lack of knowledge has been reorganized into a synthesis, a correlation of disparate parts.

THE ISLAND

It's all about opening up the hatch. (At last, a metaphor.) They have passed through the isle and out the other side. Farewell old port he writes. The species in question is the sparrowhawk, coursing over a land without shadows, without brilliance. This creates the illusion of a pensive calm. Part of him remains behind. As I walk down the steps I observe that the evening is not quite over. There is everything left to play for. Mistakes have been made and unmade. That man appears to be frozen solid (the eternal resembles gold). He came with his own version. A magnificent death can take a lifetime to unfurl. Who was found living in a remote cabin high in the Swiss alps?

KEENING

Some of the references are becoming obscure. He gets up from his knees. The promised letter is *l*, or *L*. This formula comes closest to postulating a discrepancy between the absconded and their reappearance (from some flower-vice of crystal dark, and suchlike). I can't decode. A friend leaving for good is but a small dying. The mood is recovering. Native oxides, brackish pitchlike masses.

THE KILLING HOUR OF LOW TIDE

I repeat. All other priorities are rescinded. Language obscures the purity of things. The day will come when what. He has made his own transition of the plays. (Surprised and resentful, was he?) There will be nothing else to do. (O he did, did he?) I can't complain. And there is security. And you come to me with a proposal like this? I don't mind that noise. It's taken straight from the logic: place a man on the brink of an abyss et cetera. What event is probably the same thing? I thought to send an object to you. I am planning to row around the island myself, to see if what's rumoured is fact. We'll be hearing more signs. He hangs on a tree until dawn, gently swinging from side to side. I am mindful of the macaronic interjections of his journal. Some are void words. You could have heard a pin drop. He's an imprint, a shade—elemental and metallic. Impossible, the tale of a fabulous sea voyage, records both spoken and written.

THE LADDER

A foil of tin, for mirrors. Gaoler, officers, headsmen and other assailants. Days critical and desultory: dog-star days. The rungs correspond to chapters one and seven of the book. Therein he is referred to as the unexplained. That beating could not have been more severe. Incidental stanzas have been introduced. Relative distance also died that night. (I saw to it.) Who we are, uninvited.

LIGHT

Doom, adjusted punishment. A spark of the defined. Pure narration. This is a great history and well worth the listening to (ennui, simulations and other tendencies). Whose curve was unknown? This corresponds to the state through which all things pass before becoming an imago. The atmosphere's completely dried up. Life's feeling more and more mutual with each passing day. After that the moon did not yield. He is very general. He lived among the stage crew for a season. It was a species with long wings and rudimentary hind toe. This species is an optical counterpart, or a perfect. The court is under siege. Things are becoming imitative.

LUCK

A scrappy fit or seizure. A high-hanging one, hands hooked, suspended from a gambrel. (Have you brushed your teeth?) His job is store detective. That's not the way I heard it. These subjects are very spread out in space. Find a heading, a rare passage without editorial comment. Produce the effects of a metalanguage. Be precise and uneven. Why speak of today. This book is become frusty. Incite the men to commit a crime. For years I remained alone in my thoughts (by ones, by twos). There's good reason to suppose that the subject will soon become obsolete. Removal leaves the opening tender. There are phenomena. I refuse to call 'atoms of light'. Lucky, lucky, lucky, lucky, lucky.

MAKER

Also known as mercator's projection. I've got the works. Remember in the days, when. A huge gob of grease sits on the back of his head. This verse is composed of simple phrases culled from the wife's conversation. We talked about the runners and the players, the outfield (Hercules, the stray bullet and so on). We drink. Reinvent your own role. There's plenty of room. I had only a brief cameo. What are your expectations. (Nil.) What are your exceptions. I have lost my context. It's the killing hour of low tide. As the arc edges inwards it is exposing the real. The gaseous compound we propose to use is of our own manufacture. (What sort of insect will emerge from all this?) Molten lead drips from the rooftops. Those capsules have not moved for centuries. Now they fall and split open, shells of chrysalides. Look at what happened this weekend. Break the seal. A solid body is to be constructed and fixed in place. Everything survives, notwithstanding the assaults. He says in earlier chapters there's too much *pk, pk, pk*. I want to go back to see his death. My own rules of propriety make me uneasy. We cancel out each other's deficiencies. Digging down twelve feet we found a complete tree intact in the clay. It's a spectacular story, a rather romantic one, as it turns out. The corporation collapsed from the burden of our combined weight. The source of the forgery still isn't known. Once the text goes past double figures, it doesn't seem to know how to stop. The gem in question is a ruby the size of a cricket. On its clockwise side is a permanent shadow. This account is somehow disconnected with what people are thinking. He had so much more crucible experience back then. Gold, in strictly chemical terms, is radiating onto the pitch today. Species at inventory include ruby-wasps, the swelling lobes of dead man's thumb, cuckoo-shrike. (I forget precisely who he was talking about.) Honestly, my eyes are really starting. He was appointed curator of ends. I read marketeer. There was a mage out there today. I could have been wrong. Substance is analogous, with sulphur for oxygen.

MAN

Listen, I have to tell you something, everything. There's only one possible opening along the way. Its exoskeleton is a tight cellular body. Form is an elongated oval. (I can't believe anyone needs to hear all this detail.) It's made of calcium. Never, in our object, have we arrived. Shape is achieved by inarticulation. It's always been here. For this reason the artefact is made of mother-of-pearl and stopped with a plug of wax. That's the first junction of opposites dealt with— steerage, the lowest fares. Is that clear. Substance is rarely crystalline. She carried her child down to the shore, whispering back. I have just reached that place inspired by an anecdote. I don't know why, listening to him, listening to you. Regional metamorphism has developed a cleavage along closely-spaced planes. I hear he went back to the oracle once himself.

MANTLE

This account discusses an inheritance of atoms. (And men might axe why that misericorde and pity is so revealing.) Suits of apparel were formerly worn. But most animals retreat from fire, yes? This is the nearest I've ever found myself. A distant relative died attaining: china sea, restored to form, the penultimate syllable of a word. Erase puncture.

MERCIFUL

Ebb tide. Gravitational lens quasar in Pegasus, the Einstein Cross. Mercury does not compute (it's all about the imbalance). And you will, you will do it, because you can. Memory's making a comeback. When I force an attempt I always get the original. Now there's no signal. He says he's a fugitive from the law. Sight conjures hearing, and vice versa. If it were possible this hour might pass away. He has been dragged to the well many times. (Sound of distant hammering and drilling.) It's rumoured he is patron saint of eloquence and trade. Now for an indepth view of your own personality, your possibilities and options. Its gigantic eye burst open and fluid gushed out. History conspires against us. If something were at all possible it would not be permitted. Those textual notes are a facsimile. The billows have mass.

THE MOON

Logomachy. Close all the hatches behind me. I'm never coming back.

MOUNTAIN

Helping difficult people or sick. I have reached the third junction. We're entering a steep descent. I see names historic and names temporal. He dropped dead outside a night, clutching the head. And what exactly am I supposed to be losing? This constitutes a subtle rearrangement of our miserable shared lives. The various cortices are hardened by carbonate of lime and phosphate. I saw you last of all. Stepping out of the capsule, I held my breath, straining. The anchor had a mushroom-shaped head. Consider the rudimentary phase of any insect. Sextile aspect Jupiter, Neptune.

NIGHT JOURNEY

On signs. A memory of splendid. One model which he fundamentally will never renounce. (You're just playing at psychoanalysis.) An absence of meandering has been detected. The journey's recurring theme is the forced march. This section is purely about writing. Now just how are we going to go about this. We're anticipating the next hatch of legal cases. I am declared unlimit—that which has been lost already, that which must be given up. Penalty and transgression are declared equals. A fault or breach of engagement has just occurred to me. Go down to the shoreline. I am expected. It yields just before sunrise and just after sunset. The accused survived on a diet of carbolic smoke balls. Adopt the default position. Exhale a few breaths. What are today's instructions. The revelation is incomplete (cluster of gulls, the horizon, small stones too numerous to itemize). Foreknowledge is on the increase. I can at last reveal a loudness. At the other end of the scale we find subliminal rapport and functional interaction (telepathy, telaesthesia, ecstasy, hypnosis). Terrestrial coverage simulates interest. There's a wall of yellow stuff. What are today's elevations. The foil is best removed. Money has become a by-product. When necessary, to make the sense clear, the truncated quotations have been amplified. Two planes are colliding in this one tiny space. Substance can devour, gnaw, eat up or into, or corrode. The infrastructure has vanished. We struggled to introduce words appropriate to the description required. Temperature alone makes us aware of distant bodies. We fail. You can't help looking. Enormous radio lobes are situated at opposite ends of the visible galaxy. Philosophy combats such an 'also'. It weighed over two kilotons—a local name from the shape of the tubers. A froth is secreted by the fog horror, on planets, surrendering the larvae. Dead-melt.

NOCTURNAL REVENANT

Death by firing squad. Hold your position for a minute longer. He has a shocking record of disregard. The assistant animal wrangler is missing. A convincing character exists, independent of the recognized channels of sense. Alas, his brains are forfeit, knees precious—because the day et cetera.

ORPIMENT

It's just that opening sequence. And the page suddenly snapped. A noun means a man or someone else. I thought it sounded a bit strange. I can't get away. I am foreign to myself. Cite one of the mysteries associated with the name. Modification is composed of the dichotomy *some/other*. There's been a shortfall in typographic error. Bright mineral substance is found native in soft masses. Fauna is rock-hopper, crushed. How many pieces have you coughed up today? The olfactory nerve is the best conjuror of reminiscence. How many among us will live to see a second and a third imprint? I think you boys have everything covered. It cannot be equalled. I think you boys have had enough. Who was enclosed in an envelope of flesh.

Another magical moment. False report and rumour, that absurd story. What about this whole business of tradition. It contains words, phrases, clichés, anecdotes, ideas—pleadings and odd rapping noises, scraps of munitions, scribbled memoranda, fractures and strange shadows. Half of his blood has been drained into basins, strategically placed on the flagstone floor. (Believe me, these are the best of the lucky nomenclatures.) I'm the least of your problems. I already exist among you. He's not looking terribly healthy. The machine was spinning like the teeth of a toothed wheel. An endless chain of buckets is busy raising water. He's an official ancestor. The story is already dead on its feet. There's someone behind me in the room. He meant himself to be recognized. (Trust the want of imagination.) We ignored their demands. Only fusion of the spectrum produces the necessary tincture. A rescue package is being put together. Rattling noises could be heard to the east of the escarpment. A campaign is underway. They will rescue him from hostage. Things are set in motion—it's the gravity. We're one man down already. It was the star did it. I rarely look at purgatory, so many light-seconds away.

THE OVERWHELMING EVENT

A certain class of news. A collaboration. What flourished gently above the beaches? I would appreciate the option. Well, let's talk about killing it. First allow me a brief digression. A man hangs upside down with rays emanating from his skull (by desperate thoughts against et cetera). I don't know how to proceed beyond this point—and he swings, I forgot to mention that he is swinging. Gather inside me he said, horror has everywhere. Natural flare is well beaten in any contest. This one event crept up on us all. You do not even have to understand. He whispers my orders are assassinate, assassinate—candidates for the book-as-guide, for example.

PANEGYRIC

Zone of perdition. Someone who could make me believe that it was worth speaking. A eulogy of tripartite structure. Utter loss and ruin. The imperative that the law must be enforced becomes meaningless. We move about bound together in pairs. Great distortions to the north and south. We shuffle step by step, crabwise. The planetary positions in the houses express the destiny of facts. You have my sympathy. It's really hard to talk about this with your mouth. I see only appearance. I no longer know what I am doing. The same rhythm has to thread through every hole. Look, he is sitting at home and feeling morose. There's no single reaction to the question begged. The source of one account is the murder of the legend. There was a big spike about twenty-two years ago.

Seventy-nine disappeared. If you could take one single object with you to a desert, what would it be. She has been overshadowed ever since. There is neither blame nor censure. Kittly-benders simply means running on thin bendy ice. I am reincarnated in the stone keep.

PAROLE

Between metaphorization, which takes off on its own. I don't understand why this is taking so long. We're found at the very centre of identity. It is spelt that way for the market, the longest street in Europe. Five-pointed figures are attached to a continuous line of fortifications, an endless knot. He looks as though he's carrying something about inside his belly. The ratio is the square root of five to one. It's madness to style oneself doctor concerning such things. The peak frequencies are steadily being reduced. Then a sudden taste, a folding of the tongue, stretched body with head in brace. I had intended to say trance but could not. And what is the word that once meant curving away? Imagine an absence of adversaries. (I think he got sacred of the vastness.) What teaches the population nothing. I treasured those pages—today's transits, previsions, incompatibilities. Fourteen days are left.

PILGRIMAGE

A recurrence of the space symbol. Iceblink. They mean strangers. This is the only section that appears mishandled. It slowly moves up and down, skirting the edge of the platform before toppling in. (I've always liked that ridge.) Then she crawls into the corner and will not budge. Tell her to hit the grids. It's about being inside something, not outside something. Suddenly the space of the room is oddly compressed, as if the walls were buckling and shrinking. Guide them in, within a narrowing portion of the former region. There were a few stragglers, a ribbon of sand with foam and breakers, driftwood washed up. This part may only be attempted through a reliable medium. There seems to be some confusion over the numbers—the seven watchers, for example. Young were raised following the precepts. The nucleus is variable, i.e. a charnel-house. O, why bother.

PILLAGE

What we demand of our illuminati (short controlled bursts). Location, an unfortunate string of islands. In process of time, well after the end—all the days of the years of my yes. This is also the signal track. Does that not inspire you. We approached from opposite ends and met somewhere in the middle. He is unsure of me. I cry out. This is the utmost degree attainable, dialectically opposite to zenith. These are the stations of my great ambition. It is of doubtless beginnings, the place and state whither things are going. (I don't see any method at all, sir.) We've been wandering about for forty days. A crowded brig sails on the day of our arrival. There is an entire race squeezed within him. This is the lowest point—nadir, perhaps the final syllable of a word. He is hair-triggered. I have lost count. There's a coil at the interior. I will press on until I get bored. You are simply wrong. The spectators are dwarfed because of the perspective. Anyone caught waving a flag risks arrest. They take him. They reshape him. He's a member of an abandoned order. He is renamed and sent out into the world again. Obituaries appear in all the papers. He is the man who discovered everything. They are overwhelmed by the consequences of their acts.

POET

At the threshold where visibility ends. (Cramps bout the noise it must be so hard for you.) This passage contains errors. He has now stopped. He was arrested at the outskirts—do you recall the limits? I'm like you. I remember everything. We have arrived at a remote trading post. Mister equals rain in some language. This is clearly a forgery. Be cautious, in case it is work, disguised. The small sac of blood exploded on his chest. Behind the counter stands the double, or ka. And I speak *that which I have to say to him*. Whose throat stank for lack of air? I have life (8). We are stationed at the lip and it is night. All the drama is missing. Stars come out, semée film at the farthest rim of the cog. What imprint.

PRECOGNITION

That's easy enough to say. This is where strange things start pouring out of the fridge. And the part where he escapes from prison. The men have standing orders to dispatch him. This takes us right back to the very beginning. Stop capitulating. The answer is easy. It is the name of a kind of shell—at times factual narrative, or the figure of a man used as a column. In the unlikely event that he does not fall in, what then? Or the diverse, that is to say, of indivisible substance.

PROFIT

Things are moving on a pace. It is said. Some may never leave the base. His condition is normal. The physical state has been renounced (dizziness, deafness, double vision, loss of blindness, insight). Despite the title of the book he is less good on twins. I plan to denounce you in the most uncompromising manner. Historical tumours equal inauthentic experience. They sought in this philosophy only a reconciliation with the results. Defend yourself. And he says to them, take me up and cast me into the sea. This looks like a dead reel. And he says for me all writing is very common since the war. It's made of the same stuff.

PROOF

We are now approaching. You have no authority. I am erasing as much as I'm adding on. The two qualities are opposites. Of course they cancel each other out. I suppose what I object to is this. It's quite straightforward. The construction and deconstruction theme is subsequently abandoned. They are using the service shafts to navigate about the ship. We are mapping the genome. Sometimes the simplest option is the best. (Remove this when there's more time.) I couldn't believe that frail body had so much blood in it. It might even come to something worse. These formulae are precisely those to which you should pay least attention.

RANK

Yes just done it. Printing for you your moon, on gemini and ascendant aspect. Here lives one of the remaining customers. We can expect a lot of spectacular optical effects, the bending of light. See how you feel about yourself in the morning. (It is said.) The lift cage is steadily moving up and down. Some among the fifty million kept coming back for more. Tense is intuitive. Contained within these very remarks are indicators. An adjustment has been made. Try to account for the sharp rise in disinterest rates. Etymology is obscure. Consider, when contemplating the stars in the night sky, that you are looking down. A position sixty edges apart, also.

REBELLION

It says proceed cautiously. Stop checking these. Physical repulsion augurs well. I have to read more closely. I'm actually pleading now. Whatever it was, it was big—white marble scored with red spirals. Understand is disharmony. A central portion had been cut out and removed. That man's an obscurantist. There are also many negatives. I didn't want to overlook anything. Three months passed. She returned to her own kind. (O isn't that beautiful.) A blood fine is levied for every hour erased. The favoured metal is an alloy of copper and zinc. A cylindrical mass of rock was once extracted from the bed of the ocean. Now, take a sack of gravel. Grind it, cook it, treat it with new reagents. See, once again, the perennial fascination with being buried alive. I have been appointed official vaunt-courier—a position, albeit one that moves. Let's hope at least four minutes is left. We are due to self–destruct. Never rely on an intercept, or if in transgression, the against. We have done nothing with our lives, really. Blush, monster. All this, this here.

RECEPTACLE

Without comment he returned in the morning. He has the two halves of the shell in his sack. This is taking too long. When did he first realize that a form could be described? He is every day waiting, attending time. The first spirit is called quicksilver (thou that art under the earth et cetera). I may have misaligned. You're not here for my entertainment. Stone posts were dotted about the landscape. I have worked my way into your own private box. We were trapped inside this tiny paranoid space, feeding off each other's rumours. In the deserted halls of the railway station and the shopping malls, assembly lines were set up. I wonder whether I might be doing too much. This is a point I never want to come back to. He feels with his fingers the forehead's cumbrous load. (Which ridge, above?) He seems to be stretching out toward an end or purpose. Significance is solely derived from the fringe. The years of age carry a sign, a triangle of dots nailed to the middle. Everything I read about this subject suggests a sort of generative nothingness. The slope indicates a temporary relaxation of the corrosive action of the sea. The promised word is astragalus. We fabricate, and are fabricated in turn. I am enveloping endless reminders. Steer clear. Location is independent of the bedding cleave. The central character should be a maker, or doer. Something is being delivered (mister I don't have time for this and I'm not in the mood). And of carrying a child to the shore and telling him in your own tongue, having lain down in death. Xenograft. Anti-telos.

RENDING

We'll have to cut off every bulkhead. Are you going for the bribery option? The species was grey with an intricate pattern of tiny writing. (O Mary I said.) We are mighty far from the source, far from the estuary. She tore at her clothes and crept along the ground. Come nightfall we lit the lamp and heated a tiny crucible to melt the lead. In the strictly English sense, these were our only amusements. She says she has nurtured. There exists an inanimate relationship with the subconscious mind. I have excluded words and syllabic symbols. This lacks accuracy. The mechanism of names is escaping from memory. Events are interwoven with fleeting characterizations. (Others connect it with lake, number four.) A uniform is left out as a disguise. Flora are small annual weeds. I rise to my feet, venture out of the cave. It's no use. I just don't know. Observe the stage he has reached on the path of recollection. O God, eyes are growing tired, of being temporarily forgotten. There is so much here, until it is perfectly fluid and no more gas is evolved. There is an entire alien within him.

REST

The everies, a walker. Brightly coloured arcs in abundance. He is not here, at rest between acts, at rest between migrations (questionable because of text immediately following). Certain vibratory states of distant objects are being detected and assessed. You don't need many words to express yourself clearly. Astronomers have hypnotized enormous red-shifts. Who was truly indicative? This is to do with a certain species of oil heater, memories of *don't use that key*. There is no room for them. It's a dull man who can spell a word only one way.

REVELATIONS WELL EXPOUNDED

Substance was found in eighty-five percent of places. The pages themselves are stitched. I watched him drop one shoulder as he swerved through. The reluctant gap equals the ratio of a conductor to its resistance. What's the point of trying to explain (howl, spun glass). Space is weighing heavy in its various senses. Or balanced, depending on one's perspective.

REVENGE

Point the telescope. Rattle the pupae in the box. The rock the head rests upon is unmarked. In two years she will remember nothing, save the number. The affair was about to be made unnewsworthy. The whole thing might degenerate into violence. Things are looking up. Dreams alone are empty of meaning. It's too early to let this go. Converse with that abundant energy. Who glowed through the sad terrestrial curtailment? That woman is full of deeds. She straightens her head in the rear view. It's too late for vengeance. If you don't get a letter at every port, you start to wonder. The stone I carry everywhere in my pocket is a sucking stone. Gnarled and stunted trees are widespread on these coasts, bent back. Contention exists about words, or in words. These are the preliminary things that I wanted to say to you. And in terms of matter?

SADNESS

An abstract field of a yellow resembling pollen. Not your type of meaning. Insects swarm in the humid air. Send an electric engineer and the equipment. Until now I had never thought about such things. Another could have screamed out loud. Just the preparatory work might be enough. Someone present disagrees. He appears to be grieving. No other boy has so completely deserted the community of work. (Believe me, that's important in Scorpio.) He has high social embers. It was threefold, one hundred and twenty degrees apart, hence malign. After three moons have passed they will start fighting back.

SHORT STORY

The name of a fictitious country. That day has not turned out. According to others a city, mythic head, the perfect organism. A single character has been written into the history (*qi*). You may denote an injunction to prevent a possible future act. I have consolidated things from the very beginning. You, I know all your names. Who is the one who arrived and brought snow? The light is short because of the impending darkness. Nonexistence was the material cause. A vibration drums through lips and teeth. He/she fears. Let pass these things. Events dissolved into each other towards the end. He was buried up to the elbows (law). The root is baked and eaten. We fermented and drank the rest. He says I never asked for this. Words form themselves into sequences and recognize each other—note the nacreous internal layer of the adjective. (You mean breathing, no?) Something is always written after something else. Psalms. Pleasant Sunday afternoon. Property. A pseudonym. Betoken, attach as signature. Did mine too and also our incompatibility.

SIRIUS

Land simply ran out, with energy spikes varying after brief intervals. An indication that you did not need to look.

SMOKE SCREED

Now you promised yourself. You mould it to the ear like so. As soon as one starts making selections from memory, this is fiction. An amanuensis penned that. Note the grainy images. Velvet curtains are draped about the edge. Drive those bystanders away. He possesses a peculiar animus. His feelings are dominated and geared toward the ideal. He likes water, sea voyages. He likes odd people. This could have been a noble genre. Any broken bones were reset. You can trace everything back to that horrible day. (Think about it.) Our task is simply to express the universal quality of a specific phenomenon. The distance between the text is the thinnest of membranes. The world is not only the genital-social. For some, any barrier is a brick wall. There was a moment of silent reflection. Refer to things always without explicit mention, with the merest suggestion of further associations. The planet is uninhabited. You were once my lucky star. This continues throughout the space of two to three lightyears. There's time left, enough paper.

SNATCHING AT A SEVERED PART

No, we're still collating. They're everywhere, disguised as things. Some are quite rigid, brittle. They have a tendency to count out loud and list obsessively. Everywhere time is being repealed. Perform only the natural fluxions of the body. Who else was alive upon the earth at the time? When you have made an end of reading, that's it. What is typos.

SOVEREIGNTY

He was a man seemingly devoid. And he had a secular motto. You still don't understand what you're dealing with, do you? All he does is imitation (repulsive offertory). The saltpetre remains liquid and fusible. It's a peculiar sort of target, squirming along the narrow passageways. Silence is not necessarily received as silence. (Room eighty-seven, please.) It was like looking back, or reconsidering an action once done, and which cannot be undone. Every event has been allotted a particular date. A glimpse is usually enough. Poisant.

SPIDERGRAM

Larger squares were subdivided into narrow strip-fields. And then he says this is the original chess move. Nox, our enemy, is thinking along time. He is obviously wondering whether to surrender. This is the chapter in which we recognize a very special type of human being. The highest bidder has withdrawn her offer. The artifact was fashioned from a type of clay. There's not much life left in the old mythology now. Just a word fight.

THE SPOILS

Not exactly a story. Aleatocracy, rule by die—the sinking of the signal. A good sleep will resolve it. Can the external world be proved at all. A hundred times hitherto has spirit as well as virtue flung. Substance is supposed to possess the most miraculous powers. Tell them the vehicle is black market. Block his application to settle on the surface of the planet. I recommend burial and eternal slumber. I'm going to have to sacrifice something, the separation. The skin was crisscrossed by continuities. It's a desolate place. There are surfeits, steerage by lot. The first marks set down constitute the main body of the work. Conjunction Sun, Jupiter.

SQUARE FACE (I REMEMBER)

I just skipped fifteen years. If she had known their destination she would have strangled her fellow traveller on the spot. Limbs may be extended infinitely. I've found myself in this particular dimension before (organ mass heavy and grey, open sores). The top of one digit had been sliced through like razored garlic. There's the obligatory. I am stuck within the parameters of an oscillatory system. What equation represents the degree to which any object can be identified? We're on the wane. We're losing them, outside us. This polemos or war lies at the centre of translation: men in the rain, the taut bows, curbing.

THE STARS

I can't lie to you about your chances. He says he would like to come down and meet us. Any course that follows a constant compass bearing should be represented by a straight line. Take a stick and write upon it. Strip the bark and wrapped it about a staff. He is not picking up his feet enough. The head is not for sale. Rank is that of guizer, i.e. subordinate. Who had difficulty concentrating on any job? Nervous strain is rupturing the viewer's spatial order, the boundaries. I have exquisite taste. Such amplifications are shown by the use of brackets.

THE SUN

All other priorities rescinded. It's frightening, the ease with which this has been accomplished. But it's alarming from a gravitational point of view. I watch the shadows lengthen daily, count the grains of sand in the hourglass. He can't believe he has done it. We are pushing beyond a limit, pushing beyond a surplus. Labour is independent of its particular useful character. The raw material of this experiment are the walkers. All other participants are outdone and discarded. It was like one of those big transformers attacking planet earth, what's called a material uncertainty. Think of your hand pressing against a fragile screen that stretches to infinity. He reckons this is an odd thing to do altogether. He is not saying. One woman wrote his pathos and his defiance. So saying, mister hid the letter in his inside pocket.

SUPERABUNDANCE

An outstripping. Physically, it's very hard to disagree. Compete with the materials at hand. It was like the sound of a shell deep within the sea. It is rather massive. After its death, the exquisite. (Bargain books are non re-orderable.) It had a faulty noose. At this late juncture it's felt the entire work needs redoing. Only six of the spirals actually have centres. We decided to draw lots. One among us is a professional rememberer, though would not care to compete with the men of the past. It is to be devoid—not acts, but rather the swift-as-death son, the irony of his words, spurting forth. I've lost all track of time. We're witnessing an attack of opinions. The aim is simply to survive. Space has been reined in. There are allusions in the corpus to gnostic rejections. A new cut of idiom is becoming popular. It is pointless for me to write you any further. I can see. The game's up.

A TABLE OF EVENTS

The action of or entry into mannerism. Always go with the briefest account. I am not really a place you would ever want to find yourself. You need consonants in untimely places. We are making good the empty. They are probably on their way. Poetry has suffered. I have one commodity. It should devastate about two square miles when it detonates. (I love a good gossip.) There is no other way of doing this. It took me six months to get used to this tide thing.

TABOOT

The male is yellow and black, the female silver-grey with flashes of mauve. Both have large metallic heads topped by a bristling crest. They forage while others sleep. Look, it has unwoven itself. At least try to avoid a shameful defeat.

TEST

An account of how orders should be given, on strategy in general. You two go down into the valley. Take care, by occupation they are makers. Just add water to the powdered ram's horn. We have the following statement: I am the one who gave birth to himself and who made his own name. There you will find. Leave one as forward watch. Retreat to a safe distance. On the banks of a stream we witness. Erase all memory of these events. I have denied myself. After this, I don't think you'll be needing me any more. All writing is dictation. There is nothing alike. I penned a tragedy. Grab all the supplies you can carry. We're sounding a reversal. Wait, I have to give you this. I turned the key anticlockwise and pressed the button. This is the product of a misinterpreted word. Ominously, the date of the flight arrives. We are trying to create a new country in this product. Swiftly, he improvises a shelter of branches and ferns. Tar was once used. I have nine more pages left for you to read. Gosh, it's accelerating, I think. And sure enough, light is set against light in three equal ranks (sixth by old reckoning). Perhaps a separate word expressing surprise, also spelt as a pair, especially of eyes. And the solitary current, the unacceptable.

THAT WHICH IS UNBECOMING

Some new lines. Where the heretics go. She is alone in a room. Just give us a summary of tonight's plot. The cell is small (no conscience, no remorse, no delusions of morality). There's a pallet bed on the bare concrete floor. The empty is only reached by admittance to the most abandoned places. On the front cover the figure depicted is wearing a hat in the shape of a boat. That is to say a gift, withdrawn. A forerunner was sent in advance. Morbid abnormal impressions were reported, as of sense received from a distance. We're running two models in parallel. She is delayed on her journey. The end.

THOSE WHO ARE ABSENT AND THAT WHICH IS PAST

Death sentence. This idea does not displease him. He reflects. Perhaps I could have done this at an earlier time, much earlier. There's a gap opening up. Take it in turns with the probe. A band of migrants is roaming the countryside. I spoke of earlier. Unjoint the hour. What have I forgotten. We're at the stage where things start to unravel. (Publish and you're dead.) I have moved that little bit closer. Are you working. I hunt them down and corner them. The whole affair is rather noisy. He spent a few quiet moments walking around in circles. We're back in times past now. I can wait. I forced him to drop to the ground. It was quite a coup. I told him to lie still. He growls whenever anyone approaches. Then he loses consciousness. Then he dies. I have gone out and bought a ridiculous. O and that money, that money thing is private. That is all I am going to tell you. I have become still. The subject appears to have slept off his trauma. That plastic tube is a saline drip. I wish I could sleep myself. Tomorrow I have no morning. Your body goes on a big high, then it drops. I have left them behind. Where can I find the poison letters? I have recycled the tin. I have recycled the meat. How anything is best described? The reason for this cairn is not clear. They are starting to stir. The map shows restlessness. They have burned off any excess (let the eternal enemy have no power over her et cetera). Leave the hatch open. Now for the cup of grace. When all's said, it's your brain, the memory of a haemorrhage. That is a long time to go without an explanation.

THUNDER

These parts of a man's economy are not shut up in the tomb for all eternity. Allow space for the lightning rod. Yes, we'll need new blood cells. He is also known in these parts (fabulous-winged, scaly-armoured, firebreathing). Often is a guardian, ravaging the countryside. And watchful, like a paper kite. This also applies to lizards and plants. One of the northern constellations is shaped like a scythe. Note how the ring material has mixed with the interstellar medium. Despite its brevity, I worked on this section for many years. Anti-huff is a substance used to adulterate cheese (cf. anti-contagious-diseasist, anti-pent-agonist). It's alarming, from a solar point of view.

UNBELIEF

A sleeping transmitter has just sent three different packages. One reads hallo are you all right. The second, you'd better tell us where the fucking money is for your own good. We are being held in this spectacular house. The affirmation of an autonomous precipice has been completely lost. We dart in swift caricature, across the floor on sliding hoofs. (Pass the flame.) Looking up I see the underside of gentle pink webs patting on the glass roof. This has no shape. The outer skin or shell has been abandoned. The third reads I'm in love again. It appears that liberties were taken. There is the danger too of being intent on movement. We may not wait for the right time. Sympathetic magic is the answer to all our problems. She needs the heads right now (how else). I am because of use while kneeling. It took the form in which it is now recognized more than twenty years after the war. Whence? (High above stage.) It was formed by depositing the product. There's not a trace of doubt in my mind. It can be identified by its beautiful colour while dying, the so-called brittle-at-red-heat. Next time it'll be all right, every time, and it isn't. See, a star cluster, wrapped in the glow of a nebula, in dorado. Antisyzygy.

UNBELIEF, AGAIN

Definitely disco. The cadaver is the basis of a whole pharmacopoeia. Yes, that's right, two life sentences crammed into the span of one. The composition of man greatly favours a belief in apparitions and ghosts (viz. his splintered arm). Fifty feet from the door a dozen headlights suddenly illuminates a bizarre and tumultuous scene—witless wandering to and fro, the wrongness of edge.

UNCANNY

Bottles, rags and petrol are changing hands. Into the tunnel said I. The temperature in the cell plummets. All along we've been expecting something like this to happen. Frantic rustlings pass close by. A small localized area of dead tissue has been identified. I am beloved, probably, yet free to depart. Advance upon the barricade. The text has left behind an indelible mark. Sinews, flesh and skin once covered every surface. There's a rumour. We're all to be given names. The burst sac was full of blood and pustular matter (all things being equal). Keep that thing away from the sphere. I have become forgetful and clumsy. Someone is scraping at the outside of the building. Wednesday is my birth. Good idea or bad idea? You're wrong. I am right. There's a sensation of ringing in the ears and slight numbness. I am undercapitalized. A body has been washed up. Is that an upgrade on unspeakable? Are you busy later? Two instants were crushed together in time, circling one another. A party of us went down to the riverbank to investigate. One would have thought he had cherished that girl, surpassing. Everything has lost a little, an imperceptible fraction. Reflect upon the obscure and insignificant word *tain*. Mister presiding judge, at this very table sits the miracle. I count myself among the contemplatives. They have misused, misread. There is a third machine.

UNCONSCIOUS

It should reach the frontier in about six weeks. In the same species growth-promoting metabolites have been discovered. Remember that the dogs in this experiment may not be right in every instance. Time should stand still. Perception of objects or conditions can take place at a great distance (e.g. nailfile). Reflect upon the general principle of atrophy. A cluster of tiny birds is gathered at the shoreline, perfectly still and facing the horizon. Consider the act of mistaking endless choice for autonomy, the no-remote.

UNDERCARD FIGHTERS

Back to one of my favourite constituencies. It sketches with a slender claw in the gravel of the driveway. I am safely down the well. Far more stringent technical restrictions apply here. I am up to my neck, and no more. I find observation reassuring. The price paid will come in human form. There are shadowy fingers, footfalls crunching on the path. The days of the siege are unfulfilled. You have sixty minutes before the countdown begins. Regard the aspect of two floating bodies, as seen from the surface. The sea overwhelmed our enemies. Threefold moon situated midheaven.

UNJUST

He refers to her as a statistical beauty, an enigma. We have the coins to prove it (not the slimmest of next). We have a basalt statuette, so calm, so past. This represents. Tell us our name. You were advised to hire a guide. This is hearsay. Who was a maker of irrelevances? Objects were brought into form out of nothing. Restrain me. We have to go. I am doing my best to appear corrective. You are income. I must return myself at some point. I did not want to let him go, drifting off into divers places. Establish immediately the foundation of a baseline existence. Seven hundred tins were piled into low pyramids half a metre high. All memory of this event must be erased. We've come this far, we have to go on. In the face of the enemy, I miscounted. A possible explanation for the absence of proper graves is that the coast was once visited by aliens.

UNTITLED

This contribution is about what happens in the morning. The meridians are represented by straight lines set at right angles to the loop of the equator. One last provision seals the compact. It's possible that the word had then some other meaning (storehouse at the tower). My shins ache. He has this knack for finding lost spaces—possessed and dispossessed, parceling out the body into various masses. He often describes his entry into the world of literature as a terrible mistake. Patience is already nonspirit. We've got less than thirty seconds to go.

VEIN

With flakes of burning hemp falling all about you. Try to avoid the sounds of others' happiness. Who could resist. Surely time for another injection of mercury. I've been too reticent. You she says. (Better it is eternally to be conversant with immortals.) Signs are mutable. It is possible that you may have suffered from some slight strain and shyness. A shrouded figure, tightly bound, plummets down the cliff-face. It threatens to strike the wall of chalk, but does not. The sea is in the distance. There are eleven of these falling men. Reverie is broken by the crack of a knuckle bone against a marble table top. I always welcome distractions, as at the end.

VESSEL

By the sound of it. They must be on this floor. Clearly there's an awful lot of space left. It exists in between our limbs. Picture a semi-translucent body to which cling yellow papules—moss too, and several kinds of lichen. Time was a drastic tactical change in our existence. The way the goal has been constructed and executed is quite simply alarming. In their minds I have already made an end of writing—vested disinterest, mighty real in the final et cetera. This understanding extends to all things.

VICTORY, THE

A watery spot, or elevation. In this account the enemy camp is infiltrated. References are made to hot wax. The era is that of lost geometries. Allotments are still in dispute. The deceased became dissatisfied with all actions and events. Whisper it: this could only be done by burying the four porcelain figures. The interloper was disguised (head severed). Forgive me the ebb and flow against the shore—the bones appear to have welded together. The titles have nothing to do with it. I presume one still might do this kind of thing once one is dead. Allusion, where a river ran.

WADI

An anonymous face at the window. Why is this happening. What's the name of the legend. The process includes simulated drowning. I am simply reacting to secular conditions. It looked like a body of quicksilver, an unbroken surface of liquid metal. He is one of the northern saints. I replied a hundredfold—give it away, immediately, even the eyes. In one direction sits a perfect circle of light. We are distant from each other one third of a zodiac. The beaked end worries at a bone that has dropped from the sky.

WARSHEET

The device was fitted with a mirror set at an angle to the line of vision. My chemical is unresolved. One character is depicted with an upturned face. (I welcome flatness.) It was a vector in Hilbert space, symbolled. I'm no use to you. It's statute. This chapter was overlong, for conspicuousness and ease of use.

WHERE

An dog. Two tongues. A stony place. Excursion. A fight to the death. Discovery's extravehicular capsules are spheres nine feet in diameter. Undersea cables were accidentally severed. Then an enormous sheet of flame. Of all the ceremonies the most important was the opening of the mouth and the throat. Now a return journey is most improbable. My fingers started moving that bit quicker. A remote voice is urging. My response is almost anatomical. (Press the button once the timer's running.) Again we are moving. No punctuation was used, except for stops, represented by a triangle of dots. I was a bit disappointed, I must say. There is extant human voice. Consider one of three ports, hard to the east. There isn't much time. Strike the fear of sudden death into them. Whatsoever he called every living creature that was the name thereof. Simple. That was what we wanted. It was never published. I'm not going to wait around. What a terrible afternoon. A ballot is mooted. Who discovered late in life that he was a telepath? I look back with regret at the many gilded opportunities I've missed. The subject was then embalmed and wrapped in a flexible sheath. This is clear from the present text. With a little luck the network will pick her up. That which is positioned at the head of all names is your name (titled genius and mobocracy, yes, but genteel). Who was co-creator, employed to react against the things? Those buried alive were later disinterred for the sake of plunder.

WOMEN, THE

Certains in a state of decay gather and forestall the calamities to come. I believe that is a chair over there. Thoughts have no parallel. In the second episode the sentry returns. This is misleading. Cylindrical map projections appear to float through the air. We heard the crash on the ground floor. In this experiment the subject is motionless and takes no food. (Can't I be wrong.) Dissolve me she says, quick. The timekeeper has returned from its trial at sea. It has even been suggested. This stage lasts up to fifty thousand of your earth years.

WORD, RESCINDED

The radiant activity of any new body. The subject is in his room less than one hour before panic sets in. No matter preceded or followed this second. Everything is written in an unaccountable hand. Covering the courtyard is a surface of liquid glass, crystallizing into irregular pyramids. Who bowed low in homage as they came toward thee from the underworld? He drove a stick into the ground and attached a few snacks. The object has not suffered any recognizable damage. (That's a very mean question.) I drift from town to town. All along I meant the actual concrete act of utterance. The man flipped up the collar of his army greatcoat. Take another stick and write upon it. Play the same tune over and over again. It was like some elliptical train of thought. To cut a long story short, too much is happening at the same time. (Hallo, spectral class, the spark chamber et cetera.) It struck high at the temples. On the organs of speech this is not easy—compound of mucus cells and the calcite from its nacre. The white package flipped rapidly in space, from head to tip, toe to head. Click on a planet for more information. Who was startled out of reverie.

XXXI

Stayed in to watch the silence. He says I'd prefer these notes to be left unread, or better still forgotten altogether. Scanning down the instructions it seems this part is to be rededicated. The time is four years before release. Such figures in memory are bodiless connections. What material was always without earthly abstraction? Numerous forces are in operation—gravity, magnetic fields, stellar winds. A shearing effect is caused by their revolution. I might have given them better names. I might have treated them as unconsciously as I pleased.

Here he is pictured leaning on a balcony beside his attractive. He looks so much better with a human face. There are obvious hints of collusion. He's the hermit in the pack. I find it hard to look. It's miraculous that he's still alive. We will never abandon. The wick cannot be detached. Yse-schokkill is an obsolete type of icicle. Suchlike arrangements of syllables spill from the mouth. There are obvious hints that someone has been sent to collect. It'll be all right on the night.

Ibex box.
Note the wisps of vapour. It's technically fiendish. It has been written in a surprisingly neat hand. A form of waterwheel was once used in Egypt.

He or she
An identical, yet indifferent. Which historical figure was never reconciled with the idea of confusion? From his inner pocket he draws a fragile root, the dried claw of a bird. He's a stonemason by trade. Those conical hives are common to the heel of the land. (Our bonus has been cut.) These items are material to chew on. Since reading I've made a mental note. Never complete an action. It's partly this and partly that. Carefully trained predestination has been detected. About here the river forms a perfect an ox-bow. It's like the credits. Is there something I should have done which I have not done? That and which have been misused.

Familiars are invited to distract people. I need to reach a decision before you come back. The proposed motion represents the estate of a quantum system. I need to reach a decision before he leaves and the other comes back. There exists an instrument for viewing objects not directly before the eye, the so-called.

It's to be restructured. You get the picture. No, I will read out the first bite. They appear close. (Nothing is nothing like it was.) He will soon be unable to write anything. People exclaim. That's him. I have. My problem is. I was unrequested. I am of repute. In all readiness, I am at hand. I'm not any good at that. I'm not good at this. It should always be written as a single word. He never writes anything else. I always tell people what I'm thinking. I always tell people when I'm thinking. He has an amazing voice, the other. I've got photos that resemble these. I always tell people when I'm writing. Which work is the worse of the two? Now I want to tell you of my dream panel. Time was spent in a kind of purgatory. It was more like a remote railway station. I have a reputation to deflate. I could have died. I like that, the physical effort required. I can only say what I know to be true. Only that which is collected in passing can be considered. (Is this the same thing?) I have returned the found item. It had wings. The tree had a white, hydrogenous bark. Alpha Crucis is at apogee, helium blue. Newsmen are watching. From time I have named these found things. Sursum corda equals lift up your hearts. I invent words then forget what they mean. Each morning a considerable number of people were reported missing.

Her face says it all. She is cut into. Some people talk with their hands. Every cell just seemed to implode. I spat out my share—place without place, or rather. A sublime sacrifice shamed the verdict. This embodies of course, for a moment, the cessation of work. (Sorry to spoil it, but they don't.) Yes, voodoo zombies can be controlled. Pass me that receptacle. Pass me the speculum. One was given a sentence of forced labour.

Improper use is impossible. Plumes of yellow smoke swirl about the chamber. I am not thinking clearly. Stand still before the object. (Mister sands is in the building.) I am sorry. Now stand back. Remember him. The only means of escape is to scrape away the surface. From his pocket he takes a bill and cuts it neatly in two.

The wired room.
The volumes in this impressive library correspond to a system of numbers. I am not forgetting the future. Somehow this cannot be correct. The number eight is particularly significant. Suddenly I can't concentrate. Insurrectionists are gathered outside, occasional gunfire. We have moved away. The meridian shifts due to precession. A hole was dug deeper, to be filled with moist clay and earth. A battered chaise-langue is lowered gently, from above.
I have written little since that time. The cell faces north. That man writes with his back to the sea. The cell is a rumour. Visitors are rare. There exist familiar marks by which anything is known. Another unusual combustion occurs in the following piece. The further they go, the faster they leave.

I read that he ended his life by drinking antifreeze. The last reversal, another charge is ordered. (Which begins?) Patrols have been established. He says that's a question only stupids ask. I can no longer afford to be generous. I'd laugh if I could. I can no longer afford to deal with this. It's been an interesting distraction, all these years. (She is not the girl that did undone.) Everyone knows the dissonance quartet. He is a master of the power of speech and is considered possessed. The scalp was split open from ear to ear.

Chamber, harmonies.

I'm at a loss. They are dug in beneath. You don't know what we know. The possibility of changing the past is unlimited. I am listing, usage of the odd word. (Nis is a contraction.) There is none fairer than he was. It's body appeared bathed in blood. I desired her because I was alone. Could the houses have been abandoned as they are now? And so on. It's only necessary to raise the water a few feet. You'll be visited by three ghosts et cetera. Hammer, hammer, hammer.

The original meaning is a sounding together. There was a determined pursuit. It should feel very warm in the strong sunshine. The body is turned carefully to lie on its stomach. Surrounding objects have been sterilized. The needle is aligned with magnetic north. Terrain has been cautiously mapped. It's our thirteenth anniversary. I am tired now, sapped. We're huddled against the driving rain in the lee of a drystone wall. I can't imagine listening to him without the mumbled accompaniment. He clearly does not know his right from his left. That white dust must be from two years back. Totality doesn't really suit me. This has me thinking of the man rattling his dice. You see it how works. Suddenly we found ourselves in a tunnel beneath the Dolomites. A miscarriage of speech, from unconscious. I.e. to join in aspect.

Birdland, limefill.

I am there and then I am not. I have had a jolly good day. I know from experience. Let's say the time is some time this evening. I imagine the seal looks red and waxy, like a scroll of some sort. The audience will break the spell here. The dungeon was lined with white tiles, the garden fence topped with razor wire. The owner has invited a number of friends to a banquet. Helicopters hover above the pier. (These are not strictly a part of the situation.) Heraldry is a subject under study. There are inquisitive machines, lots of cheap. There is no other show in town. Open up your own network. She says she wants a baby, anything will do. He was writing a book just before he died. The voices are unaccountable.

We don't know when this was composed. Presumably events took place during the summer. It survives as originally set down. Much of the text is spoken. The title means pillar of his mother, but this must be a later corruption. He writes that he's not happy with the job on offer. Grains of pollen were trapped in the spine. Objects can become injurious by creating confusion. Every word turns out a sentence (gentleman usher et cetera). He was held in a grim struggle with a phantasm. How can this be, anything.

That black ink was like velvet. Since she stopped seeing him the world has turned to ice. Fear was writ big. The earth flips about on its axis. I had nothing to gain by waiting. And her voice, the air she exhales. What signifies a most deformed and frame-shaken changeling?

Someone is tapping on the ceiling. The signs in the early notation combine several tongues. Various flames form one symbol. Before the art can be followed, preparations must be made. Often is prefixed entirely, penetrating, with assistance. It was nothing. It was something I had never seen before in my life. We're still on he and she.

Stillicide.

Under roaming law, stripped to fail. The first tribune of the notaries. Who was peculiarly qualified by his dexterity? About his neck on a leather cord hangs a magnesian stone. Very shortly after sixteen hundred he prepared a light in the darkness. There are some explanatory notes. Perhaps it is talc. This is not the type of progress we require. Exile the subject from the day. The flesh appeared bruised (what with his self-righteous). It parted from the godhead. Since all cognition is akin to recognition, it should not come as a surprise. Set on the table a small censor.

Interpret.

It errs. An everlasting heedful. Let this man's mimicry be unforgotten. Let this be a caution to everyone present. This weather I do not eat. I observe that they have wrapped the old Martello and capped it with glass. I saw to that myself. Space has fallen into disrepute. The book was entitled. I suggest you bit your tongue. I draw your attention the telegraph poles receding into the distance. They disappear over the horizon line. It was like a witches' sabbat. (Draw it out by hand.) The bird migrations, this is the cause. That brilliant lustre ascribed by the alchemists favours the latter view. He has made next to no headway. Indeed, it is still not understood. He says my apothecary. Ask these woods that hem us in.

We have reached the moats that bind that unhappy city in concentric circles. He crumpled up, with his shitsmeared blanket and his hair.

Substance.

Despite the semblance of its name to our familiars.

I wonder what he will do alone in his house. What will transpire within that abandoned then.

Lodelight, said to be seen above a vein of ore. How do you write one asks. The iron portion had rusted. First make a wide circuit. It is not exactly. It is close enough, the dry bed of a once torrent. The danger is that the figure will strike a projecting rock. Mine is a seven. It was a veritable writing machine. It was unaccountable. I have decided to unlearn language. We have lost conflict.

Votive fictions, 'uncensored quiddity'. Besides, it looks like rain.

Our stone is composed of the lesser numbers one and three. (Note how shapeless this philosophy is, which he *carries in.*) Remember not to exclude the sovereign triangle in your own calculations. Crystals grow inward from two directions, to meet at a spear-like aggregate. Remove yourself from here. Invade the following day. In the previous pages we have seen how they employed magical amulets, words, pictures and names. That circle of light is both the exit and the entrance to the shaft. Remember to take all of your belongings with you. (No, I've slept enough, years and years.) A mixer would not have helped the situation. A rout is on the way. If is the last thing I do. Crew dead, cargo and ship destroyed.

A reach of water, an open ditch.
He says when I write. I write about what I'm doing and what I am not doing. I miscontain. Territory was gradually recovered.

An impromptu in a flat. I can pass the days.

So is noticing a likeness seeing, or isn't it. I am calling upon you. The reclining body is moist with brackish water. The local sand boasts gritty encrustations. It feels too early. Tomorrow you are going to have to. Passage was difficult, over the rough stony ground of a dried-up river bed. The stomach was then emptied, voluntarily.

Anamorphous.
I am obsessed with a particular cathedral. It is, the text says, a brittle and friable black. (I like the bits which are true.) Consider the account of his first breakdown. He has dispensed with centuries of radiation, the so-called seven plots of earth. How am I decided. He has observed. It's a perfect day for writing everything down. Here we have dissimilar yet related concepts. There is a tendency to lean towards death. Intervals occur throughout the year and everything is semblance. At which point we simply reverse the names and everything starts up all over again. I don't mind things being one-dimensional. Some kind of rope was used on a ship. The flesh is cold to the touch. She's an expert. He doesn't. A gentle greyness of air is muffling existence. Neon is big. We're getting somewhere.

I tire. The instrument has a difficult centre of gravity. All sorts of unknowns are emerging. We are about to lay waste a land which harbours enemies. (Text us what a voice?) The theme is his cockaigne in the elder. The encompassing hills foreclose. An attachment is about to be made. Place yourself in our midst. This chapter is about how anything may be constructed. This is an exceedingly profound art. Birth can be prevented. It is about how to compose with the offhand. Whiff of dubbing and new leather in the freezing air, set loose among the still-alive. He went once or twice to visit some relatives. He says to write while locked out of time.

Azygy.
Our space-pods. Fellowless means unpaired, an organic part of the description. (Right side, esophagus above thoracic duct.) It contains two different min-

erals, the lodestone and another who shines like silver. Abandon him forthwith. I know what he means but cannot. Mandragora, nor all the drowsy serums of the world cannot et cetera.

A star that guides (tenth gulf-hole).

I wake and find I can't. It's a miracle. I am reappointed. They came barefoot with woad on their faces. I have read. Carpetbomber by trade the card said. A fetisheer.

It just keeps coming. Language can be siphoned through a planchette. One finds oneself thinking out loud, a voodoo list—heap of rags torn in shreds, a plastic doll, a puzzlingly blank stare. A passing voice says you look lovely together. The scale is an all too familiar scale. The operatic style is unconvincing. (We've just realized we're dead.) In this fragment there are further confluences, the path to the headwater. There were angels behind the windscreen. Who once said a forest of dangling chargers where the road rips into the sea? The speculators are unimpressed. One obtains what one refuses to strive for. I woke to find what. Is that all you do for a living. You have clicked in various places, for example the innermost head. I like the fact. I dissemble. Do you want to think about returning every grain of her skull? Consider the violence of each intercession. I'm glad. I don't regret spent time with you, despite all the citation. Deviations encountered in contemporary ships are still small. Hire something before it's too late. O well does no harm. Let's hear it for the death rattle.

Contained therein are smaller and larger ring-islands.

Mute elective.

He had the most uncanny blue. I remember saying exactly the same thing in the previous century. I read to forget. It looks as though there's a woman behind it. There's so much to unlearn. You'd think there would be something, even the skin tone, but nothing has changed. Could someone have a feeling for the space of one second? Break the sun's rays into their wavelengths. We are going head to head. We are going further than the landward side. The substance carried resists identification. You have a different memory of the event. They survive to continue the game. The writing room is lined with books.

Hydrocephalic.

Stretching across his forehead is a scar the shape of a centipede. He's spent another night on the beach. The wind is so strong off the ocean it blows sand against his sleeping form. Even here, a stunning plausibility. Ascend with me this dazzling apparition, and so on.

A reclining figure sculpted in translucent blue stone. Both returned to their respective planes of existence. All this has nothing to do with what I'm saying. A more straightforward consideration of analytic theory could always be made. At whose death did he succeed to the throne but was then driven from it? I asked about the reward. Who would want to be visible in such a world. Any duplicates are identified and one of the doubles is disposed of. She detaches herself. The assistant is an idiot. Damn you he roared letting go of his sister's arm. You're not going to stand up all the way are you? She declares time. The story is obvious and pressing. She is so pleased. She could have crossed herself out with both hands and not noticed. By morning, compact banks of earth have built up around the body.

The understanding (a simple misunderstanding).
Businesslike air for a time. Suddenly I'm pulled to pieces. I have made a fetish of my lists. Swap read for write, then back again. The finger was severed from the rest of the body. Everybody was there at the ceremony of opening the mouth.
Scattered ruins, mostly. The vein contains magnetic ore.

Now the story goes. (I cannot these things.) The latter is distracting, the former evil. Probability is owing to the identification. I feel guilty, like so. I want to be both animals at the same time. I was once literally. This is now the last, through a process of happenstance. There's still time to contrast yourself with the unconditional. I was not myself back then. It was extinguished and it disappeared. A delimiting term may be added to birds in flight.

Nothing endures. You always want the impossible. A word might reconstitute an object. Deposits of ash were found in a pit at the foot of the menhir. Ice was scraped from every conceivable surface. There is this tendency. Simply bear in mind that abstraction means abstract, *for us.* A contraction for ne is is not.

Short sorry.
I go bodily into the chamber and speak, calling him by name and inquiring how he has passed the night. He replies between. And I consign you back from whence you came. What do you mean by this example? Before I forget, tell me of it, now. The case remains shrouded. A project to fill up a denatured vacuum with ejaculate is underway. The following morning I notice a cigarette burn on the flesh of the left forearm.

From warsheet, the ideal. The fridge of a roof or hill.
He mastered the language of economics in a matter of weeks. Talismans were nailed to all the pillars as a preventative. In the snow the shed antlers of a stag lie half-buried. The people depicted are generally us. They are here to this day. We used an armature. I advise the administering of a compound. One element was aluminium. Specks of rust are embedded in the soap. We scraped at every surface with the scapula. Vehicles were abandoned. Survey the body laid out before us. Move that trolley. Now he must fall to pieces a little. All comfort-

ing diversion ends here. Identity has never been established—unknowable from externals, mired by encrustation, safeguards.

From these remains a jelly of phosphorous and benzine is manufactured. Every step hurtles us back in time. What a fragile lead this is. I hear the diagnostic click of dislocation. Some have a voracious desire for land, earth-hunger. A slight convexity exists upon the upper surface.

Consider a pathway. List items at inventory: ferric chloride, wood stain, coffee, tea, blood. A beam in the eye. The deck of a ship. The wing section. To arch, to arch tightly. I am filling the place of another. I cannot wait any longer. He is suffered unto. The wintergardens and promenade were flattened. But who dwells in these words, if they are uninhabitable? I have reached such a distance that the ruins are hidden from view. Consider employing a deputy or substitute (sphere of drunk). All actions are contagious impulse. Perhaps it was merely contempt. The vessel was found in a decaying orbit around the planet, Neptune.

Japans. He inserts it. He sundered. Or to exist in? And the greasy stitched-up orb. Folly indeed.

I've tried reducing the speed by ten percent and it shimmers a bit. They are no more. They are now only imagined through the experience of others.
Remnants of furlike patches and strange lateral flukes.
Tenth cranial nerve concerned and bitten into.
Remaining tooth fractured.
The art of hosting is all but lost. Symptoms include a repulsed heartbeat. The breath is out of rhyme, compulsive night wandering et cetera. This is the last thing I ever want to do. I never mention. I am inconsolable. Gram-negative rods, fixed in the present, are releasing the virus. Evidently our sides have fallen in. One flank is exposed. Reserves have been reduced to the point. Location of the source is my one abiding passion. Torn out in leathery scraps, here's the third opus of his set (from the Greek meaning pressure). There is not space or time to list the blood, the sinews, the facial tissue.

Very light.
A signal. An illuminating. A coloured flare is fired off and descends in an arc towards the horizon. Nothing is illuminated. The sky's emptying. Look at him.

Autopsi.
Circular breathing. A cubicle in a thermal complex. I took a careful step into the shallow pool. Please listen. I have not done my reading. No it's not one of those. No it's not about an insurrection, a slave revolt. I have no concept of the distinction between private and public.

This week he goes back to retrieve—nothing of himself, an ill-fortune of his own making. The monsters and demons depicted are quite plausible. And a felled warrior with attendant detail, the beautiful death. She says I have all I need, and anyway.

Just where is this state of origin. Someone will escort you back to the ridge, the saddle of the crest. A tiny porcelain figure perches on my shoulder. We lack. I can change all of this if you want me to. Throughout my time here, just one insignificant word has arisen. I do miss being close. (It doesn't have a pro-gramme.) Could you bring both versions, please, the original and the slower. I need to check out the shimmer. Someone whispers in my ear. His first fears were for the coolant. These gods place him under their protection. I too have got to thinking. I should have made an exit (the torment to which we confessed). It's too early to stop now. A hollow wheel was used instead of the wheel with pots. I have read since. Drinks should never be bright blue. Everyone knows that.

Inter view.
Death by distraction in the seventh. It sometimes occurs to me, utterance. An old woman squats on the dirt floor of the cell. Yes of course, shimmer is sort of pulsing. Will you bring yours, please. I think I may be short. On the wall is the horned relief after his tracing. Remind me she says, which is the fontal word for horse, the san-script. (Who founded these?) And which is the persistence, as generally understood? I am very impressed. I am mighty pleased. She claims to be an infamous sculpt. A sequence of impressions is perceived. The figure I saw was acephalic, with eyes in its breast. Set into the ceiling are two ducts through which various objects pass. Perhaps it was discovered—the accursed share, daily performance of the natural functions. Saint declared he had seen such a specimen. The idea is to compose something with the scope of a symphony and the intimacy of a chamber piece. As for her questions, I have no idea. I've written everything down, somewhere.

Cultural memory exists only in the present, an undertow. At rest on the ground is a company of domesticated animals. Can you guarantee the most enduring will, the most powerful and dangerous passions? She says they embody the spirits of many nations. You are thrust down into the flame. It flickers against you. When she has no more flax the soul is loosened from the flesh. I detonate one of my couplings. Warp machines indicate the levels. (Try me.) Doc-tor said death was ever-present that night. She gave me one last warmthless glance. Dozens of bare yellow bulbs outlined my reflection. The surface is a syn-thetic skin. Ambient sound puts one in mind of early experimentals. Which his-torical figure dealt in contraband? (Must have forgotten.) There's this grainy image of her raising her veil. Stay frosty people. In the void where her eyes should be turns the milky rim of an astral cog.

This business of plying variations doesn't always work. Time is beginning to evaporate. We fell into disrepute. The structure was not unlike a Martello tower. (I would never swear to that.) It's fascinating to play these complex language games. There were both notes *and* letters. Yesterday we lost heavily. She writes exactly the same thing every day. Somehow it's different. Her violence is not of the kind that explodes in a single discharge. We tried again and again. Between us we have amended the visible distribution of stars. This suggests the usual line-up of fast and slow numbers.

The accolade, a preparation of grease for proofing. For this to work, one has to withhold the page. The usual one-upmanship won't work. An impasse is possible. I have grown into something which should in reality be called a substitute. I'm kind of kicking the thing about (assail, wassail et cetera). Objects and their memories are found, not given or made. She lowers the volume to such a degree. Only broken chords and heavily decorated melodies are audible. The chosen victim is preparing for pursuit across the marshes.

If related once more, this must not include the estranged name—double carbonate of calcium and magnesium, any rock composed of that mineral. Vena azygos major. Magnesian limestone.

Some first names. The black leather bag hanging on the door. The verisimilar *that*. An urban servitude allows one's eavesdrop to fall on a neighbour. Otherwise is forbidden. Exile the subject for one night only. There are too many remarks about ice in this section. The surface is concave. A depression flutes to a hole to drain off fluids. (I mean the trolley.) It's the trumpets that bring light to the circumference. During the years the island underwent constant aerial bombardment. Lord of the two hands, dweller in the shrine is thy name, mangled about in such a puzzleheaded way.

Nothing, illuminated.
People, redressed—clusters on the riverbank, armed with knives and staves, yelling. I grew up on such sailing stories, ushering in the final years. These occasional pieces were dictated, recorded verbatim. Space is all very lyrical. (Take note, overused words are responsible for the reversal.) There is a relatively simple method of representing atoms. Sound is the lost quintet. A crack opens up in the earth. The surrounding buildings appear to bleed rust. I tried this experiment at home but it never worked. That's all I know. There's property, and then without warning, the residue evaporates.

Whereupon are found a shrine, numerous springs, a palace, towers and gates, covered channels, a radio beacon, bridges and docks, a river lock (opening very slowly), an early warning radar outpost, hanging gardens, a hippocaust, a stadium with gymnasia, and canals that lead inward to a central citadel, outward to the sea. He crumpled it up. (Quite like what?) There's sand in my boots, something concrete.

A composition for five voices, or instruments. The so-called lost.

I just poured boiling water over it and left it to stand for a couple of weeks. Most cultures acknowledge that dreams can be clairvoyant. Whenever he addresses the reader, that's a very difficult thing to do. The room housing the library corresponds to the number eight, the infinity. The whole affair is dangerous and tortuous and funny. So many of the allusions contained herein are indecipherable. Part of me wanted this to be a nonfiction account. That part lost. The accused was sent into exile somewhere really cold. (There isn't time for this.) Cadavers were cooked as late as fifty-one. It lifted its paw. There, another boom, motionless. He is always quiet, never anybody, and avoids disputes. But out of contempt for others, out of the corners of his empty eyes, as if to say.

As it turns out, every page contains hard facts. I grew weary. Cross-referencing is no longer an option. I have studied men and I know them he writes. What chance to find printed such books. Who else has written since? The outhouse was built of concrete and asbestos. It's known for sure that war took place. A word or two should be said about the cryptic letters that head certain chapters. Beneath the city spread miles and miles of catacombs. (See appendix, this past contrives et cetera.) The language I undermine denotes the limits of any world. More details have been withheld.

Horst.

Six years ago I was heisting cars around the orbital. It's the last day of my life. We're marching across the peninsula in a series of parallel lines. Ask yourself. Are you still open to visitation. There's a war on. Is this within your capabilities, the scope of your own resource? The mother state is acute, then vanishes. There is drought. Various theories have been put forward to explain meaning. (Take him earth and cherish him et cetera). He split open the taut flesh of his forehead in an unfortunate collision with a concrete pillar. He had to be recomposed for burial. He bit of his own tongue. The fact is that no one knows what the marks signify. Have yourself, engineered.

It is torn. The three senses identified may not be interconnected. The object resembled a clod of earth. Someone has been flattened into the asphalt by a passing tank. I could do with some company myself right now. (Who said our father's murmurous shade?) Science contrives to unsilence agony. This composition survives without opus number. Traditional commentators dismiss by acts of saying. This could be a good place to stop. It would be advisable for any telepathic communication to cease forthwith. We've reached a state in which death seems as lively as recovery. The best have only one word in them. The hero descended to the underworld. An accompaniment harmonizes with the surrounding air. A disquisition took place beneath the severed heads. This genus encompasses most orders of the same family. Cries mingle with an eerie jangling of bells. We're at the southern rim of the island, the terminal. Sonic phenomena are called speech acts. All this may change, of course. A shape is taking place. I dwelt within her, under law. And above all, with the terror that has us falter. Write, and no.

Nothing illuminated again.

Now I'm going to tell you about something that actually happened. (They don't, they stack.) I was deeply affected and profound. These are largely other people's words. What exactly are you trying to achieve. A purgative is the answer. It was like going back somewhere. The state is governed by divination of things found floating in the air, geomancy. The head is brittle. Character armouring won't help. Charms or words of power need only be written on papyrus. This includes the spurts of the body—the skin, the blood, the vessels and sinews, the nerve trunk with its cables and tributaries, dense filigree of bone, marrow sludge. The event was reproduced by a slow change of direction in the earth's axis. Some among them are lowing. Heads have swollen into shapelessness. I should never have returned. I am operating, the weal of the law. Any peripheral orbits.

He goes through a spell then is restored to normality by revolution. The object found had a short, sharp blade. A strip of territory stretches out from the mainland like a panhandle. The body was found dumped in an alleyway. Twice she slaps the seat beside her, beckoning the traveller to sit. She has been away with her teeth. Her odour fills the gun-carriage. You'll never get to hear my original. He says he knows, hence the name.

It moves. Every twenty-eight years the equator describes a circle around the pole of the ecliptic. He must be kept clean and separate from the things. This breaches the earlier date of seventeen. Each year I rejoice more and more. It's such a simple idea. The distorted figure appears in proportion when viewed in a convex mirror. What is happening in conjunction with any particular distraction? Thus, a making anew. The shape of bees. A decoding and scraping of the method.

A series of sudden expansions. The banks have broken. They take the path that leads to higher ground. I am expressing a failure to understand. Black water spreads across the floodplain. It's about staying here and doing nothing. That window's hardly ever open. A thing may be unmade back to nothing, amid the tapping of eggshells.

Parallax view (wave, desert, superstructure). Spend more and get more. Every chip will eventually crack. There have actually been flash mobs. It's to remind me of you. You do get mismatches, there's no doubt about that.

I find myself in a vast open field hurling a spittle-soaked ball for a dog. Then other weeks he doesn't.

A technical epithet of organic parts, still not existing in pairs. They can no longer relieve the pressure.

Still nothing illuminated.

An assembly of imperial electors gathered in a simple whitewash interior. Up until midnight everything is under control. Then its flame is deadly to your soul and your spirit and the words you embody. Seems there's still construction work going on. The slur against modern notation is discussed elsewhere. A vote was cast using knuckle bones. She says the apparent cathedral is unfinished. Two or more notes must be nailed to each syllable. It was encompassed. A voice says they have created this chaos. I suppose they could have misunderstood the reward.

Gold reverse.

A tuft of hair on the lower lip.

A pointed dome.

The so-called one.

A bottle dungeon.

An S-shaped curve in section.

The diagonal rib of a vault.

A doubtful yet possible summit.

A trunk for carrying around blank slates.

Typewriter on canvas.

Selves are uncreated (it's blood feat). The horizon was crushed by a series of explosions.

Arrival in static. Hasty and negligent irregulars. An example of my early follows, a number of meaningless marks scored with a pencil. Literally, talking arms that indicate (an obsolete liquid, a press). I read to forfeit. Wood smoke rises to my nostrils. Do you know meaning. Species include the dragnet, a marine or other large-headed spiny useless. A slang. O, obsolete and rare. Obscure all origin, all citation to rub, erode. Tell me thy name, holy.

The winding sheet.

An attempt at enigma. They say the things to make it seem improbable. There's a rumour that notes are to be phased out altogether. (I wouldn't exchange this technique for anything.) It's not the canniest way out of this mess. It's difficult to determine why they do what they do. I've gone completely the other way myself. Our explosive capability has been reduced by seventy-five. We are to be condensed into one spectacular moment. All indices are being withdrawn.

It nearly cut my leg off but it didn't. Everyone has somewhere else they'd like to be. I have a picture of him sitting in a hollow trunk with a smile on his face. Traces of grain adhere to the photograph, husk of einkorn. Real duration is something immediate. This case is apprehended as a separate manifestation of reality. Say, a composite plant, extract of root. Yes, he's screaming at the pitch of his lungs. (I lost an eye.) The beauty of this fibre is that it's future-proof.

Neolith, but only by empathy. He is, to a form, a burial mound.

The walls seem to be made of iron, unregenerate memory. A chest of files has been lost. And where dwells? And what thing is vilehead, villiago? Of this work, the reading of it probes an error. Some speculate on my origin. Time passes, entering. It is an attempt to describe an animal looking upwards, with head inclined. The text evolved out of subway directions. Any message may become garbled in its communication. We are invested in an enterprise which carries considerable risk. I can no longer speak. They can bewitch or take the life of a man by melting effigies. The library is subject to censorship. There's no choice about where to sit (a small circle of beloved faces). Thursday we start out with a new alphabet. We're surrounded. This is a new breed of English piano. And on into the eternity which cannot compass.

It's the cleft palate. This is characteristic of the fetish. A block of the earth's crust has remained in position. Bodies of blue light poured through the transportation channels. Default as you approach the end.

Imagine you're handed a name but that person doesn't exist. The action starts then it stops again. No sooner had those words left her mouth. We might overcome the evil by following the letter of the law. Sense the dangers inherent in such a doctrine. Be certain. I'm writing a play. It's about guilt and redemption, anything but the pit et cetera.

Work that's easy.

This tool is a modern copy of a much earlier instrument. It resembles a scalpel. I was recomposed towards the end of a brief life. The inconsistency of form in one place is due to a scribal error. For a guide to notes and symbols see page two.

From the strand steep steps lead down to a river. Air overrun with substance. A number has been attached. Magnesia tape records blood feud—parcel tape, brown paper, string.

Rain in the night. Back in tow, sea air fecal and sharp. Cheesewire is stretched across the causeway. One is blinded by a dagger the horseman wields. There rose a tempestuous wind, the Euroclydon. I am beating at the boundaries of the instrumental. Crises recur. We weren't covered by the takeover clause. The rearguard and the centre descend upon the trenches. I just fell on top of this minimum in the street, simply because I wasn't ready for it to be there. The pier is not either, really.

A shudder.

Here he comes, precursor. The great elsewhere—a wave, supposed to be a wrong reading. The pulp is still twenty-five seconds plus eight-and-three-quarter minutes long (mob rule). I shall use the smallest unit, the seme.

Bath drugs. A pretended deferral of opinion, one's mind already made.

A mound who is electromagnetic. Better attested readings were found and recorded. You are reminded that the salient section is now upon us. (I'll use your sharp edge here, if I may.) Expect the finale to involve ungovernable humours. It's been designed to stop people falling off the rim of the globe. Well into the evening and towards the night, again and again, come those familiar words. A cake of wax is stamped with such a figure. That rustling sound must be the shade of an ancestor. You did divide the light from the darkness, did you not. O, the same thing, differing.

What I am going to call you now. Saying so could be worse. A theory of spirit can be contrived by naming matter. (Writing makes my shins ache.) Add muscle atrophy. You are not included in this portion. There's a well-defined crater from which ejecta can escape. Adjust the lighting. Suspend thyself by thy corrupt form. They continue building the cone. How obvious was it that you were being followed.

Enter one against whose decision there is no appeal. I am state department. The exhibits include metals such as lead, zinc and tin. My witnesses are no longer causal. Matter can be cold-worked with little or no hardening. It's as if they were hovering right behind where we stood. The air slowly crystallized before my eyes. It's time. I'm a genuine. I'm found only in acts. I lay open and declare the same. I stand last. I'm found only in the event. What are you going to do with all that rubble? She asks as we're driven together. The end is unworthy of the beginning. God this winter's cold. And what was growing on the riverbanks? It enters me, flooding all respiratory cavities, canals. Of course I didn't make the world.

Number eighty-two. The bare constellation.

I'm encompassed. Type one supernovas happen. With lighting from above, unconcerned, on the playing area. This is the north, the terminal. There's a rumour that saint and saint no longer see eye to eye. (No one can remember everything.) An aerial bombardment is taking place, the politics of distraction.

Starting with today's group of three, we are all of one clock. Hydrogen from an expanding giant blasts a white dwarf companion. We need a day where absolutely nothing happens. I think myself through. We're stuck at a boundary ditch. The arrangement is little more than a broken triad. Figures are wrought: flowing claret with azure trim, Mohawk tassel, doubtfuls with red, yellow and skyblue brocade. The abstract power of society creates its concrete. Rubble and glass fragments are strewn across the mattress. Now I feel pangs of hunger. She has adjusted and it works very well. Grey matter's trapped in the floor of the left ventricle. Sometimes you need a little reminder. Now it's the long goodbye. I can't sit this way round for long. Sometimes you need a little surrender. Everything is upside down. The themes are various—unmanned drones, gaplike effects. Simply by adjusting slightly my position in space, I feel uneasy. Nothing happens untoward. You could say that originality is rather dangerous. I've been appropriated to a transferred use. Who could survive the horrors of the kanal. These things are out of joint. Substance exists in a thick stratum of discontinuity, scar tissue. The aggregate translates into a nation. Usage has always been rare. Consider the return of what one has borrowed, with disinterest. There's a brisk trade in used looks. Yes sorry, the later examples are due to mere inadvertence, what's called barking the dog. And now this catastrophic year.

What are have words, so pressed and forced they may contain my a great misshape? We watched it sink three times before we returned home. We're running out of time. The accused was sent into exile somewhere really old.

She's appointed inspectrix. You don't think there's anything wrong do you. Suddenly you're lost. This business of plying variations doesn't always work. Space has begun to evaporate, fallen into disrepute. But it's fascinating to play these complex games with notes and letters. As we get old the problem starts to slip. Exactly. The actual ceremony had tragic consequences. This primitive but still effective apparatus is known. I must have looked up. The ground around it had subsided or folded into mountains.

The feeling of time moving around inside of you.
Twenty-one miles above the junction with the river. Slump to ground at right bank. She asks. The last chapter has left us quite exhaust. The new theme is rapacity. I mean of living substance, possessed and retained. After-effects, after-image—the memory of simulation undergone by self or its progenitors. This deregulation on the model of the genetic code is limited. You just have to learn to calm your responses (less of the or what). This is where things begin to get hostile. One can't say a simple sentence, such as *You put that back in the drawer, didn't you?* There is a sound like that of birds perched along the branches come daybreak. That's it. Meanwhile she slipped into a coma. If you stop trying to engage with objects, what then. Things look bad. The skull is crushed, the brain

exposed. Must be low tide. And I think to myself, she surely must, surely. We're triggered by the friction generated where we collide.

Spontaneous, arterial.

I was watching the human centipede last night. This is by no means a radical forecast. I have this idea. A fracture is believed to exist at a depth of twelve kilometres below the ocean bed. We are broken in ranks. There is a well-defined crater. I was found standing on a vulnerable finger of land. Take passage through a more optimistic window, a simple step in any direction from an extinct edge. Molten spews from all the escape hatches. He is positioned at the same lip, albeit balancing on the other foot. (No, wait, come back.) Get to it. Are you overcome. See, a long-sought-for one who arrives at the last. The story is an intergalactic heist.

Mnemotechny, the black arts of memory, in theory and in practice.

A big square shape. They have left us with little option. But I think as a child. And they say you have three days remaining in which to open yourself up. This flings the situation into a bit of a spiral. I blame the analogue figures. (Finding myself back here, how do I convert?) The local fauna are peculiarly large animals that habitually herd together, with or without guardian.

Slip to land-fail, a reining in. Look, there's a camera on the barrel of a gun.

This part simply has to be done first. So are you enjoying the rain. Iron filings are choking up the creature's gullet. It's hard to breathe, to enjoy the normal and familiar process of respiration. My companion lies broken—the precious head, the exploding helicopter. She insisted on having the book which she had glimpsed during her spell of possession. So long as she keeps within the blind spot, the things can't see her.

How obvious is it that you are being followed?

News of his name has spread throughout the body. It's hard to remember the old country. The settlement is more like a village, or hamlet. Try to imagine the very site of the first industrial. This grants a spark of sense that cannot be named, a shudder through the spine. Everyone talks about the age. Everyone talks about those mediaeval siege monsters, the engines of folklore.

A stone of meteoric iron has fallen to earth from the atmosphere. He means through. The supplicant's face turns a shade of crimson. Heroes were once flung from heaven. Who gave birth to the signals, the acquiescence? Consider his own descent. He was left maimed. He is named after an ancient god of the storm. (Who did we think we had left behind at the moment of transportation?) Now the first tremors of a hunger are gathering in the hollow place. To my knowledge he only wrote about this once. It was fashioned of clay and spittle. There's a vehement refusal to relinquish the third person.

The mobile are mustering fast. He is pulled to pieces, the rubble. A name spurts from his mouth, all manner of sundry stuff. A name of the added name, the wearer. Scaffolding claws the chambers of the nave.

Love.

His the shining. His the silence. Passage through the same airlock, then another, then a third. In this way they sail across time and country. A hatch has been left ajar. This is a nice surprise. Drugs were commonly used at the time as a form of restraint. To our left of course we have the dock and its cargoes: bird skins and feathers, cochineal, the eye of a crane, gold and hot-forged black iron, the insect itself, jaguar and deer hide, vellum, salt and seashells, scrimshaw of whales' teeth and shark vertebrae, the sharpened bones of falcons, spinels of jade, of fire opal and olivine, spleenstone (a small subordinate vein), bracers of jet and turquoise. Now I hate to hear a person, especially if he be a traveller. I have barely warranted a mention up to now. This is my first fully-fledged experiment. It does-n't matter what it takes to win or lose a philosophical battle. The most exacting thing is not doing. If you separate, the primary aspect is lost (something about my punctuation). An arc of sunlight bends tightly across a watermeadow full of but-tercups and giant daisies. This is nice too. In regard to spelling I bow uncondition-ally. That reptile is harmless. The other is disinterested, as though this fantastic colloquy were taking place on the planet. Ditto metaphor. I never investigated fur-ther. A spiny lizard scutters across the floor of the cave. Sometimes you need a remainder—a cavity in the body, a cavity in the brain, contractile chamber of the heart, the womb. Bach said everything he achieved.

The prompter gives them prompts that tell them automatically what to do. There aren't enough of them to go round (sixty million pounding). Time is run-ning out. Some are wheeled over the cliff with reluctance. Obvious isn't perfect. The name is being changed. You have those photographs of you. I have seen: unti-tled pencil, coloured chalkface, ink, violent on toilet papyrus, the pharaonic sleep-walk. She promised to make him one of her homestead. For the hero's part we need a really good storyteller and a parley of instruments. I lack knowledge. Here are days I can't proceed. Our aim has to be the objective that never arrives, a replay of the phantom goal. I want to speak before forgetting. The green semiopaque crystal found amid the shingle has yet to be identified. You are erroneous and mis-guided and a danger to the world. I mean I want to say something before I forget.

Outside now it is evening more once. Imagine looking through the eye of a horse. Our expert is busy doing the ash flow for the gulf people. He has chained his plants to the railing, lest they're tempted to wander. Imagine that you're being unusually cynical, as well as metaphorical.

Have you snapped the cover back on.

The safety catch is off.

I'm still numbered among the living. It is my job to count the meteorites that make it to the surface. (I know what they're up to.) It turns out all the texts ever written mean nothing. I have no resistance. I have no fear. Suddenly I find myself in cherished and worthy company. A pit opens up at my feet. What business had I with hope? Some things you just can't explain. Stop wasting time. I tell myself. Approaching in the distance are itinerants, shadows of returning exile. You are unlike said he. And excuse me, darling, but what will they decide to do with us next. Under the window stand boxes of blanched bones. I shall mean anything which serves for any purpose. Pick a substitute for an object which is. By pressure against its solid sides, it quivers. In some sense, a representative or sign.

Aeromancy.
I am no resemblance at all. There is much to suggest mistaken.
To the lava fields. The police would catch us in two days. Release the valve. It's all down to laboratory effects and the exalted vision.

Across the forehead, running from temple to temple, is an embossed arc—like a rosary, a curve of string buried beneath the skin. It's the different spirit that's the thing. And wires frayed, sounds of a distant city. The ceremony of opening the mouth is depicted. I believe. I discern movement. Events are probably a lot more lethal than I imagine. It puts me in mind. It's similar to a ridge of basalt. I once saw, somewhere. The thinking is to crank up the crazy, with a view to catharsis.

Muffled gunfire on the radio. A wail rises to ear-split level. Up on the roof they mimic protest. I remember there were flags on all the lampposts the day he died. This elementary stage of development barely deserves to be called a step. A step is something taken with surety. The topography has a grotesque elegance. Blasted trees cling bent to sculpted waves of limestone. Big tidal rip. A crow in the rain. He collapsed in the bath. Granite bosses were exposed by erosion. If you're uncertain, don't move a muscle. It was quite an experience. I am forever something that should be substituted. Space was composed of different flavours and tastes (differentials, how could writing et cetera). How could this thing called forth have happened? At last, an achievement of my own. I am not owed anything. I will just punch a hole in your thicket. I don't understand. When asked I say I know nothing about the others. An achievement is being disowned. It seems we're not covered by the takeover, the cause—a professed doubt of what to say or to choose.
The difficulty. I am owed to others. Like a foghorn. On the spin of a wheel, red or black. Transit room.

The effect of nitric acid on China-wax.
What can we expect between here and the sea, here and then. It's what people call a curved vector. We have come to a place where boatmen cry out. It's time

589

for the return journey. How can you leave, with your limited resource. Their stay stretches out to encompass one lunar month. A voice says the corpse in this passage is many hundreds of years old. The durability of the poison is extraordinary. To save time we dug a fresh pit and half filled it with quicklime. (Did you say relate this to anyone else, another time, or just to ourselves?) Tell me what you need. Everything depends on the scale, doesn't it. The diachronic unity of stylistic development is demonstrated in still fragments. Any use of the word is best avoided as unnecessary and confusing. I mean the ideal of the substitute in art, the ultimate tie or bond. Time was originally a period of mourning.

Some people will decide. It is not be necessary to wait so long. Now, suspend yourself from any corrupt form. This involves a certain knot.

By contrast a dome-shaped protuberance of igneous rock is exposed. Recall the host name, composed of the opening syllables of her sons. And who would dare draw them into their nets? She has that keen desire for food which is sometimes manifest by persons just before death. (See remaining ties to earth, to one ingrained and rarely spelt.) Extinguish by a single seed in the little ear.

Battle-exe.
Into the next stadium. Of phase and anaphase (authorcop and rioter). There is just enough of a pause to obtain ourselves. Time is measured in a countdown. A digital clock erases the fiction of each second. You're like the man who's seen the man who's seen the man who's seen nothing. Horsemen were felled.

The narrative.
He escapes his assassins and takes a lover (backs to the story). Vacuum she insists. He ventures off into the undergrowth. A tortuous and roundabout refugee trail springs up. I cut open the book at a gloss of names. The opening sound is that of the narrator preparing the listener. (What's the price doing at the moment.) He emits different vocal colours. By the time of publication he's been demonized and erased. Hundreds of files of people fled flutter across the empty square. We're at the very rim of a continent. His voice is that of a flexible tenor. Do you have any idea why we're still here. We are those foremost in battle of our party. In this edition the word is translated, a place from which there is no outlet.

I, object.
I need another break. I shun recourse to shouting or melodrama, but we won't make it to daybreak. I once signalled. A remarkable portion of land is stretching out into the water. I hold letters of transit. Meaning squats beneath the threshold. You are not getting out in your own lifetime. You will drown crossing the river. The end. Usage of *diabolos* and *daimonion* becomes blurred in later years.

It doesn't bend.

You get these looks. You get these tiny hooks dug into fallow earth. We think it started somewhere in the street. It is taking up time. It is advisable. Learn the grammar of silence. You still hold rank. You were telling me all about that ring of fire. The clock reads an hour later, perhaps a little longer. I find a fragment scribbled on a blackened ember of parchment. It's numbered, of course. I'm about to discharge when I decide I want to keep everything. Reader, try reading something with due attention for once. Visit the image of peregrination, the paraquat of saint more et cetera.

It could be that he simply forgot to name this section. Questions brilliantly survived the test of observation. It crystallizes at air temperature.

Recognition.

One day she actually recognized. Which endeavour turned out to be pointless? Another day in paradise. See the thrones of the eternal triumph an so on. In principle this work has to be seen as a major contribution to the development of science. It's the outdoor nature—another day to acknowledge, with retreating stares. This sort of thing has been known to disturb. There are neurological repercussions (an absorbing form of dementia). The next stop is stonegate. She is still in the house and can still move around. I try to return her gaze. I left a message. She has her oxygen. For a while I would say that nothing is happening. But that expression keeps recurring.

The explosions seems to have worked. All the objects in the room are charged with electricity. I am unconvinced. I am checking the levels, I am checking the dials, I am checking the needles. One can isolate oneself through extreme behaviour. I need a breathing space. The wound had to be drained. I lack conviction. I am without concession. It's not about a crumbling pillar, the suspension of a sort of drape, a veil or curtain. I had no idea of the extent of the lie, the level of deception. It was largely mathematical. We cannot cross the causeway. (Where we were born?) We are due to hear from them once more at the very close of the combat. Where did you get that idea. Add names, places and dates as you see fit. This read much better before I started changing things. I have to stop (defecation, ecstasy).

Apply fingertips to eyes. It took her a while to arrive at language—dim the breaking east with her bright crystals et cetera. See, you have set a slow pace. Now she talks to any stranger.

He's not so sure. Let us step into this tangled web. No one can remember anything. Make a poultice of the remainder. Apply it to the eyelids (summit twenty-three). The crust folds into mountains by pressure against its solid sides. The shaft encloses. A circle of spikes springs up out of the ground. Penumbra shifting—love is love to whom et cetera. Your wrong. That body of fast-moving air is named Euraquilo.

After about an hour had past.

Start again. I can upgrade this for you. A name has lately been given. From time to time translucent bodies are seen to fall from the sky. Because there is no one here I have no choice. I am on the entropy, the pink one. Consider the very different western approaches to stars. The voyage will take you to uncountable tropic islands. Drumtight it was, hard as a fistula. And just when you're shaking hands with him and breathing a sigh of relief.

I can't go on, these gusts of nervous energy. Everywhere is simply passing away. Salt cakes my lips. There was a lot of time to kill before retreating inland. I folded the message up and pushed it into a crack in the wall. The other bodies were too close for comfort (and on his day off too). The item was made to order. Consider that which decides and forces us to decide. Begin from here, from this side of the mass in question. I'm not interested in what meaning may attach itself to any surface. And with a raised hand, checking the exclamation on my lips.

I had good intentions. Suffice to say, it contains carbon. Nothing is known for sure. Consider that which decodes and forces us to decode. I think if I ever met an actual writer, I wouldn't know what to say. Perhaps the flat portion on either side of the head, floating above the bone.

With the first thaw the boy returns. They have secured many fine gems. In the vulgar tongue such characters are referred to as the removed, or the axis, the skin.

Gunfire on the radio. I would not have known what to do myself. I sat up till the bellman came by with his bell. Reports of eyes plucked out by a knife-wielding horsemen. People are designated as back at work or not back at work. I'm amazed by the swiftness with which he died. Break this up. The delivery was deadpan.

No shadow of head cut across sheen.

Your mind out, it might be dangerous. Sun behind us, to the east, dipping below the familiar horizontal rent. Above the gates I saw more than a thousand raining down from heaven. An adjustable metal band secures the reed-piece to the family mouth. It is literally as if your own needs had been forever dismissed. (If I were any more earthed I'd be a fucking corpse.) He is violent, impulsive. When I say family I don't mean mine. And how exactly do you propose to rescue these characters from posterity?

It could be that he simply forgot to name this action. It took our combined efforts to talk her out of drilling him to death. It can be seen on a clear night with the naked eye, the chimp cluster. A fissure is believed to exist at a depth of forty kilometres beneath this wilderness.

Egma.

Shibboleth. Outer bract sterile, alone or alike with others. Chafflike. They cluster tightly, packed twenty deep in one place, unmoving and fully clothed. He

seizes them up, prices them out—tallies how much he can grasp by dint of
wreck. Consider that celebrated toxicophagy case, the morbid craving for poisons, voluntary blood-ruin. Yes, that's the idea, a separate vogue of consciousness. Add other facets and hint at narrative voice (true, historical anthropologies
don't have much to say on the subject either). Folk are interlarded. We separated
the tin ore from the gangue or rough by stirring the slimes in a kieve. The long
wait seems to be over. I crawled across to the others. Let's get the job done.
Everybody agrees quite willingly. There's a loud fear. It won't take long. A block
of the earth's crust remained in position. Tomorrow, a shipwrecked dog
marooned on a desert island and a trip to a rapidly advancing moon. He became
another man altogether. The ground around it subsided and slid toward the
molten core. An arm of the sea with strong currents, belonging to an image.

Séance.
What was it like being dead?
Well, he says, the best thing of all was that language stopped.

A character.
The character known as A is stationed at the junction. I remain within the
main portico (a covered ambulatory consisting of a roof supported by columns
placed at regular intervals, usually attached to a building but sometimes forming
a separate structure). He hands me his business card very politely. Language has
been carved into the marble walls. To conceal, evade or delay is falling due. I
have my suspicions. This account too remains unsettled. We could call upon the
last few pages. (And those who haunt?) My theme this mouth is attrition. The
simple fact that there are two of you together could be enough.

Tidy up. I am seeping badly. Moon hung full at apex, at apogee. It's time to
return to the ancient world. We are roughly contemporary with the product (O
thou figure of the scribe et cetera). I don't want your prizes. Labours are to be
performed in the underworld. There follows a monologue about her final
moments—brief, by her standards. Her name is often used allusively for the
female condition. Rudimentary physics reveals the context of our ordeals. The
only option was sudden death. Our prayers form a sort of index of the gods.
The details are still livid and sharp: the mountain ranges, peaks and troughs, the
textures of an arid terrain. I realize. Suffice to say, it is a point in the heavens.
There's a reason we didn't go back. He was not in the kitchen. It's as if my head
were a telescope. Knowledge is ascertained by observation and experiment.
Behind us, a little to the north, an orbiting body strikes the crust. There's no
other option. There is no way of telling. Bright, yellow and warm, it had been
emptied. Yes, that's it—critically tested, systematized, and brought under the
control of general principles. (Nominate your favourite artist.) Doubt is the
reverse of how it started out in the first place. It's time to leave. It's time to

return. There's a deep ravine between the crew and the target object. I penned a note to myself, that steady stream, straining to hear. Without X there would not be Y, that sense of the unfinished. Yes, that's it. One million. Five nights to go. No, I can't. I can't wait any longer.

A visitation.

Is it walkable. Today we're celebrating the living dead. Make something of it. Suddenly I realize I have no idea what reason to give for my visit. Think, what have you spent much of your lifetime doing? A pavement of sapphire stones spread out at my feet. Everyone applauded the first performance of his letter. (We may have to find proof of this.) May I call thee the headless one? The remaining woman will now place herself between my initials. One can be certain of this negative form, any idle observation. The causeway is lined with men wearing cloaks of spun glass armed with staves. His fame as a memory teacher was overdue, the great tooth bleed.

Clue.

It's so easy to become confused. He burst into the library with a revolver. (Who.) I can hear your heart beating. Either way they become enervated. Dense cloud cover is obscuring the mountain to the north of the city. I could always eavesdrop. It was a white-collar crime. He is speaking of a mechanical chaffinch. The speaker is a man insanely preoccupied. It seems a name has been given to the family. Nerve-force is convertible into other forms of polarity (beechwood kreosote, club moss). The species under study is a creature who delights in thresholds. Three crooked nails are perched in its voice.

He's transfigured, the soles of his feet frozen to the earth. Your double never fails to appear at crucial moments. Who came in through the shattered window? Who appeared to be composed of pure shadow? He is standing in a place where he will surely be noticed and recognized. Tiny wings sprout from his ankles. You're aware that this account leaves much to be explained, in terms of the received history of the world. I myself have plenty. This is the diagnosis. A stray bullet lodged in the wall. Even his breath was frozen. Analyse everything, one detail at a time.

Badinage.

A means of passing through, anywhere. One who traverses. A master-key. A secure hold. A certainty. Easy something.

I learnt later that it had been approaching for generations. Strips of metallic foil and bits of wire were shot into the air—refuse, worthless matter, the battering of the light et cetera. Bands of pagans raided the pilgrims on route.

We are going back to deliver the rudiments of education. These are my remotes. The part of the prince has been left out for this one night only. Under big billowy clouds, a permanent impasse—worn stone, glittering.

Who was rumoured exceptionally lucid?

Magnesia, sulphur and mercury are proportionate by nature.

Who was made most perfect?

An historical fact cannot be reduced to something else. It's not about the family.

Dogs have no sense of themselves. They are just trying to be helpful. He runs back to the café terrace, and embraces me.

Tone.

Quietism. Time for my sleepwalk. Better do this the other way around. (Homer's had two penalties.) It's shared ownership from genesis. Thank you very much indeed. I call it random choice. Once you get to five, the forms start to resuscitate. You're successful. Enjoy for a few moments. Silence is signified by a narrow strip of white page. An existence is to be had. Contemplate the subtle tension between the press to act and the press to remain idle. We have to take another look. The instructions urge a peek inside the ibex box. Voice says there is no point. What shock can loose this laboriously gathered, relentlessly pursued material? I didn't want to be a parasite. Can we order more cells, please. Is there a frontier around here, a boundary. The child might understand better if he affected an imitation. Do you remember me. Consider this a worthless gamble played with cards and dice. The frontier issue is gathering momentum—mummery as far as the eye can see, elaborate signs without known usage. The tense shifts, warm jets of evening air. I'm non-referable to any root. I am ever on the surveillance, on the contrary. I will tell when there is a more convincing sense.

Platinum bars (bag one), contamination (bag six).

An inarticulate, with closing of the tongue, partly. A keeper of goshawks. He has rediscovered the lip. (And who poked around the ruined cities of Spain?) Among the most pressing questions are whither thou shalt, and why I came. Who dwelt among the cedars and was overcome? Once again, love, do you hear me. A sound is piercing through the rain. Do not quake like the earth et cetera. All the talk is of an external body taking over—polyphonic kyrie, fearsome doubles with octaves and a lattice of scars on their forearms. Fiendhead is you. You will not find a more flattering treatment of this material. It's all about love, death and insurrection. One or two lost weekends, of all the earth.

Patent montage harrier.

A discursus around a chosen subject. This is what I really wanted to do all along. We were discussing insomnia. Yet beyond is still, weighs heavy—stuttering, backwards in forwards, without achievement. The view has been magnified. At low tide, skull crushed, brain exposed, with eye resembling. The fragment demonstrates. There really is a new and different way of calculating time. It was shaped like a giant centipede. We need to crank things up for therapeutic reasons. I wrote this on index cards. Now it is moving away from the earth once more. Nominate your favourite author.

The sense that unfinished.

If only we had those three extra rooms. None of the objects can cast a shadow. Command was safely rotated. You may pull out the transducer now. Clearly this machine does not appreciate excessive motion. What would an idea be like? The stage is set. Daughter chromosomes are drifting toward the poles of the spindle. Maybe it's the separation that is too heavy to bear. Redundant games have been unearthed. Slash office.

A scouting party for the infected. Repeats. Aerolites out of the sky. Logistically it is not possible. The game is up. (Rise to replace, then fall back into position again.) I have examined the poisoned arrows brought back ninety years.

It must be terrible down there. Each contestant has his own serrated beak. The heavier particles are not allowed to settle. (Swallow hard.) See, you have at last set a slow pace in motion. Radar signals were deflected.

Synchronicities.

A replica. A shot in the fogness. Sound exactly simultaneous with image. We shall now speak of this major boundary. The various surgical layers lie above. We need to get into that space. Come to yourself. You were possessed. The four rudders refer to the four quarters of the earth, the four cardinal points. Take things one at a time. There are three types of sentence (long, short and life). For reasons which must remain obscure, the most bizarre story has been invented. I picked up a flyer ('the half and the hole'). Who knows which is the first, the second, the seventh act—or how to build characters and so on. I try to read between the lines. The question of dialectics is also very important. From the pavement I pluck a tiny plastic soldier, his right arm raised to shield his eyes. It's unclear from what. He's green, like that worn pebble on the beach. I am waking up. Things move in and out of focus, then discharge. I think you can look at anything in the same way. The book says an eidolon is a phantom or apparition. This figure had disappointment and regret written all over it. He says his own son has been in the house and stolen his share. In the silence they were recognized. I think this is getting very close to the end. I don't like looking at things. I cannot have. Which one of us do you think will be going home next week. A confusing reflection has arisen from semblance, counterfeit. I'm actually not very good at dreaming, believe it or not. (Not the same green mind.) Blocked keys are what were described. Only the void is entitled. Girls are more realistic. I hear rounds of applause floating through the wicker gate. Writing's an ordeal, an irresistible torment. And I am not very good at beginning. (That's just too big.) I'm recognizable but sound completely wrong. He said you mean the beginning and the end. All you can see is what you're looking at through your visor. I'm swallowing my words. My brand is new. I am swallowing your words.

Her disciples call her the wanderer, the seducer, or the sorceress. (Not all at once, one or the other.) I pertain to an afterimage. You she says are self-regarding. Events are characterized by descending chromatic laments. The season is grainy, plague-stricken. Another circuits about saying yes sir no sir. She squeezed his arm. You are being evasive about the department. A sooty black rain beat against every window. It's a disease that can destroy living cells. What always follows upon the immediate effect of a stimulus? Each time fresh subjects are picked and reused. They are ejected before they can regain consciousness. I'm always relieved when it's cancelled. Contemplate a perfect system whose energy replenishes itself along the boundary of a circle. We are well under the limit of my personal two thousand. Easy has destroyed many lives. (Click of bathroom lightswitch.) I am contiguous with below—the grey commissure, final discord. After this I have cracked it. Now it's brightening up. That's all I want out of life. It's notable how rarely anything remotely familiar ever happens. Here at the suture of junction, a bundle of fibres disconnects two nerve centres. We extended upcountry, as high as the aqueduct. The fauna can only be described as hydraheaded. Motion-cycles occur simultaneously. Ragged serfs beg alms in the snow. One was chosen to be a sacrificial victim. A balance for guessing substance in water was used. The liver and the heart were assessed and weighed on the scales. A deep lateral fissure in the cerebrum opened up. I observe closely. All doubt is determined and cut away. Had I as many mouths, such an answer would stop them all in their tracks. Yes, two nerve centres—the real person or thing, second war soviet.

A broad sheet of muscle in the neck, the flat piece. Tuck your mind in before. And the head's attempt at enigma: jaeger, peddler, packman, cobbler, tinker. Free withdrawal symptoms. To click, apply by die sinker, to the striking of a melted letter lead. The proof or cast obtained, in disorder.

Sea latterly. Grey commissure. He is the chief actor in the play of his own resurgence.

Kino in the woods.
The roof is made of chalk. Grains of charcoal are embedded in the ice. Other items at inventory include yellow earth, linseed oil, buckets of oxblood. (Why can they not recognize each other.) Strategically positioned containers catch the rainwater granted access via innumerable leaks. The runoff tastes bitter. He may have suffered a paralysis of will due to excess. Of your dear father, it is writ in your revenge. I don't have the time to do this right now. The singular

and peculiar life is bound up. There's a thirteen-year-old back-story here. Calculate the wave-front scattered from the numerically defined object. I managed to shift his arm a couple of centimetres to the right. This word shall be brought to pass et cetera. It's like that game, quietism.

The bodily movements of each worker are represented in relation to a timescale. They are not found within the organism itself. The indeterminate is a crucial element. Five or six small convolutions are concealed within each fissure. (Is a slave a slave when not in use?) He is alone now. He is 'all one word'. It was a footnote to mediaeval Europe. Tomorrow we alter our course for the sun. Wire us. A majestic performance can take place in an instant. I have organized a box of matches for those among you who can count. The contest is to take place in the world-famous ballroom. A ditch full of water runs around the arena. Details, details, are always deciding the game.

Great show without reality, foolish ceremonial. It's the only known cure for sleep. In extended sense, a gadget.

All the information is in the public domain. A precedent has been erected by a landslide. There's too many of those italic titles, copies of originals. Consider a man of lasting obsession. Our theme is the reflection of the heart as aesthetic purpose. He has gone for good. I am to be scourged for my wrongdoings. It was like the cracked windows in a disused plant. Now I wish to wake from this, the frontier. And literature, whereby the horrors of the water crossed to get here are relayed to the outside world.

He cannot acknowledge the recovery of the body. Smaller figures reside therein. There's an illegal traffic in sacred things—objections, the archival tide. To obtain a vision make a drawing in biro on your left hand. Envelope said paw in strips of duct tape. Welcome to the world of archaeo-acoustics. I'm told I talk in my sleep by someone reliable. The voodoo lady says the devil has finally left the child's body. Never abuse your tools or expose them to unnecessary damage. Despite this there remain some spatial deposits connected with the root of a certain cranial nerve. White feathers are flying about the room, an overpowering stench of oxblood and tar. We felt deluded and betrayed. A pool of petrol creeps across the forecourt. These details are unpacked from moments that spring from his best work. (Which people were persistently ruined by the uneasy?) The last lights go out. He had the foresight to build himself a spare. The reference is number two hundred and thirty-one (s.14). He's offering tacit support to the private. His imagination's been ignited in some special way. In desperation he hires a ruthless moron with no style. A woman walks her dog on the beach. He gets there first. This demonstrates that there really is a new and a different. A man is in a drama. He staggers about the forest with bleeding sockets. That thing reminds me of a raw nerve. He drops a nearspent match. That's enough. I don't remember the rest very well. (It's opera, stupid.) Exhumation of the bulb itself led to the extraction of an alkaloid.

This paragraph constitutes a direct stimulus to the theory of his origin. It's the key to the whole damned book. Entropy I can't.

The frontier.
But any vibration inside the ear would have had a similarly shattering effect. How could an umbilical have created a direct link? It's uncanny, right down to the copied dash. I can't live if living is without you. The frontier issue is now gathering momentum. A uniformed official enters, loosening the writing desk which has almost sunk into the floor. It seems like he discovered how to write half way through the book. Maybe that's how he wants it to appear. Which of you has previous experience. (This sounds just like one of his shorts.) Of what, one asks. Which of you has previous experience of being sacrificed to a mythical sea monster? I rarely look at paradise. Who enclosed the alphabet a long time ago.

Dense sonority characteristic of flatlands. She is cancelled if the vibration is not exactly right. Ghost impact brilliant day, image bleed toward the edge. I am examining. She is analysing current naming practice and the outcomes. I take notes. We have begun to realize just how desperate the situation is. (Who once said when hyenas and wolves howl for prey?) I am waiting for her to make the first move. I invent a strange childhood. After being strangled and thrown into the lake there's solace in the final grouping, the play of resistance.

We (a family) cross an endless snowscape on foot. I told you I have taken much from the long walk. First I must find a job and a place to stay. I have been living out of a staircase. That morning in the bathroom mirror I noticed a tiny coil of metal sprouting from the flesh of my cheek.
Except she can't stand the idea he said. These eaves are no place to drop from.

They continue building the cone. I am with unknotting to mean: screed, sememe, escrow and so on. A deed in the hand (one third). The tense is the conditional unfulfilled, hide clicking with to burr. I dream I'm at work on a distant planet. After complex negotiations I'm allowed to return to earth through a wormhole that runs through intergalactic space.

Swoopstake.
I'd say it had eyes, once more. You have to be systematic. Costard's attempt is on page three one seven three. You could simply get rid of all the remaining wood. I waited for a few more hours to pass before I gave up. One outcome is an irrational prime number. The passers-by are about to witness a shocking incident.

Rescue this and I'll pay you livery. One by one they are set silently to rest. I get up to leave. A simultaneous cycle can be operated with the remaining fingers. In this story someone's always watching. Summer's an endless barbecue. I think I'm going to faint. I know what I have to do. On the wall hangs a chart in which the bodily movements of each worker are represented. We exist only in relation to an historical precedent. The two objects are linked by their collision. The laboratories are reached by interconnecting corridors. A spiral staircase leads up to a jacuzzi full of cuttle ink. One among us breaks off, soaring away from his companions. He leaves in his wake a great ribbon of air. The neural canal behind the chord is visible in some vertebrates. With its blue eye it resembles a wolf. Star archaeology is misleading and could well be dropped.

Check them. Seal up all the hatches with molten wax. I'm searching for a style which is both detached and inelegant. The opening has had to be camouflaged. Twenty-four masters gathered together in one place. (In that case I might as well stop talking.) You'll have heard the story. This is an unusual occurrence. Make a box ten cubits long and five cubits wide. Flank it with sheets of glass set into frames by means of pitch. I am eminently skilled in anything, especially art. There is not a lot of room in here. But he did not want to leave. He positioned himself at the fireplace. Consider the sacrifices that have been made. First there began a period of echolalia. Then a second heresy, founded on ascetic reaction in favour of the discipline. The robot bomb is a potential hazard. Who was thought one of the universals? A name has been applied to many passerine birds. The satellite turned about on its axis and approached the earth at great speed. There's an illegal traffic. Detection is stymied, the severance.

Trees of this variety tend to have a flattened top. Herein are vignettes reminiscent of classical painting. The rhetorical device of beginning successive sentences with the same word should be adopted. A space created by the removal of an entire fin remains empty. He alone knows what he means. (I am so sleep.) There are numerous spirals, the sound of letters being said. The trouble is we don't have anything to throw into the balance on the opposite side. Cold monster, that is a dead.

Aside from the mysterious splash, no, I don't remember. You have to take a good look at places. It's reassuring that there are things to do in the world. Isolationism's no longer a practical method of policing. Everything is empty. Now it's not. Next it's empty again. I mean the meaningless imitation of actions and events. I did not know what to do that day so I did nothing. The landscape is stunning.

He brought the mnemotechnic out into the lay world. Lost and starving in the frozen wilderness, who was sheltered by an indigenous? And due to what fact that.

Crystallomancy.

Both are transparent bodies, through which they may view each other's antics. Their limbs have remained for some time in the positions in which you arranged them. Collect your possessions and leave. The canon has been composed such that each variant, having arrived at an end, can begin all over again. Some of these repetitions are idiotic. This recurrence concludes indefinitely. He says he wants to express the sheer mass underlying existence. (See ms one seven four.) The utterance of pain is not connected. Bounded by faults on all sides, the outer borders of the two fields of subsidence begin to approach one another. There is shadow to spare.

Coda.

Spinal crest and fornix. A linguistic unit has that meaning. Muffled phrases decay into the distance, those sighing half-steps. (Didn't you leave without paying the bill.) The structure resembles an arched formation, a hollow place in the brain that bends like a bow. I harbour a grand love of glance (36). It was raised up to an extremity, suspended from nylon cords attached to innumerable hooks. I speak approximate. Scales line an orifice in the convex shell, the excavated part. (I mean the upward-facing.) From this elevation the aqueduct is clearly visible. A canal connects the third and fourth sectors. It's believed the weight is no more than twelve point nine nine grammes. Detect and document any anatomic relationships. Half of it has been stolen. The code is code red. (I meant still-eyed back there.) The others are creeping around in their quest for some unsuspecting reptile. I haven't heard a word and I'm dying to know what happens. Three of our company expired on route. It makes me want to press on, despite the frost-bitten fingers and thumb. Applied kinesics can be used to identify food allergies. It's black plastic and the head moves.

On speaking. No enigma, no envoy, no page. First he's asked how he can possibly function under these conditions. He answers. (Wish I'd got that book with the Chinaman on the cover now.) A familiar lengthy brass-note is sounding out. Something bad is going to happen. (Speak without saying et cetera.) I wouldn't discount anything at all here. We are still on track. He is convicted. Hopefully I can be productive without losing the necessary edge. Grant me some license. We are not told who the two women are. Retreat. All the zones under our control are enveloped in smoke. Are you trying to archive beyond yourself? He represents the late, a crucial stage in cell division. I am so far away from everything, an absent father, or the state.

Before our every eyes. Repetition of the same word in successive clauses is taking place. This is mere happenstance. The daughter chromosomes move apart toward their opposite poles. Transformation, not action, is found to create form. To be on the safe side I remain rock still. This portion has four dimensions, including an intercession for the dead. Then again, he says.

Aerolites combust in the stratosphere, flashes of permanent red.

To read laboriously, letter by letter. To make out and unriddle. Import the amount to be contemplated. Express or hint at desire, the indifference. Late anaphase.

Nor shall they acquire vast sections of the earth in exchange. Saying they had not stolen the lead from the roof was an outright lie. Nonetheless, I am health and held in spirit. I can tell you nothing new about yourself. Why don't you just commit yourself to one small movement. Nobody is going to believe you anyway. Fierce dispute attends every erasure.

He holds the trump card, the U of infinities. One passes through a figure of trespass, thence into the craw of birds. These images are found inside us all. I'll be talking about my findings in more detail below. For example, their name is derived from an object. The European limb has been salvaged on more than one occasion. In his negative aspect he also plays the intellectual oppressor, the head who burst open with light and feathers. The major arcana may be viewed in sequence. We cannot reach agreement on his mysterious insights into other people. Perception is required for this to be fathomed. Commence with the unnumbered, then conclude.

Sylvian fissure.
He is resolved to sacrifice. It was divided between night and day. Imagine seeing through the wild eye of a horse. Whose face is that behind him? He writes of a flaring light at peripheral vision.
And he pursued them unto a city called H, which is still found on the left hand. (I only know to do.) Who hurled themselves into the sea? Did I want to witness things. They rose a hundred feet off the ground and then dropped back again, suspended.

A silent game with cards or dice, not a word. An inarticulate sound with closing of the lips, partly, to murmur, to mask. Starting again from the beginning.

XXXII

This is a relatively short episode. I'm disturbed to hear of the rapacity of your decline, all that empty. I am ashamed I thought so ill. Why this irrepressible need to isolate. Once an operation begins it must come to an end. (If it's useful, it'll come back.) This chapter concludes with a disarming corral. We're searching for a water-yielding stratum, a system of aquiferous pores—a dialectic form of something, somewhat.

Who was winner of the off-world competition in eighteen seventy-one? Where you can, use simples. Avoid a portentous tone. I'm still finding my way around in all this. There's still a chance I might improve. We've been misused, extinguished. (I'm drunk.) Item, the last day.

Huge choral forces are combined in a vast echoing space. It is indeed a horrible thing. Everything is accident. By accident he dies, by accident he is consumed in a sacrificial hippocaust. Now I have to rely on my intuition rather than what I can actually hear.

He tells me that.

Without trepanation of the concrete, rainwater builds up inside the skull, causing it to crack and splinter. He rules out a regular polygon of seventeen sides. He wants this inscribed on his tombstone. The mason refuses: it would be indistinguishable from a circle. He kept a diary of his discoveries, a reflection on contradictory images. He is marchman, borderer—a back formation from morphine, as non-track or barred path.

There is an alarming conversational tone developing in the writing. The unconditional appears to amplify existing traits, while erasing others completely. It seems to me that those who have been kept alive are the unfortunate ones. Surviving activities include trigger projects: combat, the familiar struggle on three fronts. He says history would not have been possible or even conceivable. (Go for this.) I regret that I know no remorse.

To renew.

Look stranger, the correct number is probably one of the tickets in your pocket. I am trying to conduct myself as though still in a situation. As soon as anything is touched by the idea of justifying itself, it disintegrates. I am conducting myself as though still in a productive situation, rather than a terrible one. Saint was merely a feeble amateur in the art of terror. He had set himself the task of studying modern policing techniques.

They wear green triangles, our astrologers. In the compound thorn-bearing trees and shrubs are ruled by air. (Sometimes Arian selfishness can be exacerbated by stubbornness.) A very absurd and bad book was once written. This already tells us quite a lot about the personality of the native. And there will be an inclination. Reject either fault whenever it is mentioned. Part of my job is inherited guesswork. The conscious part inflates and floats off like some grotesque dirigible.

An army of ants marches across the topsoil as we speak. Everything fails completely in the end. The one who is dying can still move his fingers. I am drifting into a sound repression. This is not a genetic condition, but still—it serves to sharpen the mind, to illude. Anything that triggers another strain of action.

Archaeoastronomy (from he cannot acknowledge, achieve et cetera). There is always someone who divines opinion on that front.

A narrow funnel of light descending through a gap in the cloud.
This is an enormous day, the event of collecting. I can hear five or six stitches clacking at once. It's my job to glue together and carefully archive the things. The collection of anything is a sequence of discrete events. I am reclassified as foregoer—either of two branching, a reminder. And a hand reaches down. Existence is the obsessive action of gathering, collation and storage. The poor honoured the god by a simple procession. Or no numeral at all, number not revealed. A species of trauma.
Do I engine this. Did I write. Neither of the two trees survived the conflagration. (What is called the remnant?) Separation of the sister segments has begun to take place. The whole region is a corpse-factory.

Tumultuous scene with personifications.
It is not the finished particle. The square is still to be triangulated, circled. Someone has taken the trouble. A complete set of reading tasks has been printed in several tongues—tales of living men, prodigies related to the early days of the island. Impressions are interwoven with the voices of the dead. And behold the head, as lightning flashed convulsive in a final gesture. A foreshadowing, stretching equivalence, stretching eloquence.

A contusion of horrors.
The wonderful monster child. Signs of early form occurring prematurely, probing the root of to see, the root of I am saying. Synchronized control of diverse operations—none of which fools anyone, in spite of the absent mind. We have reached the moment when he first peers over the wall at the approaching rabble: nomadic herdsmen with human bite marks, panniers crammed with gravel and black sandglass. Wickerwork shells encase the archers, all armoured up at wrist and hip. Samples of speech follow, thick and opaque. Congratulations, you have been pulled out from the hole. A vacuum dam, roiling basket-heads.

The outskirts of.

Snagstone with tooth embedded at the temples, as clay. Modifications have been made. The wire anode is surrounded by a cylindrical cathode in a chamber of gas. Map contours are visible throughout. Note the distinctive marbling effect covering every surface. And in one place, a source.

I would like to change some of the things that are said around here. I have inherited. By this I mean autonomous objecthood. Imagine, who said all things are circular? No, I'm not angry, just in a hurry. The mob is back beneath the window, exhaling.

Descending, scales from the eyes.

I did not say they were mere herdsmen. He bought a strip of land in a poor region far away. Now we're in a time that takes place much earlier. (It is easy this in a book, you just say it and it happens.) Economy of null. One cannot choose but wonder at the hissing and the cracking immediately behind, the implosive thud on the collapse of my flesh. Divination takes place entirely through the agency of sound. I amuse myself by waiting at meal-times and other skivvying. Gravel cascades from the roof. The voices here belong to one quite unprepared. I mean the mangling of an old woman in black by the noonday tram. One remove from swoopstake.

The world's most explosive bicycle.

A surprising tripartite intervention. Just what I've been looking for all these years. You'll need these lines of guidance, tracery in the sky. You'll need that strange thing in the forest. The geiger clicks. (No way those are innocents.) Life decayed by a few hours. It resembled an arch. I can be amplified for work, a sadistic gangster story. He speaks. A single particle passing through releases a massive electrical discharge. He says writing connects the past, present and future.

A revival is taking place. Knowledge is imported, along with a cluster of operatic scenes, half-hearted solutions. A brace of organs opens and shuts at the entrance to the orifice, as if crossing each other out. This is a veritable relay team—lace of shell-body, decorative silvering. When is sudden?

Now it's eternity he would say. Nothing else can. Entry of the answer occurs before a subject can be completed, overlapping it. This is a way of increasing excitement, a supplement.

Hello is everything all right up there.

This will have to do. Are you enjoying yourselves. Now for the centre fold. In the middle of our era the sentence was transmuted to judicial torture. Rapid eye movement was repeatedly interrupted. (State is inappropriate to situation.) The idea met with some resistance. A brief elongation of the corolla may be observed. This book is of first importance for the study of figures. A shafty hollow usually envelopes the stamen. I keep telling you. I'm a distinctive type of sleep. The language game lacks substance.

Within an older order of birds, comprising more than half, and dwelling in the same place. These three shall have dissolved, not into rain water.

The machine does not appear to enjoy motion.

I can't lie to you about your chances. At the moment there are many people here keeping me company. I did not request. (I was trying to make a non-place that felt like a place.) This takes us down a wormhole straight to another galaxy. I must prepare myself. I wake to find a large circular bruise on the upper surface of my left hand, knuckles skinned and raw. There's a frequent siren, the call to work or arms. I write I feel terrible. Bitter, because I can do nothing for you despite all the love. A rock collided with her head in one dream. I've composed you a letter. It's about everything. A red welt appeared the following day. The inmates pass code via a book about a big fish—tapering upright cones, congregated blossoms et cetera.

0.38 hours.

News of the hostage release comes over the radio. I embody a puzzle, the transmutation of goods into commodities. (This must be moved elsewhere.) I lack the wherewithal to do. Today I appear to be right-handed. All the timings have been stripped back. It's the electromagnetism. He says he will come again and measure the resistance with a machine. I seem to embody. The angle is the problem.

Ambulant.

Crushed gull embedded in asphalt. Some light from behind. Volumes have been written on the different meanings acquired. White beads and fluorescent yellow gravel are strewn across the paving stones. It's a shame. I am what she is unable to imagine. I have been reclassified as a mortal extreme. This scenario reminds one of the tank and the passerby. She says I have been very much engaged in war in my time. Stern necessity usually permeates indirect action. No room is left for such a game. Atoms of light are absorbed by the dust and reflected back into my eyes. This is not the ideal circumference. This means I cannot. None present could have foreseen. There's a limit to what can be done. Or was there something else about eldritch? Stay a while.

His forbearance to obey is alarming.

The use of a word, such as it do. Avoid repetition of an ancestor, a soup of letters—the offering up of elementals. Still he responds to my every concern. Note that he is unarmed and unnamed. He was found wandering in the desert. A greyish-white crust clung to his scalp. It's said he resembles the lemur. The blind cracks. He is now called That-Which-Supports. I can't keep up with all these changes. He sits in a cave with an hourglass in one hand and a beard. The lower jaw is pierced by a spike which links the ears. Gills flap on opposing flanks to expose the face. We're under strict orders not to accept. Words are no safeguard. The overlapping of demons with angels was the idea. (Bring on the alarm.) Picture in your mind a sign. The operation of excising the nerve is underway.

Allow me to ruin some ideas by you.
The attack, as described in his delirium. For safety's sake, subjects there's no knowledge of shall be ignored altogether. Very small insects float without wings at all. There's a hand-grenade on the floor at my feet. I will leave or I will forget. (It says here.) The seven earths are joined to the seven heavens by vast hooks attached to their rims. The consequent vibrations propagate in spirals and circles. A glass bottle hanging on the lab wall contains a chemical to be broken. (Why should any of this concern me?) Obviously the plan was. It's the only way.

He's been taking low doses of strychnine to immunize himself. It's an erratic course of action, but the only option open to us. First I'm going back to where I was born. I didn't recognize you. My inventiveness is inexhaustible. I am going to speak people. I am back living with the old, the timers. Objects click and rust audibly. Give me a number from one to ten million, please. The girl does not understand.

Perhaps the worst thing is that it doesn't actually kill you. Book one is the text under study this evening, those variations. Keep exposed the regions to which something belongs or retreats into. The creature was bought against its will—or failing that, is executed. The one who is dying is speaking of excrement. If you want to go in, just go in. My first thought is always to write.

Within time, clinging to a bundle. Something with faint allusions to roomness. The common fracture, the by now familiar disconnect. I am operating now at the lip, the earth's crust. Fifty-two little boats set sail to commemorate.

The years.
Rubedo as insurrection et cetera. You can't have too much of the same thing in one place. It was the worlds he refused to take part in.

Intercellular space, patterns of cross-stratification (as witnessed in diffident actions).
The concluding section of a book is called the epilogue. We have discussed the programme. The whole threatens total collapse. (Who was the bereft?) He says he can only do one to six. All these possibilities fall within the scope of irrational explanation. Pegged outside in the wind is this big blue with rope and anchor entwined, cracking open the salty air. (I meant equivoque.) I felt old. There is something called tact involved in these proceedings. This is very important when working with other people. I am derivative of step seven. I am

endeavouring to build a really solid state. I have a stone in my shoe. It's our secret.

More cling, shrinkage. It is because. We are not trying hard enough to distinguish between works. I am not temperamentally suited to anything on offer. I once had the intention, even before extracts were around. Now we find ourselves back in that terrible year. (Give detail of this.) Muskets in the air, and the town presented more the appearance.

He emerged from his cellar to find the three adjacent houses had been hit. Underground, a variation in the ripple-crest pattern has been detected. Citizens have been loaned. Voices commonly express themselves. You have of course been milking the situation. (Long live the enraged et cetera.) The orchestration thickens. I am just being honest. Even the way we touch hands, the eye contact.

The surface of the world is so smooth. It stands steadily by itself, manifests as it is. We have a single task, to survive on this island. We have a moral. We are flung back to the very beginning, but with completely altered dissonances and suspensions. Then, selecting a little side gallery, I made good my escape. I subvert. The fighting begins: the roar of a puma, spilled contents of the inner sac—now to devour their flesh and suchlike. It's slow work sifting through the rubble. The little people soon tire. Words are accompanied by a photograph entirely disconnected from the cell in question.

Picture a meteorite crater in a desert. (Slowly, mind.) Typical acid structures visible. The cone is composed of flows lying parallel to the outer slopes. Only two of these aspects were actually planned. One is the variation in surplus of sediment. The other is the quality of the cuticle, a thin waxy film. Keep sound out of this, needless to speak.

It seems to me he says. Produce an original from which copies can never be made (blacks like the velvet, o yes). Separation of the segments is beginning, the intercession of saints.

Sea below.

Restructure this from every aspect. It's blightening up. The official letter is known as mu. He has the number eight tattooed on his back. Naming begins. We're fucked—often mad, usually angry. Not too much movement up ahead. Music plus drama is melodrama, right? Either way, I should be doing nothing right now.

Respond. Enter in at the narrowest slit. The hatch bangs open and shut in the wind. This is never a comfortable situation. People pass by. Has remains the same. It was a strange setting for our story. I do not wish to think. We are often. We are usually. I ask myself. Did I make the right decision. We are both looking at this in the same way. On the day we met we knew immediately that we had to form a trio. There's a difference between I don't know you and you don't know me. The only other object in the room is an ikon, facing due east. You stand without. You manifest something that didn't exist before. The amplification factor of the valve is nil. This is a major contribution. We're both looking at things in a different way. It's a miracle. Let me tell you what I have to do. At that moment you began to knock at the door. Bodily movements convey information in the absence of speech.

Roles I've been dreaming of undertaking, rules we've simply ignored.
I am found. Is that for me. Animals without backbones have been unearthed. Latent energy lies between the anode and the grid potentials. I am a necessary. I maintain. Current is mined at some confused value. There's an abundance of used sound trapped in the atmosphere. Oil is consequent. Deformation accompanies the rise of salt from its source. We're probably twenty thousand feet underground. A voice suddenly burst out from the adjacent wall. Steep wrinkles are cut by numerous small faults. The Orpheus reference is that I don't look back. (Be forever dead et cetera.) You see, it represents through the yellow prism: an Abraham, those distinctive circular corn stores that punctuate the landscape, all the forgotten chemistries. A group of substances can arrest growth—extracted, pressganged into workaday use. And from the wick their light is withheld. (Whose name was hanger?) And she said I will not go. Behold, I stand here by the hell of water.
Or at least to lose oneself in anomalous considerations.

Bitter poisonous principle in the seed. Decalcification is taking place. I'm unique to the specified thing. A red staining fluid was used throughout history. You can tell it's ambiguous and erotically explicit because of the grammatical structure. At one time I might have ended up over there myself. I had not read on far enough to participate.
The only possible way to preserve is to repeat. I meant this is a source book, a primer, living and dying. Without guile, without climax.
Yes I have. Return to the same point again and again. I have at the centre, a nervous system of unwrapped zones, utter exhaust. The core is infrequent. Nothing is satisfied in the sedimentary sense. Then I read your request for something fairly straight, which is fine too. (Massive it is, the quartz.) I want to expose a number of alternative endings. Moral cavities may be lined with spores, contaminated pockets of possibility. This isn't really the time to be doing this. We don't want to find ourselves flung back inside the third person. We're doing a picture of the world, are we not. Nor can he be expressed or conceived, since he is neither.
Output pulses are triggered by ionization of particles in the gaseous tube. Note the sprinkling, well-formed crystals of feldspar and beryl. On and on and on the questions roll. He is speaking but saying nothing. Let me know when you think. It's basically a free creative state. Note the absence of internal organs. But egg is not regressive, on the contrary, it is perfectly contemporary. There is desiring or celibacy. In the centre is a horse with short, jointed paws. Law stems from the genitive plural of the appointed men. Any statute that constitutes or glues

together is worthwhile. I am projected froward by a childlike simplicity. For example, that comment about the geese.

I hope you will enjoy this. I can hear in the drums, in the seventh floor guardroom. Via the emergency chutes.

Under his green visor. All right the clerk says at last from learned reflex. This isn't the Savoy. Today you are invited to hose down our levers and triggers before they overheat. The subject is regularly deprived of sleep. (Anyway is probably drug residual.) Every text is a forgery. The previous woman is being researched. We've got a problem. Who in the story turns out not to be? The subject is regularly deprived of the opportunity to dream. We've run out of gas canisters. They peered into her cunt and everything. Seventeen rounds per clip.

Just let me know when you need me. The skull-bolsters and cylinders you ordered and are in the post. What is turret she asks. And that flag is the one they used in flight.

I have rigged the alarm. For once is belonging—without from sun-up, the preventer valve. So far no one's told me much about anything. Think of the sheer amounts that are being cut. On that day there occurred a total eclipse. (Alfred ordered me to be made said the object.) Send the hangers up. Then something resembling an arch in the sky—that particular species of whither, a bleaching of the image until it disappears altogether. Here are three of his tenebrae responses. I think I should have eaten something first. When you open them up, they're like some great bird, heavy as a stone.

Yes they like it.
Toward a new centre of gravity, rushing through corridors before and aft. He had a disjointed season last year. Your idea of a hero may be different to mine. I now have the space to read your perfect book. (I wish I could, but seem cursed to write about everything.) A snide trumpet blast comes before the final crush, the entire populace. We cannot be certain of him. We cannot contain. (Cannot *uncertain* him is something different.) And I can't help feeling your minimal is a repost to any density and complexity of purpose. Breath is escaping from inside the body. Tiny frozen droplets hover in the air, one bystander silent beside another. I am containing. A man balances a chair leg on his chin, tottering. There is a hardboiled egg in the composition. None of this will make any difference the girl says.

Seine.
Now I am going to wait patiently and listen. Legend has it. The composition harks back to the very moment of incarceration. An object is never realized. Sergeant said dio mio are you sure. Count out loud from zero to ten. A large wax candle burned before the altar. Four terrible entities were unleashed to cloud the

brains. The walls were made of paper-pulp. Parts have been ignored. It's reassuring to learn that such monsters still exist. I am today pondering those bruises, the oxygen mask. It was caught breeding, tiger to horse. I held an ingot of tin from the straits over the flame—crystallizing the tendency, countering the goal.

Do you stand by the signal.
One: the time has got to be right.
Two: a focal chord parallel to the directrix of a cone (right or perpendicular side).
She clambers onto the bed to listen at the wall, ear vacuum in glass.
There is a one and there is a two, but there is no three.

Laid out flat on the shingle, the hissing of stones. An if wherein people speak to one another. Hence, indiscriminately.

Crop circle, one of those time-pressed people. An episode foreshadowed by a dead.
It is the same lower back. He murmured lamely that he saw nothing. (It is politick writing refuse of book.) It dangled from the arm of a clock-face, scratched and withered. The backdrop consists of knives, hammers, and a meat cleaver. By habit they crush in boredom. It's the signal to leave and never come back. One has crossed over from the other side. The name released is that of a southern constellation, the iliac crest. These objects have nothing to do with planets. Hence the following restrictions have to be carefully mastered.

The use of the letter L as a special contraption for will.
Call for help—summon back, recall. I've tried that but it gets confusing. I am no longer a recognizable place. Disorder, we raise ourselves to them.

Locomotor magic, night apparatus.
Row zed. Hell for leather. Big fat hard impossible tomes, ill-founded. I am happily disinvented (true). It's about word of mouth, really. It had an uncanny quality. On the contrary. Then the words faded into the light.
This is the only way in which anything can be discussed. It was doubtless shining white, with an hundred eyes. The true name begins with the letter M. She's found to have a loaded pistol on her person.

An archaic.
I mean turning awry. Self-willed. Perverse. Unreasoned. The opposite of standing still. A small book of hours by laymen. First reading book. Two obsolete sizes, approximately.

Cilia notes.
A name was given to the plant based on uncertain evidence. (Geist in chaos it said in crayon.) Moisture splits open the belly, the unripe binding. The possessed pos-

sessed many talents—something like the headless wild of folklore. The surge is a tactical success but a strategic failure. And if both lines of communication run in exactly the same direction? Each side has agreed to a bizarre and extravagant process of redaction. We find ourselves at a place where Europeans are prominent. The murders were ritualistic, systematic to the last detail. During that journey the pilgrims experienced fits of giddiness. There's a gigantic monolith spray-painted grey. The locals call it the artifact, Gabriel's lament. The moon then came up and spread its own brand of light. The buildings in the background have been spraypainted black. And such a clattering sound that resembles shells striking against each other.

Sorry to add to your sorrows. I must inform you of a dismal flight into exile that's to take place very soon. I myself am not going anywhere today. I remember that shop. I remember that café. He seeks to draw parallels between the two. This was explained during an interview at the time of release. A band of nerve tissue disconnects the hemispheres, the two sides of the spinal cord.

Count down to the last, the line where the upper and lower eyelids meet. Three times seven from previous, i.e. the segments. Where unframed dwells and so on.

She was slain instantly by a bolt of summary lightning. Our hostess is thereafter exhumed and examined in detail. These microbursts, as you shall see, all share a scandalous nature. She was having me sought after everywhere. It's hard to know how serious. The hymen was found intact.

The lost ear of embalming.
Waterhole, abyss, pit of hell. I presume your typesetting should override everything. First things first. It was buried in the earth then it came back. I'm actually subverting myself. Lemures were once ancestral spectres. My trademark concerns include dregs and paranoia. I feel just that little bit shell-shocked. I like people like you. Psyche has served its purpose and must die. If you could see the things I'd seen you wouldn't try to stop me. It's an unfortunate fact that all the texts possessed are comparatively late.

A mythed figure, perhaps himself. A fresh disease, a complete representation of the ills of the soul. A viscid brown liquid is seeping out of the hold. These are the new, or those moved to make room for them. Mould is next below the abacus of capital. The reason for use of a word has been variously conjectured. To recover, neck a draft of acid. The more something changes the more it's the same thing (no superficials or apparition). Strap racks to every available spine. The temperature of a house ranges from about seventy-five to ninety degrees. Transport the glass vessels produced in the manufactory. Attach rubber valves to all the remaining casks. This must be delivered in a voice. It's time now. (Who is what he says.) The residue was intermediate in tint between burnt umber and raw. I volunteered for suicide watch. All about us in the forest the cries of sacred brutes. Waste clings to the joints, emptied words. Who shall dwell in these worlds if they be inhabited? What wanes thou to expostulate matter? The spectators sway from side to side and scoop up the sulphur with their bare hands. Now make the deceased say something to the figure that was called forth. It is time— bulls, panthers, crocodiles. There's never been a day like it in the domestic household. I still hold an affliction. Recollections are simply as one knew them across the span of years. I should think a good service done. All chaos is set loose. You see, I have surpassed, in respect of the period of origin.

At last.

It's possible. They moved me out of the corridor by simply unlocking a door two yards away. Bridges fashioned from creepers bisect space to span the chasm. Massive blacks can form at the centre of a galaxy. We are no longer visible from the air. Limbs were fashioned of wire and wood. I propose to build my names, an armature.

Would you like to say more about that?

No, it's perfect as it is.

What she hears next.

Will we lose you then. He wrote chamber in his spares—slowly getting over the breakdown, staring through space at the garden sunlight. It is lyric (hunterlike the bow she bears, the flock flies with the wind).

Eerie November. There had been eleven degrees of frost in our town. He understood it. Seizing the key he rushed to the door, unlocked it, and burst out of the cell. The ground was crushed with ice. (Do you play insurance?) Nebulae have urged astronomers to look.

One born to compose and resurrect. Really, the huge disorder of perching birds. One who has imperfect knowledge.

A projector on a plinth whirrs and chunters (r for are is used with great effect in phrasing). We felt them an uplifting.

Things could still get worse.

Following the solid black surface signals. The S components must be sorted in alphanumeric order. It looks like a good atmosphere though, the crowd. We found ourselves on a deserted plateau. Spatially this recalls the complex layers of an oil painting, cross-sections of remote and incomprehensible lives. There were these strains of disapproval. The surface of the plain, when tilted on edge, is believed visible from the moon. (See rumours I have introduced and nurtured.) Refer to the instance of nonconformity cited in Figure 113. I wish I had loved her more when she was alive. All gathers well, for a few moments. A supply of signs is predicted. The numbers were chosen at random.

An explosive thud as each tree bursts into flame. She has kept the letter. There is little time left for reflection (ten minutes). I.e. in an averse direction, on a path away from the point currently occupied in space. Fro and suffix ward.

The forehead is scarred and has aged. The motif splits here into two distinct heresies. This performer has a volatile quality that keeps you on the edge of your seat. (Of course he is right, half of the time.) I find myself at work in an interim space, only the periodic table for company. Who were the primitive elect? Joints must be sealed against any escape of the embalming fluid.

Ripples of sullen applause. I didn't ask for this. Things are conjectured. The panther is a melanic form of leopard, I hear.

Anything more would corrode the statement. The text found me, was always finding me. It was like touching feathers. I remain stationary while the field itself revolves. (It sounds like a funeral march, a brand of ecstatic melancholy.) I may be likened, the innocent possessor of a magnet. A powerful was introduced. The subject is suspended in a bath of carbon dioxide. This is not looking good. Yes, two never centres, from we, the family.

See note tattooed on bone. They had lost control over the means of production. As one plodding, torn.

A man, watering.
Nothing is truly synthesized. We have now reached a stage that superficially resembles. Like some other books, this one didn't really end, or start for that matter. (No one anywhere is making his own atoms.) For some reason I don't think we're going to make it home tonight. Camouflage is swirling in the head, the medic. A hypothetical vanished.

X.
To tear flesh like dogs, to speak flesh. Do not take if you have connective tissue. There is a chronic disease of unknowns. Cause is characterized by the formation of nodules in the lymph, lungs, skin et cetera. For some reason I didn't think that you were ever going to show. Form is stolen from form.

He values the protection of a pocket to operate within.
An injection, pure adrenalin of expectation, directly into the eyeball. The text says as little as possible, while incorporating thousands of used words. He turned on his side, a very slight stiffening. It's nine years to the minute. Only the smallest items survived the conflagration. The structure is tiered on all three sides, and sealed. It's a question of combinations. This example is from a buried horde. An amazing compound just occurred. It's a question of combustions. The colour is

amazing, more Adriatic. It's nine years in the making, a chink of life. I hunger. It's a question of momenta. It is clumsy day, what with the gentle drip of things. Organs are dribbling, pecks of glass here and there. I can't believe I'm still doing this.

He writes.

A flaring light, a tiny history, is harboured. The chosen object is flag-blue. It would normally have hardened into dirt. The outermost border has a denticulate edge. In my hand I hold an astrolabe. Careful observations of the transit were taken from widely separated points on the globe. (Remember, the same passion led to her big break in comedy.) But these merely give an apparent accuracy, which is not in fact achieved. Love of my naked place constrained me.

He ponders things deeply and speaks in obscure riddles. (Liar.) Once you held the sceptre and the drone. The interchanges that take place between these elements can only be guessed at. Not a brick of the original building remains standing. He releases the book and we take our leave. I don't know. Don't you ever lie, never.

It was spasmodic. A quadrant, or the like. Lauds, with gradual extinction of light.

I don't really see that italic. Splashes of black very noticeable. One lives in shadow, one in the glare. The subject sits himself down and waits—he could take you apart without thinking about it. I couldn't have slept for more than a few minutes.

Dig deep, convulse, then calm yourself. The chintz opposite quivers, then still. All eyes in the room fasten onto him. Objects are losing their upright shape, dissolving into currents of silver-white light. We are unable to date the stele. Part of me wanted this to sound like an autopsy.

Birdlike the jag near arrow of head.

Constriction between the seeds.

A pod that breaks in pieces.

Connective tissue unmuscling sheath.

Fracture of limbus.

Pernicious mummy.

Yes, I'm right. I don't usually structure (hysteric). A vein of the stuff runs right across the roof of the cabin. The objective is to erect a system of rigid scientific code. The manner of composition is amnesia. (It's your first time, isn't it?) He has become afraid of the smallest things. A disembodied voice says the others owe us what we imagine they can give us. Igniter fuel is good for removing ink.

To wait for a person at the appointed place and time.

I meant somnambulistic.

Not convinced by that.

Today is symbol G. Convention is inserted in place of the disused, in lieu of ordinary sound. I demand only a few hours in which to learn everything. Units of magnetic flux play a part in our destinies. It makes that noise when you give up the ghost. Let me introduce you to the tesla ray.

I am equal. All your citizens have learned to live, to reason, and then to die. Note the loss of control over the means of production. (Yes, but the Egyptian too.) At dawn on the fifth the disloyal ignite. A bit of antimatter lurks in every object out there. This is alluring, my love, and those phantasms of the living.

Who reacted so strongly. The king is gone said he many years later and sighed. Who threw a piece of paper with something written. Because the object has been kept in a box all these years, it has become a complete thing of beauty. I'm sedated, head lying toward the stern of the vessel. At the same time, the executive.

Speed up, psyche.

A stricter methodology. Whose powers then may subvert, demon? By contrast, the white muslin—I pale-grey, without. And racemes of blue-lilac, papilionaceous blooms. An encircling stripe of differing colour, of differing substance. Quite a giant of a man ran through.

Another is seen throwing stones at a dog under water. Only the last chapter had been cut open and read. Painting is something no one could ever bring to an end. The text is inscribed in straight-crested ripples. (Are you still, eyes.) I sit snug in my own corner, moving north. Next a new list consisting of only one word.

Veinstone.

Everything's under control. Everything's a descendant of language and magic. I enjoy stating the obvious. Your plot is thin. Everything relies too much on coincidence (cf. the waves). It puts your story beyond the bounds of believability. I learnt too late in life to remember, unless absolutely essential.

An ironic youth in turndown collar. Bound in frost, a strip of black ribbon. The spit of land in the upper part of the photograph connects. (He is rendered hell in the old England.) It's a long journey back to the beginning of the book. The current produces torque. Female without wings.

Of things, by and by.

She bears witness. It was cut into sections and towed away. The suspect is found to possess no person, no noun. It is an impossible. Consider an isolate (chiefly zinc, dilute sulphuric acid).

Spiral or sickle-shaped pods, short racemes, including. From the phrase in ablative of border.

A meteoric crater in a desert.

Striated stones will become rounded. All the ingredients weathered, but there are clues. He gave us a very gentle nod. We knew it was the end. (A probe may be imitative.) There is light enough to see.

A limb with five digits. A tiny, redundant thumb sprouting from its fully-formed cousin. Blood Rorschach on well of stair, on paving of flagstone, on causeway of basalt columns. I ask myself the question. The conductors are mounted on an iron structure, a would-be musical instrument. Hold the object tightly in your hand from the moment you go over the wall.

Tension cracks. He is waiting on an error. (Don't get sarcoma with me et cetera.) And the fall of a pin might be heard. I am drawn exiles.

A horizontal athwartship magnet, whether permanent or an induced softness. The cause is deviation.

Each contestant is appointed a personal assistant to bring him back to life. Space permitting, some of the remaining words could be explained. Are you aware of what you are about to lose. In those days we were living in a vacuum state. (Enormous pressure now.) Another version of the same story comes next.

There are more than two hundred such salt domes along the gulf coast. A word is meaning host.

The ground about the mineralogist's feet is scattered with silicate of beryllium. Inside which object were they supposed to seal the young dauphin? The polymer semi-automatic 6.5mm is used by most law enforcement agencies.

Where the ocean now is, posited to explain the distribution.

Two men stand on either side of a chasm. This scenario is a projective test. No one wanted to remember. The subject's reactions to random ink blots and fungal shapes are analysed and found wanting. Arm, shoulder and leg patterns are a typical hindrance. Our findings are used to plot a course through the land-scape. The tale relates the adventures of a seeker of heresies. (Cup was his jocular rendering of skull.) He replied it is broken. And why haven't you brought back the figments. He continued. But what about the voices you hear in the head—a certain quality of hospitality, satanic humour? I hear you ask. Are you going to charge anyone with raising the equivalent? They are just staring at that white line in front of them, stock still and doing nothing. Props include a tank of carbon dioxide. The burning of a horse in sacrifice is on the programme.

A hypothetical machine.

Phantom visitation, revenance. One may or may not has been invented. It's all about the numbers. People travel from the future to commit sabotage. (I've got myself a new sponsor.) Should we place a bet against the outcome tonight? I'm accompanied by an ill-deserved reputation. I compulsively strike forehead to floor, floor to forehead. There are no seasons anymore. When dried in the sun and its shell rubbed off, the local earthworm is quite edible. In terms of my general shape, I am either off or on. This occasion is a thousand times better than drawing any conclusions from within the world itself. A man is dragged along the floor by means of hooks attached to long poles. An instant is a state of delight that may prove fatal. Acid gas crystallizes to a hexagonal system, more pockets of impossibility. Above, vapour congealing feathers—into helix, into backbone. I blink and miss everything. Partly through the fault of O, bits of the translation are missing. This hypothesis amounts to a freeing of the spatial. We've come across this maxim before. Why doesn't he do this sort of thing more often. Sometimes I forego.

The belonging-somewhere of the ready-to-hand.
Not of stone, but paper, chewed to a mash and spat out. The planetary veil of oxygen. Two anterior petals formed a keel. Very slowly the tin melted.

Being which one heads toward.
Ambiguous or equivocal appearance. Deep third hand, obviously not breathing from the diaphragm. Would someone else like to have a go. I've run out of saints. Examples include threadlike fibres. What people don't get a good sense of is the years.
A process of the temporal bone behind the ear, also. Any unsatisfactory place of consignment or oblivion, the uncertain or indeterminate state. Person.

Yes he says all day I crate them up and they're sent off all over the globe. They come from outer space, I think. Don't we all. Who decided the fates. Please allow me to introduce myself.

The eighth day.
Spines of life. The pelvic arch. A brutal mismatch. She says I hate the smell of sperm. When section is complete the blade of the knife emerges zero point five millimetres beyond the corneal side. The declared aim is a sort of limbo. (They told me I was liable, that's all I know.) Swollen veins render the forearms planar. This commentary is brutal, yet delivered with such sensual economy. There is tactic at play.
Sun directly overhead. Heat radiates from the concrete platform through the soles of her feet. We have reasoned our way back to an earlier time. A thick sequence of undisturbed events is taking place. We were slowly roasting her back to life.
It's admirable. Your eldest is foredoomed. As I speak, a piano is shunted into the room. A metal plate with holes from which plastic filaments protrude is expressed. In the background are the French windows which lead into the garden. The guests are now leaving. If I had only known yesterday what I know today.

Each contestant has a separate official to resuscitate her once the trial is over.

He-will-be.

I-am unwilling.

She-will-be.

We-are unwilling.

As-it-will-be.

They-will.

I'm no longer in a recognizable place. The reader may go unnoticed. One point nothing—the name of one of the asteroids.

Thanatoseros.

Phantom throb. An uninvited word. When dissolving into sleep this square of dark emerges. He says I'm a haven of sorts. He was very upset about losing his mind. I never would have come had I known.

Barren precipitate in schism of tilled earth. I am returning the silence. Allot to every linguistic element its function and synaptic relationship. My own acceleration is due to gravity, a revolution in miniature. I am taking up my station inside the limits of the place and time named, to the precise day.

Should he wish to flee.

Why this reluctance to move. I can only see my pessimism growing, gaining in strength and resolve. The iron bar should be gripped tightly with both feet, hands parallax to hips apart, with abdominal remainder. (Bless you.) In this paragraph I do not feel particularly close. It's been a week of musical decadence. Nonetheless, it is clear to the touch. This is a close race, as the emptiness registers. Sometimes he comes in the guise of curative substance. The fossils found embedded in the boulder clay are of a species never seen before. The rest of our company hovers at the brink of sleep. Eyes are heavy. I'm humming a tricky little love song. Thou shalt not be afraid of the destruction that lays waste at noonday et cetera.

Nothing is sheltered from the radiation. She says I once exalted in a perpetual state.

A genus of repulsive-looking leaf-nosed bats. Embracing anthropomorphism.

Eyes like sorcerers. He sits beside herself and recites a favourite tale. This fact constitutes an additional argument in support of reconstruction. She sleeps. She probably dies in it. Finally, a striking image of him crossing the treacherous bridge. There are still pieces of this missing. Only in the meantime has a given context a name. I was drawn to her because she was exile. Both hands are now occupied.

Of refuelling in space.

By the way which make was it. Luger. I'm in deadly earnest, stunned in time after the ancestral type.

Trucage.

That name sounds like a hat. For it is rooted in gesture, in iconicity, in 'radical insularity'. But the whole work suffers from prolix and pedestrian writing and metrical ineptitude.

Every chip will eventually crack.

She says she once existed in a perpetual state—a haven of sorts, apparently on the wane. I am waiting on an arrival. It seems that things are more like now, plausibly deceptive.

Various parties rally and ridicule one another with scurrilous extempore verses. I fear lest my change of name and condition prove insufficient camouflage. The latter includes one of the inquisitors.

Academic discourse on the execution of a trumpeter from a painting.

A piece of bloodied tape I once drew out of my gullet. Letters were printed thereupon. This unexpected publication of the voice-box spelled out all future states. Times are hard in the aftermath. Magic was wedded to abstract ideas of political liberty. (The eyeball easily pops back in again.) Folk became brittle. This demonstrates how fast the brain can actually work. It's a written rule that you can't appeal after looking. The title is a proper name. A bold stroke was impersonated by another character at an earlier part of the play. Hardy buds sprout from cracks in the rock. Simony is universal. The minerals are arranged in a more or less parallel manner.

He's kept in a big box in the dark. Sometimes this works. No superficial or apparent change alters the essential nature. The direction from, or time when, are later extended. Platelets in cleavage.

Evaporite.

The beginning of the final chapter is magnificent. Clay contains an abundance of fossils. All the lenses are trained. It's like artificial grass. I had become a mere bystander. Crime today is like a chemical reaction. (You never know how it's going to work out in the shadow.) He looks the part in his cape and hat, armgaunt. Maybe I never had powers of horror, after all. It's just like any old garden. The psyche does not believe he exists for that purpose.

Lids red from sleep, they handle each other the remarkable. Then one says, as you think. In the wilderness, a hunter's station, an aimless wandering beyond bounds.

Concentrate, crystallize, dry it with the pump. Wash and recrystallize. So you are, no.

Oxyrhynchus.

Flycatcher. Papyri depicting tyrant. Which surmounts the ram's head on the instrument used? The plan seemed to work right up until the final moment of execution.

A list of unforced errors.

No, he can't possibly walk all that way. The power of speech is all but dead. It's like the all-important moment in a novel. The species under study has a wormlike tongue and an acute bill. He communicates through an alphabet board, a cross between abacus and planchette. Another has lost the use of a leg (see plate fifteen). We've waited a long time for this. If I blink I miss the action. The animal depicted holds in its right paw a cube. A strip of catgut and plastic resonates to the human voice. On the ground lies a freshly clubbed doorkeep. Painting is something no-shaped.

Much summer lightning. Horses dragged us the rest of the way. Ropes were attached at ankle and wrist. What do you make of all this.

As the scattered bolts boomed overhead et cetera.

An obsolete ordeal.

It's said an event once took place. That man drank his savings. We decided to pack and lock everything up and leave. I don't want to risk being passed by, overlooked. Mneme can't be limited to organic substance alone.

Terminate and liquefy. No identities can be disclosed at this time. Velocity withers from thirty-six to eighteen names per second. Perhaps the worst aspect is that in the later stages the subject is fully aware of and can observe his own fracture and disintegration. Demise is beautifully written out.

Abstract artist of aphorism.

Life, according.

(We morons o outraged.)

Blood, sweat, tears and lots of other things.

G-force, wooden stake at the ready.

This is another example of seeing according to an interpretation. We must stop here. I promise to do quieter stuff in future: misuse as supine of to take.

I am unequalled. The one who is dying is speaking. The golden rapacious is the foremost of its kind. We are no longer in control of our gestures or our fate. An overseer conducts all men possessed. (Others feel a together shows elements of observation.) An emergency has appeared: passive devotional contemplation, extinction of the will, a withdrawal from things. Discharge of acquittance. The city is crisscrossed with underground galleries—unsaid happenstance, dispeopled streets. Air cells of the mastoid process.

The disinherited.

Stoic. Markings are not always present. Almost all of the body is hurting. I remember that ruptured street. Something slight yet bothersome is recurring. Even the musical phrases, touched by the archaism of the chord, were broken. His of almost.

A tiny clock made entirely of glass and a length of bandage were extracted from the sinus cavity. I am on my way toward the forbidden part of town. Part of me has begun play-acting. Consider in your calculations the measure of the turning effect of a tangential force.

O the heat. You're making me think, aren't you. A well-known property of the sap is to enlarge the bull of the eye. The so-called axeman's stroke.

Mute, yet it has stamina and shape, from the lid skyward. He follows or diverts the path, leading the patient toward the good, the object. Encircle, effect the ceremony of opening the mouth.

The marked vagaries of my own body.
Moulded into the air. Bystanders devour every atom. The executed scholar might be proof of such attacks. This is becoming quite a little story all on its own, isn't it. Are you aware of what you are about to lose, of what you could always lose? I am exiled from the stations of life. Where is ancestor. Some among us are yet possessed. Anything can happen and everything does. It must still be alive out there, hobbling on its crutch. It is interesting to note that the other is not mentioned. The fact seems to indicate influence. I meant hurling—a dog, a stick.

Their ages lay initially in the ratio of sixteen to zero. The company thrice lead a respectful circuit around the dead. (The incriminating letter is on the floor, if you can find it.) I do know that this is no longer concerned with the things of memory. Tendrils hung down on either side in twists of unequal length. A magnet shuttles between two poles.

A sunwise turn.
It was stored in its original box, unopened away from the light. In scanning down the group note the increase in metallic character. He says I sense you have travelled from far Sirius. What was said possessed an intrinsic logic which had no means of halting. In any case, arriving must be regarded as an impermanent condition. This year has been pretty easy. He too is having a hard time stopping. In a few million years there should be several hundred stars out there.

It was fenced in at the muscular partition between thorax and abdomen. It was about so big in business. A mass was represented. (He flashes forth in sinister lights et cetera.) The intensity of his eye is impenetrable. I sense torsion in the orbit. Hold back your nerve. The corpus of the state is unfathomable. This specious reasoning is nevertheless false.

You're not happy here on this planet, but it was your decision to leave. The question is not one of promises mutual. As well as this he knows the name of the man who answered.

Bring everyone. Stop. Bring the money. Stop. Bring reinforcements. Plus other deviations from universally accepted dogma.

How much fucking more of this is there.

A big V of swarming birds swoops down in a cloud then rises up again, before finally settling on a ledge of rock exposed at low tide. (Semi-colons, good or bad?) The sky curls back, sinuous-crested feathering high in the air. Dissident structure in eye of stalk.

This atmosphere is familiar. We stand at the foreshore and gaze out to sea. All words were drawn from a common pool. We're waiting for something to happen.

A recurring dream. I'm in an enormous foreign. We are waiting on hazard. A hollow pierces through my foot, astragalus to sole. The pencilled annotations are part of my original.

Consider prehistoric, the vertebrae. Curved recess in shell.

Actus reus.

Estuarial. In a nearby café a man with a double-bass bangs his companion's head repeatedly against a marble table. It's free improv night. A testing ground, figures snared in needless motion. How much were you listening.

Part of the surface is raised to form an upwarp. A face was painted on the corrugated iron roof. Previous reports of death have been proved wrong. And the distance to the nearest star?

He has become edibly nervous. Insects pour out of the abdomen. We are at the halfway stage. There is not much that can be done about this. He is attracted to voids, attaches himself to nothing. (Could you drink out of another man's head?) Another moment is switching to the depths of despair and suicide.

I would perceive in the massing cloud intimations of outlines mirroring the maps I hungered. A luminous white halo was seen opposite the sun during his reign. The following litany was found inscribed upon a linen screed. Also dromedaries, avian swarms, cracked and peeling varnish. The hatch was left slightly ajar. (And of the three who once enveloped?) The illustrations were too uncanny to publish. Diagonal shadows are now casting east. The semblance of a tidal bore to the movement of running cattle is long established. Look ye to oxygen, move.

Gigantic fossil ungulates from county.

She is itself. I wonder what it's like back in the England. Near the top there's a lake in which the wrecks of ships float to the surface. She is a more than capable slayer. Fragmentary organic remains are formed by evaporation of salt—or gaunt limbs, but probably an error.

Notes on the solar eclipse found behind the sofa.
We'll have to go through the whole process again. It's a long walk back to this very second. The third and most violent blizzard hurled itself out of the north. He leapt up and started running towards an open space, where the light is. Foliage had contrived a canopy.

The disc in question was projected against the wall of the cell. Note how the interior of the head has become molten. (They've got a war on their hands.) The volume of information that can be transmitted by radiation is enormous. I'm drawn to exiles, worn to resemble ordinary sediment.

Arguably this is not the abandoned chamber. And what is left within him. Somewhere under the shadow of this act a good few minutes remain—by extension a rent, a split or cleft. The manuscript seems to have gone missing in the interim. I once read of a big sea crossed by a causeway, its breadth being the hole beneath. Maybe it's time. Certainly is far less. What is the opinion of the commandant. Indigo blue is frequently found coating copper.

He says I feel so full of days. I'm glad I wore steel toes, for fear of levitation. All the profundity is concentrated in the second movement. (Very nice indeed.) A is now safely back in A.
In less than one hour we've seen the complete range of human emotion and experience. Publishing was in fragments. I can now recommend atrophy. This is an extraordinary moment of flux. That apparent lid is called the sky. (It was the town of our choice and right on the lake.) I am recommending a self-loathing which is quite legitimate. This is feeling rather fructuous. Their seductions, he abandoned himself to them. Once the musicians had taken up their places in the chapel we could commence.

On leaving this existence behind for good.
I am recommending the end of the story, a demise. This is like no other place in the world. There, I've said it. I think that's solved that little problem. How much further.

Another option is to compose an inventory of all the used books and other objects in the cell. (I hear loves lists). Consider the faking of works of art as a topic for discussion. What sets this apart from any spoken language?
Sinter is cinder, a deposit from ember. Powdered metal. Sometimes the momentary is under pressure, to the melting point. Appearances are levelled, binding together any stray atoms. Your diversity is invalid.

Air-filled cavity in the bonus of the skull, narrow straits through which pus is discharged. A notch or indentation. Scylla and Charybdis. I often dreamed that I opened the doors. I had brought form to my own voice, into solidity and bloodhood. The sky turned black is prosaic.

Of the unit, or primary delta.

War exhaust. A quick thumbnail decryption. There's a whole dimension that's currently missing. I believe in you, as in 'the watered heads of old the jugular'. What's going on is required reading. He's to be executed come dawn in the republic square. A night-guard is stationed outside his cell. Objects have been sealed up. Pleasure is without use. Sell everything by date he demands.

Odour of humans and their kak beneath the colonnade. Changes had to be made to accommodate me. We're testing being at its parameters. Each of the intercepts is cancelled on its own axis. Now for a quick break. Recollection is disordered and perverted in memory. He has become visibly nervous would have been too obvious.

I recall of the meaning—a retelling, where my usually ends. The sense of déjà vu is unequalled. I admire. Events are told again and again in rapid secession. The tide gradually turns. He is mistaken for the face. (A beach is a place et cetera.) The story gradually reverts to future, to past, to haphazard tense. The level of the ocean sinks to the level of the lake. It's said he relied on librettos that were second-hand and third-rate. The tip of a mast breaks the surface. An outflux of water ceases.

Thankyou I enjoyed reading the blue book is beautiful in its coffin box. Sharpsnouted and spit-nosed epithet of fish, sacred with esteem, that lunge into again.

Imagine that, the one who was standing next to me all along. Backlit, the dream about the dream. The replies. A questionnaire from the clinker store. Conversion in the mountain. Letters. A poll station, uncrossed. (Poetry doesn't impose, she exposes.) Speech. The occasion of receiving the free heuristic prize. The meridian. The lost address to the Hebrew. Appendices. Introductory notes. Translations and blockages. Sources. Words have the same root in our language.

I mean the one who was standing apart. I understand I do. Everybody is run aground on my back, torn into a knot. The shadows he was supposed to have chased away. Brain cell is frieze.

To spread a net. To set a trap or snare.

Also to set in place, in any position whatsoever. This thing called more, showing a perfect when. Perhaps with gaunt limbs. Perhaps worn with armour, but still probably an error. The place of origin of a people without language.

I will never forget my first full march into long space.

We chanced upon a pyramid of skulls, a relic of the island's sinister past. The size of the atom increased. She will be here for three centuries more. I defy any one of you to offer another explanation (café gourmand—deathbed—the green house—the metro). Instead of one table of card players suddenly there were two. In any case, I couldn't assign an exact moment to my answer. She shares with all else.

Man, high-skulled, by the yard. And far far greater than the amount we can communicate by ordinaries. The effort jerked them both away from the brick wall.

Themes for solitary contemplation.

Boolean ring. The usage of books, creaking gently. A riot of birds. Salt is mixed with borax and molten lead. Appearance is indirect, or by recommendation only. This is an operation dependant on the application of algebra. You can feel the tension everywhere. You wander. The phenomenon is unnamed. Put simply, AB means a *and* b. Spatial racemes play exactly the same role. I.e. the memory-like capacity of all living matter. Haemorrhage is checked by twisting the severed end of the artery.

Substance found in moon as glassy fragment. A constituency of fines and breccias. Editorial comment: potassium, phosphorous, rare earth elements and unusual iron stills. Barren is the order, with faultless, cunninghead.

This is how. He lures people in. I am worried. He physically seems to be. Add newtons throughout.

Hence retarded, belonging to two families. Priest touching state of deceased with instrument. Probably they wanted at the last minute. Force the voyager to take them all with him.

News from where.

A man is engaged in sinking an artesian well. There's a taut feeling to the air. I think I've found your spectacle. (Good instincts, which occasionally has happened.) It's doomsday once more. These are great numbers, part of the mysteries associated with the written name. It proceeds with a silence when filled. This is an estrangement, an incident of pure fiction.

No deliberation. A moment of category and law, a moment of forsaking. I'm the kind of person who would never say love you to death. I do all the time. Out of this apparent flux emerges a persistent theme. Well sometimes, naturally, but not very often.

Brother calls mother is dying. He never could grasp geometry. Speech is distorted, as though the mouth had been injured. Publication came in fragments. It's as though no one is belonging. Text is fled, mutely, like the gentle rocking back and forth.

I meant atrium, in the background, murmurhead.

Obituary.

An instrumental maker. Speed and harness can be measured by the size of each indentation. Stuff is product of atom, poison. The apparatus consists of a glass tube neatly filled with alcohol. It's time for another intermission. Steps must be taken to ensure this never happens again. No hardening of the air was ever recorded.

Zero pressure, gravitation nil. Coalesce under heat without liquefaction, a precise whisper.

Night in pieces, where P is the test load in grams.

Tide low, channel muddy. That's an oyster catcher. The elderflower is out. The distilled sap of the root is a sovereign remedy for eyes. Nonetheless, she was mortally wounded by summer lightning.

Sky heavy under cloud, topped with vents of magnetic origin. Boardwalks winding everywhere. People cluster. No one takes any notice. I'm reminded of apocalypse. (Memorize what's written around the inside of the cylinder.) I have adapted a new proof of what is already known. I'm reminded of the unnecessary word. The action is simple. He's back in the garden in his working clothes. Listen to this. One influences the other. List his injuries, observations of flora and fauna.

Windpipe crushed.

Teeth are cut.

Hand fractured, the lip condemned.

The time has come for an infamous revival. Without, the daylight fades. An inventory of the scattered remnants could be drawn up. Hints of the boneyard encumber our paragraphs (one who writes in decays). A long narrow plug is drawn from the inner ear. At one end sprouts a thick tassel of fur. Welcome back. This is quite unlike any gumshield I have ever seen before. How can bricks be unforgiving.

For example.

A body of men. Countless night-hinged phantasms. Never settle for long on any particular topic. They exist in a lineage stretching farther back. A single dramatic chord ceased without warning. Before is restlessly moving on. He died on the day. This is from me, personally.

Mine arm is out of lith.

The term has been extended to cover not only the iron core but also the wires attached to it. His perfectly preserved body was found years later. A veil of cloth was wound about the head. Primeval matter is the original stuff out of which everything collapsed. (Fame, hopes, horrors.) You still have to pay up front. It's like a mediaeval panorama. The masons rejected one of the stones. Then that unmistakable voice again. In fact, the word means belonging to an executioner. Only the eyes were left uncovered.

Lexicon.

Dial now while it's free. There's no security of performance on either side. He has lost his remaining disciple. We heard the litany of saint mouth on the radio. An epithet can be applied to favourite orators. Now, what became a kind of surname.

Shattering corpsicles. (An old sobriquet for what, you don't say.) Reconsider all the positions, all the available options. I believe he was hiding in the crowd all along. Look, a fixed star of the first magnitude. He took a studio in a part of town where anything could happen and usually did.

Titanium.

The graphic form of the last apparition. I must have made mistakes. A visible fragment is trapped at the root of the jaw. I'm exiled because I want nothing. I don't know he says, I may never know. Since they cut the power, dog is our only pastime.

Alpha Centauri.

She sits alone in the garden. (I can't say she looks the part.) Memory's not what it is. Sunlight batters at the high Elizabethan wall—the temperature in the enclosed space soars. A ridge runs between us, sliding steeply to embankments that stretch to the floor of a ravine. Where do I know you. Two areas of depression rapidly descend. The intruder's footsteps were disguised. We are torn apart. A voice remains, delicately hinged.

We have what we shall extinguish she says. We reach our destination, an abandoned city that can only be reached by a bridge of creepers spanning water. This is my calling. (Surely it dies even now.) True she said with a start. Why did I not come before. I am unnerved. The intruder rushed out of the room and there was a sacrifice in the passage. I had no idea of time. It signals itself as stem theatre. I ought to have been met said sir entering. In making use of a common word, it is often likened. (I know they are.) The bodies were hastily embalmed. Some complain that they cannot breathe. The airways have compressed, plus allergic reactions, such as skin. I feel a bit radio rental. And it was assumed that, as a result, the same things came to pass.

The funeral chapel with its yellow light through hazy windows. As soon as he lets go, it opens up again. You must be able to act independently. Insects are pouring into the compound.

He refuses to undertake. The operands take on the appearance of a valve. The diode is the best and the biggest, they say. It is never closed.

Four thousand miles to freedom, the story of one of the most journeys ever made by a man in a desperate circle.
But not from that book, the reveille, the trumpet call to waking slumber.

Can't put that there.
A force of motion, foresaid in a single gesture. From my foot I dig out a tubular plug of flesh. A black tassel is attached at one end, the tips of which were visible on the surface of the sole. This is what first drew my attention. Things get so much easier once you break. I now possess the colloquial impetus. A brightness appeared between the adversary and mine own eyes, embodied.

The climax of a struggle.
No water in this sandy expanse. We have arrived at that moment when suddenly and dramatically one is face to face. The custom of touching the ground with the forehead is a crucial gesture, an interweaving of action and reminiscence. All operations are dependant on the correct application of algebra. And they kept watch for any green thing that might tell of rainfall.
An indefinite fluorescence, stalked. Gamma rays from outer space. Temperature is sound, the cinder track.

The what.
Within our remote dislocations. We've been set worlds apart. This is simply pragmatic (viz. shaking palsy, Saint Elmo's fire). I was once so happy she said. In biology scrotum equals bag or sack. Books gather dust. I think this complaint is going to revisit us again and again. I have never lowered myself to publishing anything. I still operate under a pseudonym. (Mourning, believe me.) I know what I'm talking about. Something must be specified, made clear. Here's not time enough. The blue guide says this sacred site of the heads was guaranteed by a crocodile.
Metal, and thy fingers shine in the dwelling. A disease of the nervous stem is speaking. The name belongs, originally and properly. I mean the past found in our being-within-one-another. An unconvincing fulcrum.
I will never forget the thinness, so encompassed.

Chrysocracy.
If the word had survived its form would have been unsound. Like those gusts and blasts and battering storms that beat against thy wall. Narrative is the lynchpin of millennia-long hegemonic social structures based on the presumed signifi-

cance of instructive myth and storytelling. The angular direction of the second-ary (B), as distinct from the primary (A). Not firm or solid, clicking.

Thunderhead summer tumulus. It's a hexagon. (But now can no man see.) None is more elusive. I felt something brush against my shin, against the hollow of the thigh. A ring of soft wax was fastened to the tapering edge of the body frame. Facts he says are objects—events and phenomena: portable surveying instruments. Highstacked, not solid.

Document any defoliated metamorphic rock. The traveller is looking for a compartment where he can bite the carpet in solitary spleen. A faker of works.

I often find that I don't like what's written in brackets. There's a high rate of sedi-ment supply nearby, potential suicides. But hold on. I like the appearance of the voice I hear within me. Every act performed is noted down in a journal, then forgotten.

The thing of the dog in the water, earlier. I'm told it should read for, not at. (See undercrop.)

Risk-related.
Everyone will, there can be no exceptions. I don't know why he says, I am never here. I always thought bludgeon had a spur-of-the-moment sound. We're outnumbered by two to seven. He was always the more daedal partner. Gold is the colour of a winner—existence at the end of the plot-line. The event is retold again and again. It is always beginning, is the same, the emptiness of repetition. The smell of fading flowers and correction fluid.

The assemblage of actively swimming organisms in a sea, lake et cetera.
She says it felt like living a novel. The wind bit inside me. Where do you live now. I thought you'd never ask. It's a perfect ten. Peering into the hollow, I could see daylight through my foot.

This part is about the corridor, when fatefully he looks back. It's just a single moment in time. (Another stymie, it must be said.) All of a year has passed us by. What will your own approach consist of. A small piece of ground, I think, solved. Language arises biologically, from below.

Small claims court.
Till then, goodbye. Saturday night is opera night. One-act numbers. A savage-ness in unclaimed blood, of general assault. Like mountains, this reinforces a limited defence. Energy is drawn deep from the surrounding volcanics. Some-how he forces his opponent back inside the chalk circle. (Lo, it is he who infects all the world.) There are in fact two circles. The smaller, of white marble, is raised a little above the surface of the earth. The larger is pitch black and of far

greater circumference. It is the cast shadow of the former. Bullets pluck at the elevator. He sits silently within this compass for a spell, before answering his inquisitor. They called it the Nile in the sky.

Old stuff this really, once seen.
They dare. A revival in the night, your signs. On the pavement is a galaxy strewn of white stars. Any director worth his salt conducts by remote control.

That fateful glimpse: cheap silver penholder and snuff box with masonic star. Solemn acoustics. Murmuring they dare not he returns to sleep as usual. Who is this man who without death ventures through the kingdom et cetera.

Omnibus. Hagioscope.
I did enjoy the felt-tip moment. Also that day spoke saint afire, saint anomie, saint assassin, saint botched-execution, saint chorea, saint colostomy, saint day-release, saint disease, saint dog, saint do-it-yourself, saint dweller, saint easy, saint edging, saint encephalitis, saint errant, saint evil, saint fictitious, saint fold-of-the-integument, saint forever, saint gloria, saint greatless, saint grievous-bodily-harm, saint half-hearted, saint hangmen, saint incurable, saint involuntary, saint irregular, saint less, saint lily, saint luke, saint mucous-membrane, saint mothman, saint mouthful, saint neural, saint null, saint quicklime, saint rare, saint riotous, saint sectioned, saint sniper, saint socialistic system, saint tippex, saint torn-to-ribbons, saint un, saint whither, saint without, saint xenomorph.

Stricken, as if with a blow to the head. An absence of effective antibodies. Dregs of melted tallow at turn of road before the city gate. Black-clad, she scrapes up, semi-liquid. It's so easy to make a mistake. You cannot simply ignore the material that emerges.

Stranger, in shape or nature.
Elements of the shell or skeleton are not secreted by the organism itself. Dishonour in reference to the fact is evident. Time shrinks because of us. They may be able to sell the letters printed on their backs. You see, there is this sense of indebtedness, though I don't know why. (So where is it, if not right here.) She sits at her wheel, spinning. Wars against external enemies have traditionally propelled individuals. I mean strange in error for empty.

A tomb cannot be representative of one medium alone. Rarities never recur, except in composition, or in the act of fermentation. Much earlier, a chunk from under the chin. Allied to what.

The patriots, having completed their ghastly work at the abbey, decamped. Do take these events one day at a time. You must contact a pragmatist if your symptoms worsen. Hello, I'm an omega minus, caught in frightful solitude.

But at the same time there was no longer any need to dispel the darkness.

And not only by the reputation, the fierce eloquence of his jealous discourse. It must have been easy back then to mesmerize people with your words. Some books still live in attics. A recurrent theme appears to be the hero's persecution. (I have composed another paragraph.) He always prayed that one in minor orders would simply open up for him. And which group gained their livelihood by the labour of their own spleen? You are not sure of having been understood, are you.

There is a difference between this sweaty, earthbound boredom and a few judiciously chosen syllables. I have completely forgot the thing of the glass, the timely plummeting of spectacles. A picture of legal domestic bliss.

Mens rea.
Encamped in the bend of a river, beating the ground with bamboo staves, until they come. These decorations hold great significance for the journey. The popular conscience does not permit the enjoyment of any act whatsoever. Passes must be presented before extending in any direction. He was once content within his isolation. In future, remember it's preferable to be cut straight from the living wood.

It was one of those bizarre and exciting glimpses through the fog. In many countries it's thought to take up solid form. Shake the letters all together, gather up your belonging, and leave. Journalists quivered outside the courtroom door.

The key to everything.
An exploding horse on a deserted beach (he has this equine thing going on at the moment). This is valid for any operation of logic. Work it out on the digits of a severed hand. There's a car chase and some shooting. Are you really going to take a bow at this crucial stage. In a single generation the city was transformed into a capitalist death-camp.

False signifiers to boot.
Each of the intercepts was cancelled on its axis. It's time for a break, disordered or prevented memory. The outflow of water ceases. Watchword was exhaust.

She came to this place for purely elliptical ends. I could not respond and thus the circle was closed. But the real catastrophe is to be sought in total success. (This is going to be a bittersweet moment, isn't it?) She speaks. Just for me, cause something to remain, suspended. The way only you can.

New sets and costumes were introduced. Everywhere she goes she carries her property qualification for citizenship in a little sack made of bird skin. A police takes a bullet in the arm. Now we know what she's capable of means. That's all I can say about this episode right now. The monster that guarded the entrance, at least.

Illustrative reconstruction of the anatomy of an angel.
Rearing up in a grey void. Powdered nothing. Ash of cipher. (No it doesn't.) We're at the point in an orbit which is the greatest distance from the ground. I too am at the heighth of my power. A cleft stick three feet long is embedded in the ground right in front of me.

He's magnanimous in defeat. I must exchange names. I feel more at home within, more becoming. We never arrived at thoughts. Finding myself ill-disposed, I retreat. What is the essential law governing the separation, that which swerves to bypass.

Landscape with ribcage, petrol dumps, abandoned shells. I've been offered work in stains. I have three opinions (trader, dweller, extinction). Only through the erasure of all ownhood can you become channels. Yet another crosses his path. He quickens his step to spare himself the spectacle. There is this ongoing need. Safeguard by ensuring.

Atoms are dangerously massing together under these conditions. The guidelines have stated. The latter can no longer tolerate the inessential. This type of plot device often crops up in opera. We are founded on a score of distractions. On either side of the causeway, shimmering salt-flats. Abruptly her teeth chattered. Here, people absorb experience at one remove.

She endeavours to reassure the trio that she was only pretending.
One sits too close. She hands me a note. They set off on a pilgrimage to a noted sanctuary (Alpha Capricorni). A viable improvised explosive device was defused. In the routine of work, the glory of her inertia begins to fade. I release the flap and she spins off into the cold of interstellar space. Seal the hatch. Vision begins to fade. I am forever too close.

We are looking back at the word clairschach this week. We will never see the like again. This is not yours. End the electrons at the rotational poles, an hourglass slope. This is not your business. Changeling. Episcopal. The rest is too obscure.

On his holding life cheap or to habit.
Distinctly steeper stretches of land, known as rises. These strips of earth lie parallel to and above (a carrying back, a referencing back). I have remade your slaughters.
The valve of an insect's thorax. Hail of gravity from the rooftop. An edging away. A medium for the culture of micro-organism. The spinning distaff, unsighted.

Not seeing at all then, really.

Its magnificent chestnut head is caught in a turn to three-quarter profile. And the rain has finally arrived. I have been ill all these years. We shall never see the like again. He has vanished from the radar. It's a shame, I was growing to like the old bastard. Under hypnosis, I recollect something like a stratified well of sound. It's all done with red filters. The effect is one of endless flights of stairs interweaving on different levels: wheezing accordion, the tolling of a distant bell, a shred of stocking, someone counting out loud, the head of a discarded doll, the loop of noise, the consequence of your actions, the scraped vocal, the anomaly, the rusty hinge, the bolt of green-lightning, the key on the cuttlebone, the camera obscura, fingernail on blackboard, the penultimate whistle, the jaw harp, the tooth fracture, the radio on, the consequence of your mistakes, the twisted dial, my echolalia. Oxygen lost.

It drowned.

A shoot bends low to earth and takes up root. Do not improve within ten days. (Deceive them that dwell.) I am busy reclusing he says, an absence of quantity. Something on which an operation is performed.

Ironing him out in the half-light, she says the hotel may feel cold and dead, but you know every inch of it.

Thank God for that.

All this amounts to is a deep scratch in the soil. (They say chicken tasted human.) The visitation, it faded. An involuntary, spasmodic grin is consequent. The corners of the mouth retract into an unmarketable smile. Without, a voice. The riverran she says, inert. Some morbid condition, evidently.

Still exhaust. The feeling that the present is a fragment of past experience. Our orders say mould the problem to fit the solution. Equal to known, none.

A skewing of the emotional constellation of the moment.

Silt and needy. On the beach, dim memories of warfare are compared. Two, three, sometimes four lofty waves pursue each other. I am left without visible means. The solution is simple.

Resort to magnetic force, the countless dislocations. The internal shell can be used for toothpowder, polishing the metal parts, and sharpening beaks. In both versions we're told that men and women came into being. The nation has united in one spectacular event. (Grab something you don't usually look at.) I always wanted the complete set. He lacked readers rather than ideas. To begin with I found it easy to devote myself to the overthrow.

The name of an ancient sophism. A dilemma.

Can air be taut. This part complements the aforementioned framing device. Here he causes. Here he judges. Here he effects. Here he judges the members of his court and causes them to fall from heaven. We really need someone who's a little bit obsessive. Eleven is the answer to the number, by the way.

They have nothing to eat. In memoriam she's declared an impact player. We are looking back at clarinets this week. I have come with the address of the hours. You are the changeful shape that creeps forth from fate: he mummy, the fainter member of the pair.

She has made a study of mute conversation. Chains were worn in self-mortification. You can feel the vibration running down her arm. I try to keep my repertoire up to the minute and abreast of musical decline. I saw it in my head, the familiar. Out, good admirable. What thinness.

The yield is not sufficiently coarse nor chemically akin. I am sometimes extended, as in French to unsteady. A name given in spat, apparently, because of the abundance.

If you fail to read this book you will miss an unforgettable experience. Observe, wired in hamstrung. A lifetime passed, much greater than the lifetime of the usual drill lightning.

A round building with a conical or vaulted roof.
Sometimes you make things worse by panicking. Go through it one more time in your head before you speak. Stored within is a diamond indenter of unspecified shape (pyramidal). I am burdened by an unknown load. Straightening the body and drawing up the vertical scales made the underside concave. An after-effect, the coil of an ancestor, a disaster.

He is never happier than when caring for his objects.
The acute fold of the present, the surrendered impression. As if involuntarily pouring itself forth.

Last paragraph but one. As predicted we're now in complete control, despite all the errors. Sudden death usually means a change of plan. The basic principle is if it's going down, move it up. If it's going up, move it down. If it's too cold, heat it up. If it's too hot, cool it down. If it's moving too slowly, speed it up. If it's moving to fast, consolidate it. I meant telepathic. You get the idea.

A sphere of molten metal revolves at the core. There's less iron than believed. Look, it's hazy out there. The rest of us are somewhat in storage. Time remains, albeit oppressed with acts and suspensions.

Contraction of each jaw, titanic spasm—speech in xenolalia. Shoreward, the ossuary.

I am cornerhead. Diversion ends here. Atrophy of volunteer emotion, neural tremor of limb, the spun globe.

Bright-fracture. Last word, go on.

Saint dogstar. Active by day. It is uncertain which it was. Levelled, his rays full of head.

XXXIII

Having given the reader, I hope, a general idea of classification and its principles, I shall now discuss the ways in which the more prominent linear ideas and arguments have shaped themselves. The dominant position is a kind of evaporating (viz. believe nothing, everything's wrong, you're going to die).

A month of morphosis follows, a veritable haunting: the ruined castle, the wrong man et cetera. It was possible that later he might be in need of something, and then he would return. He has the address. Sound is an eerie screech, lying distant somewhere between brake and gull. What is it now. One could be forgiven for asking. Look, one of those chainlike things under the surface of the skin. A plaintive lull, cairned by the moving air.

You are still a long way from home. Do you not recollect. There are rumours of a tragicomic fall from grace. The symbols and logic used don't represent arithmetical qualities, being forcibly named, after all.

For thirty seconds longer he studies in the mirror the fleshy profile of the man standing behind. He waits for a while before constructing an immediate memory of the situation in which he finds himself. The other does not, or cannot, reply to this. You often affect a sideways movement with your hand. There's much I can't remember of this episode.

She dare not move. Unhinge this instant by the force of digression. I feel one of those cavity moments coming on—like the maturing of a voice, or watching a phantom limb slowly emerge from one's own torso. Defeat at this juncture would be a defeat.

The candidate resembles none of the other objects in the room. We too are unalike, of this much I can be absolutely certain. Her name is a palindrome. I thought you would need lots of extra things, she says, like light.

This can also be employed as a place of punishment—a binding together through an intermediate layer, cellulose or acetate. It's the evening of the day.

Double one, double two, double three and double four. I have seen you, previous to this moment in time. Just then a flying beetle, red and black, alights on my sack. It's an excuse for further speech, the lost art of conversation. There were always companions. I remember you.

No, that's the real one she says, the penultimate, the one who comes before the last.

I chose the correct object. (Any event can be mishandled.) We zigzagged across a ploughed field so vast it revealed the curvature of the earth. The time for quotation is past. The number is eight, doubled, which yields seven.

Be you so kind as to list, the recomposing of every detail. The harpist and singers form a sort of partition running down the centre of the room. Barely a splash is heard, or seen. They are remember.

She doesn't answer all at once, then mumbles something. This is why I have made up my mind to leave. Don't risk sardonic (3).

Polyhymnia (which I no longer recognize).
In the middle of a dense wood, at a boundary, I come upon a gigantic tree standing alone in a clearing. The circumference of its trunk must be several metres. It's made of a material at once stone and wood, its colour a lustrous goldgreen. I touch it with the palm of my hand, and at the same instant tilt my head to gaze up into its branches, which form a perfectly circular canopy. On the flat disc of ground beneath, nothing grows. Within the foliage a ring circuits the trunk, opening to the sky, a portal to the apparent.

Mist with fine rain which has the appearance of aerosol. Waves of false modesty. He drowns. I worry over the last words, the ballast of lineage. (A palpable hit, even if the book isn't you.) What do you think about having a go at astronomy today. Aesthetic appeal grows from any manifestation of both and neither.

The plain stretches out as far as the eye. Enormous unseen forces are present on the concrete platform. I'm not anticipating many paydays from now on.

The imposter returns. He's grown hands. He has stayed away so long that people think he's dead. They gather together all that is his and bury it in the desert.

I can't say. During these three years it has become so much like myself that it is not. Welcome to an evening—a substitute for the present, the last surviving trace. Tense is the infected passive: is or was called. I am named from to call.

Delta.
Home thoughts from abroad, from the mouth of a great river. A mysterious box has recently come to light. The shell is elaborately carved, the wood expertly cured. Not a single alteration is accidental—only hazard knows such accuracies. It's forbidden to utter the name of the tree of the wood. B or B are generally acknowledged to be the gods.

Mustn't quibble murmurs the other in a deceitful whisper. Incarcerated in his cell, he has lost the habit of consecutive thinking. (You'll never finish this in time et cetera.) Plaster has been scratched from the walls, cables slung from the false ceiling. Clues were once pencilled, fine concentric circles.

Under the spectacle of fearsome events.
I'm cast afresh. The validity of my method has been confirmed. High up through the tiny square window can be seen the only tree for miles around. It has a crooked trunk and corymbs of greenish-white flowers. She steps forward: fauna, the night-heron, formerly called the night-raven, twisting to hook out a name.

A sudden resemblance. The shock of combat, head couped and erased. (The things I thought mattered don't.) I have acting, the victim pleads, abilities. A complete cycle of twenty-four hours, a night and a day.

Held secure in his cell, the condemned affects a poisonous aristocratic elegance. (I don't know myself, I only saw its eyes). Listen, ear to track, the vibration of approaching steam. And through the lens: spangled helmets, grinding wheels, funeral barks, siege engines with battlerams, a mountain of used garb and redundant shoes, spectacles and amalgam. I was sleeping in my orchard when it happened, the custom always after noon. I stayed put and played dead. The others formed a circle. They wear wreaths of white flowers around their necks.

News of an explosion at the hydroelectric dam. This looks like nothing that has yet existed. Whoever does not feel capable of sustaining should say so right now. (Quote the sum total of the absence.) Three are found who are willing to separate off and escape. Four is ideal, two illegal.

Something has broken through. Shaggy mountain goats are dotted about across the lava field, bursting. Writing can only be about itself from now on. She says that word, you can't use it. I reclaim the hollow, a convenient nothing, the easy scope. Which individuals were treated like serfs and dogs (from the key to everything).

Her companions wear coarse animal skins. She was left to die on that mountain. Try to keep the instruments clean. I hope the duplicates survive, the bargains and the compacts. Prevent the wound from festering. I hope the indents survive. What's so unsettling is the yoking together of indifference and malignancy.

Going firm. I like the sound of that. She says she has a soft spot for columns—anything that forms itself without realizing. Just a glimpse, ecstatic beneath a breach, an end.

Grey and sunken, dazzling white light. Mass burial formed the aftermath, the flight line.

Just below the concrete apron, two men with staves are slugging it out on the shingle. They have responded to the invitation to do whatever you like. You can't just keep writing like this. People are watching. I tell myself. The book acts as an eternal frame of reference (homage, shelter). An ex-place. It's no longer, really.

He says we are become something disparate. But there remains a long gap in the history—the sudden disappearance of the forms, a crack that opens up between two uninhabited worlds. You can't imagine how dangerous it is to make a mistake out here. The aim was to conduct a house to house search, every ancestor. Will I then be allowed back he asks.

Now who's that racing on the outside lane. You, he says, place a great deal of emphasis on the texts that were in existence before you came. The following morning strange rumour spread across the city. What is unforgotten.

Inert metallic estate, poorly earthed.

She was born two hundred ago. I place my bet on the number three, while it's still in my head, and within my power to do so. The wheel spins. Do I think I really know what happened (no). I am manoeuvring for a change of occupation. This involves blowing and sucking on straws simultaneously. I wear an orange jerkin. (A little foresight and reflection is required here.) The work-gangs are watched by an overseer. Never go in close, I'm told—long-term performance, or even reality, can be deceptive. Have you ever owned an alarm like this? She says those without are considered less sane around here.

It was the odour of that bleeding brain that started it all, total haemorrhage. In the distance over the bay a winged figure plummets silently into the sea.

Was and persistent.

He has beaten about the bush long enough. What a team. He tried to sell me the dog that started it all for five hundred. I went to meet them but it rained and now his wife. I draw the go-to-jail card. I would complain but time is agin us.

Yes, bright idea. Describe a crime scene in waiting. I took along a book for solace. The corridor had been stripped. Garish fluorescent lights leant at angles, punctuating the bare walls. The ceiling had been removed to reveal a galaxy of wire and string. Birds inscribe the surface, between fist holes that batter the brittle plaster.

Act, the driver (a). Cut off cleanly before reaching the edge, ordinaries.

Frantic violins. We've reached the number fifty-seven. Plastic sheeting is fixed to the ground with duct tape. The spared men are here. We're escorted by groundlings carrying candles and lanterns. A sledge is drawn by two ibexes. Each hand holds the symbols (permission to act and instability). My heart is on fire: perpetual motion, the inability to stand still.

An ancient boundary stone. Be called a command, a retired place.

Metaphysics and its deliberations on the fundamental.

That does not mean that I'm even half-way toward understanding them. An absence of regulation persists, spine-tingling delicacy. I feel a duty towards the original. He requires me to touch the ground with any part of my body. (Which is another way of saying objectify one's objectifying relationship.) He's a freak of nature, a herald of what's to come. Locate your spot, the taunt.

One of eight, two of seven, one of six, and one of five points is frequently used. On the road we met fabulous and divers survivors. I could not count them because he dropped them into the mortar all at once.

On the return journey I pass an elegant courtyard in which a man is busy chopping something to pieces with a ceremonial sword. Imbalance allows effort to be minimized.

The pinks, including the marvel of Peru.

That monkey skull and femur studded with plastic bees. Properly, night blindness. Sleep-movement in the planets—the joint effects of change, generally located in the anatomy of Sagittarius. Water lapped my ankles, Venus and plough encircling.

He says our cooking depends upon shadows and is inseparable from darkness. Now for more on the only names (the I and the it). A pathological attempt at refrigeration.

They spoke quietly as men do speak at night. Penetrate, form recesses. You're forbidden to use that word. It's the point of ingress that's the problem. I think so highly of myself it's caused my eyebrows, top lip and gums to retract. My face finds it hard to frown. Some reiver has my tooth. I wear a permanent scar. A limb was once severed by a shower of shattered glass. (Perforce, it was large.) The resulting aspect changes a hundred times a second. I used to throw my weight around. I rarely have. When it was a child its mother called it tin-ribs, or crackdog.

Aping, she says. Always aping. Imitation, simulation, mimicry. Nothing is explicitly stated or expressed. Deny communication in favour of another mode of communication. (Which won.) I have the conviction that it would be wise to leave shortly after having arrived. This must be something like losing an old friend she adds.

Radiation from the margin. Abdominal migraine. From not seeing anything at all in the dimness, really. Unmistakable whiff of lilies. Insurrection was rumoured.

On closer inspection they're found to resemble starfish. We had journeyed here to found a museum. The contestants slid down a big rust chute and through the glass target before plummeting into the sea. In a nearby shop window hangs a perfectly preserved horse-suit, complete with teeth, bared. This is a vivid and instinct memory of myself, rescued from another time. A misprint, forgathered. Then I realize he's fallen asleep and has failed to answer my question.

The simple unspoken, yet overheard. The name of a meteor in a shower. Simple too or continuous is the tense of I. Because it is a Tuesday we're performing as a group of four. One is missing. Consider the inherited and instinctive impulse of every individual. A certain quality is underrated. (My favourite number at the moment is eight.) All that comes to pass renders me unplayable. We have arrived at a radiant point in the constellation.

Low surface brightness. Note its proximity to the brilliant first magnitude, only twenty degrees away. He says I decry the vacuous allegiance owed. Give up everything, we're on the wrong track. Now, what of the undeniable influence of the interpreter? A constant succession of contrasts becomes just as boring as constant repetition. They are weary, full of hope, displaced. I mean the misuse of the sublime. It's the name of a real person we're after, rather than a fictional character.

Celeste.

Magnifying strength, or a lens possessing it. Something was transferred. I'm not sure how you spell it (recess). You can't keep writing like this.

Plague of locus.

His place seems empty, dog and spouse fled. And when your feet take one step into that city, the child shall die et cetera. Let it be so for the present, to fulfil due observance. He's been hit hard this season. Disease has led us up a blind alley. The guards' aim was as inaccurate as ever. Several volleys had to be fired. All that remains is a small troupe mounted on outpost duty. Herein we have reached the heights of linguistic sophistication. New rooms must be constructed. It's like a dead cell somehow preserved in life. From this moment on despair ends and tactics begin. (We've been confusing operations with strategy.) The text is cut up and shreds of words laid neatly about the circumference of a marble table. This piece of furniture appears to hover in front of a void, i.e. nothing much. A statue is carefully positioned on a pedestal and sprayed with lighter fuel. I'm hearing that cry for help for only the second time in my entire life. Facial reconstruction begins. Events are connected to redundant deities. The mode of divination involves prime numbers and a pair of scissors. Now we're getting closer to what ordinary people actually see and feel.

It's about a horse sacrifice. When I search my mind I can't withhold the memory. I can no longer tolerate the letters of the alphabet. Certain austerities have become the objective. Adoration can sound like extermination.

The disposal unit sought advice. Mourning must once have taken place in the distant past. How long have you been a maker yourself. I am right now busy explaining. Answer the question. This is among my favourite book, of feldspar abundant in tilled fields. How long have you been a market. Often is confused with rock.

Some notes on my evidence. Concerning morphallaxis. (That's a shame, shadows are important.)

Up, and to the surface all the morning. Ever found yourself writing a single comprehensible line? We vacuumed up the ashes and shook them into the sea from a tupperware box. Moments of one and the same voice relay without solution. In the end it's just a piece of meat: the name's the thing. We burned the flag he came wrapped in. The time is turned pale. It's your duty to go out and find a convenient tree. One present still believes there are objects hidden in words and phrases. Are you a member of stuff, asks another. (Yes, apart from the ten-second breaks.) Someone murmurs a few lines from a big book. Should it also be marvellous in mine eyes et cetera? An exemplar of our prosperity was summoned.

Hang yourself from it. The boat docks and we all go our separate ways. Fists are thrust deep into pockets. We are plying the wrong edge. Trenchcoats.

The following morning a pair of silver funerary urns have been placed side by side on the lawn opposite my desk. Clearly it's a signal. Plentiful sound is declared for one day. To whom have you spoken.

I mean the noun clusters. Confess yourself. I am rendered without function. Nonetheless, some spite survives. Egg-shell skull principle.

Yens.

This place is a marvel. Eccentric staff, mouthing—mouths full of eavesdroppage, espionage. (Yes as in famous cocks.) If it's in the book, it manifests in the world. The engine cuts, the boat sinks. To whom do you utter, so ciphered.

See electricity. See dishonest abstractions. What's so unsettling about her is the yoking of unlikely opposites. We should have brought along a locksmith.

Interview at a boundary.

I must be careful not to misread. The discomfort we need is the coming thing. Our unit has received instructions to seek out and consume. You know the tactic well. The seedpods are like little sap cankers trapped in your joints. Time now for today's repercussion. What can you tell us, what can you see. Fluctuating temperature. Aperture in spasm. A starless night sky. A body of water which contains no life and lies three hundred and ninety-two metres below sea level. I have stitched up all my allegiances. Intuition is instinct leavened by memory. (That's one thousand, two hundred and eight-six feet.) Black oily patches rimmed by iridescence puff and swell at the surface, like the shadows of bizarre jellyfish. Alchemy too characterizes its child as a stone in the hand. This is hardly surprising.

They burst, releasing airborne spores. During the winter months he was frozen to a ledge on the ice-cliff. A schist-head, an out-slip, an opening—unpaid rent jammed into the crease or death-gauge, flipping back, softly. An aggregate of oblivions.

Everlastable.

We fly from west to east (night-sea journey). Disused bodies are staked out nearby on a naked strip of earth. There's a colonial swagger to the marshal of the yard. Your turn to be the head tomorrow, angel—the involuntary ancestral pulse. He took a long piece of root shaped like the letter Y and retied the bundle.

Consolations on Tyburn Hill.

Is it possible with well-weighing sums of gold. I am for quartering the large body. I am for the power to levy and conclude. I am for the conditions of no.

He is at this time transported. For that purpose he is obstructing. He is free and independent of cause. The state recoils with quarts of pretended legislation. Dissolution triggers static and insurrection: he has erected a net. He refuses the ascent. These foments are unsuited among men, for the sole purpose of purpose.

Convulsions within. Usurpations, pursuance and happiness. Prudence indeed is theirs to subject us to (mock heroic tone). And I declare that these unusual allies pledge to eat our lives, wherever they form—the jurisdiction of 'to say'.

Barely a splash was seen or heard. How close are they to establishing a motive for this repulsion. Inside, a whole range of gadgets magnetize the crowd into a direct flow.

Strange news from another.

He just got his ankle bones together at the right time. I don't understand a word. He did use his right arm. That circle expanding across the surface of the face is comprised of rectangular objects. Just try to explain the voices that you're hearing. Don't force yourself to possess the recollection. By this I mean a taxonomy of fear.

List, list skeletal here, please.

Decomposing light. A zone between the liminally conscious state and the totally inert. No trick cycling on the apron or the ramp. Thank you.

In the hereafter that substance is called gneiss—as mica-schist, hornblende. Such as is cleft. A scar of the first magnitude in the lesser dog.

Whiff of diesel. Place this at the centre of the work. He is no longer one of the big four. Leave them behind. Does anyone hereabouts have particularly sharp ears. (Who was left behind?) I was reared myself, straight to the jugular.

You break for me, into the desperate sweep of a story. Hear them now, delirium tremendous, smothered—breaking the hollow in which the eyeball rusts.

I resumed at three a.m. They were timed drowning. The second to be interviewed is a consumer of raw flesh. Our own name for ourselves is untranslatable. Without stopping he gallops toward the lake, into which he lets slip his victim. I didn't think you were so dangerous. The dimness was a benison. Ordinary nouns have a caste system. (Would you mind moving that light.) It's not as convincing as it seemed on the stage, is it. Nonetheless, there are some very odd things going on in here. You'll love the cat-and-mouse games at the end—in technical terms, a murderous loop. Come dusk we settled on a groyne. We're found not guilty. Frequent words falling under third grade principles have now to be thoroughly learned. Having had the worst of all possible starts in life, we were resurfaced. No hint here of the composer in popular imagination as sick and demented, is there. Accordingly. Bewilder. Direction.

The opposite is just so. I'm writing this purely out of a sense of decay. The

644

sacrifice was immediately devoured by the spirits of carnivorous fish. (Grant thou unto me the things which my body needles et cetera.) Here, time doesn't necessarily follow one thing hard upon the other. He retires into a certain chamber. He brings forth a bowl which he keeps for a purpose. He fills it with water. He makes wax ships and men of the enemy. We need the illusion that we've been around for twenty years or more, overgreen with moss, lichen. It pays to be watchful when you undertake the grand tour, the veritable split in the international. This federation does not amount to much in a workless milieu. But on the other hand is circumstantial.

Be still I must away. Don't forget, we work under licence, under duress (harmonic shifts, chromatic incantations). The relationship between voice, salt water and notation is beginning to corrode. The image of nycticorax became the sign for M.

The roads were no longer paved. I am leaving myself behind. (In contrast to the serf, who is bound to the soil, and cannot be sold in parts.) The moment we're going to hear has five fingers on each hand, as well as the obligatory thumb. A long red scar traverses the palm. Give up your illusions, and prepare for flight.

The reference to goatfish is variously explained. There's only a short period of time remaining before the dead line is reached.

He says nothing (my paraphraxia). Beach petrol, yes. The girl con my hand, substitutions and so forth. He struggles with consistency. They then ripped open the body with their bayonets. The news says we're shifting containment to the frontier.

The contrapuntal effect.
It's killed about a million already. A pair of twins are hinged at the hip. We are seven in all. Digits are grown numb and crooked. I ask only for the mere facts of the case. Time to wash the mussels, fasten the hampers, and hoist the prisoners back into the truck. The tarpaulin is covered with a layer of paint (mausoleum grey), and it seems to have stuck. All the writings, interviews and photographs have been heavily censored. I am still making change. It all begins in my favourite realm: brackish water, a kind of pus that separates feudalism from capital. Do you know anything of yourself. The first murder took place as early as page nine.

No I know nothing. I step over a bag burst of excrement on the pavement, tyre glyphs elegantly imprinted into faeces the texture of caramel. We cook and crack under the baking sun.

A blind one comes with cane and bell. The label says lighter fuel contains albumin. Each of the embryos is suspended in its own private sac. I ignite. I'm being stalked, regeneration in a changed form—brooding in every aspect, at the margin of species.

Track people.

I'm glad she's starting to scale things down a bit. We've got to make that train journey again. Our destination is some pagan moot.

There was once a man who answered yes to everything. The medication says this is what's killing you. I'm fated to mimic the action of every verb voiced within earshot. This demands an aimless existence, a committed wandering about. It's said data travels like a star. It's full-time work. Synonyms for matter, the basis of the opus, is one of the famous secrets. (By confession, sometimes day-blind.) We should have brought along a wordsmith.

I am contemplating the clear liquid state. It's a pogrom that hunts down and erases any undesirable memories. (The question of the book as ritual object must come into this at some point.) All moonquakes occur in just two narrow belts. Roles are being reversed.

Bareback through a raised portcullis, we enter a city with all its liberties still intact. It seems the beneficent hand is coming over to our side. Within sight of the ramparts a man is suspended by metal chains attached to hooks planted in the boughs of a tree. It's about time. Rumours of plague and civil. (Given the choice, I'd rather be governed by corruption closer to home.) No one else is doing this kind of thing. My fear has a root system: gristle on the spook of the brisket, perplexity in the chase.

The frozen blood shatters as it strikes the lab floor. (Can you imagine thunder with a voice like that.) Something glides by just beneath me. This is mysterious. It isn't exactly a nightmare, except the part where I'm chased across town by a gang of assassins wielding meat cleavers. Make the assumption that certain positions are adopted come nightfall. Corrupt him to a revolt, the easy scope of self-a-nothing.

The potency of a point with respect to a circle.

Within the cell this past year have been discovered three new reptiles, five unknown species of butterfly, and one of the moth. Each evening was ceremoniously sealed with red wax. Roles are being repulsed. Hybrids resulting from a cross between species have been maimed and set loose. Inflated pig bladders carried bobbing at the end of long slender canes are compulsory. Tiny triangular apertures have been woven into our clothes. (I am not so much invisible as taken in by my own disguise.) There descends a brief disconcert over our entire company. We were rather taken aback. He spoke easily and without hesitation. I had to remind myself that there could be no danger so far south of the soviet.

A chance encounter.

We will have no more of this. Only from the cord by the mouth do I feed. The clerestory windows admit oblique shafts of winter sunlight. We're enveloped by a thick freezing fog which appears to rise up out of the earth. The amnion of sleep is poised, they say.

One million, three hundred and fifty-five thousand of them, plus or minus a baker's dozen.

Abnormal difficulty seeing in a faint light.

At the very beginning of time, he says. He hated every mark he made, and won the urge to erase and destroy everything. It was this dissatisfaction, this refusal to act—this not-doing—which led to current practice, a practice motivated by finding, by stealing. (Highly approximate.) He stutters it's a fine word that word ghoul. The chimes of a clock ring out. I am mindful, a soft-pedalling at the piano one afternoon in late summer, the smell of the dank cellars rising up as we pass. The element is strontium, sometimes skyblue. Bringing us to this end, this homage.

The underwater evidence disappeared into a vault along with the lists. (Train the lens.) The sense free and unobstructed does not yet exist. The assumed divination is strengthened by the book's parallel blind story. I had been searching for a suitable symbol.

Polyethylene cross with stingray. Hammers strike at steel plates set over wooden resonators. This may demand an elevated structure, fortified playback. A defendant must take his victim as he finds: a tree of the family purge. He's hanging on till the very end.

Rumours of cattle raids.

Slash archive.

Inhabited, with wood splinter (91). I remember another ruined moon-viewing. I'd give it some thought if I were you.

This is one of her most sullen creations yet. I see your angels have been replaced by the state circus. This reader actually happened. There are contortions and everything, heads plucked inside heads, the pungence of bodies twisted through degrees. It's said one can replace, behind his own back. Four arms are of equal length. Another probes a finger inside the lung. Seven have crammed themselves into a cycle. This one grips a pole in his claw and flips back to swallow it whole. That one plunged a knife into the skull of a bear. A woman hangs from a bit clenched between her teeth, high up in the dome of the marquee. The ceiling is a toxic orange. Enough of this.

Signs of duct-cancer. But the evidence is not enough to show how, when and where the economy changed.

He has a perverse habit of shifting without warning from a tone of high seri-
ousness to fatuousness. A peasant huddles in the hollow beneath a dripstone
wall. He embodies one of those narrative interstices, an occasional corridor of
uncertainty. My knowledge of my own name is absolutely definite. At the last
moment he jumps to one side as a guncart hurtles down the counterscarp. The
men are dripping sweat. Timbre now insanely rapid, suggesting the irregular
pulse of your own heart. A glimpse of facetted jewels suggests lawlessness in the
plot. Direction says quickly.

I love sham. I love lies, everything false. This is dictated verbatim.

Night messengers. Silverfish. Which is another way of saying to become
acutely aware of one's own gaze.

It was calm we had no fun at all. I recall him having a memorable nervous
temperament. It was perhaps appropriate, the lucid choreography of a slow-
motion riot, the sea at its closest.

People dig up the earth. They peer into the pit. See that granite well, it creates
a blind spot. After dark she hurls down it the big knife. I have never been corrected myself, for aesthetic reasons. They're looking out for dead folk with bits
missing: zombie apocalypse, live action voodoo in the labyrinth. That blade had
propped quietly in a corner all its life.

I can see straight away that you are incapable of people. (Look, the past.) Sayest
thou still that the house is dark? This kind of thing is happening more and more.

What's your favourite decade. Tell of yourself, of the endless. What's in your
mind right now. E.g. the sign used to represent the glottal stop—secession from
the usual minerals that compose, torn out of to choose, or not to choose. The
completing stroke of the large circle should be carried down to the end. Namely,
starting with the odd numbers in order and crossing out every third number
above three, every fifth above five.

List.

For instance, often is abbreviated. (Keep it simple.) Examples shunt indolent,
functionless. Outside, solitude is directed into a single gadget. To whom am I
speaking.

A quaint and unassuming estate of consciousness. Improper books. Volumes
who lack propriety, poise. The pathological fear of narrative. (It was in the same
year et cetera.) One day I will finish his unfinished preparation of the novel. Mark
my words. Despite being alone all day, I'm forever talking. Note how the story does-
n't allow the reader to get close to any one character (in an imagined theatre of the
future I would be a sort of theoretician of rubbish). Not one of these revolutionary
heroes can be doubted for an instant. Consider his invention of a separator, the
ventilation stem. Thank God the distances between posts are mercifully short.

She says I will plant and cultivate a vessel at sea. I hear the knife-grinder go by. At that very instant, on the same day one hundred years ago, our postilion was struck by lightning. It's hard on my throat, the voice box. And who painted endless chains—cats, blue-birds, hares—and seldom came back? I'm evoking sparks myself, going hell for leather toward a finality. She plans to circumnavigate the sleeve and estuary, re-entering the city via its mouth.

Pluck your nerve. Never go back. Think of a moment that doesn't involve you. Well, today's the day.

I like some of these ideas. Now we're back to the theme of bells tolling in the head, at the inner ear. I am unsung by mistake. I enclose a letter for your kinship, the unhappy descendant and namesake of the great past. I am sheer bias—slanting and flowingly aslope, across and overthwart. The boat splits in two on a ledge of rocks hidden beneath the surface. These sounds place the music earlier than time.

He clears his throat for an impotent statement. No deviations from the recipe are permitted. He made enquiries. He feels guilty. He makes mistakes. He is bound by an error. I have no restraining motives left, save the fear of punishment. There is no infallible criterion by which to distinguish species. (He and I remain confused.) For example, a close-fitting suit with cells that inflate to prevent the flow of blood back to the head. This is worn by air as a defence against the lackness, any undue highs.

Tomorrow I may not he says. I am ending myself in disquiet pathos. He left a note.

Take me out, you fucking philistine. Sign the recluse form. I hope it rains on all your yester-days, your vomitings and blue wine, the exhaustion and the terror. You will apply yourself to this work and this work alone: all harmonic and architectural possibilities. Let me read the book and I'll tell you whether it's worth it. We'll show them what loves all about—some non-place hanging out of my vagina, the soft underbelly of science. And me, I too have no heart, though enamoured lately in the lemon grove et cetera. But the main reason is far more sordid. Otherwise I am yours, all yours. I open fire, confirming the existence of their creator. These memories are identical to his old memories: a column in the desert at whose apex stands a paralysed saint. And if such an art were not within the scope of his images? I may have been so impressed by the melting wax in the mystery (33). I too open fire, open fire.

Who left the other in his will, from descending, scales. This is one of the darkest pieces in C-major I think I've ever heard.

On the imperfections of the geological world, scant consolation.

This emerges from an incompleteness and a changing set of images, shifting perspectives. Items went missing from the pile of prosthetic limbs: arms and legs and saints. Once set in motion everything conducts. (I dreamt of you last night too.) Up and over. Touch the ground at the bottom of the ravine then turn back immediately. We're here to celebrate the anniversary. Commiserations.

I have no choice, a body fluid and intractable. Once set in motion, I conduct. I have my own perpetual automat, an unaccountable remedy.

Quips indeed, a perpetual nightmare in the child. A complex co-ordination of reflex actions results in achievement of adaptive ends. Which historical figure was without foresight or experience, one who deals in things of no consequence.

He is obliged to move to a locale more suited to his libertarian anatomy. He begins by teaching the locals how to levitate. (Start by placing your body supine on the ground et cetera). Reason is unknown hereabouts. In yielding up his name to the goddess, he places himself.

Grind of turning metal on metal. He has no choice. Throughout the moot you must be prepared to say sorry, again and again and again.

Now it seems we're back in the world of theatre. We need the head to heads, we need the salt-of-the-earth characters, we need the talking cadaver. (We creative artists have the utmost reverence for cadavers.) When you watch him cast off into a headwind, he has a different aura about him altogether. This one's really started inhaling, sucking in its cheeks. It's like an evening in the monstrous company. I am going to put this in capital punishment, the minutes.

The pressure's off. Trapped in a culvert up to here: the untenable day, intermediate between slavery and libertinage. A switch to daedal time is imminent. One paw's jammed in an underground channel in which electric cables rest. And there is a nice little shop in a nice little alley. I was once a famous conduit myself (and a pretty hostile reception to boot). The scene is lit by cozy gas lamps. We need the full mandate, statistics of desertion and escape. An immovable of the wilderness.

Horse hooves clatter and spark at the oily cobble. I am approaching a former self, hence the abjection. A crack is opening up between two impossibles. I'm inconsolable. I am as intended. There are strong fibres present, strings of spun lace. I mean the quality of malevolence, dis-tort within mirrors—body without tain, refractive silvering. I am insensible to pain. There is an unmistakable uniformity of enunciation. The pulse was never located, the angelic upstairs. Let's hear it they say (timely whipcrack). The excavations are sucking the house under. Check erosion and shingle drift—salt of wormwood—sail-shrouded capsules slipping into the sea. It is there, right there they say. Intention is always suspect, a rattle in the throat. No one uses a net around here.

The conifer forest stretches right up to the shoreline, where we lie side by side. (I could paralyse this music but am glad.) A gigantic craft swoops low to scoop up the sea, thence to vainly douse the fires inland. And as if rising up from the earth itself, the dullthudding of artillery at some imagined frontier. Time to hand you back.

Dissolute. Loss. Shoulder-blade. Batchelor. Exhaust. Escape. Slip. Escapade. Way out. Scribble.

That just about sums things up.

Ka, ba (nil by mouth).

Go back, you must do all this again. Did you turn off the down stare. That buzzing noise is leeching straight from the skull. (Don't tell me when you're going to do that again, just do it.) You see the same world he says.

Had he, in fact, infected anyone else before being sent into quarantine? In future, make use of the rebus principle to express abstract concepts. Then I won't anticipate the moment of my happening, will I.

The body vibrates uncontrollably. He is breaking through, one delicious and frivolous section. He is pulling out all the snaps. Is he trying to say something.

Ignition. Full thirst. He says I can intuit that.

A man passes by, pauses. An iguana rests on his shoulder. (The point here being?) I feel a caress of displaced air at the lash of its tail.

No it's a myth. The artifacts were baked brittle on Nile silt. One of the forelegs is cut off. The heart's torn out and offered. He takes the bleeding leg and touches the mouth and eyes four times. The oldest human remains bear upon them traces of bitumen. A very distinctive sound-world is being sketched. He assumes those gathered around him at the table are as limited as himself. The whole social organism is forgathered as a work of art. It still haunts me, the amount of geography present in any given situation. I have lost touch. On the other hand, there is a profound indifference of principle at play. Mediate him, fill the place of another.

Community suckback. Ciphermaker.

We're either still or shuffling magnet-wise between the same weary polarities. The operation of smelting has failed in its intended effect. I am furnished with air from without, instinctively operate away from a centre.

Do things ineffectually he says. (Inevitable.) Thank you for lending me the gloves. Surrender to indecision: vacillate, delay, put off until tomorrow. Defer.

Someone has scrawled in blue pencil the word L-I-G-H across my wall. There is a stack of playing cards. An arrow points upwards. Use your bladderman.

There is also a graphite vehicle of some deception.

Another anvilhead front crushing in.

You could be, I say. Above the pier a circle of dark cloud is pierced at the centre by a revolving spindle of vapour. The image fades imperceptibly to a vanishing point. The faint clack of flagpoles is barely audible. I remain still. Increase the tempo until the level of submission demanded has been achieved.

A glimpse of waves breaking the shore. He shuffles his hand. An icy draught cuts through the cabin. I press record. First, you have to have enough imagination to visualize the crime. All my life I've talked to humans.

This is the story that narrative can't withstand. It's rumoured there's no time. It's like the last seven minutes, a raft of medusas. Eyes hollow, caves—he submits. (There are bats on the cover of this paperback.) I own. Lampoon has an accent on its first syllable, cooling to the semi-liquid state.

Used as a scapegoat.

Can silence ever amount to acceptance. A one-sided surface is formed by joining together the two ends. Looks like a meat grinder to me, cellular tissue. What is called night-turning.

Readmission.

Industrious combustions in the suburbs. It's a lot easier on the eye out here. I'm at an all-time historic low. I disembark clutching a spray of tiny white flowers, plucked straight from the head. I'm not at all amused by the coming events. It's clouding over. Gravity is true. (What would a montaigne?) The subjects has abruptly ceased—divers palsy, paralysis of the lung and spleen, hearts and minds in surgical rapture.

Upon which objects have been painted the divine spoke a figure of heaven. So, the dna molecules themselves unpack over a hundred trillion times.

How the strings that bind her burden to the body are eventually cut.

The days are long. Time out of mind, the amniotic shroud. Halve the blood count.

The lone chair in shadow brings to mind the empty seat at a conference—an absent interlocutor, the place of one ceased. The greatest difficulty is the non-appearance of any story in the required sense, the absence of all trace. And I loathe the conversational tone. Likewise at the root of my sameness, unenviable simulations. But decisive progress has been made, compared to the analysis.

There can be no doubt that she's won a few disciples. Some of the patients are still gyrating. I have taken up the challenge. Nothing can represent the verb to forget. I walk on until long after nightfall. It must be way past our midpoint. This is most pleasing, when without an express command one automatically does what is needed. After a short pause for reflection she declared that she no longer needed any help. Right now I'm held witless at the frontier. First tremors of dawn, inevitable withdrawal.

She drains a sleepless night, writing. Love at the inert, the spine of the ear.

An early vision of a burgeoning character (antique).

The nearest continent is full of locations redolent of dead time: common rosin, a little oil of gallipoli, spirits of turpentine, oil of asphalt, of amber—phosphoric acid to etch the enamel. Think of an unforgettable vision of darkness. Say not a word to anyone. A tooth has fractured. Come back when the death-owl loud doth sing et cetera. Liver of blaspheming, by a four-beat echoic rhythm.

And what does I would have refused here mean exactly. All that remains after the gruesome are bare bones scattered across the bed of the ocean. It was his masterpiece. Justice inevitably leads to tragedy: the topgallant sail, the yardarm, passing new lashings around it.

I was born into the central markets, flyblow of a costermonger—creeping, wary under eyes. The site is now covered by a new block of faults. Standing on high ground, I'm identified with the breath. (I can always be identified.) At the same time there's a solitary insistence of sorry. Their marrow is melting. Ravel up the light. I'm sure I looked up psyche last time.

Hard nub of scar tissue under the skin, left hand upper surface (i.e. not chiromancy). Capering villagers in picaresque costumes: graphite, sepia ink, inedible pencil, bronze paint with body armour—the mask of an owl, the mask of a jackal, full tilt at the windmill. That perfect acoustic. Which question, further, must be distinctly complex and difficult. (It is, from his reply.) He claps his wings upon the table and the banquet vanishes. Down in the taproom we were dealing with something supernatural. The only sound we hear all night is those big glossy machines. I'll be closed for some time yet.

Sorry, I meant medicate, not trepan. The shell is shiny and reflects back the bands of light that crisscross every cell.

Cassation.

The trapdoor beneath her boot heel. One of those timely excesses that are not strictly permitted by law. After the ordeal she was set on fire. Feathers and straw were provided. A voice murmurs in a stage whisper. Harnessed players descend on ropes: grotesque animal-machines, bolts of electricity in every direction, chopping at the confines. Analogy and metaphor can render any discourse palatable.

Polysemblant, i.e. continually opening out to yield additional correspondences and meanings. (Have you too gazed into that glass sphere, wicked conjurers).

Enough money remains to ransom the whole lot of you. She disclosed the matter without the slightest discrepancy from what the other had said. The mask covering the man's face renders the whole scene melodramatic.

Look at that nice sinew you've exposed. I can no longer remember. Obsession provides the story with an undertone of hubris.

Long-phallic purple bloom she hands me. Here you are.

She has gauze wings. Disclosed, though dimly, by the faltering lamp. I want to go home and then come back again. (We shall by then have made use.) She needs me more than I need her. There's to be a retrial. We're joining. Last weekend was closed down. We are defiance and prosecution combined. Odyssey marine exploration has raised salvage from the seabed. An innermost membrane envelopes the embryo (my reptiles, my bird-life, my mammals, my amphibians). The peasant girl returns with a chipper little melody about starlings and caries. She had no excuse to feel any better. I wonder what I would do if I ever found myself in a situation. She snaps in two in front of my eyes. Land is claiming, pressing. I will now go into the story in more detail. Upon clambering onto the concrete platform I realized that I had arrived at the summit. The first thought that goes through my mind when I see her is assassin. (It's a bit late for that.) Some attempt to pursue their dead by means of mummification.

Indirect stimulus.

The point of entry of the optic nerve on the retina. My theory of authorship and her origin are one and the same phenomenon. Letters however remain something of a mystery. They came in handy.

This is a book about a beautiful man who wants to become an object. I enlisted, initially. I realized. I end up. I have stolen the idea of linking the confusion of elements. I volunteered. I walk through: an extra bedroom has been added during my long absence at the front. (I did not know.) The book leaves us in suspense throughout a long night. The ceiling has vanished. It reveals the canopy of fixed stars. In the cellar is a bomb-proof vault. There are three hours and fifty-eight minutes left in which to journey there and back. That's fourteen thousand, two hundred and eighty seconds. Stop me before I do something horrific. A chest freezer was the most likely source. I timed the time. With hindsight I would never have returned. Note that he has two gunshot wounds, one over each eye, aimed with deliberation.

Two-and-a-half years later and still stuck at a junction (the pantheon). One comes with a jaundiced leg. We're obliged to make an appearance. I duly manifest. The day started well. The maximum had always riled me. He cannot keep still. You are right. A bell rings at intervals of precisely forty-five seconds. Who stole my muttered insolently.

Everyone freezes and holds their position. A starting pistol cracks and we resume. (Imagine her brain in his head.) He has to keep moving, like the shark. He says I have only one of those fakes left in my sack. Things are becoming a little obsessed. O he's bleeding. I could no longer identify a decision. If you can't find it, forget about it. I can no longer make concessions. At this point a pattern usually begins to emerge.

He has a way hidden within him. Let's attempt something different. Montage, a work made cut up: institution foil, cloacal tissue, impregnations of ash and salt.

654

Illuminated liturgical manuscripts. Body colours mounted on board, sewn. I am thinking more a triple shot at overhang fourteen. I'm one of the best things that ever happened, pale hands clutching capital, schizophrenia. The famous stultify yourself is optional. Which famous belongs to this paschal lineage.

One among us is employed each morning to empty the night-soil. Note the position of the bronze horse suspended between the two vessels. Avoid all things. The rest is silence. And by the striking out of air, from allow me to ruin some.

Phantom limb, gnawed. A place, now only held in compound and idiom. The place which another had or might have been. A site. A space of time. Circumstances, to no avail or advantage. To set in a plight. To fill in substitution. Bedsteadfast. Inert. A lying in wake. Pass the speculum.

I always choose the direction that will carry me the farthest distance from point X. Shall we set off, homeward bound. An uncanny agency resides in the minds of men, at the tip of every tongue. We tire. We try to please. For example, a natural anaesthetic, a natural emetic (cloud sucking pier into sky). The horse is one of our last serious contacts. That year we took a boat on the night of the harvest moon.

Igniting the I-plate, juice of subjectives.
All very unbecoming. He crossed out some of the words in his workbook with blue crayon, rather crudely, as a blind one might. I once corresponded to the simple origin of a thing. (For weeks past this nightmare of war.) Insensibility and abstraction have been stretching nerves. Listen. The assault was successful. We crossed swords. Words were placed under erasure. This is dynamite. Give an account of the properly infinite leap. The result is unique and individual. You have to say. We have survived a week of amplified bell-tolling. We have lived to speak. I get the feeling I've seen you somewhere before (the simulations). It has something to do with those arrows. I misspent last night. I found myself contracted for several hours into a tight coil. (I am not the only one.) It had an unusual and catchy theme tune, figures that mimic the action of beating wings. Living beings include the lab mice. Some of these images could strike right through. A veritable book of hours is being built. The bells were the only noise. A sense of boundless sacrifice prevails in dealings between men.
He answers neither writing nor living, returning a nought.

Book-lung.
I wish to inform you of a temporary footage opportunity (my block is being). Heart render, memory pause. Everything secret, caressing, reassuring and false. Perfect. Perfect framework.

Will there be sound during the interim. Will I dream. (I don't know). It's totally smooth. The geophysicist was the first scheduled for reawakening. This is fate surely. They have framed us pretty well: no clues, no motives, no suspects. This is that fateful empire. This is a true echo of what I was going through at the time. The object is now watertight.

Its discarded cellophane wrapper.

She bends the tongue of influence at court. This is a landmark work. She admits love. We are benighted. Muscle fibre adopts a conical shape. I'm insensible (saint receiving stigmata—detail, copywright.) Benighted, our bodies are dipped in molten pitch. I unbolt the page and a folding takes place, straight into the dead night of names. If unsure, excise.

A cento, uncircumferenced motions. By the way, at the moment the subject is hanging suspended from the light fittings. A garble of patchwork, a studious incorporation of unspoken lines.

Suffice to say.
During an interim truce. (What collision?) She's a recent incarnation. So entrapped, they converse one with another. Welcome back to the archipelago. Go in, enter the story in detail. Overlook no fragment—include the unlikeliest sources, any oscillation. We are approaching overkill. I dream there's a fire and the things and the people have to be removed, forever.

They flee one set of dangers only to stumble across another—under the acacia trees, where sand is breeding. The colonists were sealed in aluminium capsules. Damp towels are wrapped about every head. If you do not know how to end, then do not end. You cannot wound me further. The flesh splits open and suchlike.

We suffer five years of a different style of incomplete. Effectively, he's going into competition with himself. They open fire. They reveal. I am content with the number five branded on my back. I have been granted a stay of carelessness. I am to the hilt. My petty dissipations were accompanied by remorse, tears, cursing and ecstasy. The author died of a cerebral haemorrhage on the twenty-eighth. Vast crowds gave him 'the funeral'. It only needed a mouth to complete the resemblance. We are here. We need to get there. Sensible.

We don't count. Days were strange days. More than anything.

Crack two. If you're not prepared to write, you are going back inside your cell. I retrieve the case. I get what I want, minus the two thousand. I deal. I shuffle. I am making these things the entire subject of my enquiries and reflections. The crown is not the type of crown one eagerly falls upon.

Hawk-high, better not to speak of it.

Slang.

A bone. Anything retrieved from dust, or the lake. (I did myself too but not much.) Set in strange lines, applied to the somewhat similar sound and motion of a rivulet over a stony bed. Intense spatials instead of extension of solidity.

A marginal note found in the rolls, embossed by the press of your own fingernail. Yes she said. The aforementioned crown is metaphorical, a figment of speech. It was a minor point of geography. (The ancients say the ka lives in the womb with the mummy.) Around the depiction of himself, note the finite workmanship. A metal implant consists of a heavy head and multiple lips, one whose skull is readily turned. Simply close the case and it explodes.

A calmative. Pause. Just squeeze tight the rubber ball in your socket. Remember.

First though, a rarity. Displaced ash before the denouement. The flight of vicarious, via the emergency chutes. The examples are full of hate, shallows of silent.

On that strange lump of stone with its faintly audible light.

I simply lack the ruthlessness to abandon her, to leave her behind, and I hate myself for it.

Several generations of a cursed family living in the same remote.

It was decided not to bother with the niceties of these dummy attacks. Over the door hangs a urine-filled bladder. (He's one of the least understood figures in musical history.) A hand-painted sign says the dead can sting you with a look. We collect, label, and bag every shred of evidence—I want people to feel familiar within the language. These are stored in a secret archive (afterpiece contracted in sixteen, pointless of barque, and such nonsense). We have no propulsion of our own. Diet is pure adrenalin and aggression. Entropy is absorbed. Stray heat rises up from the centre of the earth. If our calculations are correct we now have the dead sea directly over our heads. Hearsay is enough to convince the most superstitious among us. Farewell. We're over a body-length clear now. A long procession of moving objects is closing in, stretching back to the horizon. Your energy is absurd.

Being suspended hardly clear of the ground by its thumbs.

He certainly has an eye and a memory for fine detail. We are reflecting on the bicentenary of birth. This is how we see things in the current state of buoyancy.

On that persistent hissing at the wicker gate.

Every candidate is given a name. He had me wired. Return home. The sources are decaying.

Craving for depth, its inertia.

Their concourse, spindle of vortex. I should have arrested the list at belladonna. What is the name given to the part which almost survives. I have been known to reside in a statue of a dead thing, the amulet of ladder. Today's title is the world of floating pages. One of the hired men is hurling books into the sea. I stroke my companion's bare arm, inhale. Stop this now and go home, the repulse of intimacy.

Mythology, in all its original.
The sensation of things, a dismal could not. He next made the figure of a woman in wax and wrote upon it the name. Then he cut open his own.

It has absconded. It couldn't happen now, the dismissal. The signals must have exploded. Now we have come to the end of the part about structure. The lads from the neighbouring village carry off the head and set it up at the rim of their own well.

Net income gives the arsenal custodian no chance. Own-stuff, whispers inquisitor. A widow he got to know in the coach on the trip to the ruins.
Go on a little longer.
Morbid fear of the night or darkness, an obsolete spelling. A variant, mosaics from act four. Under the mad in pursuit of a leg.

They won't stop until there's barely any skin left. He will be challenging the loses in future. Finally, what's it like as a spectacle, under the lights.
Wingspan flapping at the naked stairwell. Stink-horde genius. Footfall at under-cliff beneath pallet bed. (Objects can always be disinvented, forgotten.) There'll be a lot of stumbling about going on in the dark. There's no news of a replacement. I know it's an old cliché. It's the things you notice more that don't count.
Distant rumble of wheels rolling over pitted cobble. Now I feel a knowing calm. He began to wish that the other would come soon. Which historical figure was stupefied by the warmth of the waiting-room after his long vigil in the snow? A radical calmative is being marketed.
With halts. Then die away, long pause. This must be transference, the rumours. Absolvent water has long been established in the teachings and sayings. At best only facilitates its repetition.
Undo the kingdom, the perpetual light. Allow me to interpret. I am leaving no sensation unturned, the countercharges. I am leaving a deep gash. Without myself, the shattering glass, damning back the whole breadth of the river—tendons severed, nerve-ruinous.
And sailed out over the lake. Midnight aloft—thunders, lightnings.

Place the two empty cones in there and leave a note. The magnet is the main theme in this the last chapter (in ballast to white sea). After whom it names its society? Saint fridge and saint odd were at one time supposed buried. Mosquitoes have driven us out of focus.

This is funny. He ascends rapidly through the agency. Who is described therein as regicide. All his works are disparaged and neglected. Do you know anything of this my tormentor asks. Elsewhere flies seem to have penetrated. I lie in immediate opposition to the animal, cowering behind sandbags and barrels of earth. Deep trenches have been cut, the catacombs filled with gunpowder. The sewers flood and burst. This is just one among the ranks of similar but lesser known spectacles. Crimes that would have merited, for someone born, a comparative sentience.

Admonition in waiting. Herein exists a sort of shared aesthetic, mutely ecstatic. Now, as it were fortified, at length he comes to look upon philosophy as a punishment.

An unsightly and edited performance. Bad screed. These silent characters attest to the general class of phenomena. The named thing belongs. Attention, this vehicle is turning itself inside out. No, I know nothing.

She was exiled to the surface on a technicality. We've had a good deal of bother lately, what with all the dwelling and leaving. The two men met at O in the autumn of thirty-one—mother of memories, absolute distress.
Lilting saxophone, funereal tin drum. A sense of pathos and defiance she wrote. Aggression and adrenalin. Bad seed. Squat to defecate.

The quality or condition of being here, existing as an indefinite thing. Here he comes, on winged sandal. In the hymn a supplicant receives the epithet. Submit intelligence and reason with it.

His eyelids are sinking quietly as he walks, usurped by the passing hours. Bead of rain at rest on right brow, a target. Not everything has yet been accounted for. What are we to do with all those sacks of saltpetre. I have left much material out in the cold. She watched me closely as I tasted and asked. No I said. I felt a trickle of sweat course down my forehead like an errant. (What.) There is nothing worth sharing here. What values are generally associated with the period under study? No doubt. Not a single point of identification survives the book. Self-love is harmless. The bird cited is the night-heron.

Speaks, outhinged.
He writes from a position of thinness and liquidity. The disc rotates rapidly, making a clattering noise. (Scrapple, scrapple, scrapple.) You get the idea. He drills into the body. Watchers were held at a safe distance. The state is fluidity. Then the state is solid. Then the state is gaseous. This has been carefully unkempt in disorders. We are fast approaching a combustible excuse for a close. It's evident that similitude—thisness and thatness—belongs not to matter itself.

A second barrier of ice probably forced them to retreat. He says he is trying to recreate the conditions for an impeccable unpredictability. I can't detect any surface features, unsurrendered silences.

Satraps like us.
This must be close work. Your eyes, in the sense of shut off forever. Peradventure, she never gets involved in doing. Ears, that's the worst, in raise of shallows. Loosely captured can connect us with the very edge. I admire their drive and energy, as if anything could be dismantled, as if everything were impossible. (Bolt of nailgun repeating.) This is the way. The remains were so compressed by the peat that they no longer resemble the original.

It is less than four. Wax thy head, tattoo ankh. Nothing is recognizable as itself. Thankyou for your companies. The only survivor had to replace himself at once from the hibernators.

Creak of stair they're coming.
Looking back on a mourning of disarray. I have just been realized, peeled back. That's when you start making mistakes. The lungs floating on the surface resemble giant aquatic plants. The text says in the slaughterhouse of love. I often gear up for a quick retort.

Found tidings, a future page.
You could always have yourself hypnotized and trepanned. I don't know with confidence what I'm to answer. It's said it was the first time that he had seen the sea. It is said.

By and by, a reluctance overheard, the slip of tongue. What can this mean. The vessel is unmarked, without doors or windows along its sides. (As if you saw one every day.) Do you think this knot suits the cut of my features.

Static in dark.
And the uncanny she says, what of it. A ferocious has been known to stumble about inconsistently. I am that supernal book. I read, I say.

The subject is only pretending to expire. It's the primeval fear of infection— blacked out late made visible. Partly in its odd sense of arising.

I've always been truthful about your progress. Above all don't think she says, turning and shaking her index. Sometimes you cannot find. This puts an all of a sudden end to the offerings. Survival can only take place within. Consider the perspective of a vast collective derangement. We are looking forward to your return journey. (You're right, demagogic language was inverted.) Will everyone please get off the field of play. You're only ever five inches from disaster. Wholesale is being airlifted. I am in the space of ten days. Redirect to publics. If ever, I stumbled across.

Still not to here. She threatens to abandon the compound to its fate. I am no longer ready. I am no longer relied upon. On fourteen a bomb went off as presenter was approaching.

Now to fix an indelible mark of infamy upon the flesh. This work seems to be senseless. (You're not the ancestor.) The artery can be rebuilt.

All four movements are in a minor key. I have enjoyed manifold apparitions. Case closed, shaved raw.

Before breaking stones in a quarry and dumping them into the ocean.
The sacrifice consists of a bull (or cow), a gazelle, an antelope, and ducks—lots of ducks. The bull is slain. Mind and sensation could suffice. Mythology is never truly narrative, strangely. (Thou knewest the ladder that was sewn et cetera.) A body without, in the stead of organism.

In front of the lighthouse next to the marquee. The queue. Which, creeping in at keyholes and crevices, stole around blind. You are all dressier, much than me. I have even seen them sniffing the envelopes for answers. What mellifluous voice says she, the gift of an entire, an entire. A single pierce of colour illuminates a dismal scene. I don't think the opportunity will ever afford itself again (stitched unbound, the usual controverse). I am the successful type of failure. A white thing in a white snowscape is dull, like that cliff of unpolished marble. What has become of our own private curse, glimpsed from a passing train.

A surprised aberration. You could say that he's self-radicalized. You couldn't say, with hand on heart, that he had adjusted himself completely. At first he did not understand. He assumed the other meant metaphorically. Makeup remover or oil usually works.

Crisis apparitions. Hooks, lines, sinkers.
At three hundred and thirty-five yards we chance upon a vicious mantrap. Each hostage is tied to a chair and shot five or six times. The last bullet enters the body at the exact centre of the forehead. (Dead capital, wreckage, epilogue.) Beyond, and the grey creature pointed. The TV's on very loud with insane charnel music. We're all causals now. Taboo has been left ajar. Faced with this news, I abandon him to certain ambush at the entrance to the cave. Worse is to follow. Equine pertains to horse, any horse.
Necessarily.
Assuredly.
That too must be granted.
It seems so.
Impossible.
No.

Nay, it is possible.
(An unlimited number of pianolas were all playing together, an absolute.)
Yes.
Assuredly.
So it appears.
Certainly.
I think you are altogether right.

Close of séance. Once daedal hands swing idle. Radix and scapula bruised. Outer bone in supine position. (Mollusc tongue or rasping gridiron.) It seems fitting that, having begun with angels, we should finish with them. The thoughts that have caressed my mind since I began to think could stop the earth in its orbit. You are losing your touch he says.

Note how the diatonic tone descends throughout, commensurate with the amount of moisture in the air. That arm is too still to be a living arm. Suddenly he announced a preference for the spelling of his name and certain foodstuffs. But that limb remains a limb, a disorder of the remembrance, the mute stem. Venues however can claim the legend. No one knew it was a place of pilgrimage. Decidedly, this is the correct script. Of mercy seat in the face, with discomfits.

We station ourselves five hundred metres apart. There's a sturdy trump of no. We're none too worthy in the glare of night. I should see you down, this road to the fore. We were followed.

Too much in the retelling as memento. You are one day destined to kill another yourself. He whispers, hooded in the passing. The signals must have exploded.

A long rectangular strip, one end being twisted through a hundred and eighty degrees. Consider the tragic nature of theme and hero in the great. Failure as a symbol, before the join is made.

Shadowwise.
Persiflage. Millstones of thought. I'm a great copyist, a grand inquisitor. When at last he appears we'll speak to him. Find someone to whom he can hand over that gift. Our guest is of undetermined affinities. An endgame is unravelling, a sickle shape.

And he said to me I will not have thee fearful. Climax is absent. All sense of culmination has been purged. Perhaps it was merely invisible light that was involved. Of all the potential forms and existences in the material world, it's a pit that's set before you. (Sign of shaggy goatfish perched high on bough of tree.) The commentator repeatedly lays emphasis on the fact that H does not exist within the letter of the law. On the question as to whether the author believes in emanation out of each other, it's impossible to know. All eyes are staring at the horizon, in the direction of a nearby continent. Who will replay me now, a decayed victory.

Eruptive rocks, spurious boundaries. At the lava field, the man up to his knees—tempted by the text, by the heights, by forgetting. One who carries out orders.

I really enjoyed what he wanted. I had never before shared a drink with a cadaver: cerebral, saint-errant, reptilious. Centoman. Quacksalver.

He was unhurt. Every surface received seven coats of black lacquer. Often the familiar is the stranger of the two options.

Though it's been a rather comedic evening thus far, the plot must advance. I can confirm. A prepared delay is invariably harmful. I can't live simultaneously in my head and in my body. And now for one of the best-known horror stories in the whole of pack, the ten of corners. Inheritance. Genealogy. Familial erosion. Blood lies. And at the same time the traveller passed the back of his hand over a thirsty-looking hound.

Hermetically sea.
An old moves slowly along a dim and stony road. A dress rehearsal. They can still sting you when they look dead. Numbers are still working on an unbiased production. The great objection among his supporters is to be recast as complete ciphers, empty nothings. They can still come straight in your eye.

But officer he's dead.

Book, hand, lung. The sign read.

The position of the photographer and the angle of press are what is most difficult to neutralize. (Though not impossible.) They believe that the body can only survive if the double is preserved. I have not seen his eyes for several weeks. That visor appears to be a permanent fixture.

Mobile lab and scientific recon group. Barbed hooks. Who is potlatch.

Of anatomies no longer in use.
The if—eating out the lines with acid, black-etched runnels. A decline, within a manifesto of dependence, taken from the ground up, as far up the chain of command as is necessary. All the earth will be out of kilter after this.

A landscape of petrified trees. Preferably olivine, elder and semistone, numbered among the extinct. Boreholes in the southeastern part of the field reveal thick beds of bauxite and uranium. It obliges us to answer this question. A more nice observation is necessary, though more simple. And a greater insensibility toward the observer, and the observed.

Eruptive rocks and aeroliths bisect the space within which we stand. (And your symptoms?) We are forewarned. The instruments say that giant dykes and causeways of basaltic lava lie on the surface. I am busy adjusting a used epiphany. How does the city sleep solitary that was once so full of mentals? The zinc walls of the craft were penetrated by holes of varying size and depth.

He repents, returns the money, and hangs himself. The spine itself has faded. But the margin of the lake was decorated with electric lights in five colours.

The cover shows a detail from chronicle C. I have eaten of his fate. I am indeed bewildered by these happenings. (I am on my way to discover what estrange may mean.) The span is vast in every dimension, long and broad from above and below. Pressure and repose will not be tolerated. He is spent. It's a risky peace, with dangerous pratfalls. I don't know what drew him in here. Tiny letter leads are flung into the air and collected where they land. He is one of the incorruptibles. He is enumerated. And now back to the hub of the drama.

Hazard a grab. It's off again, pursuing its own discourse. Singing glass today. Hymen. Hymenoptera (wrong). O. Exit wound, everyone.

Carbonate of lime, with delimiting consonant. Do not frame hypotheses (i.e. unverifiable speculations). Nektons.

Reconstructing the object.

A touch of cacogenics. The story is a story that refuses to begin and just will not go away. Clouds of incandescence, luminous by heat. (I'd guess at menagerie, terrestrial examples.) The irrigation system intercuts perilous quicksands and the lava curl. Pity we're never available at the same instant. I'm used up. I've lost all sense of place. Sure enough.

India ink and my fauna, the family arrowroot. In praise of shadows mister, and I always know exactly what you want. You could scoop it up off the ground by the armful.

Suck. As per meaning. Or if one saw a man of the people put to death, in the place of death.

Elsewhat.

Pissing in the back row by the drifters. Reflexions on the votive power of fire. This throws light on the obscure by means of the more obscure: a bad day at the races. You float. You sink. Compare everything with everything else. I am now seeing with my two eyes, traditionally placed side by side. He is the savant to whose memory these dejected members have been committed. Its leaves are said to resemble flattened lungs. A circular wall surrounded us, pictures of F and the others. Few seeming to touch, the very esse.

About the size of a tennis court then. Well, fuck it.

I agree to repay the full twelve thousand. A destination has at last been declared. All is clear. We have the equipment and the technique. I'm told I should see them again if I peer into the glass. A steam locomotive shunts away from the station. There's a war going on. People are dressed in clothes. They clutch battered suitcases and stand motionless beside enormous padlocked trunks. He was living cheaply in a garret with some cheese when disaster struck. The siege began. The truth or falsity of the law is discussed all night long. He procures stuff and other things for his enterprise. He buys these games. The wait takes on an even greater significance. Others have made it their task to furnish cyclical time with mythic underpinnings. On seeing this the father gave way to grief at the supposed loss of the son. Don't touch. I can't touch you. Whose leaves is it said resemble.

Use more rigorous arguments.

What we have to do is to secure the acceptance. Why am I reading the debacle I have no idea. And who put an end to his own life. (Whisper it.) The quality of the fluid coming from the drainage tube does not justify its removal. A similar law decrees, down on the frontiers. It reveals itself, this dreadful summit: base intersea, an exit stratagem.

Vacillate, delay, put off. You've got to go much quicker, the same with the accident bit—right through whistle to hiss. To which he replied but no, I could never live in a house like that. There's no news of the replacements. Native arsenate of copper recurs in the crystals.

If he can find a difficult and convoluted way of saying something, he will. First, a rarity. I'm making the following the subject of my enquiries and reflections.

Material bent spirally upon itself into a cylindrical form, nearly.

A list especially of names.

A wavelike flow.

To move like a bell, wheel.

To sway on an axis in the direction of a notion.

To turn away.

To move in on or like the waves.

To wander into sound, with a circular sweep, as the eyes.

You are no longer obliged in time. His disciples are discharged. (One is no longer oneself.) He has now been enumerated. Devil take your reticence he said slamming shut the trapdoor. Or rather, this superimposes itself on *any* objective explanation.

I like contact and am open to other people. Come the morning I could barely walk. Nothing the next day brought could have worsened our circumstances. An ailing wing impedes the long march. I had an effigy mounted on a wooden box in the market square.

Cacoethes loquendi. Cacoethes scribendi.
You are invited to observe us: the utter itch, the scribble ditch. The outer

boundary or face of anything—that which has length and breadth but no thickness. A foil of air.

To regain consciousness.

To rise from the bed and stroke the ceiling.

When deflated he looks like a man-of-war floating on the surface—a mere border effusion, the threshold. Mortars finish off any remnants (potassium nitrate, magnesium burns).

I felt the day break in my bared bones. A language is not so much lost as still to be written. I have passed through many filters. Yes, yes, and yes.

You are house, abode, ken. Especially disreputable: happenstance, or con with seceding. To yield or relinquish to another.

Life-seized effigy. Retrieval of the object from refusal.

She is buried at the stake. Her name once meant loud-taken-pity and she was courted among the dead. (It is lost, the aerial.) Ashes are swirled around by the wind and the tidal current. False knowledge may be bargained from a strategy of digression.

Ancient coinage. A character. A key without chromatic modulation. Our old friend gnawing on his tragic. A sense of betrayal. A curse, a play on *manes*. F flies up from the stage. The curtain falls. The audience applauds. The pair shared a keen interest in genealogy, antiquarianism, poetry and many other subjects. (I mean ancestral spirits, not horsehair). On one side of the bladder stood M and on the other R. The A seems optional.

Ha. The inside of the wardrobe. Stocking up on medicament sap, the fluid part of any animal body—electric current, petrol vapour—a crab-shell dropped from the beak of a gull in flight. This is catching us up quite unawares. After five long years I'm ready to perform an action at last. Fresh tarmac has been laid, steaming black stuff.

Leave house. Go to work. Undertake light reading, as the occasion may require. I exist as proof. It's the wilderness. Receipts exist to establish the connections and the correspondences. I may be transmitted whole by entire families.

Identify an isolate in this picture. (P has been restored after L.) It takes me. It sucks the breath from my living lung. The sac deflates, an intake of sharps. I am away, so away. I am outwaited, landlocked.

Static between the rain. Stations. The weather, stripping away the levels.

Described thus: if only I, could steal this share.

There is where. Under the dim light of two gigantic oriel windows. Up to the malcontent of utmost implausibility. I am writing the condemned man's penalty on his forehead (a situation but no plot). The apparition, it appears whenever the circle prepares to close. Come lightfast day, and the cull is breaking through the crackmans. He wears a loose overmantle of connective tissue. (Some people are uneasy with the idea of a requiem.) The role of the bound man is that of semi-conductor. The sky is obscene with badly aimed crows. It's the year of astronomy. I am invisible between the tenth and third months. The tale catches fire: a Greek myth, a Russian fairy tale, an Irish drinking song, ecstatic Balkan lament. I am packed up and ready to go. I am hinting at the idea of space opening up behind the chorus—camera obscura, the proverbial cannot, wormholes in space. We promise emergency maintenance, electric fuses connected to all the blast holes. It's the story of a man who's been away so long he's considered dead. I always have in my soul some vague form, an ideal pattern. Where represents me. None of this has been made by accident, I can assure you. I thought you were back, had remained in the capital, like some covert agency. Yours is a poor, feck-less and fathomless body.

O, everything.

Listen, the infliction of every single word (not one aorta). I didn't try hard enough—by youth of a violent faith in the inherent impossibilities. White china vessels and trinkets bear the crest. After delivering himself in a stage whisper his rail is cut loose. Events are governed by a pre-scientific principle. Everything that ignites must receive.

This thing of the guinea-pig, I think the wires plug into its back. My situations are being kept under close observation, a microscopic lens. It's the melo-drama. An unidentified sound releases itself and quivers about in the dank air. I'm no megalomaniac, I just have agonizingly accurate intuitions. (Crew drift off into interstellar space.) I'm in love. I am still attached to my dead hand, the phantom limb. I'm being nailed. Zinc roofing is hurled up into the sky by incendiaries. The ultras have already taken over, are poised to form their own. I dare you. I love you too.

It is found in mob and other modes of communication. Night jargon for naught, one who does or nothing. Who made it back before the oxygen ran out? They carry empty tins linked by taut sinew. Here, I is equal to zero, unconditional.

One squats on the cold concrete floor to defecate. She resembles half of me. (Which.) We are actually waiting. She is taking part in the thoroughly perilous event—one small step into spiralling inconsequence. We take over. We take cover. We discover there isn't actually anything wrong with the kitchen after all.

Don't you ever try to recognize me again.

To resurrect a corpse.

Take salt of uric acid, a silkworm, and a strip of moribund leather. Build a retreat, an inner lastage—the spilt delirious choir, hamstrung. The second element occurs alas in edge, in lightyear, in daybreak et cetera. Facetious is coined from to pay and to make.

Grammatology.

A pneumatic contrivance by means of a threshold, a perforation. Men fought each other in the open field, milling in the darkmans.

Preface.

Part of a cliffhanger about the nine subdivisions of the underworld, featuring a nameless character. (A new he will be, like we read of.) To make this book take an existing work and burn it in a forest clearing. Embers and charred fragments plume up into the air to be carried away by the wind. Catch hold of these randomly displaced parts in flight and transcribe them faithfully in the order found. Across a large sheet of paper, methodically record isolated syllables and consonants. On further pages prize from these tesserae the text of a novel.

Miscellaneous last things and events (at last).

The hacking of bone. A slack of marrow. The skin around a bird's eye. A phallus with wingspan, flapping at the naked stairwell. Hear me out when at last you return. Decide me. The drain of two months on the road came to an abrupt halt. My present fear is that I have too much matter, too many moments.

Sweet she scents, like belladonna. The patient had eaten about thirty of the berries. Her breath is closer, barely aware. Apparitions arise from the presence, drugged and unprepared. She lowers her head to my chest, claylike hand flat to abdomen. (Apologies for the unconventional science, I've had my adrenal glands removed.) Hair smells of puke and alcohol, something dead or dying, of inexpressible loss and grief. Great lines return in the hexagram. We breathe in tandem, the rise and fall of her breast et cetera. And maybe you did, did not.

More. A little more. Onto Z.

The same again. A solitary act of conscience (nothing more deadly than a fiction). Catastrophe never fails to deliver. I hate this half-light. The number six means premonition of misfortune. Mayhem has been too long submissive to the restrictions of composition. No octaves recur. The lowest frequency used is one thousand characters per second per second. The same applies, of course. A sudden and violent upheaval in part of the surface is taking place, an overturning. No multiple of any whole number occurs throughout the entire.

All my animals are dispersed. They withdraw back from whence they came. They have survived the crossing, carried over.

The remedial, rems.

Channelling a presentiment. It illustrates the second type, which projects its residue outwards. Please find enclosed a copy of the statement prepared. The chancre in any fact, just as the clock.

A dried vine with a few hanging tendrils. The massive pause. There is not one sample which has not been reproduced in writing, directly or indirectly. Who fascinated.

Svengali stuff, descent into byss and abyss. The image telescopes, severed and ever-crescent—misdread, beneath the starts that tremble. A memento of I enclose.

The fifth day.

Mercury, that is the separator, has figured and framed himself into an end. Of which the text is lost, unmade between victor and vanquished. And in the deep ocean, unkept, had all his time. Charge us with infidelity in quotation and misenglish. I thought the word, inanimating.

He allows himself to be injected with an unidentified yellow liquid. The occasion may expire.

More fire-trap than cut-up, aeolian ash: the horror of leaving an empty space in an artistic composition. Separated flake by flake, pieced together and sandwiched between sheets of glass, like the joints of a finger. Incomplete, wanting one syllable in the last step. Incomplete to stop.

Just do as I tell you.

Closer now, a shivering ascent into the patter of stars. And a reversal, upon realizing by the middle that quasars were very distant and luminous objects. Reproduction is by inversion of these barren details. You can't see them all at once, of course, the sole reference points. Heads have begun to drop, melt and fade away.

Desert, dazzling light.

Selected REALITY STREET titles in print

Poetry series

Maggie O'Sullivan (ed.): *Out of Everywhere* (1996)
Denise Riley: *Selected Poems* (2000)
Ken Edwards: *eight + six* (2003)
David Miller: *Spiritual Letters (I-II)* (2004)
Redell Olsen: *Secure Portable Space* (2004)
Peter Riley: *Excavations* (2004)
Allen Fisher: *Place* (2005)
Tony Baker: *In Transit* (2005)
Jeff Hilson: *stretchers* (2006)
Maurice Scully: *Sonata* (2006)
Maggie O'Sullivan: *Body of Work* (2006)
Sarah Riggs: *chain of minuscule decisions in the form of a feeling* (2007)
Carol Watts: *Wrack* (2007)
Jeff Hilson (ed.): *The Reality Street Book of Sonnets* (2008)
Peter Jaeger: *Rapid Eye Movement* (2009)
Wendy Mulford: *The Land Between* (2009)
Allan K Horwitz/Ken Edwards (ed.): *Botsotso* (2009)
Bill Griffiths: *Collected Earlier Poems* (2010)
Fanny Howe: *Emergence* (2010)
Jim Goar: *Seoul Bus Poems* (2010)
Carol Watts: *Occasionals* (2011)
James Davies: *Plants* (2011)

Narrative series

Ken Edwards: *Futures* (1998, reprinted 2010)
John Hall: *Apricot Pages* (2005)
David Miller: *The Dorothy and Benno Stories* (2005)
Douglas Oliver: *Whisper 'Louise'* (2005)
Ken Edwards: *Nostalgia for Unknown Cities* (2007)
Paul Griffiths: *let me tell you* (2008)
John Gilmore: *Head of a Man* (2011)
Leopold Haas: *The Raft* (2011)
Johan de Wit: *Gero Nimo*(2011)

Go to www.realitystreet.co.uk, email info@realitystreet.co.uk or write to the address on the reverse of the title page for updates.

REALITY STREET depends for its continuing existence on the Reality Street Supporters scheme. For details of how to become a Reality Street Supporter, or to be put on the mailing list for news of forthcoming publications, write to the address on the reverse of the title page, or email **info@realitystreet.co.uk**

Visit our website at: **www.realitystreet.co.uk/supporter-scheme.php**

Reality Street Supporters who have sponsored this book:

David Annwn
Andrew Brewerton
Peter Brown
Paul Buck
Clive Bush
John Cayley
Adrian Clarke
Lucy Clarke
Dane Cobain
Tony Cullen
Ian Davidson
Mark Dickinson
David Dowker
Derek Eales
Michael Finnissy
Allen Fisher
Sarah Gall
John Gilmore
John Goodby
Giles Goodland
Paul Griffiths
Charles Hadfield
Catherine Hales
John Hall
Alan Halsey
Robert Hampson
Randolph Healy
Colin Herd
Simon Howard
Fanny Howe
Peter Hughes

Romana Huk
Elizabeth James &
Harry Gilonis
L Kiew
Peter Larkin
Sang-yeon Lee & Jim Goar
Richard Leigh
Alan Loney
Tony Lopez
Chris Lord
Ian McMillan
Michael Mann
Peter Manson
Deborah Meadows
Geraldine Monk
Sean Pemberton
Pete & Lyn
Tom Quale
Josh Robinson
Lou Rowan
Will Rowe
Robert Sheppard
Peterjon & Yasmin Skelt
Hazel Smith
Valerie & Geoffrey Soar
Harriet Tarlo
Alan Teder
Sam Ward
Susan Wheeler
John Wilkinson
Anonymous: 11

Ingram Content Group UK Ltd.
Milton Keynes UK
UKHW040216050723
424490UK00017B/581